FIC C325
Carter, St
Palace council

Praise for Stephen L. Carter's

PALACE COUNCIL

"An engrossingly complex political thriller."
—*New York Daily News*

"A well-lit showcase for [Carter's] considerable strengths."
—*The Seattle Times*

"[A] literary novel-cum-thriller."   —*USA Today*

"Fascinating. . . . Damned good. . . . Carter keeps us spell-
bound."   —*San Antonio Express-News*

"Entertaining."   —*The New York Times*

"Offers a finely drawn picture of the complicated black
social world."   —*The New Yorker*

"Carter's ambitious, serpentine plot knits together revolutionary groups, the civil rights movement, McCarthyism
and Watergate."   —*Rocky Mountain News*

Stephen L. Carter

PALACE COUNCIL

Stephen L. Carter is the William Nelson Cromwell Professor of Law at Yale University. His debut novel, *The Emperor of Ocean Park*, spent eleven weeks on the *New York Times* bestseller list, and was followed by the nationwide bestseller *New England White*. His acclaimed nonfiction books include *God's Name in Vain: The Wrongs and Rights of Religion* and *Politics and Civility: Manners, Morals, and the Etiquette of Democracy*. He lives with his family in Connecticut.

Linda Library
Memphis University School

ALSO BY STEPHEN L. CARTER

Fiction
The Emperor of Ocean Park
New England White

Nonfiction
God's Name in Vain:
The Wrongs and Rights of Religion in Politics

The Dissent of the Governed:
A Meditation on Law, Religion, and Loyalty

Civility: Manners, Morals, and the Etiquette of Democracy

Integrity

The Confirmation Mess:
Cleaning Up the Federal Appointments Process

The Culture of Disbelief:
How American Law and Politics
Trivialize Religious Devotion

Reflections of an Affirmative Action Baby

PALACE COUNCIL

PALACE COUNCIL

STEPHEN L. CARTER

Vintage Contemporaries
Vintage Books
A Division of Random House, Inc.
New York

FIRST VINTAGE CONTEMPORARIES EDITION, JUNE 2009

Copyright © 2008 by Stephen L. Carter

All rights reserved. Published in the United States by Vintage Books,
a division of Random House, Inc., New York, and in Canada by Random House
of Canada Limited, Toronto. Originally published in hardcover in the United States
by Alfred A. Knopf, a division of Random House, Inc., New York, in 2008.

Vintage and colophon are registered trademarks
and Vintage Contemporaries is a trademark of Random House, Inc.

This is a work of fiction. Names, characters, places, and incidents either are
the product of the author's imagination or are used fictitiously. Any resemblance
to actual persons, living or dead, events, or locales is entirely coincidental.

The Library of Congress has cataloged the Knopf edition as follows:
Carter, Stephen, [date]
Palace council / by Stephen Carter.—1st ed.
p.   cm.
1. Murder investigation—Fiction. I. Title.
PS3603.A78P35 2008
813'.6—dc22   2007052134

Vintage ISBN: 978-0-307-38596-3

Book design by Virginia Tan

www.vintagebooks.com

Printed in the United States
10 9 8 7 6 5 4 3 2 1

FIC
C325p

To Eric, Leslie, Lisa, and John, who lived it with me

"O, that the years had language!"
—*Eloise Bibb*

PALACE COUNCIL

The Council

THE LAWYER WAS NERVOUS, and that was odd. His hands trembled on the steering wheel, and that was odder still. He had learned in the war that there was no sin in being afraid as long as the others never knew. He understood that courage was a discipline. As was confidence. In the marble caverns of Wall Street, the lawyer intimidated all around him with his breadth of knowledge and speed of mind. In the boardrooms of his clients, he had no equal. On his rare forays into the courtroom, he charmed the judges with his wit and persuaded them with his force. He had commanded a company of Rangers in North Africa and Europe. He provided his adoring wife and children with a house in the suburbs, equipped with every modern convenience. It was the summer of 1952, the era of such men as himself. The United States was about to elect a military man its President. The nation's steelmakers had just crushed a nationwide strike. The Congress was about to add the words "Under God" to the Pledge of Allegiance. American science had invented a way to phone from California to New York without using an operator. Some people insisted on calling attention to the nation's imperfections. But the lawyer believed in quiet progress. Quiet, gradual progress. The nation would move forward in its good time. So calm down, he commanded himself, annoyed to discover that he was drumming his fingers on the dash.

He tightened his grip on the wheel.

The driveway was full of cars. The house was long and low. Golden light spilled invitingly from the windows. Still the lawyer hesitated. August air, loamy and rich, drifted into the car. Clouds hid the moon, but the forecasted rain had yet to arrive. The lawyer glanced at the glowering sky and endured a shivering premonition of death. Fighting his growing unease, the lawyer focused his mind on the image of his wife's glowing face. He shut his eyes and listened to her teasing South Carolina drawl. Calmer now, he reminded himself why he was here.

Dinner and conversation, his host had said, smiling, over coffee in Manhattan. *And stag only. No wives.*

Why no wives? the lawyer had asked, not unreasonably.

Trust me.

The lawyer had been too savvy to press. His host knew people, and the kind of people he knew, knew other people. Then, too, his host had raised the return of favors to an art form. Everyone wanted to be in his good graces. As successful as the lawyer's career might have been so far, there were always higher rungs on the ladder. Courtesy and curiosity pushed him forward. When his host mentioned the name of some of the others who were expected to attend, the lawyer was hooked.

He climbed out of the car.

Laughter wafted from the house, and, beneath it, music, scratchy and low. The lawyer practiced his courtroom smile. The music was classical but fluffy. The lawyer fortified himself with the knowledge that his host was no Renaissance man. The disciplined confidence he had learned in the war was returning. He mounted the steps jauntily, ready to be the star of the evening.

About to ring the bell, he noticed a much younger man standing at ease on the grass, his face in shadow, his smooth hair pale and bright in the light from within. Odd. No aides, tonight's host had insisted. No drivers. No bodyguards. And this in a crowd whose members tended to possess several of each.

The lawyer rang, then turned to the stranger to say hello. But the blond man had vanished so thoroughly into the inky darkness that the lawyer began to doubt whether he had seen him at all.

Never mind. Focus. Scintillate. Intimidate.

The door swung open. The lawyer stepped inside.

When he emerged, it was well past four in the morning. He was dizzy from lack of sleep, and too much good food and excellent claret. He was among the last to leave. Their host had worked out a departure schedule, according to some scheme none of them understood. And yet they did as he proposed, accepting without a murmur of complaint his insistence on security against threats he refused to disclose. He had a hypnotic aspect, the lawyer decided. Mesmerizing. He would have been fantastic in the courtroom. He planned everything with care. Even the number of guests turned out to be a symbol of their undertaking.

The lawyer stood beside his car, fingers touching the door without quite opening it. The dew made the surface shine. He was shivering harder now than he had been on arrival. And not from cold. The host had unveiled his plan, and it turned out to be, like the man himself, brilliant, complex, efficient. The lawyer had sat there with the others, the whole room entranced as their host strode up and down in front of the fire, eyes bright and alive, filling in some details, leaving others for later discovery. One by one, the men at dinner had nodded. Some of the most powerful men in the country, and they had all nodded. Yes. Yes. And yes again. They were on board. The lawyer had nodded along with the rest, but his nod had been a lie.

The lawyer thought the plan, for all its brilliance, was evil.

There was no other word.

The plan might even accomplish its ends. Many evil plans did. The lawyer had seen enough of life to know that the triumph of good was anything but inevitable. The triumph of good in the last war had cost the world millions of souls.

The lawyer slipped behind the wheel. What was it about him that had made their host think he would join willingly so wicked a plan? Did the man really think so little of him? Maybe so. Maybe with reason. He thought about the men in the room, smoking their cigars, drinking their wine, nodding their heads. His career would likely skyrocket if he went along with them. The future stretched ahead of him, an endless golden band.

With brimstone waiting at the far end.

He knew what his wife would say. She was a wonderful woman,

but she had been pampered and sheltered all her life. She did not understand how, in the world of men, sometimes you had to sup with the devil at least for a while, in order to—

"Did you need anything, sir?"

The lawyer turned, startled. The blond man was leaning close, smiling politely through the open window. He had crept up on the car without giving the smallest hint of his approach. Even in the Rangers the lawyer had known no one as stealthy. The lawyer started to answer, then hesitated. The cobalt eyes said that the blond man knew his every thought. The gaze was at once pitying and spiritless, the gaze of an executioner.

"I'm fine," the lawyer said, after his stomach finished twisting and turning. "Fine, thank you!"

"Good meeting?"

"Oh, yes. Absolutely."

"Travel safely, sir."

"I will. Thanks again."

Driving off, the lawyer felt a flooding relief, as if he had escaped from Hell. His murder was still thirty months away.

PART I

New York/London/
Boston
1954–1958

CHAPTER I

Hitting the Town

(I)

HAD EDDIE WESLEY BEEN A LESS RELIABLE MAN, he would never have stumbled over the body, chased Junie to Tennessee, battled the devils to a draw, and helped to topple a President. But Eddie was blessed or perhaps cursed with a dependability that led to a lack of prudence in pursuing his devotion. He loved only two women in his life, loved them both with a recklessness that often made him a difficult man to like, and thus was able, when the moment arrived, to save the country he had come to hate.

A more prudent man might have failed.

As for Aurelia, she arrived with her own priorities, very conventional, very American, and so from the start very different from Eddie's. Once they went their separate ways, there was no earthly reason to suppose the two of them would join forces, even after the events of that fateful Palm Sunday and what happened in Hong Kong—but join they did, by necessity more than choice, fighting on alone when everybody else had quit or died.

Almost everybody.

(II)

EDWARD TROTTER WESLEY JUNIOR breezed into Harlem in May of 1954, just days after the Supreme Court outlawed racial segregation in public schools, a landmark decision that Eddie was certain must conceal some sort of dirty trick. He possessed a degree from Amherst, a couple of undistinguished years of graduate work at Brown, a handful of social connections through his mother, and a coveted job on the *Amsterdam News*, although he quit in disgust three months after starting. He had not realized, he explained in a letter to his beloved sister Junie, how very small and unimportant the position was. Junie, in a mischievous mood, forwarded his letter to their awesomely disapproving father, a Boston pastor and essayist. Actually, he was at this time in Montgomery, Alabama, helping to organize a boycott of local businesses that refused to call Negro patrons "Mr." and "Mrs." Wesley Senior, as he liked to be called, was a distant relation of William Monroe Trotter, the Negro journalist once arrested after tossing pepper to disrupt a speech by Booker T. Washington, and had inherited some of the fire of that clan. Upon his return to Boston, he answered Junie at once, sending along a surfeit of citations from the New Testament, most on the subject of hard work, commanding his daughter to share them with her brother. Eddie read them all; Second Thessalonians 3:10 sufficiently stoked his fury that he did not write his parents for a month, for Eddie was rather fiery himself. When he at last pulled together enough money from odd jobs to afford a phone, he refused for weeks to give his parents the number. Wesley Senior thought Eddie lazy. But Eddie, to his own way of thinking, was simply focused. He did not want to write about car wrecks and speeches by the great leaders of the rising movement for Negro rights. He wanted to write short stories and novels and decided, in the manner of many an author before him, that earning a living would disturb his muse. So, for a time, he mooched.

His mother sent money, cars were washed, meals were served, papers were sold. Around the corner from his apartment on 123rd Street was a Jewish grocery—that was what they were called, Jewish groceries, a reference to ownership, not cuisine—and Eddie for a time earned a second income working nights behind the cash register, reading and writing there on the counter because custom was thin. But a better offer came his way. In those days the seedier side of Harlem was largely run by a worthy named Scarlett, who had risen to power after the legendary Bumpy Johnson, king of the Negro rackets, was sentenced to prison for the third time. Scarlett owned a nightclub on 128th Street and much else besides, and was said to pay his dues to Frank Costello, the successor to Lucky Luciano and, at the time, the most powerful Mafia leader in New York. Scarlett was an elegant Jamaican who had come out of the old Forty Thieves gang along with Bumpy. He was popular along the streets. He liked to walk into shops and pull a huge bankroll from the pocket of his tailored suit, make a small purchase with a large bill, then tell the delighted proprietor to keep the change, thus cementing his reputation for generosity—never mind that a week later his people would be around to collect protection money from the very same store. At twenty-seven, a joyless term of military service behind him, Eddie Wesley was not known to be a scrapper. Still, he had a friend who had a friend, and before he knew it he was doing occasional odd jobs for bluff, secretive, boisterous men who were, or were not, connected to Scarlett. It was a living, Eddie told himself, but not his parents; it was only until he was discovered as a writer; besides, it would provide meat for the tales he would one day spin. He reminded himself, whenever moral doubts assailed him, that Richard Wright, in *Black Boy*, had confessed to a youthful life of crime. True, Wright stole no more than the occasional fistful of tickets from the proprietor of a movie house, and Eddie was carrying mysterious packages across state lines, but he consoled himself with Wright's dictum that the white man had done so many horrible things that stealing from him was no breach of ethics. And if part of him suspected that, whoever Scarlett was stealing from, it wasn't the white man, Eddie suppressed the thought.

"Where do you go all these nights?" asked Aurelia, his unattainably highborn girlfriend, whom he often wooed by reciting Andreas Cappelanus on the art of courtly love: medieval literature having been among his best courses at Amherst. They were canoodling, as it was called, in a shadowed booth at Scarlett's club, not the sort of place where Eddie's friends ever went, or, more important, Aurie's. "You're so secretive"—as though she herself was not.

"If I told you, you'd never believe it."

Aurelia was much quicker than Eddie, and always had been: "Then it can't possibly be another woman."

"You're one to talk," he said.

"I know." Sipping her pink gin fizz with Kirschwasser, the drink for which she was known throughout Harlem. She was a columnist for the *Seventh Avenue Sentinel*, the second-largest Negro paper in town, and wrote about everyone's scandalous peccadilloes but her own. "I am one to talk," she said, and leaped to her feet, tugging at his arm. "Dance with me. Come on."

"We shall be conspicuous," said Eddie, in the peculiar elocution he had developed at Amherst. His friends mocked him, but women adored it.

"We shall not," she teased, echoing his cadences, and perhaps she was even right, because Scarlett's was also the sort of place that always remembered to forget you were ever there. But before they could have their dance, one of the boisterous men tugged Eddie aside for a whispered conversation. Eddie, excited, told Aurelia they would have to make it an early night, conveying through his body English what he dared not speak aloud. Alas, Aurie was not so easily impressed: included in her family tree, as she would remind you at the drop of a hat, were villains galore, as well as a Reconstruction Era congressman and the first Negro to make a million dollars in real estate.

"You can't be involved with these people," Aurelia said as they walked through the sooty Harlem rain. She wore cheap plastic over-shoes, but her umbrella was from Paris, where her aunt sang jazz.

"It isn't involvement in the usual sense."

She knew his excuses, too: "Let me guess. Research for the great novel."

"Something like that."

They had reached the public library on 135th Street, three blocks from the apartment Aurie shared with two other women. Cars were jammed so tightly along the curb that it was a miracle they ever got out again. This was as far as Eddie was ever allowed to go. Aurelia kissed him. She had feathery eyebrows and a roundish chipmunk face. When she was happy, she looked like a playful imp. When she was earnest, the roundness hardened, and she became Hollywood's image of a schoolmarm. This was schoolmarm time.

"My family has certain expectations of me," she began. "I'm an only child. My future matters to them. A lot."

"So you keep telling me."

"Because it's true." The brow crinkled. "You know, Eddie, my uncle's hotel business is—"

"I'm a writer."

"They own hotels in seven different—"

"I cannot do it."

"He makes good money. He'll always make good money. I don't care what the Supreme Court says. We'll need colored hotels for the next fifty years. Maybe more." Eddie stroked her cheek, said nothing. "I wanted to ask you one last time, because—"

He covered her mouth. Gently. They had been arguing the point for years. Both knew the outcome in advance. Like tired actors, they recited the same old lines. "I have to write, Aurie. The muse sits upon me. It is not a matter of choice. It is a matter of necessity."

"Then you should have kept the newspaper job."

"It was not real writing."

"It was real money."

Later that night, as Eddie left the train station in Newark, a couple of thugs tripped him, kicked him, snatched the parcel in its neat brown paper, ran. They had marked him down weeks ago and bided their time until he got careless. He was told by one of Scarlett's people that the boys had admitted the crime. Not to the police. To Scarlett, who was said to have a way of loosening tongues. Eddie believed it. Maceo Scarlett's nickname was the Carpenter, a reference, it was rumored, to the unfortunate fate that had befallen his predecessor, whose right-hand man Scarlett had been, back when the poor gentleman possessed a right hand: something to do with nails and saws. A neighbor named Lenny, the dark, skinny imp who had tempted Eddie in the first place over to Scarlett's side of the street, assured him that he was in only small trouble, not big, for losing the package:

nothing would happen if he got out now. And so, when Scarlett's people offered him a second chance, Eddie respectfully declined. For a month thereafter Eddie did not read the papers. He did not want to know what happened to the boys.

(I I I)

AFTER THAT Eddie went back to washing cars and sweeping floors. He earned little money, and saved none, for what he did not spend on Aurelia he shared with friends and neighbors. He developed a reputation as a soft touch. You had but to ask, and he would turn over his last dollar. This was not generosity in the usual sense, but neither was it calculated. He simply lived so thoroughly in the moment that it would never occur to him to hold on to a quarter because he might need it tomorrow. The most intensely political of his buddies, Gary Fatek, playing on Lenin, liked to say that when the revolution arrived Eddie would give the hangman cash to buy the rope; but Gary was white, and rich, and hung out in Harlem to prove his bona fides. Aurie found Eddie's lightness with money endearing, even though it called into question—she said—his ability to support a family.

"In the fullness of time, I shall be successful."

"In the fullness of time, I shall be married. So watch out."

As it happened, Aurie made this comment, to embarrassed laughter all around, at a small dinner party hosted by a young couple named Claire and Oliver Garland at their apartment on West Ninety-third Street. The occasion celebrated Eddie's transition to published writer. One of his stories had at last been accepted by a serious literary magazine. Ralph Ellison sent a note. Langston Hughes proposed a toast to Eddie's grand future. Eddie had never met the famous writer, and was nervous. But Hughes, the greatest literary light in Harlem, put the young man at his ease. Hughes was broad and smiling, a spellbinder of the old school. Over brandy and cigars, he shared tales of a recent sojourn abroad. Eddie was enthralled. Langston Hughes lived the life Eddie coveted for himself. Running hotels with Aurelia's uncle could not possibly compare. Oliver Garland, the only Negro lawyer on Wall Street, seemed to have been everywhere, too: he and his cousin Kevin and Langston Hughes compared notes on restaurants in Florence. Eddie, child of a preacher and a nurse, knew little of Negroes like this.

Gary Fatek was also at the party, along with a couple of other Caucasians, because members of the younger, educated set in white America prided themselves on ignoring the cautious racialism of their parents. Afterward Gary pulled one of his cute political tricks, summoning a cab, climbing in with Eddie and Aurelia, then directing the driver to drop his friends in Harlem first and only then head to Gary's own place in the Village. Everybody knew that a New York cabbie would otherwise never go north of Columbia University. Eddie, always a proud man, would never have cooperated with this nonsense had Aurelia not been present; and Gary probably would not have tried. White friends were important, Wesley Senior had long preached to his children: That is where the power lies, he warned them, and where, for the foreseeable future, it will. Eddie and Aurelia sat together on the bench. Gary folded down the jump seat, and clutched the handle as the driver bumped angrily uptown. He lectured them about revolutionary politics. He was red-haired and gentle and certain. He said Eddie's short story showed the glimmering of consciousness, but only the glimmering. Aurelia, feigning a cold, giggled behind her white-gloved hands. Even back in college, where the three of them first met, everybody had known that Eddie was entirely unpolitical.

Eddie did not consider his short story revolutionary. He did not consider it anything, except finished. Entitled "Evening Prayer," the tale had been published in *The Saturday Evening Post*. It was expected to win prizes. The story recounted a single day of segregation, viewed through the eyes of a small boy watching the daylong humiliation of his proud father, a stern deacon of the church who worked as a hotel doorman. At the end, the boy got down on his knees, folded his hands, and vowed that, whatever he turned out to be when he grew up, he would never be a Negro. Eddie's mother wrote to say she cried for an hour when she read it. Aurelia had praised the story in the *Sentinel*, referring to its author as "Harlem's most eligible bachelor": her way of teasing from afar. Eddie's literary agent was negotiating a deal for his first novel. This was the story in which Eddie invented the term "darker nation" to describe Negro America—capturing, he thought, a sense of solidarity and distinctiveness. And although later the term "black" would come into wider usage, for a time "darker nation" was on upper-crust Harlem's lips.

Eddie, however, even if on their lips, had just barely scratched his way onto their lists. In those days, everything in Harlem was divided into tiers. Prestige mattered, and multiple layers separated the top from the middle, to say nothing of the bottom. Some addresses were better than others. So were some clubs, some spouses, some friends, and some parties. The social distinctions mattered little to the great mass of Negroes, but Eddie had been raised, in spite of himself, to an awareness of who was who. Although his father, the great preacher, pretended not to care about such trivialities, his mother had filled Eddie's head with stories, and he supposed some of them must be true. All through his childhood, Marie Wesley had spoken of Harlem drawing rooms so exclusive that it would not be unusual to see George Gershwin and Duke Ellington playing a piano duet. Of homes as expensively furnished as the high-rise apartments on Park Avenue. Once his short story began to open doors, Eddie could not bear the thought of not walking through them. Given the chance, thanks to his erudition, he glittered. He traveled upward. He could quote Shakespeare and Dante by the yard, but also Douglass and Du Bois. He could tease. He could charm. He could flatter. On a frigid evening in February of 1955, he attended a grand party at a palatial townhouse on Jumel Terrace, a fancy little cobblestone enclave near Saint Nicholas Avenue between 160th and 162nd streets. The party had been called to announce a royal engagement. The prince of one of the senior Harlem clans was to wed the princess of one of the darker nation's Midwestern kingdoms. Everyone who mattered was there, including several white politicians, and a number of men and women too famous for Eddie to dare approach. One of the toasts was offered by Robert Wagner, the mayor of New York. Frank Sinatra offered another. Everyone was buoyant but Eddie, who usually limited himself to a single glass but tonight drank quite a bit more. Eddie attended out of duty, and wished he had not.

He was in love with the bride-to-be.

Eddie watched the happy couple, listened as glasses were raised to Aurelia Treene and Kevin Garland. His usual geniality faded. He began to seethe. People were surprised. Eddie Wesley was always so placid, and so much fun. Tonight he argued belligerently with other guests. Finally, a young man with whose family Eddie's had summered on Martha's Vineyard in the old days was delegated to pull him aside and calm him. Eddie broke free. Harry Belafonte tried. Eddie broke free. Langston Hughes tried. Eddie broke free. A grim phalanx of Harlem men then offered courteously to put the fool out on the street, but the bride-to-be intervened. In full view of everyone, she grabbed Eddie by the arm and dragged him into the kitchen. He did not break free. People whispered excitedly. The kitchen was busy with hired help, everyone in smart, sparkling uniforms, eyes on the princess as they pretended to look the other way.

Aurelia was furious.

"This is just the way it is. This isn't your world, so I can't expect you to understand. But I have responsibilities to my family."

"And to yourself?" Eddie demanded. "Have you no responsibility to yourself?"

Aurelia was unfazed. She remained schoolmarm-stern. "How can we preserve what matters if we all keep on putting ourselves first?"

"I don't put myself first. I put you first."

"You put your writing first."

"I love you," he said, the words like ash in his mouth. "I'll always love you."

For a moment Aurelia softened. She touched his cheek. "Maybe if you'd taken that job with my uncle." Then, as if by force of will, the schoolmarm was back. "Some things we can't do anything about.

That's the way life is." To this credo, Eddie had no answer. "Now, behave yourself," she added.

Aurelia rejoined her admirers, and her glaringly unamused fiancé. Eddie decided the time had come to depart. A friend or two offered to accompany him, but Eddie shook his head. In consequence, he was alone when, thirty minutes later, he found the body.

CHAPTER 2

The Cross

(1)

EVERY CORPSE on which Eddie Wesley had ever laid eyes had belonged, once, to someone he knew, for his familiarity with the species flowed entirely from encounters at funeral parlors and what were called "homegoing services" at his father's church. His term in the Army had been served entirely within the nation's borders, and even during his months working for Scarlett he had never touched what Lenny called the happy end of the business. It was past mid night when Eddie came upon his first-ever unknown body. He was wandering among the lush trees of Roger Morris Park, across Jumel Terrace from the party, talking himself down, remembering how his father always warned against treating desire as implying entitlement. The park was closed to visitors after dark and haunted besides, but Eddie was a doubter of conventions and rules, except in literature, where he accepted them entirely. The park had once been the grounds of the most famous mansion in all of Manhattan, the ornate Palladian palace that had been home, a century and a half ago, to Madame Jumel, perhaps the wealthiest woman in the land. This was back around the time of the Louisiana Purchase, when the Haarlem Heights had been a distant, rural enclave for the white and well-to-do of the polyglot city. Harlem of Eddie's era, after sixty years of Negrification, possessed few genuine tourist attractions, and the Jumel Mansion was among the few, although its principal lure was probably the ghost of Madame herself, occasionally spotted leaning from the upper windows to shush unruly visitors and, now and then, crossing the hall before your eyes, perhaps searching for the fortune that her second husband was said to have stolen. Most of Harlem pooh-poohed the ghost stories by day, and avoided Roger Morris Park at night.

Eddie did not think much of the supernatural, considering that more Wesley Senior's realm.

He stumbled over the body in the shadow of a dead elm very near the wrought-iron fence, where a passerby would no doubt have spotted it from the sidewalk early the next morning. The stumbling was literal, for Eddie, pained eyes on the townhouse where every moment drew Aurelia further from him, was not looking down. He tripped, and his chest hit crusty mounded snow. He turned and, spotting a man lying behind him, spun, catlike, to his feet, remembering the boys who had mugged him in Newark. Even when he crept closer and took in the elegant suit and watch chain, the lack of an overcoat despite the February chill, the white skin, the well-fed jowly face, the closed eyes, and the unmoving hands, he was certain the man must have tripped him on purpose, because—on this point, years later, he was firm—five minutes ago, on his previous circuit along the fence, the man had not been there.

"Hey," said Eddie, anger fading as he got a good look. He shook the man's shoulder. "Hey!"

A fresh night snow was by this time brushing the city, and tiny twirling flakes settled on the stranger's forehead and lips as well as on the hands folded across his substantial chest. Still the man made no move.

"Are you okay? Hey. Wake up!"

But by that time Eddie had guessed that the man would not be waking. A white man, dead in Harlem. The press would have a field day. Not afraid but, for once, uncertain of his ground, Eddie knelt on the frozen ground and unfolded the man's pudgy hands, intending to check the pulse, although he had no idea how it was done. When he separated the fingers, something gold glinted and fell to the snow. Eddie picked it up. A cross, perhaps an inch and a half long, ornately worked, with an inscription on it he could not read in the faint glow of a streetlamp outside the fence. Then he realized that the words were upside down. Inverting the cross, twisting it to catch the light, he could make out "We shall," and, in the dark, no more. Maybe the next word was "overcome"? But the light was too dim.

The cross dangled from a gold chain, threaded oddly through an eyelet at the bottom rather than the top, so that, had the dead man been wearing it around his neck, the cross would have been upside down, the words right side up. Eddie wondered why he had been clutching it at all. Seeking protection, perhaps. But from what? Leaning closer, squinting, Eddie had his first hint. Around the plump neck, digging into discolored flesh, was a leather band. The man had been garroted.

Eddie shot to his feet, senses woozily alert. If the body had not been here five minutes ago, then the killer must be nearby. He listened, but snow crunched in every direction. He peered, but in the trees every shadow swayed. Eddie was no fool. A garrote meant Scarlett, or somebody like Scarlett, and the Scarletts of the world had a thing about witnesses.

He wiped off the cross, tucked it back into the cold, lifeless hands, and hurried away. Crawling through the gap in the fence gave Eddie more trouble than usual, maybe because he was trembling. Struggling toward the sidewalk, he kept waiting for the garrote to slip around his own neck. He looked up at the townhouse but could not face the humiliation of return. He plunged south. Fat Man's, the famous bar and grill on 155th Street, was open late, packed as usual with Negro celebrities. If you could get in, Fat Man's was the place to be seen, and right now Eddie wanted to be seen, as far as possible from Roger Morris Park. He called the police from the pay phone in the back, not troubling to share his name. He had a drink, but everybody seemed to be looking at him. Maybe because he did not belong. Maybe because he was trembling and sweaty. Maybe nobody was looking, but Eddie took no chances. He threw money down without counting: it must have been enough, because the bartender thanked him and even said "sir."

Home was a narrow walk-up on 123rd Street, noisy and airless, an address he seldom admitted outside his tiny circle, for the Valley, as it was called by the cognoscenti, was far from the most desirable corner of Harlem. For letters from his relatives he had invested prudently in a post-office box. Two flights up, in his claustrophobic flat, Eddie sweated the night away, perched on his lumpy but carefully made bed, journal in his lap, baseball bat by his side, watching the fetid alley they would use to gain entry to the side door when they came for him.

(11)

BY MORNING, the city was abuzz. The dead man was a lawyer named Castle. Eddie had never heard of him but read every obituary he could get his hands on. Philmont Castle was evidently a titan of Wall Street. Corporations across the country issued condoling statements. So did several film actors. Eddie turned the pages. It seemed there was nobody the lawyer had not befriended. President Eisenhower said the whole nation would miss Phil Castle. He promised federal assistance in tracking down whoever had committed this loathsome outrage—or words to that effect. The lawyer had been a major Republican fund-raiser. And a devoted husband and father. And a pillar of his church. And a guest last night at "an engagement party in Harlem."

Eddie put the newspaper down with a snap.

Try as he might, he could not correlate the smiling face on every front page with any of the Caucasian faces from last night. But there had been so many, and Eddie, if the truth were told, had stared mainly at the bride-to-be. He turned more pages. No mention of the cause of death, except that it was murder. Castle's wallet was missing. The police called it a robbery, not exactly an unknown event in Harlem, although the white newspapers seemed unaware that crime of any kind was relatively rare in those days along the nicer blocks. No speculation anywhere on exactly what a Wall Street lawyer might have been doing on the grounds of Jumel Mansion. Nothing about a cross clutched in Castle's dead hands, whether right side up or upside down. And no whisper of anybody's having noticed an angry, half-drunk Negro writer leaving the party around the same time the dead man did.

The authorities never questioned Eddie. Days passed. He could not get the cross out of his mind. He wished he had had time to read the rest of the inscription. He risked a rare letter to Wesley Senior, inquiring but not saying why. The pastor answered by return post. His tone for once was patient. He enjoyed being didactic. The upside-down cross was often called the Cross of Saint Peter, because tradition held that the leader of the Apostles had been crucified that way. The Roman Catholic Church considered the symbol sacred. Over the centuries, he added, the upside-down cross had been adopted as an object of veneration by the worshipers of Satan, or, as Wesley Senior put it, quoting Scripture, the followers of "the devil and his angels."

Eddie decided it was just coincidence.

CHAPTER 3

Emil and Belt

(1)

PROBABLY EDDIE SHOULD HAVE FORGOTTEN the whole thing. The cross might have been a mystery, but it was in no sense his mystery. He did not know the family; none of the responsibility rested on his shoulders. He had a career to pursue, a father to impress, and a relationship to mourn. He should have and very likely he would have forgotten the whole thing, but for three events, seemingly disconnected, which only with the benefit of hindsight fell into a pattern.

The first of the three events began by chance, two months after he found the lawyer's body, in a barbershop on Amsterdam Avenue. It was an April Saturday, unusually sultry for a Manhattan spring. The women of Harlem brought out their pastels. The men carried their jackets over their shoulders but did not forgo their hats. The darker nation needed this warm relief from a difficult winter. The Southern states had announced their "rejection" of the Supreme Court's desegregation decisions. All over Harlem, people shivered, whispering of a second Civil War. Then, just days ago, at the end of March, Walter White, legendary head of the NAACP, had died. The race had lost its leader. At the barbershop, everyone was lamenting. Eddie was there to have his hair cut, but others glided in and out the door because the barber was known to supply mezzroll, Harlem slang of the day for high-quality marijuana. You slipped the barber's assistant a couple of bills, and another assistant met you near the filthy men's room in the back. Eddie had no interest in the shop's sideline. He went for the history. The head barber, Mr. Pond, would fill your head with stories, some of them possibly true, of the jazz joints where he used to play piano before he cut hair—the Exclusive at 136th and Lenox, the Yeah Man on Seventh, even the world-famous Rhythm Club—and the celebrities he claimed to have barbered in the old days, from Lonnie Johnson to Willie "The Lion" Smith to Fats Waller to Jelly Roll Morton. Maybe. Maybe not. Today Eddie wore brightly colored billowing pants with a wide belt, not really to his taste, although his friends assured him they were the latest fashion. A famous writer, they said, should keep up with the times, and Eddie, although not yet famous, ruefully conceded the point. Sitting in the barber chair, characters from his next story shuffling and reshuffling through his head, Eddie heard a couple of men behind him laughing about a belt and for a terrible second burned with embarrassment. When he listened more closely, he realized that the joke was not about his clothes but about somebody whose name was Belt. *Doctor* Belt, the men said: the title emphasized and drawn out in the wonder typical of those times, especially down in the Valley, where educated Negroes were less common. Doctor Belt had come to Harlem, the men were saying, to general guffaws from the shop, and the bartenders better look out.

Eddie was not, really, a man who hung out in bars, for he had been bred, much against his will, to a disdain of a certain kind of Negro. He did his drinking in the nicer clubs and the salons instead. But so did Doctor Belt. The name was familiar. Eddie had saved the stories about Castle. Flipping through them later, he found a list in the *Amsterdam News* of prominent Negroes the lawyer had numbered among his friends. There it was, Doctor Joseph Belt, identified as a "government official." Eddie learned over the next few days that Belt was a physicist, a former assistant professor at Stanford, who now earned a nice living at a laboratory out west. Eddie was intrigued. He had not met many Negro scientists, although he himself had once hoped to be one. Albert Einstein, the greatest scientist of them all, had died in Princeton, New Jersey, the other day, and periodicals everywhere were running stories on "the technological century." Scientists had become heroes. Technology was everywhere. Polio had been cured. A new invention not only washed your dishes for you but dried them. There was serious talk of putting a man on

Hyde Library
Memphis University School

the moon. It had become possible to incinerate a hundred thousand people in a heartbeat. The darker nation was caught up in the excitement. There was an editor at the *Amsterdam News* who now and then still published Eddie's essays. It occurred to Eddie that he might track down Doctor Belt for a quick interview, a black take on the technological century.

But Belt was uncooperative. He refused Eddie's entreaties. He would not meet. Eddie was the sort of man who took rejection as a challenge. From Wesley Senior, past master of politics as well as preaching, he had learned that connections existed to be used, that people of power enjoyed doing favors to place you in their debt. So he approached Langston Hughes, who was owed by everyone. Hughes came through, persuading Doctor Belt to meet Eddie for a drink at the Savoy. The physicist refused to talk about his work, and told Eddie that, had he known this was the subject, he would never have accepted the invitation. Eddie said, no, no, he just wanted to hear what it was like to be a Negro scientist. Belt eyed him disdainfully from behind thick glasses. Science was science, he said, missing the point. There was not Negro science and white science, there was good science and bad science. Belt signaled the waiter for another Scotch. He was a distant, paunchy man, soft and dark like a chocolate Santa. Belt drank heavily but not sloppily. He drank the way men drink to forget their burdens, not to unload them. He was in town to visit friends, he said. He had missed Phil's funeral. He would pay his respects to the widow before she returned to South Carolina. Eddie kept trying to ask about science. Belt ignored him. He spent a lot of time looking at the door, as if expecting a friend, or perhaps an enemy. The Savoy was one of the most famous music halls in New York. There were as many white guests as black. A couple of movie stars had a table near the band. Smoke hung heavily in the air. The waiters did you a favor by fetching your order. Belt said people were nicer back home, but never said where home was. Somebody dropped a tray of dishes and Belt was on his feet, shaking. He looked around, embarrassed, and headed for the door.

"What are you afraid of?" Eddie asked in the lobby, where Belt

Hyde Library
Memphis University School

was buying cigarettes at the stand. The scientist said nothing. Eddie tried again. "Does it have to do with what happened to Philmont Castle?"

Belt focused on him at last, the eyes moist and rejecting behind the thick glasses. "I'm not afraid of anything," he said, then glanced over his shoulder.

Eddie tried again. "Does it have something to do with the cross?" He tried to remember his father's letter. "The Cross of Saint Peter?"

A flicker in the dark, constrained face. Nothing more. But the physicist definitely reacted. Then he snickered, and the disdain was back. "What is this, some kind of test? The devils are really scraping the bottom of the barrel if they had to send somebody like you."

"Which devils are these?"

Doctor Belt said nothing. He turned contemptuously away, then swung, briefly, back. "Tell them to stay away from me," he said, and left.

(11)

THE SECOND of the three events that set Edward Wesley Junior upon his path occurred in July of that same year, 1955—in the larger history, a few days after Disneyland opened its doors for the first time out in California; and, in Eddie's personal history, on the day of Aurelia's fabulous wedding to Kevin Garland. Eddie at first planned not to attend, but his younger sister, Junie, persuaded him. Junie was a law student at Harvard, the only woman of the darker nation in her class. From the time they were small, Junie had been her big brother's frequent muse.

"What are you trying to say by staying away?" she demanded, when he called her long-distance on a neighbor's phone. "That you love Aurelia? Everybody in Harlem knows you love Aurelia. So all you're really saying is you're too much of a cad to wish her well."

Eddie, feeling trapped, took refuge in silly humor. "What if I lose control and punch Kevin?"

"Don't even joke about that." He could feel his sister's shudder over the telephone. She had always hated every form of human violence. Back in high school, in the thick of the war, Eddie had teased her, the way big brothers do, demanding to know if she would shoot Hitler if given the chance. Junie had said she might, but would have to kill herself next.

"I'm sorry," he said now, and meant it.

"Go to the wedding," she instructed. "Give the best toast."

So he laughed, and went. For that matter, so did Junie, who did not want to leave her nervous brother without an escort. It had been a while since she had seen New York, she said, and it was time. Although the bride was from Cleveland, her family wanted to marry off their daughter in the heart of well-to-do Harlem. The wedding was at Saint Philip's Episcopal Church on 134th Street. Kevin Garland was a vestryman, and, indeed, the Garlands, grandest family in all Harlem, practically owned the place. Alas, at the last minute Aurelia's parents were unable to make the trip: her father had taken a nasty tumble, and was hospitalized. Eddie sat stoically, dying a bit inside, wondering how Aurie could marry into the kind of family who would insist that the wedding go on as planned, bride's parents or no; and wondering, too, whether Aurelia was really being pressured by her family to marry into a senior clan, or if Eddie had been only a last fling: perhaps this storybook marriage was what Aurie had planned all along. When the priest invited the groom to kiss the bride, Eddie shut his eyes, trying and failing to remember who had written that every true novel is about the love you lost.

Junie, who never missed a thing, poked his ribs and told him to stop mooning. "It's their day, not yours," she hissed.

The reception was in the ballroom of the Savoy Hotel, transformed at enormous expense to resemble the interior of a Venetian palace, right down to the painted ceiling, frieze-covered walls, and gilded pilasters. This was the style of the times. The matrons who ran Harlem society—"light-skinned Czarinas," Adam Clayton Powell had dubbed them, meaning anything but a compliment—made frequent jaunts to Europe, and returned bubbling with obsolete ideas. A good quarter of the guests were white. Eddie fumbled his toast, but Gary Fatek, his rich friend from Amherst, spoke brilliantly. Gary was tall and graceful and impressive. Even his unruly red hair commanded attention. When he opened his mouth, choirs sang. He kept the room laughing, and worked into his remarks the fact that he and Eddie had met Aurelia at the same college mixer, in November of their freshman year. Thus the celebrants were able to acknowledge the eight-year love affair now at an end, without anyone's actually mentioning it. This was Gary's element: not only speaking, but speaking in Harlem. On other days he could be found, by his own description, rabble-rousing in libraries and church basements, urging the glorious alliance between students and workers but Negroes in particular. The Czarinas sniffed that Gary had time for this silliness because he was half a Hilliman and did not have to work for a living. If the question ever arose, Gary, laughing, said he did it to pick up girls.

When the toasting finally ended, the drinking began. With Junie on hand, Eddie consumed less alcohol than he had at the engagement party. Clear-headed, he watched uneasily.

"Smile."

"I am smiling."

"Not like that. A real smile."

Eddie did his best, but he was remembering the last time he had sat among strangers celebrating the couple, and how that night had ended. He had yet to tell even Junie or Gary about finding the body.

"Get out there and have some fun," Junie commanded, refusing to allow her brother to mope. She wore him out, forcing him to dance one number after another, most of them with a young woman named Mona Veazie, Aurelia's maid of honor. Mona, at this time considered one of the most desirable Harlem bachelorettes, had been eyeing Eddie half the night, but grew annoyed at the way his glance kept following the bride, and finally switched to Gary. Rumor said she preferred white men anyway. As for Junie, she mostly sat at the table. A couple of the more daring young fellows invited her to dance, but she smiled shyly and dipped her head and declined. People pointed, and whispered. But, then, the senior clans of Harlem found her odd to begin with. The Czarinas did not know what to make of Junie, who studied law and showed no interest in marriage. Family ties might have rescued another young woman from similar strangeness: Mona Veazie, for example, was rather peculiar herself, pursuing a doctoral degree, but the Veazies, architects for six generations, enjoyed a social prominence that excused eccentricity. On the other hand, for all the respect in which Wesley Senior was held for his civil-rights activism, his family was not really—

And then the whispering stopped, because Junie, too, was dancing, not with a nobody like herself, but with Perry Mount, *the* Perry Mount, Harlem's golden boy, the young man every clan hoped its daughters might snare. A roomful of beautiful debutantes of the darker nation, and Perry was dancing with Junie. The Czarinas looked at each other in perplexity. Eddie glared. He had never really liked Perry, perhaps because of the golden boy's ill-concealed crush on Junie, stretching well back into their shared childhoods. Nowadays Perry went after everybody. Eddie was determined to protect his sister from heartbreak. It did not occur to him that Perry might, at this moment, be making her happy.

Gary Fatek, back at Eddie's side, handed his friend a club soda, then, for a while, watched him watching Junie.

"Look at the bright side," he said after several minutes. "At least you're not staring at Aurie any more."

(I I I)

THE BAND PLAYED a fanfare. Flurry on the dance floor as the guests parted, forming an aisle. Bride and groom were departing the palace, hand-in-hand, wearing their traveling clothes, and Eddie was cheering along with everyone else, because that was what one did; besides, Junie's fingers were digging into his arm. The bandleader announced that the dancing would continue until midnight for those so inclined. Eddie was not inclined to do anything but lead the charge to the exit. Gary and Mona were very cozy in a dim corner. Eddie looked around for his sister. Perry, bowing like a cavalier, delivered her to his elbow. Junie was glowing.

Eddie made himself a bet that Perry wouldn't call her for six months.

He had almost made his escape, arm around his sister's waist, when an imperious voice bade him halt.

Amaretta Veazie, the most senior Czarina in Harlem, demanded his attention. Amaretta was tall and stout and swaybacked, people said from years of sniffing down her nose. Her honeysuckle skin bespoke generations of careful breeding, for the clans admired such planning. Her tongue was the most feared weapon in Sugar Hill. Turning to face her, Eddie imagined himself being asked his intentions toward her daughter, Mona. But Amaretta was smiling: a friendly viper.

"Oh, Mr. Wesley," she cooed, sliding her fleshy arm through his. "There's a simply lovely man here who insists that he is a fan. He's too shy to ask, but he would be honored if you would inscribe a *dédicace*"—which she mispronounced.

"It would be my pleasure," said Eddie, bewildered, as she led him across the room—bewildered because he had published nothing but a short story.

"His name is Emil something," the Czarina explained as she led the way. "A white man, Mr. Wesley. He came with Kevin's cousin Derek. Enid Garland's son. Weren't you and Derek Garland in school together?"

"No, ma'am."

"I suppose they're just friends. Still, I don't know that I entirely approve of this business of men attending with other men, Mr. Wesley. Do you?"

"I haven't given it much thought, ma'am."

"Was Derek this peculiar in school? The politics and so on?" She dropped her voice to a whisper. "This Emil is some kind of artist. And you know how *they* are."

But Emil, when the two men were alone, looked more like a policeman, and Eddie was on his guard. Emil was perhaps fifty, with thinning somber hair and guarded eyes that knew you were lying before you did. He drank only water and spoke with a slight accent.

Eddie inquired.

Emil explained that he was a photographer and an artist, and had emigrated from Germany just before the war. Eddie had been trained by Wesley Senior to make every conversation with someone new about the other person. He congratulated Emil, because West Germany had just recently been declared a sovereign nation.

But Emil either had no small talk or did not care about his country of origin, because he shrugged like a sophisticate bored with trifles. Then he got to the point. "This man who died. This Castle. Did you know him?"

"I beg your pardon."

"The capitalist attorney who was murdered by hooligans."

"I never met him."

"I understood that you knew him."

Eddie shook his head. "You understand incorrectly."

"But you know his friends," the photographer persisted. "An acquaintance of mine saw you with Joseph Belt. The physicist. That was you, wasn't it?"

"What acquaintance was this?" asked Eddie, very surprised.

A Democratic Party ward boss came over to tell Eddie how much he had enjoyed the story. Eddie barely noticed. The German gave him the creeps. He did not look like the sort of man who attended weddings for fun. Maybe this was the man Belt was scared of.

Emil said, "I met this Castle. A fine man. Very concerned about how Negroes are treated here, as I of course am, along with my countrymen."

"Of course," said Eddie with a smile, but the German only frowned, as if levity was forbidden.

"I took photographs for Castle. His son was in some special ceremony. The Boy Scouts, I believe." A pause. Eddie could feel the other man sizing him up. "Mr. Castle borrowed the original proofs. Those belong to me." The chilly eyes continued to appraise him. "I need those proofs back. But you did not know him."

"No. Sorry."

"I would pay well for their return. Perhaps you might ask his friend Belt."

Eddie felt himself bristle. What had he said, that this man should assume him so mercenary? "You could ask him yourself."

"I cannot," said the German.

When he said nothing more, Eddie asked, "Have you tried the widow? She moved down south."

Emil twisted his face in disapproval, as if Eddie had committed a second faux pas. "The matter is complicated," he said.

"I'm sorry, but—"

"If you did manage to help me, you would find the materials in a large pink envelope, with a penciled number in the corner, seventeen or eighteen."

"I really don't think—"

"I would pay well," Emil repeated, handing him a business card. "Consider my offer."

"I can give you my answer now," Eddie began, but Emil was halfway across the room. Eddie watched him go.

Gary came and stood beside him. "Who was that?"

Eddie explained.

His friend waved to Mona Veazie, who was departing with a clutch of girlfriends. "Have I mentioned that I knew Phil Castle a little bit?"

An indulgent smile. "A time or two."

"His firm represents the Hilliman family trusts. Phil did a little work on some corporation we were buying"—this casually—"and, well, he and I got to know each other." Gary gestured with his glass. "Anyway, I went sailing with Phil and his wife and kids one day. Four kids."

"So?"

"So—this Emil guy told you that he took photos of Phil's son for a Boy Scout ceremony. He wants you to get the proofs back."

"Right."

"Did you wonder why he picked you?"

Eddie shrugged. "Somebody saw me with Joseph Belt. Emil thought I was a friend of Castle's."

Gary shook his head. "Phil Castle didn't have any shortage of friends. There isn't any reason Emil had to come to you. And, whatever he wants you to recover for him, it isn't photos of a Boy Scout ceremony."

"How do you know that?"

"Because Phil Castle only had daughters."

CHAPTER 4

Willed Imagination

(1)

AURELIA HAD KNOWN LIFE with a Garland would be different but had no idea just how different. Kevin Garland was nine years her senior, an executive at his father's small investment firm, with a lovely smile, a warm sense of humor, and considerable liquid assets. Naturally, the leading clans had pointed their daughters his way, but Kevin seemed happy on his own. The Czarinas could not fathom such a phenomenon. Behind cupped hands, they speculated on whether he might be one of *those*. Aurelia changed everything. From the first month of her arrival in Harlem, Aurie had attracted a coterie of suitors, and Kevin, along with Eddie Wesley, had led the pack. Eddie was smarter, Kevin was more fun. Eddie was always serious. Kevin loved to tell little jokes. Eddie was a terrible dancer and not terribly romantic, but he could teach her things about history and politics. Still, she could learn the same things from books if she wanted. Kevin sent her flowers at least once a week and danced like a dream. Unlike Eddie, he never talked down to her. He knew everybody, and could show her places no book could describe. True, Kevin tended to like things the way they were, but he could also provide for her like royalty, bringing to life the foolish dreams of childhood.

One evening during their courtship, Kevin said he had a surprise for her. They took a taxi to a fancy hotel on Central Park South, the sort of place Negroes dared not enter, even in the absence of a formal color bar. Kevin crossed the lobby as if he owned it. They rode the elevator to a suite overlooking the park. A pair of guards stood before the door. Inside, Kevin introduced Aurelia to Richard Nixon, the

Vice President of the United States. Nixon made an awkward fuss over her. He told her that the Garlands were wonderful people, that they were in the front rank in the fight against the Red menace. He clapped an embarrassed Kevin on the back, and pronounced him a future leader of the Negro people. Nixon was in the city to address the United Nations, where America at this time was feared and envied but not yet hated. He had a sad, shy, jowly face, a flat-footed walk, and a way of dropping his head without hunching his shoulders and still watching you. He smiled like a man not sure just why.

"We don't want to take too much of your time, sir," said Kevin.

"Your husband's a hero," said the Vice President, waggling a finger. "One day the story will come out." Nixon winked. Kevin looked at the floor.

"He's not my husband," said Aurelia. Seeing Kevin's crestfallen face, she felt constrained to add, "Not yet."

"Well, hold on to him. He's rich." The Vice President was famously not rich. His suit was relentlessly inexpensive. A few years earlier, he had deflected an influence-peddling scandal by assuring the nation in a televised address that his wife, Pat, wore a cheap cloth coat. "And a good man. Remember that."

"Thank you. I will."

"Hear great things about you."

"About me?"

"Column you write. Fans everywhere." The shy smile as an aide appeared to say it was time for the Vice President to depart. Shaking their hands, he reminded Kevin to call him any time he needed a favor.

Kevin glanced at his beloved, then dropped his voice. But Aurelia's ears were exceptional. "There's only one favor we need," he said—later, Aurelia was adamant that Kevin had said "we."

Nixon's smile faded. "None of my people have turned up a clue."

"We would be grateful if you would keep looking, sir."

"I'll do what I can."

Out on the street afterward, Kevin raised a hand. A blocky yellow cab stopped at once. No Negro could get a taxi in midtown Manhattan, especially at night, everybody knew that, but for elegant Kevin

Garland the rules were different. Aurie shivered, though not with cold. Kevin did not ask where she wanted to go. He told the driver they were heading for Brooklyn Heights, where he kept what he called his bachelor pad, but the cabbie had somehow guessed: although a stalwart of the salons, Kevin just didn't look like Harlem.

Heading downtown, Aurelia asked how he knew Nixon.

"Through my father."

"What did he mean about me having fans everywhere? I write gossip in a tiny little colored newspaper."

Kevin grinned. "Dick's a politician. It's his job to flatter you."

"I couldn't do a job like that."

"Don't I know it."

"Meaning what?" she asked, ready to get hot.

"Meaning, you're not much of a flatterer." His grin widened. "But I guess I don't need much flattery. I do my own."

Aurelia let this pass. "I heard what you and Nixon were talking about."

"Mmmm."

"What's he looking for? What's the big secret?"

"He used to do business with my father."

Her eyes sparkled at this intelligence. "And how does your father know him? Nixon?"

Kevin was a long time answering. "Remember the big scandal back in '52? When Nixon was accused of having this secret fund to smear his opponents? Paid for by a bunch of his millionaire friends from California?"

"No," said Aurelia, truthfully.

He patted her hand. "Well, not all the millionaires were white."

(11)

OVER A LATE DINNER, Kevin regaled her with stories of his father's years in California right after the war, one crazy moneymaking scheme after another.

"Some of them obviously worked," said Aurelia.

"And some of them should have landed him in jail."

She spent the night with Kevin—the first time—but was up for hours afterward, weeping. He was too much of a gentleman to ask why. He rubbed her back instead. When he asked her a few days later to marry him, Aurelia replied that she would need time. Kevin hid his disappointment and offered, gallantly, to let her have as much as she needed.

She returned to Harlem. Eddie took her to dinner. She let him kiss her good night but no more. She compared the two men. Kevin thrilled and pampered her, but Eddie touched a softness that Aurelia had never suspected was there. She sat in the apartment she shared with two other women and looked at the array of gifts Kevin had given her over the past year. The following night, she shooed her roommates away and cooked dinner for Eddie. She dropped every hint she knew how to drop, but all Eddie wanted to talk about was his writing. That was perhaps the largest difference between the two men. Both loved her, but Eddie loved something else just as much: their life together would be a ménage à trois.

The next afternoon, she surprised Kevin at his office. He left a meeting to welcome her. She could not help wondering whether Eddie would have done that. "Why do you want to marry me?" she asked.

At first he seemed not to understand. They were in the bullpen, the clerks all watching. "I love you," Kevin said, hand over his heart, playing to the gallery, but adorably. She remembered Eddie that night at Scarlett's: *We shall be conspicuous.* Kevin liked being conspicuous with her.

"But what do you love about me?"

"Everything."

Their engagement was announced two days later. Kevin wanted to visit her parents in Cleveland to ask formally for her hand, but Aurelia dissuaded him. "They can be kind of difficult," she said. "I need to handle them myself."

"When do I meet them?"

"At the wedding."

Alas, the Treenes were unable to attend: her father took that tumble. Kevin suggested a postponement, but his mother would not hear of it. Neither would Aurelia.

(III)

THE HONEYMOON was a six-week European tour. The loving couple stayed in suites at the finest hotels in London, Paris, and Rome, cities she knew only from picture books borrowed from the library. They also visited towns she had never heard of, in Tuscany and the south of France. Kevin knew people everywhere. The hotels treated him like royalty. For a week they were inseparable. Then the strangeness began. Men drew her husband aside for whispered conversations in hotel lobbies, and afterward he would look grim. Envelopes were delivered to their room, and Kevin would shake his head and sulk for hours. Now and then he would kiss her gently and say he had to go out for a while, then vanish into the starry night and not reappear sometimes until morning, cold sober and looking worried. He apologized but never gave account of himself, except to say it was business. Aurie had not been trained for this role. She did not know whether to ignore his transgressions, reproach him, or offer to help. One night, in Paris, Aurelia decided to follow him, but the doorman of the George V took so long to find her a cab that Kevin got away. Only later did it occur to her that the man's seeming incompetence had been prearranged. In Athens, she managed to grab a cab at a rank, but when her driver realized into which corner of the city her target was vanishing, he refused to take her any farther, and gave her the choice of returning to the hotel or being dumped on the corner with the rest of the whores. Aurelia went back. When Kevin walked into the suite at three in the morning, his wife was prepared to give him a really hard time, but he showed no signs of dishevelment and, later, when their activities gave her the opportunity to inspect her husband's body, she found no telltale to suggest that he had been with another woman. The next evening, to make amends, Kevin arranged a private tour of the Acropolis after it had been closed to tourists. The guide told them how the entire adult male population of Athens, thousands and thousands of men, used to assemble here to vote on important decisions. For some reason Kevin grew annoyed and distant once more. In the car on the way back to the hotel, he told her that the problem with democracy was that everybody was entitled to a say.

"Isn't that what we're fighting for? So our people will have a say?"

Her husband's frown only deepened. "There's people and there's people," he muttered.

In bed that night, Kevin told his wife he expected her to quit her job. When Aurelia lost her temper with him for the first time in their brief marriage, he softened and backed down. "I only meant you don't have to work. It's embarrassing for me. People will think I can't support my wife."

"You're a Garland," she shot back. "Nobody will think you can't support me. They'll just think I'm odd."

They foxed around, finally agreeing that Aurie would return to the *Sentinel* half-time, assuming it remained open, and only until they had children.

"When the female brain stops working," she wrote the next day in a letter to Mona Veazie.

Their final stop was London, and that was where Kevin left her alone for three days, this time warning her in advance, and explaining patiently, as she threw a poorly aimed hairbrush, that it could not be helped. The staff of the Dorchester would meet her every whim, he said. When she threatened to return to the States, Kevin dropped his eyes.

"You can do that. The concierge will fix your ticket. But I need you here."

"Need me? You're leaving me alone!"

"I mean, I need you *here*. In this suite. Please." He touched her face. "I'm sorry, honey. I can't trust anybody else just now." He kissed her. "After this, it's over. I promise."

He did not say what *it* was.

Aurelia stayed, and seethed, shopping recklessly and having the bills sent to the hotel. But she always hurried back, because Kevin had said he needed her in the suite. The mound of parcels mocked her. She had bought more than she could carry home, but she would arrive at their new apartment on Edgecombe Avenue as the most fashionably dressed woman in Harlem.

At least that was her plan.

Aurelia had always hated waiting, but waiting alone in a hotel was hell. The suite overlooked Hyde Park. She went for a walk, but everybody else was walking a dog. A couple of gentlemen tipped their caps, but most people ignored her. Back upstairs, she stalked the suite's three rooms like a madwoman. The furniture was old and heavy. The maids were subservient and never met her eyes. She wondered what they made of her. There were no other Negroes, guests or staff, in the building. She worked the *Times* crossword, getting better each time. She went sightseeing. She went to the zoo. She went to Westminster. The second day of her husband's absence was Sunday. Aurelia put on her best jewelry and attended services at Saint Paul's. Everybody gawked at her. She felt overdressed, but it was better than being underdressed. She wrote a letter to Mona on the hotel stationery. She wrote a column for the *Sentinel*, datelined London, and had the concierge send it as air freight. She wrote a long letter to her parents, but failed to post it. Instead, she left it atop the desk where anyone might see, and, every now and then, added a line or two. On the third evening, the porter appeared with a large envelope, tightly sealed. Kevin's name was on the outside. To Aurie's surprise, she was required to sign for it. She put the envelope on the dresser. The only one he could trust. Well, she would see about that. If Kevin was not back by lunch, she would open it herself.

Maybe sooner.

But Kevin was back at the Dorchester by breakfast. He slipped into the suite right behind the waiter. Aurelia leaped to her feet. Her husband's eyes were red. His clothes were dirty. "They almost didn't let me in." He rapped out an order to the waiter, then took his wife's hands and tried to kiss her, but she turned her face and made him go wash.

"This envelope came for you," she said when he returned.

"Good," he said, and kissed her. He picked it up and glanced at the flap. "Did you open it?"

"No." Kevin looked at her. "I didn't, honey." He just kept staring. She thought she would scream. "Where did you go?" she finally asked. "What have you been doing? Can't you tell me?"

Kevin sighed and shook his head, his delicate face pinched with exhaustion. "Phil left a mess behind."

"Phil Castle?"

"He did business with my father's firm."

"In Athens? In Tuscany?"

Her husband barely heard. He was riffling through the pages from the envelope. "It's a long story," Kevin said, and she knew he would never tell it and regretted what he had said already.

That night, they went to dinner at the home of a baronet, and Aurelia so charmed their host that their hostess made excuses early. In the hansom cab back to the hotel, Aurelia asked her husband how on earth he knew such a man.

"Dad knows everybody," he said.

Aurelia was a little tipsy. "He can't know everybody," she said, giggling. "It's a physical and psychological impossibility."

"Everybody," Kevin repeated, sounding glum. "Well, you'll see."

In bed that night, when she reached for her husband, he turned away. An awkward silence. Then, always feisty, Aurelia asked what was wrong.

"The honeymoon is over," he said.

A beat.

"Kevin?"

"Yes, honey?"

"Is it me?"

"Don't be silly."

A longer interlude, Aurelia wishing he would at least turn and face her in the darkness. "Did you find it?" She wished her voice would tremble less.

"Find what?"

"Whatever you were looking for."

"Not yet," he said, and slept.

The next day, they embarked for New York aboard the *Queen Mary*, in the Winston Churchill Suite, second-finest on the ship.

Kevin spent the voyage in the telegraph room, exchanging cryptic and very expensive messages with his father.

Aurelia spent the voyage wondering whom she had married.

(I V)

SOMETIMES AURELIA DREAMED of Sister Dorcas, a stocky, somber nun from the school of her youth, who used to warn at least twice weekly that lying was a sin against God's wonderful gift of speech. Once, the eight-year-old Aurie stole a cookie from another girl's lunch tray, then lied about it. Dorcas forced her to admit her double sins—stealing and false witness—before the whole class. Aurelia thought she was headed straight to Hell, but when Dorcas sent her to see Sister Immaculata, who was in charge of discipline, the elderly nun, who was said to be from Russia or Australia or one of those places where they spoke with accents, only gave Aurie a scolding and made her memorize a couplet by George Herbert about daring to be true because nothing could need a lie.

Something like that.

Yet the lesson took. As a grown woman, Aurelia had a great deal of trouble managing a lie. She could force herself to do it, especially in the right cause, but she always found, later, the words of Sister Immaculata's poem on her lips. Instead, she indulged in what she came to think of as acts of willed imagination. When forced to balance two lovers—Kevin and Eddie, for instance, back before her engagement—Aurelia never actually lied to one about the other. No. She committed acts of imagination. She created stories to keep each beau from worrying about the other. Even Sister Dorcas allowed works of fiction.

"It still sounds like lying to me," Mona had said when Aurelia tried to explain her theory.

"That's because you don't have an imagination."

But Aurie did have an imagination, an imagination as rich and fertile as any novelist's. She used it a lot, weaving works of fiction rather than lies. So, when she told her husband she had not opened the envelope delivered to the suite in his absence, Aurelia had not lied exactly. She had simply imagined a story in which she had remained a dutiful wife, never touching the envelope no matter how it mocked and teased her from the dresser. That was what she had told Kevin: not a lie, but a short story about another woman, a woman Aurelia admired but, alas, did not always manage to be.

The other Aurelia, the one who could never quite behave herself, had indeed opened the envelope, carefully tugging the flap with her fingers in a mixture of fear and worry and lonely rage, after first prudently borrowing glue from the concierge, to be able to seal it up again. The fault, this other Aurelia told herself, was not her own but Kevin's, for abandoning her on their honeymoon for what he claimed was business even though it looked more like—

Well, Aurie did not know exactly what it looked like, but she knew exactly what it felt like. It felt like her husband was engaging in a little willed imagination of his own.

And so she had opened the envelope, and pulled out a sheaf of colored papers, all of them blank, and found, in the middle, a short letter. She frowned, and, as an inveterate snoop, guessed the answer. The colored pages were to keep anybody from reading the letter by holding the envelope up to the light. The letter itself began, oddly, *"Dear Author,"* as if to a writer or a magazine.

All interrogations were negative. All sources have been unproductive. The testament is likely on your side of the water. Kindly inform our mutual friend that the debt is paid. We can offer no further assistance.

The letter was unsigned.

Maybe it was business after all, Aurie reflected, slathering glue over the flap, and hoping nobody would think to check for fingerprints.

When she was done, she crawled into bed and lay awake, waiting for morning. She tossed and turned, wondering. Her husband was receiving secret unsigned notes from people who could perform *interrogations* and had *sources* and used words like *unproductive*, people who helped the *Author* because of a *debt* owed to a *mutual friend*. He had dragged his new bride around Europe in search of a *testament* that was probably back in the States.

A testament.

The sort of thing people left behind when they died.

Now, after her husband's return, Aurie understood a little more. *Phil left a mess behind*, Kevin told her, exhaustion making him indiscreet. But a mess evidently was not all Castle had left. He had also left some kind of testament. Maybe the note referred to his will, the disposition of his estate, but her husband's frantic search suggested otherwise. No. Aurelia was sure that the testament was something else, nothing to do with money or property. And whatever the testament might be, Kevin Garland was desperate to find it.

CHAPTER 5

Again the Cross of Saint Peter

(1)

THE THIRD EVENT that cemented Eddie's purpose occurred early in 1956, not long before the publication of the novel that would make him famous. The novel, entitled *Field's Unified Theory*, was the story of a Negro physicist who spent his angry, disdainful life searching for the Holy Grail that defied even the great Einstein: the so-called unified field theory that would discover the common physical effect behind gravity and electromagnetism; and if in hindsight the inspiration for the story seems plain, it was less so at the time, at least to the public. Advance copies had leaked out. There was already talk of a National Book Award. Eddie's Harlem friends made gentle fun. They repeated drearily familiar jokes. How is a Negro writer like a giraffe? The bigger he gets, the more people laugh at him. What's the difference between a Negro writer and a Negro janitor? The janitor can live on his income. Nevertheless, they were proud of him, as was his mother, and perhaps even his father, although Eddie had only his mother's word for it.

His father had gone south again, and was busy organizing more boycotts.

Eddie hardly cared. Now New York's white as well as black salons were open to him. He had become what he had longed to be, the man on the rise. His celebrity did not quite balance the loss of Aurelia, who had become, to his confused dismay, rapidly and radiantly pregnant. One cloudy May afternoon, they happened to run into each other outside the offices of the *Sentinel* on Seventh Avenue.

They shared a distant, friendly hug, and then, eyes aglow, she asked Eddie about rumors that he had been seeing Mona Veazie.

"I believe Gary is seeing her," said Eddie.

"What about Torie Elden?" One hand saucily on hip, the other rubbing her newly rounded belly. "Somebody saw the two of you at Craig's Colony Club the other night, and—"

"I'm not seeing anybody."

"Well, you should be." She raised a hand to forestall his response. "We are where we are, Eddie. Let it be."

Her use of "we" struck Eddie as inapt. Aurelia was married to a Garland. She was pregnant with Kevin's child. Eddie felt Wesley Senior at his shoulder, thundering that Aurelia should be singing her husband's praises, not allowing an ex-beau to infer that she was having second thoughts. He asked, forcing a smile, how the great marriage was going.

Aurelia briefly dropped her gaze. "Oh, well, you know Kevin," she said.

"I'm sure the two of you are very happy," he said, every word costing him.

"I'm sure," she echoed, meekly.

Eddie's raising would not allow him to press further. They were where they were. When Aurelia, working hard, began gushing about something hilarious that Thurgood Marshall had said last week at Amaretta Veazie's salon, Eddie let her gush, and even laughed on key.

"I'm glad you're happy," said Eddie before they parted. "And, listen, if you ever need—"

"An autograph?" she teased, before he could say anything foolish. "Tell you what. When you're famous enough, I'll come beg you for one."

A couple of nights later, Eddie attended a dinner party at a Central Park South duplex owned by a wealthy white couple, patrons of the arts and friends of Langston Hughes, who had arranged Eddie's invitation. Actually, the night began as comedy. Eddie walked into the lobby still puzzling over Aurelia's meaning, and therefore failed to impress the doorman, who refused to believe that he was a guest, refused to call upstairs to check, and threatened, if Eddie would not vacate the premises, to buzz the deputy commissioner of police, who lived on the fourth floor. Hating humiliation above all things, Eddie folded his arms and stood his ground. Just then a Columbia professor arrived, a philologist of some note. He tried slipping past the contretemps, but his wife tugged at his arm and announced in a voice to wake the dead that this must be the Negro Helen had told her about.

Upstairs Eddie found only one other Negro—Mona Veazie, who arrived on the arm of Gary Fatek. Half a Hilliman or not, Gary loved to shock. Chairs had been set out in the long drawing room. A well-known pianist played a sonata. The Columbia philologist, who was just back from East Africa, discussed certain discoveries he had made about the use of participles in Kiswahili. Then it was Eddie's turn, speaking in place of Hughes, who was abroad. He was nervous: his skill was with the written word. He mumbled a few sentences about the role of the literary imagination in the movement for Negro rights, on both sides, tossing in a modest criticism of Faulkner for his portrayal of the darker nation. He graciously thanked his hosts. He was applauded.

Afterward, Eddie chatted with Gary and Mona, but it was evident that they planned an early getaway and had come only to hear his remarks. Before Eddie could manage his own departure, he was snagged by an elderly man with sour breath who wanted to compliment him on his recent success on Broadway. A swift young couple wanted to know whether he was available to do other parties. A pleasantly plump woman in her twenties flirted, asking if Eddie believed all that or if maybe it was just show.

"All of what?"

"About writing. Do you write for justice? Do you write for money? Or do you write because your muse forces you?"

Eddie took a good look at her. Her thick brown hair was tangly and unstylish, as if she didn't care. Green eyes teased him from beneath heavy brows. Her first name was Margot. Her surname had a "Van" in it. She lived and worked in the city, and was attending tonight's party with her parents, who looked prosperous and indulgent. Margot followed his gaze. She assured him that her parents lived in Washington, and were headed home tonight on the late train. Her slim mother displayed an exotic swarthiness that he tentatively identified as Greek. Her balding father possessed the same round, peppy face as his daughter. Eddie recognized the name. He was Elliott Van Epp, a conservative Senator from a Midwestern farm state, often talked of as presidential timber. Eddie was trying to decide whether the realization was grounds for backing off or pressing forward when he noticed the gold cross snuggled tightly at the young woman's fleshy throat. It was identical to the one he had found clutched in the hand of poor Philmont Castle, whose murder last year remained unsolved—and, mostly, forgotten.

Margot was wearing the same cross.

The same cross, upright this time, ornate workings unmistakable. Eddie's keen eyes could even discern the start of the upside-down inscription he had been unable to read that night: "We shall," the tiny words began once more. The rest was again lost to him, swirling around the back and into her sweater.

Margot smiled. "What are you looking at, Mr. Wesley?"

Caught. He softened. Just now, caught was not so bad. Aurelia was gone, and his other serial relationships had gone serially bad. It had been a long time. "What would you imagine me to be looking at?"

"The same thing most men look at, Mr. Wesley."

"Call me Eddie," he said, smiling back.

"All right, Eddie, but before you get any ideas, I should tell you that I'm engaged."

"A fearful malady that afflicts most pretty girls sooner or later." He bowed. "I've seen it before," he added, ruefully.

"Have you?"

"Often. But I promise not to hold it against you."

Three nights later, Eddie sat in his bedroom, examining the cross close up. He twirled it between his fingers. He had little experience of serious jewelry, but the gold was shiny and soft, its weight in his palm a growing surprise. "We shall be free," the inscription read, except that on the back the words were right side up, suggesting that the cross, when seen from the other side, was meant to be inverted.

The four points of the cross were marked by narrow arrowheads, each with a line joining the legs, as if to form the letter "A." Eddie perched on the windowsill trying to work out how this well-bred girl and a Wall Street lawyer came to own the same curiously designed gold cross, marked with the same upside-down legend. He recalled the letter from his father but could not accept the image of either Philmont Castle or Margot Van Epp as devil worshipers. Eddie suspected that he was missing something very obvious, and, being a man of action, woke her up to ask.

"From my mother," Margot said sleepily. In the darkness she was sweaty and inert. She had piously removed the cross prior to sex. "Come to bed."

"Where did she get it?"

"I think Italy. I don't remember."

"Italy?"

"Back before the war. I was a little girl." She yawned. "My mother's Italian. Half Italian. Now, put it down and come to bed."

"Are you a Catholic?"

She considered the question for a while, eyes glazing a bit because she was still a little high. Finally, she shrugged pale, sloping shoulders. "Not really. We're not really anything, except at election time." A sharp grin. Her teeth, like her famous father's, were huge. Margot was leaving town in a few days; when she returned, she would be a wife. "Then we're everything."

Eddie pointed. "What do the words mean? Are they a quote from somewhere?"

"I don't know."

"Are they from the Bible?"

"I told you, Eddie, I don't know. Come back to bed."

"Why are they upside down on the back?"

"I don't know." Yawning again, Margot looked around the cramped space. "This is stupid," she announced. "I shouldn't be here."

Eddie was too focused to waste energy on charm. "What about these marks?" Pointing. "Are they the letter 'A'?"

This time she only shrugged.

"Are there more crosses like this one?"

"I would imagine so."

Her insouciance had started to annoy him. "You never asked? You wear it, but you don't know anything about it?"

Margot finally sat up. The sheet curtained at her waist. She beckoned lazily, fleshy fingers fluttering. "Come to bed," she repeated. "Or else I'm going home."

"It's dangerous out there at night."

"It's dangerous everywhere."

"It's not dangerous in here."

"You're dangerous anywhere," she said, leaning back for him.

(11)

EDDIE LED MARGOT down the dank back stairs at five-thirty in the morning and bundled her into a waiting gypsy cab driven by his old friend Lenny from Scarlett's gang, who never slept and was amused to cooperate in these ventures, and who, Eddie swore, could be trusted absolutely. On the sidewalk, Margot took his hand but did not kiss him.

"The next time you see me, I'll be Mrs. Lanning Frost."

"And then what? First Lady in fifteen years?"

"Maybe twenty." The green eyes sparkled. "First we need to get Lanning into Congress—well, he always calls it *the* Congress, he's such a pretentious bastard—and then wait for our senior Senator, or maybe even Poppa, to retire. A term in the Senate, maybe two, and then we'll be ready."

"We?"

"Me and Lanning." She laughed. Her lips brushed his cheek. "Don't worry. I'll get the Secret Service to sneak you in. We'll have it off in the East Room."

"I'll look forward to it," he said playfully, but both knew he was anxious to be free of her.

At the end of the alley a bus guttered past. A garbage truck followed, rattling. Working Harlem, the larger fraction, had started to wake. "Eddie?"

"Yes, Margot?"

"Why did you ask me all those questions about my cross?"

He shrugged. Lenny Rouse was waving impatiently from the car. "I've never seen one like that before."

A long moment while the brilliant eyes measured him. "Yes, you have," Margot said at last, and, rising on her toes, kissed his cheek. She put her small mouth to his ear. "I don't know what you're up to, but I think you should leave it alone."

"Leave what alone?"

"Some things can't be stopped, Eddie."

"Margot—"

"And some things shouldn't be."

"I'm not going to interfere with your plans," he promised, annoyed. "Tell you what. I'll even vote for your husband."

Margot laughed, not unkindly. "Oh, Eddie. You think you're so cynical and sophisticated, but you're so naïve."

His cheeks burned. "I'm what?"

"I'm not talking about *Lanning*. You can stop *Lanning* all you want." Another peck, this one on his mouth. Then she scrambled into Lenny's cab and pulled the door behind her, the Saint Peter's Cross glistening at her neck.

(III)

CONTRARY TO WESLEY SENIOR'S FEARS, his son was not lazy. He was a prodigious worker. He simply preferred writing to everything else. Research in particular came hard to him. One of his history professors had assured him, despairingly, that he could be a brilliant student if he spent less time at his diary and typewriter and more time in the library. But Eddie did not dream of being a brilliant student. He dreamed of being a brilliant writer. Too much research, he used to preach, would dull the pen. Thus his next actions would have confounded those who knew him, had he not carefully kept them secret. He began to frequent the city's many libraries and museums. He read learned articles on the image of the cross. He browsed the collection of crucifixes at the Cloisters, the Gothic castle on 193rd Street in Fort Tryon Park, guarding the northern tip of Manhattan. He wandered Saint Patrick's Cathedral, studying images, asking questions. He contacted the Columbia philologist he had met at the party, who in turn put him in touch with a couple of medievalists. He told them he was doing research for another novel, and a part of him probably was. He even got in touch with his father again, this time actually using the telephone and risking That Voice, as he and Junie used to call it. He asked his father where the words "We shall be free" appeared in the Bible. The pastor inquired gruffly if his son imagined he had the whole book committed to memory, and directed him to Strong's *Concordance*, of which Eddie had never heard. The New York Public Library had a copy. But either Professor Strong had erred or the words were from another source, for his massive tome listed "she shall be free" in Numbers and "he shall be free" in Deuteronomy but "we shall be free" nowhere. The medievalists were no more helpful, nor were the museums, and the curator at the Cloisters kept telling him that without seeing the item in question he could not really venture a guess. An archivist at the library told him that any number of fraternal organizations—the Elks, for example, and the Rotarians—incorporated religious symbols into their seals. But none, she admitted, inverted the cross, perhaps because to do so would be disrespectful.

"To whom?"

"To anyone who believes in it," said the librarian primly, a devoted Ethical Culturist.

Harlem at this time was shot through with secret societies, service organizations, and social clubs, some for men, some for women, some for both, and some, said the wags, for neither. But both Margot Van Epp and Philmont Castle were Caucasians, and Eddie knew nothing about the world of white clubs. A friend named Charlie Bing, a dentist, knew the Harlem club world better than anyone, but when Eddie inquired about symbols, Charlie coughed, and colored.

"Nobody talks about other people's clubs. Or their own."

Last shot. Eddie got in touch with a reporter from the *Herald Tribune* who, months before, had treated him to a decent lunch near Union Square and, on promise of writing a profile, solicited his views on everything from the rising generation of "college-educated" Negro writers to the likelihood that Negro voters would continue to desert the Republican Party in the forthcoming presidential elections. The promised profile never appeared, and the paper's brief story about the "new" Negro writers had not mentioned Eddie Wesley. At the time, Eddie had been furious, and humiliated. Now he supposed that the reporter, a reasonably liberal sort, might be persuaded by the proper compound of charm and guilt to do him a favor.

"Sure, Eddie," the man said, probably to get him off the phone.

But he proved to be as good as his word. The police report on Philmont Castle's death, he said a week later over another lunch, this time Eddie's treat, did not mention any piece of jewelry found on or near the body other than a wedding band. Personal items had long since been returned to the family, but the reporter had scribbled the inventory list from the evidence vault in his notebook. He allowed Eddie to take a look. Nothing about a cross. Nothing about anything clutched in the dead hand.

"I'll tell you something funny," the reporter added as they parted. "Now, you understand, we're talking about a year-and-a-half-old murder—"

Eddie motioned this aside. "What is it? What happened?"

"The inventory list was torn out."

"Torn out?"

"They keep these things in ordinary notebooks," the reporter said. "You know, lined pages, like school kids use? Except this page was torn out. Torn out and then stuck back in with tape. Probably just wear and tear. It happens a lot." He saw Eddie's face. "Hey, is there a story here?"

"No story." But he was thinking, as perhaps the reporter was, that it would be an easy matter to tear out one page and tape in its place another, copying the list of evidence but omitting an item or two.

"You sure? Because Harlem's part of my beat. It doesn't get covered too much in this town. We should do better. A juicy scandal might help."

Eddie shook his head. He had learned at his father's feet to mistrust the yearning for outrage that fired so much journalistic endeavor. Only many years later, when the violence was out of control, would it occur to him that by telling the story to a scandal-seeking reporter now, he might have helped avoid the worst. Instead he murmured his grave thanks and returned to Harlem.

Margot's wedding to Lanning Frost made all the society pages, but Eddie could not tell from the grainy photos what, if anything, she wore around her neck.

CHAPTER 6

Czarinas in Training

(1)

"YOU SHOULD GO BACK to school," said Mona Veazie, Aurelia's closest friend. "When the baby's old enough, I mean. Get your graduate degree."

"Don't be silly, dear," said Sherilyn DeForde. "She has a Garland and a baby. All she should do for the rest of her life is bask in it."

"Actually," said the other Garland in the room, Claire—married to Kevin's cousin—"she should ignore the rest of us and do what she wants."

At which Sherilyn tittered, because she was a titterer.

Mrs. Aurelia Garland sat regally among the other women in the plush living room of her apartment at 409 Edgecombe Avenue. Regal, but terrified, and, as befitted royalty, she hid her terror behind a façade of delight. She dandled the baby. Her period of laying in was over, and she was receiving for the first time since Zora's birth. She needed to receive. She needed to be among friends. She needed relief from the endless flow of clucking relatives—none of them hers—who failed, even collectively, to compensate for the absence of her husband. She was exhausted from the work of presenting to the world the face of radiant perfection as her husband crisscrossed the country, and occasionally left it, never saying when, or whether, he planned to return.

Sometimes the telephone would ring in the middle of the night and Kevin would leap wordless from the bed and vanish for a week. And yet he could be so sweet. He took her to sumptuous dinners. He introduced her to all the great men and women she had only heard of, because the Garlands knew everybody. They gave a party for Lena Horne. They gave a party for Sugar Ray Robinson. At a dinner on Long Island, she found herself seated beside Bob Hope. And Kevin still sang, off-key, all the songs with which he had seduced her in the first place: "It had to be youuuu," he would croon, as they danced together in the front room. Or: "You maaaade me love youuu, I didn't wanna do it." One evening when Aurelia thought he was in Detroit he stepped into the bathroom as she climbed from the tub, assuaging her scream with a tender embrace and conjuring from behind his back a spray of long-stemmed roses. Two days later, he failed to come home after work, and when, close to midnight, Aurelia woke Kevin's politely demeaning assistant, Thrush, she learned only that her husband had been called away for "consultations"—by whom, or to where, or on what, Thrush apologetically found himself unable to say.

So she received instead. Sitting in the parlor, she gathered a few friends and sought good-natured advice on what she should do now. The weather was summer-sultry. The windows were open and the radio was on. This was in keeping with an Edgecombe Avenue tradition: The great joke was that some of the apartments offered views of the Polo Grounds down the far side of the hill. During a Giants baseball game, you could sit in the Garland parlor with binoculars and watch. If you raised the window, you could hear the voice of the stadium announcer, and the roar of the crowd, and then, in scratchy echo, the same sound through your radio. Kevin had romanced her with stories of baseball, a sport he thoroughly loved, and had played in college. Now that the big leagues were integrated, all the Negroes listened. The Dodgers were the favorites, because of Jackie Robinson. Kevin used to watch another great Dodger, Don Newcombe, when he played for the Newark Eagles of the Negro Leagues back during the war. Kevin liked to tell how his Aunt Cerinda had suffered a heart attack one afternoon listening to the radio as Newcombe pitched to the Giants' Willie Mays: she could not decide whom to root for.

Is that true? Aurie had asked, giggling.

Well, if it isn't, said Kevin, *it sure should be.*

But when Aurelia met Aunt Cerinda, she turned out to be forty-ish, and in excellent health. Cerinda worked in a bank in Detroit, spent every evening at church, and had never listened to a ball game in her life. In those days, Kevin's propensity to play with the truth seemed charming.

In those days.

"Kevin is so happy," said Sherilyn now, with an insider's wink. "Walking around all the time with his chest puffed out."

"You're so lucky, dear," said Chamonix Bing, with a quiet glance at Claire. "You married into the *rich* wing of the Garland family."

"Although any Garland is a catch," added Sherilyn, who had tried hard to snag one before settling for less.

"This craziness is going to be the ruin of our community," said Mona, hardly looking up. "What ever happened to marrying for love?"

An uncomfortable silence. Mona was so silly that way, always stopping the conversation with her radical nonsense.

Finally, Claire Garland spoke up, the hefty peacemaker. "I married my Oliver for love, Mona, dear. And I rather suspect Aurie married her Kevin for love, too, didn't you, dear?"

Aurelia smiled, eyes lidded with exhaustion. She sipped her sherry.

"And at least now Kevin will leave you alone for a while," said Sherilyn brightly, as if she had not been efficiently and implicitly skewered by Claire, already at thirty a sort of junior Czarina. "Men can be such a *bother* when they want a baby, can't they? So *demanding*."

Chammie Bing agreed. "They think because it's pleasure for them it's pleasure for us." She waited for agreeing laughter. When none came, she rushed on, awkward grin failing entirely to hide her embarrassment. "But it's just part of the cost of having a man, isn't it?"

"Speaking of the bother," said Mona, to Aurie, "I hear your ex-beau has been bothering Torie Elden lately."

"Eddie," clarified Chammie. "The one with no money."

"Everybody bothers Torie," said Sherilyn, who, along with Aurie, had shared a Harlem apartment with her. "And Torie bothers everybody."

"Are you all right, dear?" murmured Claire, who could read the stoniest faces.

"I'm a little tired," said Aurelia.

The women got up to go, kissing her cheek, chucking the baby's chin. At the door, Aurie laid a hand on Claire's fleshy arm and asked her to stay. Mona gave her a look—she was the one who was supposed to share Aurie's secrets—but then her good nature won out, and she gave her friend a lingering hug. Aurelia understood what was going through Mona's mind, but there was no way she could explain. She had asked Claire to stay because she needed to know the truth: did all the Garland men terrify their women, or was it just Kevin?

(1 1)

THAT NIGHT, Aurelia girded herself for battle. Kevin was in town, and would be home for dinner: she had Mr. Thrush's word for it. She gave the maid the evening off and did everything herself. Set the dining-room table with the good silver. Made a spicy chicken fricassee with dumplings, a favorite of all the Garlands. Picked out what she hoped was a nice wine from Kevin's collection. Ordered a strawberry cheesecake from the bakery down the block. Then she put on her slinkiest dress—although she did not feel terribly slinky since Zora's arrival two months ago—and what Kevin liked to call her full paint job. She mixed the martinis and crushed the ice, then sat in the parlor, and waited.

All men need a period of adjustment after a baby, dear, Claire had murmured—although admitting, when pressed, that her Oliver, Kevin's cousin, had not. *Not every man who keeps a secret is up to no good*—although everyone knew that Oliver could hardly wait to get home and tell his wife everything about his day, but only after listening to everything about hers. *If the two of you are having problems, I can recommend somebody*, said Claire, a pediatrician who worked half-time at Harlem Hospital. By this time, Aurelia could hardly wait to get Claire out of the apartment. And yet mixed in with all the useless advice came one nugget of gold: *Oliver says that Kevin never calls any more.*

He used to call?

All the time, dear. They were as close as brothers. And now they're not.

Because Kevin was too busy? Or because Oliver disapproved of whatever he was up to?

She waited for Kevin, wandering through the dining room, to the kitchen, into the nursery to check on Zora, into the guest room, into the master bedroom, then back again, another circuit, as the hands of the grandfather clock in the front hall swept past seven, past eight, toward nine. At half past ten, the maid returned and found the mess where Aurelia had dumped the untouched dishes into the sink. She heard the sobs through the bedroom door but knew better than to knock. When Mr. Kevin got home, he would have to deal with it.

Aurelia woke around one-thirty, the slinky outfit ruined, her paint job now part of the duvet, to find her husband sitting in the bedroom chair, holding a shoe in his hand as if frozen in the act of undressing. All the lights were on. Kevin had a smooth, handsome heart-shaped face, almost feminine in its delicacy. He possessed no temper to speak of, and looked rather Byronic, but tonight the poet was a demon. Her husband had never laid a hand on her, although she supposed there was always a first time.

"I need a son."

Aurie blinked. "What?"

"A son. An heir. I love you, but I have to know. Are you going to give me an heir or not?"

"What's the matter with you?"

"What else you do is up to you. It makes no difference, as long as you don't have another man's child. I need a boy, Aurelia. Zora is fine as girls go, but I need a boy." He was very drunk. He stood up, strode around the room, running both hands through his hair like a madman. "It's urgent. They won't wait. Tell me when you're ready."

He went out.

CHAPTER 7

Two Announcements

(1)

EDDIE WAS BOOKENDED by sisters. At Christmas of 1956, the family gathered in Boston. Marcella, the eldest of the children, arrived from western Massachusetts with husband and lively trio of pretty daughters, their hair flattened with a hot comb. Junie, the baby, unmarried at twenty-four (to her mother's mortification), arrived alone, still in law school, one of many mad ideas Wesley Senior and his gentle wife, Marie, waited for her to outgrow. There were not enough positions in professional life for the men of the nation, the pastor would point out: should Negro women steal the few places that were allocated to the race? Junie, more lanky than graceful, had little of the easy allure of her older sister, or, for that matter, of her brother. The day might come, she said, when she would marry, if she met the right man. If not, not. Her secret plan, the one she used to whisper to Eddie when they were yet small and she would crawl into his bed after midnight to talk, was that she would become the first Negro and the first woman to be elected President of the United States. Imagine, Junie would say, the changes we could make. She told no one but Eddie, because she knew her big sister would tease her and her parents would gently nod at the follies of the imagination, then pile upon her strong back a heavier burden of chores in order to give her something to do.

At Christmas Eve dinner, before the late service at Wesley Senior's church, the conversation was as thin as in any other year. Father and mother were shaking their heads over Representative Adam Clayton Powell's surprise decision to support Eisenhower rather than the Democratic nominee, Adlai Stevenson, in the just-concluded election, for Powell, pastor of the largest church in Harlem, was at this time probably the most influential Negro in America. He had campaigned hard for the Republican President all across the country, drawing huge crowds. Eddie had no interest in politics. When Marcella brought up the year-old Montgomery bus boycott, which had ended just four days ago, following a ruling by the Supreme Court, her brother responded with vaguely remembered jargon from his courses at Amherst: the powerful were only fiddling with the superstructure, he said, hoping he had the terminology right. For the great mass of their people, nothing had changed.

Wesley Senior eyed his son coldly. "Your attitude is inexcusable, Edward. A young man whose career is at last succeeding should view the world through the lens of gratitude, not cynicism." This was the great pastor's way of acknowledging the critical acclaim that greeted his only son's first novel, published six months ago, for the family had never evolved a proper etiquette for expressing pride.

In the general silence that followed, Junie surprised the table with the news that she had secured a clerkship with a federal district judge in Chicago. Nobody but Eddie knew what she meant. Nobody but Eddie congratulated her. Marie covered her mouth. Marcella, busy breaking up a dispute among her children, paid no attention. Her husband, Sheldon—known among the family as "the undertaker," and the marriage itself inevitably "the undertaking"—turned mournful eyes Junie's way as though measuring her for a casket: perhaps her madness might take a fatal turn. Wesley Senior vouchsafed his son a foul look, then grumped that they had spent far too much money paying tuition for his daughter to serve as a mere clerk. Actually they had not. The deacons each year took up a special collection for the amount of Junie's tuition. There was never a shortfall. The congregation was large. Wesley Senior was much respected, and his family was much loved.

Junie started to explain that judicial clerkships were few, and much sought after, opening the door to fantastic career possibilities, but her father ignored her. If she insisted on this law nonsense, said the pastor, she should at least get a serious job, working perhaps for one of the large firms in the city. Junie pointed out that few of them had ever hired a Negro lawyer. She doubted that even her forthcoming Harvard degree would change their attitudes. Her father colored. He did not want excuses, he said. He wanted results. Eddie objected that prejudice was fact, not excuse. Wesley Senior repeated a favorite story, about the Negro who went down to a radio station to apply for a job as an announcer. He failed. Asked why, the man said, "B-b-b-because I'm b-b-b-black." Nobody laughed. Everyone had heard it too many times. One of Marcella's daughters made the unfortunate choice of this instant to display her uncommon gift for mimicry, replicating her grandfather's words with near-perfect intonation, if without any sure knowledge of what he had meant. Marcella snapped at the child. Marie said not to be so hard on her. Wesley Senior's voice at once cracked like a rifle shot: Do not, he said, correct the mother in front of her daughter. Junie snickered and, when her father's heavy gaze burned her way, pointed out that he had just done precisely what he told his wife not to.

"When I do it," he rumbled, "it is not the same. I am master of the house and head of the family."

"But our duty to honor our mother and father," she shot back, "does not end just because we grow up. Marcie owes Mom the same duty of obedience that Mom owes you," Junie finished, although she believed in neither. Smiling sweetly, she told the shocked assemblage what she had learned in a legal-history class, that in some of the colonial towns disobeying one's father had been a felony, punishable by flogging or worse.

"I should have been alive then," the pastor rumbled, struggling to lighten the mood.

"You would have loved it," Junie agreed, which won her a dramatic rolling of fatherly eyes.

Marie announced dessert.

(11)

AFTER DINNER, Junie decided to skip church and return to Cambridge. The family was stunned. Nobody, not even Eddie, had ever dared do such a thing. But neither orders nor entreaties swayed her. Her brother walked her to the train. A fluffy early-evening snow dressed the sidewalks in cotton batting. The two of them kicked at shallow drifts and giggled as they had in the old days. Eddie told Junie about finding Philmont Castle's body, and about seeing the cross around Margot's neck, two secrets he had shared with no one else.

"That sounds pretty terrible," Junie said, and shivered. "Finding the body."

"It was."

Then she laughed, and touched his face delicately, the way she used to when they were children, the only gentle member of a tough, frosty family. "You certainly lead an interesting life," she said.

"That's one way to look at it."

"It's funny about you finding Phil's body."

Eddie caught something in her tone. "Why is it funny?"

"Why you? Do you believe in coincidence?"

"If the alternatives are conspiracy and God's will, yes, I generally do."

"Draw it." She rummaged in her purse, found paper and a pencil. "The cross."

He did, and handed it back.

Junie frowned over the drawing, then popped the page into her bag. "I'll ask around." She saw his expression. "It's Hah-vahd, my dear. Somebody will know."

They stopped to watch a band of carolers drifting from house to house through the snow. Warm childhood memory rose in them both. Then the carolers strolled off in one direction, Eddie and Junie in the other.

"Sis?"

"Hmmm?"

"Why did you call him by his first name before? Castle?"

A sad smile. "Perry knows him pretty well. Knew him. He used to talk about him a lot." Junie glanced at her brother. "Perry Mount. Remember him?"

"I remember you danced at Aurie's wedding," said Eddie neutrally.

"Well, Perry's at Harvard now, doing international relations. He thinks you don't like him, Eddie." Eyes soft. "He's so sweet. Remember how we used to play with him on the Vineyard before the war?"

"I remember that, the games he wanted to play, neither one of you was old enough for."

"Well, I never played back," she said tartly, and fell suddenly silent. After another block she said: "Do you really think it's hopeless?"

"Do I think what's hopeless?"

"What you were saying at dinner. Our situation. The darker nation." The pixie grin came and went. "Your novel is so depressing, Eddie. Like there isn't any hope. I don't know, bro. I went to law school because I want law to make a difference, and maybe it will, but—well, maybe it won't."

Eddie hugged her. "What brought this on?"

"I don't want to waste my life."

"Is being a lawyer a waste?"

"It is if you can't make people stop and listen."

Eddie considered. It was unlike Junie to seek reassurance. "The world will change, sis. We might have to push and tug. But it's going to change."

"Even if we have to lift the world by its ears," she murmured, eyes on the middle distance.

"Sounds painful."

"Maybe it will be. Sometimes only pain makes people pay attention."

"I thought you were going to be President." To his surprise, his sister failed to smile. He glanced at her face. She looked miserable.

They walked in silence for a few minutes. At the entrance to the subway, Junie kissed his cheek and then, suddenly weepy, told him she was pregnant.

"Who's the lucky man?" he asked, hugging her, too bewildered to think of kind words instead of clever. His own troubles were knocked right out of his head.

"You don't wanna know."

"But I do."

"Nobody. Somebody."

"Not Perry."

"Yuch. No." A sad grin, and Eddie remembered the old days on the Vineyard, how the children used to sit in the backyard reading Shakespeare aloud, Junie as Miranda in *The Tempest*, poor Perry as her hapless suitor. "One of my professors," she said.

Eddie put his hands on his sister's shoulders and held her at arm's length. Her broad face was stricken and wan. Pointy snowflakes stood out crisply on her curly black hair before vanishing. Eddie's world consisted of two sorts of people: those with whom he competed for accolades and achievements, and his little sister. "You're not joking, are you?"

"No." A slow sniffle. "The bastard says it isn't his. But I haven't been with anybody else."

"Is he . . . Caucasian?"

A sneer bared perfect white teeth. "So far that's the only kind they have down there."

Ever practical. "You can't be a law clerk and have a baby."

"I know."

"Who else knows about this?"

"Nobody. Not unless *he* told somebody."

"There's a woman I know who could—"

Junie shoved free of him and put both hands over her stomach. She looked wintry and strong. "I am not killing my baby, Eddie. No way."

"You're not thinking, sis."

"Yes, I am, Eddie. I am. Killing is *wrong*." She puffed out a lot of air. "But pain—"

She stopped. Shook her head.

"Sis?"

Without moving, she increased the distance between them. "Thanks, brother. For everything. I'll let you know when I find out about the cross." *When*—not *if.* That was his sister. About to say more, Junie turned and hurried down the steps. Eddie walked to the crowded church, where the congregation celebrated the birth of one baby and he pondered the fate of another.

Two months later, he was picked up by federal agents.

CHAPTER 8

The Coal Truck

(1)

BERNARD STILWELL CAME into Eddie's life in February of 1957, by which time literary circles had been buzzing for a year; and, like the acclaim, Stilwell never quite left. Eddie in time would grow accustomed to the flair for melodrama that accompanied their first meeting. He was eating breakfast at the counter in the Chock Full o' Nuts shop next to the Theresa Hotel, leafing through complimentary letters, when Stilwell and a fellow agent of the Federal Bureau of Investigation materialized on either side of him, flashing badges where only Eddie could see, then frog-marching him to a waiting sedan driven by a third man, who zoomed off almost before the doors were closed. Stilwell sat beside him in the back. The other agent joined the driver.

"How are you, Eddie?"

"What?"

Stilwell had sleepy hunter's eyes, and arched wispy blond brows. The pupils were very dark. It was easy to imagine him capering through Hell—one of the tormentors, not the tormented. "Famous writer like you. Must be nice, huh?"

The car headed north along the Hudson, then cut east. Eddie was bewildered. Unlike most of the Negro intelligentsia of his day, he never envisioned the government as a force, whether benevolent or malign. He hardly thought of government at all. He was too busy writing. "What do you want?"

"An autograph."

"A what?" said Eddie, thinking, absurdly, of Aurelia's promise.

"Autograph." The agent pulled a soiled copy of *Field's Unified Theory* from somewhere. "I'm a big fan."

"I beg your pardon."

"Nice little story. Very realistic. Do a lot of research, did you?"

Confusion replaced whatever else Eddie might have been feeling. He had assumed they would ask about the long-ago days working for Scarlett, and had been setting out a whole army of evasions and lies to defend himself. Perhaps they even knew he was the one who had found Castle's body. But now his dispositions were useless.

"I don't know what you mean. Research?"

"For your story. This Dyson Field. Nice name. Talk to him at all?"

Eddie laughed uneasily. Somebody's idea of a joke. "He's a character. It's a novel." No response, from either Stilwell or the men in the front. Eddie glanced out the window. They were proceeding slowly through the traffic on Seventh Avenue, at about the speed of the many parades that graced the wide, divided boulevard in good weather, as one or another colored men's or women's civic organization, all decked out in ceremonial regalia, marched forth to show the world that Jim Crow had defeated neither unity nor beauty. "I made him up," Eddie explained, wondering why he was not getting through. "Dyson Field. He's an invention. No more." The Caucasian faces disbelieved him. "Why? What's wrong?" No response. Eddie climbed up on his high horse. "Why have you detained me?"

Bernard Stilwell laughed, and the sound was one Eddie wanted never to hear again, for, if the agent had a demon's face, his laugh was the self-satisfied bray of the final betrayer in the lowest circle of Dante's mad, brilliant vision of the afterlife. He clapped Eddie on the back hard enough to throw his head forward. Eddie clenched his fists and forced down his body's instinctive response. This was, after all, the FBI.

"A lot of detail in the novel. A lot of the physics is right."

"I would hope so."

"You know any physics yourself?" The car had turned east onto a side street up in the 150s, but the driver was unfamiliar with the neighborhood. Now they were stuck behind a coal truck unloading into a basement chute, noise and dust obscuring sound and sight from outside the car. Stilwell did not raise his voice, and Eddie had to lean closer to hear. "Didn't you start out as a physics major at Amherst? You switched, though, right?"

"What does my major have to do with—"

"This is more than freshman physics." He handed Eddie the novel. "Field theory. Heisenberg's principle. This isn't F equals ma. You had a source, didn't you?"

"A what?"

"A source. For your story." Tapping the curling pages. Many had been annotated in blue ink. "All this physics. All this about security. Somebody talked to you. You talked to somebody."

Eddie sized up the federal agent, so scrawny that his pasty ankles showed above his white socks. His perpetual scowl emphasized fiery eyes. "May I see your credentials again?"

"Of course." Casually, smiling, almost without looking, Stilwell lifted a languid hand. The next thing Eddie knew, the forearm was jammed into his neck, holding him tightly to the seat, while the other agent from the restaurant leaned from the front seat and grabbed his wrists, lest he try something stupid. The driver had the grace to look uneasy, but he kept his eyes forward.

"Did you have a source or not?" said Stilwell conversationally.

"Get off me!" cried Eddie, quite surprised.

"Your source, Eddie. Come on."

"It's a story, you half-witted son of a bitch! Let go!"

Instead, the agent pressed harder. "You know who I'm talking about, Eddie. I can't prove it yet, but when I do, you'll wish you'd told the truth." Stilwell's spluttery mouth was very close. "You're a stupid little man, Eddie, and you always will be." Just like that, the heavy arm was gone, and Eddie was leaning forward, choking for breath. "Didn't you think we'd find out? Do you think we're as stupid as you are?"

Eddie lifted a cautious head. "You're crazy," he wheezed. When

Stilwell did not respond, Eddie was emboldened. "I'm going to turn you in."

"For what?"

"Assault."

"You assaulted me first. It was self-defense. I have two witnesses, both law-enforcement personnel. Who's going to speak up for you, Eddie?"

The writer ground his teeth and kept his temper. The coal truck continued blocking their path, black dust sifting through the air as the coal ran down a wooden chute. Out on the sidewalk, Harlem strolled past, none of the few pedestrians in evidence paying attention to a Negro in a car being beaten by three Caucasians. It occurred to Eddie that his first guess was wrong: the driver had chosen a side street on purpose. "I'll call the papers."

"Ever read them?"

"Read what?"

"The newspapers. Specially from out of town." The agent grinned, but only with his mouth. "Ever read them?"

He shrugged. "Sometimes."

"New Mexico papers?"

"Not that I remember."

Stilwell nodded. The driver had backed up and was executing a tight K-turn, nearly bumping a couple of parked cars. The other man in the front seat reached into his jacket, and Eddie tensed for a blackjack or gun, but the agent only drew out a newspaper clipping, which he handed to Stilwell, who handed it to Eddie.

Eddie frowned, then looked closer.

The dateline was Los Alamos, New Mexico. One week ago.

NEGRO SCIENTIST IN SUICIDE

"What is this?"

"One Joseph Belt lost his security clearance after your novel came out." He pointed to a photo in the corner. "Pretty redheaded wife, too, just like the one you made up."

Eddie studied the page. In his fury over the suggestion of a link, he had missed the name completely. Belt. Joseph Belt. Physicist. Phil Castle's friend who had met Eddie at the Savoy and refused to answer any of his questions.

Harlem's own Doctor Belt had shot himself.

(11)

"No," Eddie said. He mopped his brow with a handkerchief as he read the two columns. Gunshot to head, despondent, drinking, marriage collapsing, rumored troubles on the job. First the Wall Street lawyer, now his Negro friend. Eddie said what he thought: "I don't believe this."

"You knew him."

"I met him once in my life. I wanted to interview him for the paper."

"And what secrets did he share with you?"

"Secrets?"

"About the nation's security, Eddie."

"I don't know what you're talking about. He didn't tell me anything."

That noxious laugh again. They had reached a Puerto Rican neighborhood. The car turned south once more. They were driving in an oval, roughly navigating the perimeter of Harlem. "Sure thing, Eddie."

"I'm serious. I didn't know he worked at"—a glance at the paper—"the Los Alamos National Laboratory. I never even heard of it."

"No idea what they make there, right?"

"Actually, no."

"Oppenheimer. Heard of him?"

Eddie shifted his weight. "Sure. Father of the H-bomb. You people railroaded him. Took his security clearance."

"Had his due process first. A hearing. Buy the transcript at your local bookstore. Professor Belt testified in his favor. You didn't know that, either, did you?" The agent did not wait for the answer. "Why did you pressure your publisher to get your book out so fast? Were you trying to help Belt?"

"Help him do what?" asked Eddie, who had simply wanted to impress his father, and the sooner, the better.

The spiteful eyes blazed. "Get the book out before we could stop him. Make our work harder. Was that your idea or his?"

Wesley Senior had a way of refusing to suffer fools. Eddie copied it now. He rolled his eyes and turned to look out the window. The morning was smoky, like a battlefield.

"Come on, Eddie. We know he was your source. You met with him a couple of years ago, at the Savoy. You spoke to him on the telephone both before and after that—"

Eddie's whippet head came around. "What? I did not!"

"Eddie, Eddie." Gently. "We're not complete incompetents. All those late-night clandestine calls from bars in New Mexico to bars in Harlem. You think we don't trace calls out of the base? With everything the Reds have been up to down there? You think we can't dig up the bars where you hang out? Joseph Belt was your source, we got on to him, and he shot himself, just like in your novel. But you didn't know anything about his work, did you? You have a magical power to make your stories come true. Or do you just see the future? Is that it, Eddie?"

Eddie felt cornered and did not even know how it had happened. "It's a coincidence. That's all."

"One Negro physicist in the whole country with the right security clearance, and he commits suicide a couple of months after your novel comes out." Stilwell was looking out the window at a barge on the choppy gray water. "After meeting you the previous year." A shake of the head at the iniquity of men. "Wait! I know! It must be those nasty racists at the FBI making trouble for the Negroes again, right?"

"The thought had crossed my mind."

"Yeah, well, relax, Eddie. You're not important enough for us to waste time smearing you."

Bristling, but not sure how to greet this insult, Eddie said, "Then to what do I owe the pleasure of your hospitality?"

"We have a deal for you. You tell us everything Doctor Belt told you about his work, you don't write any more about national security, and we can maybe forget this little incident." The voice remained casual, but the eyes bored in. "We live in dangerous times, Eddie."

"He didn't tell me anything about his work, Agent Stilwell. He refused to say a word. You can be very proud of him."

"Are you mocking me?"

"Probably."

Stilwell already had his elbow cocked, but the driver muttered something, and Eddie wondered whether they were playing good-cop, bad-cop, or if he had incorrectly guessed who was in charge. Outside, the fog was thickening instead of burning off.

"Know any of his friends?"

"No."

"Did you know this Philmont Castle? The lawyer who got himself strangled?"

Eddie barely hesitated. "We never met."

"They worked together, Eddie. Castle and Belt. And it wasn't just the two of them, Eddie. We're trying to figure out who else might have been in on it. Maybe Castle's wife."

"I'm sorry, Agent Stilwell. There is no way in which I can be helpful."

"What about Aurelia?"

Despite the ache in his neck where Stilwell had elbowed him, Eddie sat very straight. "I beg your pardon."

"Aurelia Garland. Your little chippy. Loose thing like that. Was she part of Belt's scheme?"

Eddie tried to hit him. Stilwell was federal, and the car was cramped, but still he tried. His fist barely flickered. The agent had his arm pinned before he could get any energy behind the punch.

"Naughty, naughty, Eddie. Assaulting a federal officer is a year in prison, minimum."

"You're a sick bastard, do you know that?"

Amusement in those devil's eyes. "Job's a job, Eddie. But I guess you know that, don't you?"

The car had stopped on a side street three blocks from his apartment, and the man from the front seat had the door open for him.

"Goodbye, Eddie." Stilwell handed over a card. "Call me when you change your mind."

"About what?" said Eddie, rubbing his neck.

Stilwell winked, and shut the door.

CHAPTER 9

The Fine Old Truth

(1)

MEANWHILE, Aurelia was betraying her husband. Not with another man—she had not yet fallen that far from the wife she had always imagined she would be—but she was betraying Kevin's trust all the same. She had chosen today because Kevin was in London. She knew he was because she had the telegram confirming his arrival. So here she was, on her knees in his private office in the suite kept by Garland & Son in the Thirties off Park Avenue, not far from the Morgan Library. She was twirling the dial of the huge safe, manufactured, the door proclaimed, by the Mosler Safe & Lock Company of Cincinnati and New York. This was where her husband kept his secrets. If anything ever happened to him—so Kevin frequently told her—everything was there.

Everything.

An hour ago, Aurelia had never dreamed she would get so far: it was not as though Kevin had entrusted her with the combination. She had arrived at the firm with no clear plan, other than to stand in her husband's office and will the answer from the air. At first it had seemed she would not even make it over the threshold. She had tried to talk or bluff or scold or tease her way past Thrush, the unctuous white assistant whose job was to keep his master's secrets, but she had failed. Fortunately, Kevin's father, Matthew, was in today, one of his rare visits from his palace on the Hudson River near Dobbs Ferry. Matty Garland was possibly the wealthiest Negro in the United States. The investment firm he had founded, a gnat by the standards of Wall Street, had nevertheless achieved remarkable success. Garland & Son employed thirteen clerks, all but one of them white, and the other was the son of a South American land baron. Matty Garland was not an easy man to charm, but he adored Aurelia. And so, when he came out to investigate the commotion and found his daughter-in-law sobbing, and Mr. Thrush ineffectually fluttering his hands, Matty waved everyone away, slipped a powerful arm around her, and led her into his own capacious office. He sat her on the sofa, offered his handkerchief, and asked her what in blazes was going on.

The story poured out, and Aurelia found, to her surprise, that her tears were now entirely unfeigned. When she was done, Matty considered. He leaned against his cherry desk, strong arms crossed, barrel chest ready to burst through the braces.

At last he said, "Do you know what I like about you, Aurelia?"

She only stared. Wasn't it obvious? She was married to his son. But this seemed not to be his meaning, so she shook her head.

"You're like me. You started with nothing, and you were determined to get whatever you could."

Aurelia hardly knew what to say. "You didn't start with nothing—"

"Why? Because my name is Garland? Where do you think the Garlands came from? My father was a preacher in Hartford, Connecticut. Not a very good one. He never had a dime, but he sent his boys to college. My late brother Mark—he graduated. He was a professor for a while. I dropped out, because I wanted to do this." Flipping a hand to indicate the office, and what it symbolized. "I saw which way the economy was pointing. I knew what the war would do. I moved to California. I made some good guesses, I had some good luck, but, mostly, I worked my tail off. Same as you."

"I don't understand, Matty."

"You think I didn't have you looked into?"

Silence.

"Come on, Aurelia. I know why your parents didn't come to the wedding, and if he has half a brain in his head, so does Kevin. You don't have any parents. You're not from some big colored family out there in Cleveland. You're an orphan, and the nice Catholic sisters put together the money to send you to college because you're smart.

Don't start crying again. I don't have another handkerchief, and you ruined the first one. You think I care about any of that Negro-royal-family crap up in Sugar Hill? Who went to what school, who's married to whose son? Why the fuck do you think I live in Westchester? Excuse my French. I'm nobody." He pinched his skin. "Look at me. Dark as a field hand. That's what those Harlem biddies would say about a man like me if I didn't happen to have a few million in the bank. And if not for all those hints you kept dropping about your parentage, and your buddy Mona vouching for you in colored society, they'd say the same about you. I'm nobody and you're nobody, so now there's a pair of us so don't tell, or however the fuck it goes. If those biddies knew the truth about you, they'd throw Kevin out of society for marrying down. Me? I'm happy, because I know he married up. Kevin always had it easy. He needs a striver in his life. You're better than he is, Aurie. Don't ever forget that. Don't you dare settle for being Mrs. Kevin Garland and going to the parties and the salons, raising a bunch of kids who are gonna care about skin color and where somebody's parents went to school. Don't you dare, Aurelia. Those Catholic sisters expected more from you, and so do I."

He buzzed for a clerk, took the startled man's handkerchief, gave it to his daughter-in-law, kicked him out. Aurelia did not know why she could not stop crying.

"Tell you something else. I don't know what's going on with Kevin, any more than you do. He comes in when he wants to come in, he leaves when he wants to leave. He's a lazy so-and-so, and he always was, but I figured, a new wife, a new baby, he's busy. So I left him alone. Now you tell me he's overseas half the time, and I don't even know about it. Probably traveling on my dime, too. I'll have to find out. Maybe dock his pay. Now, Kevin's my only boy, and I love him. No matter what he's up to, I'll always love him. But you're worth ten of him, Aurelia. Twenty. You want to check and see what's going on? Be my guest. Don't tell me about it. I don't want to know. Just fix it. That's the girl."

(11)

TELLING THE STORY LATER, Aurelia could never quite remember how she wound up alone in her husband's office, the combination to the massive safe in her hand.

She had to do the numbers three times before she got them right. She kept expecting Kevin to burst in, his shoe in his hand, demanding to know if she was ready to give him an heir. Finally, she heard the tumblers click. She thought she would never be able to budge the heavy steel door, but it swung easily on its hinges.

The safe was almost tall enough to walk into. Hunching over, she could slip inside. There was a small ledge for sitting, and even a light switch. She found file cabinets, but they were full of financial papers. One of them disclosed her husband's net worth, a detail he carefully kept from her, and her eyes goggled at the figures. Others related to transactions for the firm, and she could not make head or tail of them, but the amounts of money involved were large—larger even than Kevin's funds. She wondered just how much Matty had. She wondered if white people even knew there were Negroes this rich. She wondered if Harlem did. When she was finished with the last drawer, she had found nothing to suggest what Kevin was doing. She sat on the ledge and pondered.

She could stop now. She could put the files back, close the vault, go home, raise this child and the next and the next, go to the parties, live in luxury, spending her husband's money. She could do all the things Matty Garland had just warned her against. All the things the Catholic sisters had not raised her for.

She thought about her imaginary family, the one all Harlem thought had bred her: the jazz-singing aunt in Paris, the uncle who owned hotels. If only they existed, they would tell her to relax, to enjoy the life she had sought and married into.

She imagined the nuns looking over her shoulder. *Check your answers one more time, dear,* Sister Dorcas used to tell her, tut-tutting whenever Aurelia finished her test before the other children. *Check them again, dear. You want to be sure you have them all exactly right.*

All right. Fine. Check the answers one more time.

Aurelia delved into the records again, and, as if in reward for her renewed labor, she found at once what she had overlooked. The bottom drawer of the second cabinet. The file folders were higher than in the other drawers. Once she realized that, the reason was apparent.

There was a false bottom.

A sheet of steel exactly the size of the drawer. It was not attached in any way, just weighted down by the files themselves. The casual observer would never notice. Aurelia took a peek out into the office. In for a penny, in for a pound. She emptied the files onto the floor. Several tries and two broken nails persuaded her that she could not pull up the false bottom with her fingers. She scrounged in her husband's desk, finally took the letter opener, and pried up the steel without difficulty. Beneath, she found a small cloth sack and a thick manila envelope.

The envelope was sealed with cellophane tape, and Kevin had signed his name over it, so that he could tell if anyone got in. But Aurelia, at her husband's instruction, had been forging his name on checks from the day they returned from their honeymoon, and by now she was willing to bet that not even Kevin could tell the difference. She peeled off the tape, pulled out the documents inside, studied the first, glanced at the second, and had to admit that she understood none of it:

> 34—Term 1—Resistance (probably war, see 27–29, 41)
> 35—Term 2—Palace Council to reconsider timing
> 36—Day 20—Shake the throne (tentative—per Author)
>   ("6 mo" + F : ix, from 1010)
> 37—Pandemonium on inside? (tentative—per Author)

On and on in that vein, for several pages. The words were typewritten, and mimeographed, and could have meant anything. Terms 1 and 2. Terms of the academic year? Presidential terms? Congressional terms? Terms in an equation? Aurelia shook her head. Who or what was the Palace Council? And Day 20. A date of a month? Was the reference to war metaphorical or literal? She played around with abbreviations and anagrams and found nothing.

Behind the mimeoed pages was a note, scribbled in an unfamiliar hand on stationery from a famous Florida hotel that admitted no Negroes:

After PC, problem. Too soon. Ask KG to find testament. He can have

And there it stopped.

Well, KG was obviously her husband, and PC had to be Philmont Castle, and here again was the testament mentioned in the note delivered to their London hotel. She was right. That was why Kevin was running around the country: he was searching for the testament. But why would anyone who could get into a fancy segregated resort—that is, anyone white and rich—care about the testament? And what was it that Kevin could "have"? A reward? Assistance in the search?

Puzzled, Aurelia crossed to Kevin's desk, took paper and pen, and copied the pages. There were eight altogether. She sealed them back up, retaped the flap—which had plainly been taped many times—and, letting her fingers relax, signed her husband's name across the cellophane.

She put the envelope back, then opened the bag.

Inside was a single item of jewelry—a man's signet ring—and set into the ring was an inverted cross.

Memory brushed her.

Eddie, sitting with her at Chock Full o' Nuts on Seventh Avenue a few weeks before the wedding, his thin face determined as always, asking if she had ever seen anything around Harlem bearing what he called the Cross of Saint Peter, then showing her a drawing he had made. And Aurie, after telling him, no, she had never seen anything like that, had rebuked him for looking so sour. Cheer up, she had told him. Cheer up and go find somebody to love.

"Already did," Eddie had said, judging her with those gentle eyes.

Not sure whether to slap him or kiss him, Aurelia had settled for instructing him to grow up. Then she left in a huff.

Now, sitting on the ledge inside her husband's office safe, holding in her hand a cross just like the one in Eddie's drawing, she wondered. Eddie had never told her where he had seen the cross, and she had never asked. Did he have some kind of connection with her husband, some secret the men shared and she did not? Men were like that, and Harlem was chockablock with clubs and societies with passwords and symbols and odd names. Perhaps Eddie and Kevin were members of one. Maybe Eddie wanted to join Kevin's.

Closing the massive door, Aurelia laughed mirthlessly at her own pretensions. She knew nothing. That was what Sister Dorcas used to call the final truth, except that a much younger Aurie always thought she was saying "the fine old truth." And the fine old truth was this: She had all but broken into her husband's safe and found his secret compartment—and still she knew nothing. But she was surer than ever that there was something to find.

(I I I)

"FOUND WHAT YOU WERE LOOKING FOR?" said Matty, ushering her out, beefy arm around her shoulders once more. "Good girl. That's the way. I'll clear up the evidence, don't worry."

"There wasn't anything," she said, faintly.

"Lying for the cause. Don't blame you, really. Done it a time or two myself. Keep the secrets, that's the thing." His voice was booming, as if he didn't care who heard him. As they crossed the open, airless room where the firm did its trading, the clerks all managed to turn the other way. "Don't worry, my dear. Things will work out. Husbands, well, we get up the damnedest nonsense from time to time. I do. My sainted Daddy did. My sainted brother did. I bet even my sainted nephew Oliver does. Wives, well, your job is to understand us. Civilize us, my Daddy used to say. You're a good woman. Better than my boy deserves. Things will work out," he thundered.

At the elevator, Matty kissed her forehead. Only later did it occur to her that he was helping establish an alibi for her visit.

Aurelia sat up smoking half the night, and spent the next day with her slender fingers creeping toward the phone, then curling back. She wanted to talk about it. She thought of Mona Veazie—Mona, who had known Aurie's secrets since college, and come up with the imposture that allowed her to be introduced to society—but Mona would demand every detail and then laugh her head off. She thought of Claire, but Claire would tell her to be patient because husbands need time. She thought of Eddie, the person most likely to take her seriously, but she was a married woman and part of society and could no more call her former beau than she could fly to the moon.

Wait. She remembered something in the mail, went to her writing desk, tracked it down. An announcement of a lecture.

Yes.

Maybe she could talk to somebody after all.

CHAPTER 10

Friendly Advice

(1)

EDDIE DECIDED to tell Gary Fatek. Gary might have been a man of the left, but the Hilliman family was solidly the other way, on excellent terms with hard-line Red-baiters from Walter Winchell and Joseph McCarthy on up. Or so the newspapers insisted. Even if the stories were exaggerated, Eddie was confident that his classmate would number among his close relations people who knew the people who could call off the dogs.

They met not in Harlem but at Gary's home, the top two floors of a three-story brownstone in Greenwich Village, not far from Washington Square. Mona, who was doing her graduate work at nearby New York University, hung around most evenings, but tonight was off somewhere with her parents. They sat on mats in the back room, overlooking the garden, because Gary, having recently visited Japan, had decided that furniture was a decadence. He listened to his friend's tale, glassy eyes blinking owlishly because he was smoking a bit of genuine Harlem mezzroll. He offered some to Eddie, who declined.

"This whole thing is pretty funny," said Gary when Eddie was done.

"How so?"

Gary unlimbered himself, striding around the empty space, one hand holding the cigarette, the other tousling his own hair. "You're thinking you just have a practical problem. How to get this Stilwell character off your back. Well, that's nothing." Waggling his fingers to dismiss this triviality. "My aunt can make him go away. She can make anybody go away."

"She would do that for me?"

"Of course not. She hates Negroes."

"I see."

Gary, quite stoned, offered the boyish grin the privileged learn young. "Don't worry. She'll do it for me. I'm her favorite nephew."

"I see," Eddie repeated. Gary wanted Eddie to understand that *She'll do it for me* meant *I'll do it for you.* That was life. If he did not want to owe Gary another favor, there was no reason to have come.

"We'll make him go away," Gary repeated, examining the fingers he had been waving. "Far, far away."

"Wonderful."

"But that's just the practical problem. You have a bigger problem."

"What's that?"

"Well, Belt is dead," said Gary, his glance sly.

"Yes," said Eddie after a moment. "They said he shot himself."

"They also said Roosevelt didn't know about Pearl Harbor in advance."

"He didn't."

"My aunt says he did." Another giggle. Gary was easing his guest toward the door. "My whole family says he did. That's the kind of family I have. Bunch of paranoid fascists. That's why they can help."

"I should meet them sometime."

"You should. They'd make great characters for a genuine Wesley novel." As they stood on the front step, the chilly night air blew all the tipsiness away. Gary's face was slack but concerned. "You know, Eddie, even if my aunt can get the Bureau off your back, you still have a problem."

"Yes. You mentioned that."

"Belt is dead," said Gary, again.

"So?"

"So—I think you might want to be careful." Gary's eyes were stone sober. "Look at the facts. The Federal Bureau of Investigation seems to think you know something about Professor Belt. You should consider who else might think the same."

"Who else? You mean the Russians?"

Gary shook his head with stern impatience. "You're small potatoes, Eddie. I'm sure the Bureau doesn't think you're a Russian spy. They might be fascists but they're not idiots. Believe me, I know how they operate. I've been investigated a time or two. No. All that Russian-spy stuff was just show."

"Then what do they want with me? What do they think Belt and Castle were up to?"

"Obviously, something else."

(11)

EDDIE TOOK THE SUBWAY HOME. There was at this time a Harlem tradition of judging class by where people disembarked from the A train. If you got off at 125th Street, you lived in the Valley, and were discounted accordingly. If you got off at 145th or 155th, you lived on Sugar Hill, the highest point in Harlem, among the truly wealthy of the darker nation. The Valley was vast, and Sugar Hill was small. In between the two, like a demilitarized zone, sat Strivers Row, policed by legions of the upwardly mobile who had not yet made it to the top. For most of his time in Harlem, Eddie had detrained at 125th, and looked down his prominent nose at the bourgeoisie, who stayed on board. Tonight he stayed on. After publication of the novel, he had moved to a spacious apartment at 435 Convent Avenue, near the heart of Sugar Hill. Different addresses carried different degrees of prestige. The doyennes of Harlem society decided which addresses were which. Number 409 Edgecombe Avenue, top of the list, had been home to such Negro leaders as Thurgood Marshall, W.E.B. Du Bois, and Roy Wilkins. Now it was the home of Mr. and Mrs. Kevin Garland. Next along in prestige was probably 555 Edgecombe, the Roger Morris Apartments, not far from Jumel Terrace. Number 435 Convent Avenue ranked fairly high on the list that

Eddie had once derided. He did his best to ignore the irony. The apartment was beautiful. The ceilings were high. The rooms were large. The dining room had a chandelier from before the First World War. Across the street were townhouses built by such luminaries as Henri Fouchaux and Frederick P. Dinkelberg, back when the neighborhood was white. The Czarinas decreed that young Mr. Wesley needed a wife to serve as hostess in so wonderful a space, and already the applicants, so to speak, were piling up. Gary Fatek had taken one look at the new place and announced that Eddie had joined the ruling class.

"Permanently, I hope," Eddie shot back.

He began dressing better. He widened his circle of acquaintances. He began to hang out with scholars, physicians, other writers. He received a letter from Bertrand Russell, praising the novel and asking him to join the international campaign against the bomb. He dined in Westchester County, at the home of Adam Clayton Powell, who did not maintain a residence in the district he represented in Congress. Powell advised him to get out and see the world. There was so much more, said the Congressman, than Harlem. The struggle was everywhere, said Powell. But never forget you are an American first. You have to do both, the Congressman said. And always be willing to carry the heavy end of the log. Eddie nodded. Powell kept peering at him with those meaty eyes, as if he believed the two of them shared some sacred knowledge not available to ordinary mortals. Later, Eddie recorded the dinner in his journal. He had an idea for a novel about a Harlem politician, although he was at a loss to invent a life more colorful than Powell's.

Two nights after his conversation with Gary Fatek about Agent Stilwell, Eddie emerged from the train at 145th Street as usual and began walking up the hill toward Convent Avenue. He passed restaurants and storefront churches. He slipped into a tiny bookstore that catered to the paranoid left and had a friendly chat with the madwoman who ran it, because she had sources Eddie himself could never tap. When he stepped outside, Emil was leaning on a parked car.

"Have you located my photographs?" the German asked without preamble. His powerful arms were crossed. He looked fit and confident, like an angry cop.

"I never promised to do that."

"I would pay well for their return."

"I'm not really—"

Emil shoved himself off the car. Another white man inside opened the door, and, for a silly moment, Eddie feared they would, in the manner of Stilwell and his companions, invite him in. But the only passenger tonight would be Emil, who was snapping out orders as he sat. "Remember, Mr. Wesley. A pink envelope, a number penciled in the corner, seventeen or eighteen."

Watching the taillights, Eddie remembered Gary's parting words. *The Federal Bureau of Investigation seems to think you know something about Professor Belt. You should consider who else might think the same.*

CHAPTER 11

The Summons

(1)

IN THE FIRST WEEK of May 1957, Eddie went down to Washington to deliver a lecture at American University. His subject was the responsibility of the intellectual. Before his address, he did some sightseeing. His parents had dragged their three children around the city frequently. Junie and Eddie used to make fun of the exhibits behind cupped hands, but their older sister would take careful notes, because their mother was bound to quiz them later, and Marcella did not want to hear Wesley Senior, in That Voice, lecturing her for inattention. The sightseeing left Eddie thoughtful. At this time Washington was a segregated city, so much so that when Thurgood Marshall and the other lawyers from the NAACP argued *Brown v. Board of Education* at the Supreme Court, they had to run across the plaza to the train station for lunch, because the Court cafeteria did not serve Negroes. Neither did the congressional dining room, unless you happened to be a member of Congress. But even members of Congress were not allowed to bring Negro guests. Adam Clayton Powell had overturned that rule by bringing to lunch whom he liked, and nobody had dared challenge him. The nation was changing. This was an article of Wesley Senior's faith, and of Eddie's. His Harlem friends argued that it was changing too slowly, and Eddie supposed that he agreed, but he had less interest than others in protesting and battling. He wanted to write. He tried to explain that writers needed space away from life's bustle, but only Langston Hughes really understood.

Eddie's lecture went poorly. The audience went away confused.

Perhaps Eddie had parsed his point too finely. He insisted that the intellectual should devote his mind to the movement without sacrificing his reason. One should not pretend, said Eddie, that intellect pointed where in fact it did not. One should not suppress inconvenient facts for the sake of victory. A bad argument in a good cause, said Eddie, is intellectual prostitution.

Applause was tepid.

Eddie hardly cared. His mind had hardly been on the talk. He had been distracted throughout by the unexpected presence in the audience, three rows back and four seats in, of Mrs. Kevin Garland. Eddie had hardly seen her these past two years. His literary rise had been meteoric. Aurelia had retreated. True, she still wrote the occasional piece for the *Sentinel*, but mainly had thrown herself into her new role as Garland hostess and Czarina in training. What was she doing here? What was she even doing in Washington? Inspired, he reached rhetorical heights he had not previously suspected, and his carefully organized lecture suffered from his efforts to impress her. Afterward, Aurelia emerged from the throng of admirers to offer a cool cheek and explain herself. She was in town for her sorority's annual convention, she said: four days' worth of what would later be known as networking, as well as listening to inspirational lectures, voting on inscrutable bylaw amendments, and, most important, changing into a different gown for each night's event, and don't you dare wear anything that even resembles what you wore last year. When she saw that Eddie was speaking, she naturally had to come, to congratulate him on his great successes.

He thanked her, even as he sensed that there had to be more.

She burbled on about how all the Garlands admired him, and so did her family back home in Cleveland, and Eddie basked not in her words but in her attention. She asked if he had time for a drink with an old friend. Naturally, he agreed. But when they were seated in a back booth at a small Capitol Hill bar that served Negroes and whites alike, she did not, as Eddie half expected, propose any extramarital intimacy. Instead, she downed her pink gin fizz in one quick gulp.

"I think I'll take that autograph now," she said, and Eddie, remembering their conversation outside the *Sentinel* last year, knew there was trouble.

And then she told him why.

(11)

AROUND MIDNIGHT, Eddie was wakened by a ringing phone. He was dozing in Aurelia Garland's arms. Most of her sorority sisters were in hotels or private homes. Aurelia had a friend, a divorcée, who lived in a small apartment building on East Capitol Street: what used to be called a woman of speed. Her friend was out of town, and Aurelia had borrowed the apartment. She had offered no reason for rejecting the hotel, and her friend had not asked. They had known each other a long time.

Actually, things had progressed further and faster than Aurelia planned. She wanted the apartment so that she could talk to Eddie in peace. She had not reckoned on the dangers of being alone with him. True, they had not had sex, or even kissed, and were still fully dressed. Nevertheless, they had spent a long time holding each other as they sat together on the sofa after she told him some—not all—of the story. Aurie had talked about her husband's strange behavior, and mentioned, in passing, his search for the testament. But disclosing these marital intimacies made her feel like the hussy the nuns never wanted her to be, so she stopped before telling about breaking into Kevin's safe. Now, waking on the sofa with her head on his shoulder, she felt two feet tall.

"Oh, shit," she said—and not about the ringing phone.

She had been a fool to bring him here. At least she was awake now, and could send him back to his hotel. She pushed him off her, hurried across the room in her stocking feet, picked up the phone, started to say that Janine was away, then listened, muttered, and, no longer sleepy, handed the receiver to Eddie.

"Nobody knows I'm here," he whispered.

"Somebody obviously does."

A male voice asked if he was Eddie Wesley, then told him that a car was waiting for him downstairs. Eddie tried to brush the cobwebs from his mind. "A car?" he mumbled. "What car?"

To take him to his meeting, said the voice.

"What meeting? You mean now?"

But the voice had hung up.

Eddie considered, then brushed his hair and picked up his jacket.

"Where are you going?" asked Aurelia, looking for her shoes.

"No idea." He explained.

She thought it over, then padded toward the bathroom. "In that case, I'm going, too," she said over her shoulder.

"I'm not sure that's a good idea."

"Whoever it is already knows we're up here together. If you're getting arrested, I want the story for the *Sentinel*."

(I I I)

The car was a dark Ford, shiny and inconspicuous, and the crewcut driver refused to take Aurie until Eddie made him understand that in that case he was going back upstairs. The car had a two-way radio beneath the dash. The driver murmured code words, listened, said "Check." They headed due west, past the Capitol, then along Pennsylvania Avenue, passing the White House, turning north again on Connecticut, eventually ending on a leafy street of grand houses somewhere in upper Northwest. Eddie looked at his watch. It was almost one in the morning. The sign said Thirtieth Place. The car stopped. Another crewcut led them into the garden and along the front walk to the house. A third opened the front door. He asked if they wanted anything to drink, which they did not. Out in the hall they heard cross words being exchanged, and Eddie had the shrewd notion that the driver was being upbraided for bringing Aurelia. One of the identical crewcuts, red-faced, stuck his head into the room and invited Mr. Wesley to please follow him. He informed Mrs. Garland that the wait would not be long, and invited her to make herself at home. There were books, a Victrola, a bar. Eddie, more bemused than worried, followed the crewcut down the hall. The young man knocked once at a heavy door, then stood aside as Eddie walked in alone. The man shut him in. The room was a library, dark and depressing, and behind the desk sat a stout, angry man who barely glanced up as he ordered Eddie to sit.

"I'd rather stand," said Eddie, recognizing his host.

"Up to you. I don't give a rat's ass." His burning gaze was studying a sheaf of papers, and Eddie saw his photograph clipped to one. "Mr. Stilwell tells me you were enormously helpful to him in the investigation of the traitor Joseph Belt. Mr. Stilwell vouches for you absolutely."

The interview had just begun, and Eddie had already been left behind. "So you're sure Joseph Belt was a traitor?"

"Did you really think he lost his security clearance because of your little story, Mr. Wesley? Is your ego so large?" J. Edgar Hoover turned a page in the thick dossier, then another. People said he looked like a bulldog, and people were right. He had a wide, fleshy canine face and a low, round brow. His hands moved like swift, efficient paws. "Had a call from somebody who had a call from somebody who had a call from somebody." The jowly face said he disapproved of such calls. "Said maybe we should give you the chance to avoid a trial."

"For what?" said Eddie, more loudly than he intended. "A trial for what?"

The full gaze, doleful and warning, flicked over him like a prison searchlight, then returned to the papers. "Espionage, Mr. Wesley. What we electrocuted the Rosenbergs for."

Eddie sat down, hard.

"We can link you to the traitor Belt. A child could connect the dots. The jury won't have any trouble." Despite Eddie's efforts, no words of indignation or protest poured forth. Hoover was playing with a pencil. "Let me fill you in, just in case you didn't know what you were passing along. What they build at Los Alamos is bombs, Mr. Wesley. Hydrogen bombs. The traitor Belt was one of these characters who thinks he's an idealist when he's really a misfit. He did not approve of the H-bomb, even though he was paid to work on it. I am told the man was a genius. I wouldn't know about that. Oppenheimer was a genius, too. Belt testified at Oppenheimer's hearing. That's the other reason he was in New York when you met him at the Savoy. He was waiting to testify. One traitor helping another."

Eddie said, "Oppenheimer wasn't a traitor. You people made that up."

"Don't blame me. Blame Teller. Anyway, that's ancient history." Hoover turned a page. "Let me explain how their little scheme worked, Eddie. After we got the Rosenbergs and Greenglass and the rest of those Jews, the Soviets had to come up with a new way to steal our secrets. The new way was to insert an agent into New York. What we call an 'illegal'—not a diplomat, in other words, but somebody who blends in, pretending to be an ordinary citizen."

"I know nothing about any of this," Eddie protested, belatedly finding his voice again.

"If you keep interrupting me, Mr. Wesley, you'll be away from the lovely Mrs. Garland's bed a whole lot longer."

"We weren't in bed," he began.

Once more Hoover rode over him. "This is how their scheme worked. Belt would take information out of Los Alamos. He would get it to his friend Castle, who is also conveniently dead. Telephone. Letters. Photographs. There are lots of ways. Castle would leave the information in a dead drop, which would be cleared by the cutout, a man we have in custody, a stupid little Finn who used the name Maki. Ever met him? No? Maki would deliver the information to the illegal. He knew the illegal as Mark. Met him? No? Listen. The Soviets are outstanding at this sort of thing. They love conspiracies. It's the heart of Leninism. Maybe you knew that already. The Soviets know how to organize a network. Belt knew only Castle. Castle knew where the drops were, but not who cleared them. That's why we call him a cutout, Mr. Wesley. Maki does not know who leaves what he collects. Maki delivers the take to his control—the illegal agent, Mark—whom he has met face-to-face only a few times. Maki might possibly be able to pick Mark out of a lineup, but even that isn't certain, because Mark was usually disguised for their meetings. And of course Maki has no idea what name Mark is living under, or even whether he lives in New York City. We have to find the illegal agent."

"I had nothing to do with this," Eddie said woodenly.

"Nobody thinks you did, Mr. Wesley." A hangman's smile of perfect charity, but his heavy gaze was on the file. "Not tonight, anyway. But if we send you to trial, everybody will think so. If we send you to trial, you and Castle will turn out to have been best friends for years."

"You wouldn't do that."

"You and I are small men, Mr. Wesley. Neither one of us is important in the grand scheme. The meaning in our lives comes from attachment to a great cause. You're not a God man." Hoover's fleshy fingers had found the page. "Good for you. Neither am I. Well, now and then. But my great cause, Mr. Wesley, is the security of this nation." Pouchy bulldog eyes lifted. "What is yours, Mr. Wesley? What do you care about?"

Eddie was, for a moment, startled. "Justice. Justice for my people—"

"Nonsense. Save it for your fans. Your great cause is yourself." Tapping the folder. "Did you know that the leadership of the so-called civil-rights movement is chock-full of Reds? Did you know that, Mr. Wesley?"

Eddie's chin rose. "You seem to think a Communist is anybody who disagrees with your point of view."

"I'm not a philosophical man, Mr. Wesley. I don't have a point of view." He glanced up. "We have sources among your people, Mr. Wesley. Sources who are in—what did you call it?" A glance at the page. "The darker nation. I like that phrase, Mr. Wesley. I like it very much. And, right now, the darker nation is at terrible risk. Being led astray. Because of the infiltration by the Reds. What we want, Mr. Wesley, is an informal sort of arrangement. You'll work for Mr. Stilwell, and Mr. Stilwell will report directly to me. All we want you to do is keep your eyes and ears open. We're not asking you what preacher has his hand in the till, or which leader can't keep his pants on." Hoover had pulled another folder from the gigantic stack beside the blotter. His flattened pate shone in the spill of the desk lamp. He inclined his shiny round forehead, as if to indicate that the more sala-cious aspect of the community was already covered. "What we want from you is occasional reports on whatever may threaten the nation's security. In particular, signs of Communist infiltration in the leader-ship. Or any other radical influence. Especially violent radicals." A fleshy hand lifted to forestall the loudly rising objection. "We're not asking you to make anything up, Mr. Wesley. Just report the truth. Analyzing it is our job."

The anger took him. Eddie was already shaking his head. Fiercely. "You have the wrong man." He was surprised to find him-self on his feet. "Even if I sympathized with your goals, which I do not, there is no possibility—"

"That you would ever work for us." Hoover, voice perfectly calm, was back at his folders. "Isn't that right, Mr. Wesley? You would never work for the hated Federal Bureau of Investigation."

"I'm sorry if that offends you, but the record of the Bureau—"

"Of course, you already worked for us on Belt. You look sur-prised. Don't be. It's all in your file, Mr. Wesley." Tapping the pages. "You were kind enough to give Mr. Stilwell a good deal of useful information on the traitor Belt, information that was crucial to the investigation. At the time of his suicide, he had already lost his secu-rity clearance and been questioned four times. The man knew what was coming. That's why he shot himself." Hoover's round face was grim. "All because of you, Mr. Wesley. All because of the information you provided."

"That's a lie! I never even met Stilwell until after Belt was dead!"

The director nodded. "You're suggesting that Mr. Stilwell has filed a false report. I fail to see why he would have done so. A false report is a very serious matter, Mr. Wesley. For a false report, a man gets fired."

"For espionage, a man gets fried," Eddie shot back.

"Yes, that is true, Mr. Wesley. Most countries of the world, civi-lized or uncivilized, ancient or modern, Communist or free, will exe-cute you for turning their military secrets over to the enemy. Perhaps that is why you informed on the traitor Belt. You are a patriot. You informed on him for the good of your country, and he shot himself, and then you profited from your betrayal of a friend by turning the story into a novel." Hoover turned a page. "Perhaps you are wondering how it is that you do not recall what it is that you told Mr. Stilwell about the traitor Belt. I cannot speak to the accuracy of your memory. But you are welcome to correct the record. We want no errors in the archives. I have your file right here." Holding it up. "This is the only copy, Mr. Wesley. If I make a change, that change is permanent. Do you want me to make a change? Do you want to tell me how, in a courageous stand on principle, you refused to cooperate with Mr. Stilwell's investigation into the traitor Belt?" Hoover let the folder fall with a snap. "The choice is yours, Mr. Wesley. If you tell me you had nothing to do with what happened to the traitor Belt, or that you never spoke to Mr. Stilwell until after the traitor Belt was dead, I will make sure that the file reflects this."

"In that case, you'd better get a long pencil—"

"Wait." Holding up a soft, manicured paw. "Before you decide, Mr. Wesley, you should be aware that the gentlemen who brought you here tonight are prepared to take you into custody. We have considerable evidence of your role in the scheme, enough to put you in prison for the next thirty years." As toneless as the weather report. "The only reason we are not prosecuting you for espionage, Mr. Wesley, is that you cooperated in the investigation." He picked up the pencil, licked the point. "Now, Mr. Wesley, if you would like me to correct the record, this is the moment to ask."

Eddie's fists were balled very tightly. He said, "You're very clever, do you know that?"

"Yes, Mr. Wesley. I know that." Hoover closed the file and drew a fresh one from the stack. "I also know that you are a man of integrity and principle. I admire that. I would not want it any other way. We're not blackmailers, Mr. Wesley. We want you to help us voluntarily. Out of love for your country. Should you choose to say no, and face the consequences, we would certainly understand." He opened the new file. The photograph, upside down, was of Aurelia. Eddie stared. Hoover gave him plenty of time to look, then opened another. Mona

Veazie. A third. Margot, now Mrs. Lanning Frost. "Of course, Mr. Wesley, there is also the matter of your accomplices in your treason. The network of traitors who assisted you and the traitor Castle and the traitor Belt." Eddie was, for once, speechless. "We at the Bureau are not philosophical men, Mr. Wesley. But we would naturally have to clear out the entire nest. A painful process. Now and then the innocent are harmed." The Director shut the folders one at a time, giving Eddie a long look at each photo. "An occasional report, Mr. Wesley. Nothing more. Keep your eyes and ears open." He drew a new file from the stack. This time the photograph was of Langston Hughes. "In particular, keep your ears open for any mention of an organization called the Agony, sometimes referred to, if our information is correct, as Jewel Agony."

"I've never heard of it."

"You haven't heard of it. You will. They might ring your doorbell. They do a lot of recruiting among your class of people. Educated people. Jewel Agony plans to do terrible things, Mr. Wesley. We plan to stop them."

"What kind of a name is—"

"You see, Mr. Wesley, Jewel Agony is run by philosophical men. They have ideology. They will use violent force to achieve their means. I think you and I can agree that a turn away from peaceful means would be a disaster for your people."

Eddie sat there, fists clenching and unclenching. He felt trapped, and furious, and wishing he had somebody to punch.

"Please apologize to Mrs. Garland for me," said Hoover, eyes on the pages once more. "It was not my intention to have her wait so long."

"You can't do this."

"We'll be in touch," said the Director, not looking up again, and somehow the door was open and Eddie was out in the hall with his escort.

(I V)

BERNARD STILWELL STOOD at near-attention before the Director, admiration in his eyes. "Do you think he believed it?" the agent asked. "Do you think he suspects?"

Hoover was already pawing at another file. "That I don't give a rat's ass about that hydrogen-bomb rigamarole? Of course he suspects. Don't make the mistake of thinking Mr. Wesley is stupid just because he's a Negro, Mr. Stilwell. He's an intelligent man."

"Yes, sir."

"He's intelligent, but he is also ambitious and envious and wants to stay out of trouble. Those are qualities to cherish in an informant." He rolled the pencil between his fingers. "On the other hand, he ponders. He obsesses. These qualities make Mr. Wesley unpredictable. Be careful."

"Yes, sir."

The agent thought the interview was done, but the Director had a further point to make. "His book isn't bad. The novel. You should read it when you have the opportunity."

"I will, sir. Thank you, sir."

"This character of his. This Dyson Field. He risks everything for love." The tone made affection sound like a vice. He turned a page. "If events turn as we expect, you'll have to keep a closer eye on our Mr. Wesley."

"I'll have help," said Stilwell.

Hoover never lifted his eyes. "The details I leave to you," he said.

CHAPTER 12

The Junie Angle

(1)

THE FOLLOWING WEEK, Eddie went up to Cambridge to visit Junie. Her condition was obvious now, and he wondered how long she could keep avoiding her parents, and persuading her friends that she was simply fat. She had decided to skip the commencement ceremony, and in that way avoid the gathering of relatives whose gossipy eyes would spot the truth at once.

He took her out to dinner at a stuffy place both hated. "And is everything . . . arranged?" he asked nervously.

"Taken care of," Junie confirmed, eyes aglow.

"And you're sure you wouldn't rather just . . ." He trailed off.

His baby sister laughed at him. "Too late for second thoughts. She's coming on into the world."

"She?"

"Could be a he. But I'm hoping. There's enough men of our nation already."

"Of our nation?" he echoed, smiling.

Junie smiled back. "I didn't like the phrase at first. But it's growing on me."

"Thanks." He took her hand. "And you won't tell me what arrangements you've made for the . . . ah, for my niece or nephew?"

She shook her head, eyes mischievous yet sad. "Come on, bro. If I have to go through life not knowing where she is—or he—well, you should be able to manage it, too."

"Does it bother you? Giving up your . . . your baby?"

"Of course it bothers me."

"Then why—"

Her voice was slow, perhaps with pain. "I'd like to have babies, Eddie. Maybe even a husband. But that's later. Much later. For now"—perky once more, but it seemed forced—"well, for now, the baby would only get in the way of my work."

Eddie hesitated. "Have you thought about postponing your work?"

She touched his face. "I'm not a writer, Eddie. I don't get to set my own schedule. My work has to be done now, and I'm the one who's been asked to do it."

Back at her apartment, they had coffee while Eddie told his sister about his encounter with Hoover. Junie listened gravely. Her apartment was cluttered: books, old newspapers, used crockery, dirty clothes. Eddie, who loved order, could not have lived here for two days. He wondered how Junie could stand it. But she did not share the family obsession with neatness. Her only obsession was her career. She also made coffee that was simply terrible: the burned taste of fried dregs. Eddie, who for reasons of solidarity took his coffee black and for reasons of machismo added no sugar, poured in everything she offered in an unsuccessful effort to drown the flavor. Junie seemed not to notice. When Eddie was done, she asked a couple of small questions to clarify the details, then told him what she thought, straight into his face, the way the two of them had always talked to each other.

"You know this is all fixable, right, brother of mine? And won't even be that hard."

Eddie admired everything about his baby sister, but what he liked best was her innate confidence. There was nothing she considered impossible. At Harvard she had missed the Law Review by a hair, and missed magna cum laude by another. Now her secret heart was set on becoming the first woman and second Negro ever to clerk at the Supreme Court of the United States. Some of her professors ridiculed the idea, others were actively opposed, but a handful were pushing her suit. Chief Justice Warren, Junie said, had already taken an interest. As always, she cruised from strength to strength, buoyed along by an effortless cheeriness Eddie loved. And yet he could not guess where the conversation was going.

"Right now, the way it looks to me, I don't have much to fight with."

Junie covered his hand with hers. Her apartment was on the ground floor, not two blocks from the campus. Windows were open to the loud and muggy night. One leg of the kitchen table was shorter than the other three, giving the surface a tendency to shift without warning. "Silly man. Different battles require different weapons."

"What are you, a commando?"

"Maybe later. Right now I'm closer to being a lawyer." She paused, and, for a moment, her face crumpled. It occurred to Eddie that his sister was very tired, and very frightened. She did not really want to give up the baby, and did not really see a choice. Her once-slim cheeks were puffy and full, along with the rest of her. Eddie marveled that nobody had guessed his sister's condition. Then he wondered why on earth he assumed nobody had.

"Are you okay?" he asked, gently.

She nodded, took a long breath. "Sooner or later you'll be turning this page, brother of mine. As you plan out your future, you might want to pay a little bit of attention to avoiding vulnerabilities."

"Are you trying to run my life?"

"No, dear. J. Edgar is doing that. I'm a lawyer. Well, almost. You know what lawyers mostly do?" The table rocked back. Junie seemed not to notice. "Clean up the messes that could have been avoided had our clients consulted us before opening their stupid mouths."

"So clean away."

That knowing, frisky smile. Junie was herself again. She went to the chipped counter, poured herself another vile cup, then returned to the wobbly table to fix everything.

"I've always thought there are two ways to look at life, Eddie, disaster or Godsend. Right now, you're thinking disaster. You're thinking Hoover's got you, you'll have to spy on your own people, file reports for years, even track down this Perpetual Agony or whatever he called it—"

"Jewel Agony."

"Right. Funny name." Scrunching her nose. "Where was I? Right. You're worried that one day, somehow, even if all you ever give them is junk, even if you make up every word, sooner or later it'll all come out, and then you'll be ruined. Nobody loves an informer, not even the people he informs to. You won't have a friend left in the world. Of course, I'll still love you, but I'm weirdly reliable that way. On the other hand, I'll be so famous and important by then that I'll probably be forced to disown you, whether I love you or not, because I'm not about to give up my power for the benefit of my big brother the snitch. That's what you're afraid of, right? Maybe doing the wrong thing—informing for the FBI, naming names—but, what's worse, being caught naming names. That's one interpretation. Disaster. The way the great Eddie Wesley always looks at the world. What we can call the Eddie Angle. Shut up." Stirring her coffee. "Now let me tell you the way the great June Cranch Wesley looks at the world. The Junie Angle. Okay? You think Hoover has you by the balls? Wrong. You have Hoover by the balls. Know what he's done? He's admitted to you that his agents have filed false reports. He's left them in the files because it's helpful to him to have them there. You're thinking, so what, it's your word against his. Know what I say? As your lawyer, I mean? I say, so what? Does he really want to tangle publicly over this? What if it turns out that the worst he could pin on you is that you helped him break up a whole network of Soviet spies? Not kids who march for peace. Real spies, the kind who steal real secrets."

"But I didn't help. Those reports were manufactured by—"

"You mean, you didn't help yet."

"Yet?"

June nodded, rubbing her belly. "Mark. The illegal resident Hoover told you about. The one who got whatever poor Joseph Belt smuggled out of Los Alamos. You give them Mark, and they back off."

"I don't know Mark."

That marvelous brain had sailed on ahead. "I think you do. I think you met Mark after Castle was killed. I think he was desperate, and so he showed himself. I think he gave you his business card."

Eddie blinked. Oh, but she was quick. "Emil. The German at the wedding."

"Emil. That's correct, brother of mine. I think it must have been Emil. You don't need to tell them he showed up with Derek Garland"—protecting, as ever, the borders of the darker nation—"but that's not the point. The point is, you know who Mark is. You trade. You give them Mark, Hoover lets you off the hook on the Agony or whatever it is. You're thinking, that kind of trade just lets him get the hook in deeper. You're naming names. But it's not the same, brother of mine. It's not. Look. Do you really think J. Edgar Hoover gives a—what did he say?—gives a rat's ass about whether Eddie Wesley ever files a report? He might want to discredit the leadership, but, Eddie, dear, I'm sorry to tell you that you're not all that important. Sure, he'd be happy to have another ear out there. But, believe me, if you don't help him go after our leaders, he's got lots and lots of other people who'll do it happily. He won't want to fight this one out, Eddie. Not in public. Especially because it might cast light on his own sympathies. Hoover's been running the Bureau for something like three decades. I don't think he's ready to retire. And, believe me, Eddie, that might be the outcome, if it gets to be public knowledge that he's out to get the civil-rights leadership."

She continued to march around the room, spinning theories. Her brother ached with pride. Junie would be a formidable lawyer.

"Don't get me wrong," she resumed. "People won't turn against Hoover because they like us. They'll turn against him because he scares them. The same way McCarthy did. You wait and see. Hoover's not a fool. He doesn't want a fight. He wants to scare you into doing what he wants. So you get up in his face, Eddie. You work out a compromise, like I said. You give him Emil, and he lets you off the hook. And, yes, maybe you're right, maybe he won't ever let you off completely. But you'll have a tiny hook into him, too. That might not be a bad thing. One day you might need a way to get information to the top. You're going places, Eddie, and you're going to meet people. You never know. One day, believe it or not, you might actually like having a friend who's head of the FBI. This is the Godsend part. You keep the contact. You promise to keep it open. He promises to keep it open. You just keep him from pressuring you, because you have the power to pressure him back. And, just to make sure, you call up some of your funny friends on Hoover's own side of the street. You know who I mean. Aurelia's right-wing buddies. Nixon and those. Make them what we might call the guarantors of your little arrangement. They'll help. Know why? Because they also know you're going places, and they want you to owe them a favor. There. We're done. See? Not disaster. Godsend. The Junie Angle."

He smiled back, and was about to say more, when the telephone rang. To Eddie's surprise, the fun ran out of his sister's face, and she looked, suddenly, droopy and old and unhappy. She excused herself snuffily and, turning her back, snatched up the heavy black receiver.

"Yes? Yes, operator . . . Hi . . . No . . . Not yet . . . I told you, I'm fine with it now. . . . Yes . . . No . . . You don't have to worry about . . . Not yet . . . He's here now, and . . . Okay . . . I can't . . . Okay . . . Okay . . . Yes."

Hanging up without saying goodbye.

It was a moment before she could turn around, and Eddie was not about to make her.

"I'm sorry," she said, face pinched.

"Was that—"

"You'd better go."

"Is he coming over?" Eddie demanded, feeling oddly fierce.

Junie laughed. "Coming over? Eddie, he's never coming over again. Believe me. He wouldn't want to. And I wouldn't want him to." The smile vanished. "I don't know why I ever—" She stopped, rephrased the point. "He's evil, Eddie. Just plain evil."

Suddenly she was in her brother's arms. Her belly bumped awkwardly against him, and there was laughter in the tears. At the door she offered him more advice.

"You think evil is obvious, Eddie. It usually is. But be careful, brother dear. Sometimes evil is invisible, except to God alone."

Then the mischief was back. "Now, get yourself a lawyer and fix your life."

She shut him out.

(11)

IT TOOK SOME FANCY FOOTWORK. As his sister had directed, Eddie got himself a real lawyer. He sought a recommendation from Oliver Garland, the crisp Wall Street attorney who was Kevin's cousin. Oliver sent him to one of the top litigators in Manhattan, a slim, courtly man named Lloyd Garrison, who had represented Oppenheimer. Sitting in his spacious Park Avenue office, Garrison heard Eddie out. Let me make some calls, he said. A week later, without making a point of it, Garrison took his new client to lunch at a club known to admit no Negroes. Nobody wanted to argue with the lawyer, because he was likely to sue or, worse, resign. Garrison explained the deal. Following his sister's counsel, Eddie sat and listened. He did not argue or question. He just nodded. Eddie spent two days meeting a pair of agents, neither of them Stilwell, one of them obviously very senior in the Bureau. The meetings took place in an apartment in Riverdale. His lawyer and a court reporter were present. When they ran out of questions, the agents thanked him gravely. The next day, they had his statement ready for signature. Eddie hesitated. The document would come back and bite him, he was sure of it. The senior agent held out a pen. Garrison whispered encouragement. Eddie knew that the mess was of his own making and that this was the only way out but still found that he was scared. He heard Junie's confident words: *Hoover doesn't want a fight. He wants to scare you into doing what he wants.* Garrison asked if Eddie needed a minute. Eddie shook his head, took the pen, and, boldly, signed.

Three days later, very quietly, the Federal Bureau of Investigation arrested an artist and photographer named Emil Goldfus who had his apartment and studio in a ritzy building on the Upper East Side of Manhattan, and stored his equipment in a warehouse in

Brooklyn. They charged him with espionage. Within a week, the arrest was public knowledge. Eddie saw the picture on the front page of the paper. The caption said that he was a colonel in the KGB, that he had operated under a pseudonym, and that his real name was Rudolf Abel.

(I I I)

THE CELEBRATION, such as it was, remained muted, because almost nobody knew what was going on. Aurelia, whose husband had still not returned from abroad, found an excuse to go up to Boston to visit a sorority sister, and joined Eddie for lunch at Junie's apartment in Cambridge while supposedly out shopping. Junie disliked the women of the Negro sororities of that day, even though her mother and big sister were in one. Fortunately, she hit it off with Aurelia, who could charm the snow off Everest. The two women spent more time laughing and chattering with each other than either did celebrating with Eddie. Eventually, he decided to take himself off for a walk through Cambridge, a town whose vibrancy he loved. The afternoon was sultry. He took off his jacket and slung it over his shoulder. He strolled down to the Square to buy a couple of overseas papers and listen to the street music and the odd undiscovered poetic genius declaiming on the sidewalk for pennies. The madcap afternoon energy seized him. He felt freer than he had in years. He was spending time with Aurelia and loving the risk. They never even touched. They did nothing but enjoy each other's company. Eddie did not know what his behavior meant. He wandered into a bookstore and found a couple of copies of *Field's Unified Theory*. He was about to track down the manager and offer to autograph them when he glanced up and saw, attacking the vast mountain of travel guides, Margot Frost.

Grinning her toothy political grin at him, the one she inherited from her father.

Friendly hug. Quick polite conversation of ex-lovers.

"What are you doing here?"

"Lanning is meeting some of his old professors. They're going to teach him everything there is to know about foreign policy in three hours." The same sparkling mischief in the dark eyes. "What are you doing here?"

"Visiting my sister. You look great, Margot."

"So do you. I read the novel. I loved it."

"Thanks. How are things with you?"

"Spectacular. Lanning is running for the House next year. I'll tell you a secret. Daddy's retiring. He's anointing Lanning for his Senate seat in '62."

"So the White House can't be far away."

"Having it off in the East Room."

"That's right." Both of them joking. The spark, for a thousand different reasons, was dead. Margot was still a handsome woman. But he noticed changes. Her hair was now perfectly coiffed, as befitted the future First Lady. Her tidy nails bespoke countless hours at the manicurist. She was wearing a loose summer dress, but the cross at her throat was silver and tiny and right side up.

"Call me if you're ever in Washington."

"Call me if you're ever in New York."

Walking back along Massachusetts Avenue, he wondered why Margot had not asked him what his sister was doing in Cambridge. Maybe it was liberal politeness, not wanting to embarrass him when it turned out that she scrubbed bathrooms at night. Maybe it was something else.

On the subway ride back to Boston, Aurie asked him what had taken so long.

"I ran into an old friend," he said.

Or she ran into me.

CHAPTER 13

More Friendly Advice

(1)

"YOU'RE AN IDIOT," said Mona Veazie.

"I figured that part out for myself."

"Why didn't you ask me before you went down there, Aurie? I would've told you what would happen. I know how you are about him and I know how he is about you—"

"We didn't have sex," Aurelia whispered.

Mona laughed—or, more properly, hooted. They were in Mona's bedroom, for she still lived in her parents' mansion on Edgecombe Avenue. Her mother, a distant Garland cousin, was the most prominent Czarina in Harlem. The view was of the walled garden, and the rear entrances of other houses. Mona sat at her dresser. Aurelia was lying on her back on the bed.

" 'We didn't have sex,' " Mona echoed. "You should put that one in the *Sentinel*. Everybody would believe it, right? 'What recently married Harlem hostess spent the night alone in an apartment with her ex, then denied to this reporter that they had intimate relations?' I can see it now."

"We didn't spend the night together. The driver dropped me at Janine's and then took Eddie to his hotel."

"The FBI driver."

"Yes."

"So the two of you are probably in Hoover's files by now."

Aurelia rolled onto her side. "Stop teasing me, Mona. I'm in trouble. I need help."

Mona's eyes sparkled. "If I believed you, I'd help you. I know how much I owe you, honey. But you never needed help in your life. You're just up here whining because you don't want a lecture."

"I don't want a lecture. That's true." Aurelia propped herself on her elbow. "What am I going to do?"

Mona rubbed her temple like somebody with a migraine. She was wearing slacks, as she almost always did, even as she topped thirty, when skirts and dresses were de rigueur among Harlem women of a certain class. Mona was about to receive her doctorate in psychology, and had lined up a postgraduate fellowship at the University of Chicago, where she would teach a little, do some research, and hunt for a full-time faculty position worthy of her credentials. She was the smartest person Aurelia had ever met, and also one of the wisest. They had been friends since the day they met. Mona, the great rebel, had a string of men behind her. Aurie was more choosy, even though Harlem believed otherwise. Eddie was not the first man with whom she had found herself sexlessly entwined.

"You're a married woman," said Mona, with her mother's chilly authority. "You have a child. You're not going to do anything. Eddie was over the day you said yes to Kevin."

"Eddie thinks that we—"

"It doesn't matter what Eddie thinks."

"We could have a harmless lunch now and—"

"You saw what having a drink almost cost you."

Aurie frowned. "When did you get so hard? You never followed anybody's rules."

Mona grinned. "I never got married, either. Respect the institution."

(11)

THE ARGUMENT with Mona took place after the trip to Washington but before the trip to Boston. For days Aurelia wondered. At that time Kevin had been gone for almost two weeks, without any serious effort at explanation. He did not seem to be respecting the institution—not the way Aurie thought the institution was supposed to work. Bewildered, she walked little Zora in her carriage, visited other Harlem wives, wrote the occasional column for the *Sentinel*. Several times over the next couple of days, she was on the verge of calling Eddie—surely there was nothing wrong with a *lunch*—but her hand always froze before she could lift the receiver.

Then she ran into Eddie one night at the salon maintained by Shirley Elden, and when they happened to pass in the empty hallway—no doubt a coincidence—she asked him, matter-of-factly, how the business with Hoover had been resolved. Eddie explained. Flushed with relief, she actually gave him a congratulatory hug, and kissed him on the cheek. The intimacy was dizzying, and it was in that moment of weakness that she whispered that she would try to meet him in Cambridge for the celebration with Junie—a choice she did not regret until she got home.

Anybody could have seen her.

Was she out of her mind?

Then it got worse. Two mornings after her return, Aurelia had an unexpected visit from her father-in-law, who stopped by on his way to work. He brought along a box of imported chocolates. She made coffee, and dandled the baby on her knee while they talked.

"My boy's not perfect," said Matty calmly. "Not by a long shot. I don't imagine living with him is all sweetness and light. I understand that. He married a beautiful younger woman, and he leaves you here alone for weeks at a time. Bad situation all around, Aurie. Very bad."

She could not meet his eyes, and so played with Zora, who was nibbling on an animal cracker but mostly smearing it on her mother's blouse.

"We're the same, you and I. That's what I love about you. We're the kind of people, we see something we want, we go after it, and nothing will make us happy till we get it. Right?" Still she said nothing. He did not want her answers or her agreement. He wanted her attention. "The only trouble is, Aurie, people like us get bored easily. We work and work till we get what we want, and then—as soon as we get it?—we want something else. You know how the Bible says, hold tight to that which is good? I'm not sure people like us are so great at that one." He raised a hand to forestall her response. "Me, I don't judge anybody. Live and let live. Besides, my life—well, it's not a model for anybody to follow. Except for one thing. My marriage. My Wanda. That's the one thing I've done right in life, being true to my wife and taking care of her."

Aurelia was shaking her head. "I've never cheated on Kevin, Matty. Please believe me. I never have, and I never would."

His eyes were wide with feigned surprise. He laid a hand over his heart. "Oh, no, honey, no. Did you think that's what I meant? I know you would never hurt my son. Never. Not that he doesn't deserve it, goodness knows." He leaned over and chucked Zora's chin. The toddler tilted her head back like a Czarina in training. "What I'm saying is, I know this has been hard, the way Kevin is acting. Believe me, Aurie, when he gets back, I'll be giving him a serious talking-to. Just what I told you, honey. Holding tight to that which is good." He was on his feet, hat in hand. "You remember, Aurie. You're worth ten of him. He needs you more than you need him. He's not so bad, really. Try to meet him halfway. My wife does that. I'm hell on earth to live with, and my Wanda's a saint. But you don't have to be a saint, honey. All I'm asking is that you give my boy a chance. I'll talk to him. And I'll tell him, Aurie. If he ever does anything to hurt you—really hurt you?—I'll pay for the divorce myself and give you what I'm leaving to him in my will."

Aurelia had never known a man who could make her cry so easily, but Matty was a salesman and could wring tears from a statue. By the time they walked to the door, she had recovered sufficiently to ask a question.

"Matty?"

"Yes, honey?"

"Have you ever heard Kevin talk about shaking the throne?"

His fleshy face crinkled in bewilderment. "About what?"

"Shaking the throne. Pandemonium. Anything like that."

"Sounds to me like the music you kids listen to." He kissed her on the forehead, and was gone.

(1 1 1)

KEVIN RETURNED from London the following week. From Idlewild, he went straight to the office, and arrived home several hours later chastened and apologetic, bearing a beautifully wrapped box from the royal jewelers, Garrard & Co. of Bond Street. He hugged her desperately. He told her he loved her. He made promises. He would never again go away without telling her. He was sorry to have frightened her. He would never hurt her again. What he called "the bad patch" was over. He was done with his mysterious travels. Aurelia wondered whether his promises meant he had located Castle's testament. Kevin was still talking, holding her close. What they needed, he said, was a second honeymoon: the chance to begin anew. After that, a house in the suburbs, so that the children would have a yard to play in.

Aurelia felt her childhood dreams gathering gently around her like clouds of triumph. A well-off husband who would never hurt her again. A grand house full of children. She remembered the orphanage, the nuns doing their best amid the crowding and the dampness and the fear. If the bad patch was really over—

She studied Kevin's earnest face and chose to forgive him.

That night, they got to work on the new baby.

A month later, opening her eyes one morning to find Kevin smiling down at her as the Tuscan sunshine poured through the windows of the rented villa, Aurelia decided that the revival of his former tenderness was real. They made love. On the second day after their return to Edgecombe Avenue, she waited for her husband to leave for work, then went into the tiny sewing room that served as her office. She gathered the notes she had made from the documents she had found in the safe, burned them in an ashtray, and threw the ashes out with the trash.

CHAPTER 14

Quonset

(1)

"I DON'T READ CONTEMPORARY FICTION," said Aunt Erebeth, patting Eddie's hand with papery fingers. It was like being touched by a ghost. A tongue so pale you could almost see through it emerged from the ancient mouth, sliding over invisible lips. Snowy hair was straight and brittle, as if she was afraid to let her maids touch it. Gary Fatek often said, laughing nervously, that his great-aunt was about six hundred years old. Just now, Eddie could believe it. "I don't read anything written after Trollope. A little Dickens now and then, you understand, but I'm more a Milton woman. You'll have read Milton back in college, of course, won't you? Every real writer has." Malicious confidence glittered in the old eyes. "You are a writer, aren't you? Gareth says you make the critics swoon. But Gareth voted for Stevenson, not Eisenhower, the ninny, so we know what his opinion is worth." She coughed, spraying Eddie with the remnants of dinner, and left unclear exactly who was the ninny. Eddie was seated on her right, the place of honor, across from Gary, and on the left of Tamra, whom Erebeth described as her minor domo. The dining room of Aunt Erebeth's Quonset Point redoubt was an ill-lit cavern. The polished rosewood table could easily seat thirty, but tonight there were just four of them. The gloss was so high that Eddie could see himself, in full color, each time he bent over for a bite. It was early June. The windows were open to the murmuring night sea.

"I am indeed a writer," Eddie agreed, wondering how on earth he had allowed Gary to talk him into this weekend. But one did not ignore invitations from the likes of Erebeth Hilliman.

"I've never heard of you," she snapped.

Gary looked at his plate: Limoges, custom-designed with the family crest. Tamra looked at Erebeth. Eddie longed to smile but fought the urge. Aunt Erebeth, according to Gary, hated two things in life: levity and the Democratic Party. "My career is young," said Eddie, hoping to sound modest.

"Eddie's first novel won all these awards—" Gary began.

"If I wanted your opinion," said Erebeth, "I'd have borne you myself. But that ninny Stella had you instead, and your father was Father's chauffeur, so I would suggest you keep your stupid ideas in your head." To Eddie, sweetly: "What awards were those, dear?"

Liveried servants cleared. Erebeth commanded the party to the library. The corridors were dark, depressing wood. The sconces were muted, because Erebeth's eyes were sensitive to light. Tamra pushed the wheelchair. She was big and blond and forty and looked as if she should be riding horses. According to Gary, Erebeth hired a new minor domo every six months or so, but Tamra had lasted more than twice that, maybe because none of the others had ever fought back. Erebeth did as she pleased. She was the only living grandchild of Major Hilliman, founder of the family fortune. The Hilliman trusts expired on Erebeth's death, and she was charged with rewriting them, so nobody denied her anything, including years of their lives.

Tea and cakes were served.

"I admire you people," said Erebeth as they sat beneath long portraits of prominent ancestors. Two were royalty. One was a President. Everybody was sipping Darjeeling except Erebeth, who guzzled a foul-smelling elixir from a plain brown bottle. Gary whispered that it was supposed to keep her alive forever. Eddie suspected that her various hatreds would be enough to keep her batteries charged. "Negroes," the old woman clarified. "I admire you Negroes. Only a hundred years out of slavery, and look how far you've come. Still on the bottom!" Erebeth cackled at her joke. Gary waggled a warning finger at his friend, but Eddie was stone. I keep my politics under wraps at Quonset Point, Gary had told him earlier. Easier for everyone that way.

"Stop it," said Tamra. She had a square jaw and a gaze of disconcerting directness. You had the sense that lies were beneath her.

"I'm just having a little fun, dear," Erebeth sulked.

"Apologize," said Tamra.

"I shall do no such thing." Then she brightened and, in her way, apologized after all. "Actually," she said, touching Eddie's hand again, "I like the Negroes. I do." Shifting her gaze briefly toward the disapproving Tamra. "I write checks to the NAACP," Erebeth added, mournfully, as if disclosing the family shame. "Gigantic checks. I'm their biggest donor in the country."

"In Rhode Island," said Tamra. "And only the third biggest."

(11)

THE TWO YOUNG MEN were walking on the beach, managing, rather nicely given their considerable inebriation, brandy and cigars. The ocean was inky dark and triumphant. Distant lights were boats, or buoys, or optical illusions. Erebeth owned the sand, a mile in both directions. She was said to own the legislature, too, which had granted her by statute the needed exemptions. Eddie wondered what it must have been like to grow up this way.

"Aunt Erebeth wants me to run her foundation," said Gary tipsily. "She's a greedy old bitch, and she'd leave her money to herself if she could, but the lawyers seem to think it's impossible. So she's creating a foundation. She's naming it after herself, and she wants me to run it, and she'll rewrite the trusts so I'll be in charge of them next generation."

Eddie marveled at life's twists. The fabled Hilliman trusts contained more money than any but a handful of American corporations earned in a year. The trusts provided for the needs and caprices of the scattered Hillimans, and provided uncountable wealth for the single member of each generation assigned as their custodian. Gary's aunt was asking the self-proclaimed radical to take control of the family.

"Are you going to accept?"

"I don't know. The foundation will give money to promote international understanding. Peace in our time. You know the kind of thing." He hesitated. "Erebeth is the last of the third generation. The fourth—my mother's generation—all died. There's fifteen of us in the fifth."

"Your cousins will hate you."

Gary seemed not to hear. He gazed into the ocean, and found distant misty memories. "My grandfather—Erebeth's older brother— wanted sons. He kept marrying new women, and they kept delivering daughters." He laughed. Angrily. "I think my mother ran off with the chauffeur just to shock the family, but he was a great dad. Grandfather wanted to cut her off, but he couldn't change the trusts. Erebeth—well, she's different. More modern."

"Modern?"

"I know, I know, you think she's a big right-winger. But, Eddie, this idea of hers, the foundation, has lots of promise for the issues that you and I always . . ." He sighed, ran down, said nothing. "If I don't . . ." Again he stopped. He shook his head, muttered something vulgar. His shoulders slumped. Temptation, temptation. "The cousins hate me already. Because of my father. And—well, because they do."

Eddie stood with his toes curled into the wet sand, thinking of his childhood on Martha's Vineyard, and perfect worlds destroyed by the hard truth that we either grow old or die young. He thought about Aurelia. And about his sister and her baby. "Why did you bring me here, Gary? I can't help you decide what to do."

"Erebeth wanted to meet you."

"Why?"

"She wouldn't say."

"I don't understand."

Gary took a long look at him, then laughed, the perennial outsider, and tossed his brandy snifter as far out as he could. They listened but heard no splash. "I don't understand, either. She said she wanted you to come for the weekend so she could take your measure.

She was very insistent, Eddie. She's Erebeth Hilliman. She doesn't give reasons. She gives orders." He took Eddie's glass, threw that one, too. Eddie had only been sipping, so brandy sloshed everywhere. Gary laughed again. "Maybe she plans to write you into the trusts."

(III)

THE GUEST CHAMBER was big enough to dock an ocean liner. At four in the morning, Eddie woke to a rapping at the heavy door. Opening it a crack, he found Tamra peering at him, wearing a housecoat, blond hair awry. It took him a groggy moment to understand that the minor domo intended nothing lascivious. He was being summoned to the telephone. A servant stood behind her, a heavy terry-cloth bathrobe at the ready. There was an extension on the landing. He heard the familiar voice and sat down hard on the wicker seat.

"I can't stand this," sobbed Junie. "It's so unfair. Why do we have to make these choices?"

She cried for a while, even though he could not work out from the few incoherent sentences she muttered what she was crying about. Second thoughts, he supposed. She did not want to give up the baby. He wondered whether she had been drinking, and remembered reading that some doctors thought alcohol was bad for the baby, and others thought it usefully relaxing for the mother. He calmed her down. He told her he loved her. He told her he could be in Cambridge in two hours. Weeping, she assured him she was feeling better and there was really no need for him to come, but he could not bear the thought of her pain. Upstairs, under Tamra's supervision, the servant was already packing Eddie's bags.

"Gary was always her favorite," the minor domo explained. "That's why the cousins all hate him, Mr. Wesley. Erebeth has no children of her own, you see." A ghost of a smile. "I very much doubt that Gary will be having children any time soon."

"But he's engaged to—"

"That governor's niece. Yes. I read the papers. And yet I rather suspect that they will never wed."

A driver was waiting. The household assembled to see him off. Gary sent Junie his best. Erebeth's glittering eyes said she had his measure. Tamra looked sad. When Eddie arrived in Cambridge, Junie was dressed, perky and smiling, and big as a house. He sensed that his sister was putting on her best face for him, and wished that she would not. She allowed him to buy her breakfast and wash the dishes, for the apartment was messy as ever. She refused to explain her crying jag, beyond referring to cold feet, and by midday had sent him on his way as if expecting a more important caller.

In Harlem two days later, he stole a few minutes with Aurelia, who laughed and told him pregnant women were always emotional. "I used to cry before every meal," she assured him. "And half the time I was ready to wring Kevin's neck. I didn't need a reason." But to Eddie every phenomenon had a cause.

(I V)

THE BABY GIRL arrived in July, scant weeks after Junie turned twenty-five. She sent Eddie a note to say that her "gentleman" had done his part, and everything was fine. She had subsequently gone up to Boston to visit their parents, and, in response to Marie Wesley's pronouncement that she seemed pale and shaky and had gained weight, told them that the rigors of law school will do that to you. Marie wanted to send her to their family doctor for a checkup, and was surprised by the vehemence of her daughter's resistance. But the temper, too, she put down to the same pressures. *I admit I still feel a little bit guilty*, Junie wrote, *but I feel the future opening wide before the whole darker nation. I can hardly wait to get there.*

Me, too, Eddie wrote back.

A month later, June Cranch Wesley left Cambridge with a girl-friend, the two of them driving to Chicago in a borrowed car, Junie to begin her clerkship at the federal courthouse, her friend to look for work.

They never arrived.

The car was later found at a rest stop in New Jersey, locked, undamaged, and packed tightly with their belongings. Both women had disappeared.

CHAPTER 15

The First Investigation

(1)

THE REST of the year passed in a slow-motion horror. At first the family clung to the possibility that Junie, always headstrong, had run off with some guy: nobody but Eddie knew about the baby, and Eddie was not about to tell his sister's secrets. The trouble was, unless it was a double wedding, there was still the problem of explaining why the girlfriend, too, had disappeared. Had both run off with the same guy? With each other? The two families wondered, dithered, at last rejected the thought. The pendulum swung the other way. They were dead, no question. The Klan had done it. The New Jersey State Police. A wounded boyfriend. A crazed murderer who roamed the countryside. No. No. Never give up hope. Congregations all over Boston prayed for Junie. Big politicians stopped by the house, because Wesley Senior was connected. John Hynes, Boston's mayor, promised his help. So did the formidable Joseph Kennedy, whose empire was said to extend into spaces so narrow not even the Scarletts of the world could wiggle in. Everyone kept clapping everyone on the back. Everyone kept insisting Junie would turn up. She would write a letter from Mexico, she would call for cash from Seattle, or, at worst, some kid would stumble over the remains in a ditch.

Everyone said so.

The police at first were solicitous. So was the press. Wesley Senior was a preacher of considerable prominence. In Boston, his endorsement meant thousands of votes. Detectives, captains, even the commissioner assured the family that their opposite numbers in and around New Jersey were doing all they could. Reporters, meanwhile, played up the story, at least locally. The family refused to give up hope.

But time passed. Summer stretched into fall. No information was no information. There were other crimes for the police to solve, and other stories for reporters to write.

The family did what they could. They called in favors and wrote letters. They buried the emptiness beneath a flurry of activity. They demanded, they cajoled, and finally they begged. The world marched on. In the end, so did the family. They had lives to lead. Marcella still had children to raise, and still had her undertaker to help. Wesley Senior still had a congregation to run. Eddie still had literary fame to pursue. Marie still had the rest of the family to worry about. By the start of 1958, the family's closeness had begun to fray, as if Junie, the least reliable of them all, had been the gravity that drew them together. As the mystery faded from public memory—just another disappearance, these things happened, this, too, was life!— the mourning, too, receded, just as surely as the hope, and siblings and parents began to call and visit each other less frequently.

Eddie, as it happened, was capable of an investigation that the others were not. He spoke only to Gary Fatek, who urged him to try. And so Eddie returned to Cambridge, where he had any number of friends. People he had never met willingly opened their doors upon learning that he was who he was, and the older brother of the vanished June Cranch Wesley into the bargain.

Eddie spent the better part of two weeks nosing around, and, applying to a single purpose all the force of his personality, he was able to gather together the disparate strands of his sister's law-school life. He chased rumor until he ran into blank walls, he distilled innuendo to find the powdery truths that precipitated out, he tracked snickers and jokes to their sources, finally uncovering the name of the professor with whom Junie had conducted her moderately clandestine affair; and who must have fathered, therefore, the vanished baby. Because he possessed an infinitude of energy but a micromitude of tact, Eddie decided, after a trio of unreturned telephone calls and a failed attempt to flirt his way past a protective secretary in Langdell Hall, to beard the gentleman on the doorstep of his small-ish Tudor in Newton.

The meeting went poorly.

The professor, a youngish married man named Mellor, tried several strategies to avoid letting Eddie in the house, including a threat to call the police, and Eddie in his turn invited him to do so, whispering, however, that if he was going to be arrested in any case, he might as well be hanged for a sheep as for a lamb, and therefore would barge into the kitchen, where Mrs. Mellor was sewing, to explain to her that the scrawny but charming Professor Mellor had fathered a child by the lone woman of the darker nation in the Harvard Law School class of 1957, now vanished. So they went into Benjamin Mellor's closet-size study instead, the poorly polished desk their only separation as Eddie asked his questions and the law professor told his lies.

No, he did not really remember a June Wesley.

Oh, yes, he did, she was in his contracts class.

Yes, yes, that's right, of course, she was in his seminar the following year.

Now that you mention it, yes, that's true, she did serve as his research assistant during her second summer, but only for a few weeks—still protesting—because she spent the rest of the summer interning at a law firm in the Midwest, and—

Well, yes. She did research for him in the fall of her third year, too: it is just that there are so many of them, and it is so hard to keep—

How many? Over the summer? Counting Junie?

Well, ah, one.

No, he never touched her, he was a married man.

Yes, well, ah, they hugged once.

Fine, there was also a kiss, he was human after all.

All right, yes, perhaps the kiss did take place in her bed.

And so on.

"You'll ruin me," Mellor complained, speaking in the self-pitying whisper he had adopted ever since the collapse of his resistance at the door. The window gave onto an overgrown garden and a stone birdbath slopping with filthy water. "My career, my marriage, everything," the father of Junie's baby continued unhappily. "It's not just me. I have two children."

"You mean, two *other* children," said Eddie coldly.

"That baby wasn't mine."

"How do you know?"

"Look. She came after me, not the other way around, okay? I know you think your sister was an angel, but, believe me, she was"— he hesitated, glanced at Eddie's furious face, changed course—"hard to resist."

"And I have no doubt that your weakness of will shall serve as great comfort to both your dean and your wife."

Belatedly, the professor remembered his station in life; and Eddie's. The gray eyes went flat and disdainful. He was a lawyer after all, and a Harvard professor. He would talk his way out of this. "What exactly do you want, Mr. Wesley? Money? Is this a shakedown? What?"

"I want to know what happened to the baby."

Benjamin Mellor shrugged, smirked, shrugged it off. "Your guess is as good as mine. She said she was giving it up for adoption."

"I know that much."

"Well, then, you know as much as I do. I have no idea what they did with it."

Eddie leaned forward and laid his hands on the blotter, fixing Benjamin Mellor with one of the looks he had learned from Scarlett's hard men. "Let's do that one again," he murmured.

"Which one?"

"What happened to the baby?"

"I told you, I don't have any idea."

"Yes, you do."

"What?" By now Benjamin Mellor had shrunk against his aging chair, hands instinctively lifted, palms outmost, as though to ward off a blow. "How would I know where the baby is?" the professor whined. "It wasn't my problem. It was her problem. I told her to get rid of it. I offered to pay. She wouldn't. Don't look at me like that. I have a family, and a career, and—"

And that was as far as he got. Eddie had a knee on the desk and a firm grip on the professor's collar and another on his necktie. Eddie jerked him forward so hard that he bit his tongue, then jerked him backward but yanked the tie before his head could strike the window. For Benjamin Mellor it was like being punched twice, but Eddie knew what he was doing: the chair never even squeaked, and the professor's wife, two rooms away, never heard a thing.

Eddie leaned close and whispered in the stunned man's ear: "You don't have any idea what *they* did with the baby. That's what you said, right? But you know who *they* are, don't you? Junie said you did your part. You couldn't take any chances. Who were *they*, Professor? Who helped Junie?"

Benjamin Mellor showed an unexpected pluck. He removed Eddie's hand from the crisp white shirt and stood to his full height. He might have projected the perfect image of the brilliant scholar he no doubt was, but for the tremor in his voice, and the fear in his eyes. "Your premise is mistaken," he said coldly. "I wasn't the one who helped her do whatever she did. When I said *they*, I was referring to your sister and that girl who disappeared with her. Sharon Martindale. Her white friend. I don't know where they took the baby, but they went together."

"She must have told you something," said Eddie, ready to grab him again.

The law professor stroked his goateed chin. "Your sister came to see me before she left for Chicago. Came to my office. She said she was sorry about the way things had worked out. I said the same. She said she was sorry to have gotten me into this"—he saw something in Eddie's face, and raised a hand for calm—"and I told her I wouldn't have missed it for the world." He hesitated. Caution? A fugitive emotion? Eddie could no longer tell. "She wished me well in my career. I wished her well in hers. She started to laugh. Then she started to cry. And then she said"—another instant's hesitation—"she said thank you." The professor dropped his eyes. "I never saw her again."

(11)

THE *THANK YOU* BOTHERED Eddie Wesley, and he suspected that the professor was romancing. Benjamin Mellor, after all, had done Junie no favors. He had not even helped place the baby for adoption.

Eddie remained in Cambridge for two more days, asking more questions. Benjamin Mellor came from a distinguished academic family. He did not have a reputation for fooling around with his students. People described him as devoted to his family, and enormously ambitious, hoping for more than a Harvard professorship. An affair would thus carry double risk. What would make a man like that choose Junie? Or make Junie choose him? There were depths to his sister that Eddie had yet to plumb, but at least he was making progress.

CHAPTER 16

The Other Half of Truth

(1)

EDDIE FELT NO SENSE of triumph. He had not even found his sister's baby, let alone his sister. He returned to Convent Avenue, but Harlem was cheerless. The same disordered energy that had long excited him now exhausted him. He stood in the huge crowd outside Abyssinian Baptist Church, paying his respects to W. C. Handy. The great composer, in his eighties, had finally succumbed to the after-effects of a stroke, and Eddie thought there might be an essay in it. Afterward, he sat in the window of his study, staring at the brown-stones across the street, pencil in hand, notebook at the ready, and nothing came. He breakfasted at Chock Full o' Nuts, he lunched at the Colony Club with Kasten, his literary agent. He dined with his friend Charlie Bing, the dentist, and his wife, Chamonix, at their apartment on Saint Nicholas Avenue, but their beautiful marriage wounded him. At the salons, he picked fights with famous intellectu-als over differences he could scarcely articulate. Gary Fatek dragged him to a couple of rallies at Union Square, one against the bomb, the other against the American invasion of Lebanon. Eddie listened to the speeches and felt himself distinctly unmoved. He spent what lit-tle money he had saved on a firm of private detectives, who took his retainer and reported no trace. The detectives had visited every adoption agency within four hours of Cambridge, but the few who could be persuaded or bribed to open their records had no mother named June Wesley, and nobody remembered two girls, one white and one black, coming in together. Frustrated, Eddie shouted at the head of the firm over the telephone, but the man had heard worse.

"Who are these people?" he said to Aurelia, when she took the time to try to cheer him. "How are they doing this?"

"Doing what?"

Eddie did not know how to articulate his growing suspicion that some malevolent force was at work, and Aurelia was not prepared to tease it out of him. Zora, at one and a half, kept her pregnant mother busy, and by all accounts aglow with happiness. But Aurie heard of Eddie's state and managed to steal a few minutes for a walk on Riverside Drive on a sunny afternoon. She pushed a shiny stroller from the midst of which, swaddled in pink-striped blankets, peeked her daughter's plumply innocent brown face. Eddie gazed down at the child of another man and felt the earth heave. Everywhere he looked were women pushing strollers, some of them mothers, some of them grandmothers, some of them nannies, and none of them Junie, or pushing Junie's baby, or, for that matter, his. He turned to Aurelia and saw a beautiful foreigner.

"You have to move on, Eddie," she was saying—whether about Junie or about Aurie she left unclear. "You still have a life to lead."

Eddie nodded but said nothing. He was trying to keep the sidewalk steady beneath his feet. Aurelia was a year older than he, but spoke with an authority and a diffidence that suggested a greater span.

"You need to write," she said. "The muse."

He managed a flickery smile.

"Oh, and, darling," she continued, "you should get married."

"To whom?"

Aurelia gestured upward, past the parkland lining Riverside Drive, toward the apartment towers of Harlem. "Any of those silly girls you dated in between me."

Eddie only shook his head. He glanced at the stroller. To proclaim his love for Aurelia would seem, in the current situation, fatuous. Instead, he told her the other half of the truth. "Right now, I need to find Junie."

She touched his arm, the sanely compassionate soul delivering bad news. "You mean, you need to find out what happened to her."

"No. I need to find her."

Aurelia's face slipped gently from schoolmarm to imp, and, for a moment, he supposed she probably did love him after all.

"If you need to find her, then find her," she said.

"I can't. I don't know where to look."

Practical, practical: "Either you go search for Junie, or you go back to your life. You can't have it both ways."

"I'll have it any way I want," he said, astonished at his own sharpness, and probably wanting to pick a fight.

Aurelia, however, was now all mother. She seemed sturdy and confident. Battling an ex-lover was beneath her dignity. She stepped lightly away, her body between him and the stroller. She adjusted the blankets as if afraid her daughter would overhear. "Not that you care," she murmured, acting with her back, "but I meant to tell you. You know that cross you asked me about years ago? Well, Kevin has one just like it."

It took Eddie a few seconds to remember what cross she meant. Castle seemed several lifetimes ago. "You're right," he said. "I don't care."

Aurelia's eyes narrowed. "I see."

Eddie could not stop. "It's easy for you to be blasé. You have everything. And Junie—well, she's my sister, not yours."

"I adore Junie."

"It's not the same, and you know it." He saw her face. He softened. "I'm sorry, Aurie. I shouldn't take it out on you. I'm just not good company right now."

"No," she said. "You're not." He expected anger. Reproach. Maybe even a slap. Instead, Aurelia favored him with the old smile. "Call me when you are."

He watched her join the crowd, one more mother in the parade, the darker nation displaying with fierce pride its hopes for a richer future, a future Junie had hoped to spend her life helping to win.

(I I)

EDDIE'S OTHER FRIENDS were full of advice. Kasten, his agent, proposed that he battle his demons on the typewriter. Eddie dined with Gary Fatek and two of the millionaire's many adoring women. After dinner they walked through the park, the women up front, the men trailing like bodyguards. Gary had broken off his engagement to the governor's niece, just as Tamra has predicted. Eddie was not sure where matters stood just now with Mona.

"I never had a sister," said Gary, "and the cousins hate me. But if I did have one? I'd like her to be like Junie." He slipped an arm across Eddie's shoulders. "And I'd always fight for her. I'd never stop kicking down doors."

Eddie glanced at the two women, vibrant and young and white, treating Central Park, even at night, like their own front yard: the purpose, in fact, for which Frederick Law Olmsted had originally designed it. Once upon a time, the police had patrolled to keep the riffraff out, limiting its use to the rich who lived along Fifth Avenue.

"You're a Hilliman, Gary. You've never had to kick in your life. You just raise your hand to knock on a door, and somebody will always open it."

"You know I don't believe in that system of—"

"I'm just saying, it's easier for you. It's different for me."

Gary was aghast. "You can't be thinking of stopping. Eddie, you can't. Your sister needs you."

Eddie had a different thought. "If she wanted my help," he said, "she'd have found a way to reach me."

They had drinks at a trendy café on the Upper West Side. The extra girlfriend wanted to go somewhere, but Eddie didn't.

(I I I)

BY THIS TIME, a few of the bolder tabloids had picked up the Los Alamos story. NEGRO WRITER FORESAW SCIENTIST'S DEATH, murmured one, on an inside page. A paper aimed at the darker nation was more alarming: WESLEY'S TALE SPARKS SUICIDE, it pronounced. Another, its readership mostly supernaturalists, engaged in what journalists call burying the lede: NEW PSYCHIC IN HARLEM! Eddie encouraged the nonsense by refusing to comment, a refusal that Kasten, his agent, called wisdom itself—even though Eddie's reasons had nothing to do with his career. Meanwhile, at Kasten's insistence, Eddie attended a dinner party down in Greenwich Village hosted by his editor. At his table was a *Times* reporter named David Yee, just back from North Carolina, where he had visited the heavily barricaded town of Maxton, the site of a pitched battle a couple of months back between the Lumbee Indians and a band of Klansmen and camp followers variously estimated in the hundreds or the thousands who were trying to burn a cross near the town, which was mostly Negroes and Indians. The Lumbee ordered the Klansmen off. The Klansmen resisted. Shots were fired. The Klansmen fled. David told the table that there was nothing much to see. The town was just a town, the empty field was just an empty field. The Indians did not want to talk about what had happened. The Negroes were grateful but equally stinting in their willingness to divulge details. It was, said David, as if the entire incident was already falling down an Orwellian memory hole. But Eddie, who now carried his leather-bound notebook everywhere, scribbled a summary in case he later wanted it.

David Yee said he had heard that the Lumbee resistance was largely organized by a group called the Agony, or something similar—had anyone heard of it? Eddie did not raise his hand. But a woman at the other end of the table asked if that was the same group that had firebombed the offices of a right-wing tabloid in Saint Louis. A college kid piped up that one of his professors had mentioned it—didn't they blow up an empty police car in Texas or someplace? Eddie stared at the college kid and remembered Hoover's claim that Jewel Agony would recruit the young and the educated.

I'd keep kicking down doors.

At the end of March, Eddie went up to Boston, only to find his mother shrunken and his father without fire. He was astonished. His own depression he had accepted as a matter of course. He was a writer, and young, and therefore possessed an entitlement to moodiness, even despair. But he had always seen his parents, whatever his differences with them, through the eyes of a child. They seemed to Eddie larger and more powerful than life itself. It had never occurred to him that they could be defeated by it. They pressed desultory questions about his life in New York, and asked him to remember them to various friends. They prayed over dinner, and again before bed, as in the old days, but the words, even from Wesley Senior, sounded rote. The silent breakfast was even worse. Their listlessness somehow swallowed his, and Eddie found the spark rekindled. *If you need to find her, then find her.* His parents were old, he realized. They were no longer capable of doing what had to be done. Someone had to continue the search for Junie, and that someone had to be him. Wesley Senior and Marie were mourning, persuaded despite their optimistic words that their daughter was dead. Eddie decided he would accept that opinion when somebody showed him her grave.

On his second evening at home, he sat with his downcast father in the study.

"I would be grateful if you would telephone a friend of yours on my behalf," Eddie said.

(I V)

AT THIS TIME, Joseph P. Kennedy, Sr., was among the richest men in the United States, and therefore in the world. He had investments in real estate, in Hollywood, in transportation, but the crown jewel of his empire was the Merchandise Mart in Chicago. Some people whispered that he had made a good deal of illegal money during Prohibition, but so had everyone else. There seemed to be nobody in politics he didn't know, and nobody who didn't owe him favors. Kennedy himself had been Ambassador to the Court of Saint James's, and his eldest surviving son was planning to make a forceful run for the Democratic nomination for the presidency in 1960, two years hence, even though experts did not see how the Republicans could lose. Yet, for a man who exercised such influence, Joe Kennedy was surprisingly unknown. He maintained a modest suite of offices in a run-down building on a claustrophobic side street in South Boston. Not many Negroes visited this part of town, but Eddie was an old hand, and driven besides. Close to seventy, Kennedy retained an athlete's slimness and a general's personal force. Hard eyes watched the world with satisfaction from behind round rimless glasses. He had the long fingers of the pianist and the powerful wrists of the laborer. He had enjoyed a famous affair with Gloria Swanson. Everybody addressed him as Ambassador.

"Edward. Great to see you."

The Ambassador rose from behind his desk and led his guest to a table by the window. The river was a distant smear. Eddie had expected aides to be present, but the two men met alone. Kennedy was a busy man, but Eddie knew from years of listening at his parents' table that Kennedy owed Wesley Senior any number of favors. Over the years, a coalition of Negro preachers led by Eddie's father had turned out thousands of their congregants to vote for Democratic candidates. It was this debt that Eddie intended to call in now.

"Your parents must be very proud of you."

"I hope so, sir."

"Take it from a father. I know they are."

Eddie nodded his thanks. Around the room were photographs of Kennedy's many children, from Joseph Junior, the oldest, who had been killed in action, to Teddy, the baby, now a lawyer, with whom Eddie had occasionally played in the old days on Cape Cod.

"I'm so sorry for your loss," said the Ambassador, eyes watchful. "June was such a wonderful young lady. The Archbishop has the whole Diocese praying for her."

"We're grateful," Eddie assured him. In point of fact, Eddie believed in the efficacy of prayer even less than he believed in the existence of God, and he believed in God not at all; but he knew that the Joseph Kennedys of the world—like the Maceo Scarletts—liked it when you felt gratitude toward them.

"As I told your father, I would do anything to help." The eyes appraised him from behind those round glasses. "And that's why you're here."

"Yes, sir. That's why I'm here." Time for the pitch. "This is a terrible time for a mother and father." Inclining his head toward the photographs, because two of the pictured children were dead. "The pain of loss is terrible enough. The pain of not knowing is worse."

Kennedy nodded, dragging it out of him.

"Mr. Ambassador, let me be frank."

"By all means."

"They say you know people everywhere. They say you have connections where others have no idea that it is possible to have connections. They say you have sources of information others could never imagine."

"I know a few people," said the Ambassador, and Eddie had the sense that he was enjoying himself.

"What I would like to ask—as a favor to my father, in return for his services, and also as a favor to me—and I, too, would place myself in your debt"—Eddie felt himself botching the carefully rehearsed lines, but it was too late to turn back—"what I would like to ask, Mr. Ambassador, is that you use your sources of information to discover whatever you can about what happened to my sister."

For a while they sat there, studying each other, the old pol and the young writer, using the shared silence to feel each other out. At last Kennedy got to his feet. He waved Eddie to remain seated, then ambled over to his desk. "I'd be a fine one to wait to be asked," he said. "I owe your father a great deal, and whatever meager resources may be mine to command, they are at his service at any time." He took a folder from the blotter and sat once more, crossing one leg easily over the other. "Understand, Edward, I think you exaggerate my capabilities and my connections. I'm a businessman. Nothing more. Of course, I have my people." He opened the folder, studied a page, but Eddie knew it was all ruse. Kennedy already knew what was written there, and he expected Eddie to accept that this single gift, whatever its contents, was all: after this, the debts he owed Wesley Senior were paid. "My people have made certain inquiries. Understand, I did not want to bother your father in his grief."

"I understand."

"I have associates who are in the business of transport," Kennedy said, without specifying precisely what they transported, or how. "My associates tell me that friends of theirs might—I emphasize *might*—might possibly have been involved in transporting a young Negro woman who may or may not have fit your sister's description, at approximately the time of her disappearance." Having shrouded the facts in sufficient uncertainty to make it impossible for Eddie to testify that he ever had any actual knowledge, the Ambassador put the paper back. "These friends of my associates believe—only believe—that a substantial fee might well have been paid for their services."

He stopped, making Eddie ask. His hand was trembling. His voice was hoarse: "Transported her where?"

"It is possible—again, I emphasize, only possible—that she was dropped at an address in Nashville, Tennessee."

"And do they—do you—know the address?"

"The possible address," said the Ambassador piously. He drew another sheet from the folder, handed it over, and waited while Eddie memorized it and handed it back.

"Mr. Ambassador, I don't know what to say."

Kennedy had an arm around his shoulders, walking him to the door. "You do understand, Edward, the odds are that this is a wild-goose chase."

"I understand."

"It was probably another girl."

"Yes, sir."

"I can't vouch for the accuracy of the information."

"I understand, sir."

The Ambassador studied him, thinking, perhaps, of his own children. "She was lucky to have a brother like you."

"No, sir. I was lucky to have a sister like her."

Only when Eddie was out on the street again did it occur to him that both of them had used the past tense.

CHAPTER 17

An Unexpected Meeting

(1)

"IT ISN'T ANY of your business," said Mona Veazie. So smoothly did she tip the porter handling her bags that Aurelia almost missed it. Mona's mother, Amaretta, Czarina-in-chief, stood stoically several yards away, a dark, tiny woman beneath a mountain of fur. An animated Gary Fatek stood beside her. The platform was two levels beneath Manhattan. People bumped and jostled, all of them heading somewhere, or wishing somebody was not. Steam curled as engines started up. Pantographs sparked electricity. If her daughter's imminent departure for three years in Chicago caused Amaretta Veazie any concern, she hid it well. "No matter what Eddie does," Mona continued, fingers resting lightly on her friend's shoulder, "it isn't any of your business. Can you try to remember that while I'm away?"

Aurie dropped her eyes. "I wish you weren't going."

"Why? Afraid you'll make another mistake without me around?"

"Another mistake?"

"With Eddie." Mona touched Aurelia's swollen belly. "Don't forget who you are now, honey." She was up on the step. She glanced at her mother, who nodded indulgently at one of Gary's jokes like a woman not straining to overhear every word of her daughter's conversation. "Junie is Eddie's sister. Not yours. This is Eddie's problem. Not yours."

"I know people. I could help."

"And get yourself in more trouble."

"You don't think much of me, do you?"

"I think the world of you, honey." A kiss on the forehead. "And I know I owe you. If you need me, I'm just a phone call away."

"And a long train ride," said Aurelia, grumpily.

The conductor called all aboard. Hugs all around. Gary kissed Mona on the lips. Then he did it again. Amaretta turned red. She was known to believe that the millionaire was sowing his wild oats before marrying someone white and important. Aurelia secretly agreed, and suspected that Mona did, too, or she would not be leaving. Gary gave Amaretta his arm. Mona was not the sort to linger in the doorway waving last giggly goodbyes. She had vanished before the train cleared the platform, riding onward to greater things, starting with her postdoctorate fellowship at the University of Chicago. Aurelia felt left behind, in more ways than one.

Amaretta stood between the two young people. "There's only one reason people ever run away," she said.

"What reason is that?"

"Because they don't want to get caught."

Gary, for once, did not offer a ride, pleading other business. The two women, today's Czarina and tomorrow's, shared a taxi uptown. They spoke little. Aurelia wanted to ask Amaretta whether she had been speaking of Junie or her own daughter, but you did not ask questions of Amaretta Veazie. Unless you wanted to be frozen out of society, you listened to her wisdom and you did what she told you. Challenging Amaretta, Langston Hughes liked to say, was about as much use as challenging the Pope.

As the cab began to climb Sugar Hill, the older woman grabbed her hand. "It's not young Mr. Wesley who needs your help, dear. It's your Kevin."

Aurie's turn to blush. Amaretta had heard after all. "I'm afraid I don't know what you mean, Mrs. Veazie."

"I believe you know exactly what I mean."

"No, ma'am."

Amaretta's eyes were pale green and unforgiving, the eyes of Judgment Day. "We need Kevin. And, yes, young Mr. Wesley is a writer, and his father does civil rights. There are hundreds of Negro writers, Aurelia, and thousands of preachers for civil rights. There is only one Garland heir."

"Oliver and Derek are Garlands, too. And there's Cerinda and her brood out in the Midwest—"

"There is only one heir," Amaretta repeated. She pointed toward Aurelia's womb. "By the grace of God, you will bear the next."

(I I)

ACTUALLY, MONA HAD CAUGHT an earlier train than the sleeper she originally intended to take. Kevin Garland had expected his wife and her best buddy to spend hours out on the town before departure time. Thus he was unprepared for Aurie's arrival at Edgecombe Avenue shortly after sundown. She decided to be quiet, to give her husband a nice surprise. She did not know what Amaretta had been blabbing about. She did not want to know. She would make love to her husband and, for now, forget everything else. She remembered the night Kevin had snuck up on her in the shower when she thought he was out of town. Now she would pay him back. In the hallway, she glanced around, then undid a couple of buttons on her blouse. She slipped her key in the lock as silently as she knew how. She gave the door a quiet shove. It was jerked away from her, and Aurelia tumbled into the apartment. She would have hit the floor, but a strong hand was already clamped around her wrist. A white hand. Four men sat in the parlor where she did her receiving, two of them black, two of them white, one of them Kevin. All four heads were turned, astonished. She stood before them, humiliated, blouse half undone. The fifth man, beside the door, was still clutching her wrist. His face was pleasant. His hair was ash blond, and smooth. His eyes were as chilly as the grave.

"Let go of my wife," said Kevin, with a force that secretly impressed her.

Her captor looked to one of the seated white men. Wispy hair, paler than his flesh, made hopeless designs here and there on his mottled head. His voice was all quiet authority. "Please do as Mr. Garland says, Mr. Collier."

At once she was released. Kevin advanced toward the door, furious. His eyes bulged. Aurelia had never seen him this way. She shrank away, fumbling with the buttons, but she was not the target of his ire. "Don't you ever lay a hand on my wife again—"

The blond man inclined his head. "Sorry, sir," he murmured, voice steady but amused, as if he wanted the room to know how little the show of anger bothered him.

Kevin tried to put his arm around his wife, but she squirmed away. Everyone looked embarrassed. Kevin did his best. He said, "Of course you know Perry Mount," but Aurelia had already recognized Harlem's golden boy, the most desirable bachelor in Sugar Hill now that Kevin was spoken for. Perry nodded and smiled as though they were old friends, and Aurie nodded back, but secretly he gave her the creeps. A glance passed between Perry Mount and the strange Mr. Collier, a complicity she neither appreciated nor understood. Kevin, meanwhile, continued working hard to smooth things over. "And may I present Senator Elliott Van Epp, and his son-in-law, Congressman Lanning Frost. Senator, Congressman—my wife, Aurelia."

Handshakes. Apologies. Murmurs about how rumors of her beauty failed to do her justice.

"And Mr. Collier is the Senator's bodyguard," said Kevin, still seething.

Aurelia had never heard of a Senator with a bodyguard. She wondered whether a member of the Senate had ever been assassinated, and it occurred to her, disloyally, that Kevin would have no idea, but Eddie would have the answer off pat. "Well, Mr. Collier is good at his job," Aurie said, still rubbing her wrist.

"He won't ever be allowed in this apartment again," her husband promised.

"I don't actually give a shit," she assured him with a chilly smile.

"We should get going," said the Senator, eyes kind. "Thank you for your hospitality, Kevin."

"I don't want to interrupt your meeting," said Aurelia.

"We were just about done."

Lanning Frost shook his head. "I thought we still had left to discuss the way to resolve whatever problems we've decided, or else to establish whether our present difficulties in relation to long-range concerns."

Aurie stared. She had heard that Frost planned to run one day for his father-in-law's Senate seat. His face was strong and attractive, his voice was flowing and mellifluous, but his mind was mutton.

"We're done," the Senator repeated, with more force.

Congressman Frost nodded sheepishly and apologized again. Perry had everybody's coats. Mr. Collier was already in the hall. Aurelia wondered about that look between them. Two minutes later, she was alone with her husband.

"I'm so sorry, honey," Kevin began, arms open with awkward affection. "It's just work. Something for my father. If I'd known you were coming back early, I never would have scheduled a meeting—"

"I want to move."

Kevin seemed not to get it. He tried to help with the buttons. She slapped at his hand. "Move? Move where?"

"Out of Harlem. Forever."

"Honey, what happened? What's wrong?"

"We can keep the apartment. You can use it when you have to be here on business. But I am not raising my children around these people."

Aurelia checked on Zora, then went into the bedroom and locked the door. She began changing her clothes, and was down to her slip when she felt the new baby kick. She looked at herself in the mirror. She folded her hands over her roundness. She had no complaints. Not really. Kevin loved her, and she—well, she appreciated him. Kevin had not lost the capacity to surprise her. The people he met. The people who wanted to meet him. She knew little of her husband's business, and did not really want to know more. What she wanted was his children.

She stopped smiling, and sat down, hard.

She remembered Amaretta's words in the taxi just minutes ago, and, a year and a half ago, Kevin sitting beside this very bed, holding his shoe, and announcing that he needed a boy. An image swam upward in her mind, swift and unbidden. The purpose of tonight's meeting. And she knew, in her bones, that the image was accurate, even if she did not yet understand exactly what it meant.

One heir was being introduced to the other.

Heirs to what? she wondered. But there was nobody she dared ask.

CHAPTER 18

The Twenty

(1)

EDDIE OWNED a car befitting his station, a long red Cadillac De-Ville convertible. He told everyone he needed time on his own, and everyone agreed. Everyone wished him Godspeed. Everyone needed time away from him. His second novel would be published in October, they told each other, and a vacation would do him a world of good. Charlie Bing listed people he should try to see. Gary Fatek offered his friend the use of the Kentucky compound built by the Southern branch of the family, then called back, chastened, to say that the Southern branch had vetoed it. But Eddie had never counted on it. Old Mr. Pond, the barber, who had not been south since the 1930s, warned him not to drive at night down there. Kasten urged him to take copious notes. Only Aurelia guessed that her ex-lover's purpose might not be what it seemed, but she was too busy mothering to tease it out of him, and, besides, she was pretty sure he owed her an apology.

He left Harlem on a Monday, in August of 1958, a bit more than a year after Junie's disappearance, and four months after the birth of Aurelia's second child. He motored south. At this time, it was still difficult for a Negro to count on hotel accommodations. When planning a car trip, especially south of the Mason-Dixon Line, it was best to have friends at the ready. Eddie stopped overnight in Baltimore, where he stayed with a cousin of Charlie's, a member of the city council. The cousin turned out to be a fan. They sat up talking about revolution. In the morning, he was off. He stopped again in Richmond, this time at the home of a prosperous Negro lawyer who tried civil-rights cases on the side. The two men had never met, but the lawyer had written Eddie a complimentary note when the novel came out, Eddie had written back, and so had begun a friendly correspondence. The lawyer possessed contacts in Nashville society. He knew the McKissacks and the Campbells and the other prominent Negro families. He gave Eddie letters of introduction. Eddie continued south. He reached Nashville three days after leaving Manhattan. All the clans gracefully received Eddie into their homes. They wanted to talk about his novel, about the Harlem literary scene. Had he met Arna Bontemps, who hailed from these parts? What about Richard Wright? Perhaps even the greatest of them all, Langston Hughes? Eddie tried to engage in polite banter but was not able to hide his impatience. They directed him to the address Joe Kennedy had supplied.

It was a vacant lot in a Negro neighborhood, house recently destroyed by fire.

Eddie asked around, but in a different tier of black society. In the barroom of a colored hotel, he found a couple of half-drunken witnesses. They were interested in getting drunker. Yes, they said, but a lot of young women had been in and out of the house, along with a lot of young men. They were too far gone to recognize Junie's photograph, and Eddie wondered whether they were only remembering what they thought he wanted them to. They argued vehemently with each other over when the fire had occurred. The next day, Eddie presented himself at the offices of the city's largest newspaper, but was told the archives were for employees only. The public library was closed to readers of his nation. The local Negro weekly had covered the fire, but its bound volumes were haphazardly kept. Finally, he found the story. The house had burned just this past March, around the time of Eddie's argument with Aurelia on Riverside Drive. Nobody had died. Nobody was injured. Early reports blamed "an incendiary device," although the paper misspelled the adjective, switching the "n" and the "d." In the next edition, the fire marshal labeled the blaze accidental. The residents were squatters, the articles sniffed. Nobody owned the house, which had been condemned by the city as a firetrap. At the home of his patient hosts, Eddie sat up half the night, worrying over his notes.

Maybe.

Maybe not.

He realized that there was a question he had neglected to ask. The following night, he tracked down his new friends from the bar. No, they said, they had no idea what had happened to the residents. But there was this rumor, said the livelier and more inventive of the pair, that some of them were white. The other man said this was ridiculous, nobody white would live in the neighborhood. As the two men fought, a woman across the bar caught Eddie's eye, beckoning with her head. Eddie left the pair and sidled into her booth. She was taller than he, and older. Her name was Marva. He bought her another drink, but when he asked her the same questions, it turned out that Marva had invited him over merely in the line of business. He pressed her anyway. The house was only two blocks away. If she plied her trade in this area, she must have seen something. Marva flirted on general principle but found her mark unresponsive. She was ready to leave the table, but Eddie kept at her. At last she admitted to having befriended a couple of the girls from the house. Eddie passed her Junie's picture. Marva studied it for a long time, and he felt a surge of excitement when a spark of recognition leaped in her eyes. But she handed it back with a shrug.

"I really couldn't say."

"It's important."

"I can't help you, baby."

Eddie put into his voice all the sincerity he could. "Please, Marva. I'm her brother."

Marva shook her head. He offered her money. Offended, she handed it back. Eddie knew a brick wall when he saw one. Junie, in her sweetness, had always touched a fierce protectiveness in those around her, but Eddie knew better than to construct a positive from Marva's negative. Maybe the reason she said she did not recognize the photograph was that she did not recognize the photograph. There was a line in *Field's Unified Theory* that seemed to apply. Heading back to the nicer part of the Negro community, the same pair of headlights locked on his tail the whole way, Eddie quoted it to himself: "Neither hope nor love provides evidence of truth."

(11)

EDDIE LEFT in the morning but did not return at once to New York. Instead, he drove east and southeast. He took his time. In a couple of towns he found colored hotels. Another night he slept in his car at a truck stop, but was rousted by the police, whose manner suggested that lingering another hour in town would prove hazardous. He wondered whether they had been ordered to roust him. On the fourth day, he reached Charleston, where the Civil War had begun. In the middle of the twentieth century, Charleston was probably the most segregated city in the United States. From his hosts in Nashville he had the address of a Negro woman who rented out rooms. Through her he found a Negro lawyer. The Negro lawyer introduced him to a reasonably liberal white lawyer, who helped him to find the lawyer he actually needed, a balding man named Witter, who agreed sniffily to pass an envelope, unopened, to his client, who in turn, to Witter's surprise, agreed to the meeting.

"This is against my advice," Witter said.

Eddie said that he understood.

"Don't you say anything to upset Mrs. Castle. She's been through a lot."

Eddie promised to behave.

The meeting was not at the lawyer's office, or at the Castle residence near the harbor, but instead at the blinding-white Methodist church near the town green. Leona Castle seemed to be sending a message, even if it was not clear to Eddie who the recipient might be. They sat in pews near the back of the sanctuary, the widow, several church sisters, the pastor, a deacon, and not one but two lawyers. Eddie wondered whether any black congregants ever sat here. He would have preferred to meet with Mrs. Castle alone, but this was Charleston, not Manhattan, and there was no point in asking.

Eddie had prepared an entire speech. Condolences. Admiration for her husband, especially his activism on behalf of civil rights, a tiny part of his oeuvre, although Eddie planned to overblow it considerably. And, slowly, slowly, rounding toward his true purpose, the pink envelope of which Emil had spoken at Aurelia's wedding: the bargaining chip he needed.

Leona Castle presented him no opportunity. She was a small woman, less pretty than porcelain, her head covered because she was inside the church, the very picture of what Eddie thought of as Southern weakness, except for black eyes of a curious intensity. Eddie sat one pew ahead of her, meaning he was forced to turn around in order to speak. He had barely made it through his condolences when Leona lifted a delicate gloved hand, signaling silence. Then she leaped immediately to where he least wanted her to go.

"You are very kind to come visit me, Mr. Wesley," she said, her accent almost as deep as the lawyer's. "I know how busy your schedule must be. But let's not pretend this is a social call. Your note said you had information about my husband's death. I would like the information, please."

Eddie glanced at the others, six or seven unfriendly Caucasian faces.

"No, Mr. Wesley," said Leona. "We will speak in front of my friends, or we will not speak."

The porcelain face was now hard. He had heard that her family had once been among the largest slaveholders in the state, and here in South Carolina that competition was fierce. He supposed that, for all her whispered liberalism, Leona Castle did not suffer Negro resistance.

As it happened, Eddie had arrived equipped with several other evasions and prevarications. But circumlocution was not natural to him, and, besides, he sensed that the wounded woman sitting behind him would not sit still for a burst of misleading eloquence. If he lied, she would walk out.

"After your husband died," he began, "I met a man named Emil." He told her of the visit to the wedding, the questions about the envelope, the claim that he had taken photographs for a Boy Scout function, the second appearance outside the bookstore. He did not mention Joseph Belt. He said nothing about his sister, or the FBI's interest. Instead, he said that the envelope surely held the key. He planned to ask whether she might have found it among her husband's possessions, but Witter cut in first like a trucker in a hurry.

"Mrs. Castle's property has been subjected to three searches by federal agents," the lawyer said, "and her husband's estate has twice been inventoried by court order. Those inventories do not include a pink envelope, with or without a number penciled in the corner. We have also had several requests by private parties to—"

Leona lifted the glove again, and the lawyer fell silent at once. Eddie recognized that the tiny woman seated before him possessed an influence, if perhaps in a smaller circle, not unlike Erebeth Hilliman's.

"Was there anything else, Mr. Wesley?" she asked.

"No, ma'am."

"So—you do not know who killed my husband."

"Not directly, ma'am. No."

"You are here under false pretenses."

Eddie hesitated. "Ma'am," he began.

The glove came up again. Southerners, Eddie had noticed, tended to settle themselves comfortably before long speeches. Northerners, slouched in whatever position they might find themselves, simply launched in. Now Leona was a moment settling, and Eddie had the wit to wait.

"My husband was a very intelligent man, Mr. Wesley. Very careful. Very prudent. Philmont believed in prudence the way I believe in God and Jesus Christ. Prudence was his lodestar, Mr. Wesley. He did not make many mistakes, and, most certainly, was cautious in selecting those with whom he would do business. He was even more so in selecting friends. He had few. He would never have been involved in any way with a pushy little German like your Emil. I am afraid that your Emil was lying to you. Why he chose to involve my husband

and my family in his lies, I cannot say. That problem is yours to resolve, Mr. Wesley. Not mine." She was on her feet, the entire company with her. "I am so sorry about your sister, Mr. Wesley. I do hope that you find her alive."

Long skirts rustled as she left the sanctuary, accompanied by her church sisters, the deacon, and the younger of the two lawyers. The pastor lingered, along with Witter.

The lawyer said, "It was kind of you not to mention what happened to her husband's colored friend."

Eddie said, "I assume you are referring to Professor Belt."

Witter seemed puzzled. "No, no. I mean Shands. The jazz fellow." When Eddie only stared, the lawyer added, "The one who died in '54 of an overdose. That was difficult for Leona also. Shands and Mr. Castle were very close."

Eddie could not hide his surprise. "Philmont Castle and Ralph Shands were friends?"

Witter was packing his wide leather briefcase, although God alone knew why he had brought it along. "Jazz is not to my taste, Mr. Wesley. But they tell me that Ralph Shands was one of the best jazz pianists ever."

"He was," said Eddie, distantly. Two prominent Negroes, both among the best at what they did, both friends of Philmont Castle, both dead in secret circumstances, nobody else around.

"I am sorry your trip was in vain, Mr. Wesley," said the lawyer. He favored the pastor with a significant look, then departed.

The pastor was a young man, perhaps in his mid-thirties, with thick glasses and a brown cowlick that made him look unserious. He invited Eddie back to the office, where another church sister, eyes downcast, served lemonade, then left them alone. The pastor, whose accent was New England, seemed embarrassed to be waited on. Eddie looked around. Stuffed onto the bookshelf among Bibles and hymnals and volumes of inspirational thought were books by Niebuhr and Barth. Eddie shifted around in his seat. Religionists made him uncomfortable, but liberal religionists were the worst, because they were less interested in saving your soul than in being your friend. Any minute he expected the young pastor to begin talking about civil rights. Instead, the pastor reached into his desk and pulled out a copy of *Field's Unified Theory*.

Eddie was surprised. He said he had understood the book was almost impossible to find in Southern stores.

The pastor nodded. "I picked it up on a trip home. I don't dare keep it on the shelves." He asked Eddie to inscribe it. While Eddie wrote, the pastor explained. Leona had mixed feelings about her husband. Philmont Castle was in most ways a good man, but, according to Leona, had allowed himself to become involved with people less good than he. He wasted much of the money the Lord entrusted to his stewardship. He had been tempted, said the pastor, by the easy answer. The devil's answer. The young man's tone grew more somber. Eddie tried to hand back the book, but the pastor ignored him. "Leona did not know exactly what Phil and his new friends were up to, but she saw that it was work that could not be done in God's good daylight, and that was reason enough to oppose it. Her husband would not be dissuaded. Still, he told her a little. He said there were twenty of them. He called them the Twenty. He spoke of a Project—capital 'P.' He spoke of its importance. Not to him, Mr. Wesley. To the country. To the future of America. Leona could not reach him. I have been pastor here only four years, but this is the congregation where she grew up. Her spiritual home. She came to me for counseling. This was while her husband was still alive. She told me that he was laughing in God's face and inviting the devil into their home."

The pastor's eyes flamed behind the comical lenses, and Eddie knew that, liberal or not, this man was every bit as fervent in his beliefs as Wesley Senior was in his. Searching for a way to slow the tumult, Eddie said, "She was speaking metaphorically, of course."

This the young pastor did not deign to answer. He was toying with one of the drawers. "You are not yet a believer, Eddie. I can tell. Sitting in the church made you uneasy. Sitting here and listening to talk of God and the devil makes you more so. But you do not have to believe in the devil for him to get to you."

Eddie looked at him. "Do you have to believe in God for Him to get to you?"

"When God wants you, you cannot keep Him at bay."

"And what does God want of me right now? That I go back to New York and forget about what happened?" A thought occurred to him. "And why did Mrs. Castle mention my sister? How did she know anything happened to Junie?"

The pastor opened the drawer and pulled out an envelope.

A pink envelope.

While Eddie stared, the pastor talked. "This has been in my possession for three years, Mr. Wesley. Leona found it before she left New York. She entrusted it to me to keep it away from prying eyes." He smiled. "There has been a lot of prying, Eddie. Not just what Dave Witter mentioned. Three break-ins at her home. And a couple of visitors, like you, asking questions. All of this in addition to the FBI, of course."

Eddie was staring at the envelope. "She lied to the FBI?"

The pastor shook his head—not in rejection but in refusal. Whether Leona had lied was no business of Eddie's.

Eddie acknowledged the point. "So, why me? If Mrs. Castle would not turn over this envelope to the federal government or any of the other visitors, and if she knew enough not to keep it at home, where it might be stolen, why give it to me?"

"To tell you the truth, Mr. Wesley, I am not entirely sure. All I can tell you is that when she received your note, Mrs. Castle wanted to make sure that you are the same Edward Wesley who lives in Harlem and writes novels."

Bewildered, Eddie accepted the envelope from the pastor's outstretched hand. "Do you know what's in here?"

The pastor shook his head. "I haven't opened it. I cannot say whether Leona has."

Back at the rooming house, Eddie set the envelope on the dresser and tried to decide whether to open it. He already knew what he would find, and the knowledge depressed him. Photographs, just as Goldfus/Abel had said. They would be gobbledygook that would translate to equations and technical diagrams he could not have fathomed on his best day. The pink envelope was numbered seventeen, and Eddie was willing to bet that there were sixteen before it. Sixteen what? Well, interpreting the diagrams might require a genius, but a baby could work out the logistics. Joseph Belt, enticed by Phil Castle, stole the information from the Los Alamos National Laboratory. He slipped it to Castle, who somehow transferred it in bits and pieces to Emil Goldfus.

What kind of information? From what Eddie had ascertained, the scientists at Los Alamos had one major purpose.

Building hydrogen bombs.

Eddie stood up and strode around the threadbare carpet. He imagined Junie marching beside him, whispering, laughing, counseling. He explained the problem. The contents of the envelope would prove that J. Edgar Hoover had been right that eerie night in Washington, and that Bernard Stilwell had been right that foggy afternoon in Harlem: that Joseph Belt, rigid, disdainful Joseph Belt, the only Negro physicist in Los Alamos, had been a traitor.

"I don't want to know," he said.

Junie said that was too bad. He had no choice.

"That's easy for you to say. You're not really here."

Junie said what she always said, that he was a little brat.

Eddie stopped pacing. His face was warm. He might have burned the envelope, contents unread, but for the memory of Stilwell, asking what he could offer in return for the Bureau's interest in Junie's disappearance. He needed a chip to stay in the game, and Philmont Castle's legacy was the only chip he had left.

So he opened the envelope and drew out the contents and knew at once that everybody had been had—the Bureau, Colonel Abel, everybody.

The contents had nothing to do with nuclear weapons.

First Eddie withdrew a note card and, pinned to it, what appeared to be a seed pod, the kind of cockle that used to prickle his legs when, as a child, he would wander the high grass along the dunes of Martha's Vineyard. On the card were four words, in block capitals:

HIS WIFE HAS IT

Eddie put the pod aside. His wife. Whose wife? Castle's? But he held in his hands what her husband had left. And the rest of what? Meaning eluded him, no matter how he tried to conjure it.

Eddie pulled out a second card, similar to the first, with more words in block capitals, written in a slightly different hand:

NOT AS IN A TRAGIC AGE

Curiouser and curiouser. The cards surely constituted a message, but Eddie doubted that he was the intended recipient. Were they to be read together? If so, in what order? Were the references to the Bible, perhaps? To a play he should recognize? He studied the cards as if hoping to unlock the secrets of the universe.

But in another sense, sitting in the colored rooming house in Charleston, fiddling with the seed pod as dusk drew in the day, Eddie Wesley was only teasing himself. The treasure trove was the cache of letters snuggling just beneath, all but one undated. He picked up the first:

> *Dear P:*
> *You were right. I had a wonderful time. I knew it was important, but I had no idea it would be so much fun. Thank you so much for inviting me. I hope you-know-who doesn't find out.*

A second:

> *Dear P:*
> *Maybe what you say is true. Maybe there is a way to do it without getting caught. But do you know what I have realized? Not all of us are meant to be happy. Sometimes we are drawn into things we never expected, and we enter them with joy, but continue them out of ennui. Do not misunderstand. I am not ready to quit. Not even close. But I get the feeling that you are.*

A third:

Dear P:

Of course I understand your position. You have a wife and a family. But it seems to me that what you are proposing requires a commitment. I see no reason that I should be the one who stays true while you flit back and forth between one commitment and the other. You have to choose, P. Or else the choice might be made for you.

And the last, the only one with a date—late January of 1955, three weeks before Philmont Castle was killed:

Dear P:

You have made your decision. Now I must make mine. You say that you are acting out of love. So am I. The difference is that you are willing to long and lament. I am not. I have always been a woman of action. Probably you will not see me again. Never make the mistake of believing that giving a gift entitles you to anything.

An affair, Eddie realized dully, flipping back to the start. Nothing more. Whatever the meaning of the cards or the seed pod, this much was clear: the late Philmont Castle had been having an extramarital affair, and Leona wanted Eddie to have the proof. Eddie and only Eddie. He supposed he should examine the letters again, in case he had missed anything, but could not bear the pain. He considered burning them in the grate. Instead, he refolded them, returned them to their envelope, and consigned the envelope to his briefcase. He left the next morning for the long drive north, having slept poorly, peering into the gray darkness, conjuring possibilities, explanations, theories—wondering about the lies. He could never share the envelope with Stilwell. He possessed no bargaining chip after all.

The letters were from Junie.

PART II

New York/Washington
1958–1959

CHAPTER 19

On the Difficulty of Progress
Without Aurelia

(1)

AND SO THE TWO MYSTERIES, the murder of Phil Castle and the disappearance of June Cranch Wesley, were linked. Driving north, Eddie admitted to himself that he had been wrong. If his vanished sister and the late investor had been having an affair, he might indeed need to know what had happened to the one in order to figure out what had happened to the other. The lawyer had been involved with nineteen other men—the Twenty—in something called the Project. If he found the Project, perhaps he would find his sister. Upon his return to Harlem, he would apologize to Aurelia, and ask what she had learned about the Cross of Saint Peter, and why Kevin Garland possessed one.

Except that Aurelia refused to see him.

There was, Eddie supposed, nothing surprising in this. She was twice a mother, and married—to a Garland, no less—and dallying with a former lover could only risk upsetting the life she had been raised to lead. Besides, the last time they had been together, when Aurie, at what cost he could only guess, had walked with him in the clear light of day, he had been rude to her. No. No. He refused to fool himself. He had been not rude, but mean. He had hurt the woman he loved, and now had to woo her afresh, but lacked the means to do so. He could not send flowers or even flowery notes to the Garland apartment at 409 Edgecombe Avenue, and Aurie was currently on leave from the *Sentinel*, ruling out the possibility of his hanging around the entrance and hoping for his chance, a course that would in any case very likely force to public attention that which she needed most to hide.

Very well. He would bide his time.

He returned to the salons, and everybody remarked on the changes. The wit was back, the flattery, the charm, the fire, the almost ferocious willingness to suffer disagreement, to argue into the night over marvelously abstruse questions—all the qualities that made him a sought-after guest. In the fall of 1958, his second novel was published, *Blandishment*, the story of a black youth who is radicalized as he works his way through a New England college as a waiter, the semi-autobiographical coming-of-age novel that editors used to say everybody published second, after working out, in the first novel, fantasies of lives unlived. The critics liked it less than *Field's Unified Theory*, but the public liked it more, perhaps because the reader was not required to wade through all that physics, or, for that matter, to admit that a book by a Negro author might challenge not just the conscience but the intellect. Eddie accepted the accolades and the sudden fortune with a quietly impressive grace. As one of his biographers would later note, it was as though he was trying, through force of will, to be the man Harlem expected him to be. He wrote speeches for politicians, chief among them Senator John Kennedy of Massachusetts: a favor for the Ambassador. It never occurred to the Czarinas that the Kennedy people had come to Eddie. They were unaware that Eddie owed the Ambassador any favors. They assumed that Wesley Senior, known to be close to the Kennedys, had finagled his son the job. Nevertheless, the connection opened the doors of still more salons. At Harlem parties, asked about Kennedy's chances to win the presidency the year after next, Eddie frowned importantly. And he attended parties aplenty, downtown as well as in Harlem. He spoke on college campuses. He even dated, for a little while, the suitable daughter of one of the senior clans, a blushing, virginal creature called Cynda, who even after their breakup extolled, starry-eyed, his gentleness. He used to recite medieval love poems for her, said Cynda, not mentioning whether the recitations occurred in bed. And yet she sensed in him, Cynda told her girlfriends, a secret and quite different self beneath the happy surface.

An angry self? they asked. A jealous self? For they had heard all the rumors. Not angry, said Cynda, marveling. Determined. Devoted.

But devoted to *what?* the girlfriends asked, unable to restrain themselves. Devoted to *whom?* To *Aurelia?*

To a larger cause, sniffed Cynda, very satisfied. To love. To his sister.

But his sister's *dead*, cried the girlfriends, thrilling to the notion of a morbid obsession at the famous writer's secret center. (After all, it was not as if he had dated one of *them*.)

He doesn't believe it, Cynda answered. He thinks she's alive. He has all these notebooks and files and thingies. He sits up half the night going through them. He's always calling people on the phone about her and writing on his yellow pads.

And how do *you* know what he does half the night? the girlfriends demanded. Shame on you! they giggled, swooning.

He's a good man, was all Cynda would say, smiling complacently. I wish I had a brother like him. She did not mention how he would spend hours at his desk, neither working nor relaxing, but frowning at a tiny seed pod in the middle of his blotter.

(11)

As FOR EDDIE, he found himself suddenly short of confidants. Aurelia was inaccessible. Gary was busy balancing protest marches, visits to Erebeth at Quonset Point to be trained for his new role in life, and visits to Mona in Chicago to keep in touch with his old one. Craving forward motion, Eddie dropped in on the Columbia philologist he had met at the party two years ago on Central Park South. The philologist introduced him to a biologist, who in turn referred him to a specialist in deciduous trees, who examined Castle's prickly seed pod and told Eddie at a glance that it had fallen from a London plane tree, a variety, unfortunately, as common as cheese in the New York area, and, indeed, all across North America. It was an unusually sturdy tree, she explained, able to resist many forms of blight, a feature that helped explain its popularity. Eddie decided that it was the fact of the seed pod, not its species, that carried whatever message the lawyer had been trying to convey. At such a moment he craved Aurelia, not only because she lifted his spirit but because she served as so excellent a foil for his ideas, and was always buzzing with ideas of her own. And because she worked crossword puzzles. It was at this time that Cynda observed him sitting up in his apartment, twisting the pod this way and that, hoping to work out its meaning.

If you need to find her, then find her.

Eddie had another thought. Hoover had shown him a photograph of Langston Hughes. Just routine harassment, or did the Bureau know something? Eddie dropped in on the great man at his townhouse on 127th Street. Hughes, as it happened, was rather busy, trying to persuade the National Institute of Arts and Letters to deny William Faulkner its Gold Medal for Literature. Over drinks, Hughes gave Eddie an earful about the man he called "the leading Southern cracker novelist." When Eddie had the chance to get a word in edgewise, he explained, shading his sources a bit, that he now believed his sister's disappearance might be related to the murder of Phil Castle.

Hughes was amused. "Do you think Junie killed him?"

No, no, said Eddie, coloring, that was not the point at all. He thought there might have been a connection between the two while the lawyer was still alive.

"You're saying they had a fling?"

"I'm saying they had a connection."

Hughes thought this over. They were sitting in his upstairs office. The place was a mess: file cabinets and bookshelves heaped with manuscript pages. Hughes always seemed to have about twelve projects going. He was a round, solid, encouraging man, who had helped an entire generation of Negro writers get their start before anybody had heard of Eddie Wesley. He drank, he smoked, he told stories, he was widely loved, and the writing was all he had. No one ever discovered what social life, if any, Hughes enjoyed. Perhaps the books and stories and plays were his true love. His books and his plays—and Harlem. Langston Hughes, who could have lived wherever he liked, had actually moved from Sugar Hill to the Valley. The Czarinas had never heard of such a thing.

"I knew Phil Castle a bit," Hughes said finally. "Have I mentioned that? Just the last six months of his life. We met at Matty Garland's place up in Westchester. This would have been the summer of 1954, because *Brown* had just been decided. He turned out to be a huge fan of serious literature. We got to talking about this and that, and, well, he asked if we could get together sometime. He said he had an idea I might be able to help with." The writer smiled. "Usually that means somebody wants a political endorsement. I don't do many of those, as you know. I started to hem and haw, and Castle seemed to read my mind. He did not want anything public from me. He wanted my advice. That was all. I admit I was intrigued, this big white Wall Streeter asking my advice. We had lunch a few weeks later. And another lunch a couple of weeks after that, and—well, let me make a long story short. Castle was involved in something he had started to think might be dangerous. He wanted my advice on how to get out of it."

Eddie wondered if he meant the affair.

Hughes poured freshly for them both. "Even now, I'm not exactly sure what Castle was talking about. He said he was part of a group of men who were in the process of doing what they thought was great work, but which he had decided was bound to end in disaster. He called what they were doing the Project, but refused to provide any details. I asked why he came to me. He said because I knew all the Negro leaders. He said that this group came largely out of our community—your darker nation—and he thought it was up to us to stop the Project. I suppose I gave him a hard time over how conveniently he managed to exclude his own responsibility. Probably I didn't believe him anyway. I thought he must be exaggerating some perfectly reasonable scheme."

Hughes was fiddling with his glasses. He had a wide face, set low on his broad body. Eddie waited silently, remembering the garrote.

"I told Castle to go to the authorities," Hughes resumed. "That was how one prevented disaster. He said he could not. The defeat of the Project had to be handled quietly, or the disaster he worried about would come to pass. Disaster for our people, he said. I must admit, by this time I had begun to wonder whether he was entirely sane. But there was a seriousness about him, and—well, let's just say, if he was indeed delusional, he believed his delusion fully. I decided to test him. I told him that I was a writer, not an activist. I gave him names of people to see. He refused. He said he did not want to take any more risks. That was what he said, Eddie. Take any more risks. He wanted me to serve as intermediary. I pointed out that, unless he told me more, I had nothing with which to intermediate. Since he was uncomfortable talking about whatever was on his mind, I proposed a writer's solution. I suggested that he put it all down on paper, and then we would look at it together, and decide what to do next. That way, I could see just how crazy he was. Let's fill you up."

Eddie held out his glass, marveling. Hughes poured, and lit a fresh cigar.

"Did he put it down on paper?"

"I don't know what he did, Eddie. Somebody strangled him before our next meeting."

Eddie needed a moment to collect his thoughts. Again he sensed a malign intelligence behind all that had occurred. He remembered his father's note about devil worship, and shuddered. "Did you tell this to—to the authorities?"

"Of course. I called the police the same day I heard the news."

"And?"

"And they did what they always do. They wrote it down in their notebooks, and that was the last I saw of them."

Riding home on the A, Eddie saw his sister's letters to the lawyer in a fresh light. Maybe she was writing about an affair, yes. But maybe she was writing about whatever Castle had wanted Hughes to share with the Negro leadership.

The conspiracy that portended disaster for the darker nation.

Maybe Junie had been a part of it.

Back in his apartment, Eddie looked over his notes. He kept coming back to the same two points: the information from Joseph Kennedy, and the report in the Negro newspaper in Nashville.

Somebody had paid a "substantial fee" to move Junie—if it was Junie—to Nashville. And an "incendiary device" had destroyed the house where Junie—if it was Junie—had lived while she was there.

This did not sound like a couple of young women off on a lark. This sounded like somebody who had access to both money and bombs.

Disaster, the lawyer had warned Langston Hughes.

An idea was forming in Eddie's head, an idea with its roots in Eddie's own experiences when Junie was still a cheap train ride or an expensive phone call away: an idea he wanted to reject but suspected, more and more, might be the truth. Two days later, Eddie drove over to New Jersey, to look for the umpteenth time at the rest stop where Junie and her friend had vanished. He parked where the car had been found. The trees were brown and leafless. In the winter, the nearly empty lot seemed bleak and sorrowful, but it felt that way in every season, and not even the bright-orange snappiness of the Howard Johnson's restaurant could—

Wait.

The rest stop was along the New Jersey Turnpike, and the Turnpike ran from north to south. At this time in America's history, the network of interstate highways was far from complete, but the Turnpike was nevertheless a peculiar way to get to Chicago. This variation from more obvious westward routes had been discussed to death, both by the police and in the family, and the consensus was that the two women had come this way because the Turnpike was finished, and decent food was cheerily available from an integrated restaurant.

But that would not be Junie. Junie would have driven to Chicago in a simple straight line, and Heaven help the owner of any roadside grill who tried to keep her out.

The girls were headed south from the start. Maybe they had chosen this spot to meet up with the friends of Joseph Kennedy's friends, who had transported them the rest of the way, or maybe that was some other girl, and there had indeed been foul play. But even if Junie and her girlfriend had been snatched against their will, they were not headed for Chicago.

They were headed someplace else.

They. Not *she. They.*

Maybe the key was that Junie had not vanished alone.

Eddie realized at last that half-measures would not do. Sneaking up on problems had never been his best thing, any more than it had been his baby sister's. The only way he would find Junie was to look for Junie, and if that meant everybody would know, then everybody would just have to know.

He even knew where to go next.

CHAPTER 20

A Companionable Journey

(1)

KEVIN GARLAND WAS DOING EVERYTHING in his power to keep his wife happy. Yes, they could move to the suburbs. Yes, he would spend more time at home, not only with her but with the children. Yes, it was fine if Aurelia wanted to go to Chicago for a week to visit Mona. Yes, yes, yes, to everything. Aurie was surprised by his fervor, and grateful for it. But she was also perplexed. One night, as they drove back to the city from an excruciating dinner at Matty's house, she asked him, in as casual a voice as she could manage, what people meant when they mentioned the Garland heir.

"I don't understand," said Kevin, eyes on the road.

Aurie had her shoes off. She loosened her girdle, put her head back, and shut her eyes. "Our son. Somebody told me he's the Garland heir."

"Locke?" The bewilderment in his voice seemed genuine. "I guess he's one of the heirs, anyway. I inherit my father's estate. Naturally, I would divide it between the children. And you, of course."

"Of course," said Aurelia, very puzzled.

"Unless you mean—" he began, and stopped.

"Unless I mean what?" She was now awake, and alert. She could read her husband's nervousness in the dipping of his head and the way he licked his lips. She sensed that this was the moment to press. The only moment. "Come on, honey. Unless I mean what? Tell me what you're thinking."

"That night in our bedroom," he said. They rounded a curve. The lights of Manhattan loomed suddenly from the darkness. "What

I said to you, how I said it—I wasn't myself, Aurie. Please believe me."

She touched his cheek. "I believe you, honey."

"I shouldn't have said it. I'm sorry. I love both of our children the same. I really do."

"I believe you," she said again.

"It's just—in the family—there are certain traditions. You know. Passed on from father to son. My dad thinks things like that are important, and, well, we're not a family that takes well to change."

"What traditions?"

"Like running the family business. Garland & Son."

"You don't think Zora could do that?"

"It's not the tradition," he said, stubbornly, but she sensed that they had somehow veered into a different argument, and that Kevin was relieved to have distracted her.

(11)

THE FOLLOWING WEEK, Kevin had to go down to Washington for a couple of days to see some people, as he always put it. This was their new arrangement, that he would tell his wife exactly where he was going, and when he would return. Usually he asked if she wanted to go along. This time she said yes. She drove the children up to Dobbs Ferry to stay with their grandparents. Wanda, as chilly as ever toward her daughter-in-law, was delighted to have Zora and Locke.

Kevin and Aurelia took the train. They stayed at the home of a relative on Sixteenth Street, an enclave of prosperous Negroes known as the Gold Coast. Kevin had meetings the first day. Aurelia shopped with Janine, her sorority sister. That night Kevin and Aurie dined with their hosts. The second day was much the same, and the second night they had dinner at the Wisconsin Avenue apartment of Congressman Lanning Frost and his wife, Margot. A couple of years ago, there had been this rumor about Eddie and Margot. Aurelia wondered whether it was true. Margot and Kevin talked about these new radicals, Agony, or Jewel Agony. Harlem was abuzz because the group had managed to set off a bomb at a Klan rally in Alabama. Nobody had been hurt, but Negroes across the country cheered. A letter from Agony's head, somebody called Commander M, promised to target only "the most violent satraps of white reaction." A couple of newspapers had published it, but not in the South. Kevin was telling Margot that this sort of thing would do more harm than good in the long run. Margot, for whom most questions were reducible to matters of who gained political advantage, said that her husband had gone to the well of the House to condemn the bombing while other liberals were dithering over whether they should seem to be protecting the Klan.

"Violence is violence," she said.

Meanwhile, the Congressman entertained Aurelia. "The thing about the missile gap," he said, "is that, whatever might be the precise amount, our preparedness has yet to be specific to our needs." But she was getting the hang of him. Still listening with half an ear to the other conversation, she said something about civil defense and air-raid shelters, and Frost nodded enthusiastically. "Because otherwise," he explained, "everyone in America is worse off in the rest of the world."

The doorbell announced the arrival of the remaining guests. Senator Van Epp apologized for his tardiness. His wife was olive-complected, perhaps Mediterranean. The Senator made a great fuss over Aurie, and, during dinner, kept the table laughing with his stories. Margot announced dessert. Then it was time for business. Kevin and the Senator withdrew with Lanning Frost to another room. After a moment, Margot apologetically joined them.

Aurie was left alone with the Senator's wife. Mrs. Van Epp sat very straight. Her voice came out of the side of her mouth in a lipless murmur. Aurie sensed the older woman's disapproval, and wondered why. Perhaps it was true what Kevin had once told her: that the white matrons of Washington were far worse than the black matrons of Harlem. As soon as she decently could, Aurelia took herself off to the powder room adjoining the foyer. When she emerged, the Senator's blond bodyguard was standing nearby, toying with a cigarette lighter.

"Good evening, Mrs. Garland."

She refused to be cowed twice. "Will you be grabbing my arm this evening, Mr. Collier?"

"Please accept my apologies." Again he seemed amused, and even managed what must have been intended as humor. "You might have been an assassin."

"With my own key to the apartment?"

"I'm afraid my function requires me to allow for that possibility, Mrs. Garland. Yes."

His evident friendliness intrigued her. "May I ask you a question, Mr. Collier?"

"Please."

"Why does a United States Senator need a bodyguard?"

He tilted his head as if to acknowledge a good point. "Mine not to question why, Mrs. Garland."

"Meaning, you'll do what you're hired to do? No matter what? Because, I have to tell you, Mr. Collier, that idea scares the hell out of me."

The blond man gave this objection serious consideration. "If there are limits to my function," he finally said, "they are not found in the task. They are found in the men assigning the task."

"What you're saying is—"

"I am a bodyguard, Mrs. Garland. I will do what is necessary to protect my clients and their interests." The blue eyes were fierce diamonds now. "But there certainly exist people, Mrs. Garland, who are not worth protecting."

He slipped away. The Senator's wife came up behind her. "I understand you have young children, dear. You simply must tell me all about them." But she had to say it twice before Aurelia heard.

CHAPTER 21

The Other Woman

(1)

PATRICK AND IRENE MARTINDALE LIVED in a peeling wooden house on a forested lot in the farming community of Darien, Connecticut. Remnants of late-winter snow clung to the trees. Climbing the gravel drive, he saw gray flash against brown and green as small animals, and sometimes large ones, darted across the road. He was surprised that the Martindales had agreed to see him so readily, and not only because they might not want to revisit the pain of loss. As Junie's brother, Eddie was, obviously, a Negro, and it had not been his experience that the sort of Caucasians who lived in Connecticut mansions inclined warmly toward his people.

Not that Patrick and Reenie were rich—this they made clear from the moment they wafted him into their dark, paneled home, pressing upon him a cigar and various liqueurs, as if meeting at a Manhattan men's club—no, no, there had been a bit of money in the family, but old Uncle Deaver had wasted the fortune, except for the land, they explained gleefully, smiling at each other in approval of their own fiscal modesty. They were an oddly matched pair, he small and happily disapproving, she taller and fuller of figure and in some murky way joyfully unsatisfied. But they took pains to assure Eddie that they were on his side, without ever asking what side he might be on. He was black, and so they knew. They spoke of the South with a fury proposing that slavery had ended just yesterday; and of Emmett Till with a fervor that suggested they had witnessed his mutilation. They could scarcely conceal their delight at hosting a Negro in their home, and Eddie suspected that within half a day all of their neighbors would know, because the Martindales were the sort of couple who would make sure of it.

"Our Sharon hated racism, old man," Patrick explained, who had a way of speaking to a spot several feet over your head. For Saturday in the country, he wore a heavy sweater and workingman's pants splattered with paint, but his untutored hands were soft and pale. During the week, he did something clever on Wall Street, but only part-time. "She hated racism," he repeated. "Battled it everywhere. That's why she and Junie were such good friends."

Reenie picked up the theme. "Our *Sharon* hated racism, and your *Junie* hated racism"—the cadence made the words a nursery rhyme—"and they planned to *fight* oppression *everywhere*."

"With the tools of law," said Patrick. "They only ever intended to sue people."

"Or whatever *else* they had to *do* to win the *fight*," said Reenie, with her oddly spaced emphases. A floral dress hung tentatively from her body like an unfinished display. It was only midafternoon, but Eddie had a shrewd notion that the Martindales had been drinking for a long while before he arrived; and he doubted that their shared inebriation was something special they were putting on for him. Maybe it had started when they lost Sharon.

Patrick corrected his wife with a fond smile. "But only within the law," he murmured.

"Of *course*, dear," said Reenie, looking away.

They sat in Uncle Deaver's gun room, surrounded by glass cases and open cabinets chockablock with weaponry. Eddie had the threadbare sofa, Sharon's parents an adjacent pair of sagging easy chairs with a low blond wood table between. Behind Patrick's head hung a Japanese sword, a souvenir from the war. Behind Reenie was a framed flintlock pistol, together with a little brass plate attesting its provenance. As the conversation danced across every topic except the one Eddie wanted to raise, it dawned on him that his hosts had chosen the venue for a reason.

"I don't know *why* you people put *up* with it," said Reenie, as her fervent husband, now bounding around the room, drew the conversation once more to civil rights.

"Talk about the case for armed revolution," said Patrick. "If I were colored, I'd carry a gun everywhere. I'd shoot the white man for sport."

"And the white *woman*," added Reenie, as if afraid of being left out.

Her husband shot her an affectionate look. She beamed back at him. They linked hands for a moment as he passed behind her. Eddie was looking at the gun cabinet, wondering what his hosts would do if he asked for a loaner, maybe to go out and shoot the white man with. He was starting to suspect that a teeming rage lay beneath the couple's surface amity.

"You need to top that up, old man," said Patrick, pointing to Eddie's nearly untouched snifter.

Eddie dutifully held out the glass. "I'd like to hear about Junie, if I could."

"Junie was such a sweetheart," said Patrick, eyeing his wife, but this time she dropped her eyes. "We adored her."

"*Adored* her," confirmed Reenie, studying the rug.

"Sharon adored her, too." Loping around the room again. "Always said she was the smartest Negro she'd ever met."

"Negress," said Reenie.

"Colored girl," suggested her husband, as a compromise.

"They need a new *word*," said Reenie.

Patrick pointed at Eddie. "You need a new word," he proclaimed.

"They adored each *other*," Reenie explained, hugging herself with thin arms. "They were *wonderful* friends. They *planned* to be together *forever*. They'd been reading *Foucault* about the *body*—"

"Mr. Wesley won't have heard of Foucault," cautioned Patrick, not quite sotto voce.

"One of the *wives* was *talking* about him the other night at the *club*," Reenie persisted. "*Not* about *you*, Mr. Wesley." A shy smile. "About *Foucault*. How he's a *Platonist*. Or *not* a Platonist. *One* of them." A brief furrowing of the brow before Reenie decided that she was above worrying about right answers. "Foucault says the *body* is a *battleground*. It *changes*. It's a *concept*, not a *thing*."

This was how they lived together, Eddie realized. Mumbling importantly about people they barely knew and philosophies they would never attempt, then heading down to the club for a bite. What kind of daughter might they have produced? And how on earth had Sharon and Junie become best friends?

Eddie said, "When the girls disappeared—"

"Ran *away*," said Reenie, promptly.

"Or were kidnapped," added her husband with a frown.

Everybody waited. Eddie tried again. "After the car was found—"

But Patrick and Reenie were the sort who showed how much they liked you by carrying on their own conversation in your hearing. "Never really thought it made sense, old man," said Patrick. "The car locked up like that. Not what a murderer would do, is it? Wondered whether it might have been locked up after the crime, actually."

"By the *kidnappers*," Reenie breathed. "If there *were* kidnappers."

"To make it look like they ran away," said her husband.

"Or else they really *did*," said his wife.

Eddie felt as if he had forgotten to switch on his brain this morning. "What I really wondered was whether you had a theory about— well, say they did run away. Say the disappearance was voluntary, and not a kidnapping." A glance at Patrick, already primed to object. "This is just a theory. But suppose they did. If Sharon decided to run away, I was wondering where she might go. Whom she might contact. Whether there are people to whom she would turn for help."

"She would do *anything* for the *revolution*," Reenie assured him, and poured herself a fresh tot.

"She would never run away and not tell us," said Patrick, flatly. "We told the police, for all that they cared. She had no secrets, old man. Not from us. We're not just her parents. We're her friends." Waving importantly at his glass, a signal to his wife to fill it. "It was a crime, pure and simple. It was a crime, and they refuse to catch the criminals, because of Junie."

"And *Sharon*," added Reenie. Eddie waited for more, but evidently there was none.

"Still," Eddie persisted, "if she did decide, hypothetically, to, say, help the revolution"—this for Reenie—"by going underground, for instance. I'm wondering where she would have gone."

"You'd *have* to ask *Ferdinand*," said Reenie.

"It would never happen," said Patrick. "And Ferdinand was over long ago."

Eddie had the wit not to interpose a question.

"Her *boyfriend*," said Reenie.

"He was never her boyfriend," said Patrick, his old-boy calm now a fierce restraint. "Colored boy."

"He was a *Marxist*."

"They barely knew each other."

"He's at *Columbia* now."

Patrick rounded on her, the revolution temporarily on hold. "They had nothing to do with each other! They never did! The fool boy was just one of her phases!" Back to Eddie. "We don't know if the boy is at Columbia or anyplace else. We don't know anything about him." He seemed to be waiting for Eddie to write this down. Perhaps they thought he was official: one of Hoover's, say. "Ferdinand had dangerous ideas. Sharon wasn't the kind of girl to be attracted to his kind of ideas."

Eddie asked, "What was Ferdinand's last name?"

"It doesn't matter," said Patrick, jumping in before his wife could speak. "He was just a friend. Not even a friend. She barely knew him."

"She *adored*—" Reenie began, but a look from her husband silenced her.

"If Sharon needed help," Patrick declared, "she'd have come to us." He scowled at the flintlock. "Us. Her parents. Not some boy she barely knew who wanted to burn everything down."

Eddie said, "I thought you were in favor of the revolution."

Patrick seemed ready to tear his thin hair. "That boy didn't care about the revolution. He wasn't a Marxist. He wasn't anything. He just hated."

"Hated who? Hated what?"

"The world. The people in it."

"Poor boy," said Reenie, sipping. "Patrick couldn't *stand* him."

"I barely knew him, woman! It was Sharon who couldn't stand him!"

But Reenie, finger wagging, had the final word: "It's *not* that Ferdinand wasn't for the *revolution*. He just wasn't very *practical* about it. He tried to burn down our *house*—"

"Don't you dare repeat that!" Patrick snapped, but it was unclear which of them he was addressing.

"This was after Sharon *dumped* him." Reenie's glittering green eyes were focused into the past. "I *suppose* he thought *we* put her *up* to it, poor boy. Still, burning the *house* wasn't a very *nice* way to show he loved her, now, *was* it?"

"Did you report the fire to the police?" asked Eddie.

"He was drunk," said Patrick, rolling his eyes. "He made a mistake. We all make mistakes. Me. You." He glanced again at Reenie as if expecting her to argue the point. "Things happen. It had nothing to do with Sharon. She couldn't have dumped him, because they never dated. And besides"—it occurred to Eddie that Patrick was offering far too many excuses—"he didn't really do much damage. You would hardly call it a fire. Forget about it." He straightened, smiled, recovered his poise. "Thanks so much for dropping in, Mr. Wesley. Oh, but drive carefully, old man. The police out here are fine people, but some of them have as much racial sensitivity as the worst Southern—"

"Sharon was *in* the house when he burned it," Reenie interrupted. "Poor boy," she said again. "He *used* to say the only thing to *do* was blow everything *up* and start *over*."

(11)

MAYBE, Eddie told himself, driving back toward civilization, and sanity, all the while watching for stray cops as Patrick had advised. Maybe not. Maybe Sharon and Junie had been kidnapped after all. Maybe they had been murdered. Maybe they had run off together to explore the radical alternative. Maybe the Martindales were bonkers. Eddie supposed that losing your only child could do that.

Still, he now had a piece of a name and a possible affiliation: Ferdinand, a Negro, who used to be at Harvard, or at least in or around Boston, and had moved on to Columbia.

He even had a candidate. Every road led in the same direction.

CHAPTER 22

A Royal Audience

(1)

THE GOLDEN BOY of Harlem was Perry Mount. He was a year younger than Eddie, and of royal lineage, as such things were measured, on both sides. His late father, Burton, had been a surgeon who lectured at Columbia Medical School and, on the side, guessed correctly which blocks of Harlem were moving in which economic direction, and invested accordingly. His late mother, Trina, had in her day run half the civic groups in Harlem and, in her spare time, become the first Negro woman to serve on the New York City Council. Eddie had known Perry since the old days, when the families had summered together on Martha's Vineyard, and the children had sat together in the backyard, reading *Hamlet* and *A Midsummer Night's Dream* aloud because Wesley Senior trusted only the King James Bible and William Shakespeare, and despised most things written since. Perry had been a chubby boy, with thick glasses and fingers all smeary from the Baby Ruth bars that seemed to serve as breakfast, lunch, and dinner, but he could fix the gears on your bicycle and put your electric trains back together. He had not been widely liked because he had not been widely likable. They had to let him play with them because the families were friends. Otherwise they would have stayed clear, for the Perry of those days was a brooding, suspicious child, swift to find insult in your tone of voice, ever ready to drop his candy bar and fight.

But that Perry was gone. The new Perry, a Harvard degree in hand, was tall and lean, with gray eyes and a pencil mustache. Perry sported gaudy bow ties and vested suits, entirely aware of his role as

Sugar Hill's most eligible bachelor, and playing it to the hilt. Perry was at Columbia, doing additional graduate work in languages, but the work must not have been terribly challenging, because Eddie ran into him frequently at the salons, always with a different woman on his arm. It was Perry who had tried and failed to calm Eddie down the night of Aurelia's engagement party; and Perry, too, who had danced with Junie at Aurelia's wedding, and, evidently, kept in touch thereafter.

Eddie got along with Perry Mount. Eddie admired him and, occasionally, envied him. But Eddie never really liked him, perhaps because he sensed behind the clever eyes and charming words a constant calculation, as if he expected you every moment to prove afresh your worth to him. He sensed it now, as Perry sat listening, the two men in a deli on Broadway near the Columbia campus. It had taken him a month to arrange the meeting. It was March of 1959, his sister had been missing for almost two years, and Eddie had the sense that time was running out.

You knew her well, Eddie was saying, his tone polite.

You stayed in touch with her all the time she was at Harvard Law—maybe wooing her, maybe more.

You knew Philmont Castle, and talked to her about him.

You must ache almost as much as the family does.

What was my sister up to? Eddie was really screaming, only in a placid tone. *And where is she now?*

When Eddie was done, Perry stirred his tea. He asked for tea all the time in the salons, perhaps wanting you to know he had spent an undergraduate year and two years since in Asia. When he received his master's degree this spring, he would be going to work at the State Department. Harlem—their Harlem—was proud of Perry, but of course wanted him to marry first. Perry sat thinking, the gray eyes giving nothing away. The mercurial personality Eddie remembered from the years on the Vineyard was gone. This was a man who pondered and planned—the very opposite of Eddie himself.

"I'm looking for her," Perry finally said. "I don't know who did this, but I'm not going to let them get away with it."

Eddie said nothing.

"I don't like the fact that you're looking, too. You're getting in my way, Eddie. You're causing trouble. People are crawling under rocks, people I need out in the open, where I can find them." He lifted the spoon, pointing. "You're her brother. You're famous. There's no way you can look for her quietly. You should leave it to me."

About to be very cross, Eddie imagined Junie's hand on his, urging a calm response. "You're sure she's alive, then."

"Don't put words in my mouth." Testy after all. "I have no idea if she's alive, Eddie. But I'm trying to find out, and you're making my work harder."

"What is it that you imagine you can do that I cannot?"

"I know you think you have connections, Eddie. I also know you've pretty much used them up. Joe Kennedy was a one-off, and look at you. Now he's got you working for his son. Big propaganda victory for JFK, huh?" The spoon pointed again, while Eddie, very surprised, wondered how much Perry knew—and how. "You're out of people to ask for help. I'm not."

"Then let us work together."

"No."

"Come on, Perry. I know part of it. I want the rest." The golden boy went on stirring his tea. "Remember the night we performed *The Tempest*? Junie was Miranda. You were her suitor, the one her father threw in jail. Ferdinand." Still the gray eyes watched and waited. Eddie could not tell if Perry was amused, impressed, or bored stiff. "You were Sharon Martindale's boyfriend. You preached about the radical alternative. Now, tell me the truth, Perry."

A cocky smile. Perry liked being one up. "About Junie? You couldn't take it."

"Try me."

"No. Leave it alone."

Eddie sat back, confused. What was he missing here? What accounted for the hostility? And then, in the watchful, angry eyes, he saw the younger Perry peeking out, the teenager once so possessive of Junie, whom, after they did *The Tempest*, he insisted on calling Miranda.

Perry knew about the baby.

And was furious not to be the father.

"You loved her," Eddie breathed. "You still love her. This is jealousy. My God, Perry. You're jealous."

"It's less than jealousy and more than love," said Perry, still hot. "Junie was my fiancée."

(1 1)

THEY STROLLED ALONG College Walk, in the shadow of the Low Library. Young white men stared. Negroes were no longer unheard of on Ivy League campuses, but neither were they common, so if you happened to spot one the odds were good that he did not belong.

"You have to understand, Eddie. The Junie you thought you knew was not the only Junie. You're her brother, but you weren't the one who shared her secrets. I was. Don't look at me that way. You never held her head when she was throwing up in the gutter in Cambridge because she had too much to drink, and you never had her slap your face for doing it. You weren't there when the bottom fell out of her life after the baby's father dropped her, and you weren't there when she had her big bust-up with Phil Castle. To you she was this helpless innocent you had to protect, but in her mind she was conquering the world. Do you really think convention would have held her back? Did you think Harvard Law School was a convent? She took the train down to New York City almost every weekend her first year and a half in law school. Did she ever call you? Did you know she was in town? No and no, right? Junie lived her own life, Eddie. It didn't revolve around your expectations of her."

Eddie said nothing. He wondered whether Perry could sense his shrinking from this diminution of his sister's purity. Junie had told him to his face that the father of her half-white child was the only man she had ever been with. Had she lied to the brother who loved her? Had she perhaps meant that Professor Mellor was the only *white* man she had been with? Was Perry lying now? After all, when Eddie had asked Junie on Christmas Eve if Perry was the father, she had answered "Yuch." Or was the true June Cranch Wesley—as her brother was beginning to suspect—a mysterious woman to whom neither he nor Perry Mount had ever gained full access?

"We talked about you a lot," the golden boy resumed after a moment, and Eddie felt as if Perry was reading his mind. "She was so proud of you, Eddie. Proud, but also a little scared. Junie knew how you thought of her. Most of us, we're worried about living up to our fathers' expectations, maybe our mothers'. Junie couldn't have cared less about that. All she cared about was her image in her big brother's eyes. She didn't want to let you down." A harsh laugh. The anger was still very near the surface. "I'll tell you something else. She never wanted you to know. About the baby. First she thought about having an abortion, then she thought about adoption. All that she could deal with. But not your disapproval. She was going to keep the baby secret from you, but I changed her mind. I really pushed her hard, Eddie. Know why?" Eddie knew. He didn't know. He felt his purpose crumbling around him, which perhaps was Perry's intention. "Because, if she didn't tell you, she'd always wonder. How you would have reacted. If you would have loved her anyway. I won't say Junie was testing the limits of your love for her, but she finally agreed to tell you because otherwise she would torture herself worrying. That's the truth, Eddie. That's what happened."

They were no longer in motion. They were standing on the lawn, no closer than men who hate each other will, but still close enough to fight. "You said you were her fiancé," said Eddie, dully. "You said you were getting married."

Perry hesitated, and seemed, for the first time, uneasy. "All right. So I asked her at a weak moment. It still counts, doesn't it? She still said yes. I asked her when she was crying over being thrown over by her baby's father, and she still said yes. She wouldn't take a ring, she hated what it implied, and besides, she said she could never show it to her parents. I didn't understand her. I tried to tell her that after the baby came I would love it as much as—"

Perry stopped. Perhaps he recognized, as Eddie did, the moment when he crossed from angry explanation to childish whining.

"I'm going to find her, Eddie. One way or another. I don't want your help. I don't need it. If you keep trying, you'll be in my way."

"And you'll be in Asia, working for the State Department, right? What are you going to do, search Tokyo and Hong Kong?" You do it for different reasons. Pride. Fury. Fear. King-of-the-hill. Eddie had not been in a real fight since his days with Scarlett, and, before that, since the Army. But now he was suddenly up in Perry's face. "I think you're a coward, Perry. You're not looking for her. You're running away."

Eddie waited for the punch. He was not any kind of brawler, as his quick knockdown by the boys at the Newark train station had proved. No matter. More than at any time in his life, he needed to be hit, and to hit back—and who better to provoke than Perry Mount, the golden boy, who loved Junie and pretended to himself that they were engaged, who had used this opportunity to smear her memory for no apparent gain, and who used to swing his fists at any excuse when they were children, even knowing that Eddie would kick the shit out of him?

But Perry neither swung nor fled.

Instead he said, "Okay, Eddie. Unball those fists. I don't want to fight you. It's fine. You can go on searching."

Eddie could not believe his ears. "You think I need your permission? Who do you think you are?"

Perry was not even interested. He had his hands in his pockets. "I don't think you're up to it, Eddie. I don't think you can find her. But if you do, let me know. I can help you both."

"If you think for one minute—"

"Now, about this Sharon business." Glancing around, as if afraid somebody would hear them and he would lose his sinecure at State. "Yes, I dated Sharon Martindale for a while. No, I never tried to burn down the house. Why would I do that? The Martindales have everything mixed up, as usual. I'm sorry to burst your bubble again, Eddie, but it was Junie and Sharon who set the fire—by accident, smoking marijuana in the bedroom when her parents were away—and I'm the one they called to clean up the damage and make everything nice before the Martindales got back. That's all."

"Why the subterfuge? Why did you let them think your name was Ferdinand?"

A careless shrug. "Junie called me Ferdinand sometimes. Sharon heard it. She liked it, and made me use it, even around her parents. Kind of like a private joke."

Eddie frowned. He felt he was missing something obvious. It was all too fluid. Too pat. Perry had an answer for everything. And yet he and Junie were close—

Oh!

"One more question," said Eddie.

"Not about Sharon."

"No. About Junie." He hesitated. "The baby, Perry. What happened to the baby? You were her friend. You must know."

The golden boy sagged. Once more Eddie had touched a sensitive spot. "She wouldn't tell me. I wanted to help. She wouldn't let me. She said it was her problem, not mine. When her delivery got close, she went off somewhere with Sharon. The next day Sharon came back by herself. And Junie—well, Junie got back a week or so later, and she didn't have a baby with her."

Eddie pondered. His sister gone to extraordinary lengths to hide the baby's whereabouts from the few people who knew she was pregnant—from Benjamin Mellor, the father; from Perry Mount, who wanted to marry her; from the brother who loved her most of all. And there was something else. Mellor had called the baby "it." Perry never referred to the baby's sex. Eddie wondered whether he himself might be the only one Junie had told that the baby was a girl.

Perry, meanwhile, had resumed his hectoring tone.

"It's time to stop, Eddie. Stop searching. Stop turning over rocks. You don't have any idea what trouble you're causing. You don't understand Harlem. Harlem has secrets. Secrets it won't yield without a fight. Harlem isn't a neighborhood, Eddie. It's an idea. You might even call it an ideology. A force. You can't mess around with it. It has a habit of messing back."

"The cross," Eddie breathed. "All of this is about the cross. The big speech. Warning me off the search. It's not about Junie. It's about that stupid upside-down cross." Perry said nothing. "What is it, Perry? What does it mean? What are you afraid I'm going to uncover?" Another thought struck him. "Do you have one, too?"

To his surprise, Perry smiled, almost sheepishly. He looked, again, like the adolescent who had wooed Junie and never won her. "Maybe you'll find her after all," he said, tone gentler, even consoling. "If you find your sister, you should ask her. Otherwise"—the hard-faced golden boy was back—"otherwise, you need to get your nose out of things that aren't your business."

"Things like what?"

"I have a lot of respect for you, Eddie. A lot of respect. You're going to be a major talent." From royalty, crumbs for the commoner. "But let me tell you what my father always used to say. The Caucasians have no idea what we're capable of. No idea. And you know something? Half the time, neither do we." A sharp nod. "Well, you'll see, Eddie. Stay out of our way, and you'll see. One day, we'll shake the throne, and then the whole world will know."

"Shake what throne? Perry—"

But the golden boy was striding angrily away. It would be more than a decade before Eddie laid eyes on him again.

CHAPTER 23

Pink Gin

(1)

"HARLEM HAS SECRETS," said Langston Hughes with a smile. "Well, well. They'll be inventing steam next."

Eddie smiled back, but uncertainly. They were in a taxi, bumping their way along the expressway toward Idlewild Airport. Langston was heading to Paris, to oversee the opening of one of his plays. He had invited Eddie to join him, on the ground that the trip would do the young man good, but Eddie preferred to stay and keep looking. So they settled for the cab ride.

"He really said that?" Hughes asked. "About shaking the throne?"

"And that after they shook the throne the whole world would know."

The great man shook his heavy head. He glanced at his watch. "His father used to use that phrase a lot. Burton. Usually in the context of daring greatly, the way the old Leninists used to talk about shocking the bourgeoisie. Your friend Perry is up to something."

"I figured that part out for myself," said Eddie. "And he isn't my friend."

Hughes ignored this. "Your friend Perry has had a difficult life. Never had many friends. His mother was this cold, distant Czarina, and in any case died when Perry was still young. And nothing the boy did was ever enough for Burton. I'm told the boy adored his Aunt Sumner when he was little, but she passed into whiteness and disappeared, oh, twenty years ago. More. So Burton was all the family

Perry had. Then the car crash last year, and Perry was alone. And of course Burton would have raised him on those wild theories—the darker nation as a force, conspiracies, shaking the throne, all the claptrap your friend threw at you." He fell silent. Eddie watched the gray city go by. "I know what you're thinking, Eddie. Maybe Burton decided to put his theories into action. Maybe this is the Project Phil Castle wanted to warn me about." He shook his head. "It doesn't work, Eddie. It doesn't hold together. Castle was white, and no sort of liberal. Not even a spellbinder like Burton Mount would be able to tempt him into a conspiracy aimed at elevating our community. Besides, Burton was a lot of things, not all of them attractive, but he was no killer."

"Killer?"

"Well, Phil Castle was murdered, wasn't he? And that's not the sort of thing Burton Mount would have put up with. He talked a good game, Eddie, but he was an armchair radical all the way."

Traffic had slowed. They had reached the long turnaround for the airport. Hughes was patting his pockets. Eddie reminded him that he would be keeping the taxi.

The men stood beside the car as the bags were unloaded. Hughes, only half joking, warned Eddie not to do anything foolish while he was away. They shared an awkward hug. Riding back to Harlem, Eddie reflected on the great man's analysis, and spotted the flaw. The late Burton Mount, Langston had insisted, was no killer. That was why whatever Perry was up to could not be the same as the Project that had spooked Philmont Castle. But that theory made an assumption that was not necessarily true.

Burton Mount might not have been in charge.

(11)

LATER THAT NIGHT, Eddie attended a meeting of a political circle of which he had recently become a member, but the subject of that evening's lecture—the possible consequences for the price of securities should the United States ever abandon Bretton Woods and delink the dollar from the gold standard—was sufficiently abstruse, not to mention absurd, that he was glad he had warned them in advance that he would be departing early. He took the subway down to a gallery in the Village, where one of Gary's friends was opening an exhibit. For once Gary had no girl on his arm. Eddie knew that his friend remained stuck on Mona, but had heard no details. Gary said a quick hello, then was lost in the throng. Eddie wandered the exhibit. Actually, he had little experience of the fine arts, and the paintings, over which everyone oohed and aahed, seemed to him mostly gaudy slashes of one color against a background of another. He heard people praising the particularism of this one and the subversive integrity of that one, but dismissing a third as derivative in its pretensions, and he wondered whether they got together to vote on the jargon first or just made it up as they went along. He slipped away to the bar but settled for a club soda. A voice beside him said, "And a pink gin fizz. With Kirschwasser. Put it on his tab."

Eddie turned in delight.

Aurelia touched his hand, down where nobody could see. "Hello, darling," she said. He opened his mouth to answer, but Aurie shook her head. She handed him a note, and was gone.

(I I I)

TWO NIGHTS LATER, as the note instructed, he stopped at the corner of 145th and Edgecombe in a gypsy cab, borrowed from a bemused Lenny Rouse. Aurelia scrambled into the back seat and gave him the address of a girlfriend's new place in Brooklyn. After a moment, he realized that she was serious.

"You stay on your side and I'll stay on my side and everything will be fine," Aurelia said.

"That makes me your chauffeur."

"And it makes me your responsibility. Isn't that what you always wanted?"

They drove for several minutes in silence. He glanced at her often in the mirror, but she did not glance back. She had taken up smoking again, and made it through two cigarettes before he decided to speak first.

"I'm sorry about before, Aurie. I really am. I wasn't myself, but that's no excuse. I had no right to talk to you that way. Forgive me?"

She smiled at him in the mirror. "We've known each other a very long time, Eddie. How many times would you say you've apologized to me? I mean, really, sincerely apologized?"

"Fifty? A hundred?"

"I think this makes three." She looked out the window. She seemed quite content. "And how many times have I apologized to you?"

He took the bait. "Three?"

"Closer to zero. I don't do apologies."

"Oh." It was a Wednesday, and late-night traffic was light. They had already reached midtown. "What do you do?"

"Evidently, I do your detective work."

"My detective work?"

"Tell me about this cross of yours, darling. Where did you see it?"

Eddie was not sure how to explain. "Ah, I saw a woman wearing one on her necklace. A white woman."

"And that made you decide to investigate further? Or did you just want to investigate her?"

"I saw another one. The circumstances—well, I shouldn't say."

"That fits." She was looking out the window. "The cross is a secret, sacred symbol of a silly little Harlem men's club. They've got a hundred of them."

"Symbols?"

"Men's clubs, silly. Every year somebody founds a new one, every one is more exclusive than the next—you know how it goes. The password, the secret handshake, the loyalty till death or till you stop paying your dues. You're probably a member of three or four yourself, except you're not allowed to say. Kevin's in Empyreals, darling. Heard of them?"

He frowned. "They're not the most prestigious."

"Or the most exclusive or the richest or the oldest. They're not the most anything."

"So, the cross is a dead end."

She shrugged, crossed her legs, saw his eyes in the mirror, adjusted her skirt. Downward. "Or else the cross means something else, too."

"Do you happen to know if Perry Mount is an Empyreal?"

"The members aren't allowed to name the other members, darling. Not to outsiders, especially wives." The car lurched to a halt. Aurelia peered at the vast sea of brake lights ahead in the darkness. She pointed. "Don't go that way; turn left, then go down Third." She waited to make sure her instructions were followed, then relaxed. "You saw the cross around a white girl's neck, darling. Harlem men's clubs don't actually admit white girls as members. I don't know if you were aware of that." She laughed. He didn't. "And don't go thinking that some paramour gave it to her. The men in these clubs take them too seriously for that."

"If you're so smart, you explain it."

"I can't yet. But I will." Pointing at the sign. "See? You listened to me, and you're already at the bridge."

"It's a couple of blocks yet."

"Well, hurry, driver, Anita is expecting me."

Eddie's eyes met hers in the mirror. "I was hoping you were going to tell me the house was empty."

"Don't be silly, darling. I'm an upstanding member of society. They even put me in the Garden Club, did you know that?"—no Harlem women's group being more difficult to crack. "You're good at this driving business, Eddie, darling. You should try it, if the writing doesn't work out."

"I'll remember that."

More silence. Eddie felt teased, which he hated, and used, which he hated more. They crossed the bridge. Aurelia gave more directions. Eddie followed them woodenly. They made several turns, and then Aurelia told him to stop. They were on a pretty side street of row houses, less ostentatious than anything in Sugar Hill, but clean and attractive all the same.

"Is this part of the darker nation?" he asked.

Aurelia chuckled. "What you mean is, is this neighborhood seg-regated?" She touched his shoulder. "Mostly West Indians, a few Italians, Jews." She had her purse open. "Look around, Eddie. This is the future."

"What is?"

"A different kind of America."

"I don't understand."

Instead of explaining further, Aurelia opened her handbag and pulled out a bill.

Eddie's eyes narrowed. Insult to injury. "You don't actually think—"

"My girlfriend is watching from the window. If she sees me pay you, she'll never even remember what kind of car I came in." A thought struck her, and she held the dollar just beyond his reach. "Eddie, listen. This ride. It isn't just a lark. I have something to tell you."

"Tell away."

"We're leaving Harlem, Eddie. Kevin and I and the children. I wanted to tell you in person is all. We bought a house in the suburbs. The children deserve the space, don't they?" She seemed to be hav-ing an argument with herself. "It's what I always wanted. A family. Stability. I never had that. I want it for my kids."

"I thought you had all that in Cleveland, growing up."

Aurelia seemed not to hear. "Sometimes in life you do what you have to, not what you want to. I'm a wife now. A mother. I have to hold tight to that which is good, and, well, once I move, we probably won't see much of each other—"

And then the dollar was in his hand and Aurie was marching up the front walk, strong and confident and very fast, the way a woman of quality walks alone at night. Eddie drove back to Manhattan in a fog. He nearly had two accidents on the way. This could not be hap-pening. Not so suddenly. Even though Aurelia was right. He parked the car where Lenny had instructed, on a side street not far from the Columbia campus, and slid the key into the tailpipe. One of Lenny's people would pick it up later. So dizzied was he by the swift turn of the evening's events that he did not notice the black sedan shadowing his stride until it pulled up next to him, dispensing two men of his nation who obviously meant business, and whose invitation to climb in did not admit of refusal.

Again the Carpenter

(1)

THEY SAT HIM in the back, then boxed him in. No one spoke. The driver headed north along Amsterdam Avenue into the Valley. Eddie struggled not to tremble; and, therefore, trembled worse. On West 123rd Street, dead quiet at this hour, the car pulled into an alley beside a nightclub where the last guests were filing out and the neon marquee was going dark.

"Closing early tonight," said Eddie, heart sinking, for he knew whose den this was.

"Yeah," said one of the toughs.

"On my account?"

"Yeah," the man repeated, ending the conversation.

They hustled Eddie in by the stage door. Lenny Rouse stood near the curtain, eyes cold as the grave. You would never know that a few hours ago they had been laughing and joking together, when Lenny handed over the keys to the cab. Now the gangster took his friend by the upper arm and leaned in close. "Keep your mouth shut," he warned, not unkindly. "Just listen unless he asks you a question. Tell him the truth. He'll know if you don't." Lenny marched him down a narrow hallway and out onto the main floor, where he pointed to the booth where Scarlett waited, then stood aside to let Eddie make the final trek alone. Even in the days when he had carried little packages for the organization, Eddie had met the boss only once, and not enjoyed the experience. Scarlett was a bluff barrel of a man who favored fancy wide-brimmed hats and zoot suits, even as they slipped out of style. His temper was a Harlem legend. His yellow eyes were not able to focus on the same spot, so that he always looked at you with one of them as the other jittered and juked. If you reacted, you were in trouble. If you looked away, you were in trouble. If you were smart, you stared at his nose. The two of them sat alone in the booth while the waiters cleaned and the band packed up, the stale air blue with tobacco and beer and sweat, the bad eye jumping all over the place.

"You gettin out of line, boy," Scarlett said by way of introduction.

"Ah, Mr. Scarlett—"

"My man Lenny tells me you're a good listener. So listen. You went to South Carolina."

Eddie, not sure whether the gangster's remark counted as a question, remembered Lenny's caution, and said nothing.

"You hearin me, boy?"

"Yes, Mr. Scarlett. I hear you."

"Then answer the damn question."

Eddie fought down the urge to reply that he had not been asked a question. "Yes," he said, unsure of the scope of either the gangster's knowledge or the present inquiry. "I went to South Carolina."

"Went to that church."

"What church?"

"Don't mess with me, boy. Castle's sweet little wife. That white lady gave you something."

Eddie shook his head. "I asked her to, but she refused." He began to see the wisdom of the pastor. "If you had a source there, the source must have told you, she walked out on me."

Scarlett, until now airy and dismissive, was interested. The band and waiters were gone, Eddie noticed. It was just the two of them, and whoever else was out in the shadows. "Maybe she walked out on you, and maybe she more like *pretended* to walk out on you. Now, tell me what she gave you, and you can go on home."

"She didn't give me the time of day." Emboldened, Eddie embroidered. "I don't think she liked me very much."

"I don't like you, either, but you're gonna tell me."

"I already said—"

That was as far as he got. Eddie never noticed a signal. Nevertheless, out of the shadows came Lenny Rouse and one of the toughs from the car. Lenny had him around the neck, and twisted his left arm high at his back, making it impossible for him to rise. The other man had Eddie's right arm in a granite grip, pressing it to the table.

"You're gonna tell me," said the gangster again.

"What are you doing?" Eddie demanded, hot liquid fear dancing afresh through his loins. He tugged at the hands holding his. "Let me go."

"Hold him tight," said Scarlett, shucking his suit jacket, and Eddie remembered his nickname.

The Carpenter.

It was not possible that they meant to—

Except that it was.

From beneath the table, the Carpenter pulled a heavy toolbox, painted bright red, so shiny it was probably polished twice a day. He flipped the twin catches and opened the lid.

"You can't do this," Eddie breathed.

"They say you're a big man," said Scarlett. "They tell me you're famous. I guess you prob'ly think you're brave, too. But brave don't got nothin to do with it. You're gonna tell me what she gave you."

"She didn't give me anything!"

The Carpenter reached into the box. He came up with a carton of heavy common nails. He shook three into his palm, then held them in his mouth by their heads. Eddie followed every move. Never had nails seemed so scary. The hand went into the box again. This time the Carpenter pulled out a hammer.

"You're gonna tell me," he said. The second man from the car approached. Eddie made a fist. The man squeezed Eddie's hand right on the ball of the thumb. Pain slowly forced the fingers open. The pressure would not let him close them again. The palm was face-down on the table. The fingers were splayed. The Carpenter patted Eddie's middle finger, found the spot he wanted, just past the knuckle. "The meat is really tender here," he said, and tapped it with the head of a nail. Eddie flinched. *Meat*, he registered. Scarlett lifted the hammer. "You got something to tell me?"

At that moment Eddie would happily have told the gangster anything to stop that nail from going in—anything except the secret that might lead to his sister.

His wife has it.

Eddie glared at Scarlett. "She didn't tell me anything," he said.

Scarlett stopped. At first Eddie thought his tough words had gotten through. Then he realized that the gangster was looking past him, into the shadows. Eddie wanted to turn his head but was afraid to show any weakness.

Without warning the hammer came down.

It missed the nail and struck the very tip of Eddie's finger.

Eddie gasped but held in the howl.

"That ain't gonna give you nothin but a blood blister," said Scarlett. "The next one is gonna be the knuckle. I hit it a good whack, you won't ever write with that hand again. Then the nail goes in after that. Understand?"

"You can't do this," said Eddie.

"Tell me what she gave you."

Eddie fought to swallow the bile rising in his throat. "She didn't give me anything," he said.

"Tell me, boy."

"There's nothing to tell!"

The hammer went up.

Eddie shut his eyes. He waited. Waited for Agent Stilwell to burst in and rescue him. Waited for Lenny to shoot his boss and take over the business. Waited for the hammer to smash his hand to bits.

(11)

"I'M GONNA LET THIS ONE GO," said Scarlett, close to his ear. Eddie opened his eyes. His hand was whole. Turning to look at the gangster, he saw movement elsewhere in the room. Maybe the man who was signaling the Carpenter, giving him instructions. Lenny and the other tough were still holding on to Eddie now, but more loosely. Scarlett patted his own palm with the hammer. The bad eye kept jumping. "My boys gonna take you out in the alley and give you a little somethin to remember me by. Gonna trim you up, boy. But what they're gonna do won't be anything like as bad as what's gonna happen, I find out you were lyin to me. You hearin me, boy?"

"Yes," said Eddie, through chattering teeth.

"You lyin to me, I'm gonna take off some pieces. You understand?"

"Yes."

"You know what pieces I'm talkin about, right, boy?"

Eddie tried and failed to swallow. "Yes."

The Carpenter nodded. Lenny courteously held the door. The toughs from the car dragged Eddie into the alley and beat him so soundly he missed most of the action. At first he tried to fight back, but fighting was not his thing, and after two minutes he just covered up and let them do what they wanted. Lenny supervised, finally calling time. He shoved Eddie into a gypsy cab, drove him to Harlem Hospital, explained things to the doctors, who nodded. They gave him a shot. He woke up in the dreary, dripping ward and lay there, thinking, for the next four days. There was some internal problem he never quite got straight, and the doctors kept prodding him to see if it was better.

He had visitors. He had a teasing telegram from Langston Hughes, who said he had promised to stay out of trouble. He was kissed on the forehead by Aurelia, who came every day and turned every head, and frowned upon by the doctors, who waited vainly for him to take an exciting turn for the worse. Gary Fatek brought the largest spray of flowers the hospital had ever seen and offered to move him someplace better, but Eddie would not turn his back on Harlem. His sister Marcella came down from Springfield—Gary had called her—and sat at his bedside for a day and a half, mostly reading the Bible aloud, and warning him that it was time to stop carousing and settle down. Eddie smiled at everyone who dropped in and said all the right things, but his mind was occupied with the memory of Scarlett's club. Not the memory of the beating, or of the fear. The memory was of a face.

The face in the shadows, glimpsed only for a moment, the man with the power to tell the Carpenter to stop.

The man had smooth blond hair. His face was white.

(III)

WHEN EDDIE WAS RELEASED, Gary and Marcella drove him back to 435 Convent Avenue. Marcie had been staying at the apartment, and stayed on to make sure her brother got all the lecturing he deserved. A couple of girls had called to check on him, but Marcie had not taken their names or messages, because they were obviously fast little hussies, calling up a man that way. Marcella stayed another week and nearly killed him. Eddie took his sister to Shirley Elden's salon, but she sat unspeaking in the corner, gazing out on the cream of Harlem society with elaborate disapproval. She joined him at lunch with Kasten, his literary agent, but Marcie kept insisting that Eddie's novels would sell better if there was a little less sex in them. For all of that, Marcella was attentive and patient, prepared to serve his smallest whim.

She simply served a side order of lecture every time.

On the afternoon of the seventh day, his sister left. That night, Eddie went to dinner at Amaretta Veazie's. They asked him to talk about his third novel, due out early next year, which everyone knew was some sort of wry comment on Sugar Hill. He told them they would have to wait and see. More cautious now, he took a taxi back to Convent Avenue instead of walking, and found a sleekly officious white man waiting for him in the lobby, despite the hour.

"Are you Edward Trotter Wesley Junior?"

"Yes," he said, warily, wondering if he was about to be served with a subpoena, or perhaps even arrested.

"Do you have any identification?"

Eddie showed him the scrap of poorly printed paper that New York issued as a driver's license.

"I have a package for you."

"At this time of night?"

The man nodded, brandishing a manila envelope. He held out a form. "Sign here."

Eddie signed, turned away, stormed up to his apartment, put Billie Holiday on the record player, opened a notebook, and began writing for the first time since his beating. It felt good to have pen in hand again. Only when he had written for three straight hours and poured himself a one-thirty nightcap did he remember the delivery. He actually had to hunt around to find the envelope. He had left it in the kitchen. He opened the flap and slid out two glossy black-and-white photographs. There was an unsigned note. Eddie did not recognize the clumsy handwriting. *Thanks for all your good work for your country. Thought you'd like to have this.* The first photo was a crowd scene, and Eddie needed a moment to place it.

Then he remembered.

It was the battle at Maxton, North Carolina, the Klan facing off against the Lumbee Indians. One of the Indians was circled in red ink. The second photo was a grainy blowup of the same person.

Except, seen close, it was no Indian.

David Yee had said that the Negroes were not involved in the battle, but Eddie was holding in his hand evidence to the contrary. The figure was a black woman, toting a rifle like she knew how to use it.

The woman in the picture was Junie.

CHAPTER 25

A New Deal

"I THOUGHT YOU WANTED NOTHING ELSE to do with us," said Bernard Stilwell, grinning like a ghostly skull in the midnight fog. "We're the big bad racists of the Federal Bureau of Investigation, and you're the sole possessor of righteousness and truth. You can't allow your purity to be polluted by hanging around with the likes of us. Or did I miss the conciliatory part of your teary farewell?"

"Previously you were blackmailing me on the basis of your own false reports. Now I am coming to you, my government, for assistance. I fail to see the analogy."

Stilwell laughed, the same wicked tormentor's chuckle that had so chilled Eddie on the occasion of their first meeting. They were strolling east along the Reflecting Pool between the Lincoln Memorial and the Washington Monument, the water flat and cold and black in the still night. Gray mist drifted over the surface like fading memory. The Mall was deserted, for this was the season of neither busloads of protesting children nor hordes of chattering tourists. "As a citizen of this fine republic, you naturally have the right to petition your government for redress of grievances whenever it strikes your fancy. The thing is, Dorothy had the right to petition the Wizard, too. And, just like Dorothy, if you have nothing to trade, the Wizard will tell you to come back tomorrow."

"I don't think that's the way the story went," Eddie said after a moment. For the tiniest instant the April fog parted. The sky was a crisp, endless purple, the stars were bright and solid, as eternal as hope, and as untouchable. Then the moment passed. "The Wizard tried to cheat her. She kept her end of the deal. He broke it."

"Glad to hear it. Now, let me tell you the facts of life." The mist curled around their legs. They had veered off into the thin screen of trees. "Two years ago, the Director gave you the opportunity to be of service to your country, to file a report now and then, help us make sure that the leadership of your people is not being infiltrated by agitators and Communists. You never filed a single report. You hired yourself a fancy lawyer and got out of the deal. You didn't want to help. Fine. Now you come and you want to ask me a whole bunch of questions about your sister." Stilwell was much the larger man, and carried his bulk with the sure authority of the licensed bully. A growing tension in his posture suggested that he was working himself into a froth, but his voice remained as low-key and casual as ever: the tone Eddie remembered from the morning the FBI man had choked him half to death on a Harlem side street. "You want to know if we're looking into her disappearance. You want to know if this photograph"—shaking the envelope—"is real or doctored. You want to know where she is." He shook his head. "Come on, Eddie. Can you give me a single reason we should help you? When you won't help us?"

"All I want to know is whether my sister is alive."

"That's very noble," said Stilwell. They were through the trees and off in the broad parkland north of the Monument, heading toward the White House, where lights glistened smearily beyond the haze. "But, Eddie, we're grown-ups here. You understand the way this kind of thing—"

He stopped.

"The reason I'm asking might actually be relevant to the Director's concern, and, in that sense, I might be able to help after all," Eddie began, having rehearsed this part already, but the agent waved him silent. He was looking back toward the shrouded trees.

"Did you bring a friend, Eddie?"

"A friend?" Eddie wheeled around, too, but could see nothing in the fog.

"To keep an eye on you just in case those wacky feds decided to get up to their usual mean old tricks. What we call a minder." He had smoothly insinuated himself between Eddie and the tree line. His left hand was unbuttoning his overcoat. "Did you bring a minder, Eddie? Because somebody's been following us since the Memorial."

"I wouldn't know where to get a minder even if I wanted one." Eddie's eyes strained into the darkness. "I don't see anybody."

"He's out there."

"You're imagining things."

"Maybe."

"Why would anybody be following us?"

"You never know with the Reds. They can be pretty bold these days."

Stilwell took a last look behind them, then shrugged, turned his back, and walked on. Eddie tagged uneasily along, wondering who might be back there, as perhaps he was meant to.

"So what's your offer?" the agent asked after a moment.

"I'm sorry?"

"You're an intelligent man. You didn't come here empty-handed."

Eddie watched his own breath dance, then vanish. He was about to cross the line he had avoided two years ago. But abstract principle was one thing. Junie was another. "Suppose I were willing—on an occasional basis—to furnish the Bureau with reports, along the line of what the Director asked two years ago."

The fog thickened suddenly, and the park became dreamlike, trees soft and dreary, the slick grass an invisible carpet beneath their feet. Eddie turned to look behind them, but Stilwell seemed at ease. "What kind of reports?"

"There's a group called the Twenty," he began.

Stilwell shut him down much too fast. "Never heard of it."

"Fine." Eddie tapped the envelope. "Say, for instance, if I could find out more about this group the Director asked me about, Agony." The agent waited. "A reporter told me that they might have been involved in what happened in Maxton."

"We are not asking you to do anything." The tone was virtuous. "You are a volunteer. You do understand the distinction?"

Taking the inquiry as rhetorical, Eddie said nothing. They cut back toward Fifteenth Street and, as the haze parted once more, wound up on the sidewalk between the granite intimidation of the Treasury Department and the swank yet homey Washington Hotel. Stilwell said, "Wait here," and stepped toward a phone booth near a shuttered newsstand. Another man was inside, talking away. Eddie thought the agent would flash his credentials to make him move, but the other man just stepped out, handing Stilwell the receiver. He had been holding the line open. While Stilwell talked, the other man stood near Eddie. He was scrawny and tow-headed and could have been the agent who held Eddie's wrists in Harlem while Stilwell choked him.

"Chilly this morning," said Eddie.

The other man only stared.

"Nice little coup in Venezuela last week. Was that your people? Or did you prefer the dictator they already had?"

Silence.

Stilwell was back. He spoke in a murmur, very low, very fast. "The Director sends his regards. He says he was very sorry to hear about your sister. We don't know where she is, but we will certainly do some digging." The other man had climbed into the car, and Stilwell, about to follow, folded his hands atop the open door and leaned across. It occurred to Eddie that the agent was choosing his words with unusual care. "The Director says, if you want to look into Jewel Agony, on your own, it's up to you. If you turn anything up, give me a call. He also says you owe us now, and he is sure you will reciprocate when asked."

Eddie stared. They had known, he realized. Somehow the Bureau had known from the start that he would be back. He remembered Gary Fatek's warning that Hoover's interest was really about something else; and how doggedly Junie had tried to get her brother out of the Bureau's clutches.

Then he saw the whole trick.

"Hoover was never interested in atomic secrets. That's not why you picked me up that first time. That was a smokescreen. It was never atomic secrets, and it was never the civil-rights leaders." He tapped the photograph. "It was this. All along, it was this. All that talk about how Jewel Agony recruits only the well educated. The Director wasn't talking about me. He was talking about Junie. From the start. He knew she would be running off to join them, and he wanted me to spy on my own sister. My God. What kind of people are you?"

The agent, expressionless, continued to deliver instructions. "I'll expect monthly updates on your progress. You can reach me at the number you have, until you get close to them. Then we'll change the contact procedures. We'll keep an occasional eye on you, of course, but if you get into trouble we won't be charging in like the cavalry to pull you out. Like I said, you're a volunteer."

"Are you even listening to me?"

Stilwell continued to lean on the car door. "I wouldn't go telling my family just yet, if I were you. The individual in the photograph may or may not be your sister. Your sister may or may not be alive. I would wait for confirmation before burdening my parents, my older sister, or my ten best friends."

"Just tell me if the photograph is genuine."

"The most important thing we need to know is membership," said Stilwell. "Next along is funding. Every organization of any kind can be reduced to those two fundamentals. Membership and money." He seemed to be reciting from the manual. "If you give us membership and money, we can do the rest."

"Why would I even consider—"

"You came to us, Eddie. We didn't come to you. You are in no position to bargain." He let this sink in. "Aside from that, let me warn you. Your sister may or may not be a part of Jewel Agony. I don't know. You don't know. The Director doesn't know. But whether she is or not, they are dangerous people. Don't let them charm you."

"Dangerous to whom?"

The agent climbed into the car, not bothering to answer. The door clanged. The car drove off.

Eddie stood on the sidewalk, watching the taillights glimmer and vanish in the fog. Reading between the lines, he could put together the message. The Bureau did not know where Junie was. But Stilwell wanted him to know they were already looking. He pondered. The mysterious leader of Jewel Agony, the signer of their various missives, was known as Commander M. There was not a single "m" in "June Cranch Wesley," but her favorite Shakespearean character, years ago on the Vineyard, had been Miranda from *The Tempest*.

Yet it was impossible to imagine Junie as head of a violent terror gang.

Walking back to his hotel, he remembered what Stilwell had said about the tail, and often turned to look, until it occurred to him that he had no idea what to look for. Still, once or twice, in the enveloping mist, he thought he glimpsed a figure, slim and dark and furtive, moving with a tragic plodding determination, but whenever the figure drew close, the fog would close down again.

PART III

Washington/New York/ Mount Vernon 1960–1965

CHAPTER 26

A New Frontier

(1)

EDDIE STOOD at the back of the overflowing Senate Caucus Room, watching Senator John Kennedy field questions from reporters with his usual adroit mix of sobriety and humor. He used a couple of Eddie's answers—including a subtle dig at one of his primary opponents, without naming any names—and another aide, grinning, poked Eddie's ribs after another clever sally minutes later and said, "That was mine." One of Kennedy's endearing qualities was his ability, despite his patrician hauteur and the close-knit "Irish Mafia" surrounding him, to make even low-level staffers feel excited, and part of the team. You never felt you were Jack's friend, Eddie explained in a letter to his mother, but you felt you were needed. It was Saturday, January 2, 1960, and Kennedy was in the process of announcing officially his candidacy for President. Eddie, once his third novel was published in six weeks, would take a leave of absence from his writing and join the campaign full-time. Eddie would help write speeches and would also serve as liaison to the literary community, because the Kennedys were determined to line up endorsements from noted authors, to counter the charge, widely whispered in Washington, that the candidate was an intellectual lightweight. Eddie would have a pitiful salary, an inexperienced staff, and a fancy title. It had been in the papers. His Harlem buddies were impressed.

His mother wrote to say that his father was proud.

Aurelia and Gary Fatek, for their different reasons, thought him insane.

"Number one," said Aurelia, when they met secretly for coffee in

the Bronx, "you're just starting to make money. You're gaining readers. You need to keep that engine going." She stifled his reply with a
gentle kick in the shin. "And, number two, taking this job means
you'll hardly be in Harlem any more. You'll be running around the
country, sleeping with overenthusiastic coed volunteers."

"As opposed to sitting in my apartment, not sleeping with you."

"Well, I'm not sleeping with you, either, my dear, so if that's the
measure of happiness, I'd say we're both suffering."

"You don't look to me like you're suffering."

"Good. Because I'm not."

"I can't just sit around on Convent Avenue," said Eddie after a
moment. "The world is bigger than Harlem." This was the advice
Adam Clayton Powell had given him years ago. Eddie quoted it
often. Probably Aurelia believed much the same. She had risen high
in Harlem society, but had also moved beyond it. She had taken
Mona's advice and was back in school, pursuing a doctorate in literature at Columbia. She had her house in the suburbs. From his lonely
literary perch, Eddie continued to love her but, at the same time, felt
he scarcely knew her. He realized that she was waiting for him to
speak; and that he was staring at those lovely eyes. "Things are starting to change out there," he said, a little desperately. His hand shot
out at random, pointing, he hoped, southward. "The whole country's
going to be different. Jim Crow is going down for the count, Aurie.
And Kennedy—well, you have to meet the man. He's so young and
energetic. He'll be the first President born in the twentieth century.
Don't you want to be a part of that?"

No, said Aurelia. She really did not. She was just back from a trip
to the Midwest, where she had seen Mona and visited old St. Louis
haunts. "And I realized," said Aurie, "that all I want to be a part of is
raising my children, and finishing my degree. The world can take
care of itself."

Eddie didn't believe her.

"Did Kevin find what he was looking for?" he asked as he handed
her into a taxi. "The testament?"

"Is that all you care about? I shouldn't have mentioned it."

"No."

"No, what?"

"No, it's not all I care about."

"I'm starting to worry about you, moping around," said Aurelia through the lowered window. "Aren't you ever going to get married?"

Eddie smiled but said nothing. He kissed her coolly proffered cheek, watched the taillights fade.

"That's not up to me," he said.

(11)

GARY TOOK HIM SAILING on Long Island Sound. Apart from wading in the surf on Martha's Vineyard, Eddie had no real experience of the water. He had never sailed. He dressed in a blazer, expecting a party on a rich man's yacht. Instead, they went out in Gary's sloop. Eddie could not tell a jib from a broad reach. All he knew of sailing was what he had read in Jack London's essay about how the real sailor gets the salt in his bones and it never gets out again. That did not sound to Eddie like fun. But here he was riding low in the water, crashing over waves, and scampering around the deck following orders, ducking constantly as the boom swept past, and, once, not ducking fast enough.

"Your man doesn't stand a snowball's chance," shouted Gary, who considered himself an oracle on politics because his great-great-uncle had been a mediocre President. "Nixon would mop the floor with him. But it won't get that far, and we both know it. Your man won't get the nomination. It'll be Johnson or Humphrey, maybe even Stevenson. This is a vanity campaign, Eddie. This is trying to win with Daddy's money. You know that joke your man likes to tell? The fake telegram from his father? 'Don't buy a single vote more than necessary, I'm damned if I'm going to pay for a landslide'? It's true, Eddie. Without the money, your man is nothing."

Eddie ducked again. Actually, he had helped write the joke, which played wonderfully well on the stump, but he had already learned that part of the role of political speechwriter was never admitting to having authored a single word that emerged from the candidate's mouth.

"He has a good chance," said Eddie, who had looked at the numbers just days ago. The spray caught him face-on, and for a moment he spluttered while Gary laughed. "Among Democrats, he's tied nationwide with Stevenson—"

"Right. Your man is spending money hand over fist, and the best he can manage is a tie with a fellow who isn't even in the race. If you're looking for a job in Washington, Eddie, this isn't the way to get it. It's quicker to ask Aunt Erebeth. She adores you. I don't know why."

Eddie was still coughing. As a child, he had nearly drowned on Martha's Vineyard, and had never entirely conquered his fear. "That's not what this is about."

"Well, whatever it's about, it's a mistake. You're wasting your time."

But it was not a mistake. Eddie liked Jack Kennedy, and despised Dick Nixon. Like most of the campaign's early supporters, he was enthusiastic about the changes a Kennedy candidacy would work. Yet that enthusiasm was not his principal reason for signing on. He was here because of Junie.

(III)

WHEN FIRST APPROACHED by Kennedy's people, Eddie had dithered—partly for Aurelia's reasons, and partly because he feared, as the whole darker nation did, being fooled again. Over and over they had fallen for charm and promises, first from one side of the aisle, then from the other. The fear in the Harlem salons was that this Kennedy would prove another in the long line of hucksters— fine talk, no action. The man the Negro leadership wanted was Humphrey, adored all through black America for his daring speech at the 1948 Democratic Convention, challenging the party to rise above the Southerners who dragged it down: "To those who say that we are rushing this issue of civil rights, I say to them we are 172 years late." Kennedy was an unknown quantity.

Eddie consulted Langston Hughes, who had made clear to intimates that he would back nobody in the 1960 election. Hughes reminded him despairingly of how the Democratic-controlled Congress had never been able to pass an anti-lynching law, a priority of the civil-rights groups for decades now. Hughes's close friend Adam Clayton Powell had bolted the party in 1956 over the issue, supporting Eisenhower instead of Stevenson.

"Not that I expect the Republicans would be any better," said Hughes.

"I like Kennedy," Eddie insisted. "I think he could do big things."

The great man's smile was indulgent. "I was young once, too."

In early summer of 1959, still unsure, Eddie had attended a conference at the Kennedy compound at Hyannisport. The idea was to gather a few dozen potential supporters and advisers, explain the strategy should the campaign indeed materialize, and persuade them that Kennedy could actually win. Eddie saw a couple of people he knew. One was Lanning Frost, Margot's husband. The presence of the first-term Midwestern Congressman came as no surprise, because, from the little Eddie had heard, it was plain that Lanning was betting heavily on Kennedy. He was astonished, however, to find himself seated at the outdoor lunch directly across the long wooden picnic table from none other than Benjamin Mellor, the Harvard professor who had confessed to fathering Junie's child. Eddie could not stop staring. When the senior staffers went around making introductions, Eddie could only grit his teeth and offer the group a ghastly smile. Mellor ignored him. As the plans were laid out, conversation grew spirited, but Eddie said almost nothing. In fact, he said even less than Lanning Frost, who seemed to be on firm orders to speak as little as possible, lest he live up to his reputation as rather a dim bulb.

After lunch, Mellor vanished, caucusing with three or four other legal experts. The foreign-policy people went to one room, the economists to another. Bobby Kennedy, the unofficial campaign manager, took Eddie for a walk. They made a circuit around the vast lawn.

"Are you sure your heart is in this?"

"I'm sorry?"

"You seemed a little subdued."

Eddie's jaw jutted out just a bit. "I have a lot on my mind."

Bobby shook his head. "That's not good enough. Dad thinks the world of you, and you've been a great help to us so far. But we need people who are with us a hundred percent. A hundred and ten, Eddie. This is going to be a high-energy campaign. We can't have any distractions. Now, I don't know what the problem is between you and Ben Mellor, but we need you both. Don't give me that look. It was obvious to everybody in the room. We don't have time for any personal nonsense. You're grown-ups. Work it out."

Eddie almost left. Probably he would have, but for a single thought: only by staying could he keep the ambitious professor from attaining whatever it was he hoped, through this service, to achieve. He did not know precisely how he would ruin Benjamin Mellor's chances without disclosing his sister's secrets, but he would figure something out.

And so he sat down with Mellor at one of the picnic tables and said he preferred to let bygones be bygones, and Mellor just stared at him and stared at him and finally said, "You don't have any idea what's going on, do you?"

Eddie had a nice stare of his own. "Why don't you enlighten me?"

"I'm talking about this whole business with your sister—"

Had they been anywhere but Hyannisport, Eddie would have grabbed a handful of Mellor's creamy oxford shirt. As it was, he smacked a hand on the table so hard that his palm would ache for days. "It's not a business. It's a baby." The professor shut up. "Your baby," Eddie added, keeping his voice down despite his fury. Still Mellor said nothing. He seemed to be waiting. Eddie paused, trying to work out what he should be reading in the wide, fearful eyes. He tossed out a guess: "You know where the baby is."

Mellor drew himself up. "I most certainly do not."

"Then it's Junie. You know where she is."

"No."

Another shot: "You've heard from her, though."

A long silence. Then Mellor slipped a hand into his tweeds and drew out a handwritten note. "This was left in my mailbox at Langdell."

> *Dear Professor M—*
> *Thanks for everything. You're a good man.*
> *—J*

Eddie studied the single page, the handful of words in the script he knew so well, shaky, as if written in a vehicle, on plain white notebook filler paper. And his first, odd impulse was jealousy, that his sister, from wherever she was hiding, had written this man, and not her big brother. His second was a flood of relief at this hard evidence, the first since that photo of the battle in Maxton, that his sister was still alive. His third was confusion over why Junie would risk this delivery, by whatever means, to thank the man who had seduced, impregnated, and abandoned her. And his fourth was—

The Junie you thought you knew was not the only Junie. Perry Mount.

"When did she leave this?" Eddie demanded, waving the paper around. "Did you see her?"

Mellor shook his head. "I haven't seen her, Mr. Wesley. I haven't spoken with her. She left the note three or four months ago. I came back from class, and there it was. And, no, Mr. Wesley, nobody noticed whoever dropped it off."

Eddie looked away, across the sloping lawn down to the water. A year and a half ago, his sister was in Maxton. Before that, Nashville. This past spring, Cambridge. She relied on others, and broke cover at least once, to risk leaving a cryptic note. But not for her brother.

"Why are you showing this to me?" Eddie asked. He felt his anger dulling. "Why did you bring it here? Why didn't you burn it? Or give it to the FBI?"

"You're welcome to keep it," said the professor, coldly.

"Me?"

"I don't want it. I can't have it on my person, obviously. Not with my . . . career plans."

My career plans. Eddie's bewilderment grew. The Justice Department. The federal bench. Eddie could imagine the world ten or twelve years on, if the professor realized his dreams: Supreme Court Justice Benjamin Mellor. "I still don't understand. All this trouble to get the note to me? It doesn't make sense. Given your career plans, as you call them—well, I still don't understand why you didn't burn it."

Mellor was on his feet. "Maybe I'm not the man you think I am."

Fat chance. Again Eddie rattled the page. "Why is she thanking you? What did you ever do for my sister besides get her in trouble?"

Again Ben Mellor climbed up on his dignity. His tone was oracular and final, as befitted a future Supreme Court justice. "I should think that would be obvious to a man of your intelligence, Mr. Wesley."

He strode off toward the house.

CHAPTER 27

Another Side

(1)

As for Aurelia, she had married into a staunchly Republican family. Matty Garland raised money for Nixon, and called him not "Mr. Vice President" but "Dick." Matty gave a fancy dinner for Nixon at his eight-bedroom home on the Hudson near Dobbs Ferry. Through the dining-room windows you could see the river, sparkling gold wherever the moonlight touched it. Most of the guests were white. Matty seated Aurelia beside the candidate. She honored Matty's faith by turning on the charm. Kevin beamed at her across the table. Richard Nixon was not known to be drawn to women other than his wife, but Aurie kept him smiling. By the end of the meal, she, too, had secured Dick privileges.

Later, Aurelia wrote up the dinner for her column. Kevin had persuaded his father to purchase the *Seventh Avenue Sentinel*, less to give his wife a place to work than to provide a Republican voice in an increasingly Democratic Negro community. The new *Sentinel* trumpeted what it called Nixon's activism on behalf of civil rights, especially his determined efforts, in cooperation with Martin Luther King, Jr., to persuade the Republican Party to support the Voting Rights Act that topped the demands of the Negro leadership—a bill on which the Democratic Congress was unwilling to act.

The newspaper neglected to mention that Nixon failed.

In early 1960, Aurelia's daughter, Zora, was going on four. Her son, Locke, was nearly two. The family lived in a large Tudor-style house on a leafy lot in Mount Vernon, a short drive or train ride from the city. Of course, most of their neighbors were white, but the number of middle-class black families in the suburbs was on the rise. Actually, the Garlands had fought their way through several real-estate agents before finding a woman willing to show them houses fitting their station. Another major goal of the civil-rights leaders was an open-housing law, but the Southern Democrats who ran the Senate—so Kevin insisted—feared the prospect of Negro neighbors even more than they did the prospect of Negro voters.

The house was beautiful, but Aurelia was lonely. Though her husband no longer traveled quite so frenetically, he spent long hours at the office. Her girlfriends were scattered. Mona Veazie was studying at the University of Chicago and, from hints she dropped in her letters, had found herself a man. Claire Garland had moved with her family to Long Island. Sherilyn DeForde had moved with hers to New Jersey. Torie Elden, still single, had moved to Washington. Everybody was leaving Harlem, but not for the same places. Sometimes Aurelia would take the train into town and stay for a night or two at the apartment the Garlands still maintained on Edgecombe Avenue. She would visit the salons and find them ill-attended, and desultory. Harlem society seemed to be dying, and so swiftly she could hardly figure out how or why.

Matty dropped by the house often, seeming to sense that his daughter-in-law needed bucking up. He would compliment her on a new hairstyle when Kevin forgot, and somehow knew exactly when a box of imported chocolates would come in handy. They would sit in the kitchen, with its gleaming white appliances, and Aurie would listen while Matty talked politics or movies or weather, anything at all to fill the empty spaces. He rarely left without reminding her that she was meant for great things and dared not settle for less.

Kevin's mother, Wanda, who had never quite made her peace with the marriage, came by less often.

Aurelia befriended some of her neighbors. Next door lived a happy couple named Finnerty, with children of ten, six, and four. Neil Finnerty worked on Madison Avenue. His wife, Callie, was a homemaker, thickset, and blond from a bottle. All she talked about was motherhood. Whenever Aurelia tried to change the subject, Callie changed it back. They walked their children together. Locke still rode in the carriage, until he clambered out to keep up with the Finnerty kids. Callie taught Aurelia to bake pies, which the nuns never had, and persuaded her to hang a clothesline in the backyard instead of using the modern Westinghouse dryer her husband had bought. But Kevin decreed the billowing sheets an eyesore and made her take them down. Callie introduced her to the merchants downtown, and in New Rochelle, at the fancy places on North Avenue and the cheaper stores on Webster. The proprietors, chilly at first, warmed up fast when they realized how much money she was prepared to spend. Another time, Callie took Aurelia to meet her friends at the country club, but none would sit at their table. Callie was mortified. Aurie told her not to worry about it. After that, the two did not talk quite as much, except to call polite hellos as they passed in their adjoining yards, until the sultry August Sunday when a chastened Callie rang the Garland bell around seven in the evening and reported that the FBI had been asking questions about them.

Aurelia invited her in.

Kevin was out of town, Locke was asleep, and the maid was on the screened porch with Zora, playing Candyland. Aurelia and Callie sat in the kitchen sipping coffee despite the hour and the heat, because Aurelia remained a little confused about suburban proprieties.

"There were two of them," said Callie. "They made me promise not to tell, but you're my friend. It's not a crime to tell my friend, is it?"

Aurie calmed her down, and eventually the story came out. Two agents, as she said. Two mornings ago: Callie had been dithering ever since. At first they just asked how the Garlands were settling in, what kind of people they seemed to be—"I told them how nice you are"—and then they asked about any evidence that the couple was involved in any kind of radical activities.

"I laughed, Aurie. I really, truly did. I told them, Aurie's not a radical. Aurie's my friend. She's a loyal American. That's what I told them. Only they didn't want to talk about you. They wanted to talk about Kevin."

"What did you tell them?"

She cast her eyes toward the sparkling linoleum floor. "I said I don't know him very well."

Aurie was disheartened by the suspicion in her neighbor's voice. True, Kevin made little effort to be friendly, but that kind of tepid answer was likely to reinforce the Bureau's conviction that—

Well, she did not know precisely what the FBI suspected, but she did know that nobody would ever suspect her husband of Communist sympathies. So it had to be something else. She cooed and reassured and hugged, told poor Callie there was nothing to worry about, it was all a big mistake, and sent her home. Sitting up in bed that night, watching *Ed Sullivan*, Aurie thought back. She remembered Kevin's mad search for Castle's testament. She wondered if he had ever tracked it down. Certainly he seemed to have stopped looking for it. But mostly she wondered whether the federal government knew about her husband's search, and was suddenly looking for the same thing.

(11)

ON MONDAY, she decided to call Eddie. He was traveling with the campaign. By this time, Eddie was doing well enough to employ an assistant, a bespectacled woman of perhaps twenty who worked for him while taking courses at the New School. Her name was Paula, she was white and of some peculiar ethnicity, and in Harlem nobody trusted her. She spent a lot of time in Eddie's apartment, supposedly working on his correspondence and typing his manuscripts, but the Czarinas conjectured the obvious. In her worst moments, so did Aurelia. She had met Paula only once, and found her hero-worshiping of the boss frankly lustful.

"I think they're in Oregon," Paula told her.

"You think?"

"Maybe Washington. The state, not the city," she added, in case Aurie turned out to be a dunce.

"Do you have a way to reach him?"

"I have a schedule somewhere. Sometimes he calls in for messages. Long-distance." Awe in her voice, perhaps thinking of the expense.

"Will you tell him I need to reach him?"

"If I remember."

"You could write it down."

"I'd only lose it."

When Aurelia hung up, she was ready to scream, but it was time to pull dinner together, an act that always calmed her. To her surprise, Eddie telephoned that very night.

"The FBI was asking about Kevin," she said without preamble.

"Then they're probably listening to us now."

This possibility Aurie had not considered. There were times when a mild paranoia like Eddie's could be considered a virtue.

"Do you know what this is about?" she asked.

"No. But I suspect that your husband possesses the necessary contacts to find out."

The chill in his voice told Aurelia he still loved her, but it also scared her even more than Callie's news.

(III)

KEVIN RETURNED to Mount Vernon late the following night. She expected him to be furious, but he took the news calmly. They sat across from each other in the living room. The only sign that her husband was disturbed was his decision to drink a third Scotch.

"It's not worth worrying about," he finally said.

"Honey, it's the FBI."

"I'll call Dad. Dad will call Dick, Dick will call Hoover—there's a way these things work. People like us don't get investigated." He drank. "I don't want you to worry."

"And I don't want you to go to jail."

His smile was wan, and self-deprecating. "Is my wife saying that she loves me after all?"

This shook her. "I never said I didn't love you—"

"And you never said you did." He crossed to the sideboard, picked up the bottle, then put it down. He set the glass next to it. "Never mind. Look. There's really nothing to worry about. If anything ever happens to me—anything at all—you and the children will be well provided for." His back was turned to her. "Very well provided for."

"That's not what I'm worrying about—"

"I got Dad to buy you a newspaper. Don't forget that. I've never denied you anything."

"Kevin, please! What's the matter with you?"

He turned around, folding his arms. The delicate face remained placid. "You called Eddie. You told him before you told me."

Aurelia was too stunned to speak.

"That stupid little assistant of his can't keep a secret to save her life. I'll bet half of Harlem knows. Unfortunately, it's our half."

Our half. She remembered one of Matty's lessons: *I'm a conservative because I trust people more than government. Kevin's a conservative because he thinks he's better than other people. His kind seems more popular than my kind these days.*

"I—I thought he could help—"

He rode right over her. "The truth is, you wish you'd married Eddie instead of me."

"Kevin, I do not!"

"Except for the money, you'd have married him."

"That's not true!" She was on her feet but dared not close the distance. "Why would you say that? I'm with you because I want to be."

"You certainly have a peculiar way of showing it."

"I told you. I was trying to help."

He nodded, less in agreement than in acceptance. "Never mind, honey. Come on. Let's go to bed."

Their lovemaking was desperate, at least on her side. Aurelia did not know which of them she was trying to persuade. She only knew that the convulsive physicality between them was the single means of persuasion left. Afterward, she clung to her husband, whispering whatever words of reassurance she could think of. That she had no regrets. That she didn't care about the money. That she would never betray him. That she respected him and supported him.

But she never said she loved him, and they both knew it.

(I V)

KENNEDY WON THE ELECTION, the closest in decades. To the Garlands, it was a matter of faith that the candidate's father had bought votes for him, especially in Chicago. Aurelia did not know what to believe. She was surprised at how little she cared. She cared about her children, and saving her marriage. Callie had voted for Kennedy, and burbled for days. Aurelia had voted for Nixon, but only because he had been so sweet at Matty's dinner.

A week after the election, she and Kevin ran into Eddie at Amaretta Veazie's salon. Possibly this was an error: every hostess in Harlem knew better than to invite the three on the same evening. Or maybe it was just Amaretta being mischievous, because she could from time to time break just as many rules as her daughter, Mona. Still, on this particular night, everything at first was fine. Eddie announced to the group his pending move to Washington in January with the new Administration. He would still write, but he would also be working half-time as second man in the White House office of speechwriting. People clapped him on the back. Eddie grinned. Kevin, watching events, said it might be nice just once to have a President who wrote his own speeches. And his own books, Kevin added. Eddie leaped to his man's defense, but Amaretta, with difficulty, changed the subject. Aurelia walked into another room. Amaretta owned a famous collection of mirrors. Aurie seated herself beside an antique cheval and stared at her reflection, wishing she and the Aurelia beyond the glass could change places for a while. Chamonix Bing sat down next to Aurie. Since Sherilyn's move to New Jersey, Chammie was the principal gossip in their set.

"Heard the latest?"

"No."

"Well," Chammie began, and was off.

There was a rumor, she said, that Mona was pregnant, and not married—thus her mother's despair. Aurie did not reply. She had recently made a trip to Cleveland, to visit the nuns who had raised her, followed by several days in Chicago. Mona wanted to come back east, but not to Harlem. Together, the two women had plotted strategy. The move would be tricky, and Aurie was not about to share her best friend's secrets. Chammie went on to other gossip, some of it involving Eddie and Torie Elden, who had also worked on the Kennedy campaign. Aurelia offered the haughtiest smile she could manage, and murmured the proper responses by rote.

"Torie always did have a thing for him. I'm surprised she's not here tonight, the hussy, holding on to him for dear life."

"Mmmm-hmmm."

Chammie continued talking, and Aurie stopped listening. She was a married woman, she told herself. She must not think what she was thinking. She closed her eyes and tried to dream of Kevin's best smile, annoyed that she kept seeing Eddie's.

Her husband's cry brought Aurelia back to an awareness of her surroundings.

She rushed back to the drawing room, certain she would find the two men wrestling. A grinning Chammie Bing, obviously hoping for exactly that, was at her heels.

Kevin was standing in the middle of the room, swaying on his feet. Eddie was one of several people crowded close. Kevin was sobbing. His cousin Oliver was holding him. Aurelia was certain Oliver had not been present when she left the room fifteen minutes ago. She took her husband in her arms, but Kevin could not speak. Oliver had to tell Aurie the news.

Matty Garland was dead.

"His heart?" she gasped, remembering his weight.

Not his heart, and, as it turned out, not natural causes of any kind.

The body of Matthew Garland, who had missed a dinner engagement with potential investors, had been discovered in a Queens motel, not far from the airport. He had been knifed, multiple times. The motel was known to be frequented by prostitutes.

Over the next few days, piecing together the story from witnesses who heard through the thin walls, the detectives concluded that the Negro in question had refused to pay for services rendered, taken a swing at the pimp, and gotten the worse end of the deal. Several of the girls identified the victim as a regular. The police put out a net for a few known characters and caught nobody.

Wanda, the hysterical widow, kept insisting that her husband had never been with a prostitute in his life. Leaving her fancy house, the detectives shook experienced heads. Wives, they told each other. They're always the last to know.

Then the pimp turned up dead. The detectives closed the case.

CHAPTER 28

Again the Testament

(1)

AURELIA LEANED OVER THE PLUMBER, watching with grim fascination as he reassembled the furnace by the dim yellowy light of the basement bulb. At the customer's insistence, he had examined every piece, cleaning even the ones just installed at the last overhaul. He kept shaking his head. He was potbellied and mustached and unhappy to be kneeling on this concrete floor for the fourth time in the past two weeks.

"There's nothin wrong, Mrs. Garland. I'm sorry."

"There has to be."

He moved his toothpick to the other cheek. "The oil pump's fine, the filter is clean, she's drawin fine, she's firin on demand—I don't know what else to check."

Aurie hugged herself, rubbing her upper arms. She was wearing two sweaters, and lately made the children go around the house the same way. It was May, and, supposedly, spring, but she had never felt so cold in her life. "Maybe the ducts are clogged," she suggested as he screwed the panel shut.

"I checked the temperature on all the vents last time I was here."

"Would you check again, please?"

"All of them?"

"If you can. I'd be grateful."

He grumbled, but did as she asked, because Mrs. Garland was not a bad sort, and when she called in the middle of the night she paid his double-time without complaint, and added an extra fifty for his trouble. Still—as he told his wife later—there must be somethin wrong with her. The temperature was in the sixties or seventies every day, the eighties twice last week, and here she was complainin. Maybe she was one of those Southern Negroes, his wife suggested. Maybe she would feel more comfortable in the tropics. She had read about the tropics in *National Geographic*, and noticed that the Negroes who lived there wore hardly any clothes.

No, said her husband. It's not that. Mrs. Finnerty right next door says she's from Cleveland, and I guess it gets pretty cold out there. Besides, it's not cold. It's hot. I think she's not right in the head.

Well, none of them are, really, his wife agreed. Her gaze fell on *Reader's Digest*, open to a picture of Edward Wesley. This one has a sister who's some kind of mad bomber: because by this time the truth of Commander M's identity had become public property.

"I'm not talkin about crazy people like that. I'm talkin about people right here in town."

They argued on into the night.

(11)

AURELIA WOULD HAVE BEEN the first to agree with the plumber. She was not right in the head. Not even close. In the six months since Matthew Garland's murder, she had never felt warm. It was as if the sun had winked out. She had her children, and gazed at them, and felt blessed. But at night, when they slept, she found the temperature falling. No matter how high she turned the heat. No matter what lie she read on the thermostat. The house grew colder and colder. She had not realized how much warmth Matty brought. Wanda, his widow, never came by. For several weeks after the funeral, Aurelia had driven up to Dobbs Ferry every few days, trying to build a relationship to replace the one with Matty. Her mother-in-law dutifully served her tea in the parlor, sitting stiffly, staring straight ahead, bearing Aurelia's murmured kindnesses with the stoicism of the tortured. Soon Aurie stopped going.

Kevin, meanwhile, was busier than ever. He left early. He stayed out late. He worked weekends. He was the first to admit that he could never run Garland & Son as his father had. Matty had relied on charisma, on the almost physical power of his personality. Lacking his father's devastating charm, Kevin substituted intelligence and dedication. He was always exhausted. Yet, when around the house, he was always solicitous, as if his wife, not he himself, had suffered the loss. Aurelia saw the absurdity of her behavior but could not seem to help herself. Callie Finnerty recommended a new baby as a tonic. Aurie and Kevin tried when they could, but without result.

"If you worry all the time like this, you'll never get pregnant," said Callie. "Worry messes up your system."

But Aurelia had known plenty of women who had worried themselves straight into the maternity wards, and said so.

She wished she had someone else to talk to. Alas, she spent too little time at Columbia to make friends there. Her Harlem coterie had scattered, Eddie was at the White House, and Mona Veazie, her dearest buddy, was in the process of planning her move from Chicago to New Hampshire, where next year she would become an assistant professor of psychology at Dartmouth. She had borne twins—all Harlem marveled—but she had never brought them home to her mother's house, and evidently had no plans to. Mona was currently divorcing the father, Amaretta told the other Czarinas, without more than a modicum of shame, this being the modern era. He had not, Amaretta confided, treated her very well.

Mona had enough to bear already.

So Aurelia turned the thermostat above eighty, despite the season, wore extra sweaters, and spent as much time as possible indoors.

Once, Kevin had to go away for a couple of days. His cousin Derek had been beaten and arrested in Anniston, Alabama, where he was participating in the Freedom Rides, protesting bus segregation. Kevin was part of a group of businessmen and lawyers who planned to sort things out. Aurie found herself terrified that her husband would wind up in jail, too.

"Why do you have to go? He's Oliver's brother, not yours."

"Oliver won't have anything to do with him."

"Derek's a grown man. He knew what he was getting into."

"I'm a grown man, too," said Kevin, and, kissing her, went.

While Kevin was gone, Eddie called excitedly from Washington. He wanted Aurelia to be sure to watch the President's address to a joint session of Congress next week. Eddie was the principal author of his speech.

"What's he going to talk about?"

"It's a secret."

"Trust me."

"Putting a man on the moon. A commitment to be there by the end of the decade."

Aurelia was wordstruck. "Are you serious?"

"Completely."

"They're beating the Freedom Riders. My husband's cousin is in jail, and my husband might be tomorrow, and you're happy that Kennedy wants to put a man on the moon?"

Eddie hesitated. "Aurelia, listen. I'm sure Kevin is fine. But you're going to read in the paper tomorrow that there was more violence in Anniston."

The chill was seeping into her bones. "More?"

"You know somebody firebombed a bus last week, right? Well, tonight somebody put a couple of bullets through the bedroom window of the man who's supposed to be the local head of the Klan. Fortunately, the family was out at dinner, but, Aurie, here's the thing. The Bureau's telling us it was Jewel Agony."

"Jewel Agony?"

"I'm afraid so."

"Eddie, I'm so sorry," she said, knowing he would know what she meant.

Later that night, Aurelia went to the shelf in Kevin's study and pulled down their autographed copy of Eddie's third novel, published last year. The novel chronicled the rise and fall of a Harlem gangster named Redd, the inspiration obvious to anybody who knew Eddie's history. The critics had been underwhelmed, but the book was Eddie's biggest seller so far. She opened to the dedication page.

To Miranda.

Miranda, meaning Junie. She had been missing now for nearly four years.

"Poor Eddie," she said aloud. He was down there in the White House, had access to inside information, and his sister was still missing. His search had led nowhere. The best he could manage was to hear about her crimes after the fact and dedicate books to her.

The shelf was packed tight. She could not squeeze Eddie's novel back into its spot without pulling down several of the books on either side and starting over. Had she not taken down so many, she would have missed the envelope. But there it was, creamy white stationery, with her husband's name on the outside in an elegant hand. She wondered nervously if it might be from a woman.

It wasn't.

(I I I)

KEVIN ARRIVED HOME two days later, unscathed and rather proud of how much their delegation had accomplished. Aurelia listened to his stories, nodding at what she hoped were the right moments. Actually, she was pleased for him. She mixed a second round of martinis, toasted him. Running the firm was giving him so much trouble, but, somehow, Alabama had ended in triumph. Maybe his easygoing style was better suited to political negotiation than to scrabbling for fees on Wall Street.

Not that she would ever say so.

After dinner, Kevin read to the children while Aurelia watched from the doorway. In bed later, she raised the question that had been in her mind since she opened the envelope.

"Remember years ago, honey? When we went to London?"

Her husband nodded. "We should go again. We will. Just as soon as I get things settled at the office."

"That would be fun." She hesitated. Outside, the wind had freshened, a cold front moving forcefully in. Aurie loved thunder showers, and hoped for one. "But that's not what I wanted to ask." She took a breath, then plunged. "What I wondered was—well, remember how you told me you were trying to clean up the mess Phil Castle left behind?"

He stiffened in her arms. "I should never have mentioned it—"

"Kevin, please. This is important."

"What is?"

"Did you ever find it?"

"Find what?"

"Whatever Castle left behind."

This time Kevin made her wait. She knew he was turning history over in his mind, trying to recall just how much he had disclosed in London. The windows shuddered as the wind rose. Finally, he said, "It wasn't illegal, honey. If that's what you're driving at. The business with Phil and my father—well, it wasn't illegal. Not strictly speaking."

Aurelia had the wit to say nothing.

"I know I scared you back in those days, Aurie. I'm so sorry. It's just—what Phil left behind—I had to try to find it. I owed that to my family. Can you understand that?"

"Sure, honey."

"The details—well, I just went where my father told me. I met the people he told me to meet."

She hid her surprise, but had to ask. "Matty knew what you were doing?"

"I followed his instructions to the letter." He seemed, briefly, proud of himself. "As to the rest, well, I didn't know until Dad died what was going on." A shiver. She nestled closer, kissed his jaw. "I can't tell you any more, honey. I'm sorry."

"I'm your wife, Kevin. You're supposed to trust me." He said nothing. The panes rattled harder. "Please, honey. I have to know. All of this secrecy—it's driving me crazy."

To her surprise, he chuckled. "Crazy, as in curious? Or as in nuts?"

"Nuts," she said, but he had succeeded in making her laugh.

He yawned. "Why are you asking me just now? Did something happen? Did somebody come to the house asking questions?"

"No, honey. This is just me."

"What happened?" he repeated.

Aurelia sighed. In for a penny, in for a pound. She told him about taking the books down in the study and finding the envelope.

Kevin bore the news with his mother's stoicism. The first drops of rain spattered against the windows. "And what did you find, Aurie? In the envelope?"

"It was a note to you. I don't know who it was from. It just said— it said that, ah, in light of recent events, shaking the throne would have to be postponed. What does it mean?"

She felt the growing tension as her husband turned toward her. "Do you believe I love you? You and the kids?"

"Completely," she repeated.

"Good. Because I love the three of you more than anything in the world. I would never let anything happen to you. But you're not telling me the whole truth, are you?"

"What do you mean?"

The rain was lashing the house. If thunder began, the children would likely wake and run to their parents' bed. Aurie wanted things settled before that happened. Evidently, so did her husband.

"The envelope shouldn't have been there," Kevin said. "It's not your fault, honey. It's mine. I should have locked it in my office safe, but I had to go out of town to take care of Derek, and, well, I thought it would be secure in my study for a week. And it would have been, if you hadn't snooped."

"I wasn't snooping!"

He kissed her. "I believe you. You were just curious. But it never occurred to you that the note might refer to, say, a corporate merger or political fund-raising."

"Is that what it refers to?"

"You know it isn't or you wouldn't have asked. You found a note about shaking the throne, and then you asked me about Philmont Castle. How do you know the two are connected?"

Aurelia could not come up with a story. No willed imagination this time. In the distance she heard the first rising peals of thunder.

"I'll tell you why you made the connection. Because you broke into my office safe years ago and read everything." His voice was less angry than rueful. "I always suspected, Aurie. Matty gave you the combination, didn't he? You read the notes about the Project. You've kept quiet about it all these years—unless you've told Eddie—but you read them. Do you have copies?"

"No," she said, miserably.

"Does Eddie know what you found?"

"No."

"Good. That's our only break. Now, listen, honey. Are you listening?"

She felt tears on her cheeks. She was frightened. Not of her husband. For her husband.

"Yes, Kevin. I'm listening."

His face was very close. "You never broke into my safe. Never. You never opened the envelope in my study. Never. You've never heard of shaking the throne or the Author or Pandemonium. Never. You won't ever mention any of this to a soul. Are we clear?"

"Yes, but—"

"Don't say 'but.' Don't ask any more questions. I've told you what I can. Yes, there is a Project. It's gone off the tracks. Philmont Castle made a mess of things. He left a letter somewhere—the testament—and if the testament comes out, well, it could cause trouble for important people. I was asked to find it, and I couldn't. They gave the job to somebody else. That's all there is. We won't mention it again."

"Who gave the job to somebody else?"

"I can't tell you that."

More rumbling, ever closer. The rain fell like bullets. Shivering, Aurelia reminded herself that she loved this kind of weather.

"But why you, honey? Can you tell me that much?"

"Because I'm who I am." He spoke with a queer pride. "Because I'm my father's son." He kissed her again, so gently she felt lost. "Now, please, Aurie. Listen. This is important. You don't know anything. Remember that. Especially if—well, if anything happens to me."

"Kevin—"

"I'm not saying anything will happen. It's very unlikely. But if it does, well, it's like I keep telling you, honey. You and the children are provided for. Very well provided for. If anything does happen, your job is to raise the children, spend the money, and enjoy your life. Promise me."

"But how can you just—"

"Promise me, honey."

Aurelia argued for a while, but in the end promised. And just in time. The thunderheads broke over the house, the roof shuddered, and the children, right on cue, came flying into their parents' bedroom.

The four of them snuggled together until morning.

CHAPTER 29

A Choice Is Made

(1)

EDDIE LIKED WASHINGTON. It was an old city that thought itself new. Every few years it was remade in the image of a new President, who brought with him thousands of supporters to take up thousands of jobs. The Congress was constantly reconfiguring itself. And each year young people flocked into town, college graduates, their degrees still spanking new, searching for work in the federal government, or in its many symbiotic bacteria: law firms, lobbying firms, public-relations firms, newspapers. All needed fresh talent. There were major universities and minor colleges. "Anybody who can't find a job here," said Byron Dennison, a powerful Negro member of Congress whom Eddie had befriended in the campaign, "doesn't deserve one."

Eddie rented a two-story brick town home on I Street (that is, "Eye" Street), in the section of the city known in those days as the New Southwest: a featureless sea of freshly constructed if unimaginative row houses of stout brick, sprinkled with uninspired apartment buildings, all surrounded by more brand-new row houses and apartment buildings, and huge tracts recently cleared to build more of the same. The New Southwest had been constructed, through the genius of urban planning, where colorful working-class neighborhoods had once thrived. Its borders were the Potomac River, a hideous interstate highway, and a massive public-housing project. Every morning, the men rose to walk to work or take the bus or, in a few instances, drive. Eddie usually went to the White House the first three days of the work week. On Thursdays and Fridays, he also rose early, but to write.

On Friday, the second of February, 1962, he slipped out of bed around six. The house was warm. The oil furnace was new and far more efficient than the coal furnace that had heated the building on Convent Avenue. He stood in the window, looking down on the grassy median separating the backyards of the townhouses in his row from the backyards of the townhouses across the way. Last week, Eddie had spotted a man in the early hours, standing back there and looking up at his bedroom. Or at least he thought he had. When he looked twice, the man was gone. But he spotted him at other times, too. Last week, in a crowd outside a movie theater, hat pulled low to disguise his face. Last night, in a checkout line at the Safeway, head turned carefully away so that, no matter what angle Eddie took, he could not see the man's face.

"Is he there?" murmured Torie Elden, from the bed.

"No," said Eddie. "Go back to sleep."

"Are you sure?"

"Yes."

Instead, she hopped up, crossed the room, stood behind him. Her hand on his back was affectionate but tentative, the touch of a woman who knows that her man is in love with someone else, and that her own perch in his life is so precarious that the stiff wind of a single argument would blow her away.

"What about in the supermarket last night?" she persisted, kissing the back of his neck. "Are you sure that was him?"

"Yes."

"And all you can say for sure is that he's white and he has blond hair and he looks kind of familiar?"

"Yes."

Another kiss. She pressed against him from behind. "Do you want to come back to bed?"

"I can't."

"Are you sure?"

"I have to work, Torie. I'm sorry."

She nodded, her hair rubbing his shoulders. "Because in half an hour I have to start getting ready for work. It's lucky I left a few things here last time, huh?"

"Very," he said, not looking at her.

About to say more, Torie released him and headed for the bathroom. Years ago, she had been considered a devastating beauty, one of Harlem's most eligible bachelorettes. Then she had made a couple of bad bets, and now, at thirty-two, Torie was unmarried, and childless, and desperate, because as the Czarinas measured time she was already an old maid. She had her college degree and had worked on the Kennedy campaign, hoping to find true love. Instead, she had found Eddie, and even though, by dint of constant effort, she successfully penetrated his I-love-Aurelia reserve, Torie had never managed to dig any deeper. They both knew she never would. She stayed with Eddie a night or two each week. In an hour she would be off to work at the Labor Department, where she helped do the unemployment numbers, and one of these mornings, she would collect the things she had "luckily" left in Eddie's house, take them when she headed out, and not come back.

Eddie felt bad. He was using her. Torie liked to say that they both needed companionship, and were therefore using each other. But their situations were not the same, and both knew it.

Never mind. Just now, he could not worry about it. He had to patrol the bedroom windows, in case the blond man showed up. One more sighting, Eddie kept telling himself. One more sighting, and he would surely remember where he had seen the man before.

(I I)

THE BACK of the house held the dining room. Sliding glass doors opened to the cheap patio. This was where Eddie did his writing, on the dining-room table, in jeans and short sleeves. He still wrote on yellow pads. He would start at the beginning and end at the end and never go back to change a single word until he delivered the manuscript to a typist. Only then would he actually read it as a whole, for the first time. He wrote presidential speeches the same way, with the important difference that his early drafts were usually read by other people. Ted Sorensen had the final word.

Eddie had not been sure whether working even half-time at the White House would leave him time for serious writing, but his discipline kept him going. Even in the evenings, he rarely went out. Now and then he might grab lunch with David Yee, now in the Washington Bureau of the *Times,* or Gary Fatek when he came through town, or any of the old crowd from Harlem. But only lunch. At dinnertime, nearly every night, he wrote. The main reason Torie came over no more than twice a week was that Eddie wanted no distractions. Once, she had dropped by without warning him first. The wrath in his face had kept her from trying the same trick a second time. Probably she thought him cruel. To Eddie's way of thinking, it was his muse that was cruel. The next novel would be his fourth, and four, he hoped, would finally make him feel like a real writer.

While Torie dressed for work, Eddie pulled a pad in front of him, and picked up precisely where he had left off yesterday afternoon:

> *unless he wanted to be frozen out of society. Frozen out. That was what they called it. The salons were Harlem's warmth and the Czarinas drew up lists*

"I'll be going now."

Eddie turned. Torie stood in the hallway, dressed in a business suit. Her suitcase stood beside her. They stared at each other. He knew what she must think of him. He wished it were possible to touch another woman without seeing Aurelia, but it was not. Torie was the fourth woman to share his bed in the nearly seven years since Aurie's wedding. Each entanglement had been brief. Each had ended in quiet pain.

"I'm sorry," he said, standing up, closing the space between them.

"I know."

"I wish—"

"I know." A hug, sexless and sisterly. "Eddie?"

"Yes?"

"Sooner or later, you'll have to admit . . . Never mind." She straightened. Her eyes were dry. She even smiled. "Keep sweet," she said, and left.

Eddie stood in the kitchen. He almost called her back. It was a very near thing. But he would only have postponed the reckoning. Better to have it behind him.

He returned to the table. He wrote for another hour and a half, until a knock on the sliding glass disturbed him. He stopped, and looked up, annoyed.

Special Agent Bernard Stilwell was peering in.

(111)

EDDIE MADE TEA while the agent made himself at home. The dining-room table was empty again. Eddie had asked Stilwell to wait, then collected his yellow pad and put it away on a shelf before inviting him in.

But Stilwell did not seem to be in the mood to nose around. He switched on the small black-and-white Zenith television. A game show. The agent turned the knob, raising the volume, and when Eddie returned to the table, Stilwell had him sit close.

"Do you enjoy the White House?"

"Yes."

"And Kennedy? You like him?"

"I do. Yes. What do you want, Agent Stilwell?"

"You can call me Bernie." He sipped his tea rather daintily. His fingers, like his body, were very long. "We've been friends for so many years."

"We're not friends."

Stilwell smiled his devil's smile. The dark brows danced. "Have some information for you. The Director wanted to make sure you had it first, before you have to read it in the papers. The Kennedy people won't tell you."

Eddie was a moment catching his breath. "Junie? Is it Junie? Is she—"

"It's not about your sister. Oh, don't worry, Eddie. We'll find her.

We've been close a couple of times, but she skipped town ahead of us. But before too long, Eddie, you can talk to her over a table just like this. I promise. Of course, the two of you won't be hugging, with the bars between you and all."

And he laughed his nasty laugh.

Eddie spoke coldly. "What do you want, Agent Stilwell?"

"Remember that U-2 pilot that got himself shot down over Soviet Russia year before last? Name of Powers?"

"Vaguely."

"And the spy you helped us catch back in '57? Name of Rudolf Abel?"

"Yes," said Eddie, remembering the long pink envelope he still possessed, the one Abel—then known as Emil Goldfus—had tried to get him to collect. *His wife has it.* Eddie was nowhere nearer translating the phrase, although at least he knew from Aurelia what the *it* had to be. Eddie had tried three times to get permission to visit Abel in prison, to press him on the Project, but his requests had been denied. "I remember, Agent Stilwell."

"They're being exchanged."

"I'm sorry?"

"One week from now, in Berlin. They're giving us Powers. We're giving them Colonel Abel."

"You're joking."

"No."

Eddie felt the room constricting, another avenue cut off. He had imagined somehow that, with the additional prestige of his White House job, he might yet be allowed in to see Colonel Abel. Now that avenue was closed.

"I see," he said, when he was himself again. He longed to be free of Stilwell, and get back to work. "Was there anything else?"

"Tell me what you think of your President."

Eddie framed his answer with care. He knew that whatever he said would go directly into Hoover's files. "I admire him. I think he could do great things for the country."

Stilwell snickered. "Huh. Heard that one before. Great things.

They'll all do great things, if you listen to their speeches. Then they get in there and rob the place blind. How's his health?"

"What?"

"There's a story out there that he's lying about his health."

Eddie forced a calm, delivered the line already crafted for careful leaking to reporters as the question arose. "That was a campaign smear concocted by the Johnson people. The truth is—"

"So—what about the women?"

"I beg your pardon?"

"The Director is interested in anything you hear about Kennedy's women. And about his health. Anything you can find out."

Eddie sat straighter. "You can't possibly expect—"

"You want us to help you find your sister, right? Well, then, this is what we want in return."

"You're asking me to spy on the President of the United States?"

"Not to spy. To report. You never know where an issue of security will arise these days."

Eddie remembered a favored mantra of one of his professors. "You can call it reporting. You can call it Thucydides or you can call it banana peel, but it's spying all the same."

Stilwell yawned ostentatiously, then waved Eddie silent. "As it happens, we have some information for you." He pulled out another of his endless supply of leather notebooks. "Last fall, as you may or may not remember, somebody shot up a car belonging to a Klan leader just outside Tupelo. Ring a bell? They didn't hurt anybody, just shot his car to pieces. Our informants say it was Jewel Agony who did it, and your sister who got them to shoot the car instead of the man. And you know what happened? The Klan shot a civil-rights leader's car in retaliation. Only he was in it with his kids."

Eddie was on his feet, furious. "Are you saying that it is my sister's fault—"

"No." Stilwell towered over him. "I'm in law enforcement, Eddie. We always tend to think a shooting is the shooter's fault. Anyway, it's just an informer's report, and half of them are lies. More than half." He put on his hat. "Think it over, Eddie. And understand something. It makes no difference to me personally if you want to help us out on Kennedy. Tell us to go to Hell if you want. That's up to you. But remember, Eddie, we didn't have to give you a security clearance for the White House. What with your sister's situation, we could just as easily have flunked you." Arresting Eddie's reply with a raised finger: "One more thing. If you do decide to tell us to go to Hell? There's nothing we can do to force you. But the Director is a very vindictive man."

Eddie thought it over. Hoover was always trying to extend his influence. He plainly lacked sources in the Kennedy Administration and wanted them. He hoped to use Eddie's love for his sister as the lever that would crack open the Kennedy White House.

The following week, Eddie was seated in his basement cubicle beneath the West Wing when he had a call: the President wanted to see him. Eddie pulled on his suit coat and climbed the stairs. When he entered the Oval Office, Kennedy was just finishing a meeting. Eddie waited politely. Everyone else left. The President took his seat behind the Resolute desk and waved Eddie to an armchair. For a moment neither man spoke. Jack Kennedy was tall and slim, with wide challenging eyes and a way of going very still when he gave you the full weight of his attention. Eddie felt that weight now. Despite his affable and charming public persona, Kennedy was deadly serious about the work of leading both the nation and the Free World. This seriousness was part of what Eddie so admired. Yet Eddie was nervous. For all his admiration of Jack Kennedy, the writer had spent little time alone with him.

"I'd like your advice," said the President.

"Of course, sir."

"Off the record."

"Yes, sir."

"Too many leaks, Eddie. Information everywhere. Security's all to hell." He lifted a newspaper, then tossed it aside. "Every bureaucrat whose responsibilities allow him to learn the confidences of this government seems to think it's his right and duty to call the nearest reporter. We could never have won the war this way."

"Yes, sir." Eddie wondered if the President knew about Stilwell's visit. And if protocol allowed him to bring it up.

"Allen Dulles wrote me." Kennedy gestured to a letter on his desktop. "Dulles says we need an Official Secrets Act. Like the British have. They tell me it would be unconstitutional, but we have to do something, Eddie. The leaks are getting out of hand."

"Yes, sir."

"Yes, meaning, you agree?"

Eddie shook his head. "No, Mr. President. I don't agree. With all due respect to Director Dulles, I think it's a terrible idea."

"You don't think people should be punished for telling our secrets?"

"If you catch the leaker, yes. But not the newspaperman who prints what he's told. No, sir." About to embark on a disquisition about the importance of free speech to democracy, Eddie read in those thoughtful eyes the message that a lecture would not be welcome. Besides, he sensed that he was merely speaking the President's own thoughts. So he said instead, "I think you as President have the right to expect that the people in whom you confide will not pass what you say on to others. I agree with that strongly, sir."

The appointments secretary came in. The President had to run.

That night, Eddie walked for hours along the Mall, working things through. He told himself that Hoover, three years after Maxton, was only stringing him along. But even if the Director really planned to trade information on Junie for dirt on Kennedy, Eddie knew that he could not be a part of wrecking the Administration of the only President he had admired in his lifetime. And so, two days later, he resigned his post. He kept the house on I Street, but severed all contact with the White House. He publicly wished Kennedy well, and explained to his astonished friends that he needed to devote more time to his writing.

"You think you're clever," said Stilwell afterward, the two of them walking along the Mall.

"Not often. Sometimes."

"You do understand this terminates our deal."

"Yes."

"No more protection."

"Protection?" Eddie thought again of the blond man, the face so familiar. "You've been protecting me? From what?"

The agent did not deign to answer. "No more protection, and no more information."

"Maybe I'll do better on my own."

Stilwell laughed, and clapped him on the shoulder. "You know something, Eddie? Everybody thinks they will. But hardly anybody ever does."

CHAPTER 30

The Chess Player

(1)

In November of 1962, Richard Nixon's campaign for governor of his native California ended in heavy defeat. The next morning, wild-eyed and sleepless, Nixon made a surprise appearance at his hotel before the reporters who had covered the campaign. Nixon did not like the press. The press did not like him. Nixon thought he had been smeared by journalists when he ran for President two years earlier, losing to Kennedy in one of the closest elections in history. The press thought it had told the nation only the unsavory truth. Now Nixon looked around the room at the assembled reporters. He told them it was fine to give the candidate the shaft if they disliked him, but added that they should put one "lonely" man on the beat who would just report what was said. He concluded, "You won't have Nixon to kick around any more, because, gentlemen, this is my last press conference." Everyone believed him, many with pleasure. Syndicated columnists buried his career. ABC News even ran a night-time special titled *The Political Obituary of Richard Nixon*. Newspaper cartoonists despaired, for they had loved his jowly face and long, curving nose.

As it happened, Edward Wesley Junior was in the back of the room when the former Vice President made his announcement. Eddie was covering the campaign for *The Nation*, where he had a contract to write four essays a year on politics. He was not sure what to say about Nixon.

By this time, Eddie was a huge name. His fourth novel had made his literary reputation. Entitled *Netherwhite*, it told the story of an obsessive social climber who, rejected by the Negro upper classes, resorted to violence, waging a one-man guerrilla war until cut down by the police. The book opened with a line that was later so often quoted that people forgot where it came from: "Plotting revenge can be such wonderful therapy." Langston Hughes, who never stopped loving Harlem, had urged Eddie not to publish it, but Eddie's judgment had proved correct. The white critics praised its sharp satiric eye, not realizing that everything Eddie wrote about Harlem he meant literally. The critics did not believe, even after reading the novel, that a wealthy black society actually existed in the secret uptown shadows of their own. This was the liberal era in our politics, and the Negro was understood by all to be poor, oppressed, and in special need of white solicitude. The Negro was a seamstress refusing to move to the back of the bus. The Negro was a sharecropper stymied by a literacy test for voting. And for once Eddie's political judgment proved superior to his mentor's. The Harlem society biddies, as he called them not only behind their backs but also in print, were enchanted. Delighted to be the subjects of a serious novel, they played round upon round of "who's who," skewering each other happily with Eddie's furious words. *Jet* magazine ran a column guessing at the true identities of his characters—and, in most cases, getting them right.

But Eddie, as usual, put accomplishment behind him. The novel was old news. Now he was worried about the Nixon story. How could it be that he was seeing what everyone was missing? The day after his return from California, Eddie went sailing on the Chesapeake Bay with Gary Fatek. The weather was atrocious, but this time Eddie was properly dressed for it.

"There's something wrong with the way the story is being covered," he told Gary, shouting as waves battered the sloop. "People are missing Nixon's tragedy. The pathos."

"Erebeth loves him," Gary shouted back. "She still thinks the Commies are hiding under the bed."

"What I'm saying is, there's an angle here we're overlooking. We all say we hate Nixon so much. Ambitious schemer, no principles, anything to win."

"Sounds right."

"But isn't that all of us?" Eddie shouted. Gary looked at him. "Doesn't Nixon somehow represent America? We're a nation of winners." A wave drenched him. "We want leaders who win, and we don't care how they do it."

Gary handed him a rope from somewhere, told him to hold it, stepped over Eddie's arm, took it back. The sail jumped, then filled afresh. Gary told Eddie to tie down the line, and Eddie remembered, more or less, how to do it.

"This isn't about Nixon, is it?" said Gary. On their new tack, the noise was suddenly less. "It's about Aurelia."

Eddie looked up. "Aurelia?"

"Sure. She's a Nixon fan, right? A big one. Her father-in-law was a Nixon backer, so is her husband, and Aurie thinks the world of him. That's why you can't see him as a monster, Eddie. Because it would betray Aurie."

"Then why didn't I support Nixon to begin with?"

"Maybe a rivalry with Kevin. I don't know."

"Come on, Gary. You can't have it both ways!"

But the smile on his old friend's face suggested that Gary did not care which way he had it, as long as he got under Eddie's skin. Over the past year or two, the old friends had more and more gotten on each other's nerves. Gary had withdrawn from his former life. Eddie no longer had any idea how his classmate spent his time, and Gary never volunteered.

"Write the essay the way you want," said Gary as they scudded toward shore. "Just be ready for the firestorm."

And a firestorm there was. The essay ran to sixteen hundred words. *The Nation* titled it "Dick Nixon, All-American." Angry mail poured in from the right, where, interestingly, Eddie's point came across with crystal clarity: by arguing that Nixon embodied the American character, he was insulting Americans, not complimenting Nixon. But the magazine's readership was mostly on the left, and nearly everybody seemed to interpret Eddie's words the other way around: he was pro-Nixon!

Soon people who had never read the essay—and never heard of

Eddie—were absolutely certain they understood his argument. And, mostly, they hated his argument, and therefore, in keeping with American tradition, hated him, too. Thus was Edward Wesley Junior labeled, for the next period of his career, a conservative. There was even an abortive move to take back his National Book Award.

"It's not so bad," said Aurelia, when Eddie ran into her at the opening of an art exhibition in New York just after Christmas. She was alone, looking tall and beautiful and utterly devoted to her husband. "They've been calling Kevin a conservative for years."

"Kevin *is* a conservative."

"Well, yes. But the way they say it, they make it sound so dirty." Aurie brightened. "Speaking of Kevin, he's so proud of Kennedy now. The way he faced down Khrushchev and made him take those missiles out of Cuba. Personally, I was scared to death. I thought we were about to have World War Three. But Kevin loved it. He even says he might support a Democrat next time around."

"Wonderful," said Eddie, forcing a smile.

Afterward he helped her find a taxi. He was too savvy to offer to share.

"I'm sorry about you and Torie," she said, standing by the open door. "You would have been a great match."

"That was over months ago."

"The grapevine's a lot slower than it used to be." A cheery smile. "So—who's special now? In your life, I mean?"

"I'm too busy for romance," he said, the line he always used, usually when fending women off.

"Silly man," she said, and touched his cheek with her gloved hand. "You need to find yourself a silly woman and settle down."

He watched the cab drive away. He saw Aurelia dip her face into her hands, but she probably had something in her eye.

(11)

EDDIE WAS A MAN of two cities now. Despite his departure from the Kennedy Administration, he had kept the house on I Street, unwilling to be separated too far from the President he so admired. But he had never surrendered the apartment on Convent Avenue, and stayed there on his frequent visits to New York. After seeing Aurelia off, however, he did not return to Harlem at once. He had a man to see, a source he had known from the beginning he would need.

He took the train to Brooklyn, where he knocked on the door of a basement apartment in a dank, crumbling building near Eastern Parkway. Derek Garland answered the door. There were three rooms, all cluttered with books. The two men sat at the battered table sipping a Russian vodka so bland you could almost taste the potatoes. Derek was a Harlem legend. He was also a madman. His face was suspicious and sweaty. He lived this way because he had trouble holding a job, and he had trouble holding a job because his politics kept landing him in front of congressional committees, or in jail. He refused as a matter of ideological conviction to accept his family's offers of assistance, offers that lately came less and less frequently. He had announced for the last several years his impending move to Ghana but had yet to show the gumption to do it. Nobody Eddie knew lived closer to America's radical fringe, and it was to the radical fringe that Eddie, from the moment he received the photograph of Junie toting a rifle, had known he would sooner or later have to go.

Eddie began with the truth. It was he who had turned in Emil Goldfus, also known as Rudolf Abel, whom Derek had brought to Aurelia's wedding seven years ago. He had protected Derek himself out of loyalty to the cause: he knew Derek liked that sort of talk. Now he was asking to be paid back. He had to get in touch with Jewel Agony. Anticipating Derek's response, he hastened to add that this had nothing to do with turning anybody in. His reasons, he said, were personal. All the while, Derek poured and drank and stared.

"This is about your sister," Derek said once he heard Eddie out.

"Yes."

"I can't help you." He wiped his sleeve across his mouth. "Those people are crazy."

"What people?"

Derek Garland had a way of opening his hazel eyes very wide behind the thick glasses while he took time to think. The goggling look made him seem stupid, but Eddie knew he was very much the opposite. Behind that strange face was a stranger brain. He had been the many-time chess champion of the Metropolitan, the private Negro social club in Sugar Hill, before denouncing the venue as a petit-bourgeois distraction. His ascetic face wore permanent bruises, and his movements were jerky. People said he had never been the same since nearly dying in a Southern jail; and only a madman would have returned for more, as Derek Garland regularly did.

"The thing about these Agony types," said Derek calmly, as if he had not been staring into space for the past few minutes, "is that they'll shoot you. Shoot you with a *gun*," he added, in case Eddie had been worried about artillery fire.

"They won't shoot me," said Eddie.

"Anyway, I don't know any of them."

"But you know who to ask."

A pause. "Maybe." His eyes leaped at something on the far wall, and Eddie turned to look but saw only shadows and, through the window, passing headlights. "I'm moving to Ghana," Derek continued in the same even tone as before. "Or Moscow. First, though, I'm getting married."

Eddie tried to catch his gaze for a congratulatory smile. "Who's the lucky lady?"

"I don't know yet. I have to find one." His tone was perfectly serious.

"Well, I wish you well."

"I wish you well, too. But be careful, lest you get cast into the fiery pit." An unexpected burst of laughter. He laughed for a very long time, hands over his ample stomach, rocking in his tottering chair. Then, as if a switch had been thrown, he was calm again. "Not that the fiery pit is so bad. I hear the people who live down there are always dreaming big dreams. Not that I believe in God myself. Or is it God who doesn't believe in me?" He frowned, nibbling at his scarred lip, and seemed genuinely to be trying to work this one out.

"Funny thing about God. He only shows up in churches. He's never around when they're feeding His people to the lions."

"I've often had the same thought," said Eddie, very surprised.

"Then you're a damned fool," retorted Derek, with satisfaction.

"I'm sorry?"

"You think God isn't watching?" Voice rolling like Wesley Senior's. "You think God doesn't know? You think—" Just like that, Derek was calm again. "Tell you something about your Agony friends. They're not afraid of the lions or the hellfire. Martyr complex. Your sister probably has one, too."

"I doubt that very much," said Eddie, indignantly. But he wondered.

Derek was not even interested. "Listen. Met somebody in jail years ago. In there for the same thing as me, telling the HUAC fascists to go to Hell and take their committee with them. Man had this idea. Group like that. Raise some money, build them a camp somewhere. Train them. Start shooting things up, scaring people. Scare them enough, he said, and they'd do the right thing. Stupid. He wanted educated people only. College degrees. So they could see further than the huddled masses, et cetera. Serious ideological error, Eddie. Hadn't read his Lenin, obviously."

"What was the name?"

"Didn't have a name back then"—Eddie realized that Derek was talking about the group the man wanted to form, not the man himself—"but he wanted to get the Negroes involved. Prominent Negroes. White man. Professor of something."

"Professor where? And what was his name?"

"Doesn't matter. He's dead now."

"But what—"

"I'll see what I can do," Derek said. "I don't know those Agony people, but, if you have a martyr complex, too? Want to get yourself shot?—I'll see what I can do." He was escorting Eddie to the door. "Don't call me. Don't use your home phone. Not for any purpose. It's not a tap you should be worried about. They put bombs in phones these days—"

And, just like that, Eddie was out on the street.

Maybe he had put out a feeler. Maybe he had visited the asylum. And maybe he had done both.

A quick trip two days later to the Library of Congress confirmed what he already suspected: when Derek Garland and Alphaeus Hunton and Dashiell Hammett and Frederick Vanderbilt Field had all gone to prison in the early fifties for refusing to turn over the lists of those who had contributed to their defense fund, one of their fellow resisters, now deceased, had been a retired Harvard professor named Hamilton Mellor, whose son, Benjamin, had succeeded his father on the law faculty, and confessed to fathering Junie's baby.

The next morning, Eddie sat in a booth in the basement of the fortresslike Riggs Bank on Pennsylvania Avenue, across the street from the Treasury Department. Here, in a safe-deposit box, he kept the most important records from his search. He opened the appropriate folder and slipped in the jottings from his trip to the Library of Congress. Before putting the file away, he glanced for perhaps the thousandth time at a peculiar note his sister had left up at Harvard Law School: *Thanks for everything. You're a good man.*

Eddie returned Junie's note to its place. Then, after a moment's hesitation, he withdrew for another look a two-month-old news clipping from the front page of the *Boston Globe* about the tragic loss off Cape Cod of Professor Benjamin Mellor when his boat capsized in a storm.

CHAPTER 31

Attica

(1)

IN JANUARY of 1963, George Wallace was inaugurated as governor of Alabama. Addressing the cheering throng at the State Capitol, he promised to get rid of the state's liquor agents, improve education, and bring in new jobs. He then went on to his main subject, promising to "toss the gauntlet before the feet of tyranny," and adding "Segregation now! . . . Segregation tomorrow! . . . Segregation forever!" In the salons of the darker nation, everyone thought the sky was falling. In March, Eddie published another essay in *The Nation*, quoting the part of Wallace's speech the press had omitted. The governor, he pointed out, had drawn attention to the hypocrisy of liberals who "fawn" over school integration but live in segregated neighborhoods. Eddie, whose view of his country still glimmered but was growing grimmer, had a different take. Wallace had not identified hypocrisy. He had identified humanity. None of us lived up to our ideals, he wrote, remembering another of his father's sermons. The hypocrite was not the man who failed. The hypocrite was the man who did not believe he was required to try.

"So are we liberals hypocrites or not?" demanded a young man he met at a party in Georgetown, a rather decrepit neighborhood that had become fashionable after the Kennedys moved in during the 1950s. "What are you saying?"

"That's not the point of the story," said Eddie.

But innocence dies nearly as hard as ignorance. "I'm for all kinds of integration," the man insisted. "Education, housing, you name it."

"Is that your wife over there?"

"Yes."

"And how many Negro women did you date before you married a white one?"

This was an unfair shot, and Eddie knew it, but he was angry at most of the world just now. The man stalked away. Somebody else came over with a question about the gangster novel. Eddie felt hemmed in. As it happened, he was attending the party with Torie Elden. They had managed to remain friends. They had set boundaries. Sometimes Torie told him stories about the men she dated, but most of the stories made her cry. More people crowded him. He was notorious. They all wanted to be able to say that they had talked to him. Eddie had never liked crowds. He told Torie they were going. As usual, he drove her to her apartment on Capitol Hill. As usual, she invited him in for coffee. He usually declined, but tonight he accepted. He woke around midnight and realized the scope of his error. He slipped out of bed and collected his things. Torie told him to be careful driving home in the snow. Evidently the blond man had expected Eddie to stay with her all night, because when Eddie got home his occasional watcher was ransacking the place. He ducked Eddie's wild swing and put him on the floor with a single punch. It was like being punched by an anvil. When the stars cleared, Eddie was alone.

A careful search disclosed nothing missing. Either the search had been interrupted too early, or the blond man had decided that what he sought was not there.

The police report was a formality. He filed it only because not filing would seem suspicious. Alas, he told the officers, he could not offer a description. He had not seen the man's face. Not in any detail. He remembered only the blond hair.

They told him he should get himself a dog, the way things were these days.

Almost everything Eddie had told the police was true. He had not seen the man's face. He did not think he would know the intruder if he saw him again. What Eddie had omitted to tell them was that he now remembered where he had seen the blond man before.

(11)

THE VISITING ROOM of the Attica Correctional Facility in upstate New York was painted a bright yellow-green and apparently white-washed regularly by trusties, because, aside from the indelible stink of the sweat of powerful but frustrated men, it lacked the grimy prison smells he expected. Eddie sat on a folding chair, watching the empty space on the other side of the shatterproof glass. It was an April morning of delicate loveliness. Three days ago, Martin Luther King and his associates had been jailed for contempt when they defied a court order forbidding them to march in Birmingham on Easter Sunday. Six different magazines had asked Eddie to go down and cover the story. But it had taken him weeks to arrange this meeting, and he was not going to miss it.

On the way to Attica, he had stopped in Manhattan, spending several nights at Convent Avenue, for the benefit of anyone who might be, at this late date, still dogging his steps. He found Harlem increasingly sad. Not depressing—merely sad. The salons were mostly gone. The Czarinas had scattered. Shirley Elden was dead. Enid Garland was sick, and had moved to midtown. Amaretta Veazie still held forth from her townhouse on Edgecombe Avenue, but word had it that Mona, who lived up in New Hampshire with her young twins, was trying to get her mother to move in with them.

Eddie visited Langston Hughes, whose health had deteriorated but who gamely hung on in his 127th Street home. The two men talked of old times, and Eddie felt again, as he had years ago, that the great man was intentionally shying away from the subject of Junie. Indeed, hardly anybody spoke of Junie any longer, and not only because most people assumed she was dead. Even those who remembered Jewel Agony and Commander M had been forced to readjust their thinking, for America of the mid-sixties was chock-full of rag-tag sects proclaiming with timid pride the primacy of the radical alternative, some of them violently. At lunch with Aurelia the other day, Eddie had wondered aloud what it was about America that drove children of privilege to demand the culture that had given them everything be burned to the ground.

"Ennui," answered Aurelia, who lately had taken to speaking aloud the same hifalutin words that she wrote. She was now editor-in-chief of the *Seventh Avenue Sentinel*—given falling circulation, very likely the last editor the paper would ever have. She had also started work on a novel, which Eddie had promised to show to his agent.

"You think young people are bored?"

"I think young people have idle hands," she said sternly. In the background, the restaurant was playing "Please Please Me" by the Beatles, but this new-style music was not to Eddie's taste, or Aurelia's.

"The entire civil-rights movement is built on nonviolence," he reminded her.

"It's going to die of nonviolence, too," said Aurelia, paraphrasing one of the big black radicals of the day.

After that she became sullen. Probably they were really arguing about something else. When they parted, Aurie asked him not to call her any more. When he tried to frame a protest, she told him he was a fool, letting life surge past while he paddled in circles, refusing to let himself love anyone he had not loved ten years ago.

(III)

THE BOOTH across from his was no longer empty.

Prison life had been kinder than Eddie expected to Maceo Scarlett. He had somehow imagined confronting a broken man, but the Carpenter, three years into a double life sentence, was broad and hulking and confident even in his prison grays. He sat comfortably, as if Attica was simply another corner of his kingdom. His good eye glared through the wired glass with a clever malice. He knew Eddie must want something, or there would be no reason for the visit.

"Read your gangster novel," Scarlett said without preamble. The huge teeth gleamed. The bad eye wandered. "That spozed to be me, boy? Cause your man Redd didn't get up to nearly enough badness. You tryin to mock me?"

"No," said Eddie, reminding himself that he was on the safe side of the glass.

"Cause I can reach you anywhere."

"I'm sure you can."

"Good." He reached into his pocket and pulled out a pack of cigarettes, but instead of lighting one, put it on the table. Perhaps he was trying to quit. The sign forbade smoking, but at this moment Eddie would have believed Scarlett capable of anything. "Now, tell me what you want, boy, and I'll tell you what it's gonna cost you."

Eddie hesitated. But he had come here to ask a single question, and if he chickened out the visit was wasted. "I'd like to talk about the night you threatened to break my hand."

"Ain't never threatened nobody. All of this"—his thick, circling finger took in the prison—"is some kind of frame-up. The white man hates a powerful black man."

"We were in your club," Eddie persisted. "This was 1959. You asked me what I picked up on my visit to South Carolina. I told you nothing, and you threatened to smash my hand with a hammer."

"Don't remember no night like that."

"The truth is, I did get something in South Carolina. I'm willing to tell you what, right now, and you can tell—well, I'm sure there's somebody who'd like to know."

"I don't know nothin bout no South Carolina."

"And in return," Eddie continued, throwing as much earnestness into his face as he could, "I'd like to get one piece of information from you. Just one."

The Carpenter had stopped smiling. The bad eye continued to bounce and juke. The good eye drifted to a spot over Eddie's shoulder. Eddie turned around. In a glass-walled office, a guard sat holding an earphone to his head, pushing buttons. Eddie realized that he could listen in on any conversation of his choice.

"I don't know nothin bout no night like that," said Scarlett. "You up here botherin the wrong nigger."

"I would have thought—"

"I gotta get back to work." He was on his feet. "Got me a sweet job. I give out the toilet paper. Every nigger in here gets zactly one roll every month, so it isn't the hardest job in the world."

"Yes, but—"

"One roll." A snort. "Gonna be trouble over that one day, boy. All kinds of trouble." For a moment, both eyes seemed to focus on the same spot, and that spot was Eddie's neck. "Gonna write another novel about me?"

"Ah, it wasn't about you."

"Bullshit." A savage smile. "Not for those years you worked for me, you wouldn't never have gotten nothin to write about. You remember that, boy."

"Weeks."

"That spozed to mean?"

"I worked for you a couple of weeks. That's all."

Eddie thought the gangster might lose his temper, but he laughed instead, so hard that the guard looked up from his desk and pushed the button. "So—what's in it for me?"

"I'm sorry?"

The good eye went shifty and speculative. "Say there was some way I could help you out."

Eddie nodded. He had thought this over before making the drive. "I work for the President," he lied. "I'll talk to him."

"President of what?"

Eddie took out his wallet, held his White House pass up to the glass, hoping the gangster would not notice that it had expired. Scarlett hardly gave it a glance. He was reading Eddie's face. He smiled. Savagely. "You seen my brother lately?"

"Your brother?"

"You seen him lately or not?"

"No."

"You go see him." Scarlett laughed. "Tomorrow night."

He left.

Driving south from the village of Attica, Eddie turned the problem over in his mind. Maceo Scarlett had no brother. He had no living relatives of any kind. Eddie knew because of the detailed files he had created while writing his novel, carefully timed to be published only after the Carpenter began serving his sentence. Therefore, when the gangster referred to a brother, Eddie guessed he meant his right-hand man, the one who had succeeded him, briefly, as king of the Harlem rackets. That would be Lenny Rouse, Eddie's old friend, the same Lenny Rouse who had drawn him into Scarlett's gang, and presided over his beating in the alley behind Scarlett's nightclub— and to whom Eddie had not spoken since.

And this led to a fresh problem.

Lenny Rouse no longer existed—but he was now, undeniably, a brother.

(I V)

THE CHURCH HAD BEEN BUILT out of several connected store-fronts on Broadway near 125th Street, looking up at the IRT tracks. The windows were whitewashed. The sign read HOUSE OF HOLY REDEMPTION, and, in much smaller letters, BROTHER H. LEONARD PEACE, FOUNDER AND PRESIDER. The sidewalk outside was trash-strewn, but when Eddie walked inside he found the place clean. The furnishings were spartan. A bored woman at a desk peeked inside an office and said Brother Leonard would see him momentarily.

Brother Leonard. Leonard Peace.

Amazing what a religious conversion could do.

Just three years ago, Lenny Rouse had been one of the scariest men on the streets of Harlem. Now Brother Leonard was one of the most admired. He ran two soup kitchens, walked around with other concerned men at night to keep women safe, preached the Gospel to snoring winos. He had put on weight, shaved his head, grown a beard, and declared to all the world that he was starting anew.

Anything to stay out of jail, said the wags. Some whispered that "anything" might even have included informing for the feds.

He greeted Eddie with a hug, as if they were old friends, as if the last time they had actually spoken to each other he had not helped beat Eddie senseless. He was not trying to make up for his life of sin,

Brother Leonard explained when they were seated at the aged wooden table that did duty as a desk. You could not make up for your sins, he said. You could only ask the Lord's forgiveness. He had asked forgiveness on his knees, and the Lord had forgiven him, then told him what to do.

"But not until after Scarlett was behind bars," said Eddie.

The preacher smiled. "I came late, but I came all the way."

They foxed around a bit, they talked about old times, and Brother Leonard tried several times to get Eddie talking about his own faith. Finally, they got to the point. Eddie told him that Scarlett suggested he come.

"A simple trade," said Eddie. "I have some information that Scarlett might be able to use to his advantage. And you have information that I need."

"Oh, I know what you're after."

"You do?"

"You want to know who the white man was in the club that night."

"How did you figure that out? I didn't tell Scarlett."

Lenny smiled. "Not hard to guess. What else would take you all the way to Attica to visit a gangster from the old days, Eddie? When you have your cushy writing career to worry about?"

Eddie frowned, wondering if Lenny intended an insult. His former friend had always been sly, and smooth. "So, then, what's the answer?"

"First you tell me yours."

"A bundle of letters."

"Letters?"

Eddie nodded. "Letters to Philmont Castle from a woman with whom he was having an affair. That's all." He raised his palms to prepare the lie. "I don't have them any more."

"Wouldn't matter if you did, my brother. I'm not in the happy end of the business any more. I'm not even in the business." He seemed wistful. "I don't care about the letters. I'm not even going to pass on what you said."

"Why not?"

"It would be un-Christian."

Again Eddie wondered whether he was being mocked. "Then why did you make me tell you?"

"Just wonderin how badly you wanted my information." The preacher scratched his shining brown pate. "Not that you have to earn it, Eddie. All you ever had to do was ask."

"All right. I'm asking. Who was he?"

"Man name of Collier. George Collier. Don't know where he came from, exactly, but that was his name."

"You're joking."

Brother Leonard grinned. "I take it you know him."

"Not know him. Know of him." And he did. Aurelia had mentioned her conversation with Senator Van Epp's bodyguard. But Van Epp had left the Senate. Presumably he no longer needed a bodyguard. Meaning that Mr. Collier must be working for somebody else.

"I don't know why you're so interested in Mr. Collier," said Brother Leonard. "But I'd be careful."

"Careful?"

The preacher nodded. "I'll tell you somethin for free, Eddie. Maceo Scarlett wasn't never afraid of nobody. But he was scared to death of Mr. Collier."

Then the good Brother remembered that he had to go to a rally. He ushered Eddie to the door, offering travel blessings for his ride home. He made Eddie promise not to be a stranger, but both men knew their business was done, forever.

Back in his car, Eddie could not help thinking that Scarlett was not the only one who was afraid of Mr. Collier.

(v)

EDDIE HAD AN OFFICE at Georgetown University, where he taught a seminar. Without the resources of the federal government to draw on, he had to rely instead on the university's formidable staff of research librarians. Accomplished burrowers, delighted to be challenged, they had an answer for him within days. A woman in her fifties named Margolis briefed him. What George Collier was doing now, the librarians had been unable to ascertain. He was on the military's books, Mrs. Margolis said. In the Army. There the books stopped dead, without even a unit designation, making it likely, said Mrs. Margolis, that his assignment was clandestine.

"I see," said Eddie.

There was more, the librarian said. Before entering military service a year and a half ago, Mr. Collier had served as an "executive assistant" for a wealthy family.

" 'Executive assistant' meaning what?"

"I cannot venture to say based on nomenclature alone."

"This would be the Van Epp family?"

Mrs. Margolis nodded. "He was with them for almost ten years. Before that he was in Korea."

"Do you have a photograph?" asked Eddie, who had yet to get a good look at the blond man's face.

"The library does not at present possess one."

"What else can you tell me?"

"Only this, Mr. Wesley. Last year, after his separation from the Van Epps, it seems that Mr. Collier used the facilities of our library. One of our researchers assisted him in his work."

"And what exactly was Mr. Collier doing?"

"My understanding is that he was assembling a dossier," said Mrs. Margolis, saving her trump for last. "A dossier on you, Mr. Wesley."

CHAPTER 32

A Year of Moment

(1)

IN THE FIRST WEEK of November, a coup in South Vietnam over-
threw President Ngo Dinh Diem. Mona Veazie called from New
Hampshire to ask Aurelia whether her boyfriend, as she called him,
could possibly put a stop to this shit. There were only American
advisers over there now, said Mona, but the way things were going, it
was starting to look as if we might wind up owning the war. Eddie
might not work in the White House any longer, but everybody
knew—said Mona—that he had friends there. He adored the
Kennedys, and they adored him right back. Couldn't he get the President's ear for five minutes?

Aurelia said none of that was remotely funny. She cared nothing
about military advisers. She had spent an exhausting afternoon meeting with her dissertation advisers, and now was sitting in the Harlem
office she occasionally visited, staring out at the dulling city. Beyond
her desk, the newsroom was quiet, and not only because Harlem produced little news these days. Aurie had been forced to lay off most of
her staff. The pages of the *Sentinel* now carried mostly wire copy,
gossip, and editorials.

"You think I'm joking?" Mona demanded.

"I hope so."

"Because people tell me the two of you were seen together."

"It was just a drink," Aurie protested. She looked at her watch.
She would have to hurry to catch the Hudson Line commuter train
at 125th Street. "One drink, Mona. And it was—oh—four months
ago. Five."

Five months ago: June, the week after the assassination of civil-rights leader Medgar Evers, which in turn took place less than twenty-four hours after President Kennedy's magnificent speech to the nation on civil rights, a speech that heavily reflected Eddie's hand. Eddie, depressed and angry, had called Aurelia to say he would be in the city on business. When they met in midtown, he told her that Southerners were blaming the murder on the harsh language of the speech—

Mona, relentless, interrupted the moment of memory. "Sherilyn DeForde says the two of you got pretty sloshed together."

"Nobody was sloshed, and Sherilyn wasn't there."

"That's my point. If she heard the news in New Jersey, everybody else heard first."

"What have you been doing all these months? Sitting on the rumor, waiting for the right moment to spring it on me?"

"I called to warn you. After what happened week before last, Eddie's likely to be calling again. This time, you have to say no."

A tumultuous time. In late August, Aurelia had stood happily in the crowd at the Lincoln Memorial, five-year-old Locke holding one of her hands and seven-year-old Zora the other, with Kevin hugging them all from behind, the family together, listening as Martin Luther King addressed the March on Washington. Two weeks later, a bomb went off during Youth Day at the Sixteenth Street Baptist Church in Birmingham, killing four children and injuring twenty-two others. The city's former commissioner of public safety suggested placing the blame on the Supreme Court, unless "King's crowd" had done it themselves. The nation was furious. The tide was turning. Passage of a civil-rights act was thought inevitable. Until three weeks later, in early October, when a car bomb killed a prominent Alabama Klan member who had boasted privately of his involvement. Another bomb, the following week, missed its Klan target, blowing up the right car but killing the wrong man. Agony, long dormant, took the credit, insisting that it would target all those who preyed upon the helpless.

"He called already," said Aurelia.

Mona snickered. "And he was depressed again, right? He wanted comfort?"

"He was angry." Remembering his words. "He said everybody was missing the point, and nobody would listen to him."

"The point being?"

"The communiqué from Jewel Agony. All the usual stuff about the fascist parasites and so forth."

"What about it?"

"It wasn't signed by Commander M."

A long pause over the long-distance line. Mona got the point. "So, where does he think she is?"

"Somewhere else."

The two women got on to other things—Aurelia's children, Mona's twins, New England life—and Aurie managed to hang up without mentioning the other matter Eddie wanted to discuss with her. He seemed determined to discover, although he would not say why, what had become of Senator Van Epp's onetime bodyguard, Mr. Collier.

Aurelia said she had no idea.

(11)

A FEW NIGHTS LATER, Aurelia and Kevin attended a private dinner at the apartment of Richard and Pat Nixon on Park Avenue. Dick Nixon, having lost his gubernatorial race last year, had taken up the well-remunerated life of a New York lawyer. Nobody thought the change was permanent. He was widely expected to make another try for the presidency in 1968, after Kennedy trounced whoever the hard-line wing of the G.O.P. put up against him in 1964. The dinner was quiet. Neither Dick nor Pat provided scintillating conversation, because both were fundamentally shy, and Kevin, although he tried hard, was not Matty. As a result, Aurelia found herself forced to lead. It occurred to her that Nixon still had contacts, and plenty of them, in what had come to be known as the national-security establishment.

So, without mentioning Eddie's name, she raised his concern—that after this last series of bombings in Alabama, the first confirmed attacks by Jewel Agony that had taken human lives, the usual communiqué taking credit had not been signed by Commander M.

Kevin looked at her hard. Pat said something about how horrible the whole thing was, and wondered why people could not resolve their differences peacefully.

Nixon laughed. "You don't see it, do you? This is like Russia's feud with Red China. They might be fighting with each other, but that doesn't mean they're not both going to try to bury us. You know what this is?" Circling a finger in the air, presumably to signify Jewel Agony. "This is just arguing over who gets to hold the shovel. What matters is the big picture."

"Which big picture is that?" Aurelia prompted, eyes wide and innocent, an expression she could pull off at the drop of a hat.

"The nation's moving right," said Nixon. "People like this Agony whatever—well, all they do is help things along. Every time these bums blow something up, they turn a million voters from Democratic to Republican."

This was too much even for Kevin. "And what about when the Klan blows actual people up?"

Again Nixon laughed. "The Klan. Hoover will have them shut down pretty soon. That's what he tells me." He fumbled with his knife and fork. "Those Agony people, on the other hand—they're pretty clever. That's what Hoover says. Lots of discipline, lots of commitment. Hard to track down. Tell you something. Next President, whoever he is? The one after that? They're gonna face so many of these left-wingers, he'll have to put troops in the streets."

"Not in America," said Kevin. "Never in America."

Nixon put his fork down. He glanced at his wife. "Let me make one thing crystal clear. America's just a country. It's like anyplace else. Anything that happens anywhere can happen here. If it's different, it's because we make it different. Us. The good guys. The quiet people. The majority nobody ever talks about or listens to. If we let the bums run the place, blow things up, burn things down? Anything can happen, Kevin. Anything."

Before the Garlands left, the former Vice President managed to pull Aurelia aside in the living room while his wife chatted with Kevin. He dropped his voice.

"Know why you're asking these questions. Know what Eddie thinks. Saw him the other day. Listen. Hoover doesn't know where she is. Nobody knows. He thinks she's still with those bums, demoted to cleaning the latrine. Reds are big on that kind of thing. Discipline. Party line. No way to tell."

He had left her behind. "You saw Eddie?"

Nixon nodded, offered that awkward smile, head bobbing. "Never got the chance to thank him for those kind words in the magazine. In Washington on some business. Dropped in at his office. Surprised him. He's a good kid. I like him. Of course, he's with the Kennedys, and the Kennedys— Let me make one thing perfectly clear. I think Jack's heart is in the right place, always have. Got him to sign one of his books for my kids. Eddie. Maybe you could talk to him."

"About what?"

"Next year, the party runs Goldwater. Gotta get it out of their system. I'll campaign for him—do one's duty—but let me make one thing perfectly clear. I'm not Goldwater. I'm Nixon. Next time around, 1968, we have big plans. Do great things for America. Could use his help on the campaign. Your Eddie. Writes a great speech. Thinks we're the devil incarnate. Listen. Put in a word. You owe me one, Aurie."

The funny thing was, she did. All the way home in the car, half dozing on her husband's warm shoulder, she reminded herself that she did indeed owe Nixon one. He had done her a favor four years ago, giving Eddie hope in his moment of greatest despair. It was at Aurelia's desperate insistence that Nixon had sent Eddie the photograph of June Cranch Wesley toting her rifle in the battle of Maxton, North Carolina.

(111)

As for Eddie, he was pulling in every marker he could think of, and discovering how few he really held. Bernard Stilwell was suddenly unavailable. His friends in the White House gave him lunch, and pitying smiles. He knew what they were thinking: that he was raising the question of Commander M's absent signature in an effort to get his sister off the hook for this, Agony's first fatal bombing. They were missing the point, but he had no way to explain. It had not occurred to him how desperately he relied on news of the group's crimes as evidence of Junie's continued safety.

"These groups change leaders all the time," said Langston Hughes when Eddie dropped by 127th Street. "You can't attach any importance to it."

"What if they purged her? What if she's dead?"

"You can't divine all that from a single letter, Eddie. You have to be patient."

But patience came hard to Eddie at the best of times. He tried his connections again and met blank walls. He talked to a couple of in-the-know journalists, but if they knew anything about the fate of June Wesley they were not admitting it. He returned to New York to track down Derek Garland, but Derek had gone off to Ghana, and his brother Oliver seemed delighted to have no idea how to get in touch. Gary Fatek was suddenly, and suspiciously, too busy to meet.

And so, in the third week of November, Eddie went home.

Not to I Street. To Boston, to visit his parents. Life had changed in the Wesley household. Wesley Senior had turned his pulpit over to a younger man, and had become a virtual recluse. He sat with his son in the study. He listened without hearing, and talked mostly about the Book of Daniel. Was he thinking of Junie? Of himself? Or simply remembering a sermon from days past? Whatever the answer, Eddie's father was visibly fading, less a shadow of his former self than a refraction, thin and without affect. The fire had gone out of his eyes, and his manner. It was as though his daughter's crimes had sapped his life's force.

Hoping to rouse him, Eddie mentioned the Supreme Court's decision last spring, banning Bible readings in public schools. Surely this would rouse his father's ire. But Wesley Senior merely nodded. "The old ways were not sustainable," he said, and, briefly, shut his eyes. "But the new ways will be the death of our people. Wait and see."

Eddie said something silly about the wheel of history.

His father snorted. "Well, you'd say that. You work for Kennedy."

"What's wrong with Kennedy?" asked Eddie, very surprised.

"Where's his civil-rights bill?" Wesley Senior demanded, but more in despair than in ire. "We turned out all those voters for him . . ."

He trailed off.

"There's big plans for the second term," said Eddie, wishing he could communicate his enthusiasm. "You'll be proud of him, Poppa." *And of me*, he wanted to add, but dared not.

"America has been good to us," Wesley Senior said before going upstairs to take his nap. "Even when it's not, we are called to turn the other cheek." He shook his head. "An eye for an eye leaves the whole world blind." The words were as close as he would come before he died to acknowledging that Junie existed.

As for Eddie's mother, she bustled about, to all outward appearances her usual self, but, in truth, Eddie made her nervous. She did not know how to treat him—nor he, her. There was a great deal of tiptoeing around the obvious. Only on the second morning of the visit did Eddie have the chance to talk to her. They were in the kitchen. Marie had made pancakes and sausage. Wesley Senior, as was his recent habit, was sleeping late. Marie poured Eddie a huge glass of orange juice. She watched him eat, but limited her own meal to tea and a bit of toast. Wesley Senior was fourteen years older than his wife, and Marie seemed to her son to be trying to close the distance.

"The hardest days," she said, "are when the reporters come around. Usually right after some action. Isn't that what she calls it? In her letters? Action. Her people take an action, they blow something up, and then the reporters come."

"I'm sorry, Momma."

"We raised her right. We didn't raise her for this. That's what your father says, and he's right." Animation crept into her tone. It occurred to Eddie that his mother wanted to talk about Junie, and had nobody to talk to. "He's disowned her," Marie continued. "He wrote her out of his will."

Eddie would have smiled had his mother's face not been so grim, for Wesley Senior possessed no significant assets other than the house, and he had made clear years ago his intention to deed it back to the church once Marie died.

"She's a good girl," said Marie Wesley, hopelessly. "I know she is. No matter what they say, she would never have done these things. Never."

On the train ride back to Washington, Eddie pondered. He should be under surveillance. The federal government had lost track of Commander M, but keeping track of her brother would be a snap. Maybe Lenny used to watch him in Harlem, but Eddie no longer lived in Harlem. Someone had to be watching him now.

He wondered who.

Just before the train reached New York City, it shuddered to a halt. People looked out on the tracks for an obstacle. The conductor came on the public-address system. His voice was crackly and faint. But everybody heard.

President Kennedy had been shot in Dallas. He was dead.

CHAPTER 33

An Editorial Dispute

(1)

IN THE SPRING of 1964, President Lyndon Baines Johnson went to Ann Arbor to deliver the first of several speeches in which he called upon his fellow Americans to build the "Great Society" that would overcome poverty and racial division. The ruling class greeted the news dolefully, but in Harlem the remaining salons sizzled with the conviction that a new day at last had dawned. Kennedy had been a fine fellow in his way, but this Johnson, Southern cracker though he was, seemed ready to push for everything black America had been demanding for a hundred years. The mood of the Negro press was celebratory—that is, the Negro press other than the *Seventh Avenue Sentinel*, whose editor, without consulting anybody, wrote a signed piece on page one warning that such apparent gifts never came without a cost, and that it might behoove the darker nation to spend less time dancing in the streets, and more time searching for the hidden puppeteers pulling the strings. Near the end of the column, she nevertheless issued a stirring call for nonviolence. She was really very hard on Jewel Agony, and the other militant groups springing up in the wake of its notoriety. All they would do, Aurelia insisted, was bring the darker nation to grief. The Commander M of whom all Harlem reverently spoke was making a deadly mistake.

Aurelia's husband was concerned. She was saying too much, he explained, over dinner in Manhattan.

"Too much about what?"

"I think you're putting together things I shouldn't have let slip."

He slid a copy of her editorial across the table. It was heavily under-lined. "I think you were writing this to me."

Aurelia looked down. "This is about Jewel Agony."

"Is it?"

"Yes."

He was silent for a while, playing with his steak. She waited for him to make the bridge, the way he always did. "Honey, look," he finally said. "We don't have anything to do with Jewel Agony, okay?"

This set her back. "Who said you did?"

"You're implying it."

"Kevin, no. You're wrong. This is about Jewel Agony. It's not about anything else."

He pointed to one of the passages he had marked. "Then who's this? Who are the puppeteers?"

Aurelia laughed jerkily. "Honey, come on. All I know is, there's some kind of Project, and it's out of control. That's all you've told me. That and that Philmont Castle left a letter behind. Fine. I don't know what you and your—your group are up to, but, really, Kevin, I'm not accusing you of—of influencing Washington."

Her husband never so much as smiled.

(11)

As soon as school was out, Aurelia packed the children into the station wagon and drove up to New Hampshire to visit Mona and the twins. The two women spent a lot of time walking in the woods while a Dartmouth student watched the kids. Mona hiked every day, usually several miles. She walked Aurelia into the ground.

Aurie told her old friend that she was tired of the *Sentinel*. She might bear the title of editor-in-chief, but Kevin owned the paper. "I'm working for my husband," she said. "I want a real job."

"Most women in America work for their husbands," said Mona, who had been reading Betty Friedan. The two women were sitting on fallen trees, taking a break.

"You know what I mean."

"You've finished grad school, right?"

"Just about."

"So, do what I did. Teach college. I still owe you, honey. I'll help you find a job."

Aurelia shook her head and dared not say what jumped to mind, that Kevin would never put up with it.

"Maybe when the kids are older," she said. "They need me at home."

Mona snorted. "Get up. Time to walk some more."

"I can't. I'm worn out."

"You need to stop smoking."

"I need to rest."

Later that night, the two women sat up in the kitchen, watching an old movie and sharing a very fine sherry, a gift to Mona from a lover.

"Eddie's pretty obsessed with his sister," said Aurie after a bit.

"Wouldn't you be?"

"I guess. I'm just wondering if there's something I should do. Something I should say. He's in so much pain."

She glanced at her friend. Mona's face was stony. "There is nothing you can do, Aurie. Nothing you can say. Don't you dare even try."

"But maybe if I just—"

"You can't undo what's been done, honey. You start talking to Eddie about Junie and, well, you and I both know where that's going to lead."

The guest bedroom was in the rafters. Aurelia lay awake for hours, watching through the dormer as the trees swayed beguilingly, teasing her with their ability to dance in place without losing their roots.

She knew what Eddie thought about Junie. She wondered what Junie thought about Eddie.

(111)

As it happened, Eddie often wondered the same thing. He had recently published a piece in the *New York Times* on the dangers of violence in a good cause, relying in large measure on a sermon Wesley Senior had preached back in the early fifties on Isaiah 60:18. Junie had always thought it one of her father's best, and Eddie probably hoped that Commander M, in whatever hideout, might read the essay, and remember her old pacifist self. Some intellectuals on the left, however, linked the theme of the essay to the Nixon piece from 1962, and concluded that the great Edward Trotter Wesley's conservative tilt was fully accomplished.

The critics were incorrect. In the months since the assassination of President Kennedy, Eddie's essays had been moving by increments in a more radical direction, almost as if he hoped to appeal, through his public pronouncements, to his missing sister. Like a lot of Kennedy's men, Eddie harbored serious doubts about Johnson, and the Great Society proposals never entirely assuaged his concerns. In early July, the new President signed the Civil Rights Act of 1964, establishing broad protection for the darker nation against discrimination in employment, housing, education, and public accommodations. As it happened, the employment provisions also applied to women. Opponents of the Act had forced this change, hoping the patent absurdity would scuttle its chances. Eddie suggested in *The Nation* that the barely mentioned amendment might, in the long run, work a larger change in American society than the more visible rules about race. *The Caucasians will forget about us,* he argued. *We are their servants. Women are their sisters and daughters and mothers. Liberating white women will strike them as more appealing than liberating Negro men.*

Eddie received a rather droll note from his own mother: *And maybe when you and the white man are done with your feud about whom to liberate first, white women or Negro men, we can do something about liberating Negro women.*

Then in August of 1964, when the new President informed the

nation that North Vietnam had fired on a pair of American patrol boats in the Gulf of Tonkin, Eddie's skepticism about Johnson flared into anger. Although the Vietnam expedition, at that time still relatively small, had always worried Eddie, he had accepted the assurances of those closest to Kennedy that the conflict could be managed. Now here was Johnson, demanding a special congressional resolution, and implying without ever quite saying that small was no longer possible. Within days of the attack, the resolution passed the House by unanimous vote, and the Senate with only two dissents. Eddie was beside himself. Not because he thought, as his friends did, that Johnson was lying about the attack. No. Eddie's concern was that the Tonkin Gulf incident had knocked from the front pages the discovery in Mississippi of the bodies of three missing civil-rights workers, dispelling the Klan propaganda that their disappearance was a hoax organized by outside agitators. In another essay, Eddie prophesied that the battle over the burgeoning war would capture the nation's attention, relegating the battle for racial justice to a sideshow.

Toward the end of August, a young black man was arrested in Mississippi, supposedly in the act of planting a bomb at the home of a local police chief linked to racist violence. Rumor said that he was a member of Agony, but he died in his cell before federal agents had the chance to interrogate him and find out for sure.

CHAPTER 34

The Festival Day

(1)

In March of 1965, Senator Lanning Frost arrived in New York to speak at a series of fund-raisers, although everybody knew he was also testing the presidential waters, if not for 1968—when Johnson was expected to win in another Democratic landslide—then perhaps for 1972 or 1976. In his first term in the Senate, Frost had become wonderfully popular for his confusing way of interrogating witnesses: "Now, General, you're not trying to tell this committee that if we build this tank you won't be back for another one next year or not?" or "If we confirm you to be a judge, it won't be because you've been more than truthful here today, will it?" Standup comics loved him. But so did ordinary Joes, who seemed to think that one of their own had made it to the top. Besides, there were those who whispered that he was twisting his words intentionally, so that the witnesses would be bound to err in response. After all, pointed out his defenders, Senator Frost seemed perfectly relaxed when questioning the witnesses he liked. Eddie was not sure which side to believe. David Yee, at the Washington Bureau of the *Times*, had told his friend privately that he was quite certain that Lanning Frost was every bit as dim as he seemed. When he behaved himself, said David, it was because his wife, Margot, wrote his lines for him.

"How has he gotten so far?" Eddie asked, bewildered. "If he's really as thick as a post, why are people talking about him as President?"

"Margot Frost is six times smarter than her husband. She tells him what to think and what to say. If they ever get to the White

House, Lanning will be the face and the voice of the Administration, but, believe me, Margot will be the brains."

Eddie had never forgotten the cross around Margot's neck. George Collier, the man who had searched his house, once worked for Margot's father: reason enough to want a closer look at Margot's husband, the future President. In Washington, Eddie was never able to penetrate the layers protecting the Senator from contact with the world. He had occasionally encountered him at White House functions or Georgetown cocktail parties, but questions were always deflected by an aide, or by Margot herself. Never had Eddie been able to speak to the Senator alone. He did not expect to do so in Harlem, either, but Harlem was at least not Washington. In Harlem, Eddie knew everyone. He would be on home ground. If there was one place where Eddie stood a chance of piercing the protective shield of young assistants and talking to Senator Frost one-on-one, that place would be Harlem. Eddie postponed a trip to Alabama, where he planned to interview a Negro preacher who had founded a new political party called the Black Panthers, and instead drove from Washington up to New York City to hear the Senator deliver the Palm Sunday address at Saint Philip's Episcopal Church, on 134th Street, where, despite their move out to Mount Vernon, Aurelia and her children occasionally attended services, and Kevin Garland was a senior vestryman. Eddie wangled an invitation to the VIP-only reception afterward at the apartment the Garlands still kept at 409 Edgecombe for their visits to the city.

Saint Philip's was one of the oldest Episcopal churches in the darker nation. Eddie hated all churches, but found the Episcopal high-church tradition incomprehensible. The tinkling of the bells annoyed him, the clouds of incense choked him, and the secret code confused him: someone always seemed to be announcing that the lectors' guild would meet in the undercroft, which should be entered via the narthex following the post-Eucharistic prayer in the nave. The vast sanctuary, with its high ornate ceiling, was packed, and a surprising number of the faces were white, everyone jostling to see the future President in the flesh. Eddie stood along with the others for the opening procession. The thurifer passed them, the crucifer guarded by two youngsters with candles, senior vestrymen with their staves of office (including Kevin), followed by the choir, another crucifer, more candles, the deacons, and then the Senator himself, followed by the rector. No sign of Margot. Eddie strained to find her in the first row of pews. He did not have a good angle of sight. He was squeezed into the back, hoping to remain unrecognized, so that he might observe without being observed. From the way the smiling woman across the aisle was nudging her husband, however, it seemed that his plan would fail.

He continued searching for Margot. By craning his neck around an obstructing pillar, he thought he could make out the back of Margot's head, but he could not be sure. A character in one of his novels had remarked that, from behind, all white women look alike. As Eddie stretched and squinted, a voice ordered him querulously to stop blocking the view. When he turned to apologize, the woman behind him widened her eyes. "Sorry, Mr. Wesley," she said.

"I beg your pardon," he said, and smiled.

"Room for one more?" said a man at his side, and Eddie found himself staring into the playful eyes of Gary Fatek, who was excusing his way down the pew.

"What are you doing here?" Eddie whispered.

"My family likes to scout future Presidents."

"To figure out how much it will cost to buy them?"

"Or how much they're going to cost us in taxes." He lifted a finger, pointed to the hymnal. "Now, shut up and sing."

Because the congregation was singing: the processional hymn, not to be confused with the introit, although it always was. The words to the hymns always reminded him of the certitudes of Wesley Senior. Yet he did his best, because what remained of the Harlem he had known was on parade today. Aurelia was in the choir, along with Chamonix Bing, former wife of his old friend Charlie. One of the altar boys was Aurelia's son, Locke. The Old Testament lesson was read by a DeForde. And when the time came for the sermon, it was Kevin Garland, resplendent in maroon robe, who stood up to introduce the guest of honor.

Eddie watched the man who had won Aurelia. Never slim, Kevin had gained weight. He was not as barrel-chested as his late father, and he lacked entirely Matty's air of being ready to buy you a drink or tangle with you in the alley, but growing prosperity had somehow worked in reverse, tempering the hauteur Eddie remembered from the old days. It was as if every dollar he earned left him calmer and more generous. Perhaps it even did: rumor spoke of the enormous sums Kevin and Aurelia gave to good causes. One of their good causes was evidently the career of Lanning Frost, whom they supported avidly, even though Lanning was a Democrat, and Kevin was very much the other thing.

Eddie turned to look at Aurelia, sitting in the choir loft. She was beaming at her husband. The selfish part of Eddie had hoped for a look of irritation, boredom, reproach, anything to signal a crack in the façade. But she just kept smiling. Eddie tried to calm himself. There were other women. He had been with more than a few over the years. But he could not tear his eyes from the one he had wanted most. His father used to preach that jealousy and covetousness were at the root of every sin, and Eddie thought this very likely true. He all but trembled with pain and loss until Gary Fatek laid delicate fingers across his arm and, leaning close, whispered, "If you don't stop, you won't get any ice cream after"—a sentiment so incongruous and absurd that Eddie forgot himself, laughing so hard that the same woman who had ordered him to stop blocking the view now hissed at him to hush.

Gary turned, gave a little bow, and said, solemnly, "He can't help it, ma'am. It's the incense. It makes him high."

(11)

KEVIN was not an accomplished public speaker. He was nervous, and fussed with his glasses a lot as he read from the paper in front of him. He seemed not to realize that Lanning Frost needed no introducing. The buzz passing through the congregation would have told a wiser man to shut up and sit down, but Kevin droned on about the schools the Senator had attended and the offices to which he had been elected and the bills to which he had attached his name. When at last he was done, Kevin blinked in surprise, as if he expected to find another page. But his smile as he stood aside was delighted and smooth.

It was Lanning Frost's turn. He stood there, tall and trim, with sharp eyes and long pink cheeks that lent to his otherwise ordinary face a certain cheery authority, like your favorite grade-school teacher. He had brown hair lightly frosted, as if to match his name, and, at forty-three years old, as dynamic and articulate as you could wish, looked every inch the presidential timber that everyone described. Eddie wondered how much of the legend was true, if a man so phenomenally successful in so short a political career could possibly be as dim a bulb as David Yee and others insisted.

Everyone heard the stories. Everyone heard the jokes. But just now nobody in the pews much cared. This was, after all, *the* Lanning Frost. The congregation rose and applauded, and he waved them back into their seats, reminding them in his warm, calmly commanding voice that this was the Lord's day, not a time to be cheering a sinner like himself. The laughter rippling along the pews was the best evidence that he had scored already, and scored high. The Senator's delivery was awkward but endearing, like a man who has memorized the big words for a quiz, never quite mastering them.

"He's quite an act," murmured Gary.

"Mmmm-hmmm."

"Erebeth says he's a ninny."

"Erebeth says everybody's a ninny."

Lanning tossed out a couple of obligatory jokes, mangling the funnier of the pair. But people laughed anyway, because this was a future President.

"You know his wife, right?" said Gary.

"Margot?"

The Senator was smiling as he related a tale from his childhood, something about being caught cheating at a game in kindergarten. The congregation was chuckling when it was supposed to, even when Frost did not.

"You've met her?"

"Sure."

"Because there's this story I heard about her—"

"Will you gentlemen please hush?"

Again Gary turned. "My apologies, ma'am. You've heard of this new treatment for mental illness? Talk therapy? Well, that's what he has. Someone has to talk to him every few minutes. It's starting to wear me out, frankly. You can help if you like."

"Wait till she spreads that one," whispered Eddie, moaning.

"That's right," said Gary, eyes front.

The rest of the Senator's talk was what Eddie would have guessed: America a great country . . . by God's grace the greatest nation the world has ever known . . . applause . . . facing unprecedented challenges both here and abroad . . . need for leadership of vision and firmness but leavened by compassion . . . keep working to build the Great Society . . . applause . . . win the battle over Communism . . . less applause . . . ease the transition from a wartime economy . . . tackle fundamental issues of poverty and racial injustice . . . applause . . . will not allow justice to be held hostage to a handful of violent racists defending a way of life that is indefensible . . . deafening applause . . . we will work together to ease the suffering of all . . . and so we shall be free . . . we shall be free!

They were on their feet, pounding the pews, stamping their feet, Christian soldiers ready to march to the polling places.

Eddie, stunned, rose only because Gary tugged on his arm.

We shall be free.

The words from the upside-down crucifix. The short hairs prickled on the back of Eddie's neck.

We shall be free.

Maybe Lanning knew. Whatever Margot was up to that brought her the Cross of Saint Peter to wear around her neck, whatever her connection to the late Philmont Castle and the mysterious George Collier, maybe the Senator knew.

Eddie looked around. Everyone was wild-eyed with enthusiasm. There was no denying the truth. The people in this church would in a few short years be joining with their fellow citizens across the country to elect Lanning Frost President of the United States.

"I think I want to hear that story," Eddie whispered to Gary as the cheering went on and on.

(I I I)

INSTEAD of going as planned to the invitation-only party at the Garlands', Eddie followed Gary into his Bentley. Gary told the chauffeur to drive around a bit, then closed the glass. He noticed Eddie's look.

"Erebeth insists. She says if I'm going to run the trusts I have to look the part." He laughed. "I'm not allowed to stay in the Village, either. Erebeth wants me to have a townhouse on Fifth for my salon, and a place on the water in Greenwich or somewhere for my big parties. I asked her, isn't it better not to waste all that money? Erebeth told me being rich is not the same as being powerful. There are lots of millionaires who couldn't get their alderman on the phone—that's what Erebeth says. She says if you don't have the parties nobody pays attention to you, and then you can't get anything done. And believe me, Eddie, I'm going to get things done."

Eddie was still studying the car: the upholstery, the old-fashioned speaking tube, the walnut inlays, the diamond clock.

"I believe you."

"You don't approve."

"Let me put it this way. The rich have more power than the poor, and I'd rather it was you than Erebeth."

"But she *admires* the *Negroes*," Gary drawled, and this time cracked only himself up.

"Tell me about Margot," Eddie said when his friend's hilarity had died. It had been a year at least since the two men had spoken, and Eddie supposed he should be asking how Gary's life was going, but the car, and his evident intention to yield to Erebeth, were information enough.

"She's having an affair," said Gary.

Eddie was scarcely interested. He had hoped for some gigantic revelation. "Is that so?"

"That's what I hear."

"I see."

"In Harlem," added Gary, savoring his little jest.

Eddie perked up. "What?"

"She's in New York a lot. She's on a couple of charitable boards. And, well, whenever she's in town—this is what I hear—she comes up to Harlem." Gary leaned close, as if the driver could otherwise listen through the closed panel or the tube. "Sneaks up to Harlem. Leaves her driver, changes her hair, takes two taxis."

"How could you possibly hear something like that?"

"I know people who know people," said Gary, piously, as if reciting his catechism. "And some of the people who know people owe favors to the Hillimans." He laughed at himself. "Well, actually, just about everybody owes favors to the Hillimans."

"Erebeth," breathed Eddie.

"What about her?"

Eddie shook his head. No point in telling Gary that the line was not that hard to trace. What he described sounded less like rumor and more like detailed surveillance—the sort of information that might show up in an FBI report. Hoover collected dirt on prominent people, and Lanning Frost, presidential timber, was as prominent as you could be without strolling into the Oval Office every morning. Erebeth Hilliman had contacted Hoover when Eddie was in trouble and made him call off the dogs. Presumably the pipeline still existed. The agents told Hoover, Hoover told Erebeth, Erebeth told Gary. Erebeth seemed to define power as getting people to take your calls. She wanted Gary to know that, too.

"Tell me the rest of the story," Eddie said.

"Not much to tell. She comes up to Harlem in her disguises, she gets off on Edgecombe Avenue, she goes into a fancy building, she stays for hours, and, afterward, an unidentified Negro male helps her find a cab to head back downtown."

"Edgecombe Avenue? Is it 409 Edgecombe?"

Gary laughed again. "No, Eddie. Get your mind out of the gutter. If she was having an affair with Kevin Garland, I don't think he'd be unidentified. No, it's in the 500 block." They were heading into the park. Gary gazed out the window at what would soon be his front yard. "A tall man. Young. Very good-looking. Hey, that sounds like me, if I were only a Negro." More laughter.

Eddie considered. The only fancy building in the 500 block of Edgecombe was 555, the Roger Morris Apartments. Although he no longer lived in Harlem, he kept tabs on who was doing what, mainly through Torie Elden. He teased himself with possibilities, running through residents in his head. Lena Horne. Joe Louis. But he was postponing the inevitable. Eddie knew perfectly well what tall, good-looking, muscular young man lived at 555.

Junie's old heartthrob, Perry Mount. The golden boy, who had dated Sharon Martindale and demanded that Eddie stop searching for his sister.

Margot knew Perry. Margot knew George Collier. Was it absurd to think that the two men might know each other?

"I think, if your driver can manage it, I'd like to go to the party now."

"The party?"

"For Lanning Frost."

"Can I come?"

"Invitation only."

When Gary spoke, he sounded exactly like his aunt, and Eddie saw, for the first time, not his buddy but the heir. "I'm a Hilliman. I can get in anywhere."

"Half a Hilliman," said Eddie, their old joke.

But Gary never cracked a smile.

(I V)

IT WAS IMPOSSIBLE to move. Aurelia had told him that only forty people had been invited, but there must have been four or five times that number squeezed into the apartment to rub shoulders with Lyndon Johnson's near-certain successor. A couple of security men watched uneasily. Lanning himself had his jacket off and was playing the piano, while Margot stood off to one side, as if bored by the proceedings, although the sharp green eyes darted constantly. The crowd around Lanning was singing, mostly Cole Porter. He played admirably. The guests made no secret of their adoration. The room was awash in liquor. Kevin Garland circulated, whispering in an ear here, shaking a hand there. Eddie guessed he was collecting commitments for the campaign war chest.

"Thank you for coming," said Aurelia, standing beside him. Eddie turned in surprise and, probably, delight. She gave him a delicate hug. "And you brought Gary."

The millionaire grinned. "Actually, I brought Eddie."

"Oh," said Aurie, confused.

Eddie said nothing. He was, for a moment, afraid to speak. He had forgotten how she felt. Her warmth. Her scent.

So Gary spoke for him. "We came to check out a nasty rumor."

The crack woke Eddie from his stupor. He rounded on his longtime friend. Had he always mistaken this naked cynicism for good humor, or had Gary changed under Erebeth's influence? "Stop it," he said.

"What?"

"You're not funny, Gary. Go bother somebody else."

But the aplomb of the truly rich is unshakable. "No, thanks. I think I'll stay and bother you."

Eddie turned his back. He took Aurelia by the arm, drew her off toward the front hall. People were shouting out songs for Lanning to play. A prosperous Caucasian was whispering in Margot's ear. She kept nodding gravely.

"What is it, Eddie? What's wrong?" Aurelia inclined her head toward his, offered the old mischievous smile. "We can't talk alone for more than a minute or two, or people will think—well, you know what they'll think."

"I want to ask you a question," he said.

She drew her Virginia Slims from her purse, tapped one into her hand, slid it between her lips. Eddie took her lighter, did the honors.

"So ask," she said.

"How well does Kevin know Perry Mount?"

"I'm sorry?"

"What you told me about the testament—"

Aurelia stiffened. She remembered Mona's advice. And Kevin's fears. "I meant what I said five years ago, Eddie. We're never talking about that again. I wish I'd never opened my stupid mouth."

But Eddie, as she often used to say, could be a mule. "I think there's a connection among the three of them. Perry, Kevin, and Philmont Castle." He cast an eye back toward the parlor. "And Margot Frost. Maybe the Senator."

"Eddie, what are you talking about?"

"The testament your husband was looking for. I think Perry—"

"I'm not going to listen to this. I don't know what's the matter with you. I think you've had too much to drink."

"I don't drink any more, Aurie."

"Well, maybe you should. Stop, Eddie, okay? Stop trying to involve me in—whatever you're doing. I've worked hard on my marriage, and I'm not going to let you wreck it. Marry Torie. Marry Cynda. Marry somebody. But leave us alone."

She swept back into the parlor.

Eddie, following at a distance, found himself beside Margot Frost. He had no idea what to say. He did not believe for an instant that she was having an affair with Perry Mount. If she was sneaking off to meet him, the reason could only be, as he had intimated to Aurelia, that they were co-conspirators.

"Nice speech," he finally said.

"Yes," she agreed somberly, keen eyes still moving over the room, perhaps wondering in whose pocket additional contributions might be found. Was it really possible that this ambitious woman had a connection to a man like George Collier? Eddie saw no way to put the question.

"It's good to see you," he said.

"You, too."

Margot never looked up.

CHAPTER 35

A Conversation Is Postponed

(1)

AND YET Aurelia was not nearly as confident as she pretended. True, Eddie had never been the same since the Kennedy assassination. He had soured on politics and largely soured on America. He saw conspiracies everywhere. But even a paranoid could, at times, be right; and, of course, Aurie possessed facts that Eddie did not.

In particular, facts about Kevin.

She threaded back through the throng, smiling and hugging and kissing as needed, searching for her husband. She saw Gary chatting with the deputy mayor. Margot was deep in conversation with a Democratic ward boss, who kept nodding his head to whatever Mrs. Frost was saying. The impromptu piano recital had ended. Lanning Frost was standing near the bar, sipping club soda. A florid balding man was berating the Senator about the campus "free speech" movement. Lanning nodded importantly. "Well, naturally, none of us really want our once-proud universities run by the kind of situation where anybody reaches the level of controversy we need to attain," he announced.

The crowd cheered.

Aurelia grabbed her pastor by the arm, but he had no idea where Kevin was. She asked Chamonix Bing, lately divorced, who was very giggly, on the arm of a stranger. Chammie shrugged, evidently on her way out. Aurie asked one of Kevin's banking friends. He looked annoyed, pointed vaguely, went back to flattering the Senator. She finally found her husband behind the closed door of their bedroom, where he sat on a chair with his face in his hands. Kevin looked up at her approach. He was not crying, as she had feared. Nor was he drinking. He was exhausted.

"Honey?"

"I can't do it, Aurie," he said, holding her hands. She sat on the arm of the chair, bewildered. "I'm not Burton. I'm not Matty. I'm just Kevin. I can't do it."

"What is it, honey? What's wrong?" Cooing all the right things even as a sick tendril of dread began to rise. She stroked his neck. "What can't you do?"

"They're asking too much now. Oh, honey." Drawing her closer, he laid his face in her lap. "I'm so sorry. I should have listened to you. You were right. I was wrong."

"About what?"

"It's out of control, like I told you, and, well—since Dad died? It's getting worse. The whole Council is scared." He sighed and sat up straighter, although his eyes were wide and, unless she was mistaken, frightened. "After the party. We'll talk tonight."

"Whatever you say, honey."

"You deserve to know. You need to know."

"Kevin, darling, whatever it is—"

He kissed her hands, then stood up. Shakily. "I have to go back out there, honey."

"Not with that tie, you don't," she said, and straightened it for him.

"Thank you, Aurie."

"I'm here for you," she said, and kissed him.

Then he was out the door and into the laughing throng, and it was Aurelia's turn to sit, and cover her face, and wonder what had happened. The years since Matty died had brought them so close together. Kevin had never been anything but affectionate and gentle and loving, and Aurelia had been everything for him that she could. He had held the firm together when people guessed he would not, he had taken her on vacations, he had rolled around with the children on the lawn, and he had never, ever sat in a chair and told her that "they" were asking too much of him, that he could no longer do—well, whatever he was doing.

Maybe Eddie was right. Not all of it—she refused to believe that Kevin was involved in anything sleazy—but, plainly, her husband was in over his head.

I'm not Burton. I'm not Matty.

Burton being Burton Mount—Perry's father.

Maybe Kevin only meant he could no longer run the firm. Fine. Sell Garland & Son to the highest bidder. They had money enough. He could retire young, and they could relax for the rest of their lives.

But Eddie had asked about a connection among her husband, Perry Mount, and Phil Castle. So maybe Kevin had not been talking about business after all. Maybe he had been talking about the papers she found in his safe eight years ago. Shaking the throne. All of that.

She would find out. Tonight, when the party was over, she would listen patiently to whatever Kevin had to say, and together, as a husband and wife should, they would figure out what to do next.

(11)

EDDIE SAW KEVIN in the hallway leading from the bedroom, and knew that he had to leave before Aurelia came out. She was right, of course. He should marry somebody. She would never leave Kevin. But Eddie, at heart a romantic, did not believe in marrying for any reason but love, and, so far, he had not managed to love anybody else.

Not that he had tried all that hard.

And he doubted that he would be able to try, in any serious way, until he found his sister.

The crowd was thinning. The security guards were unlimbering. Eddie realized that he had waited too long to depart, and now would have to wait longer, because Senator Frost and his wife were waving and handshaking their way out of the room. Kevin escorted them into the hall. Eddie looked toward the alcove, but Aurelia had not emerged. He sensed that something important had happened. He took a step toward the bedroom, then laughed at himself. He could not speak to her there. He noticed that Kevin had not returned. Of course not. He had to walk his guests all the way to their limousine.

Only a couple of dozen people remained. The caterers looked exhausted. Somebody asked for Eddie's autograph. Somebody else asked him about the war. Here was the best evidence that the party was truly over: people other than Senator Frost could now be noticed.

Wandering into the study, he noticed the winking light on the multi-line phone. Aurelia must be on a call. He wondered if it could be related to—

Chammie Bing was suddenly beside him. "Are you here by yourself?"

"What?"

"Because, you know, if you don't have plans, maybe we could have dinner or something."

"Well—"

"We could go anyplace you want. Do whatever you want." She was so ingenuous in her insinuation that he fought not to chuckle. Chammie might be single again, but she had been married to a friend of his.

"Actually, I do have plans," he said gently, and they both knew he was lying.

Chammie's face fell. She opened her mouth to answer, and what came out was a tremendous thunderclap. The apartment shook. People screamed, including Aurelia, who came racing from her bedroom, shoes off, hair undone. She went to the window looking down on Edgecombe Avenue. They all did. The smoke obscured the view. Gary had materialized from somewhere. He was tugging at Eddie's arm and yelling in his ear. The hallway was chaos. The elevators were useless. The stairwell was packed, but they fought their way down. Edgecombe Avenue was swirling bedlam. The Senator's car was a ball of flame. It took hours to sort things out, but by evening everybody in America knew that Lanning Frost had survived an attempt on his life, the blast killing two people: the driver, who was holding the door of the limousine open, and the individual who was standing between the Senator and the car, a Negro businessman named Kevin Garland.

Jewel Agony took the credit.

PART IV

Ithaca/Saigon
1965–1968

CHAPTER 36

Reconsideration

(1)

AURELIA SAT with her arms circling her knees and her feet in the surf. The incoming tide tickled frothily over her thighs, then withdrew. She wore dark glasses and a floppy straw hat against the August sunshine, and an appropriately modest swimsuit against the stares and occasional advances of men who spotted her alone on the sand. Not that she was really alone. Behind her, Zora and Locke were building impressive sand castles with Mona Veazie's twins, Julia and Jay, named for the psychologist Julian Jaynes, one of Mona's heroes. It was the high season along the New England shore, and the beach was crowded. Taking the house in Maine for the month had been Mona's idea. She had gushed about how much fun they would all have. Aurelia understood. Mona wanted her old friend out of Mount Vernon, and as far from Harlem as possible. She would have proposed France, or Japan, if either one of them spoke French, or Japanese. Maybe next year.

For now, Maine would have to do.

Aurelia heard her son's voice, youthful and commanding, and marveled at the boy's resilience. Locke was all of seven years old, and having the time of his life. Zora, at nine, was more reserved. She tended to model herself on her mother, and knew better than her brother that Aurelia's efforts to be bright and cheery for the sake of her children were just that—efforts. Aurie wiggled her toes, fascinated by the eddies. She did it again. She was thirty-nine, and a widow, and had no idea what to do next.

Mona's son, Jay, was arguing. Only five, but already as feisty as any Veazie. Locke loved giving orders, a trait inherited from his father. Jay was resisting the older boy. Any minute the two boys would be scuffling. Mona, supervising, would let them wrestle. At that age, she said, it does them good. Let them get all their male aggressions out when it doesn't make any difference. Julia would be giggling with delight: she loved to watch the boys being boys. But not Zora. If a fight broke out, Zora would come over and sit beside her mother. Aurelia would slip an arm around her daughter and listen as the odd, observant child explained some theory about why the big waves came in bunches, or why the gulls cocked their heads to the side before diving. Since his father's death, Locke had become stubborn, wanting things more and more his own way. Whereas all the contemplative Zora ever really wanted was to talk.

Aurelia was sleepy, but if she closed her eyes, she would see Kevin promising they would talk later. Then she would feel the blast and smell the smoke.

Kevin's fortune, inherited from his father, was mostly in trust for the children. Aurelia had received enough to be comfortable, and she had no complaint.

She missed him.

"You don't get to say what to do," Jay warned.

"This is the *right way*," Locke insisted.

Little Julia shrieked.

Aurelia lifted her foot from the water, watched the rivulets run off, then dipped again. Water was so peaceful. The antidote to everything. The Bible said we began as dust and would return to dust, but Aurelia thought we came from the water and would eventually go back. Even the dust was eventually washed into the sea. She kicked, made little waves, wondered how many years it would take for the moist earth to rot her husband's ornate mahogany casket, eventually drawing his physical substance into the ground, and onward to an underground tributary feeding some surface creek, then dumping him into a river, and finally back to the ocean.

The funeral, at Saint Philip's, had been fit for a king. Politicians black and white had vied to speak. After consulting with Kevin's cousin Oliver and a few other senior Harlemites—and Mona, too—

Aurie had given pride of place to Lanning Frost, whose life, intentionally or not, her husband had saved. Another eulogist had been Dick Nixon, who had missed Matty's funeral and wanted to avoid repeating his mistake. Although the press had no sure idea who Kevin Garland was, or had been, reporters flooded the church, fascinated by the spectacle of the two men considered most likely to face off in the 1968 presidential election speaking at the funeral of the same Negro. The family banned cameras. A few enterprising photographers snuck in, and were surprised when private security guards ushered them, filmless, back out.

White security guards, the reporters complained to their editors. Hired for the occasion, and lots of them.

On the street afterward, Eddie had waited as one of perhaps a hundred people wanting to whisper their condolences to the widow. Aurelia had stood there in her mourning black, holding the hands of the bewildered children, her family's rituals of grief, like all America's in the mid-sixties, dictated by Jacqueline Kennedy. There were no public displays, tears least of all. Oliver stood nearby, and people whispered to him, too. As a matter of fact, their whispers to Oliver were often more detailed than their whispers to the widow, as if he was now the man in charge.

Aurelia was unoffended.

When it was Eddie's turn, he murmured the right things, but added that they needed to talk, as soon as possible. He lingered, imploring her with his eyes. He continued to clasp her hand. Eddie said they should get together. Aurelia said nothing. He said please. She sensed a stir along the line of mourners. People would be telling stories tonight all over the darker nation. At the funeral, of all times: couldn't the two of them even *wait*? Aurelia felt Oliver preparing to intervene. She stared at her former beau. Most of her was offended, and wanted never to see him again. But another part wanted to grab Eddie and her children and run off to—

Well, that was the problem. There was nowhere to run. Aurelia was now, forever, *the* Mrs. Kevin Garland.

"Thank you for coming," she said. "It means a lot to all of us."

She dropped his hand and turned to the next in line.

(11)

OF COURSE they had eventually had their conversation. They met for lunch on a pleasant June afternoon, in the Oak Room at the Plaza, where Eddie was staying for a few days while in New York doing publicity. His fifth novel, *Pale Imitation*, had just won him his second National Book Award. He was not yet forty. His sales remained durable if undramatic, but the cognoscenti knew him, and his essays were published everywhere.

This time, Eddie behaved better.

When Aurelia swept into the room, more glamorous than any of the wealthier women present, he stood and clasped her hand and did not hug her. He did all the talking to the waiter, as a gentleman was supposed to. He renewed his condolences, asked after the children, then asked after her.

She muttered something inane about taking things one day at a time.

As it happened, Eddie's father had died of cancer the month after Kevin's murder. Aurelia had sent flowers, and now offered her own condolences. A part of her cringed, because she had not even known Wesley Senior was ill. She did not know whose job it might have been to tell her.

Talk turned to other things. The children liked Mount Vernon, but memories were everywhere. They could not stay in the house. Mona wanted her to apply for an open position as an instructor at Cornell, where one of Mona's many old flames now ran the English department.

"I wouldn't think you'd have to work," said Eddie, the first faux pas of an otherwise impressive performance. "Kevin must have left you well provided for."

"Kevin provided just fine," she agreed. And this was the simple truth. In addition to insurance and investments, Kevin had left her his quarter interest in Garland & Son. A Wall Street giant was negotiating to acquire the firm for a tidy sum. "But I *want* to work, Eddie. Not writing gossip. A real job."

"In Ithaca?" he asked, as if she was going to Jupiter.

"That's where Cornell is."

"It's so far." *From me*, he meant.

"I haven't decided yet. They might not hire me even if I apply."

"Then they'd be out of their minds," Eddie said warmly, and, for a moment, they looked at each other the old way; then dropped their eyes.

It was Aurelia who finally centered the conversation.

"Eddie, listen for a minute. Will you listen? What you mentioned that day—the day Kevin the day he died—this theory of yours. No, no, don't say anything. I want you to understand. You've been a wonderful friend for a long time, and I hope you always will be. But I will not discuss my husband with you. Not his business affairs, not anything about him. Not now. Not ever. Whatever you're thinking about, worrying about, wondering about, don't ask me. I don't want to know. My job is to make the best life I can for my children, not to investigate the past. Will you make me that promise?"

Probably he nodded. Possibly she imagined it. Certainly he did not argue.

Out on the street, she lit a cigarette to cover the trembling in her hands. Burning bridges is difficult, especially when you have no idea where you are heading. But sometimes only the fire moves us forward.

"Eddie," she said.

"Yes, Aurie."

"There's one more thing." She glanced at him, then glanced away, because those beautiful eyes were too imploring. She was going to wound him. She did not intend to pretend to enjoy it. "Eddie. Dear, dear Eddie. I'm not the old Aurie any more. You have to understand that."

"I'm not the old Eddie, either." And this was true. He had given up alcohol the day he learned of his father's illness. Since then he had become sturdier—less impulsive, more reflective—in short, a grown-up.

"What I'm saying is— Eddie, I'm Mrs. Kevin Garland. I have certain responsibilities now."

"I would imagine so."

The kindling was set. The bridge would burn horribly, and fast. She touched his face. "There can never be anything between us," she breathed. "Not now. Not in the future. I want you to promise me."

"Promise you what?" he asked, and the hopelessness in his voice drew her. "You've already set the rules."

"That's right. I have. I'm sorry, Eddie. It has to be this way, and—and you can't ever ask me why." She had made her speech. Now she had to leave him his dignity. She smiled sadly. "Not that you'd ever want me."

But Eddie refused the easy escape that agreement would have given. "I'll always want you," he said, and, bowing slightly, handed her into a cab.

Riding away toward Grand Central, Aurelia knew Eddie would still be standing there under the awning, watching her go. She felt his gaze. She dared not turn and look. If she turned, she would stop the driver, run into Eddie's arms, and never let him go. She was *the* Mrs. Kevin Garland. She had responsibilities. And secrets. Secrets she could never share, least of all with Eddie Wesley.

Yet she could not help herself. She had been in the taxi just a moment when she glanced, as casually as she could, over her shoulder.

Eddie was gone.

(I I I)

THE BOYS WERE FINALLY FIGHTING, and, sure enough, Zora slipped down onto the sand beside her mother. Julia continued to giggle. That child giggled too much, Aurelia decided, especially around boys. True, Julia was only five, but at ten she would be a terrible tease, and at fifteen she would be a terrible flirt. Aurelia had grown up with girls like that in the orphanage, and a couple of them wound up with babies before they finished high school.

Mona had better keep a close eye on her daughter.

"Mommy?" said Zora.

"Yes, baby?"

"Why do boys fight?"

Aurelia sighed. She longed for a cigarette, but Mona did not allow smoking around her children. At night, Aurie smoked on the front porch of their rented house. Mona would sit beside her, offering newspaper clippings about the Surgeon General's recent report, and asking if she wanted to live to see her grandchildren.

"The reason boys fight," Aurelia said, hugging her daughter close, "is that they're not as tough as girls."

"I thought they were tougher."

"If they were tougher, they'd find ways to control themselves. They can't control themselves. That's what makes them boys."

For a little while, they sat there. The fight had subsided. The boys were building again.

"Mommy?"

"Yes, baby?"

"Why are boys the only ones who get to be President?"

Aurelia smiled. "Would you like to be President one day?"

"No."

"Why not?"

"I want a job for *smart* people," Zora said firmly, and could not understand why her mother laughed so hard.

Later that night, the two women left the children with a sitter and had dinner at a fancy restaurant on the water in Portland. A couple of guys hit on Mona, and a couple of guys hit on Aurelia, and a couple of guys hit on both of them at once. Their dessert was interrupted by their waitress, who said she did not want to be a bother, but she had a question.

"Ask away," said Aurie, very confused.

"Somebody said you're like the wife of that Negro guy? The widow, I mean. You know, the guy who protected Senator Frost? Gave his life?"

Aurie covered her mouth in horror.

"I'm gonna vote for him," the young woman persisted. "Lanning Frost. He'll be like the best President we've ever had? I'm so like grateful? To your husband, I mean. Can I shake your hand?"

"No," said Mona, because Aurelia was crying.

The waitress went away, looking offended. Mona bundled her friend into the car. All the way back to the house, Aurie kept her head pressed into the corner between the window and the seat. She was tired of hearing the story. About how her gallant husband had stepped in front of the car and taken the bomb. Could no one see that the story made no sense? Kevin could not have known about the bomb until it exploded, and by that time it would have been too late to push the Senator out of the way. Why did the newspapers have to invent heroes all the time?

All of this she said to Mona in a furious weepy ramble, and Mona patted her shoulder and murmured soothing sounds.

Aurelia did not say the rest of it, the secret only she knew: the other reason it was absurd to think that her husband had given his life for the Senator.

Kevin had not been an innocent bystander that afternoon.

He was the target.

CHAPTER 37

Denial

(1)

EDDIE WAS WRITING about Che Guevara. He had become fascinated by the fascination of American leftists with Marxist revolutionaries, and wondered if they really would like to live in the sort of state that successful revolutionaries tended to produce. It was early October of 1965, and Guevara had just split with Castro and left Cuba. College students could hardly cross the street unless they first demonstrated their knowledge of the difference between Marcuse and Sartre. At his house on I Street, Eddie was trying to craft an essay conveying his amusement. They were all armchair radicals, he insisted. They would all wind up working on Wall Street.

Gary said his old friend was growing cynical, but Gary was no oracle. Since Erebeth's death and his takeover of the Hilliman trusts, he had retreated behind a wall of skepticism. About politics. About people. About everything. Gary's perennial good humor had somehow twisted into sardonic malice. It was not, Gary often explained, that he had rejected his former leftish views. Rather, he had decided that ideology itself was a bad idea, that the only ethical and dependable human attitude was doubt—

The doorbell rang.

Annoyed, Eddie looked up from his work. He was not expecting anyone. The bell rang a second time.

He answered, and found a couple of young people, white, college-age, looking lazy yet alert. Eddie assumed they wanted autographs, or instruction in the mysteries of the universe. Both kinds dropped by without invitation, and both had to be sent on their way swiftly; if necessary, rudely.

"Mr. Wesley?" said the girl, smiling prettily.

"Yes?"

"Could you maybe go for a ride with us?"

"I'm terribly busy right now," he began.

"It's about the woman you've been looking for," said the boy.

Outside in his driveway, the door to a car stood open.

(11)

EDDIE CONSIDERED THE BLINDFOLD MELODRAMATIC, and said so, concealing the deeper truth that he was terrified. Even in childhood, he had never liked having his eyes bound, secretly afraid that he would go blind, like his Aunt Carrie. The car was full of kids. From what he could tell before they bound his eyes, all were white. It occurred to Eddie, too late, that he was entirely at their mercy. He had no doubt, no doubt whatsoever, that he was in the hands of Jewel Agony.

They drove for an hour or so, and he tried to figure out whether they were heading into the countryside or just circling around to confuse him. The car clunked and rattled, and the young revolutionaries on either side kept bumping against him. Twice they braked hard enough to slam his face into the vinyl seat back. Another time they pushed his head down toward his lap as if to hide him. At last they stopped someplace noisy and bundled him into another vehicle without unbinding his eyes. This time they slipped glasses over the blindfold. The new car sped off.

"Nobody's following me," Eddie said calmly. "You may safely dispense with these precautions."

"Nothing need be true," said a new voice from the front seat, a male, probably white, certainly much older than the kids, "as long as it persuades." The man was quoting Eddie's novel *Netherwhite*, but the author felt more threatened than flattered.

"You believe me to be a liar?"

"I believe you should shut up."

The anger rose in Eddie, but he squelched it, not least because it would do him no good. If he ripped off the blindfold, they would throw him out of the car. He had chosen this road: the road to Jewel Agony, and to Junie. Having petitioned for entrance to their world, he could hardly complain of his treatment. Eddie was taking a risk, but theirs was greater. He was the famous writer with powerful friends to protect him, and the kids beside him on the seat lived every second in fear of the helicopter overhead, the battering ram against the door, and the rest of their lives behind bars.

"Why are you doing this?" the new voice asked after a moment. "Why are you making all this trouble?"

"You know why."

"You want to join us?"

"No."

"We don't want you."

Eddie smiled. "I don't want you, either."

An intake of breath around the car, but he had said nothing anybody could argue with. "Then why?" the voice demanded.

"I want to find my sister."

"Who's your sister?"

"If you didn't already know that, I wouldn't be here."

A sullen silence stretched. He had the sense that they were crossing a bridge. He heard banter with a toll-taker, and wondered why nobody noticed him blindfolded in the back seat. Then he remembered the glasses, and supposed he was meant to seem blind. An hour later, the car stopped. The doors opened, and Eddie heard twittering birds. Two voices whispered, an argument he could not quite make out, except that he was pretty sure somebody wanted to send him back. He heard lowing cattle. Farmland. Northern Maryland? New Jersey? He assumed the journey was over, but they led him into another car.

"Don't say a word," said the same male voice, this time alongside rather than in the front seat.

He did not.

"There's no such thing as this Jewel Agony, okay?" the man said. "There never was. The pigs made it up."

The pigs. He had noticed this term filtering into the language of the young: a peculiar catchall for police, federal agents, anybody representing law and order.

"Just sit still and be quiet," the man said.

Eddie had the sense that the decision was still being made, even without a spoken word. The car started moving. The silence was thrilling, a tease. She was in the car. Eddie trembled with certainty. His sister was in the car, maybe right next to him, and if he just reached out—

"Don't *move*," said a female voice.

Not Junie's. Caucasian.

Eddie frowned, turned the other way. Then he remembered: the older man was sitting there. Maybe the front seat, then. But as he tried to lean, the man grabbed his head and made him face the woman beside him.

"You work for *Hoover*," said the same female voice. He had never heard it before, but he would have known it anywhere. "*Everybody* knows that. You and Nixon are *buddies*. You're a spy."

He had the wit to obey his original orders. He remained silent. They were climbing a hill, very steep. Maybe they planned to toss him over the side.

"You're *crazy* to come here," the woman told him, but he already knew that. "Don't you read the *papers*? We kill without *compunction*. A federal *informant*, sent to *spy* on us, do you think we'd *hesitate*?"

Still Eddie kept his silence.

"Feel this," said the male from the other side.

Eddie felt.

A gun, pressed into his side, just above the kidney, where even a small-caliber bullet would do a lot of damage.

"You're a *dead* man," said the woman. She sounded just like her mother. "You shouldn't *be* here. Your FBI friends will *lynch* you."

A chuckle from the front seat, although nothing was remotely funny.

"You shouldn't *be* here," she repeated. She was not, he decided, quite sane. "Do you really think *she* would want you here? Don't be a *fool*."

"This is our commander," said the man, and Eddie took the meaning at once: hers was the final authority. From whatever sentence she pronounced there would be no appeal.

"She's not *here*," the female voice continued. They were headed downhill again. "She's not *anywhere*, okay? I can't *believe* your FBI friends didn't *tell* you."

Fear has a way of working its way upward, hotly, from bowels to stomach to throat, like rancid food. And, in the end, it comes vomiting out of your mouth. "Are you saying she's in custody?" he demanded, rounding on the woman beside him. No answer. He turned the other way, toward the gunman. "She's dead? Is that what you're saying? Junie is dead?"

The car screeched to a halt. Doors flew open. Somebody dragged him out and thrust him to the ground. Grass. A field of grass.

"Don't turn around," said the gunman, prodding the back of his neck.

Eddie nodded. Although already blindfolded, he shut his eyes. Maybe this was the end after all.

"He's *serious*," said the madwoman. Eddie wondered what Irene and Patrick would say if they could see their daughter now, waving guns and promising death: the new Commander M, "M" for "Martindale," not "Miranda." "M" for Sharon, not Junie. "If you turn *around*, he'll blow your *head* off."

Eddie nodded again.

"*We* didn't blow up that *bomb*. *We* didn't try to kill *Frost*. That was the *pigs* trying to *frame* us."

"They killed Kevin Garland to frame you?"

"That fool was like collateral *damage*. They wanted to kill *Frost*, and then we'd *really* be in the *shit*."

He let this pass. "Please tell me about my sister."

"She's a *wrecker*. We don't put up with *wreckers*."

Eddie was trembling with fear, but not for himself. Wrecker. He knew that word. A term Marxist regimes used before purging dissenters. Sometimes the wreckers were expelled. Sometimes they were liquidated.

"What are you trying to say?"

"We didn't *want* her any more. We don't want *you*, either. Don't turn *around*."

The gun remained on his spine. Fingers from behind removed the dark glasses and lifted the blindfold. Eddie blinked in the moonlight, careful not to turn. He was on his knees on the grass. The grass was sprinkled with bird shit. The gun withdrew. He heard the car doors slam. The engine gunned. The car sped off. He waited a full minute, then raised his head.

He was on the grassy median on the other side of I Street from his house.

They had driven him in a circle.

CHAPTER 38

Aurie's People

(1)

By the autumn of 1966, life in Ithaca had settled into routine. For most of Aurelia's life, routine had been her enemy, excitement her friend, but the roller coaster of the past ten years had persuaded her of what most adults pretend to have known all along: children need stability. In Ithaca they had it. The house was a cavernous Victorian half a block from the long pedestrian bridge that swayed gently several hundred feet above Fall Creek Gorge. In the morning, Aurelia laid out cereal and milk and fruit, then dressed while Zora and Locke ate. She walked them to the school-bus stop, taking along Crunch, the shivery beagle they had saved from the pound, who generally did his business on the way back. She left Crunch in his pen behind the house, then headed for work, leaving the station wagon in the garage because spaces on campus were expensive. She crossed the bridge, climbed the steep wooden stairs set into the muddy slope opposite, and strolled through the campus to the English department in Goldwin Smith Hall. She taught her classes, she met her students, she argued obscure literary theories with her colleagues, and about once a week she was asked to justify her presence in the faculty women's bathroom. By three-thirty she was done, and hurried home to meet the bus, because the school day was arranged, in Ithaca as everywhere in the country, around the assumption that a mother would be home to receive the children.

There were faculty parties, too, some of them mandatory. The sitter was a gangly teen from next door who played the flute. One of

Aurelia's friends was a lecturer named Megan Hadley, who had been in her year at Smith. Megan taught early-modern literature—that is, literature from three hundred years ago—and her husband, a goateed anthropologist called Tris, short for Tristan, frequently hit on Aurie, who had been hit on by husbands of friends for much of her adult life. Another suitor was a chubby engineer named Bergson, a shy man who seemed happy simply to moon over her at the occasional lunch. She even had a flowery letter or two from Charlie Bing, ex-husband of her friend Chamonix, insisting that she let him buy a drink whenever she next came to Manhattan. And then there was Lawrence Shipley, the only black professor in the history department, brilliant and beautiful and devotedly single, whose playful overtures she one tipsy night, and never again, found herself unable to refuse. Loneliness can do that, but Aurelia was humiliated. She did not want to be a notch on the handle of a campus Lothario's gun; and Lawrence was known to talk about his conquests. Mention this one, she warned him as she dressed, and she would have some of her old Harlem friends trim him up, as it used to be called; and Lawrence Shipley, who had never set foot in Harlem in his life, promised.

She figured he would keep his promise for at least a month.

Every so often she heard from Eddie. He usually called late at night. Over the scratchy long-distance lines, they kept a careful emotional distance from each other, devoting their conversations to family news. He would ask about the children, and she would ask if there was word of Junie. There never was.

One afternoon, as Aurelia returned to her office after lunch, she found Megan Hadley camped outside her door, holding a clipping from the *Times:* had Aurie seen it? She had not. Lyndon Johnson had nominated Oliver Garland, her late husband's cousin, to be a federal judge.

"I thought you told me the Garlands were all Republicans."

Aurelia managed a sickly smile. "They're whatever they have to be to get ahead."

But Megan wanted outrage. Outrage that any Negro in America could be a Republican. And simultaneous if slightly dissonant outrage that any thinking person could cooperate with Johnson, the great baby-killer. Aurelia's aplomb bewildered her. Oppression was everywhere. Megan urged her colleague to give vent to her feelings instead of bottling them up. It was time to reject her socialization, said Megan. Aurie thanked her kindly, and, when Megan was gone, stared out the window at the parking lot, wondering if Oliver knew what his cousin Kevin and his Uncle Matty had been involved in.

And if Castle's testament had ever turned up.

Another time, Mona Veazie came down from New Hampshire to visit—Mona, who had gotten her into the academic world in the first place. She brought her new husband, a quiet schoolteacher named Graves—white, like her old one—and the children, Julia and Jay. They looked less like twins every time Aurelia saw them, for Julia was half a head taller. But girls mature faster than boys, Aurie reminded herself. The two families saw each other often. Locke and Zora called the twins their cousins. While the children chased the dog and each other around the yard, the adults played three-handed pinochle, one of Harlem's royal games.

Later, the two women sat up in the master bedroom, watching the late movie on Channel 5 and drinking wine. Mona was maudlin. She did not love her husband, she said, but he kept her warm at night. Aurie refused to bite. She asked instead for news of Harlem. Mona prophesied doom. She was not sure how much longer to allow her ailing mother to live alone at the Edgecombe Avenue townhouse.

Oh, and there was one other thing. Maybe Aurie had heard the news?

What news?

Well, not news exactly, said Mona. A friend of hers with Washington connections had called. The remnants of Agony were said to have gravitated to the San Francisco Bay area. They were joining up with other radical groups to try to give the movement a push. The hard left was thought to be in dire straits. Hoover had informers everywhere. Three members of the Revolutionary Action Movement had recently been arrested, charged with planning to blow up the Washington Monument. Militant organizations were disintegrating. But in Oakland, a new movement had adopted as its name and symbol the Black Panther, formerly used by voting-rights activists in the South, and trying to raise revolutionary consciousness among welfare recipients, janitors, nurses, and other members of what it called "the industrial army." The Panthers scared people. They wore black berets and black leather jackets. They carried weapons openly, relying on their rights under the Second Amendment.

Aurie said, "Agony is joining up with the Panthers?"

"I don't know," said Mona. "Neither does my friend. The point is, the feds have good penetration. My friend says they expect to have Commander M in custody in a matter of weeks."

Aurelia sat for a few minutes, smoking and thinking. "Do they really think it's Junie out there?" she finally said.

"They really do."

"Can you imagine her behind bars?"

"Not really."

Aurie blew smoke through her nose. "Eddie says they'll never catch her. He thinks she's smarter than they are."

"So do I."

Before Mona left, Aurie asked if the friend with Washington connections was Gary Fatek. Mona grinned, but sadly. "Gary's way up there now. He's out of my league. I hear you have to be God, or at least a President, to get in to see him."

"Eddie sees him."

"God, or President, or twice winner of the National Book Award."

"What I'm saying is, if Gary told you that they think Junie's in California, then he probably told Eddie, too. He'll go out there, Mona. He could get into trouble."

"Sorry, sweetie. I can only take care of two children at a time."

A week later, the Bureau announced with great fanfare the arrest of a couple of members of Agony in Berkeley, California, at what the papers described as a safe house, but when Aurelia talked to Eddie, he told her that the "safe house" was an apartment full of unkempt heroin addicts, and the pair of college dropouts who were hauled in, neither of whom had ever heard of a Commander M, could not have blown up a balloon.

(11)

UNLIKE MONA, Aurelia was not a professor—not yet. She was, at the moment, simply a lecturer, a distinction that explained why she worked from a cubicle rather than an office. The department chair had assured her, however, that the assistant-professorship opening up in eighteen months would be hers if she wanted it, and she did. She liked Ithaca. She had used a small part of her inheritance from Kevin to buy the huge house on Fall Creek Drive. Few senior members of the faculty owned houses so grand, but Aurelia did not care about the whispers behind her back. She wanted Locke and Zora to grow up with all she had lacked—a yard, space, the dog, friends next door. Christmas was a gigantic occasion for the family, gifts heaped beneath the tree. Probably she spoiled them. The way they had lost their father, she could not imagine doing anything else.

Most nights, while the children slept, Aurelia prepared for class or graded student papers. Then, her professional life out of the way and her personal life on hold, she honored Kevin's memory the only way she knew. She withdrew a diary carefully hidden in one of the messier drawers of her dresser. On its creamy pages she was trying to reconstruct the documents she had found in her husband's safe ten years ago, and copied, and burned. Sometimes she would recall another word or phrase and add it to the pattern; two days later, she would decide she had remembered it wrong. And yet, slowly, the documents were re-emerging. She had copied the words *shake the throne* at least four times, so she wrote them now on four separate pages, hoping to spark a buried memory. There had been several references to *Pandemonium*, always capitalized, one to the *Palace Council*, and several more to someone named *Author*, or *the Author*, presumably the intended recipient of the letter delivered to the Dorchester during their honeymoon. She supposed it was possible that her late husband was the Author, but she doubted it. The Author seemed to be in charge of things, and Kevin, for all his virtues, was exactly what Matty had once described: a born second-in-command.

This was her secret obsession. She had told Eddie a year and a half ago that she would not discuss his theories. She had not mentioned that she had theories of her own.

Aurelia put the notebook aside. She smiled a little, smoked a little, cried a little. *It's getting worse*, Kevin had said in their last conversation. *The whole Council is scared.* Minutes later, standing next to Lanning Frost, he had been blown to bits.

Aurelia took up the diary again. She turned the smooth pages, studying her notes. She made a correction here, added a word there. Bit by bit she was rebuilding. Bit by bit she was forgetting the pain of losing Kevin, whether she had loved him or not.

The only other person aware of the diary was Tristan Hadley, Megan's husband. He had discovered the volume back when she used to keep it in her downstairs study rather than her bedroom. Aurelia had cooked dinner for the Hadleys and three other academic couples from her department. During dessert, when the talk turned to nineteenth-century literature, Tris had taken himself off to wander around the house. Like many intellectuals, he hated conversations in which he could not shine. When his absence became embarrassing, Aurie had gone searching. She found him in her study, watched by Crunch, his tangly tail wagging with peculiar canine approval. Professors enjoyed peeking into each other's home libraries, for the pleasure of critiquing the books on their shelves. But Tristan had pillaged her desk and was leafing through the diary.

"What the fuck do you think you're doing?"

"Figuring you out." He handed the book back before she could slap him. "You're so delightfully mysterious."

"How dare you go through my private things!" she sputtered, unable to come up with anything better.

"I dare a great deal, Aurie. Maybe one day we can dare together."

"Tristan—"

"What are all those notes about, anyway? The Author? Shaking the throne? It's like a secret code."

"None of your business."

His eyes lit up. "You're writing a novel. Like your friend Edward Wesley."

"No."

"Then it's the other way around. You found them somewhere, and you're trying to figure them out for some reason." One of the risks of dealing with Tristan was that his mind worked a good deal faster than anyone else's. Except when he was busily experimenting, as he put it, with psychedelic drugs to expand his range of consciousness. "That explains why there's so much repetition and so many cross-outs. A mystery." Rubbing his palms together. "How exciting. You're solving a mystery. Maybe I can help."

"I don't want your help."

He pointed to the diary, which she had tucked under her arm. "Some of the phrases looked familiar."

"Why do you do this, Tristan? Why can't you leave me alone?"

"I love you. It's as simple as that."

Aurelia groaned. "You're a married man."

"So?" He seemed genuinely puzzled. "What does that have to do with anything? Don't you know the legend of Tristan?"

"Yes. But I'm not your Isolde. Now, will you please get out of here?"

"Certainly," he said, patting her bottom as he passed, and so drew a slap after all.

Not the first time. Probably not the last.

(I I I)

THEN THERE WAS THE CONSTANT STREAM of letters from Callie Finnerty, her neighbor in Mount Vernon, the bubbly blonde who had taught her how to mother. Callie loved the word *great*. Callie's life was going great. Her husband's career was going great. Her new house in Scarsdale was great. Her three children were growing up great. Callie's only fear was that her eldest would be drafted: other than that, things were great, great, great. Kevin had always looked down his nose at Callie, and Eddie would have had a grand old time mocking her letters. But there were nights when Aurelia sat alone in the kitchen, sipping what she always swore was her last glass of wine, envying the simplicity of Callie Finnerty's life.

Simplicity. Normality.

Aurelia had other friends whose lives seemed to her normal—
Sherilyn in New Jersey, Claire on Long Island—and she marveled at
her inability to achieve the same. She could have chosen another
husband. It needn't have been Kevin, or even Eddie. Plenty of men
would have married Aurie over the years, had she given them the
smallest encouragement, and lots of them would have provided her a
simple, happy life, where she could write letters burbling about how
everything was going great.

Mona Veazie, whose degrees were in psychology, often warned
that the words *what if* were a signpost on the road to depression,
especially if you treated yourself to a couple of drinks along the way.
But loneliness is too powerful a force to be countered by mere effort
of will, and sometimes *what if* is all we have.

CHAPTER 39

The American Angle

(1)

JANUARY OF 1967 was a month of peculiar contrasts. The state of Georgia, supposed heart of the "New South," swore in a new segregationist governor. The United States Army was accused of conducting secret germ-warfare experiments, and the Pentagon announced yet another new offensive in Vietnam, and yet another new call-up of reserves. In Kenya, a paleontologist claimed to have found the oldest remains of a human evolutionary ancestor, but three American astronauts died in a fire on the launch pad, so perhaps science was not clicking along at quite the expected pace. A month later, the great Edward Trotter Wesley Junior managed to squeeze all of these events into a clever piece in *The Nation*, drawing a series of broad themes to which he referred, collectively, as the American Angle. Only Aurelia, tut-tutting over the essay as she sat, snowbound, in Ithaca, knew the source of his inspiration, remembering how his younger sister used to distinguish between the Eddie Angle and the Junie Angle. The American Angle, wrote Eddie, involved the determination to stay far ahead of everyone in the world but, at the same time, to keep everything exactly the same. We wanted endless technological progress that would never alter society one iota. We wanted to dominate the world without suffering any consequences. If America failed to change the angle from which it looked at life—wrote Eddie—then the nation was at a moral dead end.

Aurelia took the American Angle to be just another silly Eddie Wesley idea, which would pass, as all his nonliterary brainstorms did, without notice. He had written that complimentary piece about

Nixon in 1962. Two years ago, he had criticized black leaders for growing too chummy with their corporate donors. Last year, he had argued that the Vietnam War might be necessary, because Communism had to be stopped. Nobody remembered those essays, Aurelia told herself. Nobody would remember this one.

She was mistaken.

She first sensed something was up when Lawrence Shipley, the historian, mentioned the piece at a faculty seminar. The following week, a congressman from California went to the House floor to read into the record a formal condemnation of "this man Wesley." Nixon called Aurelia to say, after a bit of huffery, that under the circumstances he did not think his campaign could use Eddie after all. He still admired Eddie, and liked him, but publicly—

Aurie wanted to laugh, but it was too late. Events were rolling. A Southern legislature adopted a resolution of condemnation. A respected *Times* columnist weighed in, urging restraint. One of the news weeklies did a cover story about how the nation looked at the world: IS THERE AN AMERICAN ANGLE? Eddie's picture was on the cover, superimposed over images of Vietnam, student protests, and the *Apollo 1* fire. Furious letters to the editor accused him of profiting from the tragedy.

And, just like that, Edward Wesley was not a novelist any more. He had become exactly what he had never sought to be: a public figure. Lecture bureaus called. So did other magazines. His publisher wanted a nonfiction book, a longer version of the same essay. The idea of writing a nonfiction book, Eddie told Aurelia when he escaped briefly to a tiny stone cottage she found for him on one of the farther Finger Lakes, scared him out of his wits. So did the idea of being recognized on the street. Besides, he needed all his energy for the search for Junie. They had not said she was dead, he explained, voice rich with hope. They had only said she was no longer part of them. She could be anywhere.

Actually, they had this conversation in bed. Aurelia had finally broken her firm rule. The cottage was musty and damp and very near the water. Ice formed at the bottom of the windowpanes, on the inside. The kerosene heater worked intermittently. Aurelia had rented the place for the month of March from a Binghamton auto-mobile salesman, a hunter who would be up later in the season. She thought the cottage atrocious, but guessed that Eddie, who assessed physical surroundings differently from most people, would find it rustic and inspiring. She was right. She was showing him around the place when their bodies brushed accidentally together, once, a sec-ond time, and that was the end of resolution. She had managed to keep her promise for nearly two years.

"Don't tell Gary," Aurelia said, lying naked in his arms for the first time in over a decade. "He'll just tell Mona, and Mona would laugh her head off."

"I won't tell anybody."

"I can't believe this."

"Are you sorry?"

"No," she said, but got out of bed anyway. The heater was work-ing for the moment, and the cottage was sweltering. In a couple of hours, it might be freezing. Like marriage, Aurie decided. She found her Virginia Slims. Ten years, she was thinking. More. This was not the awkward young man starting out. This Eddie was less gentle in bed but more confident. She had started out trembling with anticipa-tion and wonder, but the look in Eddie's eyes told her he had known all along this day would come. Now she stood in the window, tugged aside the tattered curtain, and looked out at the frothy gray winter water. The sweetly acrid cigarette smoke calmed her. Aurelia watched the waves. Eddie, studying her forty-year-old body, thought he had never seen anything so beautiful.

"So—what happens now?" she asked, acting with her back.

Eddie yawned. The drive from Washington was eight hours, and he had made it without stopping. "Probably I leave the country for a while. It's not a matter of safety," he added hastily. "It's just, right now, I can't go anywhere without drawing a crowd."

"I meant, to us. What happens to us?"

"Us. Us." Savoring the word, Eddie, too, slipped out of bed. He padded over and hugged her from behind. "Are you asking me or telling me?"

"Am I what?"

"Asking me or telling me. Because, if you're asking me, I say we get married. But I have a hunch you're going to say no—"

"That would be correct." She heard the sadness in his voice but could offer no comfort. She blew a smoke ring, then a second.

"Then don't ask me what happens next," he said. He kissed her nape. "Tell me what happens next."

She turned, looked into the eyes that had yearned unashamedly for so long. "For the moment, we go back to bed."

It was late morning, she had no classes today, and the children were at school, so the moment was long indeed.

(I I)

BUT IT ALSO ENDED, as all such precious moments do. Aurelia picked up her watch from the bedside table, squawked, blundered around looking for her clothes. She promised to call him later, but the cottage had no phone. The nearest was the booth at the Sinclair station a mile down the road. Eddie promised to call her instead. Racing back to town in the station wagon, Aurelia could not believe what she had allowed to occur. This was not just some man. This was not a stupid fling, like the one with Lawrence Shipley. This was Eddie. Her Eddie, yes, from Harlem, but the great Edward Trotter Wesley Junior, too. There were a thousand reasons not to be involved with him, from his present notoriety to the fact that if today's slip ever became known, Sherilyn and Claire and the others would decide that the old Harlem rumors were true, that Aurelia and Eddie had been messing around on the side all through her marriage to Kevin.

And there were other complications, complications she could never make him understand.

Aurie cursed and reviled herself, sulking silently for much of the evening despite the children's efforts to lighten their mother's mood. She yelled at the dog. When Eddie finally called, around ten, she was ready to bite his head off. She had prepared a speech, and even managed to get through most of it, but somewhere along the line began sobbing instead. There had been a time in Aurelia's life when she never cried. Now she seemed to do it once a week.

Eddie remained the perfect gentleman, unwilling to go away, but unwilling to press. "I won't push you," he said. "I can wait until you're ready."

"I won't ever be ready," she snapped, thinking, to her surprise, of Kevin, who always used to take such protestations on her part as challenges, not warnings. She remembered their courting days. The harder she had tried to erect walls, the harder Kevin had tried to break them down and sweep her off her feet.

Not until this moment, listening to Eddie's smooth placations, did Aurelia realize how much she missed her late husband. And not until the following morning, as she bustled about, herself again, singing silly songs with the children as she readied them for school, did Aurelia realize that she had loved Kevin Garland after all.

CHAPTER 40

Two Bites at the Apple

(1)

THE NEXT TIME she saw Eddie, he was not alone. He had arrived at the cottage on a Friday. Saturday had been taken up by the children—Locke's youth hockey in the morning, Zora's flute recital in the afternoon—for Aurelia was yielding to the town's conventions as fast as she could. Sunday she had surprised the kids by waking them early for a rare visit to the snooty Episcopal church near the campus, where she spent a lot of time on her knees. The sermon was about unmerited grace, and Aurelia figured she unmerited a lot of it. Not until Tuesday did she feel sufficiently fortified. Even so, she took care to dress as sexlessly as possible, changing after classes, throwing on the worn, heavy sweater in which she lounged around the house in the wee hours. She decided to take Crunch along as chaperone, penning him behind the mesh in the back of the station wagon. When she reached the stone cottage, she found in the driveway not only Eddie's huge Cadillac but one of those tiny round modern machines made by a hesitant Japanese company called Subaru, advertised with a cute little jingle about saving money and gas.

She got out of her station wagon. Eddie's visit was supposed to be a secret. She felt skittish and irritated, as if he had broken the rules. She opened the liftback, and the dog ran barking around the back of the house. She walked over to the Subaru. The shiny blue panels were caked with salt from the roads. The plates, like Eddie's, read DISTRICT OF COLUMBIA.

No way to find out but to knock.

The rickety door flew open as soon as her knuckles touched it, and Aurelia could not suppress a gasp. A comely black woman stood there, early twenties if that, slim and green-eyed and fair, all the things the old Harlem families used to worship. She was dressed to the nines, and Aurelia was at once ashamed of her own costume. The girl said, "Hello, Mrs. Garland, please come in," and Aurelia, regaining her composure, recognized the melodious Southern voice. She had heard it a time or two on the telephone. This was Mindy, a graduate of Spelman, Eddie's latest assistant. He hired black women right out of college. People whispered that the duties Eddie required of them were considerably more than secretarial, an assertion Aurelia always laughed off. Yet the rumor mills of the darker nation never associated him with anybody else, and, stepping inside, Aurelia felt herself stiffening with what could only have been jealousy, and burning with what could only have been shame. The events of last Friday had happened to somebody else, a long time ago, and would never, ever happen again.

Over by the sofa stood a delicately feminine overnight bag.

Eddie was sitting at the plank table, reviewing a document that Mindy had obviously brought along.

"I just wanted to make sure you had everything you needed," Aurelia said, voice strained. "But I guess you're well taken care of."

"What? Oh. Make yourself at home." He had barely glanced up. "I'll just be another minute."

"No, no, I can't stay—"

Eddie was already reading again, distressed as well as distracted.

"Well, I'll check on you in a few days," said Aurie, backing toward the door. "You know how to reach me if you need anything." Again her eyes moved toward Mindy, who stared back with a guileless triumph that appalled her.

"Yes," said Eddie, going back to page one. "Fine."

"A pleasure to make your acquaintance, Mrs. Garland," said well-bred Mindy in her syrupy tone.

"Mutual," was all Aurelia could manage. To Eddie: "Take care."

"Right," he echoed, still studying the document. Then his head jerked up, and he was seeing her as if for the first time. "I'm sorry. Wait."

"I really have to go—"

"Aurie, wait. I need to talk to you for a minute."

"I can't just now, Eddie. I'm sorry."

"Mindy, dear, please give us a minute."

"Certainly, Mr. Wesley," she drawled, and vanished into the only other room, which happened to be the bedroom. The door clicked behind her.

Aurelia stood there, feeling like an idiot.

"I really can't stay," she said.

"Please sit."

"I'd rather not."

His eyebrows went up. "What's the matter with you?"

"Nothing," she snapped, hating herself in this mood, unable to keep her eyes from cutting toward the bedroom.

Eddie's gaze followed. Understanding gleamed in his clever face, and now Aurelia was ready to scream. He had always been able to read her, and she had never been able to read him. His grin was wolfish. His voice was soft. "Aren't you the one who just told me we can't see each other again?"

"My God, Eddie, you could have waited more than two days!"

"Four days, actually."

She wanted to slap him, but the act would require a dangerous proximity. She backed toward the front door. "Goodbye, Eddie."

"Wait." On his feet, heading toward her. She kept moving. "Aurie, come on. I was joking, okay?"

"I really do have to go. The school bus—"

"Won't be along for another hour and a half. Here. Sit down. Please."

So Aurelia sat, managing to look disdainful and bitchy, a side of her she knew he had always found alluring.

"What is it?" she asked coldly.

"First of all, there is nothing going on between Mindy and me. She works for me, honey. That's all."

Aurelia lifted her chin a little higher. "What you do is your own business. It doesn't make any difference to me. And I am not your honey."

Eddie looked exasperated. "Mindy came to deliver this to me," he said, tapping the pages. The folder was bordered with a dull red stripe. "Aurie, look. This file is important. I've been waiting a long time for it. A very long time. Mindy is just doing her job. She drove all night, and she's worn out, so she's staying over. She's leaving tomorrow." He saw her face move, but now he was getting angry. "Unless I ask her to stay longer." Another pause, heat building on both sides. "So now I suppose you'll ask me about the sleeping arrangements."

"Fuck you." She made the five steps to the door in about half a second, wishing he would stop her, knowing he was too proud.

His hand touched her shoulder, and she froze.

"Let's not do this, okay?" The voice was the old Eddie, the Harlem Eddie. Her Eddie. "I'm sorry, honey. I have no right to talk to you that way."

He waited. Aurelia held her tongue, waiting right back. If he said he loved her, she would slap his face for thinking she was easy. If he said Mindy was sleeping on the sofa, she would curse him out for thinking she was jealous.

Instead, he said the only words that could have made her stay.

"I need your help, Aurie. It's about Junie."

(11)

THE WOODEN TABLE WOBBLED when she put her weight on it, because one of the legs was loose. Kevin would have been underneath tightening the screws, but Eddie was immune to the need to showcase his masculinity.

"It took me years to get this," he said, putting the pages back in order. "I pulled in all the markers I could think of. Gary Fatek. Everybody I knew from my White House days. Even Lanning Frost."

"Lanning? I didn't realize—"

"I met him in the Kennedy campaign. I went through Margot, and—well, I guess I implied—I'm sorry, Aurie. I used your name."

"My name? What does— Oh." She had not considered this angle. The whole world thought Lanning Frost was alive today because Kevin Garland died in his place. Lanning would naturally believe he owed her. Aurelia supposed she should be furious at Eddie, but her anger was, for the moment, exhausted. As for the memories being dredged up—well, she would deal with those later, and alone. Eddie was still apologizing, but she waved him silent. "It's okay. I understand." She found a smile somewhere. "Really, Eddie. Tell me about what Mindy brought you."

Eddie hesitated, then reached down to pick up the red-bordered folder from the floor. The words SECRET—LIMDIS were stamped prominently on the cover. Eddie saw her looking. "They use a special paper that can't be copied. This is a set of originals. They're the ones that go to senior executive-branch and elected officials. They're redacted to protect sources, and, well, this is why I need your help."

"Elected officials." Aurelia tilted her head to one side, the schoolmarm look from the old days. "This is Lanning's personal copy, isn't it? Oh, Eddie. Why would he take this chance for you? What did you have to promise him?"

But they both knew the question was rhetorical. She gave up and reached for the folder. Eddie grabbed her hand.

"What's the matter? Why can't I touch it?"

"Let's just say this set is borrowed. It doesn't matter who from. The point is, Aurie, I have to give it back. Now, it's okay for my fingerprints to be on the folder. If there's ever an investigation, they'll already know I had it in my possession. But there's no reason for them to know you had anything to do with this."

Aurelia took her hand back. His protectiveness annoyed her. "What about little Mindy?"

"It was delivered inside another envelope, and I told her to wear gloves. She hasn't touched the folder itself." Eddie waited, but Aurie had no more questions. "These are summaries of surveillance reports. What the senior officials get. This is everything they have about Jewel Agony. And it's not enough." He banged his hand on the table. "It's not enough. There's information here, and it helps, but I need more." He opened the folder, pulled the pages apart, finger darting. "Look at this one. Junie's code name is WAKEFUL CURRENT. Don't touch. Just read. See?"

Aurelia read. And saw. And was careful not to touch the pages. The sources supplying the intermittent reports were similarly obscured: ORANGE VOLUME, SILVER APPLE, and so forth. It took Aurie only a minute to understand that the good guys—the FBI's informants—were all given code names beginning with colors. She looked wherever Eddie pointed. The pickings were as thin as he described. 1960: Wakeful Current seen passing through a safe house in Dallas. 1962: Wakeful Current overheard arguing with another commander about a proposed action. 1963: Wakeful Current believed to have left the country. Wakeful Current attends Ghana summit with heads of two other radical groups, names redacted. 1964: Wakeful Current spotted in Los Angeles, believed in Boston, moved to Georgia. 1965: Wakeful Current renounces violence, charged with ideological error, placed on trial, stripped of her authority—

Aurelia looked up.

Eddie's face was pale. No wonder he had been distracted.

"Eddie—"

He shook his head, tapped the page. "Keep reading."

She did.

The next report was dated spring of 1966, just under a year ago. It was brief and, in its toneless way, poignant:

Multiple sources report subject WAKEFUL CURRENT no
longer in contact with elements of Agony. Current
whereabouts unknown. Source GREEN SADDLE (q.v.)
reports rumors subject WAKEFUL CURRENT expelled.
Source GOLD DECKHAND (q.v.) reports rumors subject
WAKEFUL CURRENT liquidated by elements of Agony.
Rumors not substantiated. (Note: Multiple sources report
subject WAKEFUL CURRENT in the past sought
assistance on urgent matters from unknown Negro male

known as FERDINAND, surname not given, no ref, no
file. Sources believe witness FERDINAND might be aware
of present condition and whereabouts.)

Aurelia realized that she was gripping Eddie's hands. Tightly, her
nails digging into his flesh. Her arms trembled. She did not know
which of them was being reassured. When Eddie spoke, his words
were empty of emotion.

"Ferdinand is Perry Mount. It's a name from when we were kids.
Perry works for the State Department, in the Agency for International Development. These days, that usually means CIA." Aurie
said nothing. "None of my sources can get information out of that
particular vault. This is where you come in."

"Me?"

"I need to know where Perry is. I promised not to ask you about
Kevin, and I won't. But I need your help to find Perry. I need to find
him, and make him tell me what's happened to my sister."

Aurie let go of his hands. "Eddie, come on. I'm a half-salary lecturer in English at Cornell. I don't know anybody at the CIA."

"But you know somebody who will know somebody. I bet he'll be
happy to help."

"Who? You already tried Lanning!"

"Nixon."

"What?"

"Dick Nixon. You always liked him, Aurie. The Garlands raised a
ton of money for him. They say he keeps in close touch with the
intelligence people, and, well, I'm sure he'd be delighted to hear
from Matty's daughter-in-law."

"Be serious, Eddie. He's running for President next year. Even if
he took my call, well, it's not the best time to ask him to spill the
Agency's secrets."

"Would you try? That's all I'm asking." She had never seen such
pain in his patient eyes. "Please, Aurie. I need this. I'm out of ideas."

Somehow Aurelia was back in the station wagon, Crunch yapping
in his pen. Probably she had promised to try. She could scarcely
remember anything but those imploring eyes. She glanced at the

Subaru, reminded herself that Eddie's sex life was none of her business, and backed into the road. She was late, but could still beat the school bus if she broke enough laws. She skipped lights and, passing through one of the villages, touched eighty miles an hour. Aurelia told herself that she was running home to greet the children, but another part of her knew she was running away. Eddie demanded too much of her. If she allowed him to get too close, he would turn her inside out, and she would find herself telling the secrets she most needed to keep.

Odd how he had never doubted she would do as he asked.

(III)

NIGHT. Eddie sat at the table in undershorts and tee shirt. Mindy was asleep in his bed. She had left the door open, and made clear that he was free to join her, but he had thrown a blanket over the sofa and planned to make do. He was flipping through the surveillance summaries again, particularly the ones he had kept from Aurelia's view through the transparent device of not allowing her to touch the pages. He kept coming back to the same report, dated 1961:

> Subject WAKEFUL CURRENT is reliably reported to have given birth to a child. According to source SILVER APPLE, the child was taken for adoption. According to source BLUE SHEPHERD, the child was born shortly after Agony launched its unsuccessful attack on the county jail in Macon, Georgia. Further action not recommended at this time.

Eddie stared at the paper. He remembered the attack in Macon, as he remembered the details of every publicly known action of Jewel Agony. The attack on the jail—really just a cluster of shots fired from a passing truck, missing everything, even the many police cars sitting outside—had occurred in the late spring of 1959. The nation's press had announced, with the oracular imagination that never failed, even when wrong, that the incident had been timed to protest the lynching of Mack Charles Parker, in Poplarville, Mississippi, several states away. Maybe Macon was more convenient. Maybe the motive was different. What mattered to Eddie was that if the baby was born after the Macon attack, then the baby was born three years after Junie's disappearance.

His sister had a second child.

CHAPTER 41

The Domino

(1)

A FEW WEEKS LATER, freshly credentialed as a journalist for a radical monthly, Eddie took the early-morning flight from Hong Kong to Saigon. The Boeing 707 was crowded with reporters, diplomats, and war profiteers. As they swooped over the mountains at ten thousand feet, the country looked marvelously lush. From the air, the war might have been mythology, although the young executive sitting beside him kept talking excitedly about how one of his co-workers had been blown up in a café, and the pilot selected a sharp angle of descent to avoid whatever form of surface-to-air death hid among the beautiful trees.

Aurelia had come through. That was what Eddie kept telling himself, with happy wonder. She had gone to Nixon, and Nixon had discovered that Perry Mount was in Vietnam. There the information stubbornly halted, but Eddie had always believed in the power of determination. Finding the whereabouts of a single man in a country at war did not daunt him. Moreover, it made sense that Perry would be here. Philmont Castle had negotiated deals for his clients all over Europe, but Kevin had done Europe. The lawyer had also traveled extensively in Southeast Asia—particularly in Hong Kong and Vietnam, back when it was a French protectorate.

Perry was here for the federal government, yes; but he was also here in service to the Project. He was searching for Castle's testament.

Eddie stayed for a while at the Caravelle, because Mona Veazie, who had ex-lovers everywhere, had given him the name of a British journalist who used it. Mona's friend was at the front. Waiting for his return, Eddie hung out at Jerome's Bar with the movers and shakers, but the war reporters never paid for their own drinks and kept the best gossip to themselves. He had arrived in mid-April, in the middle of Operation Junction City, a massive, and successful, American assault on major Viet Cong bases in Tay Ninh Province. At first he cared little for such details. He did not know where Tay Ninh was, and was unimpressed that the North ran the war from there. But he quickly learned that his attitude was one of the reasons the press corps ignored him. Nobody cared that he had won two National Book Awards. Either you followed the war or you were an outsider.

Eddie could hardly search for Perry from the outside. And so he changed his ways. He became conversant in the details of the war. He learned who could be quoted, who could be believed, whom to avoid. Once he learned who was who, he changed hotels, moving on to the Duc, considerably lower in the pecking order, because he heard that the guys from the Central Intelligence Agency hung out there, but they gossiped even less. He saw no sign of Perry Mount. In his innocence, he had imagined blundering into the golden boy in the hotel restaurant.

Not much going on, he wrote to Aurelia, his mother, and whoever was intercepting his mail. *The best stories have all been told. Probably a wasted trip.*

He was surprised by the heat. He was surprised by the dust. Nothing was shiny but the cars of the rich, which must have been washed and waxed several times a day. Yet the city was bursting with energy. Everyone seemed to be employed by the war. The American buildup filled coffers, but also wrecked the economy, because the local currency became worthless: everybody wanted dollars. Inflation was uncountable. The traffic was impossible. Small-time business-men and big-time pimps glided through crowded streets in late-model European sedans. Motorcycles, from Honda to Vespa and most brands in between, wove through the snarls. The fighting seemed very far away, except at night, when you heard the distant whump of artillery, and sometimes not so distant; and in the morning, when you found freshly burned planes at the airport, or abandoned tanks on the ragged city outskirts. Now and then, a squadron of National Police would barricade a house, rush inside, and drag off some poor soul who, within days if not hours, would certainly confess to giving aid and comfort to the National Liberation Front, whether or not it was true.

The Americans had barricaded the center of the city, yet the safe zone they had thereby created was anything but. There was a morbid pecking order among the hotels. The Caravelle, owned by the Catholic Church, was widely acknowledged as safest: rumor said management had done a side deal with the NLF to avoid the terror bombings that intermittently shook other buildings. But rumor said lots of things. It was rumor, as much as anything, that had led Eddie here in the first place.

"He can't say for sure," Aurelia had warned, the two of them walking on the Cornell campus, where anybody could see.

"I understand," Eddie had answered, carefully not touching her. "But I still have to try."

"I know. Eddie?"

"Yes, Aurie?"

"You be careful, okay?"

"I will," he deadpanned. "But only because you asked me."

She walked him to his car, parked in Collegetown, at the edge of the campus. "Keep in touch," she said.

"I will." He stroked her cheek. She allowed it. "I'll miss you."

"I'll miss you, too."

"Aurie, about what happened—"

"I know," she said, and, briefly and lightly, kissed him.

He smiled in delight, and promptly ruined the moment. "I'll write you. If you can't reach me, try through Mindy."

Aurelia stiffened. "Certainly," she said, and left him.

(11)

EDDIE WAS RUNNING OUT of things to do. He kept spotting Perry in the crowded streets but he was always wrong. To settle himself down, and further establish his bona fides, he decided to act like a real war correspondent. He spent a week traveling along the McNamara Line with a company from I Corps, and wound up caught in a firefight on the Hill of Angels near Quang Tri. Shells landed right on top of them, blowing Eddie's brain to bits, except really they were nowhere near. Constant strafing fire meant nobody dared stand up. It had never occurred to Eddie that bullets were invisible. In the movies they always sparked when they hit metal but in real life they just knocked pieces out of objects and men and ricocheted on. Helicopters angled in through the fusillade to pick up the wounded and drop off ammunition.

When the shooting abated, a bespectacled lieutenant named Cox helped Eddie up. Eddie asked him what happened next. The lieutenant said the North Vietnamese needed the hill and would, sooner or later, try to take it. Eddie asked what that meant for the unit. We're not gonna let it happen, the lieutenant said. He looked at Eddie's empty hands.

"Ever fired a gun, Mr. Wesley?"

"Not really. No."

"Well, we're not really allowed to give you a weapon, but if they come hard, you find me and I'll see what I can do, because nobody's neutral. Know what I mean?"

But the real assault came weeks later, after Eddie was safely back in Saigon. One afternoon he visited a club Perry had been known to frequent. He did not find Perry, but he did find Lieutenant Cox. Eddie bought him a drink.

"What was it like?" Eddie asked.

The lieutenant took off his glasses. The eyes were fiery and empty at once, as if he was furious and had forgotten why. "We kept the hill," he said.

(111)

MONA'S JOURNALIST FRIEND RETURNED in early May: a bearded, pudgy Santa of a man, whose jolliness seemed to Eddie a concealment for the near-unraveling evidenced by the tremble in his fingers and the spittle on his fleshy lips. His name was Simon Pratt, and he told Eddie to take the direct approach. If you want to find somebody, said Pratt with his desperate smile, the best way is to ask. Oh, but how is the lovely Mona?

Thriving, said Eddie. If Mona had not told the Britisher about her recent marriage, it was hardly Eddie's place to disclose her secrets.

Nevertheless, he followed Pratt's advice, weaving past the walls and sandbags and machine-gun emplacements protecting the United States Embassy to ask for Perry Mount, only to be assured that nobody of that name worked there. A grinning Pratt, writing his eighth or ninth war, suggested Eddie try some of the other American agencies, but the answer was the same. Though Eddie wandered the city, he found no journalist who had heard of Perry; no landlord who had rented to him; no restaurateur who had served him.

Pratt had another idea. He positively bristled with them. He also possessed sources Eddie could never tap. Pratt was willing to do a bit of hunting, in exchange for what he called a share of the take. Eddie agreed. Pratt came up with a rumor that Perry Mount had set up housekeeping with a Vietnamese girl from one of the shantytowns that ringed Saigon. Pratt had no location or name, just the rumor, and the rumor was not well sourced. Nor could he ride along. All the correspondents in town were always on the way to someplace else, and Pratt was leaving at once for the Central Highlands, where American forces were interdicting North Vietnamese forces moving in from Cambodia. On his own again, Eddie hired a driver and poked his nose into the city's dank corners, where the poor sat blank-faced in front of tiny slanting houses that might sleep a dozen to a floor. His cover was a story for the magazine, and he even thought he might write one. He wanted the shantytowns to be America's fault, but the slums had been there forever. His driver refused to stop. Too dangerous, he said. Eddie gave the man ten dollars extra. Grudgingly, the driver pulled over at a shack. He argued with the people inside. They got back into the car, drove to another. And another. The same thing happened each time. Eddie asked what they told him. The driver shrugged.

"They don't know your friend. They say you all look alike."

At one of the shanties, two men ran out the back as the car approached, and another emerged from inside, holding some kind of knife. The driver talked to him more respectfully, and without alighting.

"He says you're American police. He says you're far from home."

Eddie could not tell whether he was being taken for a ride. They returned to the city.

Back from the Highlands, chubby Pratt dragged him to the sites of a couple of terror bombings, and at one of them, a bar that had catered to American soldiers, Eddie stepped on rancid chicken bones while craning for a better look and heard them crack beneath his boot, except that they were pieces of a shredded human hand. On the way back downtown, Pratt assured him that everybody vomited the first time. Eddie said nothing. He was thinking of the boys Scarlett had tortured into talking in Harlem long ago, and how for a few weeks he had skipped the newspapers to avoid learning their fate. He felt small, and morally obtuse. The next day, he filed a short piece on the compensation paid by the American military if a soldier accidentally killed a civilian. The leftish magazine that credentialed his trip happily ran the story, which was picked up by the wire services, and made Eddie more friends in some circles, more enemies in others.

The going rate for a dead Vietnamese was thirty dollars.

(I V)

IN THE CITY, the locals took him for an off-duty soldier. As he walked the crowded streets, or rode in a *cyclo*, they offered to sell him most things, including guaranteed North Vietnamese military secrets and genuine ancient Buddhist artifacts made of plastic. Young men whispered the tricks their wares would play on his mind. Young women in skirts of breathtaking shortness shouted out prices as he passed. He bought souvenirs for Aurelia and his mother and Marcella but could not find a story worth telling. Eddie prowled for his American Angle, and almost glimpsed it. Nobody in Saigon thought defeat was possible. The city was too thrilled, too drunk on American dollars, which everyone mistook for American power. But there was more to the country than Saigon. In reality, said Pratt, the combination of American troops and the Army of the Republic of Vietnam controlled only the major cities and a few key roads. By day you could drive from one town to the next. By night you partied behind high walls, or huddled in your bed, assuring yourself that if you closed your eyes it would be morning.

Eddie made notes but could not work the idea into an essay.

Three days after visiting the bombing site, he hit pay dirt. At the end of the "Saigon follies"—the unofficial name for the official military briefing, usually held on the rooftop of the Rex Hotel—a writer for one of the news magazines pulled him aside to ask if it was true that he was looking for Perry Mount.

Eddie said he might be.

The black CIA man?

Possibly.

Amused, the reporter pointed to a woman standing near the edge of the terrace as if in a fog.

"She's a freelance photographer. She's won a couple of awards. She's his girlfriend, or at least used to be."

(v)

HER NAME WAS TERI, and she was white and tangled and skinny as a refugee. Eddie's magical name impressed her. They went to the bar. She told her story dictation-style, the words evenly spaced, like a confession at the end of a long bout of torture. No, she said. She was not Perry's girlfriend. They were friends, she supposed, and in war a lot of things happened, but "girlfriend" was a little strong. It was only a fling, Teri insisted. The look in her war-weary eyes said she was willing to have another. But Eddie wanted Teri's facts, not her flesh. Worried about a setup, he asked if Perry still ate Milky Way bars by the bushel. Teri seemed confused. No, she said. She never saw him eat a Milky Way. But he scarfed one Baby Ruth after another, man. So she really did know him. They went to another bar and talked. Perry was genuine State Department, Teri told him—not Agency. She seemed very certain of it, although, pressed, she could not say what made her so sure. Except that he was so determined to help people. He was a good man, said Teri, eyes empty. He wanted to change the world a little bit at a time. He was involved in all these food programs. Working with the farmers. Oh, and he was totally committed to nonviolence, man.

Great. But where is he now?

He has a house in Hong Kong.

Is he there now? Or is he in Vietnam?

Those wide eyes that had seen too much darted around the room. "No idea," she muttered, into her drink.

"I'm staying at the Duc," said Eddie. "If you see him, will you tell him I'm looking for him?"

"I won't see him. Nobody sees him. He's the spooky kind of spook, man."

"Will you tell him?"

Teri might have nodded. She might not have. But she remembered, very suddenly, that she had to make an urgent call. She said she would be right back. As Eddie watched her every move, she used the barman's phone. She seemed to wait a very long time for whoever was on the other end. The whispered conversation was short.

Teri was back. And more nervous than before. She tried to nibble at a fingernail, but they were all bitten to the quick. Now she was sure Perry was no longer in the country. Eddie should try Hong Kong. She had to get going. She had forgotten an appointment. Out on the street, she asked Eddie if she could take a couple of shots of the great writer. She posed him near a street market, then shook her head and said she wanted a better backdrop. She posed him beside a brightly colored funeral wagon with its fake pagoda. No good. She hurried off, waving at Eddie to follow. She took a sharp corner, then another, and left him behind. Or thought she did. Teri climbed into a dusty Chevy about a thousand years old and drove like a maniac. Eddie knew this because his cab driver was following her. She did not look in any shape to spot a tail. The center of town was an ultra-low-rent version of Times Square. Bars were crowded, although most of the outdoor patios were closed: you never knew when a grenade might roll out of the swarm of humanity and ruin your dinner. Teri's Chevy blew past delivery trucks and sidewalk stalls. A traffic policeman in his white gloves stared from beneath the golden canopy that marked his stand. He did not interfere with the weaving caravan. He knew Americans when he saw them.

The Chevy pulled up to a gate. She said something to the guard, and the gate was raised. Eddie got out of his cab. The sign said LE CERCLE SPORTIF SAIGONNAIS: the swankiest country club in the city. He watched Teri hand her key to the valet, who stared at the rusting car in disbelief.

Eddie waited until she had vanished within the walls. He walked up to the gate, waved his expired White House pass, and bluffed and boistered his way inside.

He had heard of the glamorous Cercle Sportif, he had passed it many times, but he had never been inside. The club stood in the shadow of the heavily fortified presidential compound, just past the American military dispensary. With its green lawns and jacketed waiters, the place was a breath of European luxury in the midst of war. Teri was heading for the clubhouse. Everybody stared. At Eddie, not Teri. Slender white women were a dime a dozen at the club, but Negroes were not generally seen on the grounds, even in service. Le Cercle was home to Saigon's remaining beautiful people, mostly Caucasian, some Eurasian, or, in a few cases of absurd wealth, full Vietnamese. All the beautiful people seemed present and accounted for this morning, sunning themselves by the shimmering pool. Everybody was excited, because earlier this morning a pair of well-heeled guests at another private club, Le Club Nautique, had rented a boat and motored up the Saigon River, only to be shot dead, probably by the NLF. Can you *imagine*? Really, you would think the police could protect *us*.

Teri climbed the steps to the veranda with its gilded rails. Eddie lingered below, figuring there was no place for her to escape to. After a few minutes, he followed her up. The headwaiter stopped him, but Eddie smiled and said he was meeting a lady. He pointed to Teri, who had settled at a table in a shaded corner, between the pool and the tennis courts, partially shielded by a kiosk—not the most prestigious spot, but one of the least visible. Eddie wove his way past Saigon's beautiful people. When he was a half-dozen yards away, he realized that he had erred. It was only what she had reported, an urgent appointment, because the man sitting across from Teri was not Perry Mount. He was white, and thin, and wore a thick black beard. Eddie slowed. The man's superior way of inclining his head was somehow familiar. He looked prosperous, and Eddie thought he might be one of the European traders who flocked across Saigon like carrion eaters on a carcass. The man looked up. The haughty eyes met Eddie's.

And stared in terror.

Teri turned around.

The man rose to his feet. Not to run. To extend a hand, as if they were old friends. The stranger's natural hauteur, nurtured through years of performance in cavernous law-school classrooms, swallowed the evident fear. An instant before he spoke, Eddie recognized him.

And was too startled to shake back.

"Welcome to Saigon," said the late Benjamin Mellor.

CHAPTER 42

Various Counselors

(I)

LOCKE GARLAND, age nine, had been in another fight. His mother sat through a lecture from the friendly guidance counselor, who kept telling her how wonderfully sweet Zora was—the same Zora who had moved on, early, to junior-high school and no longer fell under the jurisdiction of the counselor, whose duties ended at sixth grade. If only Locke could be more like Zora, the counselor sighed, fingering the stems of the glasses she wore on a faux-gold chain round her beefy neck. No, no, no, she was not blaming the boy—of course not. Probably the other boys taunted him. He was scrawny, he was bookish, and he was a Negro—what would you expect? The other Negro kids were not on the honors track. Well, except Zora, and she was gone. Naturally they would make fun. They were good boys. The counselor wanted Aurelia to understand that. They were good boys, just as Locke was a good boy, and good boys got into fights sometimes. Part of learning to be a man.

Then why are we having this conversation? Aurelia wanted to ask, but did not.

"I'm a liberal," said the counselor, having decided to put the glasses back on. Behind the thick lenses her emerald eyes seemed kinder, or maybe just larger. "I believe in integration. And I'm so glad you moved to Ithaca, and we got your kids onto the honors track." *We:* as if their mother had not been forced to do fierce battle over every inch of ground. "They're wonderful children, Mrs. Garland. You should be very proud of them."

"I am."

The smile wavered a bit. "But I believe what they may need is the firm hand of a father."

"I beg your pardon."

"A man, Mrs. Garland. Your children need a man in their lives."

Her irritation boiled over. "Are you offering me one?"

The counselor wisely chose to take this as a joke, for she had been in the business thirty years and knew when a mother was about to declare war. In her way, she apologized.

"I know it can't have been easy for you, Mrs. Garland, losing your husband that way. I won't pretend to know what it's like. But I was divorced, and that wasn't so easy, either. I still found Mr. Right."

"Thanks for your advice," said Aurelia, and went out into the hall, where Locke sat on a bench. She was late to collect Zora from the gifted-children's program that had not wanted to take her either. All the way into town, Locke kept trying to tell his mother that the other boys had called him "Brillo," because of his hair, and Aurelia kept lecturing him, the way she imagined her father would have lectured her brothers, if only she had grown up with a father and brothers: *If you let them know they can get to you, they'll never stop. You can bloody every one of their noses twice a day, and they'll never stop.* Then Zora tumbled into the station wagon, all legs and teeth and excitement, babbling about prime numbers, and Aurelia, at her wit's end, told her to please just hush for once. But when she looked in the mirror and saw her children's faces, she relented and stopped at the sweet shop for vanilla malts.

It was not their fault. She was worried about Eddie. She had one telegram from him since he left for Saigon, and that was three weeks ago. She had no right to take it out on her children. The thought of Eddie in the middle of the war appalled her more than she would have imagined. And so she was rude to the guidance counselor and snapped at her children for no good reason, and made up for these sins by cravenly offering ice cream and malts—bribes, fortunately, that her children were still willing to accept.

The kids were so happy, in fact, they even cajoled their mother into going off her diet and having a root-beer float, which she had once told them, teasingly, had been invented by her grandfather.

They seemed to believe it still.

(11)

When Aurelia pulled into the driveway an hour later, Tristan Hadley was waving like a madman from his metallic-blue Ford Galaxie convertible, parked across the street. Aurelia could not believe her eyes. She sent the kids into the playroom and served Tris coffee in the kitchen. He looked the way he always looked: tall and elegant and handsomely innocent. He carried a scuffed leather bookbag, the old-fashioned kind with clasps on top, and you had the impression that he had been a serious reader before he was born.

"You shouldn't be here," she began, sharply, before he had the chance to get a real word out. "What's the matter with you, Tris? Are you on something? Because, just in case you haven't noticed, Ithaca is a very small town. You know better than this. I want you to stop dropping by my house. I want you to stop dropping by my office. I want you to stop calling me and leaving me cute little notes."

"I'm glad you think they're cute," he said, careful not to smile.

"You know what I mean." Crunch, the beagle, slunk in to see if it was time to eat. Aurelia lectured her unwanted guest over her shoulder as she crouched, filling the dog's bowl.

"All I know is I miss you."

"You can't miss me. Number one, you're a married man. Number two, we've never done anything worth missing."

"We used to talk."

"That was before you decided you were in love with me."

"A realization," he corrected her. "Not a decision."

"You're out of your mind."

Tristan's smile flashed, boyish and helpless, the man-child whom life has denied nothing. "Hey, I have something for you." He was delving in the pocket of his jacket, and for a terrible instant Aurelia was afraid he would pull out a diamond ring, a divorce decree, or both. But he withdrew only a notebook. "Remember those phrases you showed me? The ones you couldn't track down?"

"Showed you? You were rifling my desk, Tristan. While your wife was in the other room. Or don't you remember that part?" Aurelia called him Tristan, not Tris, when he annoyed her, and he annoyed her often. "Megan sat there at the table and I had to go looking for you. In my own house, Tristan. Think about that for a minute. Think about Megan."

"I am thinking about Megan." He was flipping through his notes. "She'll be getting her doctorate this spring. After that, well, the availability of academic appointments being what it is, we could wind up at different schools—"

"Don't even dream it."

But Tristan Hadley, an academic from a vast family of academics, had been raised in a world where the mark of intelligence was saying whatever you pleased. "The marriage," he declared, right hand over his heart to prove sincerity, "was forced upon me."

"With men it seems like it always is. If nobody forced marriage on men, none of you would ever get married."

"Unless the right woman comes along."

"What do you *want*, Tristan?"

The soft eyes went wounded. Tris could do hurt as brilliantly as he did most things. But when Aurelia refused the implicit invitation to apologize or embrace, he sighed, and surrendered. "I don't know if you remember, but Megan's field is the early moderns. She did her thesis on Aphra Behn. Anyway, Megan's the one who worked the whole thing out."

"What whole thing is that?"

"Those phrases you didn't understand. Megan told me where they came from."

Aurelia could not believe her ears. "You told your wife what you found snooping in my study? I'm right about you, Tristan. You've taken leave of your senses."

"Love does that to people," he said calmly. "I told her I came across them in a student paper. Why are you looking at me like that? There's no reason to think she suspects."

"There's nothing to suspect."

"That's right. Now, come around here so I can show you what she discovered." *Around here* meaning over to his side of the kitchen island, which Aurelia had prudently kept between them.

"I can see fine from where I am."

"The typeface is a little small," he said, pulling from his bookbag a cracked leather-bound edition of *Paradise Lost* by John Milton. "This is where the phrases come from."

"What?"

" 'The Author,' 'shaking the throne,' everything. It's all here."

(I I I)

IT TOOK HER ANOTHER HOUR to get Tristan out of the house. He did not get a kiss, but he did get a hug and a smile of thanks, and that was enough to persuade him to leave Milton behind. She fed the kids, graded a few student papers, then turned to *Paradise Lost*. Aurelia studied the yellowy pages of the book. Her dissertation topic had been the response of European writers to Negro abolitionists, with a special focus on Martin Delany and his novel, *Blake*. She had never read Milton. An undergraduate degree in English, a doctorate in literature, and she had never read Milton.

Her conversation with Tristan had been instructive. He had preened and pranced around the kitchen, proud to have proved himself, and Aurelia had let him do it. She rarely saw his pedagogical side, and saw why, years ago, a graduate student named Megan Feldman had found it so attractive.

"What do you know about *Paradise Lost*?" he had asked.

"Satan against God, right?"

Tris had furrowed his smooth brow, the way the learned do when confronting the Philistine. "Well, that's a start, Aurie, but you're oversimplifying a little. *Paradise Lost* is an epic poem about the danger of ambition and hubris, and the foolishness of obsession and revenge. Satan rebels against God out of pride. He rallies other angels to his cause, but he and his army are defeated and cast into the fiery pit, where Satan tells his troops they can still win. He refuses to believe that God is as omnipotent as the disillusioned rebels keep whining. Satan keeps fighting, keeps losing."

"Because he's evil," Aurelia murmured, wanting to slow Tristan down, because in his teaching mode he was too endearing. "Or because he's a fool."

The anthropologist never paused. "Some authorities think that Milton, who for his time was considered a progressive sort of Christian, shows a sneaking admiration of Satan. Not what you might call Satan's politics. His perseverance. And, you know, when the poem is taught as literature—especially to undergraduate seminars—there are always a couple of fiery arguments about how Satan was right to rebel against the arbitrary authority represented by God. My own view is that this is a serious misreading of the poem, and also of Christianity, but—"

Aurelia finally had to walk around the counter after all, because the only way she could make him stop talking was to cover his mouth. He seemed delighted at the physical contact, but when he reached for her she stepped away. "The quotes," she said, gently.

"Whatever you say." But as they stood side by side, looking down at the yellowed pages, Tristan managed to ride his hip against hers, and not just once. Unwilling to offend, she let it happen. "Over here," he said, pointing and pressing. "Here. Milton divides the poem into books. Now. Book I. As the story opens, Satan and his armies have just been defeated. He tries to rally the troops, to keep their spirits up, while he plots his revenge. Look, here's the quote about 'We shall be free.' One of the most famous stanzas in the poem:

> *The mind is its own place, and in itself*
> *Can make a Heav'n of Hell, a Hell of Heav'n.*
> *What matters where, if I be still the same,*
> *And what I should be, all but less then he*

Whom Thunder hath made greater? Here at least
We shall be free; th'Almighty hath not built
Here for his envy, will not drive us hence:
Here we may reign secure, and in my choice
To reign is worth ambition though in Hell:
Better to reign in Hell, than serve in Heav'n.

Tris glanced her way, eyes shining. "Brilliant. Milton, I mean. A genius. You see it, right?" But he marched straight on, just in case she did not. "Satan is telling them that, even if they only get to rule Hell, at least they get to rule. He does not mind being damned, as long as he no longer has to serve God. Do you see?"

"I see," said Aurelia, marveling. "What else?"

"Well, 'Author' is easy. It's simply another name for Satan. It recurs throughout the book. For example, in Book VI, in the midst of one of the battles, the Archangel Michael refers to Satan as 'Author of evil, unknown till thy revolt.' And there are others—"

He was flipping pages again. It occurred to her that Tristan had done a lot of work, trying to impress her. And she was, indeed, impressed. She had to remind herself that the presentation was mostly the fruit of Megan's research.

"Tris?"

"Yes, honey?"

"Don't call me honey. Listen. You said your wife told you all this?" Deliberately using her appellation, reminding them both. "After you showed her the quotes?"

"That's right," he said, suddenly testy.

"And you told her they were from—where again?"

"A student. A student who came across them somewhere."

Aurelia frowned. Thin. Tissue-thin. "And she did all this work? Just because one of your students was puzzled?"

"She's very conscientious," he said, piously. Then he saw his error. "She didn't do all the work, Aurie. I did a lot of it myself."

She turned a page. "Where did you get this book, anyway?"

"From Megan."

"You borrowed your wife's book? You didn't think she might notice?"

"What if she does?" Drawing himself up. "A man can borrow books from his own wife, can't he?" He tapped the pages. "I came here to help you, Aurie, and instead I'm facing a cross-examination. I resent that."

She sighed. "I'm sorry. You're right. This is all wonderful, and I'm grateful."

Tristan remained unsatisfied. "Maybe I should just go. Should I go on? Will you stop the nonsense now? Or should I just go?"

"I said I was sorry." Forcing the words out. "Please stay."

"If you insist." Grinning again, wanting Aurelia to see he knew he had outsmarted her. "Here's a part that gave us some trouble. That note you wrote about the four arrows or four letters 'A'? That one stumped us for a while." *Us*, she registered, sadly. "Then we found it. Here. Back in Book I again, Satan speaking to his fellow rebels. Read from, mmmm, line 105."

Aurie read:

> *"What though the field be lost?*
> *All is not lost; the unconquerable Will,*
> *And study of revenge, immortal hate,*
> *And courage never to submit or yield:*
> *And what is else not to be overcome?"*

Aurelia read the lines, then went over them again, registering the way the words pounded home their meaning. Unconquerable Will. Revenge. Immortal hate. Never to submit or yield. It sounded like an oath. A very angry oath.

Maybe that was it. The cross symbolized membership in some group that required—well, a very angry oath. An organization run by the Author.

Tristan, meantime, was talking again. "See how the first letter of each line lines up? They all start with 'A,' and they summarize Satan's case. And of course his pride. If you look down later in the paragraph, you'll see that this is where Satan reminds them that—from their point of view—God is a tyrant."

Aurelia had found the spot already. She followed his finger down the page, speaking the words half aloud. They chilled her blood:

> ". . . since by Fate the strength of Gods
> And this Empyreal substance cannot fail,
> Since through experience of this event
> In Arms not worse, in foresight much advanc't,
> We may with more successful hope resolve
> To wage by force or guile eternal War
> Irreconcilable, to our grand Foe,
> Who now triumphs, and in th'excess of joy
> Sole reigning holds the Tyranny of Heav'n."

She said, "What does this mean? 'Empyreal substance cannot fail'?"

Tristan returned to his notes. "Oh, right. Satan is saying that he and his angels, and his whole realm, are made of the same substance—the Empyreal substance—as Heaven. They are immortal. They cannot be destroyed. By God's own command and design, they are eternal."

"Let me understand. He's saying, as long as they are immortal, they might as well keep waging war against God? The Tyrant?"

"Exactly."

Empyreal substance, she was thinking. A rebellion against the Tyrant, led by the Author. Immortality. It fit.

Meanwhile, Tris was still turning pages. "One more thing in your notes. Pandemonium?"

"Yes?"

"That's the name of Satan's palace." He pointed. "See here? Milton refers to Satan's closest advisers as the 'council of demons.' They sit with Satan in his palace—in Pandemonium. So this other phrase in your notes—the 'Palace Council'—would have to be Satan's advisers. In other words, the Palace Council would be the leaders of"—he hesitated, grinned, shrugged—"well, of whatever it is that these notes are about."

"They're not about anything," she lied, hoping God would understand.

(I V)

THE CONVERSATION with Tristan had occupied much of the afternoon. Now Aurelia sat in her bedroom, Megan's copy of *Paradise Lost* beside her, notebooks spread everywhere.

She puzzled and puzzled. Why was "shaking the throne" mentioned so often? What did the oath mean? And, most baffling of all, why did the group identify so completely with Satan, who is doomed to defeat?

And then she had it.

Not all the details. Not yet. But she glimpsed the sweep of the Project, and understood the need for secrecy. She saw why Philmont Castle's testament was so fiercely sought—and fiercely defended. The key was the advisers to Pandemonium—the Palace Council. She stretched a trembling hand toward the telephone, only to remember that Eddie was half a world away. A cable to Saigon could wait days to find its recipient, if it got there at all; a letter already took a month.

Eddie was in Vietnam looking for Perry Mount because he believed the golden boy to be the path to Junie. But what if the Palace Council thought Eddie was searching for the testament? Aurelia had no idea what role, if any, Perry was playing in events. She did not, yet, know the fine old truth; she did know that Eddie was in terrible danger.

She sat on her bed long into the night, trying to figure out how to get a message to the man she loved, a man brave enough to wade into a war to find his sister, and careless enough to blunder into the middle of a more secret battle. She refused to allow herself the luxury of sentiment. Already she saw the ending. The Palace Council would kill him. It was as simple as that. The Council would kill the great Edward Wesley Junior to protect the secrets of its preposterous Project, and she had no way to warn him. She had lost Kevin, and now she would lose Eddie. She cried a little, prayed a little, dozed a little. Just past two in the morning, she had an idea. She padded downstairs to her study, took the address book from its nook, and, despite the hour, placed a call to New York City.

CHAPTER 43

Arrest

(1)

"You should have something to drink, Mr. Wesley," said Benjamin Mellor with that indulgent dip of the head. He had recovered entirely from his astonishment. "You need to calm the nerves." He signaled the waiter. "They do some marvelous local beers here." Pointing to the bottle in front of him.

"No, thank you," said Eddie. His voice was scratchy. He sat very stiffly. He had the sense that if he moved he would wake, and if he woke he would not hear the story, and he really did need to know why the confessed father of his sister's first baby was still alive. "I don't drink."

"Mineral water, then."

Mellor ordered two with the panache of a veteran French *colon*, even though he could not have been in Southeast Asia for more than four and a half years—four and a half years, that is, since he vanished in a boating accident off the Cape. In Eddie's files, he was listed as dead. Presumably his own family believed the same. Yet here he was, sitting at the fanciest club in Saigon as if he belonged. Teri had disappeared.

"This is rather awkward, Mr. Wesley," said the professor when the waiter had gone. "I wish I had known you were coming to town."

"So you could disappear again?"

"Precisely." He sipped his water. "You must be wondering what's going on."

"Good guess," said Eddie.

Mellor ignored the belligerence. "You thought I was dead. The world thinks I am dead. I would be grateful if you would be so kind as to leave the world with its illusions."

"You faked your death for—what? Self-protection?"

"Precisely. Everyone involved was dying—being killed—and I saw that I had better run or I would be joining them. Matty. Kevin. All of them. I ran—I had some help—and, well, here I am, established in society." He looked around the club with satisfaction. Over on the tennis court, Ambassador William Colby, said to rank high in the Central Intelligence Agency, was limbering up for a match. A Vietnamese millionaire was arguing with a famous reporter from one of the American television networks. Waiters scurried and bowed. "You can make a fortune in a war, Mr. Wesley. All you need is a little bit of brains and a little bit of guts. I think I wasted my intelligence teaching lawyers. It's the things you can do without the lawyers that make you rich."

"Everyone involved in what?"

"Sorry?"

"You said everyone involved was being killed."

Benjamin Mellor had finished his mineral water. He signaled the waiter, ordered something stronger in bad French. His linen suit was soaked with sweat. Either he had been drinking for a very long time or he was very nervous—quite possibly both. The tables nearest theirs were emptying. Eddie felt naked, and unprotected.

"Well, I suppose you're entitled," said the professor finally. "You're here, after all, and I suppose you could make trouble for me, tell them where I am." The waiter brought him a gin and tonic. Mellor lapped at it sloppily. "The thing you have to understand, Mr. Wesley, is that the Council is not the only, ah, entity concerned. So you understand my caution."

"The Council?"

"Dear me, you have fallen behind, haven't you? They call themselves the Palace Council. The group you're looking for, Mr. Wesley. Now, may I please continue?" As if addressing the classroom dunce. "Where was I? The Palace Council. Yes. The Council is searching for the testament. So are you, from what I gather. But so is somebody else. A third party, you might say. A third force, Mr. Wesley, that has not yet shown its face. And that third force is exterminating the Council members."

Eddie suffered a moment's vertigo. First Benjamin Mellor comes back to life, then he sits sipping gin and mineral water at a posh club in the middle of a war and confirms all the worst suspicions of the American left, and, at times, the right—the secret organization, behind the scenes, hiding its hand, manipulating destinies—

And, at the moment, being wiped out.

He counted on his fingers. "Burton Mount. Matthew Garland. Kevin Garland. Joseph Belt. Phil Castle—"

"And others. Quite a few others. One of the rules of being on the Council is that you designate an heir to take your place. But the deaths were happening so fast, not everybody had the opportunity. So the Council is smaller, and weaker." He stroked that luxurious beard. "You do see the point, don't you, Mr. Wesley? The Council started things in motion, then lost control of the monster it created."

"The monster being what?"

But the professor preferred to pursue his own lesson plan. "The Council lost control, and now its members are being killed."

"Is it Perry Mount who's doing this?"

"No. Perry helped me hide here. He has connections over Southeast Asia."

"Not Perry," said Eddie, marveling at how badly he had misjudged matters. Assuming always that the professor was telling the truth. "Wait," said Eddie, struck by a thought. "This Council—is its symbol by any chance an inverted cross?"

Mellor was, for once, impressed. "The Cross of Saint Peter. Yes. How did you know that?"

"It doesn't matter how I know," said Eddie. He had been right in his guess so many years ago. Poor Philmont Castle had indeed been trying to ward off evil the night he died, frantically waving the cross to signal his membership in the Council, not realizing that his membership provided the motive for his murder.

"But it does matter," said the professor. "It matters a great deal. I'm afraid you're at the center of all this. Well, no. Not you precisely. Your sister. Junie. The Council wants to find Junie, and so does this—this third force. Some of the Council members were tortured before they died. Whoever is looking is in a hurry, and willing to do what's necessary. But you—"

He stopped, drank, drank some more. Over on the tennis court, Colby was trouncing his opponent.

"Do you know where my sister is?"

Benjamin Mellor put the glass down, hard. He wiped his mouth with his blinding-white sleeve. "Don't be ridiculous."

"It isn't ridiculous to think you'd be interested in what happened to—"

"Mr. Wesley, please. Allow me to make my point." All the Harvard arrogance was back in his voice. "Whoever it is out there, looking for the testament and killing the Palace Council—this third force—well, they need to be stopped."

"We agree on that much, anyway."

Mellor toyed with his empty glass. "Don't judge me too harshly, Mr. Wesley. I'm neither as foolish nor as selfish as you seem to think. Before I tried Perry, I went to the FBI, like a good citizen. I went to Hoover, I told him what I knew—some, not all, but enough to whet his appetite."

"Hoover knows?"

Mellor nodded. "Oh, yes. I was interviewed half a dozen times. I thought, at the very least, the Bureau would offer some kind of protection to me and my family. After a while, though, it became clear to me that Hoover was never going to lift a finger. All he's going to do is sit on the sidelines and let things play out. To be sure, he was interested in my information, but only because he wanted, ah, a lever to move, ah, powerful people."

Eddie remembered Stilwell at I Street, asking him about the various Kennedy rumors. "Go on," he said.

"When I realized that the Hoover business was going nowhere, I tried Perry. And, as I said, he settled me here. So far, I've been undiscovered. As far as I can tell, even that third force out there thinks I'm dead."

"And your family?"

For the first time the professor seemed uneasy. Here was a burden his agile mind had been unable to shift. "They're better off. I was a poor husband. A ridiculous father. They have the insurance, they have the assets, or most of them."

"Less what you needed to get started on whatever you're doing over here."

A plea for understanding. "I could hardly bring them with me, Mr. Wesley. One man, on the run, alone—he can hide for a very long time. But how long could I hide my family? Or, if this third force knew I was alive, how long before they would use my family against me? You do see my dilemma?"

"I'm not sure I do," said Eddie, gathering confidence from the professor's sudden tumble toward the maudlin. "You don't know where my sister is. You said that's what this third force wants. Why are they killing off the Palace Council? Why would they kill you? If the Council can't find Junie, why would this third force of yours care?"

"It's complicated," said Mellor, again to his glass.

"I'm listening."

The professor gave the patio a quick scan. Eddie followed his uneasy gaze. A new group had settled into the nearest table, three or four women gossiping about their husbands. Two fit young men had taken over the tennis court. A teenaged girl was swimming laps, under the shouted instructions of her mother. Mellor plainly felt hemmed in. He said, "Not here."

Mellor was on his feet. Eddie followed. He chose not to argue with the hunted man's instincts, which had preserved him for four and a half years on the run.

"Where, then?"

"Tonight. Teri will pick you up at ten."

"The curfew—"

"She has a pass. Be ready."

Mellor sat again, but Eddie was plainly dismissed. Teri was at his side. She led him to the sandbagged front gate. He felt the law professor's gaze the entire way.

(11)

THE PRESIDENT of the Republic of Vietnam had ordered all civilians to stay off the streets of Saigon after nine. But this was the same President who had ordered all soldiers to stay out of the city's teeming nightclubs. For all the effect of his decrees, he might as well have been Canute. Nevertheless, Eddie worried. Vietnam might be small, but its penal code, he had learned from Pratt, was both extensive—even dancing in public was forbidden—and punitive. Benjamin Mellor had said that Teri would have a pass. Eddie hoped it was the right one.

As he left the hotel, he expected to be warned, but the porter did not even notice. The whole downtown was alight with neon. A *cyclo* pulled up at once. Eddie declined. A policeman across the street ignored him.

Teri arrived at ten on the dot.

"Hurry up, man," she said.

Teri's eyes had that empty look again, and Eddie supposed she must be pretty stoned. Her attention to the lane markings was intermittent. Outside the Notre Dame Cathedral she almost hit a *cyclo*. They were waved down by American military police, but the pass on the dashboard got them through. Roaring off, Teri began to fishtail again.

"Do you want me to drive?"

"Do you know where we're going?"

"You could tell me."

"No," she said, and kept on weaving.

"The military pass. A gift from Perry?"

"You ask a lot of questions, man."

They stopped in front of a low whitewashed building in the city center, catercornered with the huge Park Lane cigarette billboard above the Sony sign. Eddie climbed out of the car. Teri stayed in her seat. "Third floor. Apartment twelve. Take the stairs. The elevator is a death trap, man."

She sped away.

Eddie stepped into the lobby. The concierge was watching television. She never looked up as he headed for the stairs. The windows were covered in wire mesh, like windows all over the city, to reduce the damage should a shell explode just outside. If it exploded inside, there was nothing to be done.

On the first floor a couple was arguing in what might have been Khmer, and on the second floor he heard the sound of scratchy music from an old record player, but when he reached the third, silence reigned. There were four apartments, and number twelve was right next to the stairs and directly opposite the elevator, just the place for a man on the run. Nobody answered his knock, but the door was hanging open anyway, only one hinge intact after whatever had happened.

Eddie stood in the hallway listening to the silence. There should be sirens, rushing feet, a gesticulating crowd. There was nothing.

He stepped into the apartment. It was easy to follow the course. They had knocked the door off, and Mellor had made a stand in the hallway, where a lot of worthless artifacts had been smashed when somebody fell hard. There was blood in the hall and in the kitchenette, where they must have subdued him. There were two other rooms, and they had torn everything to shreds. The closet was half empty. The dresser drawers were overturned. There was no sign of a body. Had they taken him with them?

Some of the Council members were tortured before they died.

Eddie shivered. Better to have drowned in the boating accident.

Back in the hallway, he started to pick up the artifacts, to set them on the overturned shelf. He did not know why. A last salute to a desperate man who had pretended to die before and was now somewhere dying much more slowly. He stood up. Probably there were clues everywhere if he knew what to look for. Probably he was standing on top of valuable evidence, to say nothing of leaving his fingerprints everywhere.

He wondered what Mellor had wanted to tell him.

Time to go.

Standing, he noticed, in the midst of the mess, a shattered picture frame holding a photo of the Harvard Law School class of 1957.

Junie's class. He picked it up, brushed off the broken glass, then squinted at the faces until he found, in about the third row, the only black woman. He touched her image with his fingers. That this was the only Harvard class whose photo Mellor had kept spoke to—what?—an unexpected sentimentality? He took another look, and noticed, this time, that his sister was not gazing at the camera. She was smiling down at the faculty in the first two rows, and in particular at Benjamin Mellor.

After all that the professor had done, Junie had smiled at him.

Eddie decided to take the picture along. He slipped it out of the broken frame, and that was when he saw the words on the back. The searchers had looked inside the frame but, in their haste, had not studied the picture itself.

I can't stop them, Junie had written. *You'll have to do it.*

Nothing more.

Was the note recent? Did this mean Mellor knew where she was? Might he, at this very moment, be spilling her location to his captors? He folded the photograph and slipped it into his jacket. He took a last look around, then stepped into the hall, and hurried down the stairs.

In the lobby, he was stopped by two Vietnamese men in Western-style business suits. There were a lot of flashing lights outside. The men flashed their credentials.

Vietnamese National Police.

"Do you live in this building, sir?"

"No."

"May I ask why you are out after curfew?"

Eddie realized that Teri had driven off with the pass. He improvised fast, but not cleverly. "Visiting a sick friend."

"Does he live in this building?"

"Yes."

"And what is his name?"

Stuck. He had no idea what name Mellor was living under. As it happened, the plainclothesmen did not seem to care if he had any idea or not, because by this time they had the cuffs on, and were marching him toward a squad car that had materialized, spinning lights playing across the lobby. When Eddie got outside, he saw that there were actually three or four vehicles, the white-gloved officers armed to the teeth, as if expecting resistance. There might have been an American standing with them. He could not get a good look before they ducked him into the back of the car and sped off.

At the barracks, they turned him over to the jailers, who slapped him around a bit because that was the form, stole what cash he had on him but left the crinkled photo, then tossed him into a filthy holding cell to sit on the floor alongside assorted pickpockets, rapists, drunks, and druggies, until a nearsighted, frightened child from the Embassy, responding to Eddie's call, showed up to vouch for his bona fides. By that time, hours had passed. Nobody apologized. The guards returned his seized property, other than the money, but when Eddie took a *cyclo* back to the Duc, he found his notebooks missing. He telephoned the Embassy and asked for the man who had bailed him out, but the Embassy duty officer might never have heard of the Vietnamese police.

"I would like to have my property returned," Eddie said, holding one ice pack on his split lip and another on his battered fingers.

"What property would that be, Mr. Wesley?"

"Somebody will know."

The duty officer hung up. When Eddie turned around, the young Embassy staffer who had bailed him out was sitting quietly in the rickety chair beside the open window, playing with a cigarette lighter.

"I know all about you, Mr. Wesley," the man said. The comically thick glasses were gone, and he no longer looked frightened. "I knew about you before you arrived."

Eddie Wesley was oratorical master of most situations, but no words came. He stood very still, more frightened than at any time in his life since the night he was dragged off to meet Scarlett: worse, for example, than the night he was shot at on the Hill of Angels. His tongue seemed to swell. The intruder waited patiently. Outside, a tropical rain exploded into life, not a slowly increasing patter but an unannounced drenching that drowned even the noise of the geckos, and most of the traffic.

"The name is Collier. George Collier." But already Eddie had recognized him, and cursed himself for not piercing the disguise when they met two hours ago. Collier did not extend a hand, and his steady blue eyes dared Eddie to try. The lighter flicked on. Eddie's eyes followed the flame. The lighter flicked off again. Collier smiled. "I think it's time we had a little talk."

CHAPTER 44

Plea Bargain

(I)

EDDIE DID NOT WASTE TIME WONDERING how Collier had gotten into his room. He had chosen the hotel, after all, because it was practically owned by the Central Intelligence Agency. "Yes," was, at first, all he could manage. His voice was screechy. He tried again. "You look a little young for your reputation."

"Do I? Oh." Collier had long thin legs and arms, a short torso, and the shining yellow teeth of a career smoker. "I'm thirty-five, let's say. Yes. Thirty-five." Nodding thoughtfully, as if he had a lot of ages to choose from, which perhaps he did, for in the gaudy neon glow from the street he looked ten years older, but in a duller light could probably look ten years younger. "And you're—what? Forty?"

Eddie was certain that George Collier knew precisely how old he was. "What happened to Benjamin Mellor?"

"What does it look like happened to him?" A grin appeared suddenly, like a conjurer's trick. "Did he leave you any souvenirs, Mr. Wesley? The police didn't find anything on you. Maybe they didn't look hard enough."

"Are you saying—"

"Too bad about his girlfriend, though. That Teri." He shrugged. "Well, people should read the consular warnings. There are just some neighborhoods Americans should stay out of, especially in the middle of the night."

Eddie sat down hard. He tried again to get his own voice moving through its normal cadences, but without immediate result.

"What did you do to her?" he whispered. "She didn't know anything."

"True. She really didn't." Collier continued to play with the lighter. "I'm sorry you wound up in jail. It seems that the police misunderstood the situation. They were supposed to take you into custody but not lock you up. They had been told to deliver you to the American MPs, who had orders to see you safely on board the plane leaving for Hawaii at 2300. It seems you missed it." Flick went the lighter: On. Off. Eddie wondered how it would feel to be burned with it, and whether he would soon find out. He put the ice pack on the chipped desk, because clutching it felt like a sign of weakness. He would live with the pain. George Collier's flat hunter's eyes followed his every move.

"I was being expelled? Can you do that?"

"Vietnam's a sovereign country, Mr. Wesley. They can do what they want." On. Off. On. Off. "My understanding, however, is that the order was for your own protection. You obviously have somebody back home who thinks you're in trouble here and wants to get you out of it. Are you, Mr. Wesley? In trouble?"

Eddie seated himself carefully on the bedspread. He was sweating. The air conditioner was loudly unreliable. The deluging rain had yet to undo the day's long heat. Or maybe the sweat had another source. Collier seemed perfectly cool.

"I wasn't until tonight, when you had me beaten up by the police."

"You were at the scene of the crime, Mr. Wesley."

"That explains the arrest. Not the beating."

"I had nothing to do with that. Don't you read the official handouts, Mr. Wesley? The Republic of Vietnam happens to be a sovereign country. We're the guests. Certainly we cooperate with their armed forces, but we have zero involvement in domestic affairs. We don't control their police forces. I have no idea what laws you might have broken. I have no idea what you've bought, or smoked, or stolen. The police seem to think they do. Yes, they let you out, but only as a courtesy. General Loan—have you met him? No? Air Force officer, runs the National Police. Very smart. Very honest. Can't bribe him. You'll recognize him if he comes for you. Only one leg. And a very angry man, Mr. Wesley. I'll arrange an introduction if you like. General Loan owes me a favor or two. So he turned you loose. But you have to realize, Mr. Wesley"—the blue eyes were really too casual—"that General Loan can throw you back inside any time he wants."

"Then why am I out? Why are you here?" Eddie found that he had balled his fists. This afternoon, he had sat in the swankiest club in Saigon chatting with a dead man, and now he was sitting in his hotel room chatting with a murderer.

"You're a writer, Mr. Wesley. You're a writer, and I'm a source. I'm going to give you a big story, and then you're going to go home and be famous."

(I I)

EDDIE WAS A MOMENT ADJUSTING to the new dynamic of the conversation. "Why would you do that?"

The lighter flicked on again. "We share a common objective, Mr. Wesley. I believe that we can help each other."

"I doubt that very much, Mr. Collier. And if this is some convoluted effort by Perry Mount to buy me off, you can tell him—"

"I am not employed by Perry Mount." The killer's voice for the first time lost its playfulness. This time it was steel, tempered with a hint of—what? Disdain? Fury? Frustration? Then the magical smile was back. He pointed to the desk. "Get your notebook out."

"Somebody stole my notebook."

"Third drawer from the top, behind the extra toilet paper."

Refusing to show any surprise, Eddie flipped through the pages. He found them undisturbed.

"Ready?" asked Collier.

"I suppose." But he could not still the trembling in his fingers.

The eyes glittered. "I know what you're thinking, Mr. Wesley, and, if I were you, I would be thinking the same thing. But orders are orders, and I have been ordered to leave you, let us say, unmolested."

"But not Benjamin Mellor."

Again Collier pointed to the notebook. "Write this down: America has never lost a war, but we're going to lose this one."

"We are?"

He nodded. "North is stronger than we thought, Mr. Wesley. NLF won't quit. Big debate just now: can they attack Saigon or not? Most of our people say they can't. Some of us think they can. If they do, we'll drive them out, but I think they'll be here no later than January or February of next year, and after that, even if we win the battle, we won't look so invincible." Flick. Flick. "Americans like to look invincible. A battle in the streets of Saigon would be bad news, even if we win. And some of the things we're doing to try to win—well, we won't win the hearts and minds of the people that way." Flick. Flick. "I believe in this war, Mr. Wesley. Communism has to be stopped. Lose one domino, the rest fall. All right, you don't agree. So go home and vote. Maybe your side wins the next election. Meanwhile, there's still a war on, and I don't have the discretion to stop it, even if I wanted to. People are dying out there in a cause I believe is right. But I don't think we can win. I would love to be proved wrong, but I think I'm right." Was that a smirk? "I bet you hope I'm right, don't you?" Collier said. "You'd love to see us lose."

Calmed by the appeal to his intellect, Eddie took the question seriously. "I think America could use a little humility."

"So could anti-America." He put the lighter back in his pocket. "Tell me, Mr. Wesley. Your search for Perry Mount. Is this related to your search for your sister?" He saw the writer's face. "Everybody knows what you're up to, Mr. Wesley. You don't know the first thing about searching on tiptoes."

"I'm not prepared to talk about my sister," said Eddie stiffly. "Not to you."

"I don't blame you, Mr. Wesley. You're a loyal brother. Every girl should have a brother like you. As I am sure you understand, however, if I ever decide I want you to talk about your sister, you'll do exactly that." Before Eddie could object, his visitor was on to the next subject. "Do you remember the last time we met? In Harlem? At Mr. Scarlett's place?"

"I remember he was getting ready to put a nail through my hand, and you were on the sidelines cheering him on."

"I wasn't cheering him on, Mr. Wesley. I told him to stop."

"Why?"

"Understand me, Mr. Wesley. I am not a free agent. I work for others. Now, were it up to me, with all the trouble you've been causing, you'd have taken a little drunken tumble one night into one of those gorges that make Ithaca so famous."

"I don't drink," said Eddie, suppressing the shudder.

"That night you would have reverted to old habits. Depression over writer's block. Probably the reason you asked your girlfriend to help you find that little stone cottage in the first place." A helpless smile, an innocent bewildered by the ways of the world. "But it's not up to me. I follow orders. Orders are to let you run."

"Run where?" A thought struck him. "You think—they think—whoever you're working for—you're expecting me to lead you to Junie. That's why you're letting me go."

"I told you. I'm going to give you a very nice story. All about what's going on in Long An Province. The CIA is torturing people out there, Mr. Wesley. Killing them, too. You can write about how the big bad Agency is doing its usual nasty mischief. Most people will hate you, but your leftist friends will love you."

"Why would you want to stop whatever's going on out there?"

"Because it hurts the war effort. Because we don't win the hearts and minds of the people by getting them to inform on each other and torturing them to death. Do you think you're the only one with a conscience, Mr. Wesley?" The killer seemed amused. "You and I both love our country. We just see our duties differently."

Eddie shook his head. Knowing he was not going to die tonight emboldened him. "No. That's not it. You want me to run because you want me to lead you to Junie. And the Long An story—that's what Perry is doing over here, isn't it? The torturing, whatever else. Perry is a part of it. You want me to smoke him out for you. That's why you're giving me this story." A chilling thought. "He's too good for you, isn't he? You can't find him. Perry Mount is part of the Council, like his father was, and you need to kill him and you can't track him down. Not in Asia. This is his turf. You want him sent back to yours. Is that it?"

Collier was on his feet. "There's a plane at 0730 to Hong Kong. You'll be on board, Mr. Wesley, whether you like it or not. The only question is whether you want to leave empty-handed."

His manner was too lazily confident. Eddie had guessed wrong. He was not sure which part of his thesis was wrong but some part of it was. "Tell me about what's going on with you and Perry."

Again Collier ignored the gibe. He flexed long fingers. "I know what you're thinking, Mr. Wesley. You could name me as your source. You could even try to accuse me of something worse." The smile was back. "I wouldn't want you to go to that trouble. Those gorges are so deep. And the way Mrs. Garland drinks at night, when she's feeling morose—well, you see my point." He stuck out a hand. "Do we have a deal?"

"I have a question first."

The killer smiled indulgently. "Of course, Mr. Wesley."

Eddie wanted to put no foot wrong. He saw the risk of speaking up. But Wesley Senior would never have let the matter pass, and, just now, neither could Wesley Junior. "What you did earlier tonight. To Mellor. To Teri. How can you work for people who would—"

"You have no idea what I may or may not have done earlier tonight," Collier interrupted pleasantly, waggling a finger. "I would advise you not to speculate."

"But *you* know," said Eddie. "You know what kind of people you're working for. You don't have to speculate."

Collier's eyes widened. His good humor faded, and, for a moment, Eddie glimpsed the beast beneath the bonhomie. The killer rose from the chair, and the room seemed very small indeed. Eddie looked around for a weapon.

But Collier only shrugged. "The job is what it is, Mr. Wesley. Some days are more complicated than others." Again he extended his hand. "Do we have a deal?"

Eddie shook.

CHAPTER 45

Water View

(1)

TWO MONTHS LATER, in July of 1967, the magazine published an exposé, authored by the great Edward T. Wesley, novelist-turned-war-correspondent, of a Central Intelligence Agency program carrying the code name of PHOENIX, under which cash bounties were offered to South Vietnamese nationals who turned in informers or leaders for the Viet Cong. Too often, wrote Eddie, especially in the demonstration phase of the program out in Long An Province, those who were turned in turned up dead, or worse. Moreover, there was an incentive to make up stories to get that bounty, or to get your enemies taken care of, or both. Intentionally or not, Eddie wrote, America was sponsoring a wholesale campaign of torture and murder, in the guise of pacifying the countryside. The article cautiously named no names, but cited "intelligence sources." Military spokesmen ridiculed the story. Back home, even some leaders of the antiwar movement distanced themselves. Much later, when a fuller account came out in the mainstream press—Congress would not hold its first hearings on PHOENIX until nearly three years later—Eddie Wesley would be tarred for getting some significant facts wrong, although, in essence, his account turned out to be true. Already there were circles in which he was considered a hero, and, for Eddie of the late sixties at least, those were the circles that mattered.

In Ithaca, Aurelia fielded a telephone call from a furious Richard Nixon, the man she had contacted to try to get Eddie out of Vietnam when she thought his life was in danger.

"Do a man a favor and this is how he pays me back? Let me make something clear, Aurelia. A thick skin doesn't make a man an idiot. All right, terrible things happen in war. I've been in a war, so I know. But you don't bite the hand that feeds you. Everything we've done for him, and look at this mess."

"I'm sure he's just doing what he thinks is right," Aurie murmured.

"Good for him. Back in my day, a man disclosed classified information, he went to prison. Do you have any idea how this could harm the war effort?"

He finally calmed down, but by this time Aurelia had divined his true purpose. She promised him, unasked, that she would never mention to a soul the favors he had performed over the years for the notorious Eddie Wesley.

Later that afternoon, Megan Hadley, Tristan's wife, popped in, waving the clippings and telling Aurelia how sensational her Eddie was. She was so glad, she said, that he had wound up on the right side. Eddie and his sister both, she added. Aurelia was relieved to see her friend in such a good mood. Recently she had been morose. Megan had confided to Aurelia the cause of her unhappiness: she thought her husband was having an affair.

"With somebody on campus," she had said, as Aurie cringed.

At the end of January of 1968, North Vietnamese troops launched a surprise attack on Saigon, even gaining brief access to the exterior grounds of the heavily barricaded United States Embassy, after its police guards were unexpectedly withdrawn. The assault was driven off and carried no tactical or strategic significance, but American reporters, many of them caught in a pitched battle for the first time in their lives, wrote, inaccurately, that the Tet Offensive represented a powerful show of force by the other side. Back home, people began to consider the possibility that America might actually lose the war. That those . . . savages . . . might prevail. Surveys continued to show strong public support, but there was at the same time a sense of stasis, people saying yes out of habit but looking for signs that perhaps the tide had turned. Whispers began that Lyndon Johnson might actually not be re-elected. In March, the rumors came true. After a surprisingly strong showing by Senator Eugene McCarthy in the New Hampshire primary, Johnson, despite having finished a comfortable first, dropped out of the presidential race. He would spend his remaining months in office, said Johnson, working for peace. Vice President Hubert Humphrey became the odds-on favorite for the Democratic nomination. But the left saw him as Johnson's man and, therefore, the war candidate. Senator Robert Kennedy entered the race, and in the sleepy capital of a Midwestern farm state, a first-term Democratic Senator named Lanning Frost called together his backers and began to consider moving up his own run for President.

Too soon, said the wisest, including his father-in-law, a political pro recently retired from the Washington wars: The Democratic Party is going to implode. Concentrate on your own Senate re-election campaign. The rest can wait until 1972.

After certain consultations, his wife, Margot, agreed.

(11)

EDDIE WAS NOT IN SAIGON at the time of the Tet attack. As a matter of fact, he planned to leave Southeast Asia a few weeks later, taking a circuitous route ending in England, where, during the fall of 1968, aged just forty-one, he would hold a visiting chair in American studies at Oxford. Back home, the ground was shifting, but Eddie paid scant attention. Instead, rapt, he sat in his Hong Kong flat reading one account after another of the Tet Offensive. Everything George Collier had predicted had come true. The attack had been beaten, and nobody in America seemed to notice, or care.

Very strange.

Meanwhile, Eddie's desk was piled high with letters and telegrams forwarded by the magazine and his publisher, many of them from journalists considerably larger than Eddie himself. A breathless note from Aurelia contained both congratulations and gratitude for his safety. Eddie was rather grateful himself. While working on the PHOENIX story, he had managed to intercept Ambassador William Colby at a Saigon restaurant. Colby had told him nothing, and left quickly, ignoring Eddie's shouted questions. One of his minions had lingered, to warn Eddie off, whether officially or not: "This is war," the man said. "In war, people get hurt. All kinds of people." According to a dismissive Pratt, lower-level Agency people said things like that all the time. Nobody took them seriously.

Still, Eddie had returned to Hong Kong as swiftly as possible.

Now, leafing through the messages, he found himself wondering if Junie had seen the story, and what she thought of her brother. He realized that he wanted to make her proud. Pinned to the wall above his desk was the photo of her law-school class, with her note to the professor on the back.

I can't stop them. You'll have to do it.

Whenever his gaze fell on the photo, he was besieged by the same questions that plagued his sleep: Were they working together? Had Mellor known where she was? Had he told before they killed him?

Perry Mount might have the answer, but Eddie could not find him. Perry turned out to have a house in Hong Kong, just as poor Teri had said. Eddie had no trouble finding the place, over in Kowloon, on a narrow side street off Prince Edward Road, near Flower Market Road. There were very few privately owned homes in Hong Kong, but Perry had somehow managed to get title to one of them: a tiny cottage squeezed among tiny cottages, across the street from a small English church, where the burial ground around the side had headstones large enough to crouch behind. Eddie knew because he had crouched there a lot, at various hours of day and night, watching the door, but nobody had gone in or out except the Filipino amah, who claimed, in excellent English, not to speak any.

In Kowloon, a lot of the houses had names. The plaque in front of Perry's cottage read PANDEMONIUM.

Eddie asked around, but none of the neighbors knew a thing.

And so he sat in his flat and stared at the photo. The apartment had been found for him by David Yee, who now covered Southeast Asia for the *Times*. It was small but serviceable, on a high floor in one of several identical towers on a hillside, excitingly new because the units had individual bathrooms, which was not, said David dryly, the invariable custom.

But neither was it the invariable custom to have married professors father children by their students and then to have both parties act as if nothing had happened. Something wasn't right.

In early April, Eddie stopped by Perry's house in Kowloon, as he did at least twice a week. He found the sign gone, and the house occupied by an elderly Swiss trader who insisted that he come in for tea. The trader had very strong views about the war, but, alas, lacked any knowledge of the prior occupant.

The golden boy was gone. It was time for Eddie to go, too.

A few days before his departure for India, Eddie dined with Lieutenant Cox. The two had stayed in touch since their chance meeting in Saigon after Quang Tri. Then the lieutenant had been angry and tense. Tonight he was relaxed. Eddie asked what he thought of the theory behind the war, the idea that the Communist advance had to be stopped in Vietnam, lest the other countries of the region fall like dominoes.

Cox thought this one over. "I'm an officer in the armed forces of a democracy," he finally said. "It's my job to go where they tell me, Mr. Wesley. The day I decide I have a different job, that it's up to me to figure out whether I like the theory of the war, is the day we stop being a democracy. Know why? Because that's the day the military takes over."

Eddie found the answer so troubling that he walked the streets for an hour trying to sort things out. It struck him that what Benjamin Mellor called the Palace Council must have exactly the opposite theory: they had no patience with democracy, and would be more than happy to take over.

Still brooding, Eddie wound up at a jazz club in Lan Kwai Fong, soaking up atmosphere and music. He returned to his flat close to midnight and, if not for the rather pleasant buzz fogging his brain, might have sensed something amiss even before he opened the door, and certainly right after, because they had removed the overhead bulb, causing him to stumble into the room, hands out in front, searching for the table lamp beside the sofa, so that when they grabbed him he was briefly too disoriented to fight back, and briefly was all they needed. Three minutes later, gray duct tape over his eyes and mouth and around the wrists secured too tightly behind his back, Eddie was bundled into the service elevator. Struggling, he felt the floors dropping away. A flurry of well-placed punches reduced his feistiness. They dragged him off the loading dock and threw him into a truck that went jouncing off, one of them sitting atop him just in case. The ride seemed like hours but probably was just minutes, because time stretches when you are terrified. All he could think of was Benjamin Mellor. Whatever had happened to the professor was about to happen to Eddie.

The truck juddered to a halt. Nobody had spoken a word, and Eddie, mouth taped, could hardly ask any questions. When they lifted him to the ground, he kicked out hard behind him and made satisfying contact, even being rewarded with an exhalation of pain and a rich curse in what sounded more Hakka than Cantonese: Chinese is not an inflected language, which is why it sounds singsongy to unsophisticated Western ears, but hang around Hong Kong long enough and you begin to catch the different intonations. He felt a thrilling stab of pain in his kidneys and thought it was a knife, but some people's fists will do that. A clout on the back of the neck laid him flat. They carried him up a flight of stairs and down a flight of stairs and tied something around his ankles. He heard the slosh of liquid, very near. They ripped off his shirt and lifted him onto some kind of platform, and then, before he could gain any sort of orientation, just let go, dropping him, headfirst, into a tank of freezing-cold water.

And left him there.

The rope held his feet. Only his head and upper body were beneath the surface, but that was enough to make him panic. He could not twist up. He could not break free. He could not breathe. He thrashed. The iciness eased into his head, and into his bones. He was dizzy with fear but also with nearing asphyxiation. His lungs pounded. If only he could see, he might be able to think, but the tape on his mouth and eyes made pain and panic worse. If he screamed he would drown. If he breathed he would drown. Then he was up again, out of the water, dangling from the rope, struggling for breath through his nose.

A voice, Chinese but speaking English with that same uninflected accent: "Where is she?"

Before Eddie could process the question, he was down in the tank again, head and shoulders beneath the icy water, needing to gasp for air but not daring to. His chest seemed to constrict. His heart jumped and shuddered. The blood pounding in his ears was impossibly loud. His thoughts refused to coalesce. He was going to drown.

Out again.

"Where is she?"

But for the tape he would have tried to answer, just to stay out of the water, except that nobody seemed to care about his answer. In again, this time all the way to his waist, and now in the midst of his mind-stealing terror he realized that he had forgotten to inhale during his brief period above the water. Air exploded from his lungs, into his covered mouth, and up through his nose. Water burned its way in. Everything ached. He felt as if his brain was congealing, but probably it was just trying to die.

Out again, suspended, shivering, gasping not only through his nose, from which water and blood alike freely flowed, but also through his mouth, because the tape had loosened a bit. Never had he been so grateful for the simple existence of air.

"Where is she?"

Eddie knew he could never survive another dunking, and tried to signal that there was nothing he would not do or say to stay out of the vat, but he lacked any means to signal them, and, besides, he was already in again. He kicked and struggled with what strength he had left, but the amount was zero. He felt his life force fluttering weakly away. His skin was numb. His brain was numb. His lungs were numb. His heart was numb. They had to understand. He would do anything. Anything. It was not a matter of courage versus its opposite. Courage was a myth, a fantasy, an imaginary trait dreamed up by those who had never been blindfolded, gagged, and trussed upside down under the water.

Out again. In again. Out again. In again.

The next time they pulled him up, the tape on his eyes was also looser, and he could see, mistily, metal walls, a concrete floor, and, worst of all, the water, cold and dark and filthy, waiting directly beneath for the next dunking. He knew he was seeing everything for the last time. He strained to force a word or two through shivering lips but could only cough blood into the gag. He was not even sure what he was trying to say. Maybe goodbye.

Only they seemed to prefer hello.

They swung him wide of the tank and cut the ropes. He hit the floor and lay in a heap. It was not possible, gasping only through his aching, bloody nose, to get enough air, so he decided that dying on the concrete was as easy as dying in the tank.

Footsteps approached. A figure crouched beside him.

A whisper in his ear, the same voice, chilly as the water, and as willing to end his life. "You don't know where she is, do you, Mr. Wesley?"

He could not even croak. He did not think of lying. He shook his head. A rapid-fire argument took place somewhere in the room, but not in English.

The voice again, this time with instructions: "Whatever you think you know, Mr. Wesley, you do not know."

Fine with Eddie. No idea what it meant, but it sounded just fine.

They lifted him to his feet and pulled his shirt back on. They wanted him dry. That was why they had taken it off before shoving him into the tank, and why they had dunked him only waist-deep. Eddie congratulated himself on this deduction as they dragged him, coughing and choking and spitting water and blood, out of the building and into the truck. After a short drive, they cut the bonds on his wrists and yanked the tape from his mouth. "None of this happened," the voice informed him. They poured something over his face and upper body. Cheap wine. For good measure, they poured it down his throat, too. The truck slowed but never stopped. They lifted him and pulled the tape from his eyes, the pain making him cry out. They threw him out the back and slammed the doors long before it occurred to him to turn his head and get a good look at his tormentors. He landed on something squishy and disgusting. Garbage, his exhausted mind informed him. Mostly dead fish. The drenching odor was almost as bad as the water. Still, his legs were free, weak but functional. His hands were free. He could at least crawl out of the garbage. But even crawling seemed like an awful lot of work, so Eddie closed his eyes instead. The last image in his mind before darkness settled in with all the sweetness of rescue was of what he had seen on the floor of the warehouse.

A Baby Ruth wrapper.

CHAPTER 46

Yet Another Old Friend Returns

(1)

THE OWNER of the fish market found him in the morning, wine-soaked and bloody and incoherent but, fortunately if surprisingly, with wallet undisturbed, so that, from the moment of his admission to the hospital, enterprising staffers knew his name and were able to call their newspaper contacts. EDDIE'S DRUNKEN NIGHT IN HK, as the British tabloids called it, became worldwide news. The doctors decided he did not have to stay overnight. A British police inspector openly disbelieved that he had been kidnapped, and the inspector's Chinese colleague sat silently, allowing him to go on disbelieving. It occurred to Eddie that every word out of his mouth would just make things worse, so he bade them good day and asked for a ride home. The Chinese officer drove him.

"You are a very lucky man," the officer said as they fought the snarly traffic. "The triads have only warned you, not killed you. To be killed by them is not a pleasant experience."

"Not being killed by them wasn't so pleasant, either."

"They are not pleasant people, Mr. Wesley."

"It wasn't the triads," said Eddie after a moment. His voice was weak. He shivered.

"Do you have enemies, sir?"

"Millions."

The officer gave him a searching look. "Is there anything you would like to tell me, sir?"

Eddie drew a roguish grin from deep within his reserves. "Believe me, Inspector, I wish there were."

The apartment had been searched, and not by the police. His notebooks were gone. His summaries of what he had learned, and what he had guessed. No matter. Nothing was irreplaceable. He could reconstruct it from memory.

They had also taken his notes for the Southeast Asia novel he had planned. They were less replaceable. He wondered if he could negotiate, get them back.

Then he laughed at himself, realizing how punchy he must be.

He looked at the bulletin board. They had taken the photo of Junie's law-school class, and that loss hurt more than his bruises.

Later. Worry about it later. Moving to the sofa, to say nothing of the bedroom, seemed like a lot of unnecessary work. Exhausted, he almost missed the knock. It came a second time, authoritative and peremptory.

Eddie creaked to his feet and peered through the peephole, expecting David Yee or perhaps Perry Mount, dropping by with candy bar in hand, just to make sure Eddie no longer knew what he thought he had known. What he saw almost knocked him over.

He opened the door.

"What have they done to you?" said Margot Frost.

(11)

MARGOT BREWED TEA in the kitchenette, but not before making him comfortable on the living-room sofa, pillows for his head, a blanket for his body, clucking like a mother hen. She was a little softer, a little rounder, a little more somber, a little less playful. She was a political wife now, married to presidential timber, and probably could not afford to stay long in the apartment of so notorious a libertine as the acclaimed Edward Wesley Junior. But she seemed in no hurry to go. She was in Hong Kong for a week with the children and their nanny, while Lanning and half a dozen other Senators did the obligatory fact-finding tour of Vietnam.

"Everybody does one these days," she explained.

"I'll say," he muttered.

Watching her move smoothly around his flat, Eddie remembered the last time they had been together, the terrible explosion in Harlem that had killed Kevin and sent Lanning's approval ratings skyward. He remembered how everybody said that Margot provided both the brains and the ambition in the marriage. Most of all, he remembered that George Collier used to work for Margot's father.

Eddie rolled over, groaning, and not only from physical pain.

"Are you okay?" she asked.

"Not really."

She smiled.

Lanning was in Vietnam, where Eddie had been but now wasn't. Margot was in Hong Kong, where Eddie now was. The front man was away finding facts. The brains of the outfit stood in Eddie's kitchen. He watched her. Margot kept smiling and clucking and assuring him that everything was going to be fine, even though he had expressed no sense that anything would not. He remembered the Cross of Saint Peter around her neck the night they met, and how she had warned him that some things cannot be stopped.

"What do you think?" Margot murmured at one point, spooning the tea into his mouth because he was too tired to sit up. Her hip snuggled warmly against his leg. "Do you know why they did it?"

"Uh-uh."

"Were they sending you a message? Was that it? Oh, Eddie, dear Eddie, have you been poking your head into other people's business? Or just sleeping with the wrong man's wife?"

But Margot laughed alone.

"Do you think it's that article you wrote? About the CIA and Operation PHOENIX? Are they punishing you for that? Because, if they are, we should tell Lanning. We can't let them get away with this, dear."

Eddie shivered. Margot kept referring to what "they" had done to him, even though the papers had twisted the story around to make it sound as if Eddie had done it all to himself: selecting the nearest trash bin to sleep off a bad drunk. She stood up and went to the kitchen to freshen the cup. She seemed to know where he kept his tea, and where he kept his cups, and where he kept his blankets. He wondered how long Margot had spent here last night while the place was being searched; or if she might even have been in the warehouse while they took him to pieces, standing silently next to Perry as he munched calmly on his Baby Ruth.

Finally, Eddie said, "How long have you been in Hong Kong?"

"What?"

"When did Lanning leave town?"

Margot was sitting next to him once more, trying to make him open his mouth. Chicken broth this time. "Lanning flew straight to Saigon. He's meeting us back here next week." Her eyes narrowed. "Why, Eddie Wesley. I hope you're not suggesting anything untoward."

"Untoward?"

"Number one, I'm not that kind of woman." Smiling, Margot laid a finger across his lips. "Number two, even if I were so inclined, you're not in any kind of condition."

"Ah. True." He shifted position, sucking greedily on the spoon. From what he could tell, the broth was not poisoned. He closed his eyes for half a minute, or maybe half an hour, because when he opened them Margot was on the settee, reading, without permission, the draft of his latest essay about the war. It was one of the few pieces of paper left in the place. He said, "What time is it?"

"Time for me to go. Can't have people talking."

He gestured with his chin. "I'm pretty sure I left that in the other room."

"That's where I stole it from." She grinned. "You're a brilliant writer, Eddie. And you're right about the war."

"Thanks."

"You're welcome." She stood up. "We're going to stop it."

"We?"

"Lanning. Me. You. People of good will, Eddie. That's who ends most evil things. People of good will, working together."

"We'll work together," he agreed, watching. "We'll shake the throne, won't we?" Quoting Perry Mount. "End the agony, once and for all?"

Margot frowned. "I better go," she said again. She kissed his forehead.

"Margot?"

"Yes, Eddie?"

"Why did you come here?"

"To Hong Kong? To wait for Lanning and give the children a vacation, I told you."

"I mean here. My flat."

Margot had found her wrap. "Oh, well. I couldn't let them get away with this. I had to make sure you're okay." Her voice trembled unexpectedly. Her eyes glistened. "I can't believe what they did to you."

Because they didn't tell you first? Or because it was worse than you expected?

Aloud, he said, "Does Lanning know?"

"Know what?"

"About the Project."

The thick, owlish brows furrowed. "What project?"

Eddie took his time, and not only for effect. "What you're doing with Perry."

She sat next to him again, felt his wrist, the side of his neck. "I think you're delirious, Eddie." Another soft kiss on his forehead. "Go to sleep. Do you have a friend you want me to call? Otherwise, I can make sure somebody checks on you in the morning."

Sleep indeed tugged at him, but he had to finish. "I don't think Lanning knows. I think this is your own thing, isn't it? He's a . . . a stuffed shirt."

Margot bristled. "Lanning is a very intelligent man," she announced crisply, a statement for the press from an irritated wife. "You can't believe what you read in the papers."

"How true."

"I'm sorry. We're sensitive on that point. People are always saying—"

"I know what they're saying." He sighed, squirmed. "I'm sorry."

"Sleep, Eddie." She half stretched beside him, hugged him into her warmth. "I'm just glad to see you're okay," she said into his hair.

For several minutes, they held each other, although the holding was mostly friendship—if even that.

"Margot?"

She stirred beside him. Perhaps she had been dozing, too, for her voice was far away. "Yes, dear?"

"Remember Palm Sunday three, four years ago? When Lanning spoke at Saint Philip's in Harlem?"

"The day poor Kevin died."

"Yes. Ah." Adjusting position again. But nowhere was comfortable. "Did Lanning write his own speech?"

Stiffening in his arms. "I told you, he is not a dummy."

"Please, Margot. I just want to know about that one speech. Did Lanning write it himself?"

She sighed, relaxed a bit. "Oh, Eddie, I don't remember. Probably his staff wrote it. That's what staff does. Maybe I contributed a line or two. It was two or three hundred speeches ago." A glance at her watch, a theatrical rolling of dark, teasing eyes. "You did it to me again, Eddie. Just like ten years ago. Made me stay when I was all set to leave." She sat up, smiling, shaking her head. "I told you then, I'll tell you again. You're a dangerous man." He watched her climb to her feet. A floor-length mirror adorned the back of the door, and Margot stood before it, twisting this way and that, sweeping wrinkles out of her skirt and sweater so nobody would guess she had been lying down. "I'm a mess," Margot muttered, but she looked just fine, so maybe she was not talking about her physical appearance. "It was so great seeing you, Eddie," she said, opening the door and peering out to make sure that the hall was unoccupied. "I'm sorry it had to be an occasion like this."

"Thanks for coming," he said tonelessly from the sofa.

"I'm just glad you're okay."

"Margot?"

"Yes, dear?"

"Tell them I got the message. I'll leave it alone."

"Eddie," she began, and then, as if disciplining an untamed emotion, stuck her fist in her mouth, slipped into the hall, and shut the door.

PART V

Ithaca/Oak Bluffs/ Washington 1969–1972

CHAPTER 47

The Project

(1)

"Do you think he did it?" said Megan Hadley.

Aurelia, cutting into her veal, looked up in confusion. "Do I think who did what?"

They were seated in a small Italian restaurant on a downtown side street. Megan pointed at the television screen above the bar, where the announcer was reporting James Earl Ray's guilty plea in the assassination of Martin Luther King. It was March of 1969, and King had been dead eleven months.

"I think it was a conspiracy," said Megan, for whom everything was. Although Aurie was now an assistant professor and Megan was still an instructor, they continued to steal time for evenings out like this. "Ray pleads guilty this week. Sirhan Sirhan pled guilty last week." Sirhan being the man who killed Robert Kennedy in the midst of his presidential campaign. Three assassinations in five years.

"So what?" said Aurie, uneasily.

"So, it seems a little convenient. Everything wrapped up nicely for us like that." Megan sipped her water. "I'm surprised your boyfriend doesn't write one of his essays."

It took Aurelia a painful moment to understand that Megan was referring to Eddie.

"You should tell him," said Megan, waving her glass. "And tell him I loved his book. Not the novels. The new one."

Everybody loved the new book. Everybody on the left. Entitled *Report to Military Headquarters*, it consisted of essays against the war crafted for a general readership. The PHOENIX article, expanded and more deliberate, was included. So was the story of his week at the front, along with several other tales of morally shaky activities undertaken by the American government in the name of the holy struggle against Communism. *Report* had been published during Eddie's time abroad, and sold astonishingly well, but was condemned on the floor of Congress as the work of a traitor. On college campuses Eddie was in demand as a lecturer. He was seen in the company of famous radicals. Perhaps only Aurelia suspected that Eddie's sudden infatuation with the left he had always mocked was a last-ditch effort to ingratiate himself with the people who might help him find his sister.

"It should be required reading," said Megan firmly. "The President and Congress should especially be required to read it."

Aurelia smiled with difficulty, and promised to pass on the praise. The trouble was, she did not know how. Since his return from abroad, Eddie had called her only once, and had not visited Ithaca. He had traveled instead to a number of speaking engagements. That little bitch Mindy, who had waited patiently for the twenty months of his exile, was traveling with him. So Sherilyn said, anyway, and Sherilyn was hardly ever wrong.

Most of the time.

Aurie needed to talk to him. Urgently. But she could not commit her worries to paper, and there was no way she would tell Mindy what was on her mind. Instead, knowing how it would sound, she told the girl only that it was important, and that Eddie should contact her as soon as possible. His single call in response was to tell Aurie he was on the road, and busy, and would talk to her later.

His voice had been icy.

"Did they ever find his sister?" Megan asked. "The bomber?"

Aurelia spilled her wine.

"Not that I know of," she managed, coughing hard.

"Good," said Megan. "I'm such a fan of hers."

(11)

AFTER DINNER, Aurelia called home. Locke was ten. Zora was twelve. Neither believed a sitter was necessary, but, as their mother often told them, their votes didn't count. She ascertained that they had not killed each other, or the teen from next door. Then she walked with Megan to the Strand, Ithaca's only movie theater. The building was a palace in the old style. The lobby floor was terrazzo. There were marble accents everywhere. The main stage could have held an army brigade. The Strand had been built for live spectaculars. Tonight's showing was almost empty, as Aurelia would have predicted. The film was about the first black President. Going to see it had been Megan's idea.

Something about solidarity.

On the way home, the two women talked, vaguely, politics: which was less likely, Megan wondered, that a black man would become President, or that Richard Nixon would? Aurelia laughed this off. Dick Nixon, her old family friend, had been sworn in two months ago. Aurelia had gone to Washington for the inaugural ball, escorted by a black congressman named Dennison, who was trying to get the other black members to join in creating a formal congressional caucus. Representative Byron Dennison, Bay to his many friends, chaired an important House committee and was a power broker. At fifty-one, he had never been married. There was nothing romantic between them. Bay Dennison escorted everybody. They had met years ago through Matty, and kept in touch ever since. Bay was the first man she had dated since Kevin who actually knew how to dance. At the ball, people watched them twirl around the room. Afterward, as the Congressman's driver held the door for her outside her hotel, Aurie was surprised to find Dennison's hand on her arm.

"Wait," he said.

"What's the matter?"

"This has been fun," he said. "You need more nights like this. More fun."

"Maybe so," she said, cautiously, now terrified that Dennison would invite her back to his townhouse. She clutched her sequined purse tightly, just in case she needed to swat him with it.

"That's how you should spend the rest of your life, Aurelia. Having fun. You deserve it."

All right, so maybe he was proposing marriage. "I don't understand."

"I understand your friend Eddie Wesley is coming home soon."

"Next month. At least, that's what he wrote me."

Byron Dennison nodded. "Here's the thing, Aurelia. You're raising the Garland heir. That's an important responsibility. And your wonderful little girl, too." He had released her arm but was holding her with his words. "Maybe it's time to stop the other nonsense, Aurie. Stop worrying about things so much. It seems to me that you should spend your life raising your kids and having fun. You and Eddie, even. He'd marry you in a shot. You know that."

"Bay—"

"You should marry him. That's what I think. Marry him, the two of you ride into the sunset together."

"What other nonsense? What is it you want me to stop?"

"Not me." He splayed his fingers on his chest to prove his innocence. "I'm just delivering a message. From good people, Aurie. People who want you to be happy."

Bewildered, she shook her head. "I can't marry Eddie. I just—I can't."

The smile vanished, as if the Congressman had put it away until next time. "No? Well, that's your call, of course, but it's really too bad. Still, you know best."

He bade her good night.

(I I I)

SHE WOULD HAVE TOLD EDDIE, but their paths stubbornly refused to cross. She called him several times at home, but only

Mindy ever answered. She tried his office—he still held his part-time appointment at Georgetown—but she only reached the departmental secretary. She even tried through his literary agent, who promised to pass on her message. By the time of her dinner with Megan Hadley, Aurie supposed that the entire darker nation must know that the widow of Kevin Garland was shamelessly throwing herself at her old boyfriend.

At night, she still studied the notebooks where she continued the hard work of deciphering Kevin's codes, and, thrice, she even went hat in hand to Tristan Hadley, sitting nervously in his office, even flirting a bit in order to get him to pass on questions, surreptitiously, to his wife. Each time, Tris dutifully turned up on her doorstep with the answers, and Aurie gave him coffee to be polite. On the third occasion, he brought her roses, a gift she knew she should refuse. Instead, she accepted them, to keep the pipeline open. She supposed people would say she was using him. A university could be like a small town. If she wanted to keep the information flowing and the gossipy tongues silent, her meetings with Tris had to be surreptitious. Once, they grabbed lunch at a greasy diner in the far corner of Trumansburg, a working-class suburb. Another time they managed a really clever encounter in the stacks of the Olin Library, and when Tristan took her by surprise, stealing a kiss, she finally had the satisfaction of slapping his face.

Tristan only grinned, and, for the next few days, whenever Aurelia ran into Megan, she cringed with shame.

Still, by now, with Tristan's help, she was getting a detailed picture. Two or three nights each week, after the children were in bed, she locked her bedroom door and took out the notebooks. She knew that Kevin had been part of a group that called itself the Palace Council—a modern-day analogue to the council of demons and fallen angels who, in Milton's *Paradise Lost*, assisted Satan in his rebellion against God. The leader of the Palace Council was referred to as the Paramount, or the Author. Some years ago—what she had translated so far had yielded no dates—the Council had been formed to implement a plan, called the Project, that would "shake the throne." In Milton's tale, shaking the throne referred to Satan's plot to spoil God's creation, given that God Himself was beyond reach. At first Aurie had thought the matter one of simple substitution—the members of the Palace Council were black, and the throne they planned to shake was the seat of white power. But she soon realized this was untrue, and not only because of the note she had found in Kevin's safe, scrawled during the fifties in a lily-white Florida hotel. There was also internal evidence, in her remembered jottings, of a great variety of members of the Council, just as Milton numbered among the demons the gods worshiped by many non-Christian cultures.

She still did not know exactly what the Project was. She did know that it was meant to be implemented over a long period, that shaking the throne was meant to encompass several generations, and that the plan involved battle. She was not sure whether the war was metaphorical or not, but at least some of the violence was real. Everything Eddie had told her suggested that Phil Castle was a member of the Council. Maybe his friend the physicist, whose death in Los Alamos was ruled a suicide. Probably poor Matty.

And very likely Kevin.

And there was something else—the reason she had been certain, whether rationally or not, that Eddie would be killed in Vietnam. When she lined up the deaths—Phil Castle, Joseph Belt, Matty, Kevin—it seemed to her that the other members of the Council were being systematically killed off. As if everyone with direct knowledge of the Project had to go.

The Catholic in her wanted to do the right thing. Take it to the authorities. Call the FBI. Call Nixon. Call somebody. But what was she going to say? That someone whose identity she did not know was methodically killing off everyone who knew about a plot she could not describe? A plot with its roots in Eddie's darker nation? She imagined the repercussions in her community and shivered. The ensuing investigation, the explosion of mistrust between the races, would shake the throne all right—the wrong throne.

And so she kept it to herself, patiently husbanding her information, hoping to avenge her husband, waiting for—well, she did not know exactly what she was waiting for. She just knew it hadn't happened yet.

Proof, maybe. That was the thing. She needed hard evidence instead of a theory.

She needed Castle's testament.

(I V)

IN LATE MARCH, Dwight Eisenhower died. Aurelia went to Washington because the President said she should attend the funeral. She sat at the National Cathedral alongside other Garlands: Oliver and his wife, Claire; Kevin's mother, Wanda; and Cerinda from Chicago. Nixon invited her to have breakfast with him and Pat the following morning in the White House residence. The President was upset. Students at Harvard had seized the main administration building. "I thought we were past this kind of thing," he said.

"They're upset about the war," said Pat.

"It's not my war. It's Johnson's war. It's Kennedy's war. People elected me to bring our boys home, and now these bums won't even give me two months—"

He raved on. Pat looked at Aurelia, who carefully did not smile until the First Lady smiled first.

The President, meanwhile, had finished his speech. He tossed his napkin onto the table. "Tell you why you're here. You have to tell your friend Eddie to stop."

"Stop what?" said Aurelia, very surprised.

"Making trouble. Turning over stones." From a side table he pulled a copy of *Report to Military Headquarters*. "He's not giving us a chance."

"I believe he wrote the book during the previous Administration," said Aurelia, trying to keep things calm.

Nixon nodded. "Well, tell him to come see me. Set him straight. Help each other. There are plans in the works. This term, we do foreign policy. Spheres of influence. Next term—well, next term, we go domestic. Tell him."

Aurelia said that she would. She wondered if the President knew how much he sounded like Eddie himself, back when he used to defend Kennedy.

"Did he ever find his sister?" asked the President, escorting her to the elevator, where an aide waited to lead her out. "Your friend Eddie. Does he think she's alive?"

Surprised, Aurie hesitated. "Is there some reason to think she isn't?"

"No idea. No idea. Just wondering." The awkward smile. "Listen. Tell him to come see me. Have to have a talk. It's important."

Alas, she had no way to reach Eddie. And so she did the next-best thing.

CHAPTER 48

The Other Heir

(1)

GARY FATEK SWEPT into the Finger Lakes region aboard a private jet, landing at Tompkins County Airport, where he instructed his pilot to wait. His aide and his bodyguard were surprised when he told them to wait, too. Outside the terminal, Aurelia sat in the station wagon. Gary had suggested that she not get out. No point in letting anyone snap a photo of the two of them hugging. She knew what he meant. There had always been these stories that the Hilliman heir preferred black women. Some people even whispered that he was the man Mona had married in Chicago in 1959 and divorced a year or two later, the unnamed father of her twins. A gossip reporter had once made it as far as the Cook County clerk's office but found no records—a clear case of conspiracy! Meanwhile, Gary had married a famous actress, fathered a quick child, and divorced her. It was as if he was establishing a role. He was forty, and filthy rich, and intended, he had told Mona—who had told Aurie—never to marry again.

If Gary Fatek had a current sex life, nobody knew about it. Aurelia had given up trying to figure him out. His politics had whirled 180 degrees. The radical Harlem organizer had become a supporter of every conservative cause under the sun, along with a few that existed only because he funded them. The Republicans hardly made a move without consulting him. He and Nixon were said to be bosom buddies. One story said Gary had provided major support for George Wallace, the segregationist Alabama governor whose third-party presidential campaign had helped send Nixon to the White House. The foundation Gary now controlled had lately issued a report, signed by scholars from major universities, concluding that "the so-called liberation of women" would destroy the nuclear family, "the very bedrock on which civilization rests." The late Erebeth Hilliman would have been proud.

And yet he always took Mona's calls, and telephoned Aurelia the day after she had asked Mona to set up the contact. When Aurie asked if there was a time it would be convenient for him to see her, he said, tomorrow. When she explained that she unfortunately could not drop everything and fly to New York, he said that would not be a problem.

He would come to her.

During the drive from the airport, Gary asked Aurelia all the right questions about her children and her career. He understood that she had a novel of her own coming out. A romance—was that right? He looked forward to reading it. And, yes, he did see his daughter as often as he could, but, in truth, the girl's mother was better suited to raise her. It was in their genes, Gary explained. Mammals were like that. Females cared for the young. That was nature's plan, he said. But when Aurelia, biting her tongue, hazarded a glance his way, she saw Gary grinning like a schoolboy who has lied successfully about the dog's eating his homework.

(1 1)

THEY SAT in the diner in Trumansburg, because Gary did not want to come to the campus. It would cause talk, he said, and, besides, the president would hear about it, track him down, and hit him up for money.

"The president of the university," Gary explained, in case she had trouble figuring out which president he meant. "Although that might not be a bad idea," he added, and told her about his nephew Jock, who had no particular talent but wanted to attend an Ivy League college. Now that Gary ran the family trusts, he was supposed to fix problems of that kind. "I'll probably have to give somebody half a million," he concluded gloomily.

They dug into sloshy sandwiches. "I need to talk to Eddie," said Aurie, preliminaries over.

"So talk to him."

"He won't take my calls."

"Guys are funny."

"Funny?"

Gary nodded. He signaled several times before the waitress realized that he wanted another cup of coffee. "Where do you get this blend?" he asked as she poured. "I've never tasted anything quite like it."

"A & P."

When she was gone, Gary said, "Eddie's avoiding you."

Aurelia stiffened. "I figured that out for myself."

"It isn't out of spite. It isn't out of jealousy."

"It has to be out of something."

"I think it's out of love, Aurie." He stirred his coffee. He had given up on the sandwich. The green eyes had a faraway look. "Remember the first night we met? That mixer in Northampton?"

"The Smith girls and the Amherst men."

"The Smith girls and their chaperones," he corrected lightly. "There were so many chaperones, you almost had one each." He sipped, pulled a face, added more sugar. A lot more. "But Eddie told me that night that he was going to marry you one day."

"He was a romantic," she agreed, brushing at her cheek.

"He still is, Aurie. To the rest of the world, he's a cynic. That American Angle of his. But when he thinks about you, he's a romantic. He wants to be your dashing hero or whatever it is guys want to be when they're in love. He's had a woman here and there, Aurie. You know that. He and that Torie even had kind of a hot-and-heavy thing for a few months. But he's never married anybody. He's still waiting to rescue you."

Aurelia picked at her French fries. "Gary, are you trying to say that Eddie won't take my calls because I won't marry him? That's pretty childish. And pretty offensive."

"That's not the reason." He shoved his coffee to one side, picked up his water glass, frowned at the stains, put it down. "No, Aurie.

He's a romantic. He'd happily die loving you from afar. He still wants to rescue you. That's why he won't let you near him now. He's trying to protect you."

"From what?"

"I'm not sure, Aurie. Something happened to him over in Asia. He hasn't told me what. You heard about that night he got drunk in Hong Kong?"

She remembered the headlines. The photos. "Of course. I couldn't believe it when I heard. He doesn't drink. You know that. He's been a teetotaler since his father— Oh."

Gary nodded. "You see? It was a setup. We were supposed to think he was drunk. Whoever set it up didn't know he doesn't drink." He took one of her fries. "I'm not sure, Aurie, because he won't talk about it. But—from little hints he's dropped?—I think whatever happened to him over there changed him. Now he thinks there's a danger, and he wants to shield you from it."

Aurelia could not help herself. The words just leaped from her mouth. "Then why isn't he shielding Mindy?"

"Mindy? Who on earth is Mindy?"

"His assistant."

"Oh, yes, his assistant," said Gary vaguely, as if names of assistants were beneath him. "What about her?"

"She travels with him everywhere! Why isn't she in danger?"

It took him a moment to get the point. "Oh, I see. You're jealous." He spoke so matter-of-factly that there seemed no point in contradicting him. "There's no need for him to shield Mindy. What happened to him in Hong Kong—well, he survived it. I don't think Eddie is worried for himself. He seems pretty confident to me. No, Aurie. I think you're the one who would be in danger."

"Me?"

"If the two of you meet up. If whoever it is thinks you're working together. That's when the danger would arise." He saw her face. "Now, don't worry, Aurie. Nothing is going to happen. Eddie's very sure. Nothing is going to happen, as long as he stays away from you."

She turned away, gazed out the window at the bright autumn sun glinting off station wagons and pickup trucks. Ithaca was supposed to be her refuge. Hers and the children's. Aurelia remembered her conversation with Bay Dennison after Nixon's inaugural ball. *That's how you should spend the rest of your life*, the Congressman had said. *Having fun.* And then, of Eddie: *Marry him, the two of you ride into the sunset together.*

Until this moment, it had not occurred to her that the words were less a suggestion than a warning. But, then, Kevin himself had tried to warn her, years ago, after she admitted rifling his office files: *You've never heard of shaking the throne or the Author or Pandemonium. You don't know anything. Remember that. Especially if anything happens to me.*

Gary touched her hand. He spoke softly. "I can send somebody if you like." He paused. "To look after you. I know competent people, Aurie."

"But I'm not in any danger." She managed a smile. "It's sweet of you to offer, but I'll be fine. I don't think they'll hurt me, either."

"Eddie thinks otherwise."

"It's probably best if he goes on thinking that. I'll leave him alone for now. You can tell him—well, tell him we spoke, and that I'll leave him alone."

Back at the airport, Aurelia thanked Gary for all he had done, especially for Mona. He nodded and kissed her cheek. Watching the plane bank across the brilliant sky, she remembered the rest of her conversation with Bay Dennison. *You're raising the Garland heir. That's an important responsibility.*

Locke Matthew Garland, named for the writer of the Harlem Renaissance and his paternal grandfather. Locke, the Garland heir.

This was all about her son.

CHAPTER 49

Again the Golden Boy

(I)

"I WON'T BE STAYING for the party," said Lanning Frost. "To do otherwise would be ethically unjustified."

"I understand," said Aurelia, who had already heard from Margot that the Senator would not be present, and had actually hoped that he would depart before her arrival. But he was either too savvy or too well counseled to say a word about Kevin, dead now four years.

He gave her hand a practiced political pump, then swept out of the room surrounded by a bevy of advisers. The occasion was a reception Margot Frost had arranged at her Georgetown home to honor the surprise success of Aurelia's first novel, which had been hesitantly published, to token publicity, a month earlier. It was late May of 1969. War had broken out in California. That was what people called it, a war. National Guard troops with fixed bayonets had battled demonstrators in Berkeley. A helicopter had launched a chemical attack. Mona was thrilled. Aurelia was terrified. Not for her country but for Eddie, who had been out there, lighting rhetorical fires, but had evidently escaped before the aerial assault. At the reception, everybody pretended nothing was going on in the world. Aurelia's novel was a romance, and editors were certain that nobody was reading romances any more. The story among the cognoscenti was that the publication of her book had been a favor to the great Edward Wesley Junior. But somehow the novel had found an audience.

Margot shepherded Aurelia around the roomful of important Washingtonians. Since her husband's near-assassination, Margot

Frost had become one of the city's leading hostesses. People who had never heard of Aurelia until today told her how much they loved her work. A few old pals and experienced pols asked about her children. Aurelia felt hemmed in. She had been in her day quite the party maven, but since Kevin's death and her flight to Ithaca, she had grown locked-in, private, uneasy around crowds. She did not understand the success of her book. She did not see the nation's hunger for the ordinary amid the turbulence. She saw a richly furnished drawing room packed with fawning strangers, most of whom made a larger fuss over Margot, future First Lady, than over Aurelia herself.

Their inattention relieved her.

She was standing near the bar, half listening to a conversation about California, when she spotted, in the corner near the piano, the onetime golden boy of Harlem, Perry Mount—a familiar face, and the man Eddie had crossed the ocean to find. He was as tall and impressive as ever, communicating a sense of energy, a readiness to leap into excited action. Nursing a glass of ginger ale, Perry had made his own private space. Nobody approached him. Aurelia suspected that nobody knew exactly who he was, or what he was doing there. He caught her eye and tilted his glass her way. She excused herself and approached him.

"It's been a long time," she said, smiling broadly because, in his familiar presence, the old Harlem skills came back to her. She reminded herself that Eddie had told her on the day Kevin died that he believed Perry and Margot were conspiring together. Maybe it was even true. He was, after all, here. "You look well," she said.

Back in the day, Perry had reserved for women a puffy half-smile, almost a kiss, that managed to welcome and mock you at once. He did it now. "And you, Aurelia. But of course you always look good, don't you? Congratulations on the success of the book, by the way. I haven't read it, but I can hardly wait."

"When did you get back?"

"Back?"

"I heard the State Department sent you to Saigon—"

"Oh, I quit. Ten years. That's more than enough service to one's country. I'm at a think tank now. More money, less risk." His smile grew wider, but the brown eyes, huge behind the glasses, were waiting for something. "And I get to stay home. Maybe I'll start a family. I'm in my forties, Aurie. Don't you think it's time?" He toyed with his ginger ale. "I've been seeing Chamonix Bing. You remember Chammie, from the old days? Formerly married to Charlie Bing? Listen. Maybe when you're not so busy we can all do something together."

"That would be nice." She decided to be direct. "Perry, did Eddie find you? He went all the way to Vietnam looking—"

"Oh, yes. Eddie." His eyes bored into her, beseeching and demanding at once. The eyes of command. And victory. Aurelia wondered if it would be possible to hide secrets from this man. Or, if he really put his mind to seduction, to resist him. "We sort of found each other."

"Was he—how did he—"

"He seemed fine when I saw him in Hong Kong." The smile flattened. All at once the golden boy looked golden and boyish, an expression that used to drive the girls half mad. "Don't tell me your Eddie hasn't been in touch. That's rather unlike him."

She let this one pass. "Perry, if you saw Eddie, then you know he was hoping you might—"

He cut her off. "I don't know where Junie is. Neither does Eddie. I'm certain of that." He spoke with a peculiar satisfaction. The eyes were hardening. "I'm not even sure she's still alive."

Aurelia had always been bold, and she did not think this opportunity would again present itself. She felt more than heard people approaching. "Eddie says you were in touch with her. With Junie. Underground, I mean."

Perry shook his head. "Somebody's been telling tales out of school, I see. You should know I can't discuss that, Aurie. Just let me say that whatever I did, I did in my official capacity."

"You were in touch with her. You *were!*"

"My inability to comment is not a confirmation." He seemed to be quoting from the manual.

"Have you ever heard the term 'shaking the throne'?" Taking her only other shot. "Because years ago you said something to Eddie about shaking the throne, and about how Harlem has secrets."

"Did I? I was such a pretentious little bastard in those days, wasn't I?" The powerful eyes lit up, but he was looking over her shoulder. "Margot, dear. Surely you haven't come to take this ravishing creature away from me."

Margot had come to do exactly that.

Perry was handing Aurelia a business card. "Call me next time you're in town," he said, receding, with the old kissable grin.

(11)

WHEN THE PARTY BROKE UP, Margot made Aurelia stay. They had not laid eyes on each other since Eisenhower's funeral, and had not exchanged more than a word or two since Kevin's. It was time, said Margot, that they had a talk. Just two girls together, she added. But Aurelia knew that Margot Frost was the sort of woman who had never been a girl in her life.

They sat in the parlor and took off their shoes, and Margot broke out a very impressive 1947 Château Carbonnieux Blanc. Its taste was light and surprisingly rosy, and Margot said they should get sloshed together, as in the old days. The trouble was, they had shared no old days, and Margot Frost was the last person with whom Aurie was interested in getting sloshed. Aurie took small, practical sips. But Margot, fleshy legs tucked beneath her on the sofa, was gulping the wine like water, and Aurelia supposed that if the future First Lady wanted to get sloshed, her own job was to sit there and let it happen.

"You seemed pretty cozy with Perry," said Margot, teasingly.

"We're old friends."

"What about your boyfriend? Eddie? How's dear, dear Eddie?"

"He's not my boyfriend, Margot. I haven't really talked to him since he got back."

"I hear he's looking for his sister." She lifted the glass and swirled it this way and back, playing with her own reflection. "Do you think he'll find her?"

"I wouldn't really know."

"Maybe she doesn't want him to find her."

"Maybe not," said Aurelia, suddenly very wary. She reminded herself that, in order for Margot to be the genius behind Lanning, she first had to be a genius.

"Women do run from men. Happens every day."

"I suppose so."

"I ran into him in Hong Kong," said Margot. "Your Eddie. Did I mention that?" A long swallow. "He seemed—determined."

Bother while a maid came in with more cookies. Margot, without ever quite seeming to stuff herself, had finished off the tray. It occurred to Aurelia that something quite terrible was eating at the First-Lady-in-waiting. She wondered whether it could possibly be as terrible as Eddie seemed to think.

Alone again.

"You have to understand Lanning," said Margot, several times. "He's not the way everybody says. He's not stupid. He gets a little tongue-tied. Don't we all get a little tongue-tied sometimes? But he's going to be a great President. A great President." More wine. Aurelia helpfully poured. "You know, it's not easy. Your husband—he was a good man. Lanning is a good man, but, well, he's not easy to be married to. He needs a lot of help, Aurie. My help. Other people's."

Aurelia murmured understanding.

"This is what I was raised to be," said Margot. "First Lady. I mean, I'm not First Lady yet, but everybody knows I'm going to be. I can't ever let my hair down. Ever." And then, eyes sparkling mischief, she reached up and did exactly that, mussing a coiffure that must have cost her half a week at the salon. "Well, no. No. That's not right. I wasn't raised to be First Lady. But I was raised to marry an important man and to help him achieve whatever—and that's what I'm doing, Aurie. I'm helping my important man. I'm making the deals and the alliances and raising the money. Why do the newspapers say I'm some kind of ambitious schemer? Why do they write these things?" Accusatory, as if Aurelia had written them herself. "I'm a wife, that's all. Isn't this what wives are supposed to do? Help our men? Didn't you help Kevin?" Another glass. She was angry now. "It was easier for you, Aurie. You didn't have to live with all these expectations. There's nothing I wouldn't do to help my man get to the top. You believe that, right?"

"Of course."

"I wish I was more like you," Margot continued, to Aurie's surprise. "I wish I could just disappear to some little town for three or four years and come back and—well, I don't know if I'd come back or not. There's too much to do. So much to do, and so few people I can really talk to. There's Perry, of course—"

"I never realized that you knew him," said Aurie, ingenuously.

"Our families go back simply years," said Margot. Her wide brow furrowed, three neat little lines, as if more would be an offense. "They say he was in love with Eddie's sister. Do you believe that story? Don't you think his employers would hold that kind of thing against him? In government, I mean?"

"You can't control who you fall in love with, Margot."

The future First Lady seemed to find this proposition dubious. She gulped at the Château Carbonnieux and lapsed into a troubled silence. "I'll tell you, though," she finally said. "Perry's the ambitious schemer. Not me. Perry. He knows where all the bodies are buried. Literally. He's CIA—did you know that? And those articles Eddie wrote? About PHOENIX and everything? That was Perry's baby. That's why he had to come back. Why he had to leave the Agency. Eddie wrecked his career. Did you know that?"

"You're not serious."

"I'm very serious. Perry must hate him terribly." Margot leaned in closer, her breath sweet from the wine. "You know what Lanning says? Perry killed people over there."

"It's a war—"

"Not *that* kind of people," said Margot. She covered her mouth. "Oh, well. We've talked long enough, haven't we? Didn't you say you and Claire Garland had tickets to a show later tonight?"

She was bustling Aurelia to the door, and did not look remotely sloshed. All the way back to the hotel, Aurie wondered. Maybe Margot was really able to turn her sobriety on and off that fast. On the other hand, perhaps she had been trying, from the depths of whatever her involvement with the Project, to send a message.

Maybe a threat.

Maybe a plea for help.

CHAPTER 50

Conversation with a Judge

(1)

BY THIS TIME, Aurelia was coming to share Eddie's paranoia. She believed, often, that she was being followed. She would glimpse the same pale face behind her at the supermarket, or lurking in the shadow behind the statue of Ezra Cornell on the Quad, or climbing out of a car an aisle or two away when she pulled into the parking lot of the Jamesway Discount Store. Not Mr. Collier. Eddie had never explained exactly what he suspected about the former bodyguard, but Aurelia would have known his face anywhere. No. This was somebody else. Then, in the summer of 1969, her follower changed identities so suddenly that she wondered if she might be imagining things after all. That summer, the irrepressible Locke was eleven, and the quiet Zora had just turned thirteen. Their mother decided that the family needed a real vacation. And so, following their annual late-June trip to Beechwood Cemetery in New Rochelle, where they visited the grave of Kevin Garland on his birthday, Aurelia rented a small house on Martha's Vineyard, a shingled Victorian on a crowded hill overlooking Oak Bluffs Harbor, inland from East Chop, a neighborhood known in those days as the Highlands.

Her follower came, too.

This one was a woman, a sallow brunette, and her solitariness, her lack of family, made her conspicuous. So did her whiteness. At this time the Vineyard, an island off the coast of Cape Cod, was not as well known to the public as it later would be. Segregation had long ago driven the middling and upper classes of the darker nation to create their own summer colonies: Sag Harbor, near the easternmost tip of Long Island; Atlantic Beach, in South Carolina; and a few strategic and secluded spots in the western portions of Connecticut and Massachusetts and in upstate New York all had their innings. But the Vineyard enjoyed a certain durability, as well as the relative seclusion granting it an exclusivity: it was difficult to get there, and expensive to stay. Claire and Oliver Garland had bought a house in Oak Bluffs in the early sixties, and spent every summer in residence. Aurelia and Kevin had been their frequent guests, but the summer of 1969 was Aurie's first visit since her husband's death four years ago, and, this time, Aurie wanted a place of her own.

"You should buy before the prices go up," said Claire.

"I'll think about it," said Aurie, still uneasy with wealth, who had been driving the same station wagon now for six years.

The family arrived in early July. The weather was splendid. Each morning, Aurelia would wake the children for a march down to the small strip of beach below the house. She called this dawn swim "bathing," because Kevin had. More likely than not, she would spot her pale shadow at the same beach moments after arriving. Because she had so enjoyed *Funny Girl* last year, Aurelia took to calling the female shadow Streisand, and her male counterpart Sharif. Once the family settled into routine, Streisand might even be waiting for them, swimming in leisured figure-eights by the time Aurie and the children reached the sand. Or they would make a pre-lunch expedition to the playground in the middle of the Highlands, and Streisand would be sitting on the bench, reading a magazine. The children loved the dangerous spinning wooden platform with high metal rungs they would hold, shrieking with glee while Aurelia whirled it faster, faster, Mommy, faster! One day, while the children were on the teeter-totter, their mother grew bold. She walked over to Streisand, sat beside her on the bench, and offered her a cookie from the bag she kept for the kids.

Aurelia was not sure what to expect. Would the woman brandish a badge? A gun? Would she demand gruffly to be left alone, or, embarrassed, slink off into the muzzy Vineyard sunshine?

Streisand did none of these things. She lifted her eyes from

Newsweek, offered a smile of complicity, and declined politely before returning to her magazine. Aurie returned to her children. When she looked up again, her shadow was gone.

In the afternoons, rain or shine, they would walk or drive to town, where the children would ride the carousel, the Flying Horses, most of the steeds original, dating to the nineteenth century, Zora waving and giggling, Locke trying to snatch the brass ring from the wooden arm in the corner and win the free ride, Aurelia snapping away with her Kodak Instamatic. Sometimes Streisand showed up. Sometimes she didn't. Sometimes Aurelia would sit up half the night in the bedroom of her rented house, trying to figure out how much was real and how much imagined. She wished she could talk about it, but there was nobody to talk to. She could not call Eddie and was afraid to call Mona, who enjoyed, at odd moments, diagnosing her. She tried Gary Fatek, but did not enjoy Mona's streamlined access. She could not fight her way through the buffers that protected him from the hoi polloi. No matter how many flunkies promised to pass on her messages, he did not return the call.

She did manage to reach Callie Finnerty, her friend from Mount Vernon, and was warmed by the unadorned friendliness in her voice. They talked about their children until Aurelia decided they had better stop, because it was daytime, and the rates were high.

Meanwhile, the magical Garland name combined with Aurie's own growing stature led to invitations to visit most of the salons on the Island, but she turned everyone down, unless Locke and Zora were invited, too. Dorothy West, one of the giants of the Harlem Renaissance, owned a house not far away, and welcomed the children happily, even telling Aurelia tartly that she could, if she liked, send the children in her stead. Adam Clayton Powell had once summered nearby, but no longer came to this part of the Island. The house was now owned by his first wife, Isabelle—not the same wife Aurie had met in Harlem—who fed the children cookies and lemonade, and told stories of the days when the Garland family was nobody. But most of their visits were to the splendid summer cottage of Claire and Oliver Garland. The house was a rambling Victorian, fifty years old if a day, located on Ocean Park, with a lovely uncluttered view across untidy grass to the Nantucket Sound and the Cape beyond. Oliver, now on the federal bench, was able to get to the Island only rarely, even in the summer, but Claire and the four children were in residence from the middle of June through the end of August. The children ranged in age from Addison, the eldest, who was about to start college, to Abby, the youngest, a fierce little ponytailed tomboy of eight. The younger son, Talcott, obviously had a crush on his cousin Zora, but it was to Mariah, Claire's fourteen-year-old daughter, that Zora naturally attached herself. For much of that summer, the two girls were inseparable, whether hanging around one of the two houses, swimming at the beach, or strolling along Circuit Avenue in search of the perfect ice-cream cone. Aurelia found herself alone, often, with Locke, who, freed of his sister's influence, grew more serious, and asked the thoughtful, searching, utterly unanswerable questions that occur to children: "How can you be so sure Daddy is in Heaven? Don't some people go to Hell?" and "If you get a new husband and new children, will you forget us?"

One day, on a hunch, Aurelia waited for the two girls to leave the Garland house for their regular two-block walk to Circuit Avenue. When five minutes had passed, she slipped out and started hunting for them. She tracked them with ease to Darling's candy store, and the reason she knew the girls were inside was that pale Streisand, clad in shorts, was outside, fiddling with her bicycle.

As Aurie marched past, the watcher waved her hand in friendly salute.

(11)

GARY FATEK RETURNED THE CALL during the family's second week on the Island. Explaining her difficulty, Aurelia felt herself sounding more than slightly crazy. If she was not careful she would begin chattering about the Author and Pandemonium, and how the Palace Council planned to shake the throne but now had lost control of the Project. She would begin explaining why she thought the bomb had been intended for Kevin, not Lanning Frost.

But Gary, who somewhere along the line had misplaced the sense of humor they all remembered from the old days, listened to her story of surveillance with the same gravity he no doubt brought to corporate acquisitions.

"What exactly are you asking me to do?" he said when she was done.

The question took Aurie aback. Wasn't it obvious? Was he weaseling out of their friendship, perhaps on the ground that he had done enough already? "Can you find out who it is?"

"I can try."

Again she noted the wiggle room Gary left himself. She was on the screened porch behind the house. There was a plug for the extension. Zora and Mariah were at the picnic table, whispering giggly confidences. Locke was inside reading a book. Aurie thought she saw movement in the trees that screened the backyard, but suspected she was imagining things.

"When will you know something?" she asked, hoping to box him in.

He answered with a question of his own. "Have you talked to Eddie yet?"

"Eddie?"

"About why Nixon seems so fixated on him."

Aurelia needed a moment to catch up with the swift change of conversation. "No, Gary, no. I haven't had a chance."

"It's important, Aurie. We really need the answer."

We? "I told you, he's not taking my calls. I know, I know, you said it's to protect me. But he's still not taking them."

"Too bad." A long sigh, or perhaps it was just the scratchiness of the long-distance carrier wave. "Fine. Don't worry. I'll see what I can do."

About Streisand and Sharif? Or about Aurelia and Eddie? There was no way to ask, because Gary had hung up. He was too important these days to waste time saying goodbye.

That night, as Aurie sat in bed poring over her notebooks, she heard a footfall on the landing.

In the doorway stood not her shadow but her son, Locke, in his pajamas, barefoot and frowning.

"You're making noise," he said. "You're keeping me awake."

The boy's expression was distant and unreadable, reminding her of Kevin that night, holding the shoe and demanding an heir. She shivered. She must have spoken some of her hypotheses aloud. The wooden walls of their rickety house were tissue-thin. "Mommy's just doing some work, honey. I'm sorry if I kept you up. I'll go downstairs."

But Locke, still pensive, came over and hopped onto the bed. His mother snapped the notebook closed as if hiding pornography.

"Is it a secret?" he asked, hazel eyes searching her face.

"Is what a secret?"

"Your work." Her son touched the cardboard cover. "What you were doing that woke me up. Is it a secret, Mommy?"

Aurelia felt weak, silly, exposed. She did not understand who was gazing at her out of those young eyes. Somewhere she found words. "Yes, honey. It's a secret." She swallowed hard, put the book aside, took him by the hand. "Everybody has secrets sometimes, honey."

"Is it a good secret or a bad secret?" he asked as she led him back to his own room.

Oh, Heaven! Oh, help! "A good one," she lied. Locke crawled back into bed. Aurelia drew the Superman comforter up to his neck, kissed his forehead. "You'll like it, honey. I promise."

"Mommy?"

"Yes, honey?"

"I don't like secrets."

"Me, neither."

"Aunt Claire's kids say I'm going to be rich when I grow up. Am I? You shouldn't keep that secret if it's true." The lilting voice was severe. "You should tell me."

"Oh, honey—"

"I have secrets, too."

She stood in the doorway, scarcely breathing. "What secrets are those, honey?"

Her son giggled. "If I tell you, they won't be secrets."

Aurelia felt those clear, questioning eyes judging her as she pulled the door behind her. Locke liked it closed.

(I I I)

THE FOLLOWING WEEK, Aurelia and her children were invited to Ocean Park along with three or four other families to watch on television as Neil Armstrong walked on the moon. After dinner, the adults played pinochle and the younger children played hide-and-seek all through the house. The talk turned from the war to Teddy Kennedy, who, two nights earlier, had driven his car off a bridge on Chappaquiddick. A young woman in the car with Kennedy had died. People spoke of the event in mournful tones. He was our best hope to beat Nixon, someone said. Now that's gone. Oliver Garland kept a prudent silence. He was a Republican, like all the Garlands, in the tradition of the old Negro ruling class. In Harlem of fifteen or twenty years earlier, voting Republican had been nothing to apologize for, but those days were dead. People speculated on who else might run in 1972, now that Kennedy's chances seemed doomed. Muskie, of course. Maybe Frost. Not Humphrey, whose support of the war had left him damaged goods.

They asked Aurelia what she thought. Everybody knew her side of the family was close to Nixon.

"I don't follow politics," she said, eyes on the table.

Come on, Aurie, they insisted. Who does Nixon most want to run against? Who's he afraid of?

"I really wouldn't know."

Oliver changed the subject. There was a rumor, he said, that Nixon was considering taking the nation off the gold standard, a revolutionary act that would reverberate through every economy in the world. What did people think?

The answer was the special sheepish smiling silence with which we greet the warbling of the very brilliant, or the very crazy. But Zora, sitting nearby because she was bored with hide-and-seek, said after a moment's thought that it would mean everybody was just pretending to have money. Like kids playing store, she said.

Everybody laughed but Oliver, who nodded unhappily and said, "Exactly." He turned to Aurelia. "Budding genius," he murmured. Everybody laughed again, but Oliver was serious.

The raucous party wound down to breathlessness as Armstrong's moment approached. Everybody wanted to be cool and cynical, even to mumble about how the money that went into Project Apollo could have been better spent feeding the hungry, but nobody wanted to miss it. The idea of no longer being confined to Planet Earth made the whole world heady. Even the stoical Oliver Garland seemed infected by the hysterical quiet. Not a word was spoken as Armstrong drifted down the ladder, his image a grainy gray and white. His boot touched. When CBS flashed the logo ARMSTRONG ON MOON across the grainy image of a human being standing on the lunar surface, then cut away to a helplessly smiling Walter Cronkite, half the group was in tears. Everybody applauded. Aurelia felt oddly sad, as if we were not so much escaping our planet as deserting it. Conversation began swirling once more. Aurelia missed Eddie. She missed Matty. She missed Kevin. She missed her old life—

Her ears perked up.

Someone had just remarked that the astronauts were sitting where we dare not soar. Sitting where we dare not soar. A paraphrase of a passage from Book IV of *Paradise Lost.* Or were they simply the words of her fevered imagination? Tuning in once more, Aurelia could not figure out who, among all the brown faces, might have uttered the phrase. If indeed anyone had.

Later, as the party began to break up, she managed to snare a moment with Oliver, the two of them alone in the small first-floor library.

"People will talk," said the judge, but he smiled.

"I wanted to ask you about a piece of family history."

"Of course."

"It involves your uncle."

Oliver nodded. He wore glasses with gold rims. He slipped them off and polished them with a silk handkerchief. "Please," he said.

"I know this is going to sound weird, but bear with me for a minute. Did Matty ever mention a big meeting in the early fifties? Something about—well, there would have been, um, white men and black men, talking about a project—"

Another nod. "Sure. The meeting up at Burton Mount's house. Right here in Oak Bluffs, on Winemack, just off New York Avenue. Not far from where you're staying, come to think of it. It's still there. The ranch with the white picket fence. This would have been—let me think." He clucked his tongue, trying to remember. He seemed entirely untroubled. "I would guess around 1951, 1952. Yes. It was the summer of 1952, because Claire and I had married the year before."

"Were you there?"

"At my wedding, yes. At the meeting, no."

"Do you know what happened?"

He put his glasses back on. People called Oliver the Judge, with a capital "J," not only because of his job but because of the weight of his mien. In the old days, he had been Ollie. These were the new days.

"I wasn't that close to my uncle," he said. He drummed a fingertip against his lip. "Uncle Matty and Burton Mount were very close. Even when I was a boy, I remember how, after a few drinks, Burton would float some crazy idea—going back to Africa, say, or starting an uprising, in the name of racial justice—that kind of thing. Burton would float these ideas, and Matty would shoot them down. Too impractical. Too expensive. Burton Mount was a dreamer. Matty was more the realist." Again Oliver smiled. "As a matter of fact, they had an argument at my wedding. My father was alive then. It was at the reception, and everybody'd had a few. Burton said that if we really had any sense—the colored race, he meant—we'd do what the white folks do. We'd find a way to get everybody so scared they'd have to do what we wanted. Uncle Matty asked how we'd do that exactly. Burton said it wouldn't be too hard. All we needed was commitment.

My father broke it up. He said that commitment was what got people put into insane asylums. I don't think Burton was terribly amused, but—"

"There you are," said Claire, bustling into the library. She seemed alert, and nervous. Aurelia could understand that. She was a widow, and available, and had become, despite her best efforts, a woman of no certain reputation. Oliver kissed his wife on the cheek. "I've been looking all over for you, dear," said Claire. "Lisle and Betty want to say their goodbyes." As her husband slipped away, Claire turned to Aurelia. Her voice was low, and sweet. "I think Mariah would like your Zora to spend the night. Would that be all right with you? Of course, we'd love to have Locke, too. He and Talcott get along so well. You could pick them up in the morning. Even the afternoon, if you like."

Aurelia was barely listening. She was exhausted, and trying to remember why she had ever married into the Garland family. "Yes," she said, faintly. "That would be fine. Thank you."

"Not at all, dear. Not at all. It would be our pleasure. Your children are such a joy. Oh, there is one other thing."

"Yes, Claire?"

Her modulation never changed. "If I ever find you alone with my husband again, I'll scratch your eyes out."

Driving alone back up to the Highlands, crowded by loneliness, Aurelia made a detour. Even in the darkness, she easily found the house on Winemack, on a grassy rise with a view over Crystal Lake to the Cape. She climbed out of the car as the first smattering of raindrops fell. The picket fence Oliver had described lay in ruins. The grass was at her knees. The house was shuttered, and, seen up close, the shutters themselves were cracked and beaten. There was trash in the yard. She tried to imagine the scene seventeen years ago, in the summer of 1952, cars rolling up the circular driveway to discharge the powerful men who constituted the original Palace Council. She wondered who else had attended the meeting besides the names she already knew. She wondered how they kept the meeting secret. There would have been bright lights, rich food, fine wine, maybe a bodyguard or two. Aurelia struggled to picture it all. But her imagination, usually so clever, could conjure nothing except the wreck that stood before her.

Like the wreck of the Project they had conceived that night.

The rain was coming down harder. As Aurelia climbed into the station wagon for the drive back to her empty bed in the empty house, Streisand sailed gracefully past on her bicycle, the red reflector on the rear fender circling and bobbing in the soggy mist before vanishing into the night.

CHAPTER 51

Dennison

(1)

SHE COULD NOT AVOID EDDIE FOREVER; nor he, her. On New Year's Eve of 1969, they encountered each other for the first time since his return. The occasion was Byron Dennison's regular party, held in the grand ballroom of Boston's fanciest hotel. Among the well-to-do of the darker nation, the Congressman's soirée was the place to be seen, if you could only wangle an invitation. Aurie had not attended since Kevin's death, but this was evidently her year of returning to old haunts.

She had no escort, but Bay had asked her to serve, in effect, as the evening's hostess. Aurelia was more than willing. She had played this role several times already over the past few months, appearing on Bay's arm at public occasions. Let people think what they wished. Byron Dennison was funny, and fun, and knew everybody. Aurelia no longer felt threatened by his attentions. In September, Bay had told her frankly what she had already guessed: he was not a man to love a woman. Nobody on the Hill cares, he explained with the patient glee of the much-amused man, but my constituents do.

And so the Congressman gently encouraged the fiction that he was dating the widowed professor-turned-romance-novelist, and Aurelia allowed him to do so. She liked Bay, and, for the most part, trusted him. She wanted him to trust her, too. She was biding her time, and by New Year's Eve decided she had bided long enough. Tonight, with the children up in Hanover visiting Mona and her kids, Aurelia would be staying in Boston. As a matter of fact, for the sake of convenience as well as the fiction, she would spend the night at Bay's townhouse on Beacon Hill. That would be the time to ask what she needed to ask.

The party was huge, and formal, and glittering. It was more integrated than Aurelia remembered from earlier years, but still identifiably black. The band played constantly, though never too loud. The room was bright and colorful. People blew on paper horns. Balloons and streamers were everywhere. Aurelia floated from one group to the next, shaking hands or hugging or kissing cheeks as the moment demanded. Sometimes Bay was with her. Sometimes she was alone. "It's so wonderful to see you," she murmured, over and over, sounding each time as if she really meant it. "The Congressman and I are so happy you could come."

Then she saw Eddie.

He was seated near the dance floor, his bow tie already loosened, arguing heatedly with several other literary figures. Sitting beside him, her arm proprietarily on his shoulder, was a famous black radical, just recently out of prison, her Afro huge, her body angular and svelte, her fingertip caressing the back of Eddie's neck. Aurie, drifting closer to the table, could not take her eyes off that finger. The gesture was maddeningly intimate. The way Eddie seemed unaffected suggested, however, that it was also nothing new, that the seduction had been accomplished long ago.

This was just her way of letting the whole room know.

Aurelia downed her pink gin fizz and went to the bar for another. Why had the grapevine not informed her that Eddie was seeing someone? Did people think her so fragile? Or was it that they did not think she would care? Either way, she decided after all not to confront him. Eddie did not want to talk to her, and she understood his reasons. Aurelia had just started to back away when Bay materialized at her shoulder. "Go ahead," he whispered. "Faint heart never won fair gentleman."

"I'm not trying to win him." She inclined her head. "Besides, he's spoken for."

But Byron Dennison would never have risen so high had he not been deaf to the word *no*. He lifted her hand, kissed it grandly, then linked her arm through his own. He strolled easily toward Eddie's table.

At their approach, everybody glanced up.

Eddie's eyes widened. The others leaped to their feet, all but the girlfriend, who ostentatiously took her time, smoothing her gown as she rose.

"Hi," said Aurelia, forgetting her script. She spoke only to Eddie.

"Hi," he said back.

The girlfriend linked her arm through Eddie's. Smiling savagely, she reached out her free hand to shake. Bay Dennison grabbed the hand and gave a political pump, telling the woman how glad he was that she was out of prison, how the dignity with which she had borne her suffering was an inspiration to them all, his blather filling the air as he managed, without ever quite seeming to try, to bear her off toward the other end of the room, where there was somebody she really just had to meet.

He winked at Aurie over his shoulder.

"How have you been?" she asked Eddie.

"Good. Good. You? Oh, and the novel was wonderful, by the way. Thanks for sending it."

"Thank you."

"The kids—"

"They're thriving."

He dipped his head. "I'm sorry about not calling. There are good reasons."

Anyone with the last name Garland could handle that one half asleep. Aurelia stood taller, tilted her head back just so, flashed a practiced smile. "Oh, dear. It has been a long time, hasn't it? I'm sorry. I've been so busy, I don't think I noticed."

"Stop it, Aurie."

"Stop what, Eddie dear?"

"Look. You don't have to put on an act for me, okay? I understand why you're doing it, but you don't have to. I want to talk to you, Aurie."

"About what?"

"About what's been going on." A quick glance for curious ears. They stood near the bar but in a crowd. "And also about why I—"

Aurelia lifted a hand, covered his mouth. Gently. "I'm so sorry, Eddie, dear. It's wonderful to see you, but I really need to get back to the Congressman. Your girlfriend is simply lovely, and poor Bay always did have an eye for the ladies."

She left him, hoping to have been overheard.

(11)

"ARE YOU GOING to marry him or not?" asked Bay in the limousine.

Aurelia was dozing against the agreeable leather. It was almost four in the morning. She could not remember when she had last been so tired. Her shoes were off, because her feet were killing her. She had danced half the night with Bay, and the rest of the night with a dozen other men, none of them Eddie.

"Marry who?" she said, probably still vamping a bit.

"Your Eddie."

"I told you, Bay. He's spoken for."

"He's about as spoken for as you are." He patted her on the shoulder. "Eddie's staying at the Copley. Just in case you're interested."

"I'm not, Bay. Please leave it alone."

They drove in silence. At the house, he made her sit in the kitchen while he warmed a little milk. She protested that she did not need any, she was practically keeling over already. But Bay insisted that it would help her sleep.

It did. She put her elbow on the counter, rested her chin on her hand, and closed her eyes.

"Aurie?" he asked, softly.

"Hmmm?"

"What is it you want to ask me?"

She sat up, blinking. "What did you say?"

He smiled. "I'm an old politico, sweetie. I can always tell. Fun though I am, you're not here for the parties. You want something. Might as well tell me what it is."

"Oh. Yes. Right."

"Well?"

Keeping her eyes open was a strain. "A year ago. You told me about how I'm raising the Garland heir. And how I should marry Eddie and—and be happy. Remember?"

"Rings a faint bell." But his smile never wavered.

"You said you were sending me a message." She yawned. "I want to know who sent it."

"Oh, goodness, Aurie. That was so long ago." A guffaw. He slapped his cheek comically. "You can't expect me to recall a detail like that."

"Bay, come on."

The wise, experienced eyes measured her. He folded his arms and, for a moment, reminded her of Matty. "You know, Aurie, not everything that happens that's good can happen in the sunlight. Some things can only happen in the shadow. Sometimes, to make progress, we have to do things we can't talk about. The fact that we can't talk about them doesn't prove they're evil."

"It increases the chances, though." Aurelia climbed to her feet, swayed, managed to stay upright. "If you stay down in the shadows? If you never come up in the sun, where people can see you? It's easy to think you're superior to everybody else. It's easy to think you're doing good. But unless you interact with people who can tell you you're wrong—"

She stopped. She was drunk and tired and achy, and she had lost the thread. Probably she had intended to make some point about violence, but she could not remember. Besides, he might be telling the truth. Maybe he really was the messenger, and nothing more.

"I'm worn out," she said, dragging toward the stairs. "I'm going to bed."

"Don't let the tosies bite," he called after her. He laughed. "Or however it goes."

(111)

SHE WOKE FIVE HOURS LATER. She knew the time because the bedside clock told her, but also because she never slept more than five hours, even when, as now, indecently hungover. She sat up too fast, and the bright sunshine bounding from morning snow sparkled painfully. She moaned, and lay down again. Gingerly. She shut her eyes, rubbed her forehead, kicked off the blankets. She was drenched with sweat. Bad dreams. She opened her eyes again. Slowly. The guest suite was in the back of the second floor, with a view out over the tiny backyard and into a small street, with more town homes across the way. Bay had the bedroom in the front, looking down toward the Public Garden and the Common.

The two of them were alone in the house.

That was the point of the fiction, of course, to be alone with no staff to whisper that all was not as it seemed.

She sat up. Her head protested and so did her stomach, but there was a remedy she had learned from Kevin, and if Bay had ginger root and Tabasco sauce in his kitchen, she could probably mix a glass. She used the bathroom, washed her face, put on her bathrobe and slippers. In the mirror she looked old. Eddie had looked so young. But he was not raising any children. He was running around with sexy assistants and glamorous radicals.

"Stop," she said.

Aurelia stepped into the hall, and immediately heard the angry buzz of a chainsaw, even if it was really Bay Dennison snoring grotesquely. The door to the master suite was open. Aurie tiptoed over, peeked inside. The curtains were drawn. The Congressman was a huddled mass beneath the blankets. Why was the door open? Probably because, in his exhaustion, he had forgotten she was here. Bay had been, if anything, even drunker than she.

He would likely sleep for a while.

She pulled the door closed, then padded downstairs. She found everything she needed in the kitchen, and fried her throat with Kevin's concoction, but now she was wide awake. She brewed coffee, toasted an English muffin, retrieved the morning paper from the front step, settled at the kitchen counter, reading the news.

Pretending to read the news.

She waited. No sign of Bay. Neither the sound of the door opening nor the smells of fresh coffee and a toasted muffin had stirred him. She snuck back up the stairs, opened his door a crack.

The chainsaw ran on unimpeded.

Now or never.

In addition to the kitchen, the first floor held a dining room, a parlor, and a powder room. Down the stairs was the basement, where the Congressman hosted his poker games and maintained a windowless office.

Chased by the admonishing voices of the nuns of her youth, Aurelia descended the stairs. For cover she carried the newspaper. She could always say that the light was too bright upstairs after last night's revelry, and she went to the basement to read in the cool darkness.

Not that he would believe her.

The door to the study also stood open, as if he did not care who entered. Maybe he didn't. Maybe there was nothing incriminating.

With a last glance over her shoulder, she switched on the fluorescent lights. Like the rest of the house, the study was obsessively neat. Reports here. Books there. Papers neatly filed. Desktop clear except for telephone and memo pad. Depressed by the order, Aurelia was careless. She yanked open drawers, rifled file cabinets, pummeled closets. She did not know what she was looking for. That nothing was locked up strongly suggested that she would not find it.

She almost didn't.

But there was one gem, a brief note jotted on the small pad beside the telephone, a busy but organized man's reminder to himself. A reminder he either forgot or in the end did not need, because it remained where presumably he had written it.

Ask her about E. If worried, reassure. No details. Keep vague. Want her curious not frightened. Reassure. *Make her see no danger. Keep her looking. Not for P. For J. Get her to talk to E.*

Aurelia looked up at the drop ceiling, but heard no footsteps. She dropped her gaze to the note once more. Its meaning was plain. Byron Dennison, one of the most powerful members of the House of Representatives, had spoken to someone on this telephone, and that someone had given him what amounted to orders. He was supposed to reassure her, to find a way to get her back together with Eddie, presumably with an eye toward discovering whatever he was looking for. They wanted Aurie to keep looking. Presumably they wanted Eddie to do the same.

To keep looking.

Not for P. For J.

Whether "P" stood for "Perry" or "the Project," the idea was to keep them focused on J instead.

Whoever they were, they wanted Eddie and Aurelia to find Junie for them.

Junie.

She was back at the beginning.

CHAPTER 52

Reintegration

(1)

WHEN EDDIE ENCOUNTERED AURELIA on New Year's Eve of 1969, he had been back for nine months. He had touched down at Dulles Airport in March of 1969, just before his forty-second birthday, two months after the inauguration of Richard Nixon, and of a new era in politics. The American voter, as he tended to do every couple of decades, had suffered a melodramatic change of mind. Martin Luther King was dead. Robert Kennedy was dead. Campuses trembled. Cities burned. The Great Society promoted by Lyndon Johnson had turned to ashes—in Saigon, said some, or in the angry flames licking through the nation's cities. White America fled to the suburbs. After its heavy defeat in the Civil War, the apologists for the Confederacy had proclaimed that the South would rise again, and so it had, a century later, electing conservatives nationwide on a tidal wave of snickers and code words and hints. Or so Eddie proclaimed in a *Rolling Stone* interview published a couple of weeks before he set foot on American soil.

Nobody was sure what to make of him. He had been such a moderate soul, mistrusted by the left, tolerated by the right, beloved by no one other than a few literary critics. But the stuff he had written from abroad seemed so angry—particularly that *Report from Military Headquarters*, the book Megan Hadley would later praise at dinner with Aurelia. There was talk, once again, of clawing back some of Eddie's many awards. It was one thing to be antiwar, another to seem so—well—anti-America.

At Dulles he went through customs, and Mindy, back for another stint as his assistant, met him at the barrier with a perky smile and a banner that read WELCOME HOME, which she had trouble opening. In the interim she had done a little magazine writing. As for Eddie, after the events in Hong Kong, he had visited another writer he knew in India, probably overstaying his welcome, and had spent time in Kampala, lecturing at Makerere University, known at this time as the Harvard of Africa. Then it was on to Oxford for his visiting appointment, during which he had spent a lot of time deciding what to do next. Rushing back to an America he no longer understood was not high on his list of choices.

Mindy was accompanied by a neatly dressed young man of their nation, a Morehouse graduate named Zach who turned out to be her fiancé. Zach was a law student. He carried Eddie's bags. They had borrowed somebody's station wagon. Zach drove. Eddie sat beside him. From the back, Mindy prattled on about the wonderful offers that were waiting.

"So I hear," said Eddie.

"You're on all the shelves," she breathed. "In the *front* of the store."

Eddie nodded. He could not keep up with the changes. He had returned to a strange land in which white schoolchildren suddenly read books by Negro authors. The canon had been exploded, *Invisible Man* had replaced *Silas Marner*, and two novels by Edward T. Wesley made the high-school reading lists regularly. All across America, students wrote college-entrance essays on science as metaphor in *Field's Unified Theory*, or the social inversions in *Netherwhite*. His publisher was ecstatic. The public-school curriculum, his editor explained, was where the money was. The trick now was to build on the momentum. Eddie had promised a novel about a Negro in Hong Kong—a black man, as everybody said nowadays—and his editor, Stock, was the portrait of long-suffering eagerness. The new novel, she said, would be an enormous success. Fans were waiting. It had been five years since *Pale Imitation*. Kasten, his agent, demanded and received a ridiculous advance.

But Eddie was determined not to rush. He was still regaining his balance after the events in Southeast Asia. He sought solitude. He had revived his academic appointment at Georgetown. Mindy had found him a large house on Albemarle Street, not far from Rock Creek Park. All of his furniture had been moved. All of his books had been unpacked. The new house had shelves everywhere. It had five bedrooms. It was set back from the road and screened by trees. Dropping him off, they asked if he needed them to stay.

He said he did not.

Alone in an America he did not recognize, he went into the kitchen. Mindy had stocked the larder. He found an apple and stood munching in the window, looking for signs of surveillance. He saw none. But he had come to doubt his perceptions. Since the events in the warehouse, Eddie occasionally saw things that were not there, or missed things that were. A kind of mental flex, he had told the pompous psychiatrist he had consulted briefly at Oxford. A twisting of the mind, as though I am back in the tank of water. Say, once every couple of months. The psychiatrist had nodded indulgently, proposing to get to the root of the fantasy, plainly not believing that the events of the horrible night in Hong Kong had actually occurred.

Eddie had quit after the third visit.

And for all that, he had found no trace of Junie. He had been shot at, beaten, and tortured, he had discovered Benjamin Mellor and led Collier to him, but he had not found his sister. Perhaps she really was dead.

Eddie took another couple of bites of the apple, then tossed the core. He continued to watch the gray street as gray shadows drew out from gray houses. He watched until the trees swallowed them, then watched some more. Full dark, and Eddie could not stop watching.

Sooner or later, they would come for him.

(11)

ON HIS THIRD DAY BACK in the States, Eddie had dinner with Gary Fatek at a steak house on K Street. Gary's red hair was thinner, his pale body thicker. He had visited Eddie in England twice and

India once, and now, on his way to Buenos Aires, had stopped in Washington to welcome his old friend back to the States. He dug into his chop like a man too busy to eat.

"I hear you're the big Republican now," said Eddie, marveling.

"Nah. It's just, the family's that way."

"And you, personally?"

Gary shrugged. "I don't have time for politics any more. But I gather you do."

"If this is about the book—"

"Nope. Haven't read it. Don't plan to. Wars are trivial. Economies are what matter. Erebeth used to say that, and she was right. Never mind." Hunching forward. "You've met Nixon, right? I've gotten to know him pretty well. He's a weird, paranoid man who always thinks everybody's out to get him. Here's the thing. I've sat with him two or three times since the inauguration. He keeps asking if I've heard from you. He's a pretty obsessive guy, but he's really obsessed with you."

"No."

"Yes. He wants to know what you have against him."

"I don't have anything against him, Gary. Will you tell him that?"

"Sure." Back to the steak. "But I don't know that he'll believe me."

The next night, Mona Veazie called from Hanover, wanting to see if he might be willing to come speak at Dartmouth. Gary had given her the number.

"I might," he said, exhausted.

"Good. Because I've got a girl for you."

"You have what?"

"A girl for you. Named Gwen. Very sweet. You should meet her. Don't worry, she's black."

Eddie remembered that Mona's mother, Amaretta, had been not only Harlem's premier Czarina but its leading matchmaker as well.

"Not interested," he said. Kindly.

Meanwhile, the papers were full of news about Lanning Frost. His rise seemed inevitable. Nixon had been in office two months and already the journalists were handicapping his likely opponents in 1972. The Senator was described as tough and honest and hardworking.

His wife was described as brilliant.

One morning Eddie watched Frost on television, being interviewed about the war. "It would hardly be appropriate," said the Senator, "to second-guess whatever the potential outcome of strategies that I think it would be wrong of me to disclose at this time."

The enchanted look on the reporter's face told the viewers that no insight had ever been deeper.

(I I I)

THE FOLLOWING WEEK, Eddie drove north on the recently completed Interstate 95 to visit his mother in Boston. He expected to find her shrunken and weak after four years of living without her husband. Instead, he found Marie ebullient, yet guarded by an unusually pensive Marcella, who tracked Eddie from room to room as if expecting him to steal the silver. Marie prepared a huge meal, all the foods her son had loved since childhood. Eddie could not remember experiencing such contentment in the bosom of his family. Not while his father was alive, he conceded guiltily.

Later that night, he sat in the kitchen with a still contemplative Marcella, who wore a long robe and bunny slippers. She brewed tea. Marcella was tall and stolid and implied eternity, just as their father had. She and Sheldon had married the month after college graduation. They had set straight to work making babies. The siblings traded small talk for a while. They told each other stories about Junie, some of them true. They speculated about where she was now.

"I've been meaning to ask you something. I read what you wrote about the war. I mostly agree with you." Marcella stirred her tea. "Tell me something, Eddie. If you had a son, and he was eighteen, what would you do? About the war, I mean."

The question surprised him. He had never thought about it.

Even if he put aside the events in Hong Kong, memories of his own brief experience in Vietnam kept him awake many a night, the fried hand that crunched like chicken bones particularly. He had never for one moment imagined the possibility that his own flesh and blood could actually die in a rice paddy, helmet clutched to his head, or be blown to bits in a sidewalk café. Only other people's children did that.

"I don't know. I don't have a son."

"But what if you did?" Marcella persisted.

Eddie felt trapped. He waited for the flex that caught him at moments of stress, but it spared him this time. "I'd send him to Canada. What else?"

His sister frowned. "I only have daughters. But my Sarah is graduating from Boston College next year, and my Ruth is a sophomore. If they were boys, well, they'd be eligible for the draft." She dropped her solemn eyes. "I'd tell them to go, Eddie. I would hate it. I would cry every minute they were away. I hate this war. I think it's terrible. But I would tell them to go. Not to Canada. To Vietnam. It would be their duty, Eddie. To give something back." The dark eyes came up again, pained yet unbending. "America has been good to us, Eddie. Our children don't have the right not to go."

"How can you say America has been good to us? Look at the history of—"

"Look at the *present*. Where else would you prefer to raise your children?"

Eddie, who had faced this question many times over the past two years, gave his usual answer. "Did you ever read this story by Langston Hughes called 'Poor Little Black Fellow'? One of his best, Marcie, and he wrote a lot of great ones. It's about a Negro boy who's raised by a rich white family. His father was the family servant, and died in France in World War One. The white family raises the son as their own. They love him, but they make him sleep in the attic, because they think he would be uneasy sleeping among them. They look for a good Negro college for him to attend, because they think he would be uncomfortable at Harvard. They're trying to help. When the family takes him to Paris after he finishes high school, he decides to stay, because he hates America. The white woman who raised him starts to cry. She says, 'But your father *died* for America.' The young man—he's not a boy any more, he can make up his own mind—the young man looks at her and says, 'I guess he was a fool.' The point is—"

"Oh, I get the point, Eddie. I just don't happen to agree. I don't happen to think it's right to take the country's benefits and then try to make sure the burdens fall on somebody else's children."

"And suppose the war is immoral? What then?"

"You send your children anyway," said Marcella, very cool. He had the sense she had spent a lot of time rehearsing the conversation in her mind, but had not been able to have it with anybody else. "You have no right to send somebody else to die in their place. And then you do what you can to stop the killing."

"It's not me who'd be sending them," Eddie began, but his sister rolled right over him. He had never known her to be so voluble. Or insistent. It occurred to him that the mantle of head of the family had already passed.

"This is where your lack of faith makes you weaker. Not just you. The whole country. Children become a kind of talisman. Almost a possession. You do not like or trust your fellow man, and you have no one greater than yourself to whom to turn. So you engage in idolatry. Preserve your children's lives at all costs. Do not, under any circumstances, put them at risk. Not when you can risk someone else's child instead." Stirring, not drinking. "That's not terribly charitable of you, Eddie."

"You sound like Dad."

Marcella smiled briefly. "I love your novels, Eddie. I've read them all. You have a gift. The writing. It's beautiful. Last year I started reading the book about the war. The *Report*. Just the first few essays. I couldn't finish it, Eddie. I couldn't believe you felt that way about your country."

The old Eddie would have fought the point, wrecking the weekend, but the Eddie who had lived through the experiences of the past couple of years only smiled and kissed his big sister good night.

"I know what you're really mad about," Marcella said as she preceded him up the stairs, bunny slippers squeaking. "It's not America you hate. It's Junie."

Eddie stopped. "Marcie, I adore Junie."

"You do and you don't, Eddie. You love her, sure. But you're mad at her, too. Not for the bombings—the great Edward Wesley Junior wouldn't be worried about a few minor crimes. No. You're mad at her for not getting in touch with you all these years. For trusting other people more than she trusts you."

She went on up to her room.

(I V)

EVIDENTLY, ALL WAS FORGIVEN, because in the morning it was Marcella who made breakfast, not allowing her mother to lift a finger. Marie sat there beaming. Eddie ate, but only to be polite. He was baffled. His mother should not be this happy. Her husband was dead, her son was notorious, and her younger daughter was a radical bomber sought by the authorities on three continents.

Yet she was happy.

It had bothered him all weekend. He could not fathom her joy. Only as he was packing his bag on Sunday did he get it. Marcella's words on the stairs Friday night struck him like a blow. He sat down hard on the bed, remembering the note Junie had written Benjamin Mellor, still in the safe-deposit box in Washington.

No point in beating around the bush. He went down to the kitchen and asked his mother if she had heard from Junie.

Her smile was one of beatific innocence. "Goodness, Edward. I don't see how that's really possible. Do you?"

"I think it's very possible."

"But what a risk, Edward. Why would your sister take such a risk? Don't be silly."

Marcella followed him to the car.

"You were right, Eddie."

"About what?" he asked, probably more harshly than he meant, but his contentment had melted away.

"It's not that Momma wants to hide the truth from you. It's just that Junie asked her not to tell." A brief smile. "I see I have the famous writer's attention. Yes. She's heard from Junie. Junie asked Momma not to tell you, but didn't ask her not to tell me. Junie never asked me not to tell you, so I think I'm on safe ground."

Eddie was scarcely able to control his impatience through this lawyerly digression, but he recognized that he had found, unexpectedly, an ally. Marcella was talking herself into imparting a confidence.

"She got a note from Junie, oh, four years ago. Just after Dad died. You remember how the FBI was at the funeral?" Eddie did remember. At least a dozen agents outside the church and, later, at the cemetery, with police backup, in case the former Commander M decided to break cover. "Well, just after that, Momma got the first note. She was in Pittsburgh visiting Aunt Sadie, and she came back from shopping one day and found it at the bottom of her handbag. Junie said she was sorry for everything, that she didn't want Momma to worry about her, that everything was going to be fine. That was all. Not a word about Dad," Marcie concluded, with a hint of the old disapproval.

By now Eddie's analytical self was back in charge. "You're sure that's what she said? Not that everything was fine, but that everything was going to be fine?"

His sister nodded. "Then she sent Momma another note while you were in Vietnam." Brief hesitation. "Somebody left it in the slot at the church for Mom's guild. It had her name on it." Stronger. "Anyway, the second note said things were getting better, and she was happy."

"Happy?"

"That's what the note said." The tone suggested that Marcella found this as peculiar as her brother did. "Don't look at me. I'm just the messenger."

Eddie considered. The first note said everything was *going to* be fine. The second said she was happy. Did that mean that whatever was going to be fine at the time of the first note had indeed *become* fine?

He said, "I know Dad's church, Marcie, and so do you. If there was a note with Mom's name on it in her mail slot, there are about twelve biddies who would have read it before anybody called to tell her to pick it up."

"It was a day she was there."

"Mom was at church when the note was left?"

"Uh-huh."

"Did you see the note?"

"No. Momma showed me the first one. The second, well, she just told me about it."

Eddie swayed on his feet. The lie was transparent. The second time around, Junie had not bothered with a note. She had visited in the flesh. In the midst of trouble, wanting to reassure, Commander M had gone to see her mother.

CHAPTER 53

Conversation in a Coffeehouse

(1)

IN JUNE, once more in his reportorial role, Eddie attended the national convention of Students for a Democratic Society in Chicago. Officially, he wanted to see what the true radicals had gotten up to in his absence. Unofficially, he wanted to troll for news of his sister.

The belly of the beast.

On the plane, he thought about Aurelia. Her novel had surprised him. It was a throwback to another era, almost countercultural in its celebration of patience and hard work. Just the book that would succeed in an era when Nixon was insisting that there existed a silent majority of Americans who were unimpressed by the revolution in the streets. People thought Eddie had helped her publish it, but this was not true. He had not even read the manuscript. Eddie marveled at its success. A younger Eddie, without Southeast Asia behind him, might have felt a twinge of jealousy, for although *Report to Military Headquarters* had been one of the biggest-selling books of 1968, it was fiction that defined the writing craft, and he had not produced any serious fiction in five years. The new Eddie saw matters differently. His only goal was Junie. For the current phase of his quest, avoiding any connection with Aurelia was crucial. He could not afford guilt by association. The SDS types were at this time working out a theory of the need for a revolutionary assault on "white skin privilege." After Aurelia's novel, they would consider her reactionary.

Eddie wondered what they would consider him.

Just to be on the safe side, he gave Mindy and Zach detailed instructions on what to do should something happen to him.

"Something like what?"

"I'll tell you when I get back."

The Chicago meeting started out bad and got worse. Speakers were shouted down. Posters were torn down. People talked about burning things down. He was astonished to discover how the left had split in his absence—not merely the armchair radicals from the activists, but, along the fringe, sharp divisions over ideological points that he doubted many of those choosing up sides fully understood. He heard a young man screaming from the rostrum about "Trotskyites" and "wreckers," and a woman—Eddie could not tell whether they were allies or enemies—groaning about "deviationists." On the second night, he dined with a clutch of Maoists from Stanford, but two got into a fistfight over the priority of which buildings to trash: should they begin by targeting subjects that had direct war applications, like engineering, or attack the beast's lair, as one called it, the humanities classrooms where imperialist ideology was rammed down the throats of the impressionable? Eddie sat in his hotel room and wrote in his notebook that the Nixon faction had already won. The silent majority could sit back and relax. The left was dying of its own inconsequentiality. Bad ideas, he wrote, will beat no ideas every time.

On sudden impulse, he called Aurelia up in Ithaca to say hello, but fourteen-year-old Zora answered, and said that her mom was on a date. Eddie decided not to leave his name.

(11)

THAT NIGHT, doleful, he walked the Chicago streets through one of those angry Midwestern rains that strafe the land like an aerial bombardment. He stopped at a jazz club, he stopped at a bar. He listened in on the radicals with their unkempt hair down. He listened for any mention of Jewel Agony or Commander M. He heard none. Jewel Agony had been drowned in the noise of its competitors. At three in the morning, sitting exhausted at an alternative coffeehouse in Lincoln Park, where a series of poets doomed to remain undiscovered moaned into the microphone, Eddie surrendered, accepting that the convention was a dead end. He was heading for the door when he heard his own name being called.

"*You! Wesley!*"

He turned back into the gloom. Another unsung genius was heading for the mike. The waitresses had vanished. Marijuana smoke lay heavy upon the air, but the food had no additives.

Another call.

"*Wesley!*"

He found the source. In a booth near the back, a young white woman sat despondently, a roach clip in one hand, a Scotch in the other. Both hands trembled. Her hair was trimmed short, and sloppily, as if she had cut it herself. Her scruffy tee shirt displayed the American flag upside down. She possessed the painful skinniness of the badly addicted.

"Sit," she commanded, pointing, and a chubby, earnest student with a goatee and a Tufts sweatshirt hastily made room, vanishing into the shadows.

"Do I know you?" he asked.

She took a long drag. She continued to shake. Seen close up, her face was older than he had thought.

"Not know as in *know*," she explained with an addled seriousness. "We *spoke* once before. *I* spoke. *You* fucking sat there and *listened* like a *good* little boy. But we *couldn't* fool *you*. You're too fucking *smart*."

Eddie sat straighter. "Sharon. You're Sharon Martindale."

She giggled, and it occurred to him that she was either very high or very crazy, or, possibly, both. "I *was* Sharon fucking *Martindale*. I've had a *lot* of names since *those* days. I'm with fucking *Weatherman* now." Tossing in the "f" word everywhere seemed, at the moment, the largest rebellion of which she was capable. But he knew something of her crimes, and warned himself that her madness made her no less dangerous. "Except we are going to fucking *rename* it. What do you think of Weather *Faction*? Or Weather *Underground*? Because *Weatherman* has such *connotations* of—"

She stopped and took a largish gulp of Scotch.

Eddie wanted to reach across the table and shake the answers out of her. "Junie," he said, knowing she must be close. "Where's Junie?"

"Junie's *not* with fucking Weatherman. She wouldn't be *allowed*. She doesn't *believe* in the imminent fucking *worldwide* revolution." Her eyes closed briefly. "We're going *underground* soon."

"You and Junie? You were already underground."

"*Weatherman*. Don't be fucking *dense*. *Weatherman* is going underground. *Junie* is already fucking *gone*."

"Gone?" Gripping the edge of the table. "Dead?"

"She fucking left *town*," Sharon explained, with her mother's gift for speaking as if surrounded by idiots. "She *hates* meetings and *debates*. *She* believes—I don't know *what* she fucking believes. *Not* in the imminent *revolution*."

"She was *here*?"

"*Everybody* was here."

There were so many questions he wanted to ask. About Jewel Agony. About membership and money. About who tried to kill Lanning Frost. But now, presented with the opportunity, only one query suggested itself: "Where is she, Sharon? Where did she go?"

"I don't keep *tabs* on her. I'm *not* your *sister's* fucking *keeper*." She dipped her head, but not her screechy voice. "Security. *Compartments*. No two cells *know* each other." Another gulp. "It's *better* for all *concerned*."

Eddie reached over and, gently, took the clip. He put it on the table. He took the glass. "Where is she? Why did you call me over?" Sharon stared at him with her mother's crazed eyes. "What is it? What did you want to tell me?"

"We *tried* to get you to stop looking. You *refused* to stop looking. You were fucking *warned*. It was *Junie's* idea." A hiatus as her eyes lost focus. She sounded as if she wanted to fucking shoot him. A few tables away, a man with shaggy red locks was arguing about a favorite chair. No one, he shrieked, was ever to sit in his chair again. Nobody bothered with him. Sharon coughed. Her whole body rattled. Eddie turned back. "She doesn't *like* it." She reached for the glass. He held it away. "*Living* how she *lives*. She's fucking *tired*, Eddie. We're *all* fucking tired."

"Help me find her, Sharon."

"Are you fucking *nuts*? I'm no *snitch*."

"It's not snitching. I'm her brother."

"Well, then, let me fucking *tell* you something. *Families* don't matter. Brothers and *sisters* don't matter. Fucking *countries* don't matter. Only *one* thing fucking matters. What *side* you're on." Sharon snatched the clip, took a long drag. "And you and your *sister* aren't *on* the same fucking *side*."

"I'll always be on Junie's side," he said, startled.

"Yeah, well, your *sister* has a side of her *own* now. She doesn't *believe* in the *revolution*. She said the revolution turned *rotten*." She took her glass back, held it aloft, but no waitress came. It crashed back down as if too heavy for her shrunken arm. "I told her, *everything* is rotten. The whole fucking *world* is rotten. We have to burn it *down* and start *over*. *She* said, if you try to burn down the *world*, the man with the *match* dies *first*."

"I wrote that. I wrote that about Jewel Agony, oh, four, five years ago."

"She *knows* that, Eddie. She reads *everything* you write." An evil little smile. "She thinks you *hate* her."

"She what?"

"She's fucking *scared* of you, Eddie. Every time you got *close*, you drove her further fucking *underground*."

"That's not true," said Eddie, fighting the desperate fear that what he had thought of as years wasted had actually been years of making things worse. "I love Junie. She knows that. She's always known that."

"Well, your dear *sister* never wanted you to fucking *find* her."

"I don't understand."

"It's *why* she ran *away*. Because *you* were getting too fucking *close*."

But the obvious pain in the radical's shivering face gave the lie to her words. She was telling Eddie not what was true but what she wanted to be true. He shook his head. "I know what happened,

Sharon. I know about the trial. I know you expelled her. And it wasn't just this year. Please stop lying to me. Tell me where she is."

"I don't fucking *know* where she is! She wouldn't fucking *tell* me!"

"But you know why she left, don't you? Why she really left."

Sharon Martindale said nothing. She shook her head.

"Please, Sharon. Look. I know you're scared. I won't pretend. I can't offer you anything. I don't have any connections. I can't keep you out of prison if they catch you. I'm asking you for Junie's sake. Not mine. I want to help my sister. You know I would never hurt her. Please, Sharon."

He had overplayed his hand. He recognized the signs. Sharon had shrunk into her chair and was looking frantically around the coffeehouse, maybe for someone who would rid her of this quarrelsome writer.

"I remember the night the first *baby* was born," said the radical after a moment. "She wouldn't let me fucking *see* it. She wouldn't let me come to the fucking *hospital*. She got on the *train* the *next* fucking *day* and took the baby somewhere. I never knew where. I never even found out if it was a *boy* or a *girl*. Same thing the *second* fucking time." Eddie was about to object that Sharon was not answering his question, until he realized that she was. "Her *babies*," said Sharon, her voice almost gentle. "She went to find her fucking *babies*." She laughed. "What the *fuck*? If *I* had any fucking babies, *I'd* go find them, too."

And just like that, everything was clear. Strolling back to his hotel through the same drenching rain, Eddie found himself smiling. He did not know where his sister was, but, still, he had information that Sharon Martindale did not: Junie had broken cover long enough to tell her mother that she was happy. After her fall from power, according to Sharon, Junie had left Agony to track down her children.

She had visited her mother because she had found them.

(111)

EDDIE TOOK THE MORNING FLIGHT to Washington. He met Bernard Stilwell at the National Gallery of Art, in front of an indifferent Goya. The two men strolled through the crowds of tourists. Eddie proposed to trade. The trouble was, he could offer nothing the federal government wanted. Stilwell already knew that Sharon Martindale had attended the disorderly SDS convention in Chicago.

"Did you see your sister?"

"If I had, I wouldn't be here talking to you."

"You might want to do your patriotic duty."

"My first duty is to my family."

Stilwell grinned. "Do you want to know why you didn't see her? Because she wasn't there."

"Sharon Martindale said she was."

"Sharon Martindale is a drug addict. She's nuts. She's dying of about six different diseases. I wouldn't pay attention to anything she said."

"Why haven't you arrested her?"

"Because she's so easy to follow."

In the great hall, Stilwell told Eddie what he already knew—that his sister had left Agony to find her children—and then added a detail of which Eddie was unaware. "We tracked one of the babies—the first one—to an orphanage. She was adopted maybe seven or eight years ago, but get this—the adoptive parents turned out not to exist. False names, false addresses, the whole thing."

"Aren't they supposed to check on these parents? Isn't there some kind of law?"

"I guess they broke it."

"Where was the orphanage?"

The agent shook his head.

"I'm retiring, Eddie. That's what I wanted to tell you. Not mandatory age, frankly, but it's high time. I don't like what's going on in this town any more. I came to Washington to catch bad guys, and now—well, never mind. Doesn't matter. Look. In the unlikely event that you want to get in touch with the Bureau, call the same number. Somebody will answer. They might even listen."

The brisk farewell on the front step carried an aura of tragic ceremony, like the final reunion of a college class whose members have mostly passed on.

"The Bureau will find Junie sooner or later," said Stilwell, hands in his pockets to avoid the necessity of shaking. "She's out of places to run, Eddie. We almost had her in that explosion in San Antonio last year. Yes. She was there. One day soon, we'll scoop your sister off the street. After that, you can visit her as often as you want, at the federal women's penitentiary in Tallahassee."

CHAPTER 54

The Latest Gossip

(1)

"You really need to meet new people," said Mona Veazie, the two of them standing on South Main Street with several other Dartmouth faculty and a student or two. The group had just finished dinner. In a few minutes Eddie would be delivering a lecture entitled "The Left's Silly Season." A couple of the more agitable campus political groups had vowed not to let him speak. It was November, and snowflakes were swirling. The New Hampshire wind insinuated itself inside Eddie's thin jacket with frigid intelligence. "I have this really sweet friend—"

"Thank you, but no," said Eddie, irritated.

Another professor spoke up. "Give it up, Mona. He's dating what's-her-name, the big Communist."

"She's not a Communist," said someone from behind. "She's a nationalist socialist."

What a phrase. Eddie frowned at the failure of historical memory. But memory was failing everywhere. Thus his topic tonight was how Woodstock and the lionization of the Chicago Seven, on trial for conspiracy, distracted the nation's progressive forces from fundamental challenges. The left, he planned to say, had become far too interested in making fun and having fun. A big crowd was expected. Edward Wesley Junior was, after all, the author of *Report to Military Headquarters*, and it was generally assumed that Spiro Agnew, the Vice President of the United States, had Eddie principally in mind in his recent denunciation of the war's critics as "nattering nabobs of negativism."

They strode toward the theater where Eddie would speak. Mona kept teasing him, naming various women from his past. Did he hear from Torie Elden any more? Had he heard that little Cynda got married? She mentioned, in fact, everyone but Aurelia, her own best friend, leaving Eddie to assume that Aurie was avoiding him every bit as hard as he was avoiding her. He supposed he would run into her next month, at Bay Dennison's New Year's Eve bash, but—

"And Chammie Bing is getting married again," Mona went on, clucking with disapproval, the way her mother used to. "Remember Chammie? Charlie's wife in the old days? Well, guess who she's marrying?"

Gossip had never interested Eddie before his trip, and it interested him less now. "Who?" he said.

"Your sister's old flame. Perry Mount."

Eddie stopped walking. He felt the flex, the sense of reality shifting. The frigid water was everywhere. The next plunge would kill him. He clenched his fists. On the floor of the warehouse was a Baby Ruth wrapper—

"We're going around the back," said a dean of something. Eddie realized that a couple of police officers had joined them. The dean pointed. "Demonstrators. Sorry."

Eddie forced a smile. "This is what the soldiers call earning our pay the hard way. Let's go in the front."

They did. The jeers and catcalls and chants were probably outweighed by the cheers, but in the general noise, with the harsh wind as backdrop, and the water sloshing below him in the Hong Kong warehouse, it was difficult to be certain.

(11)

THEY SAT in the cluttered kitchen of Mona's house, a neat colonial on North Balch Street, at the eastern edge of the campus. Her twins, Julia and Jay, were running around in the other room. Mona offered wine, but Eddie stuck to tea.

"Sorry about the mess," she said. In the sink, several days of plates awaited washing. Cabinet doors stood open. Eddie's mother would never have tolerated such disorder. Neither would Eddie. Evidently, Mona's lifelong rebellion extended to housekeeping. "I get busy sometimes."

"I don't mind."

"Good. Great speech, by the way. Except when that guy from the Spartacus League tried to rush the stage." She munched on a Ritz. Her nervousness fluttered in the room like a live thing. Mona's life was not particularly ordered, but Eddie's presence had disrupted it. "You're really good with handling people who disagree with you. Well, except the ones who want to blow your head off." Another bite. "Now, tell me what's up. I'm assuming you're not after my body."

"I want to hear about Perry Mount."

"Perry? What about him?"

"You said he's marrying Chamonix—"

"Well, honestly." Slapping the countertop, an old Harlem gesture. "She's so sweet. I can't believe Charlie left her for some hussy. It's been six years, Eddie. Raising those kids by herself—well, I know what that's like. All I can say is, it's about time some guy realized how great she is." Mona shoved her teacup aside. A look of pain flitted over her face. Then the children ran in. They hardly said a word. They took down a box of cookies and ran out again.

"Kids today," said Mona, forcing a smile. She jumped to her feet. In the refrigerator she found a couple of beers.

"No, thank you," said Eddie when she offered.

Mona poured and drank and, for a moment, shut her eyes. Eddie realized how little he knew about her life. Here she was, Aurelia's best friend in the world, and he hardly knew her. The two women had shared some trauma years ago that bound them together, but he had no idea what it was. She struck him as terribly unhappy. She seemed to view the twins as a burden.

"I'll tell you something funny," Mona resumed. "About Chammie and Perry, I mean. She doesn't think he loves her. She says he told her she's the kind of woman his parents would have wanted him to marry. You know. Old Harlem family, et cetera. It's all very practical for him. Very orderly. But Chammie, well, when you get to a certain age, you don't worry so much about if the guy loves you or not. He said to her—I wouldn't want this to get around—but Perry told her he had thought of marrying a younger woman but she would do. That's what he told Chammie. That she would do. Well, he was always a little strange."

"I'll say," said Eddie, shuddering with memory.

Mona gave him a look. "Well, so far, Chammie could live with it," she resumed. "Yes, fine, it's not true love, but a husband, the golden boy—who's going to complain, right? Except then it got stranger." She poured another glass. "Turned out, the reason Perry thought about marrying a younger woman was because he needed an heir. It was time, he said. Past time. Like he was on a schedule. Can you imagine?"

Eddie said nothing. But he could imagine quite easily.

"And Perry told her—get this—that, marrying her, he'd get an heir quicker than marrying a younger woman. He didn't need a baby, he said. Just an heir. Her own boy—you remember Jonathan?—he told her Jonathan would do just fine. In fact, he told her Johnny was even better than a new baby, because he was eleven, and that's old enough to understand."

"To understand what?"

"His responsibilities. He told her great ideas need great thinkers first, but then they need great stewards. Perry said he was the steward of a great idea, and his son would steward it after him." Eddie wondered how many other heirs were out there, being trained to join the Palace Council. And wondered, too, who might be responsible for training Aurelia's son, Locke.

Mona looked at her watch. "Oh, dear. I had no idea it was so late. You better get going, or people will start to talk."

Walking back to the Hanover Inn through the chilly night, Eddie experienced an unexpected sympathy with his tormentor. Perry was evidently under a great deal of pressure. Well, no wonder, if the Project he was supposed to be stewarding had run so badly off the rails.

Maybe this was what Benjamin Mellor had wanted to tell him in

Saigon, before Mr. Collier got him. Not about the marriage. About Perry. He had not told Chammie that he was *a* steward. He had told her he was *the* steward.

Perry Mount was the head of the Palace Council.

(I I I)

THREE EVENINGS AFTER his Dartmouth talk, Eddie was due in New York, to speak at the opening of an exhibition of banned books. In between, he stopped in Boston to visit his mother. Over dinner they talked about the old days, mostly repeating the same old stories. Marie Wesley seemed to be fading. She told her son that the house was getting to be too much for her. She was thinking she might give it back to Wesley Senior's church and move into an apartment. Eddie did the dishes. His mother turned in early. She seemed nervous again. Perhaps Marcella had confessed that Eddie now knew that Junie had been in touch. No matter. Eddie had no intention of pressing his mother on the question. He had no intention of pressing his mother on anything. He just wanted to make sure that if and when she gave up the house, she would have the best apartment in the city.

In New York two days later, Eddie lunched with Charlie Bing, pressing his old Harlem pal on what Chamonix might have let slip about her impending marriage to Perry Mount. But Charlie was not the kind of man who paid much attention to ex-wives, of which by now he had collected a pair.

"She does seem to be in a big hurry," said Charlie. "You'd have thought Perry would've come to me first. You know. To ask permission." He brightened. "Tell you what she did say, though. Perry's angry all the time. You remember Chammie used to do a little acting, back in the day? Well, she says Perry's like an actor who has to take a minor part and watch a lesser man take the starring role. That kind of anger."

"Did she hint at who the lesser man was?"

"Maybe she still loves me," said Charlie, who had that kind of mind.

The exhibition of banned books opened that evening at the public library at Fifth Avenue and Forty-second Street. Eddie offered the expected paean to freedom of thought, and received the expected polite applause. Afterward, marveling, he perused the glass cases displaying first editions of Whitman and Pascal, Voltaire and Cleland, Joyce and Lawrence—

Wait.

D. H. Lawrence. *Lady Chatterley's Lover.* Of course. He could have kicked himself. One of the librarians, a big fan of *Report to Military Headquarters,* unlocked the stacks and brought down another copy. Eddie leafed through it. How could he have missed the clue? It was right there in the opening chapter.

"Not as in a tragic age": those were the words on one of the note cards from Philmont Castle's envelope.

Thanks to D. H. Lawrence, Eddie now knew what they meant.

CHAPTER 55

Conversation in a Garden

(1)

"HOW WELL DO YOU KNOW NIXON?" said Senator Lanning Frost.

"I've met him a couple of times," said Eddie, very nervous, because he hated when this subject arose. Still, he knew what was coming next, because it always did.

"You wrote that essay about him in the *National Review* when he lost the governor's race in '64, though, didn't you? About how he was a true American, a patriot, all of that?"

Actually, the essay had been in *The Nation*, and the election in 1962. "I was trying to be ironic," said Eddie.

The Senator nodded. Eddie had a hunch that the man could not have defined the word *ironic* to save his life. They faced each other, breath curling whitely in the chilly air. It was January of 1970, three weeks after Eddie's brief meeting with Aurelia at Bay Dennison's New Year's party. There was snow on the ground, but Lanning Frost, a Midwesterner, professed to find the temperature bracing. So they stood in the walled backyard of the Senator's luxurious house in Georgetown, where he and Margot entertained on a grand scale, befitting a President-in-waiting. Lanning was smooth, and funny, and a stander of no nonsense, having endeared himself to the left by grilling a recalcitrant assistant secretary of Defense on Pentagon cost overruns in a televised congressional hearing, and having endeared himself to the right with a stirring speech on the Senate floor calling for prosecution of protesters who burned the flag of freedom, a flag for which he had proudly fought. Usually the yard would be filled with patrons and supplicants, the champagne flowing alongside the twin fountains while the Senator's paired collies, Darrin and Saman-tha, nosed their way beneath the elegant tablecloths in search of scraps. The newspapers called Senator Frost the front-runner for 1972. Behind his back, the reporters who knew him best called him a dope.

The Senator ran a strong hand through his crewcut. He was a head taller than Eddie, and broader in the shoulders. He ran five miles a day, and made sure the press knew it. "It's early days yet, Eddie, but we expect Nixon to be vulnerable next time around. Very vulnerable."

"So I've heard."

The levity seemed to annoy him. "We're going to beat him, Eddie. We'll be organized and well funded and everything. We'll have to hold off the McGovern wing of the party, and make a deal with Muskie. But we can do it. The war is part of it. Half a million American troops are over there—more than half a million, close to two percent of the male population"—a calculation not only erro-neous but patently ridiculous, a correction Eddie chose not to make—"and maybe the President really wants to bring them home, like he said. The trouble is, he has no idea how to do it. The intelli-gence people say there are enemy supply lines running through Laos or Cambodia or—well, one of them. And, well, either one, it's a whole separate country, Eddie. What's Nixon going to do? Invade? So, no, Eddie"—as if his guest had contradicted him—"the war will tilt against him. Plus the economy. Layoffs are getting pretty severe in my part of the country. Layoffs from *jobs.*"

"Nixon's been in office just a year," Eddie pointed out, probably to be bothersome. "Not everything can be his fault."

"That's the point," said the Senator, confusing Eddie even fur-ther. One of the dogs nosed past his legs. Frost leaned and stroked the shaggy ears with a quick, practiced gesture. In a lighted upstairs window, Margot was laughing on the telephone. Eddie remembered her weeping in the flat in Hong Kong, asking what they had done to him.

"My people have put together a couple of interesting mock-ups," the Senator went on. From his pocket he drew a folded sheet. A design for a bumper sticker. Red, white, and blue lettering: GET FROSTY IN 72. "Pretty catchy, huh?"

Eddie thought the slogan ludicrous. "I wouldn't know."

"That's right. I forgot. You hate politics. You don't think it matters who wins."

Eddie answered the mockery with steel. "I did politics already. Everybody I supported, they killed."

The cornflower-blue eyes studied him. "The other thing about Nixon is, he's just not the kind of man people take to. Sure, they voted for him last time, forty percent of them, anyway"—the actual figure was forty-three—"because our party went to pieces at the convention. But, deep down, people don't trust him. That'll work our way, too." A pause. "That's where you come in, Eddie."

"Me?"

"I assume you're a Democrat. You worked for JFK."

Eddie waved this away. "I was younger, Senator."

"We were all younger than we used to be," said his host. He took Eddie's snifter. "Let me freshen that for you." They moved together to the bar set out near the French doors. The collie followed hopefully, like an orphan. Lanning poured another finger or two of ginger ale, swirled it like brandy, handed it over. "I don't want to argue with you, Eddie. Look. I'm not as bright as you are. I know that. But I try to surround myself with people who are smarter than I am—"

He looked up. "Darling," he said, in evident relief.

Margot had joined them in the garden. "Dear, dear Eddie," she cooed, presenting a rosy cheek. She wasted no time on chitchat. "What my husband is saying, Eddie, is that Nixon's people play dirty. They always have. This last election was relatively clean, most likely because Nixon didn't sense any threat, but by next time he'll have reverted to form. I guarantee it. Already he's surrounded himself with some fairly unsavory characters."

But Eddie was remembering the concluding words of his own long-ago essay: *If Dick Nixon strikes some as too prone to attack, ask yourself whether the nation that has by turns loved him and loathed him is so different. Nixon is not our national aberration. He is our national fulfillment.*

"If you say so," Eddie said, quietly, as the dog nosed his ankle.

"I do say so. And if the President is going to lash out, we're going to have to be ready to strike back." A grim smile. "Do you know Nixon's secret? Why he almost always wins? Because nobody ever thinks he can. We're not going to make that mistake, Eddie. He's going to attack us every way he can. We have to stand ready to do the same."

"Exactly," said Lanning, adoring eyes on his wife.

Eddie thought about Perry Mount, and wondered how much Lanning knew of what his wife was mixed up in.

"I see," he said.

The Frosts exchanged a look. Margot nodded slightly. The Senator's turn. "The thing is, Eddie, if Nixon throws mud at me, I'm going to have to throw the same mud back. He's a bad man. It's going to be a rough campaign. So—what I'd like to do is put you with some of my people who will help you remember . . . well, whatever dirt you might have, ah, witnessed."

Help you remember. Eddie liked that one, too. He said, "The President and I met only once." He shoved free of the dog again. Rebuffed, the collie crawled to the base of the wall and settled its long head onto its paws, sulking as it waited for some attention.

Margot again: "That doesn't matter. Just point out some general paths for investigation." A pause. "You're not the only one, Eddie. We'll be talking to lots of the President's old associates. But you're special, Eddie. You're different."

"Oh?"

"We have sources—never mind where—but we have sources, Eddie, good sources, reliable sources, sources we trust absolutely. These sources tell us that the Nixon people are worried about you."

This brought him up short. Pretty much the same thing Gary Fatek had told him. "Worried about me how?"

"The sources don't know. Nixon's people don't know. But our sources tell us Nixon thinks you have dirt on him, and he's terrified it might get out."

Eddie looked at the two political faces, the one clever, the other worried. "I don't know what dirt Nixon thinks I have. I don't know what dirt the two of you think I have. I do know there's no reason for you to have brought me down here, taking the risk of being seen with a notorious character like me, unless you're very frightened of whatever dirt Nixon might dig up on you."

Lanning stared. Nobody talked to United States Senators this way. Margot had the wit to smile. "You were always smart, Eddie. Yes. Of course there's dirt on Lanning. There's dirt on everybody. What's that phrase of yours? The American Angle? Well, we would be a better nation if the American Angle didn't include such an interest in people's dirty underwear. Unfortunately, it does. We're stuck with politics as it is, Eddie. We're in this to win. The only question is whether you're willing to help us get rid of this man in 1972, or if you want to sit on the sidelines."

Eddie's mind swirled with possibility. What could Nixon be afraid of? First guess: Nixon, not Benjamin Mellor, was the secret father of Junie's children. But no. Whatever people might think of the man, nobody had ever called him a philanderer; besides, it was difficult to imagine that even a young woman as clever as Junie could have snuck off privately to meet the man who was at the time Vice President of the United States.

Second shot: Nixon was Junie's secret protector, knew where she had gone to ground, and was terrified that Junie would get word to Eddie of his role. But aside from the even greater absurdity of imagining Junie in regular touch with the President, there was the simple point that the problem was easily dealt with: Junie need only vanish for good.

Consequently, the dirt had to involve his sister indirectly, not directly. He looked at Lanning Frost, saw the shrewd calculation in the face. Eddie was no fool. Eddie could not assume a link between Nixon and Junie simply on this powerful couple's say-so.

"I'll think about it," Eddie said.

Margot looked at her husband. "It's almost six, dear. Aren't you supposed to be calling Mike Mansfield?"

(11)

THEY WERE ALONE. The garden was chilly, so they walked into the house. The collie jumped to its feet to follow. They stood in the wide marble foyer, beneath the clerestory windows.

"You look well," Eddie said, formally, but it was true. Although Margot, never thin, had gained weight, she looked radiant, energetic, ready for White House duty. The faint crinkles around her eyes and the touch of early gray in her hair—she was in her late thirties—only confirmed the general image of maturity and confidence. You had the sense that Margot would be the sort of First Lady who had a lot of say in her husband's decisions, and that the country would be better for it. It occurred to Eddie that in another age, with women playing a different role, Margot herself would be the one spoken of as presidential timber.

"I do not." She rapped her hips. "This is what four children will do to you." Her smile broadened. "But you, Eddie—what do the Brits say? You just go from strength to strength. Every time I look up, you're either writing a new book or campaigning to get some radical out of jail."

"I do what I can to keep life interesting."

"Like whatever got you into trouble in Hong Kong?"

"Maybe," said Eddie, watching her eyes, except that Margot turned to glare at the hovering maid, who drifted reluctantly away.

Facing him again, she took one of his hands in both of hers. "Lanning doesn't know, Eddie. And I . . . I won't have him knowing. We're not one of those political couples. We have a real marriage. Oh, it was rocky at first, but now—well, now it's real. I want to keep it that way."

"I understand." But he was already wondering what the rocky parts were, and whether that might be what Lanning was afraid Nixon's people would find out. "He won't hear about it from me."

"What about your friend?"

"My friend?"

"The little guy who drove the car."

Eddie smiled, but sadly. "Ever see the photo of the moment after King was shot? All his aides pointing up toward where the shot came from?"

"Sure."

"Well, the bald man standing next to Andy Young is Brother Leonard Peace. You've heard of him?"

"We've had dinner with him several times to discuss civil rights. Lanning and I have developed—I mean, Lanning has developed—some innovative ideas that you should really—"

He waved her silent. "Well, Brother Leonard is the little guy, as you put it, who drove the car. Only in those days he was a gangster. A small-time hood."

Margot looked shocked, then laughed. "Seriously?"

"He said he had a call from the Lord, then changed his name when nobody would take him seriously. And, believe it or not, I think he's sincere. At least, if he isn't, there's no reason for him to have stood all those beatings in Mississippi in the summer of '65."

She continued to smile and, for an instant, was her old impish self. She put a hand on his cheek. "Eddie. It really worked out for you, didn't it?"

"And for you," he agreed, covering her hand with his own but then, carefully, returning it to her side.

Margot hesitated. "Eddie, about June. If there's anything we can do—"

"Your husband is running for President. What would you imagine him doing?"

"The president of Yale gave that speech about how no Black Panther can get a fair trial—"

"Junie isn't a Panther. She isn't a Black Muslim. She's not the Yippies or the Chicago Seven. She's the Agony. They've killed people, Margot. White people. They've blown things up. People are scared of them." He forced himself to calm down. "Thank you, Margot, but you and I both know if she gets caught there's nothing to be done."

"She has zero chance of a fair trial."

"And neither you nor Lanning can improve those odds."

"Eddie—"

"It's not your problem, Margot. I have my own ideas, but—well, never mind." Out on the front step, the Senator's driver was holding the car door. Eddie hesitated. "Margot, listen. I'll help you if I can. Oh, I don't think Nixon is the devil incarnate, but I also don't think he's the man we need in the White House. He's small-minded and paranoid. So—yes. I'll meet with Lanning's people. I doubt that I can be much help, but I'll give it a shot." Again he took a moment, wanting to get the words just right. Snowflakes swirled gently past the streetlamps. "But I'm going to need something in return, Margot." Eyes held eyes: steady brown on cautious green. "Something only you can give me."

The smile disappeared. If she could have contrived to do it quietly, Margot would have slapped his face. "No, Eddie. No. Absolutely not. I told you in Hong Kong, I'm not that kind of woman. So don't even suggest—"

"That isn't what I'm proposing," he interrupted, lifting innocent palms. "No. I just need you to answer a question for me."

"What question?"

"Does Lanning know what the cross means?"

A blank expression. "The cross? You mean Jesus? The Bible? All that?"

Impatiently. "The crucifix. The one you used to wear around your neck. The one your mother gave you when you were a little girl." The pale eyes never even flickered. "You know, the one she bought in Italy, with the words on it. The Cross of Saint Peter."

"I don't understand."

"You were wearing it the night we met."

She considered this, then, slowly, shook her head. "I'm sorry, Eddie. I don't remember my mother ever giving me a cross, and I don't think she ever got to Italy until my dad took her there a few years before she died." Misting up a bit. "She'd always wanted to go."

"You told me she was half Italian!"

"Mom? No. You must have heard wrong. Mom was from New Orleans."

She closed the door.

(111)

THE FOLLOWING DAY, Eddie had lunch with Torie Elden, who now worked as a deputy to John Ehrlichman, Nixon's chief domestic policy adviser. She cautioned before they so much as sat down that she was seeing somebody, and Eddie said how wonderful that was.

Then he got down to business.

"No," said Torie, when she was sure she had the question right. "I'm sorry, Eddie. Nobody in the White House has ever mentioned you. Not in my hearing, and I'm in a lot of meetings. I don't think the President is the least bit worried about you. I'm not sure he's ever heard of you." She was working herself into a fury. "People have other things on their minds, Eddie. Not everything is about you."

CHAPTER 56

Conversation in a Library

(1)

ON THE FIRST FRIDAY in March of 1970, a bomb exploded at a New York apartment house, killing three members of Weatherman, who evidently planned to blow up a military dance in New Jersey. The bomb was filled with nails, intended as shrapnel. The evening news did not have enough room for all the Washington figures competing for condemnatory airtime. The networks led with the President, and two of the three followed with Senator Lanning Frost. On Monday morning, Eddie telephoned a surprised Aurelia at her office, to assure her, and perhaps himself, that Junie had not been present.

"You know Agony has folded into Weatherman," he said.

No, said Aurelia. She had missed that bit of news.

"Junie's not with them any more."

Yes, she had heard that.

"Aurie, look," he said. "I wanted to say I'm sorry."

"Sorry for what?" she asked, because a Garland never forgot a slight, but also never acknowledged one. She was gathering together books and papers for the class she had to teach in ten minutes.

"We should get together sometime. Just to talk," he added hastily.

"Talk about what?"

"Things." He seemed about to say more, then leaped to a new subject. "Lanning and Margot want me to help them against Nixon."

"I thought she was part of your conspiracy."

Instead of a joke, an eerie pause. "It's complicated," he said.

After hanging up, Aurelia tried to work him out. Was Eddie calling to say he loved her, or to say he didn't? Was Margot Frost one of the bad guys, or wasn't she? And what about Gary's warning to stay away? She wished she could talk to Eddie about what she had learned. And yet there was the matter of her long-ago promise to her late husband: *You don't know anything*, Kevin had warned her. *If anything happens to me . . . your job is to raise the children, spend the money, and enjoy your life.* And of course there was the matter of his legacy, which she would not, without more evidence, besmirch.

No matter what he had been involved in.

Somebody was killing off the Palace Council. When she knew who, she would know what had really happened to her husband.

On her desk was a photo of Kevin. Aurelia lifted it, and kissed it, and went to class.

The following weekend, Perry Mount married Chamonix Bing at the National Cathedral in Washington, D.C. The bride was radiant. The ceremony was grand. Aurelia and her children sat with Mona and hers, beside a federal judge and behind Lanning and Margot Frost. Everyone was there.

Everyone but Eddie Wesley.

(11)

TWO DAYS AFTER HER RETURN to Ithaca, Tris Hadley called during dinner. "Any more quotes need translation?"

"No." The telephone, bright yellow, hung on the kitchen wall. Talking to him in front of the children, she felt naked.

"We could get together tonight if you want. Megan's out of town."

"No." Locke and Zora, eating burgers at the kitchen table, watched her curiously.

"I have more information for you. Really important information."

"Um—"

"Meet me for a drink."

"I can't," she said, adding, stupidly, "Not tonight." The children grinned at each other. They were persuaded absolutely that Mommy had a boyfriend, even though they had not yet figured out who it was.

"Call me, okay? When you're free. Believe me, Aurie, you'll be interested. This one is big."

"All right," she said, hating her dependency on him. If only she had come up with a way to talk to Megan directly. Now it was too late.

"All right, what?"

"All right, I will."

She hung up.

That night she called Mona, but reached only the machine.

(I I I)

SHE MET TRISTAN HADLEY on Friday afternoon. She crossed the campus in the shadow of Willard Straight Hall, the student union, recently the site of a famous occupation by black radicals. Magazine photographers had begged the radicals to hold up their rifles. Editors saw photos of young black men bearing arms and turned them into scary covers. The stories failed to mention that the shots were posed.

The meeting place was the second subbasement of the Olin Library, near the microfiche storage area, in a long alcove of gunmetal shelves, holding mostly pamphlets in painstakingly indexed boxes. Nobody ever came down here, except the occasional librarian, whose approach was usually signaled by the clopping of tired shoes.

Descending the steel staircase, Aurelia kept looking around, wondering if anybody was in the vicinity. She had not noticed either of her familiar shadows, Streisand or Sharif, since last summer. Still, she felt watched. She was as nervous as a woman rushing to an assignation. She stepped into the alcove and thought she heard a sound behind her, but when she turned there was only the soft rumble of water in the overhead pipes, and the steady ticking of some unrepaired mechanical device in the wall.

"Tris?" she said, softly.

"Over here." An excited whisper.

She found him around the corner. "I thought you weren't coming," he said, trying to slip an arm around her shoulders and lead her. She shrugged it off. He hesitated, then moved toward an ancient wooden carrel. He had several volumes open on the top shelf, along with a notepad on the desk. "Cover," he said. "In case we're caught."

"What do you want, Tristan? What's the big discovery?"

Boyish hurt. "Hey, don't I get a cheery hello? Maybe a hug?"

"Hello," she said, and kept her hands to herself.

"Fine," he said, pouting as he drew *Paradise Lost* from the middle of the stack of books. "Let's do business."

"What's that?" she said, head whipping around.

He stood beside her, gazing into the shadowy rows of gray shelving. "There's nothing, honey," he said, touching her arm lightly. "It's just nerves."

"If I'm nervous, it's because of all this skulduggery."

"Do you have a better way for us to meet?"

Aurie almost said—it was a near thing—that she did not want to meet him at all. Instead, she shrugged and shook her head. "Okay," she said. "Show me."

He glanced at her. His aplomb had been shattered. He had planned a big presentation, no doubt with plenty of gratitude on Aurelia's end when he was done, and her attitude had thrown him off his stride.

"I was thinking about the two other phrases that you wrote down," he said. "From wherever the others came from." A forced grin to show he did not mind being denied her confidence, although of course he did. "One was 'unlimited might.' The other was 'Day 20.' You'll remember I told you neither one appears anywhere in the poem."

"I remember, Tris."

"I still haven't worked out Day 20. But, in the case of the first phrase, we didn't find it because we were looking for the wrong words." His excitement was growing again. "Look here. Book VI, where Milton describes the actual war between the legions of Hell, led by Satan, and the legions of Heaven, led by the Archangel

Michael. They fight hard, but neither side can gain an advantage. There's a stalemate."

"I've read it," she said, tiredly, and it was true: she had read every stanza of *Paradise Lost* at least half a dozen times. "There's a stalemate until Satan manages to break through Michael's lines with some kind of weapon. Michael gains the advantage again, and then God sends His Son to end the battle."

Tristan nodded, impatient as any academic at the demonstration by others of their knowledge when he was itching to display his own. "But turn back," he said. "Right at the beginning of the battle. Around line 227. The reason for the stalemate. See here?"

He pointed. Aurelia heard the sound again, glanced over her shoulder into the darkness, then turned back and followed his finger.

> *Had not th'Eternal King Omnipotent*
> *From his strong hold of Heav'n high over-rul'd*
> *And limited their might . . .*

"See?" Tristan's voice was eager. "Either side might have won, except that the Eternal King limited how much force each could bring to bear. 'Limited their might.' See?"

She nodded, impressed. He had given this a lot of thought. "So when—ah—somebody speaks of 'unlimited might'—"

"They have to be speaking of removing those limits, so that their side can prevail."

"Right. But the limits are placed by God—" Aurelia got his point, and spoke more softly. "Meaning that you would have to *be* God in order to remove them."

"Right."

"God in this case meaning—"

Tristan gave her a long look, and in his fair eyes she read his long forbearance. Somewhere along the way she had forgotten his intelligence. Tris knew. It was as simple as that. Tris had always known. "Whoever they're trying to overthrow," he said.

"Overthrow," Aurelia echoed. Now at last she understood what they wanted. And why they had blown up her husband: because he was in the way. "Oh, my God," she whispered, meaning it as a prayer.

She burst into tears.

Tristan stood his ground for a moment, then slipped his arms around her. She let him. He patted her shoulder and whispered to her. She let him. He kissed her forehead—

"Hey!" he said, shoving her away.

Aurie tumbled against the carrel, confused, and saw Tristan sprinting along the metal corridor, yelling at someone to stop. She hesitated, then followed. Their feet clanged. So did the feet of whomever he was chasing. "Hey!" he shouted again. "Stop!"

Tristan disappeared around a corner into an alcove. An instant later, she heard him cry out, this time in pain. Aurelia arrived at the alcove in time to collide with another man, hurrying out. He was carrying something small and dark, and for a moment she thought it must be a gun. She had armed herself with a fire extinguisher, and now swung it at his chest. Aurelia was not strong—despite Mona's entreaties, she still did not work out—but she slowed him down. He grunted and swayed. He swung at her, catching her in the arm. It hurt like blazes. Then Tristan jumped on his back and Aurelia kicked him in the balls.

He crumpled.

They rolled him over. Not blond hair. Not Mr. Collier. She was not surprised. She suspected that Mr. Collier could have taken them both down with his left pinky.

"Who are you?" Tristan demanded, but the man was too busy moaning, so Aurelia delved inside his windbreaker and pulled out his wallet. She flipped it open and, wordless, handed it to Tristan. The man was a private detective, and the black box, which he had dropped, was a camera, loaded with very fast film to take pictures in the basement without a flash.

"Private detective," sneered Tristan, delighted to have a physical advantage over another man. "And who are you working for?"

Aurelia said, "Let him up."

The anthropologist looked at her. "But he— Oh. Yes. I see."

(I V)

HUMILIATED, she called Mona, who listened for five minutes, then told her she was talking to the wrong woman and hung up. So she dutifully phoned Megan, hoping somehow to explain that what was obviously true was actually false, but Megan hung up, too. Feeling a fool, she packed the kids into the station wagon and drove over to Megan's house, determined to make her see that there was no affair.

Megan stood in the doorway, listened grimly, then said, "My husband is in love with you, Aurelia."

"I never—"

"He says he wants a divorce. Fine with me. You're welcome to him."

The children were still in the car, faces pressed against the window. "It was just a research project," Aurie said.

"And you never noticed his feelings toward you? He never mentioned them? You never decided it was time to stop doing research together? Your research was so important you were willing to encourage him? I have photos, Aurelia. Photos of all those cutesy little meetings in the diner and the library and—"

She shut the door.

Back home, Aurelia tried to put the matter out of her mind. At least for a little while. She had tried to do her duty to Megan, and had done it too late. She could not make up for her error. She had to get back to work. To call Eddie, to tell him that Tristan Hadley, of all people, had worked out what seemed to be the goal of the Project.

They wanted to replace the man in charge.

And there was something else, an idea that had occurred to her once Tristan began talking about chronology. "Day 20." *Paradise Lost* was broken up into books, not days. But she had read her copy so often now, she could make a chart. She sat at the kitchen table, drawing red lines across the stanzas at the beginning and end of each day. She counted twenty.

And saw it all.

On the twentieth day of the poem, Satan gives up his idea of fighting against the forces of Heaven directly and decides instead to attack God's creation. He will befoul the earth.

That was the point. The Palace Council was not planning to do battle any longer. The plan was to subvert from within, by replacing the man in charge. What Eddie had feared was true.

The Council—whoever was left—was electing a President.

CHAPTER 57

Conversation over Breakfast

(1)

IN MAY of 1970, soldiers of the Ohio National Guard shot and killed four student demonstrators at Kent State University. The deadly rounds came from M-1 rifles, stripped-down versions of the weapon being used by American troops in Vietnam. The soldiers claimed self-defense; perhaps they were worried about being burned to death, for many of the demonstrators carried lighted candles. Responding to the news of the shootings, the Dow Jones Industrial Average suffered its largest single-day decline since the assassination of President Kennedy. Wall Street was betting on chaos. And for a time chaos seemed to reign. President Nixon warned solemnly that tragedies happen "when dissent turns to violence." Perhaps it was the Guardsmen who were dissenting, said the wags. Across the country, some two million college students went on strike. There were marches, formal and less so, in large cities and small towns. There was vandalism. There were battles. In New York, hard-hatted construction workers clashed with antiwar protesters, beating them with pipes and boards, putting many students into the hospital, formally dissolving the glorious student-worker solidarity still worshiped in many a campus coffeehouse. The hard hats waved a banner proclaiming GOD BLESS THE ESTABLISHMENT, and, in the spirit of the moment, tried to take over City Hall. Troops of the National Guard were mobilized nationwide, occupying dozens of campuses. And not just the campuses. Personnel carriers showed up on city streets. Army units were held in reserve around the country in case the revolt got out of hand.

Four days after the Kent State shootings, protesters descended upon the Mall. Buses came from everywhere. The night before the demonstration, the students held a prayer vigil. William Sloane Coffin delivered a homily. Judy Collins sang. The group walked quietly to the White House to leave candles on the wall beneath the wrought-iron fence, in memory of the dead at Kent State. The city was prepared for the worst. Heavily armed soldiers had taken up positions to protect government buildings. An inventive variety of barriers, from sawhorses to barbed wire to buses, augmented walls and fences.

Afterward, many of the students camped out on the Mall. Eddie was a featured speaker at the rally, but the night before, he trolled the crowd. Silly though it might have seemed, he thought perhaps Junie would be there. He thought he spotted her in the throng once or twice, but he was wrong. Eddie had a tent of his own, and helped others set theirs up: not for nothing those enforced years in the Boy Scouts. He had decided not to spend the nights before or after the demonstration at his own home. He did not want to fight the traffic to the Mall. He wanted to be nearby, just in case things got hairy. In addition to the tent, he arranged alternative accommodations through Gary Fatek, who called in a favor at the overbooked Marriott.

But Eddie preferred the Mall.

The feds, of course, were out in force, most of them no doubt dressed to look like students—he searched for white crew socks as a clue—and the protesters passed around stories of cars slipping past the encampment filled with men in suits, snapping photographs as they went.

Shortly before five, he heard a ruckus. He pulled on sweater and sneakers and left the tent, following the few who were awake and on the move. He carried his notebook. Marijuana smoke hung in the heavy air like morning fog. A knot of kids had gathered on the steps of the Memorial. Crewcut men stood uneasily around. Maybe somebody was being arrested. He slipped out his notebook, hoping to record some grit. Then he reached the front and found the President of the United States chatting nervously with the students in the predawn mist.

(11)

Eddie was astonished.

He remembered the Nixon of the fifties, somewhere in Latin America, plunging into a crowd of jeering demonstrators and being spat upon. Voters had loved him for that. Now here he was again, in the belly of the beast. Not just talking but listening. Aurelia's friend. The man on whom Lanning was gathering dirt. Eddie crept closer. A respectfully angry young man was telling the President that he was willing to die for what he believed in. Nixon assured the group that he understood, adding that his generation was trying to build a world in which it would not be necessary for people to die for what they believed in. The students looked skeptical, but seemed impressed that he was there. Nixon told them to go ahead and shout their slogans tomorrow, that was what America was about, just keep it peaceful.

Everybody shook hands.

Then, smiling shyly, the President moved down the line toward his car, surrounded by an increasing number of worried White House staffers who had come looking for him. He reached Eddie, and the political hand shot out for the automatic, quick pump. Eddie started to speak. Nixon passed on. Eddie felt deflated. He thought Nixon a terrible President, but something childlike inside wanted to be singled out for special recognition. At his car, Nixon waved awkwardly to the protesters, then turned to whisper to an aide.

"Did you see him?" said a student standing near Eddie, chest full of medal ribbons bought at a flea market. "Was that really the baby killer?"

Eddie, about to say something, felt a touch on his elbow. A Secret Service man asked if he would please come this way. Eddie was led down the hill, past the crowd, then back to the street. An instant later, he was in the limousine, across from Nixon.

"Didn't want to embarrass you in front of the kids," the President explained calmly, as if the two of them saw each other every day. "Can't have them thinking you're part of the power structure." He pointed. "We're going up to the Capitol."

"We are?"

"Never thanked you for those kind words." Nixon's gravelly voice was always awkward at expressing emotion. Actually, he had thanked Eddie, seven years ago. "Good man. Glad you're back safely from your travels. I know you're speaking tomorrow. Have to say nasty things about me. I understand that. It's politics. Do what you have to. That's what we do up here, Eddie. What we have to." Gazing out the window as they streaked along Constitution Avenue. Only one other aide was in the back, a buttoned-down young man who looked uneasy about the President's rambling. "These kids— they're great. I love the kids. All right, some of them are bums. Burning up the campuses. But most of them, they just want peace. Who doesn't? You know I'm a Quaker. When I was younger, I thought Neville Chamberlain was a hero. I thought Winston Churchill was a monster. Shows you how much I knew. But it's natural to want peace. Natural."

"Yes, sir," said Eddie, bewildered, sitting there with the President, wearing jeans and a sweater. He had left his backpack in the tent. He was glad he had remembered his wallet and his notebook. He wondered if anybody had yet liberated his sleeping bag.

"Did you see we promoted Oliver Garland to the court of appeals? Good man. Good heart. Good friend. Knows how to keep secrets. He was a friend of yours, too, wasn't he?"

"Yes, sir."

A brief silence, although he could tell at once that Nixon disliked silences.

"A good man," the President resumed, drumming his fingers on the sill. Even that simple activity seemed somehow clumsy, a little off, like an instrument out of tune. "Kevin was a good man. Matty.

All those Garlands. We need more men whose hearts are in the right place, Eddie. Especially these days. Might need your help. Man like you, a good heart, good head on your shoulders. The world is changing, and some of what we hope to do—"

He stopped. They had reached the Capitol. Nixon hopped out, dragging his small entourage past suddenly wakeful security guards. They found somebody to open the House chamber, and Nixon showed Eddie his first congressional desk. He sat down—to Eddie's eyes, happily—then sent one of his aides to sit in the Speaker's chair. The early morning grew surreal as the President told stories of the old days. Eddie felt half asleep, but Nixon's energy crackled. At the Lincoln Memorial, the man had seemed exhausted and a little befuddled. Now he was rejuvenating before Eddie's tired eyes. On the way out, he chatted with the cleaning staff. A black woman asked the President to sign her Bible. This was too much for Eddie's crowded sensibilities, and he was ready to find a taxi back to his tent, but Nixon took him by the elbow and led him to the car. The chief of staff materialized from somewhere, urging a return to the White House, but Nixon said no, he and his old friend Eddie were going out to breakfast.

"Really, no, I should—"

"You can't refuse your President," said Nixon, smiling gaily.

Minutes later, they marched past an astonished maître d' into the restaurant of the Mayflower Hotel. The waitresses stared at the President, but also at the funny little Negro in dirty jeans. Later, the newspapers would speculate unconfidently that Nixon had decided to buy a meal for some poor soul who lived on the street, a publicity stunt, maybe, to deflect attention from the demonstrations. The President and Eddie sat alone at a table. Nixon ate hash and eggs. Eddie, whose interest in food had grown no greater over the years, had cornflakes and half a grapefruit.

"You and Aurelia," said the President, digging in. "What happened there? Thought you would be one of the great couples."

Again Eddie was astonished: first, that Nixon knew there had ever been anything between them, and, second, that he cared. But of course he was an old friend of the family. Even since entering the White House, the Nixons had twice visited Wanda Garland, Kevin's mother, as all the darker nation knew.

"It wasn't going to work," said Eddie, picking his words with care.

"On your end or hers? Give her another chance. Tell you something. Knew I was going to marry Pat the night I met her. If you feel that way—" He stopped talking, started chewing.

"Yes, sir," said Eddie, bewildered.

"I know what you have to do tomorrow," said Nixon, returning to his theme. "So you just go out and do it. Flay me alive. Not a wimp. Matter of fact, I have a fairly thick skin. And I know Frost wants you to talk to his people. Do what you have to do, Eddie. Tell Frost whatever he wants to know. Doesn't matter. He can't win. Believe me. Poor guy doesn't have a chance. So go ahead and do what you have to do, but·when you're done, come see me. There's great work to be done in this country, and maybe we can do it together."

"Thank you, Mr. President," said Eddie, startled by Nixon's knowledge, and not at all sure what the man wanted of him. It occurred to him that Nixon did not know, either.

"I hear you had a rough time in Vietnam."

"Ah, no harder than anybody else." His stock answer. "Sir—"

"Johnson's war, not mine. Kennedy started it. Doesn't matter. If it happens on your watch—and we can't abandon them. Cut and run. America doesn't do that."

"Even when America's wrong?"

"Not a matter of right or wrong. Matter of reputation. They have to believe you'll do what you—" He scooped his thick head for a bite. The shy smile was almost apologetic. "Can't do it. Can't cut and run."

"It's like playing poker, Mr. President," said Eddie, hitting upon an analogy he hoped Nixon would find persuasive. "You know what they say. If you throw good money after bad, you wind up out of the game before you—"

"America doesn't cut and run."

The President's eyes shifted one way, the other way, back again.

He seemed restless and uneasy. He was said to be a brooder, a breed Eddie knew at first hand. Eddie looked around the restaurant. Aides stared back, and, beyond them, a few gawking early risers. All these smart people at his beck and call, but Nixon had pulled Eddie out of the crowd to eat breakfast. And then Eddie got it. The President of the United States had nobody else to eat with. He wanted company, and, on this particular morning, a left-leaning novelist who hated the war but had written a vaguely complimentary essay about him eight years ago was the best he could do. Nixon wanted to be Eddie's friend. Yet he had no small talk, which meant that it was up to his guest to keep the ball rolling. And Eddie knew just what ball he wanted to roll. So he took another bite and said, "Mr. President, if I may, there's a question I'd like to ask."

"Ask."

"It's about my sister."

The President shoveled another clumsy bite into his mouth. "Nobody's above the law," he said after a moment.

"I know this is going to sound very strange, sir. Please don't think me impertinent. I was wondering if you ever met her. My sister."

"You know, I understand them. The radicals." He put his fork down hard, nearly knocking his water glass to the floor. "People in a hurry. Kids today, they've had everything. My generation, we had to fight for—" He took a sip. "Grab a gun. It's natural. We fought. Now it's their turn." The glass clattered. "Not that we can let them burn everything down. The President's first responsibility is the security of the nation. Took an oath, Eddie. Against all enemies foreign and domestic."

"Yes, sir. Now, about my sister—"

"The thing is, Eddie, sometimes the methods you use to defend—well, you can't use them in the sunshine." He brightened. "They tell me she's smart, your sister. Ivy League. Must be a pretty bright gal."

"Yes, sir. She is."

"Too bad which side she ended up on."

"Yes, sir."

"She'll spend years in prison when we catch her. Sorry, Eddie.

Can't avoid that. But it's not so bad. Some of the best writing of the century was done in prison."

Eddie looked around the restaurant. Other diners continued to stare.

"The reason I ask about my sister—"

"Did you ever find her? Everybody says you're looking. Brotherly love. That's the way."

"No, sir. I haven't found her. Not yet."

"Any prospects?"

Eddie knew his hesitation was obvious. Was this really the object of the exercise? Had the President of the United States traveled to the Mall and plucked Eddie out of the crowd hoping to talk about Junie?

"No prospects," said Eddie, watching him closely.

"But you'll keep looking. Kind of thing a brother does. Good for you." Was this permission? Eddie said nothing. "Never met her," Nixon continued. "Never talked to her. All I know is what's in the reports I get. They tell me she's chasing her kids. Hope she finds them."

"So do I, sir."

"Come see me. After you make your speech. After things calm down. Come see me. There are things we can do together that would—"

He dropped his fork.

Two aides rushed to pick it up. A waiter brought a new one, but the White House staff was faster. They took advantage of the hiatus to get the President moving. Eddie stood up, not sure what was expected of him. There was no way he was getting back into that car. Fortunately, the staff had reached the same decision. A deathly pale young man engaged him in conversation, thanking him for his time, swearing him to silence, filling the air with faux-friendly babble until the President was safely out the door. Only then did the pale young man ask if Eddie needed a ride.

Eddie said he would make his own way, thanks.

The young man paid the tab. Eddie watched the motorcade depart. He shoved his hands into his pockets and began the long walk through the hazy dawn back to the Lincoln Memorial. Clusters of troops stood here and there. Eddie could not bring himself to hate Nixon, and suspected that, had he never met the man, his feelings would not be much different. Eddie had trouble finding space in his heart for hatred, even toward his enemies. He believed in justice and historical forces. He was skeptical that any problem could be resolved by finding the nastiest name to call the people on the other side. Wesley Senior had preached countless sermons on love of neighbor, especially through times of trial, and a younger Eddie used to sit there rolling his eyes. Now he was horrified to realize how much of his father's teaching had rubbed off on him.

He waved to the soldiers as he passed. One or two waved tentatively back.

A couple of students had taken over his tent. Eddie let them sleep. He retrieved his backpack and snuck off to the Marriott, where he had never quite canceled the reservation Gary Fatek had made. Eddie's real luggage was in the room. He slept two hours, then showered and shaved and, dressing, watched the morning news.

And all the while, he reflected on his peculiar morning with Nixon. Eddie considered himself a shrewd judge of character. Nixon was harder to read than anyone he had ever met, but Eddie did not think the President had lied. Nixon had never met Junie, and knew nothing of her whereabouts.

The dirt he was afraid Eddie would dig up had to be something else.

CHAPTER 58

Reunion

(1)

EDDIE CLOTHED HIMSELF conservatively for his big speech. He
had been a guest of sorts at many a demonstration, but never anything like this. He imagined his father preparing to address his congregation. Even though you shouldn't judge a book by its cover,
Wesley Senior used to say, everybody does. So Eddie wore a suit. He
was in his forties, after all, to these kids already an old man. He had
published six books, five of them fiction, and most of the kids had
read one or two in high school or college, and even written essays on
them: that made him older still. So he would dress the part. Let others wear shirts sewn from American flags or prance about in ragged
jeans. Eddie would be an adult. The suit was summer-weight, powder blue, from a tailor in Hong Kong. His tie was red, white, and
blue. He thought of a flag pin in his lapel, Nixon-style, but decided
the students would miss the irony; besides, he didn't have one.

He wondered if Junie would be watching.

Eddie took a taxi to the Mall and had to walk the last four blocks,
fighting his way through the crowd. At the assembly area, there was
bother about checking his badge. The pigs, a helmeted woman told
him, were sneaking in saboteurs. Past the barriers, the atmosphere
was celebratory. Alleged music deafened him. Kids danced in the
Reflecting Pool. Their joy surprised him. He tried to imagine Junie
at his side, smiling encouragement, but he saw her instead hiding in
some safe house, exhausted and wan. He noticed the Yippie flag,
marijuana leaves and red star. He shook his head. The left of fifteen
years ago had been ideologically serious, believing its task was to per-

suade, not to self-indulge. These kids seemed to miss the point. They had no interest in appealing to anyone who did not already agree. Yet he loved them for the purity of their intentions.

Eddie waited, listening to the superstars. Dr. Benjamin Spock spoke. Jane Fonda, newly recruited to the cause, electrified the crowd. At last Eddie ascended the platform. The writer had just returned, according to the student who introduced him, from a tour of centers of colonialist oppression all over the world. Even now, the young man continued, Edward T. Wesley's sister is on the run from the pigs—

Eddie, trembling, tuned him out.

Thirty seconds later, the introduction was done. Eddie stood behind the microphone and gazed out across the largest crowd he had addressed in his life.

Later, he would not remember a word. The events of the next twenty-four hours would prove too tumultuous. There were cheers galore, but by that time the kids were cheering everything. Public speaking had never been Eddie's best thing. He expressed himself best in writing. When he opened his mouth, especially to large groups, what emerged was often prolix to the point of inanity. He stumbled through the speech, hurried off the platform before the applause died, and practically ran the dozen blocks back to his hotel.

He decided not to stay the night after all. He would brave the traffic and the roadblocks and drive home to Albemarle Street. He had just finished checking out when an aging hippie in dark glasses, smeary hair past the shoulders of his military jacket, slouched across the lobby to congratulate him on his speech.

In a voice he knew well.

"Where can we talk?" whispered Professor Benjamin Mellor.

(11)

"HOW MANY TIMES are you going to pull this trick?" Eddie asked, steering his Cadillac up Sixteenth Street. He had no intention of taking Mellor anywhere near Albemarle Street. He was thinking of poor

Teri, and Mellor's wife, and, most of all, Junie. "What do you do, wait until some girl's in trouble and then disappear?"

The professor had slipped off his glasses. Worry had etched fine lines into his face. "I couldn't have done anything for her, Mr. Wesley. They came for me just before our meeting. I had a gun, I had some luck—I escaped. I was outside when you drove up. I was going to flag her down, but she was already down the block, and then—well, they were waiting. They had her, and I got away."

"Leaving other people to be tortured," Eddie muttered, fighting the image of filthy water rising.

"I'm not here to argue with you, Mr. Wesley. I'm going to disappear again, and this time I won't be back."

"That sounds like a very good idea."

Mellor looked out the window. The farther north they went, the thinner the ranks of soldiers and police. "I've been living here and there, Mr. Wesley. A commune. A crash pad. Here and there. I've had a lot of time to think. And I want to do the right thing before I vanish for good. I want to finish our conversation from Saigon. You'll remember, I was going to tell you—"

"Why your life was at risk. I remember, Professor."

A hard look, as if suspecting an insult. "You think you're alone. You're not. The Council itself is divided. It has been ever since—well, ever since it began to change membership from the original twenty. There are members who oppose the Project, Mr. Wesley. Good people, no matter what you think. Decent people. You have to get in touch with them. The loyal opposition, you might say. They can help you. I believe they might have been helping you already."

"Are you going to give me a name?"

"No, Mr. Wesley. That I can't do."

Eddie slammed on the brakes. They were on U Street, near Twelfth, one of the city's roughest neighborhoods. He leaned toward his passenger. "If I were to knock you around up here, nobody would notice."

Mellor visibly shrank against the door. "It's not that I don't want to tell you, Mr. Wesley. I don't know. Genuinely. I don't know who the dissenters are."

"Then how do you know there are any?"

"Little things. Things Perry mentioned in Vietnam."

"But that's not who's after you, is it? The dissenting members of the Council. You said in Saigon that there's a third force. That's who you were hiding from."

"They think I know where Junie is. I don't, but they think I do, and, well, if they catch me—you get the idea." Mellor shuddered. "Perry hid me from them. I told you that. But he can't help me any more."

"Why not?"

"Because he and this third force have thrown in together. The Council has been decimated, but Perry is trying to put it back together."

Eddie had hold of the professor's collar, but now released him. He was remembering the note he had found in Mellor's flat in Saigon. Junie had wanted Mellor to stop them. Eddie had found the message confusing, but now he saw the trick.

"You're not the father, are you? Of my sister's baby. It wasn't you."

Mellor shook his head. "It wasn't me. I was asked to step in and help."

"By the Council?"

"Essentially." His eyes grew fervent. "I believed in those days, Mr. Wesley. I truly did. I had the politics from my father. He taught me that the most important thing is reaching the right result. Fighting for justice with whatever tools come to hand. You have to understand that the group we're calling the Council—well, it's older than that meeting in 1952. The Council goes back fifty years or more. But its members were all powerful white men, until Burton Mount and my father—well, let's say they integrated it. With this crazy idea." The fire faded again. "They put their Project together. They designed Jewel Agony. They recruited your sister. And you know the rest."

"I don't know the rest," Eddie protested. "How did it all come apart?"

"My father and Burton Mount were hoodwinked. They thought

they were in charge. They thought the whole scheme was to achieve racial justice. They were fools, and so was I. The Council never belonged to them, and it never cared about justice. The third force was running things all along."

"And the search for Junie—"

"She can stop them. Or they think she can. I'm not entirely sure why, to tell you the truth. I was never a true insider at the Council." His hand was on the door. "I must apologize, Mr. Wesley. I seem to be out of time."

"Wait—"

"I know you have more questions. The best way to get answers is to find your sister. As for me"—he opened the door—"I am now out of your life for good."

He faded into the mass of pedestrians, and was gone.

Eddie drove across town and up through Rock Creek Park. When he pulled into his driveway, Aurelia was sitting in a rocker on the front porch, luggage at her feet.

She stood up. "Gary sent the plane for me," she said.

"What?"

"Dick called." Out of doors, she was unwilling to say his full name. "He said you needed me. He said I had to get down here fast. I called Gary. He knew where you were staying, and he sent the plane, and I took the kids to my neighbor, and, well, you said if I ever needed an autograph— Eddie, are you okay? Why are you looking at me like that?"

"Would you like to see the house?"

Inside, Aurelia tried to enforce her rules.

But not for long.

(1 1 1)

THEY HAD A LOT to catch up on.

Eddie had never told Aurelia about Benjamin Mellor, or what happened in Hong Kong, or the details of his suspicions about Lanning Frost and, more important, his wife. Aurie had never told Eddie about Kevin's files, or his fears the year before he died, or the translations she had worked out with the help of Tristan Hadley. They compared notes and pooled resources and, in between, rediscovered each other. Emotionally as well as physically.

"The presidency," said Eddie at one point, marveling. "Lanning?"

"Just like you thought."

"But he's a dunce."

"Margot isn't, and she's close to Perry Mount."

Break in conversation.

"I never thought of Richard Nixon as a matchmaker," said Eddie at the next intermission.

"Dick's a romantic at heart."

"How would you know?"

"I know men."

Another time, she asked what had really happened with Toric Elden. "I hurt her very badly," said Eddie, honestly. "I found it impossible to pretend."

"If you hurt me very badly, I'll scratch your eyes out."

They dozed. Played. Talked some more.

"I can't believe you didn't tell me that," each said, more than once, about their feelings as well as their evidence.

Eddie swore he had never slept with Mindy.

Aurelia swore she had never slept with Tristan.

"I was tempted, though," she confessed.

"So was I."

Around midnight, Aurelia decided she was hungry. She hopped out of bed. In the kitchen, they scrounged a meal from leftovers. As they ate, Eddie asked her why she had changed her mind.

Aurie was smoking. She took her time.

"I didn't," she finally said. "Not completely."

"I don't understand."

"Dick said you needed me. Not *wanted* me. *Needed* me." She lifted his right hand from the table, kissed his knuckles. "Kevin needed me before. You only wanted me. I need to be needed, Eddie."

His turn to think about it. "All right. I accept that. And I do need you, Aurie. Desperately, as a matter of fact."

"I noticed."

"That's not the kind of needing I mean. Or not the only kind." He took his hand back. "So, then, tell me. What part of your mind did you not change?"

"I'm not going to marry you."

"Did I ask?" he said, crestfallen.

"If I don't warn you," said Aurelia, smoking hard, "you will."

Eddie considered. "What if I said I don't want you this way?"

"You'd be lying."

(I V)

IN THE MORNING, they sat in the kitchen and put their research together and, once more, kicked each other verbally for not having done it sooner. They even worked out a rough chronology. They wrote each event on an index card, then laid the cards on the table and switched them around until the order worked.

> Early 1950s: Burton Mount and Hamilton Mellor discuss the creation of a radical organization to scare America. Burton arranges a meeting at his summer home on Martha's Vineyard to discuss this idea. Among the twenty men present are Philmont Castle, Matthew Garland, and, probably, Joseph Belt. All three are now deceased, as are Burton Mount and Hamilton Mellor.
>
> Early 1950s: Inspired by Milton's Paradise Lost, the founders call themselves the Palace Council, and, sometimes, the Twenty. Their leader is the Author, Milton's word for Satan. The first author is Burton Mount.
>
> Mid-1950s: The Council begins to bring in others, including Perry Mount and Kevin Garland, now deceased. Perry in turn brings in June Wesley, who is supposed to be one of the leaders of the radical organization, apparently because her commitment to

nonviolence is expected to provide a moderating influence. She works closely with Phil Castle, who apparently helps pay for the creation of the radical group but later has second thoughts.

Mid-1950s: Phil Castle is killed. The Council discovers that he left a testament behind, probably describing their activities. Kevin Garland is assigned to find the testament.

Aurelia needed a moment. Eddie understood. He did not touch her. Still in bathrobe and slippers, he took himself off for a walk in the backyard. As far as he could tell, they were alone. When he returned, Aurie had used the bathroom and washed her face and looked, if not radiant, at least prepared.

"Okay?" he said.

"Let's get back to work."

Late 1950s: The Council's plans are slightly upset when Junie becomes pregnant. She gives up the baby for adoption. Hamilton Mellor's son Benjamin confesses to being the father.

"Wait," said Aurelia. She tapped the page. "Mellor told you he wasn't the father."

"Yes."

"How did you know to ask?"

Eddie was delighted at the chance to show off his literary knowledge to a professor of English. "Phil Castle loved literature. Langston told me. The note in Castle's envelope said 'Not as in a tragic age,' right? And the first sentence of *Lady Chatterley's Lover* is 'Ours is essentially a tragic age, so we refuse to take it tragically.' See? 'Not as in a tragic age' means that what happened in the real world is not what happened in the novel."

Aurelia was very fast. "In the novel, the lover of Lady Chatterley is the gamekeeper, Mr. Mellors."

"Right."

"Okay. The opposite. If Mr. Mellors was the lover in the novel, then Professor Mellor was not the lover in the real world. That's what the message means."

"Right again."

"Don't give me that hangdog look, Eddie. I do this for a living."
She kissed him. "Okay. Very clever. Now, let's get back to work."

*1957: Junie vanishes with her friend Sharon Martindale. Both
become members of the radical group now called Agony, or Jewel
Agony. Junie is one of the group's leaders from early on. Sharon
evidently becomes a leader later.*

Late 1950s: Agony becomes active.

1959: Junie gives birth to a second child.

*Early 1960s: The Council becomes concerned that the
testament has not been found. Kevin Garland says the Project is
out of control.*

1960: Matty Garland is killed.

*1963: Birmingham attack is the first action by Agony to
take lives.*

*1965: Kevin Garland is killed in an explosion. The target
might have been Senator Lanning Frost. It might have been
Kevin. The authorities say Agony took the credit. Sharon
Martindale denies to Eddie that Agony was involved.*

Aurelia needed another minute. This time she asked Eddie to
stay with her. They wound up walking the yard together. She said it
reminded her of Ithaca. She pointed to a scrawny tree, its trunk gray-
white.

"It's a birch. A dwarf birch. A birch tree can't survive by itself,
Eddie. You need a grove of them. Otherwise, it's going to die." She
licked her lips. "It's so lonely out there."

"We're not birches, honey."

"I think sometimes we are."

Back to work.

*Mid-1960s: Junie Wesley is expelled from Agony after
renouncing violence. She disappears to look for her children.
Agony goes into decline.*

Late 1960s: Remnants of Agony are folded into Weatherman. The weakened Palace Council comes under the sway of what Benjamin Mellor calls a "Third Force," presumably Margot Frost, carrying out her late father's wishes with the aid of Mr. Collier. Perry Mount hides Mellor in southeast Asia, but later joins the Third Force.

Late 1960s: Eddie is tortured in Hong Kong, probably by Perry Mount, to discover whether he knows where his sister is.

Late 1960s: Congressman Byron Dennison urges Aurelia to get back together with Eddie.

"Enough," said Aurelia, drained.

"Enough," Eddie agreed, scarcely doing better himself.

That night, they went to dinner and a movie, dating publicly for the first time. Nobody recognized them, and Eddie found himself vaguely disappointed. In bed later, Aurelia told him she had to get back to Ithaca. "I have to think of some way to tell the kids."

"Kids tend to figure things like this out for themselves."

Aurelia stretched against him. Her body was warm. Her voice was sleepy and complacent. "You can drive me as far as New York. I'll fly from there."

"I can drive you all the way."

"I could also fly from here. But we're stopping in New York for a reason."

"What reason is that?"

"To pick up the testament."

Eddie sat up. "You know where it is?"

"So would you, if you did crossword puzzles."

"Where is it?"

"You'll find out when we get to the city."

No matter how hard he tickled, she refused to tell.

CHAPTER 59

The Testament

(1)

"YOU'RE A SILLY MAN," said Aurelia, turning the seed pod over and over in her smooth fingers. "Did you know that, dear?"

"It's been said."

"I'm saying it again." She put the pod down on top of the note. They were sitting in the study of the apartment Eddie still maintained at 435 Convent Avenue. They had left in the late morning in Eddie's Cadillac and arrived in Harlem just past four. Eddie was all set to go hunting, but Aurelia, amused, had told him they could not get the testament until dark.

Why not? he had asked.

Because we have to break in, she answered, eyes twinkling.

Now she said, "You should have guessed for yourself, Eddie. You're supposed to be the one who reads history. Why didn't you show this to me in the first place?"

Eddie stood in the window, looking out at Harlem. None of his old crowd remained. Langston Hughes had died while Eddie was in Vietnam. He often wondered why he kept the apartment. "I'm sorry," he said. "Which first place are we talking about?"

Aurelia smiled. "The note," she said, tapping the paper. "His wife has it."

"I know what the note says."

"And I know who his wife is. I even know who *he* is." A beat. "Which you obviously don't."

Eddie came back to the table, sat down, took her hand. She was wearing one of his robes, and seemed uncommonly brown and beautiful. A package of Virginia Slims lay between them.

"Please tell me," he said, and Aurelia found herself impressed by his ability to be gentle after all the years of searching.

She picked up the pod again. "This is a burr, Eddie. You know, a burr? Like Aaron Burr? The Vice President a hundred fifty, hundred sixty years ago?"

"So?"

"Oh, honey. How could you live in Harlem for so many years and not know? I thought everybody knew. Aaron Burr was the second husband of Madame Jumel. He stole her fortune."

He dropped her hand. "Madame Jumel? You're saying—"

Aurelia nodded, delighted at her coup. "Castle's testament is hidden in Jumel Mansion."

(11)

THEY STOOD on Jumel Terrace, across from the shuttered townhouse that had once belonged to Shirley Elden, where a thousand years ago Harlem society had celebrated Aurelia's engagement to Kevin, and Eddie had walked out in a huff and discovered Philmont Castle's body. The cobblestone street was empty. The mansion loomed white and silent in the darkness. It was surrounded by a high wrought-iron fence, the pikes very sharp. They had searched for breaks in the fence and found none, meaning they would have to climb. Old Harlem tales insisted that the house was haunted by the ghost of Madame Jumel. Standing on the sidewalk as mist swirled around them, they found the tales harder to dismiss.

Why had he not thought of the mansion before?

This was where Castle had been killed. He had not, as Eddie thought, been dumped here after his murder. He had been followed onto the grounds by whoever strangled him. The killer plainly had no inkling of the testament, or he would have searched that very night.

"I have to go first," said Aurelia.

"Why?"

"Because there's no way I can boost you over the fence."

So Eddie boosted her, and she snagged her sweater on one of the wrought-iron spikes and had to tear it to jump down. He scrambled up after her, leaped, landed badly, and hurt his ankle. They stood inside the fence, sheepish grins on their faces. "Some secret agents we are," said Aurie.

A swoosh of movement made them turn, but it was just a night bird, swooping low as it foraged.

"We need to calm down," said Eddie. "Nobody knows we're here."

"We hope."

They followed the stone walk to the mansion, studied its foundation by flashlight, selected a basement window. Eddie picked up a heavy tree branch.

"What if there's an alarm?" said Aurie.

"Then we abort."

"That should be fun, trying to get back over the fence with the police on the way."

Eddie looked at her. "It's a little late to bring that up."

"And you were a little late showing me the burr."

In response, he struck the window. It shook but did not even crack. He laughed nervously, tried again. Same result.

"The branch is too long," she said. "You don't have any leverage."

"What?"

"You were never a vandal, Eddie." Even in the darkness he could hear the smile in her voice. "That's the problem with having a dad who's a pastor. Vandals use small objects. You can't break a window swinging a branch. Either kick it in or throw a rock."

"Why didn't you suggest this before?"

"Because you're the kind of guy who'd try it your own way no matter what I said."

About to snap back, Eddie smiled. She was right. He found a rock, threw it, missed. He kicked and made a tiny crack.

"Harder," she ordered.

"You're bossy."

"Get used to it."

He kicked again, harder, then a third time. The glass did not shatter. Not at first. Instead, the whole window fell in, crashing to the basement floor with enough noise to wake the dead. Or the neighbors, if there were any.

They waited, shivering.

Then Eddie said, "This time I'll go first and then help you down."

Aurie peered into the darkness. "I think that's a good idea," she said.

(I I I)

THE BASEMENT TURNED OUT to be just a basement. Ancient and musty and dank, yes, but containing what any basement did: a furnace, a water heater, endless pipes along the ceiling, few of them insulated. Boxes were stacked here, extra furniture there. Several trunks stood near the stairs, stacked head-high.

"This is a perfect hiding place," said Eddie, despairingly. He ran the beam of his flashlight around the space a third or fourth time. "It would take us a week to go through all this junk."

"Fortunately, we don't have to."

"Why not?"

"Because the testament isn't down here."

He turned toward her, intrigued by her certainty. "What do you know that I don't, Aurie?"

She used a hand to shift the beam away from her face. "For one thing, I know better than to shine a light in my boyfriend's eyes."

"Sorry." He glanced around. "So, we're going upstairs?"

"Two flights."

Somewhere up above, a floorboard creaked. Just once, and the sound did not repeat. And then, faintly, it did.

"The house is settling," said Eddie.

"Or somebody's up there," said Aurie.

"Or both."

She shifted her beam. "We can't turn back now."

"At least tell me where we're going."

"His wife has it. That's what the card said, right?"

"Yes."

"But his wife is dead, Eddie. She's a ghost. And everyone who claims to see her sees her in the same place. Her bedroom window."

Another creak. "The bedroom," he repeated.

"That's right." She gestured toward the stairs. "Lead the way."

The basement stairs led to a door, but the door was not locked. It opened at the first push and did not even creak. They were in the grand foyer, large rooms on all sides, and the sweeping staircase to the second floor on the north wall.

"Keep going," said Aurelia. "I've got your back."

"Swell."

Midway up the grand staircase, they heard another soft creak, this time down below, perhaps in the dining room. More settling, or somebody trying too hard to be quiet? But nobody could have followed them. In the emptiness of the street and the grounds, they would have noticed.

"A rat, maybe," said Eddie.

"Or the ghost."

Upstairs, they made their way to the rear of the house. The doors were all open, except one. A moment later, they stood in the bedchamber. Closed for renovation. Their flashlights picked out the bed, a four-poster, currently without canopy. An old dresser, but not old enough. Incongruously, a file cabinet, with the look of having been moved hastily from somewhere else. So the locked-off room, like the basement, was used for storage. Aurelia moved closer. The beams found the dingy chandelier, then swung jointly toward the door as something skittered in the darkness.

They stood very still.

"The ghost," said Aurie, giggling weakly.

Eddie, struggling against his own growing fear, gestured toward the square of smeary light from the filthy window. "That's where she sits and looks out and scares the kids."

"You think—"

"It has to be here. Where his wife sits."

Both beams flashed that way, found the settee, and whatever curled on the sagging cushions rose, huge and rotten and fetid, uttering a snarly cry as, eyes redly glowing, it soared toward them through the shadows. They leaped back. Aurelia screamed. Eddie's head bumped one of the bedposts, and his flashlight went flying. The pain sent him to his knees. The ghost swooped down. Beating devil's wings struck his face. He grabbed and shoved, was clawed and scratched in return, then saw, by the light of Aurelia's beam, that he was wrestling a huge barn owl. Eddie ducked away. The owl was as scared as he was. With a final glare, the creature sailed majestically off into the hallway.

Aurelia knelt beside him. This time her mirth was genuine. She touched his bleeding face. "Want me to kiss it and make it better?"

"I want you to stop laughing."

"Then you have to stop being so funny," she said, and kissed him anyway.

They stood and crossed to the settee. It was sagging and sprung. They peered underneath, coughed in the dust, found only mouse droppings. They shook the heavy frame, but nothing fell out. They began tugging at the fabric. Aurelia pricked her finger on a freshly uncovered coil but refused to stop.

That footstep again.

On their knees, they swung around, both beams at the door. Nothing.

"We need to calm down," said Eddie.

"We need to hurry," said Aurelia.

"Why?"

She shuddered. "Can't you feel it?"

And he could, a growing pulsing miasmic stirring, as if the ancient house was slowly waking, its ancient haunts with it. The eaves whispered in the wind, and the whispers were clever and old. Floorboards creaked as the house settled, and the creaking meant that whatever evil the house nurtured was climbing the stairs. They tore faster, desperation in their hands, and found nothing. No envelope, no papers, no hidden photographs. They looked at each other.

"We were wrong," said Eddie.

"We can't have been."

"This is the window where she sits. I don't know where else it could be."

Aurelia stood up, stretched, leaned on the sill. She pointed. "It's nailed shut."

"So?"

"So—she can't possibly lean out."

"She's not real. She's a ghost."

"What I mean is, people see her lean out, with the window open. Or they used to, anyway." She leaned close. "Eddie, these nails are new."

He crouched. They were tarnished. "They're not new."

She lifted her light, ran a finger along the paint. "Look at this. Look how it flakes. See? There isn't any here. Where the nail holes are."

"You're saying—"

"Somebody drove these in just a few years ago."

Eddie's excitement grew. "And nobody noticed because the room was closed off."

"Or, if they did notice, they just thought somebody official had done it."

"So what do we do?"

She tugged. "We take the nails out."

Comedy. The nails were driven deeply into the sill, and neither of them had thought to bring a hammer. They hunted around for a tool.

"The office downstairs," said Aurie.

"I'll go," said Eddie.

"Not without me."

Halfway down the sweeping staircase, they heard the footsteps again. "No ghosts," said Eddie.

"No ghosts," Aurelia echoed, teeth chattering.

The door to the office was locked. They forced it. They found desks, file cabinets, bookshelves, boxes of souvenirs to be sold out front.

"Bingo," said Aurelia, emerging from the small bathroom.

A toolkit.

Back upstairs, the nails yielded easily, and as they lifted the lower sash, the higher one fell, very hard, nearly mashing their fingers. Glass splintered. The sound echoed. Eddie and Aurelia scarcely noticed. Drifting to the floor was a long envelope that had been hidden between the panes, covered by the wood trim where the sashes met when the window was open. Aurelia tore it open, and Eddie extracted the contents: eight pages in Philmont Castle's tight, spidery hand.

The testament.

Eddie beckoned Aurelia, but she was already reading over his shoulder. Here, at last, was the answer—and, God willing, the road to Junie. Together, they read by flashlight:

My name is Philmont Castle. I am a member of the Bar Associations of the City of New York, the State of New York, and the Supreme Court of the United States. I am writing these words in the hope that, should I not survive, someone will read them and be able to prevent the madness that I have helped to plan. I could do nothing to stop it, because my family stood hostage to my loyalty. I only pray that whoever discovers my testament will have the fortitude to stop what must be stopped. The details I shall disclose will be sufficient to put an end not only to the Project itself, but to the careers of the men who designed it.

In the second week of August 1952, a meeting was held at the summer home of Burton Mount on Winemack Street in the town of Oak Bluffs on the Island of Martha's Vineyard, for the purpose of planning a crime of grandeur, audacity, and stupidity, in the name of building a better America. The meeting began with dinner, but no spouses were permitted. Mrs. Mount was visiting friends on the Island, I believe the Powells. Two maids laid out the food en buffet and then were dismissed. Burton as usual provided an excellent repast, beginning with sautéed scallops and mussels in an excellent cream sauce, bridging the courses with berry-filled crêpes instead of sorbet. Burton next served lobster tails . . .

Annoyed, Eddie rifled the pages. How much of the testament was going to be travelogue and culinary description? Aurelia touched his hand.

"He was writing for the ages," she said. "He was conscious of his audience."

"Meaning what?"

"You never read Pliny, did you? The Romans used to write this way."

But all Eddie knew of Pliny was that Wesley Senior had once cited him in a sermon, drawing from his work some obscure evidence for the existence of Christ.

. . . bridging the courses with berry-filled crêpes instead of sorbet. Burton next served lobster tails, followed by a filet mignon, butterflied and grilled just a minute or two past medium rare. Naturally, each course was accompanied by an appropriate wine. After dinner we settled in the parlor with brandy and cigars. The maids had stoked the fire. Burton sat beside it, a cadaverous man with an angry smile. I was struck, even then, by the image of Burton as the devil, welcoming us to Hell. The image turned out to be less far-fetched than I imagined.

I was one of twenty men present at the meeting. Eight were Negroes, twelve were Caucasians. We were the Twenty, said Burton, flames at his back. We were the Council. He announced that he, along with several unnamed associates, had conceived a plan for setting America on the proper path. The plan was dangerous, he explained. The plan might lead to violence. And yet he was convicted—that was what he said, convicted—that the plan would succeed. Because of the risks, he and his associates would not move forward without submitting their idea to scrutiny. The twenty men present this August evening would judge the plan. We would weigh its merits, said Burton, with the hope of pardoning our offenses. This invocation of the liturgy was intended, I am sure, as a joke. No one laughed except Senator Elliott Van Epp, who sat beside me. Van Epp had indulged too freely in the excellent wines. If we judged the plan unworthy, said Burton, it would be discarded. Otherwise, the men in the parlor would become the overseers of the plan. Burton was a serious man. He was a spellbinder, a man of enormous charisma, and could exercise a near-hypnotic influence on those who listened too closely.

Burton himself freshened our drinks, pouring from the snifter. He asked if anyone wanted to leave. Now would be the time, he said. No records would be kept. No grudges would be held. The nervous twitter among the guests surprised me. The parlor was full of powerful men, but no one protested the subtle threat. Perhaps we were held by Burton's charm. Perhaps by curiosity. Perhaps by fear. One had the sense, sitting there, that Burton Mount commanded resources, legions, vast demonic armies, ready to be unleashed upon all those who dared defy his will. One had the sense that our only role was to approve, not to reject.

There is evidence to support this. After Burton began the formal presentation, Ralph Shands, a jazz pianist of considerable renown, leapt to his feet shaking his fist and said that God would not allow so evil a plan to succeed. Burton rang a bell. A maid appeared with the man's vicuña coat in hand, although how she could guess that he was leaving us, I have no idea. Two years later, the pianist died of a heroin overdose.

As to the presentation itself, Burton had divided it, like Gaul, into three parts. . . .

"Very well done, Mr. Wesley."

Eddie and Aurelia spun, trembling beams piercing the darkness, but found no speaker.

"Put your flashlights on the floor, please."

Eddie complied at once. When Aurie hesitated, he snatched hers and put it down, too. He recognized the voice, and knew what they were facing.

"Eddie," she began, but he waved her silent.

"Do you want us to put our hands up now?" he asked.

A shadow separated from the deeper shadows in the corner behind the chipped dresser. Eddie held Aurelia's wrist. She jerked her hand free, straightened her clothes. The shattered window allowed a sliver of light in past the decades of filth caking the panes. Not enough for them to pick out much, but the dull metal in the visitor's hand was certainly a gun. Eddie had no idea how long George Collier had been watching them.

"No," the killer said. "Just put the pages on the floor, then step over to the divan."

"How long have you been following us?" Eddie asked.

"I'm not the sort of bad guy who explains himself. That only happens in the movies. The pages, please."

"Listen," Eddie began.

"Please don't waste time, Mr. Wesley. If I have to shoot, I'm afraid I will be shooting Mrs. Garland first. Nothing personal."

"Not at all," she said, fingers digging into Eddie's arm.

The gun glinted. "All the pages, including the ones you slipped inside your sweater, Mrs. Garland."

"Turn your back."

"Now, please."

Out of ideas, hoping for a miracle, they put the papers on the floor as asked, then stepped back. "Sit," he said. They did, being careful of the springs. The shadowy figure stooped, the gun trained on Aurelia. Gloved fingers moved. The testament vanished. "Close your eyes."

Eddie refused. He stared hard into the darkness, wondering how it would feel, or whether there would even be a sensation. He remembered Vietnam, the bullets knocking chunks from the bodies of brave, frightened young men and whizzing on. A raw rubbery heat rose from his stomach. Where did professionals shoot you? The head, like Jack Kennedy and Martin Luther King? The chest, like Bobby? Aurie shivered in his arms. He was not ready to die, but he was not ready to admit it. At least he was with the woman he loved. She was whispering. Eddie held her more tightly. He heard "protect." He heard "please, Lord." A prayer, he realized, with a start. It had not occurred to him to pray. He heard "take care of them." Aurie was praying not to get out of this mess, but that God would protect her children. His love surged, and, just like that, he removed her fingers and was on his feet, closing the distance between the settee and the place where he had last spotted the gun, ready to take the bullets to buy Aurelia a precious second to jump out the window.

He dived into the darkness, hoping at least to tackle Collier to the floor before he died.

And hit the floor himself, lying on threadbare carpet.

George Collier was gone.

CHAPTER 60

Cover Stories

(1)

In August, a California judge was murdered in a botched effort to free the black radical George Jackson from prison. Every revolutionary group under the sun was accused of being involved, including Agony, which many experts thought had died. But the politicians dredged it up, listed the group's crimes, demanded that the leaders be brought to justice. FBI agents interviewed Edward Wesley at his home in Washington, duly reporting that he denied having had any contact with his sister. They believed him. In fact, the interview was perfunctory. They did not press. Probably they had decided she was dead, and wanted to close the books on Agony once and for all.

By this time, Eddie and Aurelia had become an open, if occasional, item. People were not sure from one moment to the next whether to invite them to the same party. Actually, they were considered moderately scandalous. Their arrest inside Jumel Mansion back in May had made all the papers: trespassing, burglary, and destruction of public property, pled down within a day to malicious mischief. They paid their fines and were released, but the damage was done, twice over. George Collier had covered his escape by calling the police, and telling them what to look for; and he made Eddie and Aurelia so silly and conspicuous that any effort to explain what had happened would be taken for an absurd excuse.

"Why didn't he kill us?" Aurelia had asked as they drove upstate. She was smoking even harder now. Her hands still shook. "He should have killed us."

Eddie glanced at her. "In Vietnam he told me he was under orders."

"Whose orders?"

"Whoever he's working for. I'm not being facetious. It all gets back to Junie somehow. I can't work it out, Aurie. I can't seem to untie the last knot. But they can't harm a hair on our heads as long as Junie's at large. I'm sure of that part."

"He used to be Senator Van Epp's bodyguard. So maybe now he works for Lanning Frost."

"So what are you saying? That we're alive because Lanning is still grateful to your husband?" He had another thought. "Besides, didn't we agree that Lanning is not our actual problem?"

"Maybe Mr. Collier works for Margot."

"But why would Margot want to keep us alive?"

Aurie grinned. "Happy memories?"

"Very funny."

"I'm not joking." She sounded irritated, and told him when he dropped her off that she thought they should have a little time apart.

"We just had ten years apart," he protested.

"Twelve."

"You see my point."

They were in the foyer of her house. The children were at school. Tonight, with their suddenly infamous mom back home, they would sleep in their own beds for the first time in a week.

"It's going to be different," she promised. "It's going to be fine. I just need some time to get used to things."

She kissed him to prove it.

(I I)

THE CHILDREN DID NOT KNOW what to make of her. She had left as Mommy and returned as this madwoman whose mug shot was on the front page of the papers, including their own *Ithaca Journal*. Aurelia sat them down on the bench in the foyer and told them that it had all been kind of a misunderstanding, but after something like this, people would say a lot of things about her that were not true.

Zora, going on fourteen, accepted this intelligence with grave acquiescence. She believed everything her mother said, always.

Locke, at twelve, had a question.

"Are you gonna marry him?"

"Marry who?"

"That Wesley guy. The one who got you arrested in the haunted house."

"He didn't get me arrested," she said, gently. "I told you, it was all a big misunderstanding." She hugged them both. "And, no, honey, I'm not going to marry him."

Locke squirmed free. "Why not?" he demanded. "What's wrong with him?"

Aurelia was shocked. Zora told him to stop, and he did. Later that night, Zora told her mother that Locke wanted a father in the worst way.

"What about you?" asked Aurie, fearful of the answer.

"I think you're cool," said her daughter, which was not, precisely, an answer.

Back in her office, Aurelia found concentration difficult. The students had gone on strike to protest the Kent State killings, and exams had mostly been canceled, but some of the more ambitious young strikers had snuck final papers into the faculty mailboxes, hoping not to be caught by their fellows. Aurelia's grades were already tardy. Her department chair asked if she needed time off. He spoke kindly, the way one does to the dying. In academic life, those who take time off tend to be forgotten very fast. Often the salary slot goes to someone else. Aurie told her chair not to worry. She worked double-time for a day and a half and got all the grading done.

In free moments, Aurelia pondered. The part of her that had always believed in America wanted to go public, to call reporters she knew, or perhaps have Eddie talk to his political contacts. But Eddie was dead set against the idea. With the divisions in the country, especially over race, he feared the path that public hysteria might take. Besides, he said, nobody would believe them: Mr. Collier, by arranging their arrests at Jumel Mansion, had cleverly shoved them to the political margins. Aurelia allowed herself, however reluctantly, to be persuaded.

Toward the end of June, she packed the kids into the car and made her annual pilgrimage to New Rochelle, visiting Kevin's grave. While the children fed birds around the pond, Aurie remained standing before the headstone, asking her husband for lots of advice, and, probably, lots of permission.

Two weeks later, Tristan Hadley, now separated from his wife, asked Aurelia out on a date. She refused. He asked if that meant that she and Eddie were a steady couple. She said she had no idea. Tris brightened. He sent flowers. He sent cards. She could not get him to stop. Tris pestered her and pestered her until she said yes out of sheer bone-weariness. Over dinner at Ithaca's one fancy steak house, while a woman who might have been Streisand sat nearby, Tristan produced a ring.

Aurelia almost fell out of her chair.

She told him that he was sweet but she was not a marrying woman. He accepted this, then asked if he could see her again. She said no. She said it nicely, but she said it firmly. Later that night, she called Mona. At first Aurie asked about her son's worrisome secretiveness, and his temper. Mona assured her that a degree of rebelliousness was normal at his age—especially against his mother. Then Aurie confessed her true purpose in calling.

"This whole thing is getting out of hand," she said.

"If you'd say yes to one of these guys, the rest of them would go away."

"I can't say yes."

"Then quit dating."

Aurelia decided she would. But when Eddie called to suggest that the two of them get away to the Caribbean for a few days once her children were settled at summer camp, she said yes fast.

"Just don't bring a ring," she said.

The island they chose was Barbados. A very polite police detective followed them everywhere they went. In bed one night, they decided whom to tell.

(1 1 1)

THE DRAWING ROOM had been refurbished since Erebeth Hilliman died. Out had gone the antiques and chintz. Now everything was modern and sleek and bound to be obsolete in another five years. It seemed to Eddie that there were fewer servants at Quonset Point, and, certainly, no domo, whether major or minor. They sipped fruit juice instead of sherry, because Gary Fatek was on a health kick. He did not have much time for them because his nephew Jock was waiting to see him, a spoiled preppie who was always in trouble.

"How much of this do you actually know?" he asked when they were done, folding fleshy fingers over his knee. "How much of it is speculation?"

"We can show you our notes," said Eddie. He and Aurelia were on the low Scandinavian sofa, holding hands.

"Notes on conversations with each other," Gary pointed out. "You see the problem, don't you? The central player isn't you, Eddie. It's Aurie. And the world will say she compiled these notes from two sources, both of whom she was sleeping with. Correction. Three sources, counting her husband." He held up a hand in apology. "I know you weren't sleeping with Tristan Hadley, but my sources say the whole academic world thinks you wrecked his marriage." He stood up and began to pace. "I'm not saying I don't believe you. People are dead, and it can't all be coincidence. And not by natural causes. Two or three murders, a suicide, a ski accident." He was at the window, looking out on his private beach. "And Mr. Collier. My sources tell me things about him, too."

"What things?" said Aurelia, when she realized that each of the two men was prepared to wait the other out.

"George Collier is an assassin. Well, maybe you guessed that. He's done a job or three for our government, details unavailable. His military appointment is cover. Which agency actually employs him, my sources can't find out. But he's a legend in the secret world, so they tell me. His particular expertise is making sure that every job he does is blamed on somebody else. He doesn't leave unsolved crimes lying around for some journalist to pick up later. If you have Mr. Collier as an enemy, well, maybe you should move in with me. My place is a fortress, and, frankly, I could use the company."

"I don't think he's going to hurt us," said Eddie, wondering why Gary was refusing to face them. "I don't think he's allowed to."

"Yes. You said that. But you're putting an awful lot of faith in something a killer told you in a Saigon hotel."

"He could have killed me in Saigon. He could have killed us both in Harlem."

Gary shook his head. "No, no, Eddie. You're missing the point. He couldn't just shoot you in Jumel Mansion. What good would that do? I just told you, he doesn't leave unsolved crimes lying around. He plans his murders for months, from what I hear. Maybe years."

Eddie and Aurie looked at each other. Both understood that there was something the leader of the Hillimans was having trouble getting out.

"Let's say you're right," Gary continued. "Let's say your theory is true. What do you think we should do about it? You think because I have more money than Midas I can wave my hands and make people disappear?" He was suddenly very agitated. "You don't have evidence to arrest anybody. You could say, let's beat Lanning Frost. Well, fine. I'll finance as many campaigns on the other side as you want. How's that? You dredge up the candidates, I'll buy them." A long pause. Too long. "Or were you thinking of a more direct form of action?"

So there it was.

Gary was asking if they wanted him to hire a George Collier of his own.

"Of course not," said Eddie, quite alarmed. "That's the craziest thing I ever heard."

"We're not killers," said Aurie, eyes wide as she began to understand. "You're talking about assassination, Gary."

The billionaire laughed, and turned to face them. He leaned on the sill and folded his arms. Now that he had broached his idea, the tension seemed to have evaporated. "You know, Eddie, what Lanning

Frost said to you was true. If your opponent has dirt on you, you better have more dirt on him. And if your opponent has Mr. Collier on his side—follow me?"

He offered them a guest room, but they decided to drive back to Manhattan that evening after dinner. In the carport, he told them they should call him if they changed their minds.

"Well, that was a waste of time," fumed Aurelia as they sped along the interstate.

"No, it wasn't," said Eddie. "He was delivering a message."

"That he thinks we should kill somebody?"

"No. If we'd said yes, he'd have found some excuse. No. That whole speech was to let us know he won't lift a finger to help."

"But that's impossible! He's"—a momentary stumble—"your friend!"

"Not any more," said Eddie. "We're on our own, honey."

As they drove on through the darkness, Eddie remembered his first and only meeting with Erebeth Hilliman, more than a decade ago. He would never be a real writer, she had lectured him, until he read Milton.

John Milton—author of *Paradise Lost*.

CHAPTER 61

Again the Golden Boy

(1)

THE YEAR 1970 MELTED into 1971, and still there was no word of Junie. Eddie wondered if his sister might have fled the country. There was political violence everywhere. The Baader-Meinhof Gang was robbing banks in Germany. Could Junie have joined them? The Front de Libération du Québec kidnapped a British diplomat. In Uruguay, the Tupamaros kidnapped another. Had Junie been involved? Somebody had to know. Despite his outward cynicism, Eddie, like many American radicals before and since, harbored a childlike wonder at the Godlike powers of his government. It was not possible for them to have misplaced Junie so thoroughly. Therefore, it was a plot. A conspiracy. Not human failing. Human malice. What he could not supply was a motive.

Eddie still found topics for essays. A Supreme Court decision on busing. The Pentagon Papers. But his writing had lost its sparkle, and everybody knew it. The promised Hong Kong novel languished. He roamed the huge house, unable to concentrate. Sometimes he visited Aurelia. Sometimes she visited him. Sometimes she found him unbearable.

In September, riots erupted at Attica. The prisoners took hostages. The assault by police and National Guard units three days later led to the largest killing of Americans by Americans in the twentieth century. One of the inmates who died was Maceo Scarlett, a leader of the uprising. Harlem had forgotten the Carpenter, so Eddie paid for his funeral. Only a dozen mourners showed up, but one of them was Bernard Stilwell.

Later, he and Eddie had a bite to eat.

"I never told you why I left the Bureau," said the retired agent. He was pale. His hands shook. "The Director is an old man, Eddie. He's sick. One of his sickest ideas was something called the Counter-intelligence Program, or COINTELPRO. You've never heard of it. You will soon. You know Hoover liked to collect information on powerful men. The sort of thing I bugged you for when you were at the White House. Well, COINTELPRO puts some of the information to use. The Bureau infiltrates any group the Director considers radical. Some of them are violent. The Panthers. Weatherman. But a lot of them are just people the Director disagrees with. We kept tabs on all the civil-rights leaders. I helped run the program for a while, Eddie. I know."

Stilwell coughed. His chest rattled. Sympathy welled unexpectedly. "Why are you telling me this?" Eddie asked, more gently than he would have expected.

"I don't have too much time left. You guessed that, didn't you?" Another cough. "Maybe I want to make amends. Maybe I just don't want to die with certain things on my conscience." He sipped his coffee. "Eddie, the Bureau had Agony marked down from the beginning. Those kids couldn't make a move we wouldn't know about. When your sister joined up—when she had her training sessions in Rockland County, when she was in the safe house in Tennessee—all that time, the Director had his finger on them. Their name wasn't even Jewel Agony. That was something we made up to separate out the false confessions. Really they called themselves Perpetual Agony, and, well, anyway, we had them fully penetrated. Then they got away from us. That's the thing. They got some new help, professional, somebody who knew our methods as well as we did, and we lost touch. The Director was furious. A couple of people got demoted over that one."

Professional help, Eddie was thinking. Maybe from a CIA man who used the name Ferdinand, who would have seen the Bureau's reports and wanted the woman he loved far from Hoover's clutches. Either the woman he loved or the terrorist organization the Palace Council had created, as Castle's testament put it, to scare America.

"The thing I want you to understand is this, Eddie. Until Agony got away from us, nobody ever died in its actions. This was when your sister was running it. But once we lost track of the group, Sharon Martindale took charge, and people started dying. That's what I wanted you to know."

Eddie did understand. And could have kicked himself for not seeing it earlier. The dates in the source reports he had read in Ithaca matched up perfectly with the dates of Agony's actions. The 1963 Birmingham bombing, the first fatal attack by Agony, occurred when Junie was in Ghana. Then, in 1965, after Agony killed Kevin Garland, Junie renounced violence. She was stripped of her authority, and within a year or two, she left to find her children. After Junie's departure, Agony kept on killing.

With Sharon in charge—and Perry Mount pulling the strings.

No wonder he wanted Junie found.

(11)

AT THE END of 1971, Eddie received his usual invitation to Byron Dennison's New Year's party. From Albemarle Street he called Aurie. Yes, she had hers, too. And she thought they should go.

"You're joking."

"We should talk to him."

"He's part of what's going on."

"I'm not so sure," she said after a moment. "I don't think he's a bad man."

Against his better judgment, Eddie agreed. As usual, Aurelia drove the kids to Hanover just after Christmas. She and Eddie met in Boston. In the taxi, he was nervous. "He's not going to hurt us," Aurie said.

"That's not what I'm worried about."

"Then what's bothering you?"

He showed her the clipping from that morning's *Boston Globe*, an innocuous item most readers would have forgotten immediately after turning the page. The article spanned only three paragraphs, and was buried deep in the middle of the paper. FORMER STATE DEPARTMENT AIDE TO ADVISE SEN. FROST, the tiny headline decreed. The story reported that Lanning Frost had retained the services of a veteran of several foreign postings to help develop foreign-policy positions for his likely presidential run. Of course, the Senator was being schooled by experts galore, and nobody had ever heard of the new gentleman. But already, according to the final paragraph, Perry Mount—"a Negro graduate of Harvard"—was being mentioned by senior staffers as a possible National Security Adviser, should Lanning snatch the nomination from the favored Muskie in 1972.

Aurie said, "So, what do you want to do, Eddie? Call Gary back and tell him we accept his offer?"

But her man was lost in his own thoughts, and she knew when to leave him alone.

The party was as sumptuous as always. Bay was delighted to see them, and made a great fuss. The governor of Massachusetts pumped Eddie's hand as if he consorted with radical novelists every day. Claire Garland greeted Aurie as if they had never argued in their lives. The two old friends wound up sitting at a table with five or six other prominent women. Aurelia lost track of Eddie.

Then Chamonix Bing sat down beside her, and Aurelia knew there was going to be trouble, because her old friend's last name was now Mount.

Somebody asked the obvious question.

"Perry is wonderful," Chammie enthused. "I love being married again, and to such a wonderful man. The children adore him, and he adores them. Jonathan especially. I couldn't be happier."

But by now nobody was listening to her desperate assurances, because across the room a fight had broken out.

(111)

"THERE'S A MORAL HERE," said Byron Dennison as Aurelia applied Bactine to her lover's bleeding cheek. He held an ice pack on his split lip. "Never punch a man who's been in the CIA."

They were sitting in the kitchen off the ballroom. Waiters streamed in and out the door. The noise of the party crackled. The revelers had taken the fisticuffs in stride. Perry and his wife had left.

"I wanted to do a lot more than punch him," said Eddie.

"You never did like Perry," said the Congressman. "Didn't he have a pretty big thing for your sister once upon a time? I wonder how he ever got a security clearance."

"Maybe he had help," Eddie growled, glaring at Bay.

Aurelia kissed him on the forehead. "Stop it."

Dennison's eyes were thoughtful. "Maybe you want to tell me what's going on," he said. "Maybe I can help."

Eddie was still angry, and needed an outlet. "Like you tried to help before? Getting the woman I love to steer me away from Perry toward Junie?" He brushed Aurie's hand aside, and, shakily, stood. "What was the idea, Bay? To have me keep looking so your Palace Council could find her? Yes. I know about the Palace Council. And I know Perry is the Paramount. Well, does the Council know that its Paramount has had people killed? Or what he was up to in Hong Kong?"

The Congressman seemed as relaxed as ever. None of the chefs was close enough to hear. "Why don't you enlighten me?"

"Why should I trust you?"

"Not everybody's your enemy, Eddie. Some of us—well, we don't all agree with the direction in which Perry is taking things." He nodded at Aurie. "Remember year before last? When you gave me that speech about how, when you do things in the darkness, you don't have anybody to tell you when you're wrong? Well, that's the problem with Perry. Burton was crazy, but in his heart he was a decent man. I'm not sure Perry is all that decent."

Eddie was about to say something irretrievable, but Aurelia got in first. "So, it was Burton's plan to begin with?"

The Congressman nodded. "In a way. Burton was the head of the Empyreals, back in Harlem in the old days, and that's where all those silly names and phrases come from. The Paramount. Shaking the throne. All of that. They had mimicked *Paradise Lost* for decades. Maybe they thought it captured the story of the race. I don't know.

The point is, when they all got together, Burton suggested using the same terms, and everybody liked them. And there it was. The Palace Council." He pursed his lips. "And it was a joke. A big joke on the Empyreals. Of course Senator Van Epp let the black folks run the meeting. Of course he let everybody think that it was all Burton's idea. But it wasn't. Not really."

"Burton was a figurehead," said Aurelia.

"I don't think he ever knew," said the Congressman. "Elliott Van Epp was a strange man. He'd been putting together his coterie of conspirators for a long time. He didn't really trust democracy. He thought it had to be guided. That was his big word. *Guided.* And a man like Burton, well, he was easily seduced. You see the point. Burton Mount thought he and his people were seducing the white folks in the room, and all the time it was the other way around. Go ahead, Van Epp and his friends were saying. Play your games. We're on your side—but only as long as you're useful to us."

"And they're not useful any more?"

"I don't really know what the fuck is going on. That's the truth. Perry, well, for a while, I thought he was one of the dissenters. But not any more. He seems to have signed on for the big prize."

"Why don't you stop him?" asked Aurelia.

Dennison smiled. "If I had the testament I could. Or if I had Junie."

"Why is Junie so important?" said Aurie, her hand covering Eddie's mouth.

"I'll be honest. I don't know why. But Perry's fixated on her. I think she has something or knows something that would throw his, ah, interpretation of the Project off the tracks again. You saw my notes, Aurie. I realized that after you left. You saw my notes, and you figured I must be one of the bad guys. Well, I'm not. Eddie, the reason I wanted Aurie to direct you away from Perry was to protect you. I want you to find Junie to put an end to the whole thing."

"Meaning, the election of Lanning Frost," said Aurelia. "Lanning in the Oval Office, and Perry right down the hall, pulling the strings."

The Congressman nodded heavily. "The Palace Council running the country."

"You could go public," Eddie began, and stopped. He remembered Benjamin Mellor in Saigon, describing how Hoover hoarded the information about the Council to himself. And his debates with Aurelia about the consequences for the darker nation if America came to believe that a part of its destiny was being secretly directed by a cabal of black men.

"I have to get back to my party," said Dennison. "And the two of you have to get to work." He had a hand on the swinging door. "And if you do find her—"

"I won't tell you," said Eddie. "I'm sorry, Bay. I appreciate what you've said tonight, but, to be frank, I still don't trust you."

"There isn't any reason that you should. I wasn't going to ask you to tell me, Eddie. I just meant—if you find her, make sure to use whatever she knows. You have to stop this travesty."

He went out, just as the cheers erupted. The band broke into "Auld Lang Syne." The year 1972 had begun.

CHAPTER 62

Beeswax

(I)

"A THIRD-RATE BURGLARY," said Aurelia, sliding the *Ithaca Journal* across the table. "Dick's people say it was nothing. I talked to John Ehrlichman this morning. He says not to worry. He laughed. They're not involved, Eddie. They're going to win by a landslide. Why would they break into the offices of the Democratic National Committee?"

"I wouldn't put anything past Nixon."

"You don't know him as well as I do." She lifted a forkful of eggs. Having nobody left to tell—nobody who would believe their tale—they were trying, at least for now, to enjoy their lives. "I'm not saying he's the most honest person I've ever met. But he's a smart politician. Very smart. He wouldn't do anything this stupid. He'd be run out of town."

Eddie chewed for a moment. He turned the pages of the newspaper. It was a lovely June morning in 1972. They were sitting in the kitchen of the house on Fall Creek Drive. The school year was over, and Aurelia's teenagers were sleeping in. Eddie had arrived early. Whenever he visited Ithaca, he spent his nights at the Statler, operated by Cornell University's hotel school. The children had grown accustomed to having the great Edward Trotter Wesley Junior hang around their mother. They called him Uncle Eddie, because there existed, as yet, no polite word for unmarried adult monogamy. No doubt Locke and Zora assumed that their mother sometimes slept with her beau. But Aurie, her Catholic upbringing never far away, preferred to maintain the fiction.

"I agree that Nixon is too smart," Eddie said, "unless he was really worried about something."

"Something like what?"

He looked at the newspaper again. The break-in was at a place called the Watergate, a large hotel, apartment, and office complex.

Aurelia sipped her coffee. "I talked to Granny Vee about you the other night."

"Granny who?"

"Granny Vee. That's what Mona's kids call Amaretta since she moved in with them." A moment while Eddie imagined that proud woman, once the mightiest Czarina in Harlem, living out her dwindling days in the spare room of her daughter's house in a lily-white New Hampshire college town. "Anyway, she calls me now and then. Offers me advice. I think it's because Mona won't listen to her."

"What advice did she give you this time?"

"She wanted to know about—well, about us. You and me. She asked if I knew the difference between being hesitant and being patient." Her eyes were thoughtful, and inward. "I told her I'd never given it much thought."

"What's the difference? Did she tell you?"

"She said patience is a virtue because your future lies ahead of you, but the person who's hesitant has nothing to look forward to but the past."

"Do you know what she was talking about?"

"Of course I do. Don't patronize me." Aurelia shoved her chair back, nearly striking the aging Crunch, who had shambled into the room. "Sorry, honey," she said—whether to Eddie or to the dog was not clear. "I'm just tense. I'm going to check on the kids."

Eddie was not listening. He was staring at the newspaper.

"Honey?"

"I think I know what Nixon was worried about," he said, not looking up. "Maybe he was at the meeting."

"Nixon? A member of the Palace Council? That's ridiculous."

"Why? Senator Van Epp was a law-and-order type. He was there." Eddie's finger stabbed the page. "It would be something to hide, wouldn't it? To be present at a meeting where they set up a terrorist group?"

She shook her head. "Come on, Eddie. Nixon wasn't just some Senator. He was running for Vice President. He couldn't just slip away for a secret meeting with a bunch of black businessmen."

They stared at each other.

"Matty—" she began.

"Was his friend and a big fund-raiser," Eddie finished.

"That could have been everybody's cover story. It wasn't just a friendly dinner, it was a fund-raiser for the Republican ticket."

"How can we find out?" Eddie wondered aloud. Then he answered his own question. "I'll call the Georgetown University Library. There's a woman there who can track down anything."

Aurelia smiled. "I can do it quicker."

"How?"

"I'll call Oliver Garland. He'll tell me."

"Aurie—"

"I know, I know. He's Kevin's cousin. You're thinking he must be part of whatever's going on. But I'm not so sure. He has too much integrity." She waved away Eddie's objection. "I know. I know. You don't believe in integrity. You think everybody acts out of self-interest. But, Eddie, think about it. You act out of love for Junie, right? You'd sacrifice your own interests for hers."

"So?"

"So, why is it so hard to believe that somebody could love his country or his honor enough to make sacrifices?"

"What sacrifices did Oliver ever make? He was a Wall Street lawyer and now he's a federal judge! You don't think the Palace Council could have gotten him those jobs?"

"I think some people actually earn what they get."

She went into her study to make the call. Eddie washed the dishes, dried them, put them away. The children came downstairs, first Zora, sixteen years of age, spindly and brilliant and awkward, then, minutes later, the charismatic Locke, not nearly as smart but twice as fun, and, at fourteen, already recognizable as the kind of kid who would be elected class president five times before his sister had her first date. Eddie scrambled eggs for them. Zora watched him intently but said nothing beyond good morning and yes, thank you. Locke was reading *Sports Illustrated*. He kept up a running patter, told jokes, and worked hard to draw Eddie into a conversation about Reggie Jackson of the Oakland Athletics, who had shocked baseball by growing a mustache, the first on any major league player since before World War I. But Eddie, who had no interest in sports, barely heard. He was busy watching the archway, waiting for Aurie's return. He was developing a new theory about what had happened to Junie. Much turned on the success of Aurelia's call.

(11)

BY A HAPPY CHANCE, she reached Oliver at his house on Shepherd Street in Washington. His wife had broken her arm, and the man they called the Judge was home for a few days, helping out. Aurie was touched, but Claire, before she went to call her husband to the phone, whispered that he spent most of the time in his study, working.

When Oliver came on the line, Aurelia was too nervous to engage in many pleasantries. She explained what she wanted.

"I wasn't at the meeting," he said. "The little I've heard about it all came to me secondhand. It's nothing but hearsay."

"I understand that, Oliver. I'm not asking for any details. I just want to know if the meeting was a fund-raiser for Nixon."

"Why do you want to know?"

"I can't tell you that." She hesitated. "I'm asking you to trust me."

The Judge thought this over. "I don't think much of your friend Nixon, Aurie. I never have. He's too goal-oriented for my taste. I'm old-fashioned. I believe that games have rules, and you don't switch the rules around just because your side might lose if you play it straight. Nixon's the other way. Well, a lot of people are these days." A longish pause. "I don't like what's been happening in this town the past few years," the Judge resumed. "In politics. In journalism. In anything. And I especially don't like the way that people go around digging up dirt on their opponents. I used to think that politics was run by grown-ups. Now I'm not so sure. If you want dirt on Nixon, I'm not going to help." Switching sides for a moment. But maybe integrity had a side of its own. "We're turning the voters into cynics, Aurie. The constant mudslinging is going to be the death of democracy."

"I'm not trying to sling mud, Oliver. I just need to know this one fact. I can't tell you why, but, believe me, right now, if you love your country, nothing is more important than the answer to that question."

Another long pause. For a moment she was sure she had lost him.

"No," said the Judge finally. "The meeting was not to raise money for Nixon, or for Eisenhower, or for the presidential ticket. There. Does that answer your question?"

She returned to the kitchen in time to hear Locke asking Uncle Eddie when he was going to marry Mom.

"None of your beeswax," she said, and kissed her children on their heads.

Later that morning, Eddie and Aurelia walked along Cayuga Lake.

"If the meeting wasn't a fund-raiser," said Aurelia, "then it wouldn't make sense for Nixon to be there. They couldn't have kept his presence a secret."

"So it would appear," said Eddie, lost in thought.

(I I I)

EDDIE LEFT ITHACA the following day. He made Aurelia promise to stay put. He could feel the battle lines forming. Whatever was going to happen was going to happen soon. The Watergate break-in was part of it. Of this Eddie was sure. He knew things Aurie did not. Knew them, and planned to act on them.

He had told Aurie that he was returning to Manhattan, but he needed an untapped telephone. He stopped overnight at a motel in New Rochelle. He called his former assistant Mindy, now happily married to Zach. An hour later, she got back to him with the arrangements.

In the morning, Eddie drove on to Rhode Island. This time Gary took him sailing, as if he, too, now worried about being overheard.

"It's very simple," said Eddie after the sloop had glided for a while in the splendid flat silence. "I need to know which side you're on."

"Side?" said Gary.

"Are you with Perry or with Bay?"

"I'm sorry?"

"One of the Hillimans was at the meeting, wasn't he? Look at me. In 1952, at Burton Mount's house. There was a Hilliman there. Your grandfather, I'd bet. He chose Erebeth as his heir, didn't he? The same way he chose her to handle the family fortune. He didn't care about this male-female business. He cared about who would do the best job exercising power. All those lessons Erebeth taught you. You're her chosen heir, Gary. We can't mess around any more. I don't know if you've been guarding my back or tracking my moves or both. I do know you're a member of the Palace Council."

The bright-green eyes were steady. "No, Eddie. I'm not."

"I don't believe you."

"And I don't care if you believe me or not. There was no Hilliman at the meeting. Yes, I know about it. Erebeth told me the story before she died. Her father was approached, and he said no. He kept an eye on them after that, because anybody who tried to run the country was a threat to the family interests, and nothing was more important to Grandfather. I think the reason she wanted to meet you—the reason she dropped Milton's name—was that our friendship worried her. Erebeth thought you were being groomed as a member of the Palace Council."

"Me!"

He nodded. "Erebeth thought so, and, frankly, Eddie, I think it's possible." He waved a hand. "Spare me your indignation. People are getting killed out there, but, somehow, you miraculously survive. Mr. Collier leaves you alive? With all of Southeast Asia to play around in? It beggars belief, Eddie." He subsided. They were headed back toward shore. "I know why you came, Eddie. I keep tabs on you. You want me to send somebody to protect Aurelia, right? It's already taken care of. She has a couple of shadows watching her every move."

"Streisand and Sharif."

Gary smiled. "Is that what she calls them? Well, they're good. Not as good as Mr. Collier, but still very good."

"But they're not just there to watch her, are they? You're watching Aurelia because you're afraid to watch me." A moment as they pulled the boat out of the water. "You're afraid I'm a member of the Palace Council, and I might have a couple of watchers of my own."

"Something like that."

Eddie declined Gary's invitation to stay for lunch. In the driveway, they nevertheless shook hands.

"Were we ever friends?" Eddie asked.

"We'll always be friends, Eddie."

"Even if we don't trust each other?"

"That's not such a terrible thing in a friendship."

Eddie continued on to Washington, still searching, but searching alone.

PART VI

Washington/Ithaca/ Hanover

1973–1974

CHAPTER 63

A Poolside Chat

(1)

EDDIE WESLEY OPENED HIS EYES from a dream of peaceful eternal darkness to the reality of hard angry whiteness. Flashlights were shining through the windows of the sedan. Marine guards peered in. The sign on the gate read NAVAL SUPPORT FACILITY THURMONT. Eddie yawned and looked at his watch. Almost eleven at night. The gate shuddered aside. The car rolled past a watchtower and thick foliage and several low cottages, harshly illuminated for security's sake. Hickory and oak trees danced in the night wind. At the reception building, the driver opened Eddie's door. After the artificial warmth of the limousine, the chilly late-April air staggered him. At least now he was wide awake. A nervous flunky welcomed him to Camp David. The driver was nervous. The Secret Service people were nervous. Eddie began to grow nervous, too, even though he was not sure why. The flunky let him freshen up, then led him along a path over a small hill. The guards near the porch of Aspen Lodge did not interfere. The door was opened from within. A desk stood empty. The flunky knocked and opened the inner door, not waiting for an answer. "Mr. Wesley," he announced. Standing aside to let Eddie pass, he murmured, "It's been a terrible night. Try to cheer him up." But Eddie had already spotted the shaken, shrunken figure by the picture window, gazing out on the bucolic Maryland countryside as if for the last time. Eddie, unbidden, stood beside him, and looked, too. He had forgotten how mountainous Maryland was, once you escaped the swampy lowlands where, in its wisdom, the founding generation had decided to establish the capital of the new nation.

"You sent for me, sir?"

The President stood, still as a waxwork. And, indeed, his skin had taken on an oddly shiny pallor, like plastic. "They've resigned," Nixon finally blurted, not turning. "Haldeman and Ehrlichman."

And high time, thought Eddie. "Yes, Mr. President."

"You heard? It leaked?"

"Rumors on the news, sir."

"That's all they do on the news. Rumors."

And a few facts you wish were rumors. But Eddie did not say this aloud. "Yes, sir."

"Dean's gone, too." His soft hands clenched and unclenched. "And good riddance." But the flash of anger lasted only an instant. The President sagged. The room was large, and seemed, with the heavy drapes open to the night and the interior lights off, larger still. "It's all over, Eddie."

"I'm sorry, sir."

"We had such hopes. Such dreams. We were going to change everything."

To Eddie's horror, tears began rolling down the broken face. He tried to remember the ruthless Red-baiter of the forties and fifties, the architect of the "Southern strategy" that had so skillfully exploited white anger over school desegregation in putting together a Republican electoral coalition. He saw instead the shy, friendless man who had stood in the early-morning haze, trying to persuade astonished student protesters that he was, deep down, a good guy. But he was not. He had been right, Eddie realized, in that essay back in '62. Nixon was the essential American. What he valued more than honor, integrity, all the virtues Wesley Senior used to preach about, was finishing first.

Eddie said, "I'm sorry, sir. But, you know—"

"Never mind. Never mind. Let me tell you why you're here." He glanced around the room, focusing on the shadows. "I'm under pressure," he began, then stopped. "There are things," he said, and stopped again. "He's been to see me," the President said, finally, shaking his head as if it was common knowledge between them, this *he*. "Could get rough. Why I sent for you alone instead of Aurie. How's she doing?"

"Ah, great, sir. Just great."

"Hear the two of you are quite the couple."

"Maybe so, Mr. President. I don't know. She sends her regards."

Nixon nodded, stalking around the room. He had lost the thread. "We did Russia. We did China. We did arms limitation. We tried to get the energy thing under control. All right, fine. Mistakes were made. There were problems." Whether he was referring to the energy price controls or the Watergate coverup was unclear, but the passive voice was classic Nixon. Without warning, he grabbed Eddie's arm. "We were going to do so much for your people, Eddie. There wasn't time. You understand."

"You mentioned being under pressure—"

"Right. Right." He was back at the window. "Whatever our differences, I've always been able to count on you. I want you to know I'm grateful for that, Eddie. Grateful."

Eddie, breathtaken, said nothing.

"I prayed last night," Nixon confided. "Do you pray, Eddie?"

Again taken by surprise, Eddie groped for an inoffensive reply. "Ah, not often, sir."

"You should, Eddie. Do you know what I prayed?" He had released his grip and was wandering around in front of the picture window, framed by the mountain darkness. "I prayed that I wouldn't have to wake up this morning." He spread clumsy fingers against the glass, not turning from the vista. "Can't do business this way. I need to think about future Presidents. Or do you think I should resign, too?"

Eddie, not wanting to be a witness to this unraveling, tried to keep the conversation light. "Well, Mr. President, that depends on whether you want to go down in history as the man who gave us President Agnew."

A bark of laughter. "President Agnew. Sounds funny, doesn't it?" The humor faded. "Anyway, he has problems of his own. He can't be President."

"Then you might have to stay."

"But can I? That's the question. Can I still govern? He says I betrayed the voters' trust," said Nixon, roaming again. "I didn't. I was betrayed. I was a victim, Eddie. I had bad people around me. Bad advice." A sudden swivel like a dance move. "If I resign, it sets a precedent. Do you see that, Eddie? A man makes mistakes—small ones—they add up, but still—"

He stopped, and shrugged, and smiled shyly.

Eddie spoke carefully. "I'm sorry, Mr. President. I'm not sure who it is you're talking about. The man who wants you to resign."

"Need some air," said Nixon.

(I I)

THE PRESIDENT OPENED the back door. Behind the cottage was a wooden deck, and, nearby, a heated pool. A Secret Service agent stood nearby, and, at the tree line, a pair of Marines patrolled with a guard dog. Eddie followed Nixon out. "See all this? I hate this part. The security. Not one second of privacy. And, Eddie, let me tell you something. You can try to cover up. You can try to save your plan. Do whatever you want. Try to keep the secret. But there's always somebody out there who knows the truth. Buy off one, there's always another."

Outside the lodge, the President seemed to gain fluency. Eddie wondered if Nixon was worried about eavesdropping. Surely the United States of America possessed the technical means to prevent its own leader from being bugged against his will.

"Beautiful up here," Nixon said. He stood on the concrete deck near the kidney-shaped pool. Wisps of vapor gathered just above the heated surface. He put one flabby hand on the metal rail leading to the ladder, and, leaning over, pointed at the water. "They say it's not a bad way to go. Drowning. A moment of panic, then you get this kind of peace."

Eddie looked around at the Secret Service man, who stared

unblinking back at him. Could he hear the President's mad speculations from over there by the house?

"I suspect it's quite terrible," said Eddie, insinuating himself between the President and the pool, and remembering Hong Kong. Beside the lodge, newly blossoming flowers suffered silently in the cold.

"Can't be worse than dying on the battlefield." A pause. The eyes slid toward Eddie, then away. "I was in the big one. A lot of good people died, but I wasn't a hero. I was just there when the bombs were falling." He walked away from the pool, toward a path into the trees. A pair of agents fell in behind. Another agent materialized in front, as if leading the way. Up here in the mountains, the night was achingly cold, but the cauldron of boiling emotion that constituted Nixon, like the similar simmer deep inside Eddie, generated all the warmth he needed. The President leaned toward his guest until their heads almost touched. He dropped his voice. "Things I did long ago. Not fair. Trying to help. Your people, Eddie. Tried to help your people, and now—"

A shake of the heavy, dipping head. "Sent a message," said Nixon. "Your friend. I agreed to see him because—well, I had to agree. No choice. Can't negotiate with people like this. Can't buy them off. They don't seem to want anything. Most people have a price, but not when—" He broke off. His hearing was remarkable: around the bend came a pair of very quiet Marine sentries. They snapped off salutes, which the President, vaguely, returned.

"You're right," he resumed once the guards had drifted into the distance. "Have to stick it out. Can't let Agnew be President. Man's going to be indicted. Secret, but it's true. Listen. This is the presidency. Have to stick it out for the sake of the presidency. Can't quit. We were going to do great things, Eddie. Great things. Still can." Back to the beginning. They had reached a wooden bridge spanning a sluggish creek. Nixon leaned on the railing, pouchy eyes entranced by the dark water. Maybe he was wondering again how it would feel to drown.

"Mr. President," said Eddie, finally, "what was it you wanted?"

"Ever find your sister?"

"Junie? No."

Nixon shook his head. "Too bad. Too bad."

"Yes, sir, I—"

"Maybe if you'd found her I'd know—" He started again: "Thing is, Eddie, I never really thought anybody would—" Third try: "You do these things when you're young. Follies of youth. It was supposed to be a secret. But they never let you forget, do they?"

Eddie stared at the President of the United States. "The meeting in 1952. You were there." He had not believed it. Even sitting with Aurelia in Ithaca, the two of them speculating wildly, he had thought the possibility absurd. But now here was absurdity come to life, and staring him in the face. "You were at Burton Mount's house in 1952, and now somebody is using your presence to force you out of office."

Nixon said nothing. He seemed faded and old.

"That's why you wanted me up here tonight. To ask if I'd found Junie yet. To give you ammunition to fire back. And that's the reason you kept encouraging me and Aurelia to get together. She thinks it's because you're a romantic. But you were just hoping, if Aurie and I joined forces, we'd have an easier time tracking down my sister." Eddie felt himself physically backing away. "The answer is no. I don't know where she is. And even if I did—Mr. President, you can't think I would help you. Not with this. I'm sorry. It's not possible."

The President nodded. "I'm on a schedule now. Very practical. I need to interfere in the investigation five or six months from now, and make things worse and worse until I'm forced out next summer." Suddenly he straightened. The old Nixon, confident and sly. "Unless you find your sister before then."

"I'm sorry, sir, but I just told you—"

"Know what you have to say. Understand, believe me." A wink. "Well, you don't have to worry, Eddie. The microphones are only inside the lodge."

"Microphones? Are you saying—"

The President was clapping him on the shoulder and pumping his hand. "The best thing about landing in trouble," Nixon said, "is that you find out who your real friends are."

Five minutes later, Eddie was back in the anteroom.

"Good meeting?" asked the anxious aide who had escorted him in. "Did you cheer him up?"

But Eddie was lost in thought. Nixon, without meaning to, had given him the clue.

Follies of youth, the President had said. *It was supposed to be a secret.* Eddie was all but kicking himself for not seeing it before. *You find out who your real friends are.*

He knew where to find his sister.

CHAPTER 64

Argument in an Office

(1)

SUDDENLY THERE WAS LITTLE TIME. For that reason, Eddie decided to slow down. He had the Secret Service driver drop him back home, for the benefit of anybody who might have been watching. He wanted the world to know that he had done nothing after Camp David. No calls, no visitors, no panic. But the world had other plans, because as soon as he hung up his jacket he saw the envelope with his name on it, lying on the table in the hallway.

Eddie looked around. The house seemed undisturbed. The front door had not been forced. Nevertheless, he went to the kitchen for a large knife before checking the sliders to the yard. They, too, were locked. He made a quick search of the upstairs and saw nobody. Yet the envelope was, unquestionably, here. He opened it and found a photocopy of Philmont Castle's testament.

The testament stolen by George Collier.

He did not pause to wonder where it came from. He flipped through to the last couple of pages, noted the names of the attendees. A couple surprised him. Most were dead. There was no Hilliman, just as Gary had insisted, but among the few still living was, indeed, Richard Nixon.

I'm on a schedule now. Very practical.

Eddie took his own car. He tried to put Junie out of his mind. He dared not dream of approaching her; not until he was sure that everything was over, and nobody was looking any more. He had to concentrate on tonight. He drove to a 7-Eleven and used the pay phone before anybody had the chance to come in after him, then bought a cup of coffee and got back behind the wheel. Then he drove over to the Georgetown campus. He parked the car at his building, let himself in, and checked the door twice to make sure it was firmly locked behind him. In the duplicating room, he made two copies of the testament and sealed all three in envelopes. He put Gary's private post-office-box number on one envelope and mixed it with the outgoing mail, scribbling the name of a faculty colleague in the upper left-hand corner, just in case somebody dogging his steps thought of looking here. The second he addressed to his banker, with instructions to store it unopened in the vault until Eddie came in to move it to his safe-deposit box. This one, too, he marked as though it had been mailed by somebody else. The third one—the copy he had found on the table—he slipped into his jacket pocket. He refused to wonder who had left it there; besides, he thought he knew.

When he was done, he stepped into the hall, and that was where Benjamin Mellor crashed the butt of a gun into the back of his head.

Eddie went down fast, and Mellor hit him again, then rolled him over and sat on his stomach, the gun pointing at his face. He was still wearing the hippie attire, but the glasses were gone, and his eyes were wild and frightened.

"Where is it?" the professor demanded.

"Where is what?" said Eddie, bucking. "What are you doing? Get off of me!"

"Don't think I won't shoot you, Mr. Wesley. You have the testament. It's obvious, the way you're acting tonight. You have it, and I want it."

Eddie shook his head. "You're wrong," he said gently. "I don't have the testament. Now, please. Get off of me."

"Come on, Mr. Wesley. Nixon's presidency is going to pieces. You were at Camp David tonight. It has to be you. You're setting it up. Now, give me the testament, and I'll leave you alone. It'll guarantee my safety and—well, you know the rest."

"I don't have it," said Eddie again. He tried shoving Mellor off, but the skinny man had the strength of mortal desperation. Eddie's eyes darted, searching for a weapon. The fire extinguisher was too far away. There were letter openers in the office he had just left, but they might as well be a mile off.

"You're lying," Mellor snarled. He slammed Eddie's head into the floor. "It's not as much fun, being on the receiving side, is it?" He did it a second time, and, for a woozy instant, Eddie was back in the Hong Kong warehouse. "You're an arrogant prick. You were arrogant in Cambridge, you were arrogant in Saigon, and you're arrogant now. Did you believe you could outthink me? Are you really that stupid? Well, it's over now. Give me the testament, Mr. Wesley. I'm not going to ask again."

Eddie considered. One chance. "Okay," he said. He inclined his head. "It's over there. In my office."

Surprisingly agile, the professor leaped to his feet. He backed away. "Stand up, Mr. Wesley. Slowly. Keep clear of me."

"Don't you want the key?"

"You unlock the door."

Eddie did. He stepped inside, and Mellor had no choice but to follow, or risk being locked out. Eddie leaned over his desk. His captor waited. In the lower drawer was a coffee maker. Nearly prone on the desktop, Eddie reached in, grabbed it, then rolled over and swung it hard at the professor.

And struck only his shoulder.

Mellor reeled back, then straightened, the gun pointing at Eddie's midsection. Before Eddie could scramble off the desk, he heard two quick shots.

No pain.

Eddie stood up. He had not been hit, but the law professor was a bloody gurgling heap on the floor, and George Collier was standing in the doorway.

(11)

"WHAT—" said Eddie. "What—"

"I'll clean up the mess. You have work to do."

"I don't understand."

"You have the testament, don't you?" He pointed to Eddie's jacket pocket. "Well, do what you have to do, then. But do me a favor first." He pulled out the copies Eddie had left in the mail room. "Burn these."

"But why are you—"

The assassin waved him silent. "Not everything has a neat explanation, Mr. Wesley. Do you think because I do what I do I don't care about my country? Who winds up running things? If so, you're mistaken. But we don't have time for a debate. There's a dead man on the floor of your office. You don't know how to remove the traces of what happened here. I do. Now, let me do my job. You go away and do yours." He was behind the desk, pulling down the volume where Mellor's bullet had lodged. "Don't look at me that way, Mr. Wesley. Remember our conversation in Saigon, when you asked me about what happened to Mr. Mellor's lady friend. The job I do has its nasty days. It's as simple as that." But he seemed to be trying to persuade himself. "And, yes, I know, I told Mrs. Garland years ago that some people are not worth protecting, but you can't assume that just because they ask me—never mind. You have business elsewhere. I suggest that you get to it."

"We should call an ambulance," Eddie managed. "The police."

"You really need to get moving, Mr. Wesley."

In the hallway, legs still buttery from his near-miss, Eddie paused. "I don't know what you're up to, Collier. I do know you didn't shoot Mellor for my sake. I know I'm only alive because you're under orders. You would kill me without hesitation if you were ordered to. You and I are still enemies."

Kneeling beside the body, the assassin did not even look up. "And I wouldn't have it any other way, Mr. Wesley. So, for your sake, let us hope that our paths never cross again."

CHAPTER 65

A Surprise Visit

(1)

AND STILL THE ENDLESS NIGHT STRETCHED before him. Even without Collier's gibes, Eddie would have known where he had to go next. It did not seem possible that Benjamin Mellor had just been killed at the university, but as the campus receded, Eddie found the events of the past hour easier to accept. He was on a mission. The testament was in his pocket, courtesy of a paid assassin who had decided to start thinking for himself, and there was nowhere to go but forward. Eddie forced a calm upon himself. He had to be alert for the next phase.

He parked on a side street at the eastern edge of the bridge where M Street crosses Rock Creek Parkway. He would walk the rest of the way, giving himself time to think, and to spot a tail. At four in the morning, even Georgetown was silent, the delis shuttered, the neon signs in front of the bars dark. Unfriendly shadows paced him all the way to P Street. He supposed the house would be watched, at least on and off, as befitted the home of a man constructed of presidential timber, but Eddie was not about to be deterred. Sure enough, when he reached the corner, he spotted the security at once, a sedan across the street and a uniformed police officer in front of the door.

"May I help you, sir?"

"Friend of the family."

"Name?"

"Edward Wesley."

The cop consulted a clipboard, but Eddie's name obviously was not on it. Across the street, the passenger-side door of the sedan eased open. "It's four o'clock in the morning, Mr. Wellesley. A funny time for a friendly visit. Do you have an appointment?"

"Not exactly." He pointed to a lighted first-floor window. "But I believe you'll find that I'm expected."

The officer put his hands on his hips. "You might find this hard to believe, Mr. Westerly, but I don't actually buzz upstairs every time somebody claims to be a friend of the family. Now, what I think you should do is move along, and if you want to see the Frosts, give them a call."

The front door opened.

"It's all right, Officer Craig," said Margot Frost. "I don't think Mr. Wesley has murder on his mind." The green eyes sparkled mischief. "Not tonight, anyway."

(1 1)

THEY SAT in the kitchen, with a view into the garden where three years earlier Lanning Frost had asked him to find dirt on Nixon because Nixon was finding dirt on him. The same shameless collies, Darrin and Samantha, padded around the kitchen like an encircling army. The maid offered to make tea and sandwiches, but Margot sent her back to bed. For privacy, she said, once the maid had gone. Eddie matched her steely smile. Margot, no homemaker except to the voters, barely knew her way around the cabinets, so they scrounged. Eddie nibbled on an apple. Margot gorged herself on barbecue potato chips and lemonade—not what she ate on the campaign trail, she said, and not when her husband was in eyeshot, either. So don't tell anyone, she added, grinning, but Eddie could read the tension in her fleshy pink face. He supposed his own face must look worse. He remembered the empty eyes of Lieutenant Cox, when they met in Saigon after the battle: *We kept the hill.*

"Lanning is away raising money," Margot said. "You'll have to settle for me."

"You knew I was coming," said Eddie. "That's why you waited up." He hesitated, doing the arithmetic in his head, wondering how much she knew. "You have somebody at the White House."

"Lanning does."

"A spy."

She shook her head firmly. One of the dogs nuzzled her leg. "Somebody who cares about the future of this country, Eddie. Somebody who isn't prepared to let it go down the tubes because of the antics of a single paranoid—"

He held up his hand. "Please, Margot. Save it for the campaign trail."

She stood abruptly, startling the dogs, who had taken up resting positions at opposite ends of the room. She jerked open a few cabinet doors, found a bag of Toll House cookies, smiled. "I'm supposed to be on a diet, but you know what they say"—settling once more—"the road to Hell is paved with good intentions." To the dogs: "You won't tell, will you?" She crinkled open the bag and nibbled the edge of a cookie, savoring her own inability to resist, then plunged the entire thing into her mouth. "I'm sorry. Look at my manners. Want one?" Proffering the bag.

"You know why I'm here, Margot."

"I do?"

"If you didn't, you wouldn't have waited up or called extra security. I didn't tell anybody at Camp David that I was coming here tonight. Something else must have tipped you off. Or someone else. Who called the house, Margot? Who told you I was coming?"

"Nobody called. I'm always up late. I heard the officer talking, I looked out the window and saw you—"

Eddie rode right over her. He had had his fill of lies, and this one was about to become too elaborate. "And I'm willing to bet you have no idea who went to Camp David to blackmail Nixon, either, do you?"

"Blackmail Nixon? Eddie, what on earth—"

"Never mind. Margot, look. I've been thinking about what you said in Hong Kong."

A flush crept up her throat, and she dropped her eyes. "Eddie, you know, I was just so upset seeing you that way, I didn't know what I was saying, or doing. . . ."

Margot trailed off. Eddie waited until the silence became uncomfortable for her, watched as she began fidgeting in the chair. "Tell me about your mother."

"What about her? She was wonderful. Wonderful mother, wonderful wife." Smiling wistfully, but rushing the words. "First lady of the state when Dad was in the state house, and then the Senate, and—"

"And she was . . . black."

Margot put down a half-eaten cookie so fast one of the dogs leaped to its feet, ready to assist. Maybe they really were trained guard dogs after all. A final line of defense. "She was what?"

"Black. A Negro. Colored. A woman of the darker nation. An Afro-American. Take your choice." He leaned in closer. "Your mother was black. She was Sumner Mount, wasn't she? Perry's aunt. The one who passed into whiteness in the 1930s. Very light-skinned, but black. That's why your mother looked so swarthy. That's why you could never remember whether you told people she was part Greek or half Italian or some mixture from New Orleans, although I assume by now you have your lie straight. What your stories had in common was that they would all explain skin of a faint brown tinge, not quite olive but almost. She was a black woman who raised you as a white woman. Well, that's not a sin or a crime, and it happens all the time." He saw her face. "No. I don't care about it. I'm not planning to go public. I know it would ruin Lanning. I know we like to say it's 1973, America is above that kind of thing, but the truth is, there's very little America is above. So, yes, I suppose you hide it. I understand that. By the way, does Lanning know?"

"Of course he knows." Her face had gone ashen, and she looked closer to sixty than forty. "I have no secrets from my husband."

"Or only a few."

"Yes, Eddie. Only a few."

One of the dogs had padded from the room, like a sophisticate in search of less callow conversation. The other watched, over folded paws.

"So you and Perry Mount are—what?—second cousins?"

"First. My mom was his father, Burton's sister." She lifted the cookie, studied it, put it back down. "I know what you're thinking. I eat the way some women drink. In private. Because I'm unhappy. Because of stress. Because I'm lonely." A gruesomely forced laugh, like the last joke ever. "Well, you're wrong. I eat because Lanning doesn't like me eating. He wants me thinner, so I'm getting thicker. There. Now you know my deep, dark secret. Happy?"

"I'm not judging you, Margot."

"Then why are you looking at me that way?"

"Tell me about the Agony."

"I wouldn't call it agony, Eddie. I live with pain, but it isn't—"

He lifted a hand. She subsided at once, mystified. "I mean Agony with a capital 'A.' What the press calls the Jewel Agony."

Margot tilted her head to the side, and the half-smile reminded him of the night they met. "You mean your sister's group? What about them?"

"Come on, Margot. I know the truth."

"What truth? About the Agony?"

"The name comes from Book II of *Paradise Lost*." Eddie decided that Margot pulled off perplexity and bewilderment rather well, even when it was fake. "The guardianess of Hell is talking to Satan. She describes the plight of the lower realm as 'perpetual agony and pain.' " Margot kept staring blankly. He wanted to reach out and shake her. Instead, he pointed toward her neck. "Come on, Margot. Don't play games. I'm talking about the people whose cross you were wearing the night we met, and lied about the last time I was here."

Margot flushed and looked down. "I'm sorry about that, Eddie. About lying. But, really, I'm sorry I let you see the cross in the first place. Mom was furious. I was supposed to wear the cross that night, but I wasn't supposed to be off in the corner discussing it with you."

"You were *supposed* to?"

She nodded. "Mom told me to wear it to the party. There was

someone there who was supposed to see it, she said. That was all she would say."

Someone there. If not Gary Fatek, then who? Some other fellow traveler of the Council, no doubt. Someone he would never be able to identify, because Margot genuinely did not know. He was thinking about Nixon, and the follies of youth, and finding out who your real friends are. He was thinking about heirs, and his own blindness: Elliott Van Epp need not have chosen his daughter as successor.

"Oh, no. No."

"What? What are you upset for? I'm the one who should be upset, with you barging in here."

Eddie sat back, worried. "Because I guessed wrong. I thought it was you. It isn't you. It's him, isn't it? All this time, it's been Lanning."

"What are you talking about?"

"I thought you were the contact. I thought Lanning was your . . . well, I guess, your puppet. Yours and Perry's. But when you snuck off to see Perry, that was just because he was family. Nothing else. Just saying hello." Even now he could not quite get the last piece. "I thought the same thing as everybody else. That your husband was the dummy. The stuffed shirt. That the big plan was to hand Lanning the presidency, and run the country through you and your cousin."

"Lanning is no dummy," she began.

Eddie shushed her. "I know. I know. Everybody was wrong. Lanning is no dummy. That was an act. And it was just Perry all along. You had nothing to do with it, except that you introduced them. Or maybe your father did. Perry and Lanning. And Mr. Collier did the rest."

"What rest?" Panic in those remarkable eyes. "What are you talking about?"

"Your husband. That was your father's plan all along. To seduce your husband, then pave his road to the White House."

"Whose plan?"

"The Palace Council. Your Uncle Burton's idea. You've never

heard of the Council, have you? Not the Empyreals, either. There's no reason you would have. They're a—a Harlem social club. And you were raised as a white woman. No Harlem clubs for you."

"I still don't know what you mean."

"Unfortunately, I believe you."

"I am glad that you believe my wife," said Lanning Frost, from behind. "Especially because she is telling the truth."

CHAPTER 66

The Apparent Heir

(1)

HE STRODE into the room, tall and slim and presidential. His tie was loosened, and his manner easy, casually confident. Behind him was his foreign-policy adviser, Perry Mount. The Senator said, "I am sorry Mr. Wesley has disturbed you, my dear. Perhaps you should retire and let us talk."

"Are you saying you know what this is all about?" Margot asked, displaying little of her usual smooth self-assurance. "The plan? Smoothing the path? What's going on, Lanning?"

"You should retire, Margot."

"That's a good idea," said Perry, in that tone of softly wondering innocence.

"But—"

"Go," Lanning said sharply, and, gathering her robe, she went, sparing a final glance at Eddie, part despair, part supplication, and part warning.

The remaining dog followed.

Perry closed the door and stood in front of it, arms crossed. Lanning looked at the table, scooped up the cookies and potato chips, and tossed them into the trash. Opening the refrigerator to dump the lemonade, he spoke over his shoulder. "She knows better than to eat this junk. She has to lose weight. Her weight is unhealthy."

"She can't be more than ten pounds overweight. Eight."

The Senator had already moved to the next topic. "You should never have troubled my wife, Eddie. Why would you do that? You should have come to me in the first place. Then we could have thrashed all of this out."

"All of what?" Eddie asked, sitting very still, his eyes mostly on Perry, the former intelligence officer who had presided over his torture. Perry stared steadily back.

"You seem to be against me, Eddie. I don't understand why." Washing the dishes, reciting the words by rote. "I am trying to build a better America, an America worth loving again, an America free of the nightmares of poverty, of racial injustice, and of threats from abroad. Why does that bother you so?" Drying with the towel, putting plates and glasses into the proper cabinets. "I would think you would be with us, Eddie. For all these years, you've fought for a better America. You've tried to make us look at ourselves." He leaned against the sink, folding his arms across his chest much as Perry had done. "You see the nation's flaws as well as its possibilities. I see the same thing. You see the abuse of power as well as the chance to use it for good. I see the same thing. Why must you work against me, Eddie? What have I done to deserve this?" He turned the force of his charm on his visitor. "We're going to change the world, Eddie. That is what my campaign is going to be about. We will make America stronger and safer, but also fairer, more just. We will never be content to serve as mere stewards of our national inheritance. We will transform that inheritance into something greater. Why will you not help us?"

Another glance at the stoical Perry. "Because you're a monster, Senator. A monster who's sold your soul to the devil."

The Senator whistled. "The devil. That's pretty low, Eddie."

"But it's true. You and the Palace Council—"

"Eddie, please. No more wild conspiracy theories. No more paranoia. I do not for one moment believe that your love of country is so great that you would go to all of this trouble just to save America from a President whose friends you dislike. Come on. Nixon has broken half the laws on the books, yet you and Nixon are friends. Why not you and Frost?"

"Because Nixon never betrayed my sister."

A knife-edged silence and, from Perry behind him, a greater still-
ness, like tension before a battle. The Senator narrowed his brilliant
eyes, and the decisive chin lifted a millimeter and jutted. "Didn't
what?"

"Junie. My sister. You betrayed her, Senator. Not the Empyreals.
Not the Palace Council. You personally. You seduced her, you set her
on her course, you sent her underground, and when it suited your
purposes, you had her kicked out and left to rot."

(11)

FROM THE DOOR, Perry Mount laughed in disbelief. The Senator
moved away from the sink and sat across the table. His smile was
amiable. "How does that theory run exactly?"

"The dirt you were afraid Nixon would find. I thought it was the
Palace Council you were hiding, but I was wrong. Oh, I grant you
wouldn't want that to come out, the deal you made, whatever it was,
through Perry and, I suppose, Margot's mother. But that wasn't the
big secret, was it? It all started in the fifties. You had a girlfriend,
Lanning. A girlfriend who was . . . black. That was what the Soviets
were buying from Phil Castle. Not nuclear-weapons secrets. They
collected the same secrets Hoover did. Secrets they could use later
on, for blackmail. You killed Castle to try to get the toothpaste back
in the tube, but you couldn't find the material, could you?"

"I was not even in Congress—"

"But you were headed there, weren't you? Margot's father had
cleared the way. He was at the meeting in 1952. He knew the Council wanted to elect a President within two decades." Over his shoulder: "Shaking the throne, right, Perry? His own chance had passed,
and so he arranged for an heir. And he knew just where to bring pressure, didn't he?" Eddie's laugh was mirthless. "Funny how the
Bureau's public position was always that Colonel Abel never came up
with any valuable intelligence. So how come when he went home the
Russians treated him like a hero? Could it be that they gave him

those medals because he had gathered enough dirt on potential future Presidents of the United States? Including Lanning Frost?"

Silence in the kitchen. But there was no point in stopping now.

"The summer before her third year of law school, Junie worked a few weeks as Benjamin Mellor's research assistant, but the rest of that summer she was an intern at your law firm in Chicago, wasn't she? That was where you met, unless you knew each other before. You were married, but you had an affair. It continued in Cambridge. Then, one day, she told you she was pregnant, didn't she? She refused to have an abortion, so you invented this elaborate fiction of an affair with Professor Mellor. You, or maybe Senator Van Epp. Junie went along. She even told me that Mellor was the father. But he wasn't. That was the significance of the note Castle left. *Not as in a tragic age.* It's a literary reference. Never mind what it refers to. Let's just say it makes clear that Benjamin Mellor wasn't the father of Junie's baby."

Eddie paused, expecting a crack in the Senator's granite mien, but Lanning only stroked his rugged chin. Perry was motionless. "Well, let's take a minute and figure this out," said the Senator. "Suppose I had a girlfriend. All right, it happens. I am not confirming it, but suppose. There is no earthly reason to think it was your sister, Eddie. Even if she worked at my law firm in the summer of 1956, I fear I would have been off raising money for my congressional race."

"You ran in 1958, not 1956."

"And if you think it's possible to make all the contacts, raise all the money, in just one year, you're a rather naïve radical, Eddie. Now, consider the rest. Suppose I indeed possessed the magical ability of persuasion—to say nothing of the utter lack of conscience— necessary to set up a substitute boyfriend, as you suggest. Why on earth would your sister have gone along?"

"For you, you bastard. She did it for you. She loved you, Senator. Remember that word? Love? She loved you, and would have carried your secret with her to the grave. But you don't understand love, or believe in it." Eddie hesitated, feeling accusation pointing the other way. The words were all at once a struggle. "But you couldn't take the chance." Strong again. "First you sent her away. Then, when you found out what she was doing, you got in touch. She stayed underground, she ran Agony your way—"

"Agony, you may recall, tried to kill me."

"That was a lovely moment, wasn't it? Cementing your position with the moderate voters because a violent revolutionary group targeted you. Funny how they missed, though. They killed Kevin and missed you. Those years were rough on the insiders of Burton Mount's plan, weren't they? Castle and Belt and Hamilton Mellor in the fifties. Matty Garland and Kevin Garland in the sixties." He turned toward the door. "Friends of yours, Perry. That's who was being slaughtered. Friends of yours. All to turn the game around. You thought your father was in charge of the Council. So did your father. But it was Elliott Van Epp all along, Perry. And his tame killer, Mr. Collier, now works for Senator Frost. The people who thought they were running Lanning Frost—well, one by one, they're going. They got your friend Ben Mellor tonight, Perry. Did you know that? Right in front of me. You might be the last one, Perry. Watch out. You could be next."

Silence in the kitchen. Eddie felt his hold on the story weakening. He was missing something. He could read it in the Senator's confident gaze. "Tell me, Senator, was the second child yours, too? Did you maybe resume your affair with my sister while she was running around and blowing things up?" Silence. He turned to the man at the door. "You loved my sister once, Perry. Are you going to let him get away with this?" Back to Lanning. "So—what happens now? Does Perry shoot me in the back?"

Lanning's smile was political and confident. "Oh, I think such melodrama will hardly prove necessary, Eddie. Your story, I admit, possesses the virtues of imagination and verve that one finds in the best of your fiction. Its only vice is that it doesn't happen to be possible." He leaned forward, tapping extended fingertips against each other in his excitement. "Think about it, Eddie. It's all very clever. I killed off some of my father's best friends, arranged to blow up poor Kevin Garland while making it look like they were after me—all of that. But it still rests on a single premise. The premise is that Junie and I had an affair. All right. Let's think it through. Suppose that your sister had been my girlfriend. Suppose she was carrying my baby. When exactly did the Soviets think to acquire this information? Your sister vanished in the summer of 1957. Wasn't Colonel Abel already under arrest by that time? Besides, Castle died in 1955. If Junie had the baby in July of 1957, her pregnancy began, when? Late in 1956? When am I supposed to have impregnated her? And how could an envelope left behind by Phil Castle possibly have contained that information?"

(1 1 1)

EDDIE COVERED HIS MOUTH. He had missed the obvious, and Lanning, in a trice, had found it. Eddie had been patient. For a decade and a half he had collected facts, building and building until he could finally present his thesis. And Lanning Frost, with the simplest and most basic of criticisms, had knocked over the entire structure.

"I'm sorry to have to disappoint you, Eddie. I know what your sister meant to you. Still means to you. If you're right, and the unfortunate Professor Mellor was not the father of your sister's child, then the father is still out there somewhere." The Senator grew reflective. "And the baby, too. Let's see, born in July of 1957, your niece would be going on sixteen now. Maybe you should put your indisputable energy and talent into finding her, Eddie. Maybe she needs you."

Eddie said, "I never told you the baby was a girl."

"No? I'm sure you mentioned it."

"I've never mentioned it to a soul, Senator, and certainly not to you. And I'm quite sure Junie wouldn't have told a stranger, either." He felt dizzy, confused, the way we do when we stand on the precipice poised between everything we always wanted and everything we always feared. "Junie told me. But who would have told you? I don't think anybody in the world knows, Senator. Nobody but me, and Junie . . . and the baby's father."

"So we're back to that." The smile faded.

"Yes, Senator. We're back to that."

"You still believe it? Despite your little embarrassment over the dates?"

"I can't see how it was done, but, yes, Senator, I believe it. And I believe I'm ready to use it to ruin you."

"Well, fine, Eddie. America is the home of free speech. Say what you like, to whomever you like. I won't stop you. Wild stories like this—well, you've been spreading all sorts of craziness this past decade. Call the *Washington Post.* Call CBS News. Call whom you like. Tell them the story. It's salacious, it's exciting, it's tabloid fodder. They'll consider the source and ignore it. As they should. Democratic politics are destroyed by such personal attacks. Nixon made it an art form, which is the main reason he has to go."

"I hear you're getting death threats."

"Every politician gets them."

"From Junie?"

The Senator shrugged, but his eyes shifted ever so slightly. "We'll deal with them."

"Why would Junie threaten to kill you unless she blames you?"

"I don't know, Eddie. Why do radical misfits do anything? To get attention? To deny their inadequacies? I have no idea."

Eddie burned. "We don't have to wait for Junie, Senator. I could just kill you for what you've done to my sister."

This seemed at least to capture the Senator's interest. "I suppose you could make the attempt, yes. And, lying dead after your failure, you would ensure my election." That smile again. "Especially once it turned out that you were a former suitor of poor Margot's." His wiggling fingers described quotation marks in the air. "NOVELIST WESLEY SHOT TRYING TO ASSASSINATE FROST—CRAZED WRITER LOVED SENATOR'S WIFE, SOURCES SAY. Yes. I like that scenario very much. So, Eddie, please. Go ahead and try." He laughed. "Oh, and we'd also have to be sure to tell them you were a friend of Nixon's. That would put me over the top if nothing else would."

"I might succeed."

The smile vanished. "Yes, Eddie, you might. You might succeed in killing me. You might succeed in persuading the country that a group of successful black men from Harlem has been secretly running the world. And the pogrom that would follow would then be on your head. Think of what the nation would do to your people, after a Negro assassinated the next President, and more Negroes turned out to be conspiring to do worse." He was on his feet. "And there is a larger problem, Eddie, isn't there? The larger problem is that you aren't sure you're right. And you would not want to do murder, take the life of another human being and bring all of that hellfire down on your people's heads besides, without being absolutely certain." He leaned over the table. "Let it go, Eddie. There is no point in fighting. Some things are inevitable."

"I don't believe that. People should know the truth."

Lanning shook his head. "No, Eddie. Not your version of the truth. The nation will never abide your truth, Eddie. And, in any case, your people would not survive it." He glanced at his watch. "The hour is late, Eddie. I would still rather have you as an ally than an enemy, but, in any case, I'm afraid our meeting is at an end."

"You won't get away with this."

"You're welcome to try to prevent it. But do consider the consequences." The grin turned cold and wicked. The Senator moved toward the door. His aide stepped aside. "Perry, see our guest out. Eddie, a pleasure as always. I'll say your goodbyes to Margot."

(I V)

IN THE FOYER, Eddie turned to his silent escort.

"What about you, Perry? You loved Junie once. Are you going to let him get away with this?"

"With what?" He was holding the door open. The street was empty. The sun had risen during the argument with Lanning. Now it was Sunday morning, bright and clear and cold and quiet. "The nation is going to move, or we are going to move it. Nothing takes precedence, Eddie. Nothing."

"Perry, come on. He ruined Junie's life. She committed terrible crimes—"

"Of her own volition."

Eddie ignored this. "And then he left her to rot. Searching for those children. One of them his. Maybe both."

Perry stroked his goatee. "You would sacrifice the whole darker nation for the sake of your sister, wouldn't you?"

Eddie decided not to take a swing at him, because it would never land. "I don't believe that to be the actual choice I'm facing."

"If it were, however, you wouldn't hesitate, would you?" When Eddie did not answer at once, Perry grew animated. "You've read *Paradise Lost*, Eddie. A hundred times by now, I'll bet. Remember how it ends?"

A tight nod. "Adam and Eve march off into the world."

"That's right, Eddie. They look back, and Paradise has been closed to them, defended with gates and armies and flames. They walk into the world because they have no choice. They listened to the serpent—the Tempter, the Paramount, the Author, Milton uses all of these—they listened, and the gates closed behind them. Because they must." He pointed into the house. "You think *this* is the whole of the Project? You think Lanning Frost in the White House is the answer to my father's dreams? Because, if that's what you think, you're wrong. The Project is larger, and separate. And it cannot be stopped."

"But this election—"

"Lanning Frost is an opportunity, no more. Random chance. My Aunt Sumner decided to move to the Midwest and pass into white-ness. Margot's father fell in love with her. Lanning fell in love with Margot. We didn't plan any of that, Eddie. How could we? But we would be dimwits indeed to take no advantage of it. My father began the negotiations with Elliott Van Epp. He didn't foresee all of this, but, still, the plan is essentially his. If Lanning wins, the community moves a centimeter closer to justice. And, yes, I will be there next door to the Oval Office to make sure that he does what is necessary on the matters most important to our people. If, on the other hand,

Lanning loses, the community will be no worse off. Because the Project endures." His eyes bright, gazing into the triumphant future. "The hour for stopping us is past, Eddie. Our victory is coming. Believe me. We are going to shake the throne. If not this decade, then next. You could have been a part of it. You are a worthy adversary, Eddie."

"Decades," said Eddie. "That's why you need the heirs."

"We are patient men."

"Don't touch Locke. Don't you dare touch him. He will never be a part of your Project. Never. If you try to recruit him, I'll kill you."

Perry seemed amused. "Boys grow into men, Eddie. Men make up their own minds. But that's a question for some other time." His eyes glittered. Malice. Triumph. "What matters, Eddie, is that now, at last, the Project is back on track. Lanning as President makes our path easier, but we can do it without him."

Eddie said, "I don't care about the Project. It's Lanning I want to stop."

"So stop him," said Perry. "This question of your sister is between you and Lanning Frost. We have no position in the matter."

"But—"

"We are not amoral, Eddie, nor are we entire fools. We did not kill Philmont Castle. We did not kill Belt or either of the Garlands." His eyes were bright, and confident, and insane. "What matters to us is the Project. Not Lanning Frost. Not the presidential election of 1976. Only the Project. If you can come up with a way to bring down Lanning Frost without harming the Project, we will not interfere." A wry grimace. "I cannot of course speak for the Senator himself."

"What about the consequences Lanning predicted?"

Perry Mount, leader of the Palace Council, tilted his handsome head to the side. "We could not permit those consequences to come about, Eddie."

"Spell it out."

"What you do with Lanning Frost's secrets is up to you. What you do with ours, on the other hand . . ."

"Why did you do it?"

"Do what?"

"Switch the envelopes. Make sure I got the clues about Lanning and Junie instead of whatever it was Belt swiped from Los Alamos. You got Leona to make a switch. Or that pastor. The Russians weren't buying secrets about presidential contenders. That entire scenario was for my benefit. How would they know whose secrets to buy, so many years in advance of an election? No. They wanted nuclear secrets from Los Alamos, and Joseph Belt supplied them, just like Hoover said. Somebody in Charleston tossed the photos the Russians wanted and replaced them with the letters and the note from Phil Castle. Then, later, somebody else added the note about D. H. Lawrence. But only after you were sure I would be coming to get the envelope. The first note—'His wife has it'—that was from Castle, wasn't it? He wrote it for Langston Hughes, so in case anything happened, he'd know where the testament was. The Council intercepted the note but couldn't solve it, so you left it for me. And the note about the tragic age—that was your handwriting, wasn't it, Perry? Your insurance policy."

A smile might have flickered over the tired face. It lasted no more than half a second, and, later, Eddie could not have said for sure. But it looked that way. "I really don't know what you're talking about. I was in graduate school."

"You wanted me to know. You wanted the information out there, just in case Lanning got out of control."

"You give us too much credit, Eddie. Or too much blame."

"It's been you all along. Spreading the breadcrumbs for me to follow. Even when you tortured me in Hong Kong. You weren't trying to make me quit. You were hoping I'd be so angry I'd keep looking. I hadn't found any confirmation in Vietnam, so you did what you did to me to give me confirmation."

Perry might have been stone.

"That's why you're giving me permission, isn't it? You *did* miscalculate. Frost *is* out of control. You *do* want me to stop him." He covered his mouth briefly. "You don't want Lanning to be President, do you? You believed the clippings in the paper about how he was a dope. Everybody did. Only he turns out to be smarter than you thought he was. More independent. More—" He saw it. "You're scared of him. He's a killer. He hired Collier to find the testament, and now he has the whole list. Everyone who was at your father's meeting. And you can't touch him, can you? All those wonderful reasons he gave me in the kitchen, reasons why I dare not kill him or even try to bring him down—he was talking to *you*, wasn't he? Reminding *you* who's really in charge!"

"Speculation," Perry snapped.

"Maybe. But why else would you waste all this time with me, instead of ordering me into the street?" Eddie laughed. "Okay, maybe I have it wrong. Maybe George Collier doesn't even work for Frost. But if he does, the Palace Council is in terrible trouble, isn't it? The monster turns on its maker? Or maybe you're living the scene at the end of *Paradise Lost* when God transforms Satan into a serpent permanently, and all he can do is crawl around on his belly and hiss. That's you, isn't it? You're crawling and hissing and hoping I'll do your dirty work for you. Oh, Perry!"

When the retired intelligence officer kept his face professionally blank, Eddie turned and stalked out into the morning cold. He swung back around, meaning to tell Perry that he was nobody's pawn, but the door was already closed. It was nearing six. Across P Street, Sunday gawkers had already begun to gather, along with a lone protester, whose sign proclaimed that the right to burn the flag would be the last to go.

(v)

EDDIE WALKED ALONG P STREET to Twenty-seventh, then down to Dumbarton. There was a church there, of stout red brick, First Baptist of Georgetown, founded by a former slave in 1862, and still thriving, even though the surrounding community from which it had once drawn its congregation had turned white, and uninterested. Eddie was just in time for morning services. Peeking around on the off chance somebody he knew might notice, he slipped inside, sat in the back, and waited. After a moment, Aurelia joined him.

"What happened?"

"I failed."

"Failed?" Grabbing his arm. "Failed how?"

He sat back, closing his eyes. "Nixon is out, but I didn't have anything to do with it. He'll resign within the year. I'm sorry, Aurie."

"And—and Lanning?"

Eddie was a long moment answering. "Lanning Frost is going to be the next President of the United States."

CHAPTER 67

A Promise

(1)

A YEAR AND A HALF LATER, Eddie and Aurelia sat on the sofa in the back room of his house on Albemarle Street, watching the disapproving countenance of America's most famous newsman reporting President Gerald Ford's pardon of his predecessor, Richard Milhous Nixon.

"Poor Dick," said Aurelia, who had never forgotten his kindnesses.

Her head was on Eddie's shoulder. He was playing with her hair, worn lately in a large Afro after the style of Angela Davis. Eddie kissed her forehead. "He wasn't a good President."

"He didn't deserve what happened to him."

Eddie considered Nixon's two secret selves, both betraying his love of conspiracy: the paranoid worries that, together, led to the series of misdeeds known collectively as Watergate; and his presence at the meeting at Burton Mount's house when plans were laid for the creation of Perpetual Agony. Perhaps Nixon had joined the Project for Elliott Van Epp's reasons, persuaded that the existence on American soil of violent revolutionaries would help slow or even reverse the pace of social change. Whatever Nixon's motives, Eddie knew what Wesley Senior would have said: Richard Nixon had sown discord, and, predictably, reaped the whirlwind.

"He did deserve it," Eddie said, marveling at what a spellbinder Burton Mount must have been, to win liberal support for his mad Project by talk of racial justice, and conservative support by talk of turning the nation back to its traditions.

Aurelia bit him on the neck. "Worse men than Dick have retired with honor." She considered. "And gotten away with a lot more."

Eddie decided not to pursue it. He kissed her again, then hopped to his feet. Aurelia, lounging in a robe, watched him taking a couple of books from the shelf, reaching behind them. She sipped her wine. She knew what was coming. She was sitting in her robe. Her legs had been curled beneath her, but now she put her feet on the floor, firming her will for the obligatory scene. It was late August. Aurelia's second novel, another romance, was selling briskly. Locke was on the Vineyard with Claire and Oliver and their children. Tomorrow Aurie would drive to New York City to pick up Zora, who was interning for the summer at the *Times*. The next day she would pick up Locke on the Cape. A week later, Zora, who had skipped a grade, would return to Radcliffe for her sophomore year, and Locke would begin his junior year of high school. But first there was the obligatory scene with Eddie.

On the television, Lanning Frost was talking about restoring America's greatness. The Senator had grown remarkably articulate over the past two years, but nobody seemed to notice.

Eddie switched off the set.

"We might be facing eight years of him. No need to start now."

"Second the motion," Aurie answered, but weakly.

She sat very straight, watching the man she loved pull the neatly wrapped box from its hiding place. He had not offered her a ring in almost a year. It was time for him to ask her, time for her to refuse even though she could not tell him why, time for him to grow first hurt, then angry, time for them to exchange words that could not be withdrawn, time for them to spend a chilly night in separate beds before she left at first light.

Aurelia steeled herself as he settled beside her, box in hand. He did not extend his arm.

"Eddie," she began.

He kissed her gently, to shush her, then kissed her again.

Aurelia turned her head away. "I'm sorry," she said.

But Eddie was smiling. The box had not budged. "I'm going to give you this," he said, "in December."

"December?"

"Right after Christmas. It'll give you something to look forward to."

"Please, Eddie. Don't do this."

He kissed her again, taking his time. "Remember what Granny Vee told you about how patience is a virtue because your future lies ahead of you? Well, she was right. We can be patient, Aurie, because in December you'll say yes. Right after Christmas."

"No, Eddie. I won't."

"You'll be going to Mona's, right? Like you always do?"

"Probably," she said, feeling soft and vulnerable, irritated at the ease with which he could make her feel this way.

"I'll meet you there."

"Why?"

"Because I know why you won't marry me."

(11)

FOR FOUR MONTHS, Aurelia wondered. She taught her classes, she tried not to hover over her son, she made notes for a new novel. But at night, as she lay alone in bed in the house on Fall Creek Drive, sleep eluded her. Aurelia had never been a night owl, but now she conducted clandestine conversations with Mona in the wee hours. Eddie doesn't know anything, Mona assured her over and over. He's bluffing. He's just trying to rattle you. But Mona sounded rattled herself. "You're the one who dragged me into this," said Mona one windswept October night. "I'm not sorry, sweetie—I'm glad—but you're in a funny position to come to me with second thoughts."

After that, Aurelia called less often.

That fall, she saw Eddie twice.

The first time was in late September, when they served together on a panel at Duke on the future of Afro-American fiction. Everybody knew of their relationship, of course, and their hosts had offered to let them share a hotel suite, but they took separate rooms.

At the panel, the two famous authors disagreed heatedly on whether the writers of the darker nation should simply tell stories, as Aurelia thought, or use their work to push an ideological agenda, as Eddie insisted. The astonished audience wondered what had happened to everybody's favorite literary couple. That night, their lovemaking was so fierce it was almost combative, and afterward, Aurelia asked Eddie what he was fighting against.

"The past," said Eddie, dressing to return to his own room. "The present."

"Not the future?"

He shook his head. "Our future is going to be wonderful."

"Eddie—"

"I promise. After Christmas, your last excuse will disappear."

The second time she saw Eddie was in late October. She had just finished her graduate seminar, and was crossing the Quad in the company of a student. The woman was white and flaxen and dedicated to the literature of the darker nation, which had been virulently suppressed, as she put it, by the white male literary establishment, which saw black people as simply a lower form of woman, or perhaps the other way around—Aurie could never get it straight. The student gesticulated wildly, raving about how the poetry of Eloise Bibb had never been sufficiently appreciated. As they passed the brooding statue of Andrew Dickson White, the university's co-founder, there was Eddie, lazing on the crumbling stone bench with its optimistic inscription: ABOVE ALL NATIONS IS HUMANITY.

"The poetry of Eloise Bibb," Eddie said—to the graduate student, not to Aurelia—"is unappreciated because it is entirely derivative." He smiled at the young woman's confusion. "You should select another topic for your dissertation."

In her office in Goldwin Smith Hall, Aurelia fought to keep from laughing. She glared as hard as she could. "You've never heard of Eloise Bibb in your life."

"True."

"Bibb was a genius. Especially for her time, writing in the South."

"If you say so."

"You know Nancy recognized you. Poor thing. The great Edward Trotter Wesley just told her to pick another subject. Now she'll have to start over."

"You're the great Aurelia Treene Garland. You can set her straight."

Aurelia sat down. Another part of her was still angry from North Carolina. "What do you want, Eddie? What are you doing here?" She shoved papers around on her desk, frantic to keep her hands busy, lest they hug him by mistake. "I thought you were going to Zaire for the fight. Aren't you doing an essay for *Rolling Stone* or something?"

"For *Saturday Review*. I'm leaving tomorrow. I wanted to say goodbye."

"Foreman is going to destroy him." She did not know why she could no longer have a real conversation with the man she had loved all these years. "Ali could be injured, Eddie. Seriously injured."

"Aurelia—"

"I can't stand the thought of him going out this way."

"Will you stop for a minute and listen?"

"All right. What is it?"

Unbidden, Eddie moved a stack of student papers and sat in a rickety chair. "I wanted to tell you, before I left. I've done the cleanup work. It's over."

"The cleanup work?"

"I went to the Vineyard. The librarian was very helpful. She pulled the newspapers from the summer of 1952. The Council was smarter than we thought. They hid the meeting in plain sight."

"How? It wasn't a fund-raiser for Dick. Oliver told me. You remember. I don't think he would lie."

Eddie smiled briefly. "I think Oliver was having a little fun with you. True, it wasn't a fund-raiser for Nixon. It was a fund-raiser for Elliott Van Epp. Nobody on the Island would pay the slightest attention to a Republican Senator raising money from his rich buddies."

"But Nixon—"

"He isn't mentioned in the stories, Aurie. Not until a couple of weeks later. It seems he was an unannounced guest. In more ways than one, I'm betting. I'm sure Matty brought him, to impress Burton." Serious again. "Not counting Nixon only two of the men mentioned in the testament are still alive. I've visited both. They won't talk. They're afraid. They're old, and they're afraid."

Aurelia was playing with a gold pencil. "Maybe they should talk. Maybe we shouldn't sweep it under the rug." Then she saw his point. "You and I know what happened at that meeting, too. Should we be afraid?"

"There's nobody left to be afraid of."

"Yes, there is. The same person they're afraid of. Lanning Frost." She remembered Eddie's empty face when they met at the church. "You said he can't hurt us—"

"He can't."

"How do you know?"

"I'll tell you in December."

"Eddie—"

"After you say yes."

Aurelia rubbed her forehead. She felt a migraine coming on. "Please stop, Eddie. I'm not saying yes. Not now, not in December, not ever. I can't."

His smile was weatherproof. "Well, kiss me goodbye anyway." She did. But only for a while.

(111)

THE FOLLOWING NIGHT, at a dinner party in the suburb of Cayuga Heights, she found herself seated beside Tristan Hadley, now happily divorced, who still on odd occasions came sniffing around her. Tris dominated the table, as he always did, and tonight he wanted to talk about Lanning Frost, whom he planned to support for President next time around. Aurelia suffered in silence until somebody pointed to her, reminding the table that her late husband had worked for the Senator.

"Kevin just raised a little money for him," she muttered, hardly lifting her eyes.

After dinner, Tris Hadley walked Aurie to her car.

"That was clever of you," he said.

"What was?"

"Pretending that your husband was less than he really was."

Aurelia, who had been keeping half a step ahead of him on the leaf-strewn street, the better to avoid his hand on her elbow, stopped and swung around. His self-important blue eyes had a hungry flicker. Steady, she told herself. Calm down. Tris is just having his fun. You've seen the names of the men who were at Burton Mount's meeting, and none was a Hadley.

"Kevin was a Republican all his life," she said. "As far as I know, Lanning was the only Democrat he ever supported."

"What your husband did for him was a little bit beyond the call of duty."

Again Aurelia swayed on her feet. But no. No. Surely he only meant what everybody else believed, that loyal Kevin had thrown his body in front of Lanning's.

"He wasn't a hero," she said. "He was just there."

"All I'm saying is, I see why you're anti-Frost."

"I'm not."

"Sure you are. It's in your eyes. Your voice. You can't stand him. It's because you blame him, isn't it? For Kevin."

"What?"

"I understand, Aurie. Believe me. I'm here if you ever need to talk."

Aurelia should have wept. Or slapped his arrogant face. Instead, she laughed. To their mutual surprise. Threw her head back and howled at the magnitude of Tristan's error.

"You're a silly man," she said, more warmly than either of them would have expected. At least he had made her feel attractive, at the very moment when she had begun to wonder. "Sometimes you can even be sweet." She got up on her toes and kissed his cheek. "But, please, Tristan, dear, try to get it through your swelled head that I am never, ever going to bed with you."

She slipped into her car, leaving him on the sidewalk. Heading back to Fall Creek Drive, Aurelia wondered what Eddie thought he knew, and how he intended to make her marry him. She remembered the night back in college when Mona had taken too many pills. Aurelia had dragged her unwilling friend to the hospital, bearing her bleary invective. A week later, fully recovered, Mona had promised Aurie that when the day came, she would do as big a favor in return. A few years ago, Aurie had finally asked. Mona had come through. Hugely. Secretly. Aurelia shivered. If Eddie had somehow uncovered the secret—

But it was impossible.

She hoped.

(I V)

EDDIE WAS AWAY for two months. After Zaire, where Muhammad Ali unexpectedly knocked out the formidable George Foreman in "The Rumble in the Jungle," Eddie returned to Kampala to lecture at Makerere University, but by this time the college once known as the Harvard of Africa had fallen under the sway of President Idi Amin, who had exiled many prominent members of the faculty, and Eddie left after just two weeks. Depressed, he wandered. He spent a few days in London, a few more in Paris, and a week visiting friends near Toulouse, where he was thinking he might buy a cottage. At each stop, American intelligence took a look, because he was still on their watch lists. His sister, the dangerous radical, had never been found. Although her organization had died, and the search for her officially stood down, there remained the hope that she might turn up. And Eddie, who knew exactly what was going on, had his fun leading the watchers into the dankest alleys in the chilliest hours of the wettest nights, only to return to his bed without having spoken to a soul.

Nobody guessed that Eddie was following the itinerary of Aurelia's honeymoon with Kevin Garland nineteen years ago; and not even Eddie could have said just why. He supposed he must have hated Kevin back then, and a part of him had nearly hated Aurelia for marrying him. But Aurie had stayed with her husband for ten years, and Eddie refused to believe she had been after the Garland money. No. Aurelia had come to love her husband. She had, unknowing, even changed him. She had turned Kevin Garland from a supporter to a skeptic of the Council's mad plan, and he had been blown to bits for his doubts. So much horror, for the sake of success. Wesley Senior had been righter than he knew twenty years ago, when he had written his son that the upside-down cross might be a symbol of devil worship.

Eddie's only bad moment came one night in a bar in Marseilles, where he was buying drinks for suspicious Corsican sailors, soaking up color for a scene he was considering for his next novel. He was struggling to memorize a wonderful story one of the men was telling in several languages at once, when he thought he saw, off in a shadowy corner, a lighter flicking rhythmically on and off before a hard white face topped with blond hair, but when he looked again the man was gone. Later, awake in his hotel room, longing for Aurelia, he told himself that George Collier had no reason to follow him. The man in the bar had been somebody else, and only Eddie's nerves made him imagine the killer's face. Collier had handed back the testament, shot Benjamin Mellor, and pronounced his own part in the proceedings done with. Yet, if he had lied—

The questions and doubts chased Eddie into sleep.

CHAPTER 68

The Opposite of Truth

(1)

ON THE SNOWY SECOND MORNING after Christmas, Eddie arrived at Mona Veazie's house on North Balch Street in Hanover, New Hampshire. He had gifts from Africa for all four children: colorful kente wraps from Bonwire for Julia and Zora, a Masai warrior's headdress for Locke, and an Umkhonto spear for Julia's brother, Jay, who, to his mother's chagrin, was keen on joining the military.

For the two grown women he brought nothing.

The seven of them lunched in town, Eddie's treat. He kept looking at Mona's children. So did poor Locke, whose crush on Julia was palpable, and hopeless. Julia, already a flirt at fourteen, played to him shamelessly, but Eddie knew neither mother would ever allow a relationship to develop.

Too risky.

After lunch, the children went off in Mona's four-wheel-drive to ice skate on Occom Pond. Eddie announced that he and Aurelia were going for a drive. Mona looked grim but only nodded. She had known this day was coming. They all had. Three minutes after leaving the house, the occasional lovers crossed the Connecticut River on the stone bridge connecting Hanover to Norwich, Vermont.

"Where are we going, honey?" Aurelia asked several times, but Eddie never answered.

The house lay just north of Main Street, on the western edge of the village green, a small, neat, whitewashed clapboard that could be lifted from any New England town and dropped into any other with nobody the wiser. They sat in the driveway for a moment. The mailbox said G. CULLEN.

"What are we doing here?" said Aurelia. "Whose house is this?"

"It belongs to a woman named Gwen. Gwen Cullen. She teaches art at the local elementary school." Eddie glanced at his beloved, who was staring wide-eyed at the house and nibbling on a fingernail. He had never seen her so nervous, not even when they faced Collier's gun at Jumel Mansion. "She's a friend of Mona's."

"A friend?"

Eddie nodded. "Mona's been wanting me to meet her. I assumed she was trying to set me up."

"Set you up? You mean, with a girlfriend?"

"That's what I thought. But now I'm pretty sure it was guilt." He opened his door. When Aurelia followed suit, he put a hand on her arm. "Wait here."

"Why?"

"I think you know why," he said, and got out of the car.

The walk from the driveway to the front steps was probably fifteen feet, but it was the longest of his life. Through the window he saw a neat living room, all chintz and fluff. A chubby black cat watched incuriously from the sill. It took him a year to lift his hand to the doorbell and the rest of his life to push. The sound was a melodious twinkle. When nothing stirred, he rang a second time.

Still the house was silent. But somebody was home. He had spotted a car in the garage, and a shadow at an upstairs window. He would wait. Standing on the step, hands on hips, he glanced across at Aurie, who was nibbling harder on her nail. His breath gathered and danced and vanished in the crystalline air. He wondered if—

The chain rattled, and Eddie spun in place.

The pale woman who opened the door had put on a lot of weight since Eddie had seen her last, but last was almost two decades ago.

"Hello, sis," he said.

(11)

THEY SAT in the chintzy living room surrounded by abstract water-colors, pale pastels in soft New England shades, many pierced unsubtly with bolts of bright red. They had not hugged. They had barely spoken. Junie had selected an overstuffed armchair, and waved Eddie to the sofa. The cat was in her lap, and she was letting it paw at a bright-blue ball that she would then snatch out of its reach.

"Her name is Mira," said Junie.

"Hello, Mira," said Eddie, less sure of his purpose than when he first rang the bell. Maybe the Beretta his sister had been holding against her hip was the reason. The gun lay now on the side table.

"It's short for Miranda."

"I figured."

Another long moment, Eddie watching his sister tease the cat. She had done a lot of teasing these past seventeen years, leaving notes for poor Benjamin Mellor and for her mother, but never once contacting her brother. The room was thick with books. The shelves were packed, and volumes were heaped on the tables, most of them fiction. Eddie spotted none of his, but both of Aurie's. There were no newspapers. There was no television. This was Junie's world: novels, the cat, her own artwork, and days spent teaching small children. She had constructed a shelter of the imagination, protection not only from the past but from the present.

And she had a gun in the house. At least one.

"What are you doing here, Eddie?" she finally said, not looking up. "What do you want?"

For a moment he was wordstruck. Wasn't it obvious? "You're my sister. I wanted to find you."

"Did it ever occur to you that I might not want to be found?" Before he could answer, she made a sound of disgust, somewhere between a snicker and a spit, what their mother used to call snup-ping. "I told them it was a stupid idea. I told them we wouldn't fool anybody."

"By them, you mean Mona and Aurelia." When Junie said nothing, he added, "And you've fooled everybody for a long time. I don't think anybody else knows."

"Except whoever's following you."

"Nobody's following me, Junie. That's all over."

"My name is Gwen." She had given the ball to the cat, who had leaped from her lap and was chasing it around the throw rug. "And I stopped believing in the Easter Bunny a long time ago."

"You have to tell me." He did not budge from the sofa but struggled to cross the space between them. "It's been almost twenty years, Junie. I know most of the story. I need the rest. No matter how terrible it is, I need the rest." He considered telling her how he had almost died looking for her, but decided he would evoke no sympathy: his sister had surely been through worse.

"Terrible. Right." She laughed without humor. Her hair was twisted into a long ponytail. From the table beside her chair, she took a pair of glasses. She did not put them on but toyed with the stems. "You don't know what terrible is, bro. You don't know what it's like to huddle in a safe house waiting for the battering ram that announces the arrival of the pigs, and then have the house blow up the next day, while you're out buying milk. To crawl across borders with your chin in the mud because you're on your government's classified shot-while-attempting-to-escape list. To know that one of your own bullets—" She stopped, bit her lip, eyes following the cat as it tumbled around the carpet. "Terrible. Right. It was terrible."

"Junie—"

"I knew you'd figure it out. I just didn't know it would take you so long." Her tortured gaze came up. "Or did Aurelia peach?"

"No. She kept your secrets."

"I told her to marry you. She said she couldn't marry you, not with this on her conscience."

"She was keeping me at a distance. For your sake. If she married me, how could she keep me from finding out?"

Junie made the snupping sound again. "That wasn't it. Aurelia's great at keeping secrets. She fooled you in Harlem, talking about her parents and her childhood. She might have fooled you about me for the rest of your life. She was just afraid, if you ever did find out, you'd be furious at her for not telling you. That's why she wouldn't marry you. She was afraid you'd hate her. Do you hate her?"

"No, Junie. I love her."

"Gwen." She tilted her head. "She's in the car?"

"But she didn't drive over. I did."

Junie nodded. "Mona called. You must have known she would."

"I thought she might."

"She warned me to get moving, but I spent ten years on the run. I'm not running any more." She tapped the gun. "And I'm not letting them lock me up. I've done prison already."

This surprised him. "When did you do prison?"

"One of the countries where we hid for a while had this idea that we— Never mind. It doesn't matter." Suddenly she smiled, bright and gay, Junie of the fifties. "Eddie. Look at you. The writer you always wanted to be. Famous around the world. Friend of Presidents and Prime Ministers. Are you happy now? Having everything?"

"I don't have everything—"

"No kids. No wife. That's because you're a silly romantic. Remember the Junie Angle? Disaster versus Godsend?"

"I remember."

"Well, your life is a Godsend. You decided to pine over Aurelia. That was a silly choice, but it was your own choice. You could have married anybody." Her face closed down again. "My life is a God-send, too. I want you to understand that. Not disaster. Godsend. I was in a mess, and God led me out. I have a job I like, I'm near my children"—almost, but not quite, a sob—"and I'm enjoying it. I'm their silly old Aunt Gwen. I get to watch them grow up, I paint my pictures so I don't go out of my mind, and I wait for the pigs. Eddie, what are you doing here? Please, go away."

"Junie—"

"I know what you want to ask. Was I Commander M? Yes. Was the first baby Lanning's? Yes. Yes. Whose was the second? Not your business. Who suggested this idea? Your girlfriend. We hit it off, Eddie. Back when I was pregnant the first time. We used to talk on the phone at night a lot. Then I graduated, and, well, after that, we kind of fell out of touch. When I wanted to come out, I got in touch with Aurie. Arranged a meeting. I wanted to see my kids. I didn't want to go to jail. There were things to arrange. Documents. A place to live. A job. It took almost a year, Eddie. By that time, Aurie had talked to Mona, Mona had agreed—okay? Happy now?"

"Why didn't you get in touch with me?"

"Because everyone in the world was watching you. They probably still are. Plus, you would've disapproved of what I've been doing. You don't know what it's like, bro, to face your disapproval. When your jaw juts out and your lip curls? It's worse than That Voice ever was. No wonder Torie Elden couldn't stand you." She softened. The cat was back in her lap. "It wasn't a lack of trust, Eddie. And it wasn't a lack of love. But it wasn't a good idea. It still isn't. I'll probably be arrested tomorrow." Her nervous eyes cut toward the window once more, then down at the gun. "Maybe tonight."

"You won't."

"You don't know that."

"I do."

Another long moment, the siblings finding uncomfortably little to say to each other. Three women, he reflected. Three brilliant, beautiful women who should have been the champions of the darker nation, all sacrificing, and suffering. Aurie never marrying again. Mona raising Julia and Jay as her own, calling them twins to put everybody off the scent, marrying a succession of white men she did not love so that everyone would think her obsession explained the interracial kids. And Junie herself, alone with the cat, the art her only therapy. All those watercolors, New England peace pierced by jagged red arrows of pain.

Eddie said, "There's a part you're not telling me."

"There's a whole lot I'm not telling you. There's a whole lot I'm never gonna tell you."

"I mean, about your babies."

"What about them?" Defensively, almost snarling. Even the cat noticed.

"Your daughter. Julia. She was born in 1957."

"So?"

"So, you're still protecting Aurelia, aren't you? No wonder my private detectives couldn't find any trace of the baby at the agencies around Boston. Little Julia was in the Midwest, wasn't she? Maybe even being raised by the same nuns who raised Aurie." He was talking half to himself now. "Then you went underground. You got pregnant again—maybe you were still seeing Lanning, maybe it was somebody else—and it was two years later. That's when you got in touch with Aurelia again. Not when you wanted to come out. You wanted to make sure the kids were taken care of. You had the baby—Jay—and somehow you got him to Aurelia. Maybe Perry helped. I know you won't tell me. But you got Jay to Aurelia, Aurelia got him to Mona, and then they went to the orphanage in Cleveland to get Julia, so they could be raised together. Mona told everybody in Harlem they were twins, and then she went straight to New Hampshire so nobody could see that Julia was bigger than Jay. She stayed away for years, and by the time she came back to visit, she could just explain that Julia was taller because girls mature faster than boys. Mona must have known the truth, but—"

"Are you done?"

"Done?"

"Done proving how smart you are. I know you're smart. That's the other reason I never wanted you involved. There's such a thing as being too smart, Eddie. Too curious. Sometimes you have to leave things as they are."

"Yes, but—"

"I'm not going to talk about this any more, and I don't want to listen to you talking about it, either."

Eddie nodded. He said, gently, "I'm just glad you're all right."

"Thanks."

"And you are, aren't you? All right?"

"Sure." But the eyes were haunted again. "I'm fine."

"Do you need anything? Can I help you somehow?"

The snupping sound again. "I earn my own money."

"That's not what I meant," he said, although it was. He realized that he was talking to a stranger, that the little girl who used to crawl into his bed and whisper her dreams was gone forever. The special connection between the two of them had died long ago, everywhere but in Eddie's own rosy memories.

"If you want to help," she said, oddly belligerent, "you can use some of your connections to get Sharon Martindale out of prison."

"My connections don't run that high any more."

"Or you think she deserves to stay in." He said nothing. Probably Junie was right. "She's no worse than me, Eddie. The sooner you get that through your head, the sooner you'll see why you shouldn't have come."

Before he could answer, the telephone rang in another room.

(I I I)

WHEN JUNIE CAME BACK, she did not sit. She had changed into a thicker sweater, as if talking to her brother had chilled instead of warming her. Her arms were crossed, and her eyes were lost. "It's time for you to go," she said.

"Junie—"

"Gwen."

"Gwen. Who was on the phone?"

"The FBI. The CIA. My boyfriend. My girlfriend. What difference does it make?" She pointed to the front window. "Aurie is out there worrying. Probably freezing, too. You should go."

"We could invite her in—"

"No."

Eddie clenched his fists, fighting the frustration. He did not know what he had expected, but he had not expected this. "Junie— Gwen—look. I'll come back. As often as you'll let me. Every week, every month, whatever suits your—"

"No."

"No, what?"

"No, you can't come back."

"Sure I can. It's not that far, and—"

Junie lifted her palm and covered his mouth, the way she used to.

A ghostly smile danced across her lips. "That's not what I mean, bro. Sorry. This time I'm the one who has to be selfish, not you." Her hand fell to her lap. The fingers trembled. "I'm sorry, Eddie. I am. But I can't let you get close to me. If you come up here once, well, fine, you're visiting Mona. You come twice, and all your friends—the Bureau, the Agency, Lanning, everybody—they'll wonder why. A third time, and everybody will come sniffing around. My cover's good, but not great. What keeps it intact is, nobody has any reason to look behind it, and, well, nobody has the resources to investigate every woman of my age in the country. The easiest plan is to follow you until you lead them to me."

Junie crossed the room, tugged the curtain aside, peeked. She did not turn back toward the room. Her shoulders shook, and Eddie supposed she was crying, but he knew better than to offer comfort. It occurred to him, far too late, that among the many reasons his sister had kept her distance all these years was the undeniable fact that he had indeed once served as an informant for the FBI, in the capture of Rudolf Abel. Junie herself had arranged it.

"I'm where I am, Eddie," she resumed after a moment. "I've made my peace. I can't have my old life back. So I have this one. I do my art, I teach my students, and, every now and then, I see my kids." She let the curtain fall. "The alternative is to go to Algeria or some-place, or else to go to prison. They've got indictments waiting for me everywhere."

"But you didn't do anything," Eddie protested, a bit stupidly. "You were just—the whole thing—it was imaginary."

"Agony did a lot of things," said Junie.

"You didn't do them personally."

"I was the commander, brother of mine, and that makes me liable." A harsh laugh. "And, besides. You have no idea what I did." She swung around and, for a moment, the gray eyes went flinty. "No idea," she repeated.

Eddie could not meet her gaze. It implied too much that he would rather not envision. He wondered whether she ever confided in anyone, but knew at once that she did not. These despairing arguments with herself were all Junie had. Life alone is a terrible thing.

"Okay," he said.

"You should go." This brought his head up. Junie's cheeks puffed out with the effort of holding in whatever she was really feeling.

"I just got here," said Eddie, his limbs in any case too leaden for him to rise.

"You still should go."

"I have a question."

She shook her head. Her voice was steel. Commander M. "No, brother of mine. No questions. I'm not going to tell you where I've been or how I got here or who else helped me. I'm not going to tell you the names of my six best lovers or my six worst enemies." She read something in his face. "What do you want me to do, bro? Go to the newspapers? Call my congressman? I'd be dead before anybody answered the phone."

Eddie saw this quite clearly. "What I want to know is—Junie, look. I've read the memo. Castle's testament. I know about the meeting at Burton Mount's house. I know who was present. I know why they picked you to lead Agony. They were looking for somebody who would see to it that no real harm was done. You were a pacifist, Junie. Wouldn't hurt a fly. That's why they picked you."

"I'm not going to discuss it," she repeated, and turned stubbornly away.

"I'm not asking about the history, sis. How you got involved in Agony, any of that. I just have one question, and it isn't about the past. It's about now, Junie. I want to know if you're still a pacifist."

"It's late, brother of mine."

Still Eddie could not budge. "Those threats against the Senator. Those are genuine. Those are from you." Junie said nothing. She was playing with the cat again, tickling its nape. "You're just keeping him off balance, right? You don't actually intend to do anything about it." The cat was occupying all of her attention now. She caressed it with both hands, calling the creature sweetheart and baby and snookums, and the cat mewled and stretched with pleasure. Eddie tried again. "You don't want him to forget what he owes you. What he did to you. That's his punishment, right? Not being allowed to forget?"

"He ruined my life," said Junie, mostly to the cat. "Yes, mmmm, yes, he did, the bad man ruined Mommy's life, didn't he, sweetheart?" She shook the cat's cheeks. "He ruined my life. Look at me, bro. He ruined my life, and he deserves to suffer."

"Yes. He does. To suffer. That's all." He quoted Wesley Senior, who had measured his daughter's crimes not according to the Bible but according to Gandhi: "An eye for an eye makes the whole world blind."

"Uh-huh."

"Uh-huh, meaning you agree?"

Junie stood up, the cat now on her shoulder. "You better go," she said, and her smile was like an unforgettable but hopelessly distant summer. "Before the bad guys start wondering where you are."

Their hug was brief, and felt like mourning.

(I V)

WHEN EDDIE CLIMBED BACK into the car, face stony, Aurelia started to speak, to apologize, to explain. Eddie covered her mouth with his hand. He kissed her. Then he leaned across her and opened the glove compartment. Inside was the jeweler's box. He handed it to her.

"No more secrets," he said. "That's the only rule."

Aurelia looked at him. Feeling queasy, she opened the box and took out the ring. It was old and heavy, and she guessed it must be an heirloom. Perhaps it had belonged to his late mother. She looked at him again, pondering. Time for the fine old truth. Mira the cat watched from the window. Gwen was nowhere to be seen.

"This time I'm not changing my name," Aurie said.

The Retirement Party

(1)

ON THE SECOND SATURDAY in March of 1975, Edward Trotter Wesley Junior married Aurelia Treene Garland in a private ceremony at the bride's home on Fall Creek Drive in Ithaca, New York. The groom was attended by Gary Fatek, the bride by Mona Veazie. There were few other guests. Marcella represented the groom's family. Nobody represented the bride's, but her son and daughter jointly escorted her down the aisle. The afternoon was unexpectedly warm, so the small reception was moved out onto the lawn. Gary led off the toasts, just as he had at Aurie's first wedding twenty years ago. Mona watched him closely. Of course, there were still people in the well-to-do corners of the darker nation who believed that the Hilliman heir was the father of Mona's children, but the rumors would die with the generation that had spawned them. Black America was so spread now. The trickle of the middle class out of their segregated neighborhoods had become a flood, and the younger generation would spend less energy than their parents on what Langston Hughes used to call colored *sassiety*.

Eddie watched Gary, too. He now understood his old friend's furtiveness. He had been caught between the proverbial rock and hard place. Gary must have been the other link, the person who had helped Junie escape, and whom she had refused to name. That was why Aurie had been so upset at the thought that he might have betrayed them. It would have taken money and connections to set up Junie's emergence from underground. Gary had both, and, back then, would have done anything for Mona.

Including allow those rumors to spread, the lie so juicy that nobody would imagine a different truth.

By five, the weather had cooled a bit, and the guests had departed. Zora left early, for the drive back to Cambridge. Locke, on spring break from school, left with Mona and her children for a week in New Hampshire. The honeymoon would be in the Caribbean. Eddie had already packed his wife's station wagon for the quick jaunt to Tompkins County Airport. Waiting downstairs for her to decide she was presentable, he walked from room to room. The house was so big, but this was where Aurelia wanted to live. She loved Cornell, and she loved Ithaca. She had blossomed here, and did not want to risk unblossoming. Eddie was a man of the city, but he supposed he could write anywhere. Besides, Washington held no further attraction for him. He was through with politics.

For a moment the pain rose, the realization that he could never see Junie again. But he wrestled it down, as he had every day for the past couple of months, and he supposed he might have to wrestle it down every day for the next thirty years.

Never mind. Junie was past. It was as simple as that. Junie was past, and Aurie was future. He had to live in the future.

He stood at the bottom of the sweeping staircase. "Are you almost ready?" he called.

"One minute, honey."

"You said that half an hour ago."

"Get used to it, buster."

He checked his watch. "We'll miss the plane."

"There's another one at nine-thirty."

"We'll miss our connection. We'll have to spend the night in New York."

"Then leave me alone and let me dress."

Eddie smiled. He took an apple from the fruit bowl on the dining-room table, then settled onto the bench seat in the foyer with a copy of Toni Morrison's latest novel.

The doorbell rang. Eddie put the book down, supposing that a late gift was being delivered.

He was wrong.

George Collier stood on the front step.

"Let's walk," the killer said.

(11)

"WE HAVE A PROBLEM, Mr. Wesley."

"We do?"

Collier nodded. He was wearing a windbreaker and jeans. The jacket was zipped but loose and bulky. Eddie wondered what it concealed. "I've decided to retire from my current line of work. Time to turn it over to the youngsters."

They had reached the suspension bridge. Collier stood aside, indicating with a sweep of the hand that Eddie should precede him. As they traded places, Collier glanced up at the house. Eddie had no need to do the same. He had told Aurelia only that he would be right back. He knew she would be watching from the window.

"The trouble is," Collier resumed, "that a man who does what I do doesn't generally leave witnesses around. People who can get him into trouble."

"I can see how that would be a problem," said Eddie, hoping the blond man's attention might slacken for a moment, giving Eddie a ghost of a chance to shove him over the fence, down the two-hundred-foot drop into the gorge.

"You could get me into serious trouble, Mr. Wesley." He pointed over his shoulder. "So could your wife. If she has any sense, she's hunting for her gun right now."

"She has a lot of sense."

"No doubt. However, I have her gun." He patted one of the many bulges in the jacket.

"I see," said Eddie, waiting. They were standing in the middle of the bridge, leaning on the rail, the surface rocking slowly in the wind.

"You're thinking I'm here to kill you."

"The notion crossed my mind."

"That would be silly of me, killing you in Ithaca. If I wanted you dead, Mr. Wesley, I'd wait for you and your lovely wife on Eleuthera. Honeymooners drown all the time." Collier patted Eddie's shoulder. "No. I'm here to offer you a deal."

"What kind of deal?"

"I told you the people I was working for insisted that I keep you alive. Now I guess I know why. They didn't dare harm a hair on your head, did they? Because she would do something about it. Expose their secrets. Their connection to Agony."

Eddie rounded on him then, furious and fearful. "You—you didn't—"

"But I did, Mr. Wesley. It's your own fault. You left plenty of clues. I've been to Norwich. Don't give me that look. You sister remains"—he seemed to search for the word—"undisturbed." A pause. "For the moment."

"What do you want, Collier?"

"A simple exchange. You leave me alone, I leave you alone."

"And Junic?"

"You mean Gwen. I leave her alone. I'm going into retirement, like I said. I have a farm, and I'm staying there. I'm even getting married. Oh, and, by the way, congratulations." That yellow grin. "You do see the point, don't you, Mr. Wesley? If the FBI drops in on me one day, if one of my former clients sends a hit squad after me, well, I'll know who sent them. I can find you. I can find your wife. I can find your sister. Follow me?"

"Yes."

"Good. Then I wish you a pleasant honeymoon." The killer stuck out his hand. Eddie did not shake. Collier shrugged. "You're probably right. We're not friends. We're not anything, really." He adjusted his jacket. "Well, all right. We won't meet again, Mr. Wesley. One last job, and then I'm through."

Eddie's eyes narrowed. "One last job?"

Collier nodded. "You don't want to know."

"True. I don't."

But he was remembering what Collier had said to him after killing Benjamin Mellor: *Do you think because I'm a hired gun I don't care about my country?* And his words to Aurelia, at Lanning Frost's apartment years ago: *There certainly exist people, Mrs. Garland, who are not worth protecting.*

"If and when it happens—" Collier began, and stopped.

Eddie took his cue. "I won't say a word."

"That is correct, Mr. Wesley. You won't. Because you know what happens if you do." He straightened up. He said, without turning, "It's all right, Mrs. Wesley. You can put down the knife."

"My last name," said Aurelia, "is Treene." But she lowered her hand.

"All the way down, please."

At a nod from her husband, she let the knife clatter to the concrete surface. Never looking back, Collier gave the knife a kick. It bounced, then spun, then slid beneath the fence, tumbling toward the creek below. Eddie watched it glisten bravely, then vanish suddenly, like the hopes of youth.

"Do we have a deal?" said Collier.

"Yes," said Eddie, arms now around his wife.

"Yes," said Aurelia.

"Good."

Eddie met the killer's pale eyes. America was so violent a country. Assassinations had become almost commonplace. People expected them. The television networks loved them, because everybody tuned in. Horror and disaster were the nation's most popular spectator sports. Perhaps that was the true American Angle. People watched, and cried, and hugged the familiar ever closer. Wesley Senior would have called it holding tight to that which is good. Eddie found himself drawing his wife into his protective embrace. Lanning Frost, to whom next year's election had been all but conceded, was a terrible man who had done terrible things. His march to the Oval Office was fueled by violence. Yet he, too, had a family that loved him. More than that, there was a way to stop such men. Indictments. Impeachments. Trials. The country, in an agony of righteousness, had turned one President out of office, without resorting to murder. Might there not be energy to do it a second time?

Maybe. Maybe not.

"What you're planning," said Aurelia suddenly, "is wrong." So she had been thinking along the same lines.

Once more the killer bared his teeth. "*Wrong*. I like the sound of that word. Short and to the point. I wonder what it means." He shrugged. "Tell you what, Mrs. Wesley. The day America looks up the definition, and cares? I will, too."

He turned and, for the last time, left them.

AUTHOR'S NOTE

THIS NOVEL, although spanning twenty years, is about the sixties. I mark the sixties as two decades, not one, the era beginning with the Supreme Court's decision in *Brown v. Board of Education* in 1954, and ending with President Richard Nixon's resignation in 1974. *Brown*, like the Cold War and the Apollo Program, was a product of the nation's buoyant postwar optimism. Nixon's fall from power reflected the nation's newfound pessimism. The Vietnam War formed the bridge between the two. Like so many wars, Vietnam began in idealism and certainty, but ended in cynicism and doubt. Vietnam was probably the greatest foreign-policy calamity in American history, and we have not recovered from its domestic effects. The end of the war in 1975 marked the beginning of the end of rule by the World War II generation, and the dawn of modern America—the mean-spirited America of me-first, trust-nobody, sound bites, revile-anyone-who-disagrees, and devil-take-the-hindmost. All of this misbehavior is a mark of our timidity, not our confidence. Americans across the political spectrum cannot bear dissent, because we lack the courage to meet it squarely.

And yet, within that collapse of American self-belief, individual stories of triumph are possible. I have tried to manufacture one here, without slighting the truth. In particular, I have worked hard not to exaggerate the violence of the sixties. With the exception of the crimes that I specifically attribute to Agony, all the attacks that I describe actually took place; and I have listed only a fraction. In our rosy memories of the era we might readily forget how much terror really occurred, with true believers on the left and right sharing responsibility.

I have not, however, been entirely true to the record. The opening chapters of this novel rest on a slight anachronism. The Harlem society in which Eddie Wesley moves was more characteristic of the 1940s than the 1950s, and of the 1950s than the 1960s. By the time Eddie Wesley began to come to prominence as a writer, the trickle of middle-class families out of Sugar Hill and into midtown Manhattan and the suburbs had become a flood. Some matrons tried to maintain the whirl of the grand salons, but by the early 1960s, even most of the artists and writers had moved out, although Langston Hughes himself stayed on in Harlem until his death. Indeed, even the world of the forties and fifties was less intellectually fierce than had been the salons of the Harlem Renaissance, notably that of the millionaire A'Lelia Walker, the only child of Madame C. J. Walker. A'Lelia's was surely the greatest of the salons, and one can date the end of the Harlem Renaissance from her death in the summer of 1931. After that, the tradition continued, albeit soon concerned less with the intellect and more with social position. And, as I say, by the sixties, it was practically over. But I needed that strange and wonderful and terrifying social world to last a little longer in order to create a plausible spread of ages for the novel's protagonists, and so I chose to fiddle a bit with history. My only excuse, other than the needs of the narrative, is that I have tried to reorder the decades in a way that does honor to my subject, for, whatever the weaknesses and contradictions of Harlem society in the middle years of the twentieth century, it possessed the singular virtue of so many efforts at solidarity: They tried. At least they tried.

I have shoved around a number of specific historical events to fit the needs of the narrative. For example, the security hearing for Robert Oppenheimer occurred in April and May of 1954, not March and April of 1955, but I needed it to fall around the time of Aurelia's wedding to Kevin Garland. Future Director of Central Intelligence William Colby began his second tour of duty in Vietnam in 1968—not in 1967, as in my story—but that would have been too late for Eddie to meet him. The program that became known as PHOENIX did not get that name until after Eddie's departure from Vietnam. The Soviet agent who masqueraded as Emil Goldfus has gone down in history as Rudolf Abel, but that was not his real name either. I moved the FBI's arrest of Goldfus to May of 1957 because Eddie had other things to do in June, when the arrest actually took place.

Allen Dulles's efforts to persuade President Kennedy to recommend an American version of the Official Secrets Act came in the spring of 1961, not the winter of 1962. Virginia Slims cigarettes were not introduced until 1968, but I could not envision Aurelia smoking any other brand. Similarly, the Subaru was not sold in the United States until two years after little Mindy drives one, but the car just seemed so right for her. Aurelia's theory about dwarf birches is wrong.

Eddie could not have worked in the office of speechwriting at the White House during the Kennedy Administration, because the office did not exist until the Nixon Administration. But it seemed an appropriate job for him, so I cheated. Langston Hughes's effort to deny William Faulkner the Gold Medal for Literature occurred in the early 1960s, not the late 1950s. Lloyd Garrison's offices did not move to Park Avenue until the 1960s. At the time Eddie met him in the 1950s, he would have been closer to Wall Street. But I wanted to avoid too great a profusion of Wall Street lawyers. The references to Foucault in chapter 21 are moderately anachronistic, but they were utterly irresistible. At the time of Eddie Wesley's meeting with Agent Stilwell in 1969, the federal women's penitentiary in Tallahassee had not yet been constructed. I moved the seizure of the administration building at Harvard ahead a few days to make it coincide with Aurelia's visit to the White House the morning after Eisenhower's funeral. I moved President Ford's pardon of his predecessor forward by a few weeks. I made certain minor alterations in the geography of Ithaca, New York, and its environs (including Cornell University) to smooth Aurelia's life a bit. The alert reader will no doubt discover additional examples where the story diverges from sober history. I hope that most of those you might spot represent my decisions, not my mistakes.

On the other hand, many historical instances that might seem to the reader to be my inventions actually occurred. For example, the story of the Lumbee Indians and their shootout with the Klan at

Maxton is true. The summer 1959 meeting at the Kennedy compound on Cape Cod, intended to persuade various movers and shakers that the young Senator could win, actually took place. Richard Nixon really did negotiate with Martin Luther King, and try to persuade the Republican Party to pass a voting-rights act in the late 1950s as a way to break up the New Deal Coalition. But Eisenhower would not go along. In addition, Nixon really did sneak out of the White House in May of 1970 to talk to the antiwar protesters, and, afterward, went to the Capitol to reminisce in the House chamber and, subsequently, stopped at the Mayflower for breakfast. And although, for dramatic reasons, I have moved the events from daylight to nighttime, Nixon, by most accounts, really did cry after Haldeman and Ehrlichman resigned, and really did stroll by the swimming pool in a mood that made aides fear he might try to take his own life.

The basic theme of Eddie Wesley's short story "Evening Prayer" is drawn from a favorite tale of the great raconteur, great lawyer, and great human being Thurgood Marshall. Adam Clayton Powell's advice about carrying the heavy end of the log was actually delivered toward the end of his colorful life. I had hoped to find space for the fascinating Powell in this novel; but that story will have to wait. A handful of lines in the novel, as well as the characters of Irene and Patrick Martindale, are intended as an homage to the great John le Carré. Those who admire his work as much as I do will understand why.

The Harlem apartment building where Eddie Wesley lived, at 435 Convent Avenue, was once among the most prestigious addresses in all of Harlem, rivaling the fabled 409 Edgecombe Avenue (home, in my story, to Mr. and Mrs. Kevin Garland). Among the many well-known residents of 435 Convent Avenue was Adam Clayton Powell, Sr., one branch of whose family remained there across generations.

Readers of my novel *The Emperor of Ocean Park* may notice certain minor alterations in the structure of the Garland family. But I did not know the Garlands as well then as I do now. Similarly, the lives of Mona Veazie and her children are not precisely as Julia recalls them years later in my novel *New England White*. But time plays tricks on us all.

Many people have made contributions to this novel, particularly by sharing their memories of the Harlem of the 1950s. I would like to single out in particular the reminiscences of my father, Lisle Carter, and of Mrs. Constance Wright. I was greatly assisted by the staff of the Morris-Jumel Mansion on Jumel Terrace in Harlem, a splendid museum I highly recommend. The many alterations I have made in the interior geography of the mansion are my sole responsibility. (By the way, the staff denies that the house is haunted.) I relied for my research on sources too numerous to mention. I hope that I have correctly absorbed their teaching. My marvelous editor, Phyllis Grann, and my outstanding literary agent, Lynn Nesbit, once more managed to rein in my flights of fancy without interfering with the integrity of the work.

Finally, I would like to thank my children, Leah and Andrew, who continue to inspire me, even as I slowly grow accustomed to the fact that they are no longer upstairs slumbering as I write; and my wife of twenty-six years, Enola Aird, my first and best reader, my partner and cheerleader, and, truly, God's gift in my life.

Cheshire, Connecticut
December 2007

ALSO BY STEPHEN L. CARTER

THE EMPEROR OF OCEAN PARK

In his triumphant fiction debut, Stephen L. Carter combines a riveting novel of suspense with the saga of a unique family. *The Emperor of Ocean Park* is set in two privileged worlds: the upper-crust African American society of the Eastern seaboard and the inner circle of an Ivy League law school. Talcott Garland is a successful law professor, devoted father, and husband of a beautiful and ambitious woman, whose future desires may threaten the family he holds so dear. When Talcott's father, Judge Oliver Garland, a disgraced Supreme Court nominee, is found dead under suspicious circumstances, Talcott wonders if he may have been murdered. Guided by the elements of a mysterious puzzle that his father left, Talcott must risk his marriage, his career, and even his life in his quest for justice.

Fiction/978-0-375-71292-0

NEW ENGLAND WHITE

Lemaster Carlyle, the president of the country's most prestigious university, and his wife, Julia, the divinity school's deputy dean, are America's most prominent and powerful African American couple. Driving home through a swirling blizzard late one night, the couple skids off the road. Near the site of their accident they discover a dead body. To her horror, Julia recognizes the body as a prominent academic and one of her former lovers. In the wake of the death, the icy veneer of their town, Elm Harbor, a place Julia calls "the heart of whiteness," begins to crack, having devastating consequences for a prominent local family and sending shock waves all the way to the White House.

Fiction/978-0-375-71291-3

Nonfiction
The Culture of Disbelief, 978-0-385-47498-6

VINTAGE AND ANCHOR BOOKS
Available at your local bookstore, or visit
www.randomhouse.com